ALSO BY ERNEST LANGFORD

Rendezvous at Dieppe

The Apple Eaters

Survival Course

Rosie & Iris

The Wax Key

Necessities of Life

Valley of Shadows

Oh, Patagonia!

The
EXISTENTIALIST

*signed with
best regards
Ernest Langford*

Ernest Langford

A Novel

Battle Street
BOOKS

BATTLE STREET BOOKS
175 Battle Street
Kamloops, BC
Canada V2C 2L1

Publisher's note: This book is a work of fiction. Characters, places and incidents are the product of the author's imagination, or are used fictitiously. Any resemblance to actual places or persons, living or dead, is coincidental.

Canadian Cataloguing in Publication Data

Langford, Ernest,
    The existentialist

    ISBN 1-896452-30-2

    I. Title
PS8573.A555E9 1999   C813'.54   C99-910586-8
PR9199.3.L323E9 1999

Distributed by Gordon Soules Book Publishers Limited
1354-B Marine Drive
West Vancouver, BC
Canada V7T 1B5

Cover and book design by Warren Clark

Printed in Canada

To C

To you I owe a debt
that cannot be repaid.

I have existed on hope whose
fruition so long delayed has
by your sweet charity
granted my heart relief
and through your firm constancy
sustained my self-belief.

CHAPTER

1

ON A BOISTEROUS AFTERNOON DURING THE SECOND WEEK of April in the year 1916, Arthur James Compson, a sergeant in a British cavalry regiment, met Sylvia Elizabeth Wiley at a tram stop in the seaside town of Tambourne situated around a wide bay in the English Channel. Arthur Compson was in the final days of convalescing from leg wounds, and Sylvia Wiley was doing her bit to win the war by working as a volunteer nurse's aide at the Tambourne General Hospital.

From this chance meeting came a rapid courtship, a quick marriage (disapproved of by Sylvia's bank-manager father, her class-conscious mother and a social-climbing elder brother) and a three-day honeymoon. After this brief respite, Sergeant Compson was re-posted overseas and the young Mrs. Compson returned to the hospital where, to escape her mother's reproaches and her father's insults, she doggedly continued to work until an onrush of labour pains landed her in the maternity ward. There, after seven hours of sweating, moaning and terminal screaming, she gave birth to a six-pound, four-ounce son whom she named Arthur Edward, the former after his father and the latter after her own unappreciative father who implacably refused to visit his daughter and only grandchild.

Sylvia dutifully announced the birth of their son in a letter to Compson, who eventually read it months later in an army hospital where he was recuperating from an acute case of gonorrhea given him by a Cairo whore. While the army physicians cured his complaint and told him henceforth to avoid whores, they did not know, and consequently could not tell Compson, that the disease had wrecked his chances of ever fathering another child. Being hospitalized also prevented Arthur from joining his regiment in the great Allenby-led offensive against the Ottoman army in Palestine. Instead, he was enrolled in a course on explosives and demolitions, then posted to serve in northern Arabia with a short-tempered, impatient officer named T.E. Lawrence who, among other things, had taken to wearing Arab dress and to carrying on extended quarrels with the army general staff and the colonial office. In northern Arabia, Sergeant Compson became a camel-train master, though he loathed the animals. He also assisted his senior officer in demolishing bridges and railway lines, for which Compson later received a military medal, and he was present when the triumphant Arab forces entered and laid claim to Damascus. He was there, too, when Allenby arrived and imperiously swept aside the flimsy Arabian claims to Damascus and Syria, but then, unfortunately, came down with a severe attack of dysentery. This landed Compson back in the Egyptian hospital from which he was eventually discharged and shipped to England, where he spent what was left of the war years slowly recovering from the disease which had so debilitated him.

Finally, in 1919, he was discharged, given a small pension and returned to Sylvia who, grudgingly supported by her parents, was living with their toddler son in a rented house in Ponnewton, a small riverside Hampshire town. Once, before sand and eroded soil from the nearby Royal Forest had slowly but persistently drifted down to construct a barrier across the river mouth, tall-masted ships had entered the placid little river on the incoming tides, unloaded cargo at the town wharf, reloaded timber and charcoal from the forest, then departed on outgoing tides. That had been the town's heyday and explained the existence of the broad High Street lined with fine houses once belonging to maritime merchants, the bow-windowed shops, the porticoed town hall and the lofty steepled church. Inevitably, the day came when the sand bar at the river mouth became so enlarged that ships were unable to enter the river, even at the height of the tide, and when that happened, everything changed. Merchants went bankrupt, and within a few years the town was transformed from a thriving port into a dull backwater where only small centre-board sloops and shallow-drafted motor boats lined the town wharf and the height of commercial activity was the conversion of an eighteenth-century Methodist chapel into a cinema.

There, Sergeant Compson joined his wife, and for several months did little except eat, sleep, drink the occasional pint of beer, get acquainted with his son, and engage Sylvia in extended bouts of making love. Although maternity had slightly broadened her hips, Sylvia was still physically far more attractive than the whores on whom Compson had formerly expended his abundant sexual energy. Sylvia expected two things to result from their reunion: that their intense lovemaking would bring about another conception, and, that after a short rest, Arthur would obtain employment and relieve her of the humiliating necessity of depending upon her parents to support them. Neither of these occurred. Sylvia did not become pregnant, nor did Arthur demonstrate the slightest inclination to get meaningful work, or even talk about getting a job.

While little Arthur was napping, Compson would stroll to the nearest pub for a pint of mild-and-bitter, then return to sit at their kitchen table. While puffing on and stubbing out cigarettes, he would tell Sylvia how he had followed his half-crazed senior officer past Turkish sentries; both were loaded with explosives which they then stowed under railway lines before scurrying back past the sentries and scrambling up the scrub-covered hill. There they rejoined the Arab tribesmen, who waited impatiently for the moment when a locomotive passing over the charges would blow up both train and bridge, freeing them to charge down the hill to slaughter the hated Turks prior to looting whatever remained. Whenever Compson narrated these stories, sweat would accumulate on his forehead, fall onto his high, prominent cheekbones, and roll down his cheeks to rest on his thick black mustache.

Another story concerned an Arab chieftain, whose youngest son had been buggered and then impaled on the sword of a sadistic Turkish pasha. Thereafter, the chieftain would force captured Turkish soldiers to kneel while he drew out his long, curved sword. As the terrified peasant soldier (the Turkish army consisted largely of conscripted peasants) wept, pissed and shit himself, the chieftain would circle him, fingering and testing the sword edge and then suddenly dart forward to split the crouched man from crown to gut, sometimes slicing off his head.

These tales, told after a pint or two had loosened the locks of Compson's memory, terrified Sylvia, who, through the thick and thin of the four-year war, had clung to her belief that, while men in battle shot to kill, once the fighting was over they were invariably decent in their dealings with prisoners, the wounded and their fallen enemies. But then, Sylvia had been raised on a literary diet of romantic prose and poetry in which warriors saluted foes or praised them as they lay dead while simultaneously glorifying their own gallantry in battle. In any case, from Sylvia's point of view, Compson's tales of his exploits in Arabia did not pay the rent, nor put coal in their grate or food on their table.

Eventually, after almost a year had passed, Sylvia's mother, who had indirect but influential connections, procured for Compson the position of a forester (though he knew nothing of silviculture or management of plantations) in the Ponnewton Royal Forest, an area which had been established as a royal hunting ground by one of the Norman kings. Originally, the area covered approximately one hundred thousand acres, but throughout successive centuries the boundaries had been whittled away to the point where the original forest gates were now miles from the forest boundary. Internally, the forest had fared no better. A plat of the forest revealed that parcels of it had been given outright to royal favourites, others had been fenced in and arbitrarily possessed by local inhabitants. Custom held that any forest land so fenced between sunset and sunrise became the property of the encloser and his successors.

These holdings were accompanied by certain traditional "rights," which allowed the owners to graze ponies, pigs and cattle on open land and to gather bracken for cattle bedding and heather for roof-thatching, though these cutting rights were seldom exercised any more. The financially valuable part of the forest was divided into carefully fenced wooded enclosures, and Compson was responsible for overseeing three of these enclosures—there were about eighty in all—which were composed of English oaks mixed with stands of American white pine and Norwegian spruce, plus a thousand or more acres of heather- and bracken-covered moor and marsh land. There was also a furze-speckled Common, adjacent to the village of Hasterley, on which animals were grazed. The villagers, whose ancestors had lived on the site long before the arrogant Norman king requisitioned it, had pruned the name of the village to Asty. Over time the name had come to be used to refer not only to the village itself, but also to the Common and to the fenced enclosure of spruce and pine which wrapped the village so tightly on three sides that when gales from the Channel swayed the trees, the tall, dark columns appeared as though they would march forward, obliterating the inhabitants and buildings in their path.

That is how it came about that Arthur Compson, the former cavalry sergeant, and his wife Sylvia packed pots and crockery and the few pieces of furniture they'd managed to pick up at second-hand stores and moved to the village of Hasterley, where they settled down with their small son in a house owned by the forestry commission. Of course, Sylvia knew that her relatives looked down on her because, as one cousin reported to another, she had married "beneath her." Even her own mother had told her that she had "chosen her bed and must now lie on it;" but, while Sylvia clearly understood she had plummeted downwards socially in marrying Arthur Compson, she nevertheless thought her mother's choice of words inappropriate since she herself had no objection to lying with her husband in their brass-framed bed; in fact, she thoroughly enjoyed it, although she continued to believe that the sole reason she did so was to conceive another child. While Sylvia knew that "good" women avoided sex unless it was thrust upon them as a marital duty (her mother had told her this), she couldn't deny that she rather liked having Compson's swollen "thing" pulsing and vibrating inside her body. She had no objection to feeling her husband's hand beneath her nightgown, then moving up her legs and over you-know-where onto her tummy before he parted her thighs and did "it" with her. However, in keeping with her upbringing, she was circumspect in the way she responded and never allowed herself to demonstrate any more than a slight quiver of her body and a small sigh of satisfaction to stir the night air above her parted lips. She had not forgotten her mother's grim warnings about prowling men who take advantage of feminine weaknesses, although she was never able to reconcile her mother's cautions with the delicious sense of anticipation that flooded her whenever her husband's hand prowled the outskirts of her nightgown. There seemed to be a contradiction somewhere, and she wondered if the way she felt was common among women warned by their mothers to beware of the perfidies of men.

The villagers accepted the arrival of the Compsons, and the family was split into "The Sarge," "Missus Sylv'a" and "Little Artie." Whenever any villager stopped Sylvia in the lane and asked how "Little Artie" was doing, she bitterly regretted she had given her son a name that could be reduced to such a ridiculous diminutive, even telling herself that a certain king, mythologized by the poet Tennyson, had borne the same name did nothing to reduce her discomfort. Sylvia also grew tired of explaining to villagers why her three-year-old son would unexpectedly faint and remain unconscious for an hour or more, occasionally for an entire day. But of one thing Sylvia was certain: Her son did *not* have epilepsy. When Dr. Robertson, the local physician, after examining the unconscious boy on the first occasion he lost consciousness, raised the possibility, Sylvia flushed and angrily replied: "My Arthur certainly does *not* have that complaint." The physician, who lived with his wife and daughter in the only other decent brick house in the village, and who didn't much care why the boy lapsed into periods of unconsciousness, shrugged and remarked: "We'll keep and eye on him," further enraging Sylvia and confirming her low opinion of the doctor. Surely he should have known, merely by looking at her and hearing her speak, that she always kept a watchful eye on her young son. Sylvia thought the one sensible thing the physician had said on that first visit was that Arthur might be developing too rapidly, and though she had told the doctor at least three times that her son seemed to have learned to read all by himself, simply by turning over the pages of his Mother Goose book, he repeated that she must not push her son ahead of what was normal for his age and that she should make sure he got plenty of exercise and fresh air.

Although she distrusted Dr. Robertson, Sylvia faithfully followed his advice and made sure that her precocious son had plenty of exercise and fresh air. Every afternoon, regardless of the wind or rain so plentiful in the area, they walked through one of the forest enclosures. On days when the sun shone and spring breezes had transformed the yellow-flowered, prickly gorse bushes into a rippling yellow sea, they would run into the wind, flapping their arms, pretending they were reincarnations of the buzzards that came to circle the broad common that lay between the village and the road to Ponnewton before they flew the opposite way, to far-away places like Salisbury, Southampton and London. Arthur knew a little about each of those places: London had a bridge that had fallen down; Salisbury had a church spire that almost touched the sky; and Southampton had many boats, because it was a great port from which passengers were carried across oceans to truly far away countries, like America and Africa. He and his mother agreed that some day they too would travel to these exotic places.

Sylvia urged her husband to get their son a pony and couldn't understand Compson's lack of enthusiasm for her suggestion that once little Arthur had his pony, he could accompany his father around the forest enclosures. "You can teach him how to look after the forest," she said. While young Arthur finally did receive his pony, which he named Mary, he never did accompany his father on his rounds through the enclosures, the reason for which was explained in a note pushed under the back door of the Compson house one day informing Sylvia "the Sarge fucks other women in Asty." The paper was cheap, and the letters were as ill formed as the message was crude. Sylvia read the message over and over again, then put the scrap of paper into the kitchen fireplace and watched it burn. She wasn't sure how she felt about the information and therefore uncertain what she should do about it. She knew from her reading of novels that a woman finding herself in this position had alternatives. She could rush back home and confirm maternal suspicions about male infidelity, or avenge herself by taking a lover, perhaps scream and yell and throw pots and pans at her treacherous husband, or coldly announce her intention to seek divorce. Sylvia did none of these things. Instead, she let her husband know she was aware of his deceitful behaviour by refusing to let their son ride out with his father.

"No!" Sylvia firmly said, her face mottled with red flushes, when, after Arthur had received his pony, her husband suggested their son ride out with him one morning. "He's staying with me! I've changed my mind. I won't have you dragging him through the village dirt." Compson guessed that Sylvia had heard he was regularly making the rounds of women in the village and was indirectly telling him that, while she might not be able to change his behaviour, she would do everything in her power to prevent her son from being contaminated by his father's promiscuity. Besides, Compson knew that regardless of what Sylvia had heard, she would never break up their marriage or deny him rights in their marriage bed. Although he wasn't an overly intelligent man, Compson's country background as a child and his army experiences as an adult had led him to the conclusion that his wife's class pride, coupled with the impulses natural to all women, would force her to try and demonstrate her superiority to the local women.

Compson's success with the village women was easily explained: it was the outcome of his prolific sexual energy combined with his military background which worked hand-in-glove with the traditional system of hiring forest labourers. He formed the labourers into squads, then discovered that while one squad could work all the time and three squads some of the time, no matter how he juggled the enclosures and the available men, the labourers couldn't all work all of the time. As an experienced military man, Compson knew that idleness breaks down discipline and efficiency, so he introduced his own system. Instead of hiring the village men to fell trees, mend enclosure fences, clear rides and clean out ditches, he forced them to compete for work and pay him, though not in specified ways, to retain employment. No one could ever be sure, even the Sarge himself, how using labourers' wives and daughters entered the equation. Still it happened, and within months of becoming forester, the Sarge would ride off each morning on his pony Jack, circle the village, tie the pony to a tree, then make his way through the trees to enter a cottage where a labourer's wife or daughter would offer her body as payment for the Sarge's guarantee that a husband or father would have regular work in the forest enclosures.

Some people may wonder how one man could come to dominate a village of a hundred souls so completely, but it wasn't really surprising considering the isolation of the village and the economic hardships that prevailed there. Compson's system was simply another version of the feudalism that most believed had vanished from England centuries ago, and while some labourers privately resented their servitude and a few women their prostitution, most accepted the regime. After all, it provided men with full-time jobs, though meagerly paid, which suited everyone, not the least the women, happily relieved for six days a week of morose husbands underfoot every which way they turned.

But Sylvia, knowing nothing about the labour contract her husband had worked out with the villagers, merely knew that Compson had demeaned her and the sanctity of their marriage by being with women she regarded as her social inferiors. She came to believe that her husband was indirectly telling her that the secret places of her own body, into which she permitted him to intrude only because they were married and she wanted to bear another child, were no better than those of the village women. On afternoon walks with her son, if she met a village woman, especially if the woman asked how "Little Artie" was doing, she felt like slapping the woman's smirking, subservient face. Yet on nights after encountering a villager whom she knew Compson regularly visited, she would, by gesture and tone of voice, let him know he could have what he wanted from her. Of course, she hated that part of her body that drove her to surrender herself, no matter how hard she fought again the impulse; and when she felt him settle between her thighs and press his warm belly against hers, she swore the day would come when she would revenge herself and invite other men to occupy the place he was at that very moment entering.

She came to hate the sexual act itself, but masochistically enjoyed her surrender, though she had to bite her lips to prevent herself from reaching a climax, which she was successful in avoiding for the rest of their married life. She found that the easiest way to do so was to imagine Compson "doing it" with whichever woman she'd seen earlier in the day. She pictured the woman as having a gross, foul-smelling body, which enabled her to hate Compson even more for believing he had the right to her own still slender, sweet-smelling body. The way Sylvia felt and behaved in bed at night with her husband so conflicted with everything she had been taught and believed about herself that at times she thought she had surrendered her body and soul to the devil, and sometimes, when resolution of the mind battled with the rising delight of the body, she peered into the darkness and saw the horns of the devil on the forehead of the man possessing her. At such times, she told herself that she must leave her husband, but there was nowhere for her to go except back to her parents, and that was unthinkable. And so, instead of confronting Compson's whoring, the two of them skated around it, in part because they wanted to avoid doing or saying anything that might bring on one of Arthur's spells and worsen his condition.

Apart from that, the Sarge was also beginning to suspect that the responsibility for Sylvia's failure to conceive another child lay with him because so far no village woman had ever slyly said: "Yer know somethin', Sarge? I'm in the family way, and wot're yer goin' ter do 'bout it, eh?" Well, he had a ready answer for them if ever it was needed: a pay raise for the husband. To be sure, the increase wouldn't be generous, because Compson had little room to manipulate wages; the most he could do was dock a shilling here and a shilling there after condemning a labourer for sitting on his arse and smoking fags when he should be working nonstop. Apart from keeping his squads in line, he liked to accumulate a few extra shillings because it enabled him to purchase his son a story book on the Friday afternoons when he rode into the forestry office in Ponnewton to collect his own and the labourers' wages. And there was another reason for buying Arthur gifts: It appeased Sylvia and helped her to forget his infidelities, at least temporarily, by emphasizing their mutual devotion to their son. But it was only temporary, and while Sylvia didn't openly reproach her husband, or deny him "marital rights," she let him know he wasn't getting off scot-free through the slapdash meals she prepared and the holes she burned in his shirts. One day, she broke their only teapot, which meant that for a few days, until Compson could go to Ponnewton on the Friday, his afternoon tea was brewed in the pot in which Sylvia boiled cabbage. Yet, Compson didn't reproach her.

Taking the matter further, Sylvia hinted at undergoing a medical examination to find why she hadn't conceived again, to which Compson simply nodded. Once, when Sylvia raised the topic after a menstrual period, he offered: "Better luck next time," a comment that didn't go down well with Sylvia, who was now beginning to think that her husband was sowing fertile seed in other furrows, while dumping empty seed packets, so to speak, in her own. She remembered herself as a child, handing brightly coloured packages of flower and vegetable seeds to the gardener and receiving back empty ones after he had dribbled the seeds into carefully prepared furrows. Somehow that image seemed to fit with what she now got from her husband: as the earth readied itself for seed, so she prepared her womb and offered it to her husband, but received nothing in return. Still, Sylvia never went beyond hinting she might have a medical exam. Her dislike of Dr. Robertson prevented her from seeking his advice, and she was also fearful of what Compson might say or do if she openly suggested that the responsibility for her barrenness lay with him.

Lying behind Sylvia's reluctance to blame Compson and his seeming disregard of Sylvia's concerns was their unspoken, shared fear that any child they jointly conceived might suffer from the same affliction as their son, and while they didn't understand how such a thing had come to pass, they felt themselves to be somehow contaminated and unable to bring forth anything but "bad fruit." When Arthur had his next spell, Sylvia swept him up in her arms and lay cool damp washcloths on his forehead, weeping all the while, while Compson, who could not cry, assured her their son would soon grow out of it. "You'll see, Sylvia. Young animals often have problems, it's only natural," to which Sylvia, still sobbing, replied that her little boy was not an animal; and though her husband, a country boy, knew otherwise, he didn't contradict her. In his own way, Compson's love for his son was as great as Sylvia's, and it tore at his heart to stand beside the bed and look down at the unconscious child. His impulse was to gather him into his arms and breathe life back into him. He had seen too many still, dead bodies during the war and hoped he himself would die before he would be called upon to gaze upon another; and it didn't help to tell himself that their son was not dead, that within a hour or two his eyes would open and he would smile up at them. He was such a loving little fellow who, after an evening meal, asked for nothing more than to climb into his father's lap and lie against his long brocaded waistcoat.

"That's Arthur's great treat for the day," Sylvia always remarked. During such evening hours, she would come close to forgetting how much she longed for another child, a daughter whose hair she would arrange in braids and tie with ribbons, and whose lovely little-girl body she could dress in frilly petticoats and gaily flowered, lace-trimmed frocks. She adamantly refused to have Arthur's dark brown hair trimmed, and when his father complained his boy was beginning to look like a girl, she denied it. "Arthur's got your high cheekbones," she told Compson. "Put your faces together. See? You're as alike as two pins." Knowing he resembled his father delighted little Arthur. He still believed that his father could do anything he wanted, which meant that he, Arthur, could do all things too. He longed to repeat his father's exploits, such things as single-handedly (according to his mother) defeating the Turkish army and capturing the great city of Damascus, though some other man received credit for it because, as his mother explained, his father became ill and was sent back to England to recover.

Years later, Arthur came to understand that the greatest gift his mother had bestowed him was a vivid imagination and that most of what she had told him about his father had been produced by this. Of course, Sylvia never told Arthur his father was a compulsive womanizer who had copulated with practically every woman in the village, including Belinda Robertson, Dr. Robertson's wife, whose rosy-cheeked, bronze-haired, skinny-legged daughter Arthur adored from the moment he had first seen her skipping along the village lane with her mother. Sylvia once told Arthur that she and Belinda Robertson were third cousins: they shared a remote aunt, the daughter of a Lord, who was the second son of an Earl, whose mother was the daughter of a Duke. From that point onwards, the genealogical path Sylvia followed became so torturous that Arthur finally gave up trying to follow it and merely nodded when she concluded: "So that means we are related to the King and the Prince of Wales, just think of that, Arthur." And while Arthur did his best to think about these distant relations, he was unable to see how they fit into his own and his parents' lives; indeed, as a child, he had concluded that these relatives were irrelevant as far as he was concerned, a conclusion which later experience and thought confirmed.

In after years, when a certain woman with whom Arthur had formed an intimate relationship asked where he had been schooled, he replied: "At home. By my mother." When she then asked if his mother was a qualified teacher, he explained that he had learned to read on his own when he was three years old. (Arthur had been four when he mastered reading, but knocked off a year to impress the woman.) Actually, Arthur had no clear memory of having been taught the alphabet, although perhaps his mother had helped him, but he recalled reading Mother Goose rhymes on his own and also working his way, word by word, line by line, through the tales of the brothers Grimm. When he was six or seven years old, he started reading the Bible and closely examining the coloured illustrations in a book of Biblical stories that had been his mother's as a girl. And it so happened that Arthur was in the midst of reading *The Song of Solomon,* substituting Heather Robertson, the doctor's daughter, for King Solomon's beloved: "Come my beloved, let us go forth into the field; let us lodge in the villages," when a school truancy officer came to the house, who, after inquiring Arthur's age, asked why he wasn't attending the village school.

Arthur, sitting at the kitchen table, watched colour suffuse his mother's usually pale face. "Do you think for one minute I would allow my son to enter that place?" she demanded, to which the man replied it had nothing to do with what he thought—it was the law. "To hell with the law," his mother said, blushing as she uttered the oath she had never used before. "My son is frail. Besides, he can already read and write. Would he like to hear him read?" She then grabbed the Bible, dropped the open book in front of Arthur, pointed to a line and ordered him to read it. Arthur, grasping that a vital issue was at stake, obeyed, carefully enunciating each syllable and word: "Judges 20. Then all the children of Is-ray-el went out, and the con-gre-ga-tion was gathered together as one man, from Dan even to Beer-sheba, with the land of Gil-e-ad, unto the Lord in Miz-peh."

"Yes, yes," the truancy officer sighed. "That will do. Is your son doing his sums? Adding and subtracting?"

"Of course!" his mother loftily claimed. "Arthur, what is 13 plus 16?"

"Twenty-nine," Arthur dutifully replied.

"Read from there," his mother ordered, dabbing a finger onto another Biblical passage.

"And the chief of all the people, *even* of all the tribes of Is-ray-el, presented themselves in the assembly of the people of God, four hundred thousand footmen that drew sword."

"That will do," the truancy officer interjected. "I'm impressed by your son's ability to read, though not by his reading matter. A boy your son's age should be reading a variety of books."

"You don't approve of the Bible?"

"Madam, I most certainly do, but parts are unsuitable for children. The battles, the killing and so forth."

"I disagree," Arthur's mother said disdainfully. "Completely." She then proceeded to fabricate a lie. "I was allowed to read everything when I was a child, and it didn't distort my outlook on life."

"There're exceptions to every rule," the officer replied as he edged towards the door. "You and your son may be two of them."

"I agree." Having won the battle over Arthur's schooling, Sylvia could now afford to be generous. "Do visit us again some time," she invited.

"I will." The man laid his hand on the door latch, then turned to say: "Keep up the good work, sonny."

One day, many years later, when Arthur was around fifty years old and sitting beside a great blue lake in a far off mountainous country, he suddenly recalled that afternoon, and a subsequent one, when the truancy officer returned to listen as Arthur read several paragraphs from a book the officer had brought from the village school. Afterwards, the man had sat with his mother at the kitchen table to drink a cup of tea while Arthur, nibbling a cream biscuit, crawled under the oilcloth-covered table to enjoy the pocket of warm, muggy air beneath it. He heard his mother's high voice and the man's baritone reply; he saw his mother's shoes and part of her cotton stocking-clad legs; he saw the inspector's brown, muddy boots (village lanes were always mud-covered) and the lower part of his trousered legs. Then a large hand suddenly appeared below the table, which, from Arthur's viewpoint, seemed unconnected to anything. The hand moved, almost touching Arthur's head before it migrated to his mother's knees and, as he heard his mother telling the man how her husband provided work for every man in the village, the hand lifted his mother's skirt and disappeared beneath it. "He's an important man in the village. This house comes with the job."

"Hm-hm," the man commented, while Arthur now leaned forward and to one side and saw that the hand underneath the table was joined to a wrist and that the hand was moving between his mother's legs as though it wanted to get past the point where broad elastic garters held up her stockings.

Arthur heard his mother say: "My husband usually comes home about this time," and immediately the hand scurried away from his mother's legs and disappeared from Arthur's sight, reminding Arthur of a spider scooting along the floor of his bedroom before vanishing beneath the baseboard.

"Perhaps I'll come by earlier another day," the truancy officer said.

Arthur heard his mother laugh before saying: "Oh, I don't think so." She then called, "Arthur, where are you?"

"Here," Arthur replied from beneath the table.

"For God's sake!" the officer exclaimed.

Sylvia mother laughed again. "That's Arthur's favourite spot. He spends hours there, don't you, dear?"

In later years, Arthur was able to think about his mother objectively, but in childhood, he mythologised both his parents: his father was a war hero; his mother, the most beautiful woman in the world. His idealization of them was harmless, and of course he had no idea what went on in their adult world, so he couldn't have known that his mother, by smile and gesture, had invited the truancy officer to place his hand on her knees. Nor would he known that the officer, who visited the village each week, would call at the house again while Arthur was having his daily nap, or in later years, out riding his pony. Arthur preferred to believe that during his childhood years his mother's behaviour was morally impeccable, but as an adult he suspected that might not have been so, even though his mother would have felt herself justified when she compared whatever she did with her husband's prodigious infidelities.

One evening, not long after the visit from the truancy officer—and he retained a particularly clear memory of this evening—Arthur was sitting on his father's knee, using his forefinger to trace a path through the embroidery on his father's waistcoat, imagining that he was a great explorer discovering islands, continents and archipelagoes among the coloured threads. He informed his father that he wanted to be an explorer like Captain Scott, whom he had read about in a book Father Christmas had left in his stocking. His parents had laughed, and his father had said, "Just make sure you don't get lost."

"You have such a vivid imagination," he remembered his mother saying to him that night. "Did you find any hidden treasure on your journey, dearest boy?"

At that point, Arthur's memory failed him, but had he been able to remember the rest of the conversation, this is what he would have heard:

"We must get Arthur a copy of *Treasure Island*. Call in at Smith's on Friday. Order it, if they don't have it. It's by Robert Louis Stevenson."

"I know, I know. I read the book as a boy, but I always thought *Kidnapped* was the better story."

"I never read that one," Sylvia had admitted, surprised her husband had read a book she hadn't. In fact, she'd thought he'd never even read one.

"There's Kingsley's *Westward Ho,* too. Arthur might like that. I'll see what I can dig up."

"Oh do," Sylvia cried. "I want a whole row of books set on the dresser here, so if that horrid truant officer comes again, I can tell him Arthur's read every one of them. A horrible man, he insinuated we aren't looking after Arthur properly."

"Did you tell him about the—you know—about the spells?"

"Certainly not. That's none of his business. I only said Arthur's condition was fragile. Then I got Arthur read to him from the Bible. I'm sure there's not another child in the village school, even the grammar school in Ponnewton, who can read as well as our son."

"Maybe," Arthur's father said, "it's hard to say." And that was certainly true, it *was* difficult for Arthur's parents to know what to say or how to assess their son's intellectual and physical development. Sylvia's love for her child was close to being obsessive and, as she observed the way her husband caressed his son's head as he sat on his knees, she never doubted that he too dearly loved his son, and so between them that evening they finally decided to have Arthur examined by a specialist.

The next day Sylvia discussed the matter with Dr. Robertson, who agreed that seeing a specialist was a good idea. He told her that he had interned with the doctor who was now the resident neurologist at the

Tambourne General Hospital, and as a kindness he would undertake to telephone Dr. Stephenson and give him an overall outline of Arthur's medical problem. He expected and received effusive "thank yous" from Sylvia, who then timidly suggested he give her a letter explaining everything. "Oh no, that won't be necessary." Robertson waved dismissive hands. "My call will do the trick. I'll arrange it for tomorrow. Be there at eleven."

To be on time, Sylvia and Arthur had to leave the house before seven, walk to the main road to catch a bus to Ponnewton, and from there travel on another bus which carried them, so it seemed, along every road and down every lane between Ponnewton and Tambourne. When Sylvia and her son eventually arrived, no one seemed to know why they were there, since the referral from Robertson had gone missing. As a consequence, Sylvia and Arthur ended up sitting among people whom Sylvia knew, having worked at the hospital, were "the down and outers," on whom interns practised their limited diagnostic skills, all the while hiding their appalling ignorance behind long white coats and frequent *hm-hm's* and *ha-ha's*. By that time Sylvia knew she wasn't going to see Dr. Stephenson, and her instincts told her to get up and leave immediately; but a sense of duty to her son bound her to the hard wooden bench, where Arthur was bunched up against her. She told the nurse in charge she had worked in the hospital during the great war, but that didn't seem to help, the nurse simply stared at Sylvia as though she was speaking a foreign language and moved on to attend to other patients.

Never, never before in her life, until that day, as she sat on the bench for what seemed like hours, had Sylvia experienced the ignominy that pervades the lives of the poor and downtrodden. It numbed her to be in such company, and when her name was finally called, at first she didn't hear it, and blushed with shame when the nurse impatiently said, "Didn't you hear your name called? Come on, come on, don't keep Doctor waiting." Then, "Get your boy undressed" as she dragged the flimsy curtain across the cubicle into which she had led them.

Ten minutes later, the curtain was pushed aside, and a man, whom Sylvia judged younger than herself, entered to sit a small table and stare at Arthur who, naked, was perched on Sylvia's knees. "Well? What is it?" he barked, and immediately Sylvia sensed that the hours she'd spent getting to the hospital were going to be a waste of time. Still, she tried. She started out by explaining she had seen Dr. Robertson about her son's "spells"— that was as far as Sylvia got before the physician interrupted.

"How often does the boy have fits?"

That this embryo doctor should utter the prohibited word broke Sylvia's determination to make the best of it. She moved Arthur off her lap, grabbed his clothes and boots. "You fool!" she hissed at the astonished man, then pushed open the curtain, ran through the waiting room to the hospital entrance where she dressed Arthur in front of two student nurses and several coughing patients, then announced: "I'm never coming to this terrible place again!" She did her best to exit with dignity, but by the time she had pushed open the doors, her shoulders had slumped and she was crying.

As the crow flies, home and husband were only twelve miles away, but it took Sylvia almost twelve hours to reach them. Had she not loved her son as much as she did, she might have blamed him for missing two buses to Ponnewton, but she had to find a place for him to empty his bladder, then get him something to eat because he complained of being hungry. She lost track of time in the tea shop, and when she looked at the clock, she found it was past four. She dug a sixpenny piece from her purse and hurried Arthur out and along the street to the bus stop. There she waited another hour before the Ponnewton bus drew into the curb after she had frantically waved it down. The bus reached Ponnewton at half-past six, and she waited there another hour for the bus that she assumed would take her home, but, being the final bus of the day, it travelled no further than the junction with the main highway to Tambourne, where it waited 30 minutes for passengers before returning to Ponnewton. This forced Sylvia to get off the bus, and she had no choice but to carry Arthur the rest of the way home, a distance of four miles. By the time she got home and Compson had lifted Arthur from her arms, she was hysterical and could do nothing more than collapse on a kitchen chair, put her arms and head on the table and wail.

"I'll put him to bed," Compson said, and went up the steep narrow stairs.

Sylvia's limbs and jaw were shaking from exhaustion and humiliation: How could people from her own class treat her as an inferior! "Scum, that's how I was treated, Arthur. Scum!" she sobbed after Compson returned to the kitchen. "And Dr. Robertson! He was no use! I hate that man! He didn't notify the hospital, so nobody knew why I was there. And they didn't care! They put us in an awful room. Nobody cared! Oh God! I can't bear to think of it. I tell you, Arthur, Robertson is not coming near my boy again. Never. Never. I'll die first. And there wasn't even a specialist, just a young fool in a white coat who didn't know anything."

Arthur, who had much experience of battle shock, made a pot of tea and forced Sylvia to drink several cups heavily laced with sugar; and when she lurched away from the table, still sobbing, he grasped her arm, guided her out into the darkness-clothed garden, raised her dress waist-high, pulled down her knickers and supported her in a squatting position so that she could relieve herself. The odour of feces surrounded him as she wailed: "I wasn't able. All day."

"Hush, hush, Syl, it doesn't matter. Don't worry. I'll see to it in the morning. Come on, let's get you to bed."

Afterwards, whenever gossip about her husband reached her ears, Sylvia would always think of the night of her terrible breakdown. She remembered his kindness, the way he helped her back into the kitchen, poured hot water into a bowl, then undressed and bathed her, beginning with her tear-drenched face, then moving downward, over her arms and shoulders, which ached from carrying Arthur such a distance, then further down, over her tummy and hips and—well, moving everywhere—to rinse away the day's accumulation of sweat, dirt and humiliation. And then, after he had finished drying her, he changed the water and got her to sit with her feet in a bowl of fresh, soothing warm water while he knelt and washed her tired legs and feet. These attentions made Sylvia feel like a new person, like the snake she'd once seen in the lane that had sloughed off its old tired skin and was wriggling out, shiny and new. Sylvia was so grateful for Arthur's tenderness that she didn't mind him seeing her so utterly naked and defenceless as he sponged and dried every part of her exhausted body. Every part. She would later wonder how many women in the world had experienced being intimately bathed by their husbands. If any other woman had ever felt the touch of a washcloth guided by her husband's hand, moving over her breasts (hers weren't as firm as they used to be before she breast-fed Arthur) and around her tummy and hips, then over and under her bottom and nearby places. Oh, when something such as that happens to a woman, when a man gently washes the grime of a humiliating experience off her body, then brings her a nightgown and lowers it over her head, the woman knows that while she may not love the man, and may from time to time hear tales about him going with other women, still she knows that she can trust him. During those hours when she reached the lowest point in her life, her nadir, he tended and comforted her and let her know he valued her above all other women.

Sylvia always remembered the events of that day at the Tambourne Hospital, and the night that followed, because they changed her. She, who had once believed in the sanctity of the particular social system into which she had been born, now didn't believe in anything, except her son and her husband, certainly not the medical system which had treated her and her son so shabbily. So, when the usual childhood diseases arrived to afflict Arthur, Sylvia resolutely refused to have Dr. Robertson attend him, forcing Compson to consult Robertson on the sly and become his medical amanuensis. The first time Compson went to see the doctor after Sylvia's disastrous visit to the clinic, Robertson assured him that he had indeed referred little Arthur's medical problem to the head neurologist at the hospital, but somehow the necessary paper work hadn't been done. "I should have given Mrs. Compson a note. Tsk, tsk, tsk. I could kick myself for not doing so. I mean, those chaps in the outpatient clinic weren't qualified to deal with a case like little Arthur's. Tsk, tsk, tsk."

Compson had felt like obliging the doctor by giving him the swift kick in the buttocks he had asked for, for his opinion of Robertson's medical skills matched Sylvia's, but since the doctor was the only source of medication for his son, Compson, former army man that he was, had no intention of allowing personal animosity to cut him off from his single source of supply.

"So your boy seems to have the measles, eh?"

"That's what it looks like."

"Of course I should examine him, but since I can't, I'll tell you, there's no medicine that'll cure it. So what you and Mrs. Compson must do is keep the room dark, that's to protect his eyes. If he complains about the itching, dab him with camomile lotion. And since he'll run a high fever, give him plenty of water. It's a serious disease, though most children get through it nicely. It'll take two weeks before the spots fade. So . . . dark room, camomile lotion for the itching and lots of water. That'll be five shillings."

Compson paid the fee, and went to the front of the house where Robertson's wife stood at the door. Belinda Robertson always let in patients and bade them goodbye, though, to most, she felt like saying good riddance. She smiled conspiratorially at Compson. "Good afternoon, Mr. Compson," she said, followed by a whispered question: "When will I see you again?"

"Soon," Compson replied, then raised his voice and continued, "Little Arthur has the measles."

"Oh dear. I'm so thankful my Heather's gone through all those children's complaints." She lowered her voice. "Tomorrow afternoon he's away in Ponnewton."

Compson smiled, said nothing, then left the house. Army experience had made him a dab hand at dealing with people seeking favours, and he knew what Belinda Robertson wanted from him was something she'd never get from her husband, if they lived together a million years. Oh yes, it hadn't taken the former cavalryman long to find out that what Belinda Robertson wanted was to be broken in and ridden like a horse; she wanted a halter over her head and a bit in her mouth; she wanted to kick and prance and throw her head back and forth, as he, holding the reins, forced her to circle around him by slapping her heavy buttocks with his whip; Belinda Robertson wanted to be a sweating, bucking filly that finally bows her head and allows her master to saddle and mount her. Oh yes, she wanted to be broken to the bit. He'd seen it happen time and again when he was in charge of a breaking-in: the fillies, sweating and shaking and dribbling piss, finally signified their submission, and afterwards he always made sure the beauties were blanketed and given an apple or a few sugar cubes to let them know that the men who had broken their spirits also loved them.

Sometimes Compson thought he cared more for horses than for his own kind, because horses were simple, beautiful creatures and never demanded anything from him other than a dip of crushed oats and a pitchfork of sun-sweetened hay. He had spent his childhood among them, his father being in the business: horse trader and knacker. As a youth, he'd crawled among their legs without ever once being harmed. At age ten, he had hoped to become a jockey, but at fifteen knew he was too big. The night before he left home to join the army, he had got into his fourteen-year-old sister's bed and persuaded her to let him play jockey to her horse. The ecstatic experience changed Compson's life, and left his sister pregnant, and while he would go from woman to woman for the rest of his life, attempting to relive the ecstasy of his initial physical awakening, his sister, unable to explain to her parents why she was five months along, would be driven from her home to end her life by loading her coat with rocks and jumping off a bridge into a canal. Because his sister had never told their parents where the child in her womb originated, Compson was able to attend his sister's funeral and demonstrate to everyone present that he had all the makings of a good soldier by standing erect in his new uniform beside her grave, without once lowering his head or producing a single tear. But Compson's stoicism didn't mean he was not affected by his sister's death. The contrary. His sexual encounter with her, followed by her suicide, had in fact so profoundly affected him that he spent the remainder of his life trying to find a woman like her, and because he wasn't a man inclined to introspective thought or examination of motives, he was never to realize that his wife Sylvia, except for her middle-class accent and mannerisms, came as close to being a physical duplicate of his dead sister as he was ever likely to find among the millions of women that walked upon the face of the earth.

CHAPTER

2

AT FIRST ARTHUR WAS FRIGHTENED WHEN HE DISCOVERED how easy it was to imagine he was inside another person's skin and know exactly what that person was thinking and feeling. It was as though he were actually standing in the other person's shoes and experiencing everything that person saw and did from his or her perspective. It was especially easy if the person were a woman, which seemed odd, because he thought it should be easier for him to imagine being a boy or a man.

One day, after one of his spells, Arthur stood by the little window in his bedroom which overlooked the small paddock where he could see his father's pony Jack, Heather Robertson's pony Billy and his own darling Mary, gathered together at the fence as though waiting for him to appear, as he so often did, with apple cores and peelings left from a pie his mother made. He always meticulously divided the leavings so that each pony received the same number, while making sure Mary received the largest cores, Billy the smallest. It wasn't that he disliked Billy or even that he had any objection to Billy sharing their paddock with Jack and Mary so that his father could teach Heather how to ride and how to take care of her pony. Arthur adored Heather and wished she would occasionally smile at him, but she always ignored him and didn't even bother to thank him for giving Billy a share of cores and peelings. His mother said Heather was very stuck up, while his father said she'd never make a good horseman because she treated Billy like an animal and not a good friend.

As he stood at the window, an image appeared and he recognized himself lying unconscious on the bed, his parents huddled beside it, looking down on him. He lay there motionless, but otherwise looking much the same as the reflection he viewed in the small mirror above his dresser each morning while combing his shoulder-length hair. His mother always recombed it after he finished washing his face and hands at the kitchen sink, but he enjoyed looking at his reflection and remembering how his mother once said he resembled Lord Byron. "You never know," she dreamily said, "maybe somewhere, way back, we're related to Lord Byron." But while Arthur was sceptical about any ancestors his mother might try to tack onto their coat tails, he could think of no reason why he might not one day be a poet, and he carefully examined himself in the mirror each morning to find out if eight hours of sleep had made him more "poetical-looking."

As he stood by the window, it was easy enough for him to imagine what his parents had said as they stood beside his bed, looking down on his unconscious self:

"No, I won't," his mother said. "Not after what I went through at the clinic."

"I'm thinking of the boy," his father replied.

"Are you saying I'm *not* thinking of him? That I'm thinking only of myself? Well, let me tell you, Arthur, I'd give everything I have in this world to have my son cured."

"Everything?" his father quietly replied. He never raised his voice. Never.

"Yes. If someone told me I could have my son cured in return for my life, I'd accept the offer. Do you think I enjoy seeing him lying there?"

Even as a child, Arthur would ask himself if it were possible for him to become unconsciousness deliberately, so that his parents would be forced to express their love and concern for him. Did he secretly enjoy having his father kneel beside the bed to embrace him once he'd awakened? Surely he wouldn't do such a thing. Coping with the excruciating headaches and physical weakness that inevitably followed his spells was not something anyone'd wish for. When he was younger, maybe three or four, his mother would bare her breasts and hold him against them, and later, when he'd asked why she'd done this, she had blushingly replied: "I really don't know, except that you were helpless, and I needed to make you strong. I don't know. Maybe it was to comfort you, maybe it was because I wanted another child. I don't know. I did a lot of silly things in those days."

Even during childhood, Arthur had sensed a special quality within himself. The knowledge had come to him as he worked through the books he read, such as the Bible with its wild and wonderful stories of prophets and kings. When his father had asked him if he'd enjoyed *Westward Ho*, he'd answered that the story didn't seem "real" to him. Later on, as a more or less established writer, Arthur would spend time thinking about what was "real" in fiction and what wasn't, and how best to achieve authenticity. In his early novels, Arthur went to great lengths to ensure the "realness" of the characters and the events he created, but he remained uncertain of the precise method by which he conveyed this elusive quality through the words he transferred from his imagination onto paper. Was it accomplished by setting down every detail about a man or a woman? Was authenticity realized when an author revealed, for example, that a man during his pubertal years abused his developing body, or a nubile woman had daydreamed of lovers gratifying her heated, pulsing loins? Or was authenticity better achieved by portraying individual quirks and mannerisms? He wondered if creating fictional characters was similar to what painters did when they planted seeds of life into the eyes of portraits of people, thus persuading viewers that behind the eyes dwelt not only a soul, but also a vault in which stored memories resonated from the ecstasy of heaven to the torment of hell. If that were so, then an author's solution to the problem wouldn't lie in exposing every detail and nuance of the characters' lives. Instead, an author would have to be suggestive, allowing readers to flesh out the characters with their own desires and memories. In that way, every male reader could become the hero, every female reader the heroine, and although the names and the accoutrements of their daily lives changed with the generations, the corn within the husk remained the same.

Arthur started out life believing literally everything his parents said. Thus, when Arthur asked his father where he had come from, and his father, after a pause, answered that he and his mother found Arthur under a savoy cabbage leaf, Arthur spent many hours searching the vegetable garden, raising cabbage leaves in the expectation of finding an infant. And, amazingly, his innocence coexisted in a village where children commonly greet each other with "Fuck you," and boys regularly wagged their droopy penises at girls and girls their bare bums at boys.

"Those children!" Arthur's mother would often say to Compson. "You have to wonder what'll become of them." To her question, Compson would faintly smile, because he did not have to speculate how or where they would end up. He knew. A percentage of the lads would remain in the village to replace their fathers as forest labourers, the rest would drift away, some into the army, others to work on farms outside the forest, some to the prison population. And the girls? Well, some would stay to maintain the village population, the rest would go off to scrub floors or walk streets in the great naval and commercial seaports on the eastern side of the forest. Compson, knowing more about the villagers than Sylvia, was able to look the children over and have a pretty clear idea of who would remain and who would leave. Those among the boys he labelled "leavers" tended to be the cheeky, slightly impertinent kids, or those who slyly watched him from the corner of their eyes, letting him know they despised him. Things were generally reversed with the girls: the cheeky ones ended up pregnant and married by the time they were sixteen and remained in the village, while the shy, docile girls departed to survive as best they could in the external world. It was a curious situation, for while the Compson family lived among the villagers, Sylvia and her son remained separated; only the Sarge, due to his position, knew all the men by name and a fair number of women by how they felt beneath him, as well as a sprinkling of older girls who, encountering him by chance in an enclosure, had no idea what was in store for them when they accepted his invitation to get behind him on Jack for passage through the enclosure.

Arthur, cloistered with his mother and isolated by the strange complaint that afflicted him, actually knew very little about village life. True, he walked the village lane to Hasterley's single all-purpose shop with his mother, and on Sundays rode out with his father and with Heather Robertson when she was home from boarding school. While Arthur continued to adore Heather, he resented her presence on these outings because when he and his father were alone, they would ride through the enclosures and emerge onto the heath over which they would gallop until they reached its crest, crowned by a clump of wind-battered Scotch pines. This was Arthur's favourite spot, and there, when he and his father were alone, they would sit on their ponies and look southward and westward beyond the forest toward the English Channel and the Isle of Wight, sometimes spotting a liner emerging from behind The Needles, slowly increasing speed as it advanced into the open channel. His father told him the story of how the supposedly unsinkable Titanic, racing through fog off Newfoundland had struck an iceberg and sunk. Hundreds of men, women, and children too, were drowned because the liner did not carry enough lifeboats, which seemed terrible to Arthur. But when his father told him about the army transport which had carried his regiment and horses to Egypt and how the mounts had suffered terrible seasickness in the Bay of Biscay, Arthur's eyes filled with tears as he thought of Mary and Jack.

"At least we men knew what was wrong with us," his father said, "but the poor animals could do nothing but groan. I tell you, son. It was hard to bear their suffering."

"I'd never let that happen to Mary," Arthur told his father, who replied that the horses had quickly recovered once on land.

Oh yes, when no one else was there, he and his father had a marvellous time. But when Heather Robertson appeared for riding lessons, Arthur always felt his father's interest slip away. What was more, Heather demanded his father's attention by pushing her pony between Mary and Jack, never once glancing at or speaking to him, but continuing to chatter to his father about her friends at school, as if his father cared about a bunch of silly, shrieking school girls. Worse, though Arthur wasn't certain it had actually happened, one afternoon when his father and Heather galloped off over the heath, leaving him behind trying to get Mary into a canter, he thought he saw his father lean over and kiss Heather. Afterwards, he decided he was mistaken, because when he finally reached the clump of pines, his father was pointing to an oil tanker in the Channel, telling Heather that oil tankers were floating bombs and how, during his journey to Egypt, he had seen a tanker explode after being hit by a torpedo. Hearing his father tell Heather a story that he, Arthur, hadn't heard caused him to feel even more resentful of the girl's presence, and he could hardly wait until her school holiday was over.

"Here comes slow-coach," Heather said, when Arthur finally reached the clump of pines.

"Blame Mary, not Arthur," Compson said. "She's got fat and lazy. Arthur gives her too much sugar." Of course that wasn't true, Arthur thought, he always gave the three ponies the same number of everything, though he had to admit Mary was a little lazy and perhaps took advantage of him, knowing he would never slap her, but still, Mary was only half the size of Jack and smaller than Billy, and everybody knew small ponies couldn't gallop as fast as large ones. Besides, Arthur couldn't understand why his father played up to Heather. He himself never did, though, being in love with her, he had every right to try to please her. He even dreamed that one day—after becoming a famous poet—he would marry her, but at the moment, he was only eleven, which meant Heather was fourteen, and because it was unlikely he would become famous until he was at least seventeen or eighteen, that meant waiting six years, by which time Heather would be twenty. He wasn't sure at what age people married and made a mental note to ask his mother about this. In the Bible, girls married when they were young, often to men who ended up living a long, long time. He made another note to check the ages of Biblical men. He recalled reading that "all the days that Adam lived" were 930 years, and that Methuselah had lived 969 years before he died, which would mean that he, Arthur, had many years ahead of him and plenty of time to marry. He thought Heather looked older in her jodhpurs, black cap and white shirt, especially the shirt, because it set off her square shoulders and showed her developing breasts, which Arthur wished he could see and he felt jealous and resentful when he noticed his father glancing obliquely at them.

"Time to go," his father announced and slapped his rein against Jack's neck. Arthur attempted to swivel Mary before Heather turned Billy to position herself at his father's right side, but the manoeuvre didn't work. Instead of responding to his rein and rib-kick, Mary slowly pivoted in a large circle, taking them further away. For one frustrated moment, Arthur wished Mary had been shipped off to the knackers, but immediately felt remorse for such disloyalty and leaned over to whisper an apology in Mary's ear, which she accepted by gurgling in her throat. His father and Heather rode ahead, but when they reached the enclosure gate Compson left Heather and galloped back to swing Jack around and halt beside Arthur.

"Everything all right, son?"

"Oh, yes," he replied.

"Shall I slap Mary's rump to liven her up?"

"Oh, no. She's doing her best."

His father suddenly laughed and reached out to ruffle Arthur's hair. "You don't think you can ask more from a filly, son?"

"I don't know. Mary told me she's going as fast as she can."

His father laughed again, then said, "Never believe what a female tells you, son."

As they neared the gate, Compson pointed in Heather's direction. "Look at that girl," he said. "She's so impatient she can't wait for a minute to pass, let alone the sun to rise and set. But she'll get knocked down one of these days." He brusquely called to her: "Open the gate." Heather obeyed. "Don't forget to close it," he ordered as he and Arthur rode through into the enclosure. Arthur could feel fury radiating from Heather as she dismounted to close the wide gate and knew how angry she really was when she rode behind them, instead of alongside, sulking until they got home, where she quickly unsaddled Billy, hung the saddle and bridle in the stable and stalked off without saying a word. His father winked at him, turned down his mouth and said loud enough for Heather to hear: "Give Billy his oats, son. His mistress has forgotten him."

Arthur happily agreed; and he and his father laughed when in the distance they heard a thin, high voice shriek: "I hate you!"

"She'll mean that 'til tomorrow. That's women for you. One minute they hate you, the next it's forgotten. Not like men, they store their hatreds."

Arthur spread a dipper of crushed oats in the trough his father had nailed together from three pieces of wood, and the three ponies jockeyed for positions to get at the feed. As always, Mary was pushed aside by the other two ponies and forced to take what she could get from one end.

"Mary should have her own trough," Arthur said, as he tried to push Billy away from Mary's share of oats.

"She doesn't do badly all things considered," his father said. "Maybe we should get you a bigger pony."

"What about Mary?"

"We'd sell her."

"No!" Arthur protested, realizing that selling Mary meant she would be sent off to the knacker's. "No! I won't! She's mine. I love her. Next to Mother and you, I love Mary most of all in the world."

His father hesitated. "We'll see, but don't forget in a few years when you're astride Mary, your feet'll dangle on the ground."

"I don't care. I won't let her go. I won't ride any more."

"We'll see," his father said. He patted Arthur's shoulders and after putting hay into the trough, they walked from the paddock through the vegetable garden, where Sylvia carried on a running battle with rabbits and the occasional fallow deer. At the house they washed their hands and sat at the kitchen table to eat their Sunday afternoon tea of salmon sand-wiches (Arthur's favourite), canned Australian peaches, slices of warm currant cake and cups of strong tea into which they poured canned milk. Though fresh milk was available in the village from a man who owned a two cows tethered in the grassy spot on the Common, Sylvia, having learned as a nurse's aide that milk was an active carrier of tuberculosis, was con-vinced the local milk teemed with bacteria and refused to use it. Most of the food the family ate was bought from vendors who called at the village households two or three times a week: The baker arrived every other day, the butcher every third day, the greengrocer once a week in the winter and every other day in spring and summer when fresh vegetables, greens and fruits were available, and the oilman, from whom Sylvia bought candles, paraffin and soap, came every other week.

The fishmonger rattled into the village on a motorbike twice a week, and from his sidecar took out a board on which he arranged a selection of fresh herring, mackerel, Dover sole, sometimes trout, even—with a whis-per and a wink—cutlets from salmon netted in the Ponnewton River. Mr. Jones, a Welshman who had abandoned his homeland to eke out a living in southern England, fascinated Arthur when he twisted the corner of his lips and whispered to his mother: "I wouldn't sell these lovelies, except to a

lai-dy like you, You know 'ow ter cook 'em. A little butter, a hot pan . . ."
And Sylvia, who didn't much like fish but who was victimized by his
flattery, would purchase the fish and the next day dig a hole in the garden
and bury it. "I really don't know why I buy it," she said to Arthur as she
shovelled soil into the grave. "Do you know why I buy it, darling?"

"To eat?" Arthur suggested.

"I intend to cook it at the time. I really do. And Mr. Jones is so anxious
to sell the fish. That's what it is, I worry that the poor man won't have
enough money to buy petrol for his motorbike unless I buy it." She pressed
the soil down with her shoe while saying: "Least said, soonest mended."
Sylvia used this adage to bridge gaps in conversation, and as a gesture of
reconciliation when she feared a discussion might develop into a full-blown
argument. Arthur spent much time observing his mother's habits. After all,
he had no other company. He enjoyed watching the way she tilted her head
and pursed her lips when she was about to criticize someone; the way she
pushed her fingers through her carefully coiled hair when she was upset;
the way she glanced sideways at him whenever she spoke about his father;
her habit of uttering incomplete thoughts, yet demanding to know if he
had heard what she'd said; the way she stood, walked, raised and lowered
her shoulders while periodically muttering "hm-hm-hm," as though carrying on some internal conversation. He even enjoyed watching her sudden
flashes of irritation when she ordered him to go outside and clean his boots
before entering the kitchen, or her telling him not to get in her way, or
calling him in from the garden when she thought it was too cold or raining
too hard, then forgetting the command and shooing him out again. Although Arthur wasn't sure what these mannerisms implied about his mother,
he knew with certainty that he loved her more than he did his father, and
that one of the greatest pleasures in his life was to stand beside her and
inhale the aroma that emanated from her body, although sometimes she
would become irritated when he pressed his face against her clothes. Some
of the scent came from the Pears soap, which the oil man procured especially for her. But the part of his mother's smell that Arthur loved best, and
which he had associated with her since his toddler years, carried a faint
whiff of sun-warmed grasses. "Why are you sniffing at me like that? Go
away. Do something useful. Read a book. I can't stand it when you hover
around me, like a fly buzzing 'round a jam pot." Then, after he was back at
the table, his nose in a book, she would abandon her housework to hug and
kiss him and tell him how much she loved him while he leaned against her
and perversely wished he could have a spell so that he might awaken and

feel her bare breasts which, out of love, she might uncover, as she had when he was a child.

It seemed to him as his birthdays piled up, that the need to be consoled increased in proportion to his realization that his spells might seriously handicap his life in the future; and because he couldn't speak of his fear to his parents, he confessed it to Mary. At thirteen, Arthur was too big to ride Mary, but he still talked to her, convinced she understood his problems and was attempting to reassure him when she nudged her soft lips against his cheeks. If Billy should happen to butt into the discussion, Arthur purged his resentment of Heather by slapping the pony's nose and telling him to bugger off. When Heather was away at school, he adored his memory of her, but when she came to the paddock, he hated her, but couldn't prevent himself from rushing from the house to open the paddock gate for her as she trotted Billy out, then kneed him into a canter.

"I hate Heather," he would tell Mary, but when Heather reappeared, he hungrily returned and watched her swaying hips and vibrating breasts as she accommodated herself to Billy's short-gaited trot. His mother had taken to calling her "Miss Stuck-up."

"Does Miss Stuck-up ever speak to you?" she asked.

"No. But I don't care."

"Hm . . ." Sylvia had seen Arthur race from the house when Heather could be heard calling Billy. "She could at least be polite. Heaven knows, she chatters away to your father. I'm going to speak to her. And to your father."

"Please don't, Mother. Please."

"All right, darling. But I don't see why somebody shouldn't set her straight. Our family's as good as hers."

Arthur didn't want to hear his mother wade through the rip tides of relative family importance. "I know we are, but please don't say anything. Please." Arthur had good reason for not wanting his father involved in his feelings about Heather Robertson. The onset of puberty had brought with it an increase in the frequency and intensity of his spells. These were now intermingled with episodes in which he appeared to experience a separation of mind and body. He wandered around in a kind of limbo with his body in one place while his disassociated mind drifted off in other directions. However, Arthur kept this strange phenomenon to himself, knowing that if he told his mother, she would try to prevent him from ever leaving the house.

One afternoon, in the midst of one of his new limbo episodes, Arthur wandered into the Hasterley enclosure to lean against a tree while drifting in and out of consciousness. Time was suspended. The sun stood still and trees and birds appeared painted upon a dense background of sky. The trunks and leaves of trees were transparent, which enabled him to look from one end of the enclosure to the other. He saw ponies standing docile by a path, cropping tufts of grass and, off to the side, beneath a dark canopy of Norwegian spruce, a man holding and kissing a girl. He couldn't under-stand why the ponies and the man and woman were not transparent like the woodlands. He saw the man unbutton the girl's blouse and unhook her brassiere to nibble and kiss her breasts. He felt himself move forward to become the man who pulled down the girl's jodhpurs and white undergar-ment, motioned her to kneel, knelt himself, then penetrated the girl from behind. There was no sound, not even the call of a wood pigeon or the creak of saddle leather. Nothing. It was like a shadow play, or a dream. The man and girl then stood, straightened their clothes, mounted their ponies and rode along the path, while he, Arthur, returned to his motionless body and somehow got himself back to the house where he lapsed into uncon-sciousness. In the days that followed, Arthur began to speculate about what he had witnessed in the forest and eventually came to believe he had seen his father raping Heather Robertson.

Not long after this, on a Sunday afternoon, when Arthur and his father were standing at the paddock gate feeding carrot and potato peelings to the ponies, his father turned to him and out of the blue said, "I want to talk to you about something important, son," then without further ado he laid out the physiological alterations that transform boys into men. After tell-ing Arthur things he had already observed in his own body, his father con-tinued: "I think you're having more spells now, because you're making all man's spunk in your balls, which day-dreaming's not going to help. You've got to put your spunk where nature meant it to go. You've got to help yourself keep well by keeping your cock quiet. Understand what I'm say-ing?" Arthur miserably nodded. "Now, son, you know the dressmaker, Dot Perks? Are you listening? Don't turn away from me, son. This is impor-tant. I've spoken to her, and you're going to visit her once or twice a week, depending how things work out. She's expecting you tomorrow afternoon, so don't let me down, son."

Why should his father suggest that his failure to visit the dressmaker would let his father down? After all, he had visited Dot Perks' cottage many times in the past with his mother, patiently waiting while his mother tried on a skirt or dress that needed altering. He himself had felt the dressmaker's hands adjusting and pinning and buttoning his clothes, while telling his mother that his trousers needed taking out at the waist, or his jacket had got too short for him and she would do her best to lengthen it. Dot Perks' husband had joined the Citizen Army in 1914 and been killed in the Battle of the Somme, and she had been forced to take up dressmaking—and apparently something else too—in order to support herself, To Arthur, Dot Perks seemed quite old, but at the time he first went to her cottage as dictated by his father, she was thirty-two.

"So what can I do for yer?" she asked.

"Father said . . ."

"Oh, that's right. Yer daddy said yer needs a glove fer yer number eleven finger. Yer do 'ave a number eleven, don't yer?" When Arthur mumbled that he didn't know, she raised her eyebrows and said: "'ow many fingers do yer 'ave on yer 'ands, 'andsome?"

"Ten," Arthur said.

"Well, I bet yer 'as another finger somewheres. Ain't that so?" She leaned over the sewing machine. "I knows yer does 'cuz yer daddy asked me ter fit me glove around it. 'E said as it'll 'elp yer 'ealth. So why don't we do that, eh? Will yer drop the latch on the door?"

Arthur never forgot his first visit with Dot Perks. He remembered trailing her into the small bedroom and obediently taking off his clothes while she drew the curtains and folded down the blankets on the bed. "Ah, just like yer daddy's," she said when she turned to look at him. "A big one." He stood at the foot of the bed, watching her undress, unsure of what was expected of him, and afraid, yet fascinated by the size and contours of her white body. "Well, come on then," she said, as she lay on the bed, opened her thighs and indicated he should get between them. It really was quite simple. His thing went into her, and when he stirred his hips to make it go in further, his spunk shot out, and then all he could do was lie upon her, sucking her brown nipples until his thing stiffened again. He remembered every word Dot Perks said and could even project an image of his skinny self, beating against the curves of her belly, desperately trying to obey his father and rid his body of its frightening affliction.

"That's me boy," she said, when he began stirring again. "That's me boy. Slow down . . . take yer time. There ain't no 'urry. Yer got all afternoon. That's what yer daddy paid fer. Get 'im ter work it out, 'e said," which reminded Arthur of his mother vigorously stirring cake batter or whisking egg whites. When it was over and he rested between Dot Perks's accommodating thighs, he dared to believe that in fact his father's sug-

gested therapy had worked and he would now be forever rid of his affliction; but in fact a much more profound change in his life occurred, one
that left him feeling deeply disturbed.

The encounter with Dot Perks had altered the way he perceived his
mother. She was changed from a maternal presence who prepared meals,
cleaned house, washed clothes, and made beds into a woman possessing
all the physical elements he had observed in the dressmaker. Now, when
Arthur sat at the kitchen table while his mother stood at the stove, turning
slices of bacon and frying an egg and hunk of bread in the bacon fat, he
didn't see her skirt or dress, or whatever she wore beneath it, instead he
looked straight through her clothing and saw her stomach, her breasts and
her buttocks, and when she turned from the stove holding a plate of bacon
and eggs and fried bread (which Arthur adored), he didn't see his mother's
smiling face, or the apron that covered her from shoulder to skirt hem.
Instead, he saw a naked body like Dot Perks', and because he had never
thought of his mother as like other women in the village, he began to resent her, then to criticize her privately, and finally came to dislike her for
being no better than the village women; moreover, he wanted to make her
admit she had deceived him, and he let her know she had betrayed him by
pushing away her hand when she reached out to caress his face or make
some other gesture of love.

Hurt and confused by her son's sudden rejection, she spoke to Compson
about it. "I don't understand what's come over Arthur," she said. "I don't
do things different than before."

"He's not a child any more, Syl. He's almost fourteen. Practically a
man. I joined the regiment when I was fifteen and thought of myself as a
man."

"Arthur's not like you."

"You're wrong. He's as much like me as he's like you." They were in
bed, carrying on a whispered conversation, and, as always, her husband's
right hand moved beneath Sylvia's nightgown, touching her breasts, belly,
genitals and thighs; and though Sylvia remained unaware of it, she had
become so habituated to being stroked like a cat that it took her much
longer to fall asleep when, for some reason, Compson failed to reach out
to raise her gown and caress her with the rough-skinned hand she had
licensed to venture wherever it pleased. It was as though the hand tracing
her body was applying the glue that bonded them together. While Sylvia
knew of Compson's carrying-on with village women—she was neither
deaf, blind nor a fool—nonetheless she didn't believe, deep in her heart,

that he had ever stroked a village woman as he caressed her when they lay together in their dark bedroom. Thus, when Compson told Sylvia that he'd become a man by age fifteen, she took him to mean that fifteen was the age at which he had begun going after women, perhaps thinking that becoming a soldier had given him that right. And oddly enough, Sylvia did not object to Arthur transferring indoctrinated military protocols to his civilian life, because regardless of how people talked about the armed forces in peacetime, she had come to believe that soldiers existed to kill, then to gather the spoils of victory by taking their enemies' women. When her son began reading the Bible, she often leaned over his shoulder and been shocked to read accounts of wars in which entire armies and cities were destroyed, kings were hanged on trees and women and children mercilessly killed. When she compared the behaviour of Biblical warriors with her ex-soldier husband's dilly-dallying with village women, the latter seemed almost harmless.

"I wish you hadn't sent Arthur to Dot Perks," she said.

"I thought it'd quiet his spells if he got rid of his spunk."

"It turned him against me."

"He'll come back."

"It hurts when he pushes my hand away." She began to cry. "I feel as if a knife's going through my heart."

"I'll speak to him."

"No, no. He mustn't know he's hurting me."

"Nonsense." His fingers moved through her pubic hair, up over the little rolls of belly fat to probe and tickle her navel. "He must respect you." Army service had inculcated respect in Compson for men senior to him, and he couldn't imagine a relationship not based on it. He expected Sylvia to respect him and expected their son—though he was marred for life with his strange illness—to respect Sylvia and himself. He moved his hand up to follow the lines of her breasts.

"Please don't say anything. Promise me?" She felt him nod and gratefully pressed his hand over her heart at the place where she often experienced palpitations, which she attributed to a childhood bout of rheumatic fever that, according to her parents, had left her with a slightly enlarged, weakened heart.

"It's still beating, Syl," he said, then added. "I've watched men die. The first time it happened I thought it was wrong they died and I went on living, but when I got shot in the leg, I was glad to be alive. And if I was dead, I wouldn't have met you. In Palestine, I saw other men go under and that told me there had to be a reason I stayed alive. Like that bastard I served under. *He* thought we stayed alive only so long as destiny had a use for us."

"Did you hate him?"

"I was scared of him. And in a way I'm scared of our boy, too, because he'll do things in life I'll never be able to." He moved closer, and Sylvia raised her hips to provide him with easy entrance, and though Compson thought he had fucked every drop of spunk out of his testicles earlier in the day, he was able to vigorously thrust another dollop into Sylvia, who sighed with mingled pleasure and regret, having long ago given up hope she would conceive another child. She then waited for him to retreat, rolled onto her side and fell asleep.

Chapter

3

ARTHUR BECAME OBSESSED WITH DISCOVERING WHAT WAS hidden beneath the jumpers and long skirts his mother habitually wore. He wanted her to be different than Dot Perks; he found it almost impossible to look at her and think that parts of her body resembled the dressmaker's. Endless imagining tortured him. He wanted to think of his mother with pure white, unbroken skin, like a statue, while he, her son, had emerged as a chick from an egg or, as his father told him, had been found sleeping under a cabbage leaf. He was prepared to believe anything rather than accept that what he did with Dot Perks was duplicated by his father with his mother, because that in turn meant his mother resembled Dot Perks.

The dressmaker wasn't above maliciously gossiping about other village women after Arthur had completed his spell-prevention exercises, though she was careful not to say anything about Sylvia. According to Dot Perks, everybody knew the doctor's wife carried on with other men and her daughter wasn't much better. Oh yes, she'd been told Heather Robertson had been packed off somewhere because he had more in her tummy than liver and lights. Well, it proved cod was cod, no matter how you sauced it up, and when the fancy knickers came off, you couldn't tell a queen from her scullery maids. Oh yes, women would try to deceive themselves, but when it came right down to brass tacks, they all wanted what Dot Perks was giving Arthur dirt cheap as a favour to his father.

Arthur hated her for saying these things and despised himself for being unable to stay away, and worse, for having evil thoughts about his own mother. He began following Sylvia around the house, trying to observe her during moments when she was unaware she was being watched. But even though he crept around in stocking feet, she always seemed to know he was following her and would turn to smile. "Ah, there you are, dear," she would say. "Why're you carrying your boots? Are they muddy? Well, scrape them off outside. Oh, that horrible, horrible blue mud!" Sylvia was required to spend time each day removing the effects of the layer of blue clay on which the village sat. When damp, it seemed to move of its own volition onto boots, and when dry, turned to dust which drifted through window frames to settle on furniture and porcelain plates sitting in cupboards.

"Where did you walk this afternoon, dear?" she might say, then leave the sitting room, return to the kitchen, open the oven door and peer at a sizzling roast, while Arthur followed and watched her, tortured by the suspicion that his mother's air of quiet authority was a mask which hid a woman physically identical in every detail to Dot Perks. "If you've nothing better to do, peel the potatoes. Don't stand there looking at me. I've done nothing to offend you, have I?" But Arthur was incapable of answering the question because he no longer saw Sylvia as his perfect, always available mother. Part of him wanted to express love, but even as the words formed in his mind, he saw an image of himself between Dot Perks' thighs. He turned deathly pale and remained mute.

"Are you all right, darling? Tell Mother you're all right."

"Yes, I'm fine."

"You sure? You're so pale."

"It's nothing," he mumbled, remembering how he'd gone to the earth closet that morning and before sitting over the hole had looked down into the pit, wondering if something his mother had left there would provide a clue to her physical identity. In his toddler years, Sylvia had toilet-trained him by demonstrating how to sit over the hole and grunt, then she supported him while he fruitlessly tried to imitate her.

In the evening, when he climbed the narrow stairway to the bedrooms, he refused to look into his parents' room because seeing the bed reminded him of what he did on Dot Perks' bed. Imagining his mother sprawled out on his parents' bed made him sweat with terror, while at the same time aroused in him sensations similar to those he experienced when Dot Perks crooked her finger and said, "Come on, 'andsome, get to it."

One morning, after he'd been to the paddock for his usual chat with Mary, he returned to an empty kitchen and assuming his mother was paying her post-prandial visit to the earth closet, he went upstairs to get his copy of *Bleak House*, the novel he was currently reading. The year before, Arthur had decided to work his way through the classics, and each week walked to the Ponnewton library and took out as many books as he could comfortably carry home. (This week he was reading Dickens.) His bedroom door was open, and as he entered the room he saw his mother leaning over his bed, straightening a sheet. The sight of her protruding hips inflamed him, shattering all reason and self-control. He sprang forward, knocked Sylvia onto the bed, pushed up her skirts to tug at her pink underwear, tearing it and exposing part of her bottom. After letting out a shriek of surprise and terror, Sylvia kicked at him, hitting his testicles. He recoiled and fell away from her to lie at the end of the bed, clutching himself, trying to contain and quell the pain that filled his groin. Arthur heard her whisper: "What do you think you're doing?"

Understanding that any answer he gave would not make any sense to Sylvia, he finally said, "I . . . I thought . . . you were different."

"Different? Different from what?"

"From others."

"What others?" Her voice had never been so cold. She repeated: "What others?"

"Women . . ."

"What women?"

"You know."

"No, I don't know. So tell me—what women?"

He tried to avoid answering. "You hurt me."

"You deserve to be hurt," she said, then repeated her question. She waited, and when he didn't answer, she said, "I'm your mother. I'm made like other mothers . . . like other women."

"No!" he shouted. "No!"

"Yes. I'm made just like that slut Dot Perks."

"No!" he screamed. "No!"

"Yes. Is *that* why you've been following me around? Well, is it?" She got off the bed, lifted her skirts and pulled down her torn underwear. "Look. There's no difference." He pressed his face into the bed covers and refused to look. "The difference between me and that slut and Belinda Robertson, who thinks she's a cut above the rest of us, is that I have some self-respect. I've never cheapened myself by running after the first man who winked at me. And I never thought I'd have a son I couldn't trust." She lowered her skirts. "Heaven knows what your father'll say when he hears about this."

"Don't tell him. Please, Mother. Please."

She ignored his pleas and continued her jumbled complaint. "It's all happened because of your father's crazy notion that having you work off your . . . well, your energy . . . would calm your spells. Of course, he did it because he loves you. Oh yes, he really loves you as much as I do, so I'm not saying his intention wasn't good, but you're too young to be doing something like that. I told him we ought to encourage you to have a friend, a nice girl you could walk with on Sunday afternoons . . . hold hands . . . gradually do things . . . exchange kisses . . . the things girls like doing. But no, he must have his own way and foist you onto that slut! I could have guessed what would happen." On and on she went, spilling out reproaches and beyond those, her underlying resentment against her husband and her jealousy of Dot Perks. How dare that cheap whore benefit from everything she had done for Arthur from the moment of his conception! She had suckled him beyond the time mothers usually breast feed their babies, she'd bathed and dressed him in clothes she'd patiently stitched until her eyes ached, she'd suffered anguish when he had a spell, and now she was faced with a son who had tried to rape her because going with a cheap whore had made it impossible for him to distinguish right from wrong. Of course, Arthur knew she was deliberately magnifying his offence. She wanted him to weep and turn away his head so she couldn't see the shame that blanketed his face. But he continued to stare at her as though he could not believe she existed. It unsettled her so much she had to leave the room.

He got up to stand at the window. Mary was at her usual place at the paddock gate, waiting for him. He saw a rabbit enter the garden, squeezing itself under the wire netting and watched it hop toward a cabbage and begin to nibble it. The rabbit was fully grown and could be used in the rabbit stew Arthur loved so much, with potatoes, carrots, onions and smooth gravy. The door re-opened, and Sylvia entered the room to stand beside him at the window. "There's a rabbit in your cabbages," he said.

"Oh, drat it! Did you see how it got in?"

He pointed and said, "By that clump of grass."

"I'll tell your father to set a snare."

"We could catch it if we stood in front of the hole."

"You think we could?"

"We'd have to run across the garden before the rabbit got there."

"Well . . ."

"We could try." Arthur desperately wanted to do something to normalize their relationship.

"All right. We'll have to be very quiet."

They went downstairs to the kitchen and looked through the window at the rabbit sitting in the garden sat with its back to them, nibbling a cabbage leaf, ears twitching to pick up any threatening sound.

Sylvia leaned against Arthur to whisper, "Cheeky rabbit! Coming into our garden as if he owns it."

"Shush," Arthur cautioned as the rabbit's ears moved. "Shush." Their faces were very close.

She turned her head and kissed him, then whispered, "Forgiven and forgotten," and he returned the kiss with the words, "I love you."

They crept to the back door where Arthur picked up a heavy hawthorn stick, carefully opened the door, quietly made his way to the garden gate and opened it. He then nodded at Sylvia, who ran diagonally across the garden while the rabbit bolted away, hit the wire netting at the end of the garden and careened from end to end, chased by Arthur swinging the stick without once hitting the rabbit, which suddenly turned and ran straight for Sylvia, who stared at it, eyes and mouth wide, before she drew back her right leg and kicked it. They heard a thud, the rabbit squealed, rolled over and lay quivering at Arthur's feet.

"Oh . . ." Sylvia gasped. "Is it hurt?"

Arthur lifted it by its hind legs. "I think so." Then, as he'd seen his father do many times, he struck its neck to sever the spine.

Sylvia stared at the dead rabbit. "I've never killed anything in my whole life."

"Except flies and wasps."

"They don't count," she said.

Arthur looked down at the rabbit's hairless belly and saw fluid dribbling from a tiny nipple. "It's a female," he said.

"How can you tell?" He pointed to the moisture and, after frowning and biting her lip, Sylvia said, "I won't have it in my house. Bury it. And fix the fence." She walked past Arthur, head averted and went into the kitchen.

Arthur fetched a spade from the shed, buried the rabbit, then cut a notched stick to pin down the netting. Afterwards, he went to the paddock gate and told Mary about the misunderstanding with his mother in the bedroom and about her reaction to having killed a mother rabbit. As always, Mary understood everything and proffered sympathy by rubbing her nose against his face.

For a while, Arthur was hopeful that the close relationship between him and his mother had returned, but then he began to notice the absence of endearments and touches, little gestures of affection he'd always taken for granted, and their disappearance ate into the way he felt about himself. Whenever he entered the kitchen and saw his mother sitting at the table drinking her mid-afternoon cup of tea, the melancholy droop of her shoulders and the sadness in her face generated such feelings of guilt in him that he felt he should kneel before her and beg forgiveness. But this did not happen; the most Arthur ever did was stand on the other side of the table and stare at her mutely, or else utter a commonplace about the weather. He slowly fumbled his way into the realization that a catastrophe, whether in the natural world or in human relationships, cannot be corrected by minimal actions or tepid gestures, and after a while he came to understand (vaguely) that the only way to eliminate one catastrophe would be to replace it with another. He considered suicide, and though the peacefulness of death appealed to him, especially during the recovery periods after his spells, he realized that to die would be self-defeating since he would neither know if his sacrifice were successful, nor be around to enjoy the restoration of the relationship with his mother. (Had Sylvia appreciated the degree of her son's physical and emotional trauma, she might have knocked down the wall of reserve she had erected around herself and reached out to succour him, but being a woman of average emotional and intellectual capacity, she was incapable of understanding the lengths to which Arthur would go in castigating himself for his behaviour.)

In addition to contemplating death, he sharpened a special knife to castrate himself, though in the end he was unable to make the cut. He did, however, for a short period, go into a dark place in one of the forest enclosures and beat his recalcitrant loins with a lash made from birch twigs. He stopped doing this only when Sylvia asked if the blood on his bed sheets and underpants was evidence of hemorrhoids. He had also discovered that while beating himself might temporarily force self-detestation into retreat, the feeling rebounded with even greater vigour when the beating ceased. In the end, he found that he could do nothing but continue to wander around his limited world, enclosed in misery. He had no one on whom to drape the adoration he formerly bestowed on his mother, who had closed all her emotional doors, and even Heather Robertson was no longer available, for she had stopped coming for riding lessons. That left only Mary, though Arthur, in the throes of adolescence, had come to realize that Mary's devotion to him was directly proportional to the quantities of oats and hay he fed her. He continued his visits to Dot Perks once or twice a week and invariably left hating his body's need that drove him there. Sensing the way he felt, the dressmaker would say: "Yer needs a real girl. Yer don't want me no more. What yer wants is a girl, like that Heather, the doctor's daughter. She ain't been 'round fer a while. A real, strapping girl. 'Er mum used ter 'ave me let out 'er frocks. Yer don't know where she is, eh?"

And Arthur, lying on Dot Perks's bed afterwards, responded that all he knew was that Heather didn't come to the paddock any more and the knacker had collected her pony.

"One thing I knows about 'er," the dressmaker said. "'Er couldn't stand 'er mother. Ooh, them two was like two she-cats squabbling over a Tom. Yer wouldn't think a mum and her girl could 'ate each other like they did. Mind yer, under 'er frock 'er was a real strappin' girl. Big enough ter do things. Yer know, like yer, when yer first come 'ere." Dot Perks' heavy breasts and belly vibrated as she laughed. "Remember me fittin' a glove over yer finger?"

Arthur felt like slapping her, quickly dressing and leaving, but he remained on the bed and refuelled his self-detestation by listening to more gossip. He knew other men with a few shillings to spare made use of the dressmaker, but he couldn't bring himself to ask how she rated him compared to other men, though the unspoken question was on his lips whenever he lay with her. He compared her to a Biblical whore, for surely, the seventeen-year-old Arthur thought, Dot Perks had to be something more than a war widow prostituting herself to make ends meet, so he transformed her into a Biblical harlot: she was like Rahab of Jericho, who hid Joshua's spies with stalks of flax on the roof of her house before lowering them to the ground by means of a scarlet cord in exchange for a promise not to harm her family ("Thou shalt bind this line of scarlet thread in the window which thou didst let us down by . . . and she sent them away, and they departed: and she bound the scarlet line in the window"). It was not sufficient that Dot Perks simply stripped and allowed men to wallow and lurch upon her—there had to be more than that, for surely no woman would willingly suffer such physical degradation unless she believed her sacrifice was necessary to redeem her husband's dead soul.

At the time, the notion of living people unconsciously sacrificing themselves for dead ones was so nebulous that Arthur, being immature, dismissed it, and it wasn't until more years had passed that it finally crystallized in his mind as a possible explanation for certain human behaviour and henceforth became a common theme in his work. But then he was too young and too wrapped up in his own pain to stand back and attain the objectivity necessary to cope with so problematic a theme. What he had wanted was a quick solution to the problem of his own health and the restoration of his relationship with Sylvia; he wanted his afflictions, physical and emotional, to go away forever. And the fact that Dot Perks complemented him on his good looks didn't help, he still hated himself. Whenever she told him he was handsome, Arthur would screw up his features and tell her to shut up, but he was always careful to agree when she said: "Yer may not believe it, but I use ter be real pretty meself."

He wondered why she had not had children. "I tried with Bert 'fore 'e went off and got 'isself killed. But I ain't never got in the family way, so there 'as ter be summat wrong with me insides."

"My mother was only able to have me," he told her.

"It 'as summat ter do with the war. Women ain't goin' ter 'ave kids with all that killin' goin' on. They thinks as there'll be another war in twenty years' time, so the kids they 'ad in one 'll be called up and killed in another, and that makes their insides shrivel."

"You really believe that?"

"Yer bet I do. Yer goin' ter fuck again? If yer ain't, I'll get back to me sewin'. Yer want me lyin' on me tummy for a change?"

While kneeling and pummelling at her immense, soft buttocks, Arthur resurrected the image of himself in limbo that day among the trees as he watched a man he believed was his father thrust himself against a girl he believed was Heather Robertson. And it was true, as Dot Perks said, that Heather's disappearance from the village mystified everyone. Explanations for it ranged from her going to live with relatives in America to having been murdered and buried in the forest. Sylvia claimed Heather was attending an expensive finishing school in Switzerland. "Belinda's out to marry Heather well," she said whenever Heather's name came up. "Heather wouldn't stand a chance if she was left unfinished." She appealed to her husband. "She was so gauche, don't you agree, Arthur?" who shrugged and said, "No worse than any girl her age."

"Mark my words, one of these days we'll see an announcement in the paper that she's engaged to some high-and-mighty. Mark my words. How old is Heather now? Arthur's almost seventeen, so Heather's twenty. It wouldn't surprise me if Belinda doesn't try to get her presented at court."

"You can't blame her for wanting to push her daughter ahead."

"I'm not blaming her. I'm just saying, she's the kind of mother who'd do practically anything to get her daughter married to a man who'll inherit a title."

"What do you think happened to Heather, Dad?" It was a daring question for Arthur to ask.

"Don't know. She never said anything to me about leaving home. I doubt she knew what she was doing. I mean, if I'd known what I was doing when I was fifteen, or whatever age Heather was, I doubt whether I'd 've enlisted."

"I thought you always wanted to be a soldier."

"No. I was raised with horses. So the cavalry was an easy out for me;

but if I'd known I'd have bullets shot through my legs and my Sammy riddled with machine gun fire, I would've run t'other way. You should've seen my Sammy, son, he was a first-class jumper. If they'd've allowed it, I'd have entered Sammy in the Grand National. He'd have cleared Beecher's Brook with no trouble, but the captain wouldn't let me risk a broken leg. So, where did he end up? In France, lying in a field, with a bellyful of German machine-gun bullets, and me beside him. I put a bullet through his head to stop his pain. I cried over that."

"I don't think we should talk about the war," Sylvia said. "I thought we were talking about Heather."

"A passing comment," his father said.

Not long after that exchange, Arthur introduced the subject of his father's army service while he and his father were preparing the garden for Sylvia to plant vegetables and, as his father slyly remarked, to fatten the rabbits.

"Best forgotten," his father said. "If you don't, you end cursing yourself for being foolish enough to risk getting killed for a bunch of—" And there Compson stopped and went back to spading the soil, but Arthur knew what his father had been about to say because, coming from the working class, Compson had no inhibitions about letting other people know that he had no time for the upper classes. Social pretensions in the Compson family were all on Sylvia's side. She always made sure her son never used the local dialect and had pressured Compson into speaking correct English in the company of her son. She was not going to let people discriminate against her family on the basis of speech. That was one reason she had encouraged Arthur to read the Bible. "You can't go wrong if you speak like the Bible," she told him, and became irritated when he pointed out that many county dialects were liberally sprinkled with *thou's* and *thee's*. "That's different," she said. Every once in a while, Arthur teased his mother by dropping his aiches and saying "yer" instead of "you" and he rather enjoyed watching her face redden and hearing her angrily order him never, ever to speak like village boys. But the crudities of the local dialect were stored in Arthur's mind, as were the configurations of the dressmaker's body, although until he began writing novels, he had never contemplated using the information and, then, everything he'd seen and heard in the village seemed to flow directly from his memory to his pen and, later, to the keys of his typewriter as naturally as water coursing down a hillside. (He actually wrote an entire novel in village dialect, but discarded the prose as turgid.)

The catastrophe that Arthur had vaguely envisioned as a means of repairing his relationship with his mother actually arrived. His father died.

Compson failed to come home from work one evening, and after Sylvia and Arthur had gone outside, repeatedly called his name and conducted a rudimentary search, a team of village men combed Asty and within an hour discovered Compson beneath a chestnut tree hidden in a plantation of Norwegian spruce. He was lying face down, coat off, britches around his knees, Jack hitched to a nearby tree. The official story was that he had gone into the plantation to empty his bowels and died of a stroke, but the tale circulating the village was that he had met a woman there, and died while fucking her. The woman, they said, had panicked, leaving him alone to die. The rumour never reached Sylvia, but Arthur heard it from Dot Perks, and while he angrily refuted it, he privately thought it was true.

He walked behind the coffin to the small village graveyard adjacent to the church. One of the two curates who conducted biweekly services in the church read the service and the final prayer at the graveside. Arthur threw a handful of dirt into the grave (Sylvia was too distraught) then watched as the two men who functioned as grave diggers, shovelled gravel, clay and soil back into the grave. Mother and son waited until the final shovel of soil had been added to the mound, then placed a wreath of arum lilies on it. Clasping hands, they walked back through the village to their home.

Two weeks passed before a clerk from the forestry commission office came to the house, and after expressing the commission's condolences, went on to explain, as Sylvia no doubt understood, that the house would now be needed for another forester. "Yes, yes, of course," Sylvia agreed. But it was clear she didn't grasp the implications of the clerk's request, though the realization came immediately after he departed and she was left to sit, trembling, at the kitchen table, while Arthur boiled water to brew a pot of tea. Then she cried out, "What will we do? Where will we go? What will we live on?"

Arthur Compson, the former calvary sergeant, had not earned much more than the labourers to whom he meted out wages each Saturday, but since the house he lived in was rent-free, his wages together with his army pension enabled Compson to provide for his family. But nothing had been put aside, because Compson never thought beyond the next pay day; and Sylvia, disposed to let Compson take care of money matters, resolutely denied any possibility of bad times ahead. The result was that Sylvia had barely enough money to purchase a coffin for her dead husband, to pay the two men to dig and refill the grave and to provide a gratuity for the curate to read the burial service. That emptied her purse. So, added to the genuine sorrow she felt for losing the man she loved, was the uncertainty of where she and her son would live and how they would get money to live on. Her parents had been dead for years, and everything had gone to her elder brother, whom she would never, never approach for help, nor would she ever accuse her husband of being improvident, or even let anyone think it. Oh, no. Her husband had been a good provider and a temperate man who never drank more than a half pint of beer, nor smoked more than two Woodbines in the evening to get his bowels working. She clutched at Arthur's hand when he bravely announced she mustn't worry and that he would find money for them to live on, though it was clear Sylvia took little comfort in his words, because she kept saying: "What will we do? Where will we go? What will we live on?", hanging onto his hand when he left his chair to stand beside her. Arthur could feel his mother's body trembling, but could think of nothing to say or do to reassure her, except to pat and stroke her head and shoulders now draped with a black shawl to signify her status as a widow.

"Your father was a good man," she said. "A good, hard-working man. I know people gossiped and said things that mostly weren't true, but he did everything he could to be faithful to me. I know that, Arthur, because a wife can always tell when a man's going after other women. She always knows. But I could tell how he felt about me."

Arthur, who did not want his mother to reveal intimate details of her relationship with his father, and who feared she might resort to lying in order to exonerate herself and clear his father's name, tried to shut out the sound of her voice, but it filtered through the barrier he erected and every word she uttered was recorded in his memory.

"I knew how he felt by the way he touched me. There was never a single night he didn't caress me and let me know he'd not changed toward me. And I always welcomed him. You're old enough now to know what that means, aren't you, Arthur? I needn't feel embarrassed telling you that, need I? Mother talked about it being a wife's duty, something a wife suffered, but I didn't feel that way about your father. And our last night together, I welcomed him. I lifted myself up to him. Oh, what'll I do? What'll I do?"

Fortunately Arthur did not have to reply because Sylvia continued to talk: "If Mother could see me now, she'd say I told you so, though if Mother and Father were alive, I'd never ask them for a penny. Never. Even if I was starving. Don't forget, Arthur, your father was a finer man than my father, much, much finer. Mother only said those things because she didn't have a husband who caressed her and made her feel worth having. Promise me when you marry—I'm sure you will, one day—promise me you'll let your wife know how important she is to you." Arthur, aware that the second catastrophe in Sylvia's life had wiped out her memory of the first, agreed that once he had acquired a wife he would pass on the traditions established by his father. It was simple enough for Arthur to say this, because he knew, even at that age, how easily promises are broken.

Sylvia couldn't stop talking about her marriage, and Arthur observed that the more his mother talked, the more she altered his father and herself, until it came to a point where they bore almost no resemblance to the parents he had known. His father became highly intelligent—Arthur inherited his father's brains *and* his good looks—and he would certainly have been a general had he elected to remain in the army. Sylvia herself became even more modest and respectable, though always a highly responsive wife who welcomed her husband into her arms despite his occasional infidelities, which she forgave him. Furthermore, her husband's marital derelictions weren't his fault, but were caused by loose women like Belinda Robertson—oh yes, she knew all about Belinda—who gave him no peace until he . . . well . . . until he gave them what they wanted. They were shameless creatures who—Sylvia blushed to hear herself say it—took off their knickers for any man and flaunted what young women in *her* day had been taught to conceal before marriage, and dole out parsimoniously after it.

Sylvia's narrative continued as Arthur haphazardly prepared for the day on which they must vacate the house. Sylvia ignored the deadline, preoccupied with recreating and reliving the first moments she and Compson had met. Fate had brought them to the tram stop, she told Arthur. Sylvia would never know that Sergeant Compson, up for re-posting in a few days, intended to spend his battle-earned money on a prostitute, but spotting Sylvia Wiley at the tram stop, decided to save his money and go after her. He had reconnoitred the Tambourne municipal park earlier in the day and knew it could be a simple matter to "ground" her in the darkness, behind some convenient bushes. The sergeant was a relentless pursuer of women, and in the first moments after he followed Sylvia from the tram and spoke to her averted face, it seemed as though he were speaking to his fresh-faced sister. But she would have none of going to the park with Compson, though she had fallen in love with him instantly and, after learning he had only three more days of leave, forced him to accompany her to the hospital chapel, where, unbeknownst to her parents, they were married. Compson then rented a room in a cheap hotel where he spent the next twenty-four hours energetically copulating with his inexperienced bride.

Two days later, after waving her husband back off to war, Sylvia returned home to face her table-pounding father and accusative mother. She held up her marriage certificate to prove she hadn't wasted her maidenhead on a lowly private, but it didn't help. "A sergeant!" her father bellowed. "A sergeant! Couldn't you find a captain or a major?" Sylvia's mother was no more supportive: "Suppose you've become pregnant? Suppose he's killed?" Sylvia substituted romance and hope for unbearable truths, and it was no wonder she continued to modify the truth after her husband's death. She thought she could hear her father shouting at her: "You idiot! What're going to live on? Eh? Eh?"

Sylvia now spoke to Arthur as if he were no longer her adolescent son, but a grown man, and while Arthur packed dishes into boxes, she sighed and spoke of her longing to have another child, preferably a girl. "Would you love her, Arthur?" she asked, and he agreed that of course he would love any child she bore. His mother's meandering was beginning to frighten him; it was as though she was in the processing of divorcing herself from reality while she sat and watched him ineffectually trying to organize their belongings. She even sat on the bed and talked while he packed his father's clothes and only returned to the present when Arthur spoke of giving them away. "How dare you think of giving away your father's waistcoat? How dare you speak of a village labourer soiling your father's coat? You should feel proud to wear his clothes!" She had then ordered Arthur to remove his pullover and put on his father's braided waistcoat and riding jacket. "There!" she said. "You look just like him!"

Finally the morning arrived when two village men arrived with a truck to load and transport their belongings to a small three-roomed cottage which Arthur called "the hovel," located along the village lane three cottages away from *The Old Oak,* the local beer house. The cottage was cramped and damp with a fire grid that held no more than five coals and a small oven that was either red hot or stone cold. The last occupant had slit his wife's throat, used her blood to write a note saying he couldn't bear life any longer, then hanged himself. Arthur never knew what rent his mother paid for the cottage; he only knew it was owned by the publican at *The Old Oak,* who appeared every Saturday morning to sit at the kitchen table and look at his mother as though he wanted to eat her. "You don't have to stay, Arthur," Sylvia would say. "Mr. Smithson and I have business to attend to." But how, Arthur wondered, was his mother going to pay the rent when they were almost penniless? Much later, he decided that his mother had paid by opening her legs and allowing the publican a glimpse of what lay between them. After all, it was well known that women in desperate circumstances will resort to any expediency in order to house and feed their families, so why would his mother be an exception? Smithson may have even paid extra for his mother to do more, for Arthur had noticed Sylvia always seemed to have a shilling or florin among the pennies and farthings in her purse. But Arthur, with his vivid imagination and ability to attribute all manner of thoughts and feelings to people, couldn't quite bring himself to the point of contemplating that his own mother prostituted herself— that was going too far.

Years later, however, he imagined a scene between his mother and Smithson sitting across from each other at the kitchen table, with Smithson saying, "Listen 'ere, Missus Sylv'a. Yer 'usband uster fuck my woman, so why shouldn't I 'ave a piece of yer, eh? I'll let yer 'ave this place cheap and give yer a couple of bob as well. 'Ow's that fer a deal?" He imagined his mother, brought face-to-face with penury, responding: "All right. Five minutes, five shillings and free rent," then, during the embrace, mumbling acts of contrition like a devout Catholic clicking rosary beads: "I'm doing this for Arthur, this is for Arthur. I'm doing this for Arthur, for Arthur," as she watched the long hand of the clock slowly tick the minutes off. In the end, in an attempt to uproot the endless round of speculation that circled around in his head, Arthur worked Sylvia's widowed circumstances into a novel, published the year after her death.

The idea of writing had come to Arthur one day while out walking, feeling thoroughly miserable about their poverty-stricken life and what he thought of as his mother's "decline." He happened to see sheets from the Ponnewton weekly newspaper blowing along the village lane, so he ran and picked one up, read a few articles and an editorial and decided he could produce articles equal, if not superior, to those he had read. He would write articles, maybe stories, about the forest, its moors, its bogs, its woodland and its people and, more to the point, he could try to get payment for them. Within days, he had composed two 500-word articles, the writing of which was easy. The more difficult and nerve-wracking part came when he entered the untidy newspaper office. During his walk into town, he had measured and timed his stride by repeating "Nothing ven-tured, nothing gain-ed," though drumming this refrain into his head hadn't prevented him from pausing before opening the office door and charging forward to meet his destiny, which presented itself in the form of a thick-bellied, grey-haired man sitting behind the counter, who raised his head from papers he was examining to say, "Yes?"

"You the publisher?" Arthur asked.

"I'm everything around here," the man said.

Arthur thrust out the articles. "Will you publish these?"

"Depends." The man took the sheets of paper from Arthur and read them with a rapidity that impressed Arthur. "You appear to know your subject."

"I should. I've lived in the forest all my life."

"You don't look like a greybeard to me. How old are you?"

"Old enough to write articles about the forest," Arthur replied.

"I could use an article or two as filler."

"How much will I be paid?"

"Paid! Now listen here, son—"

"Don't call me son. I'm not your son." Impelled by a picture of an anxious, worried Sylvia sitting at home, Arthur continued: "I won't work for nothing. Give them back."

"Hold your horses, young man. If you want to get ahead in this world, start listening to what other people have to say. These articles 'll be fine with a bit of editing. If you provide me with a weekly piece, I'll pay you fifteen bob each."

"Thirty."

"A pound, not a penny more."

Arthur knew by the sound of Bythe's voice that he would offer no more. "Agreed. A pound an article. You have two articles there, 500 words each, so you owe me two pounds." Arthur was surprised at himself; he hadn't thought he had it in him to bargain.

"What's your name?" Arthur provided it, and as the man wrote it down, Arthur realized his name would now appear in print. He was on the verge of becoming a published author. The man went into an inner office and returned with two pound-notes, and Arthur's hands trembled as he fingered them before shoving them into his jacket pocket. "One thing more. From now on, the articles must be typed and triple-spaced."

"I don't have a typewriter."

"For God's sake! How can you be a writer if you write everything out by hand like a school kid." He went into an adjacent room and came back carrying a black case, which he placed on the counter and opened to reveal a portable typewriter. "Good as new," he said. "Two shillings a week to lease."

"I can't. I need the money."

"Please yourself." He started to close the case, then stopped. "What about five shillings a month?"

"Four."

The man scrutinized Arthur, gestured and said, "Oh, for God's sake, take it and pay whatever you can. You'll need typing paper." He felt beneath the counter and came up with a thick wad of paper which he placed on the counter.

"Thanks," Arthur mumbled.

"Forget it." The man put the paper on top of the machine and closed the case. "Wednesday is layout. Your deadline is Tuesday."

"Thank you," Arthur said. He felt so grateful that after a momentary pause he added the word "sir."

"The name's Harry," the man said, "Harry Blythe, owner, publisher and managing editor of Ponnewton's one and only weekly. See you in two weeks' time, preferably Tuesday morning."

Arthur felt immensely blessed at having emerged from his cocoon of isolation to become a writer of newspaper articles who was actually going to be paid for his work. He strode along High Street, head arrogantly raised, wanting to shout out at anybody who passed that he was on the point of being launched into the ranks of such immortals as Swift, Dickens and Zola. He could hardly contain his joy and wanted to bellow: "Two pounds! Two pounds! I've earned two pounds!" He walked past the chemist's and on impulse went inside and purchased a small bottle of lavender water for Sylvia. He would have a pound a week! Think of it! A pound a week! It was almost too much to bear. He left town and marched along the highway, chanting: "A pound a week, never again will I be meek." He arrived home after six o'clock just as an anxious Sylvia, thinking he might have had a spell, was about to go out and look for him. When he laid the money on the kitchen table, she sat down, hid her face in her arms and began sobbing. "I told you I'd get us money," he boasted. "And I did."

She pulled Arthur down into her arms and feverishly smudged kisses over his face and head. "What I have done to you?" she whimpered, "what have I done?" He assured her that she had done everything for him and that he asked for nothing more in life than to be with her. "Oh, my God, oh my God!" she cried. Familiarity with his mother's and Dot Perks' little quirks had filled Arthur with the assured wisdom of a youth of seventeen, so he already knew (or thought he did) that women experienced random agonies unknown to men and, when beset by profound emotions, call upon

God to explain why they must dwell in such misery, much as dogs without warning raise their muzzles at night and howl. After a while, Sylvia calmed down, put the money away and made tea, and they sat together at the kitchen table to drink it and eat slices of bread and butter.

Arthur recounted how he had demanded a pound an article while Sylvia chorused: "How brave of you, darling." She began to speak as though Arthur were an adult, which flattered him. He couldn't get enough of his mother's admiration, and he strutted and preened himself before her. For a while, it almost seemed as if he were courting her.

They finished eating and Sylvia had washed up when Arthur remembered the bottle of lavender water. "Not since I was a girl. My darling! How did you know I adore lavender water? It's so ridiculous of me to behave like this." She sobbed as she opened the bottle and dabbed some on her dress in the vicinity of her heart. "There," she whispered, "that means you'll always be in my heart. Always."

"And you in mine," Arthur responded, but became uneasy when she raised his hand and kissed it.

"I'll have to repay you somehow," she said and looked at him as though she were seeing a different person. "You seem so mature. You've grown up." She laughed and sniffed the lavender water again. "It's quite intoxicating. Come here, darling." She held out her arms and Arthur entered them. "You're so like your father, except for the mustache." She outlined Arthur's upper lip. "I'm being silly. Do you think I'm being silly?" She parted her legs and he moved between them to lie against her. "When you were small, I'd lie with you on my breasts. It was so wonderful to have you there, your skin against mine, so wonderfully smooth. Now you're almost a man. You *are* a man. It's amazing. You don't know what will happen, or what is happening. It's all the feelings inside you when your husband holds you for the very first time and you're not sure what will happen. Oh, my darling, you're a man now, aren't you? Soon you'll hold a young woman in your arms. Your wife. Women want to be loved. Your father used to kiss my neck and under my chin. Then I'd lift myself up to him."

"You've told me."

"Have I?" She seemed dazed and unaware of where she was. "I suppose I did. That was when I thought I'd conceive again and have a little girl. I had dreams about her, bathing and dressing her—little girls are so beautiful. I'd see her in my mind's eye, skipping around in frilly dresses and lace-trimmed petticoats and panties." Arthur always became uncomfortable when his mother spoke of the daughter she had never borne. He wanted to destroy her romantic, unrealistic picture by telling her that her daughter's frilly dress would be smeared with blue clay and her lacy panties filled with stinking shit. "But how could a beautiful little girl live in a place like this?"

"I have," Arthur told her.

"But you're strong, like your father. Remember, he fought in Arabia and demolished railway tracks and bridges and rode camels and slept in the open desert." She stared vaguely at the typewriter case. "Where will you put that? You'll need somewhere to put it. How can you be a writer in this place? A writer should have a study where he can work. Did you say you'll get a pound every week? Every week?"

"Yes. And I'll try and get more."

"It's wonderful." Her hands feverishly moved over him. "I wish I had more to give you, to make you so strong you'd never have another spell again. You know, sometimes when I look at you, I feel I'm looking at your father. He was a strong man. Do you feel you're like him?" She focused on the typewriter case again. "I have to find a place where you can work."

"I can put the typewriter on the table, right here. That's why it's called a portable. You move it around."

"No, no. You must have a little room where you can work. Oh, I know. We'll take down your bed and put the table . . ." She pointed to a folded gate-legged table she had long ago purchased at a second-hand shop, claiming it was a genuine Sheraton. ". . . in your bedroom, with your father's chair. You can share my bed. There's absolutely nothing wrong with you sharing my bed. It wouldn't be the first time you've slept with me. And you'll have a real work room."

"I don't want . . ." he began, but Sylvia didn't hear him. She was intent on completing the furnishing of his workroom.

"I wish we had a little rug to keep your feet warm. Writers need floor coverings—Persian carpets—and walls lined with bookcases. Oh, I knew the minute you began reading before you were two years old . . ."

"I thought I was four."

"Oh no, it was just before your second birthday. I remember it clearly. I was making your birthday cake and putting the batter into the pan when you—you were sitting in your highchair—suddenly began reading "London Bridge is falling down" from your Mother Goose book. Hm-hm. I was so astonished I dropped a spoonful of batter onto the floor. Thank goodness it was a small spoonful, or it would've been a mess. Hm-hm." Her hand had settled on his right buttock. "You can wear your father's britches."

"I'd rather not."

"We'll need a picture for the wall. Oh, you'll need a lamp too. You can have the kitchen lamp, and we'll use the other one in here. If you're earning a pound a week, we'll have enough to buy paraffin for two lamps."

"Mother—," he began. He wanted to escape from her hands, from her projections of his future; and while he had no objection to wearing his father's waistcoats or the long, heavy riding coat, the cord britches were too intimate a part of his father for him even to consider putting on. And of course, he'd never wear his father's grey serge cap, never. His intention, when he could afford it, was to outfit himself in grey flannels, open-necked shirts and a tweed jacket, clothing similar to that worn by the sons of prosperous Ponnewton families. Of course, he hated those people with all the concentrated fury of a resentful, have-not adolescent, but that didn't prevent him from wanting to emulate them.

"We'll fix the room right now," his mother said, overriding his protests. "Now, now, remember least said, soonest mended." She went into the tiny, damp room where he slept and began taking apart his bed. "Bring in the Sheraton," she called, while Arthur stood at the kitchen table, chewing his lips, wondering if the dampness of the cottage and the dreariness of their daily lives had driven his mother mad. She appeared in the doorway carrying folded sheets and the three flannelette blankets he needed to keep warm at night. "Hurry, darling," she urged, "it's almost bedtime."

So what could Arthur do, except carry the table into his former bedroom, place his father's armchair at the table and put the typewriter on it? When his mother brought the lamp from the kitchen and put it on the table, even Arthur had to admit, if he ignored the iron bed frame, springs and worn mattress stacked against the wall, that the glowing lamplight and the stacked paper on the table had transformed the cold room into a quiet study where an inspired author could write a masterpiece. His mother clasped her hands like an excited schoolgirl. "There!" she cried. "It looks wonderful! I just know you'll write great stories in here. I feel it in my bones." She put an arm around his shoulders and hugged him. "You know, Arthur, for the first time," she solemnly said, "for the very first time, in my heart, I feel there is hope for us. We won't be trampled down and forgotten, will we? We'll do something with our lives. Do you feel that too, darling?"

What could he say? How could he disillusion the woman who had him reading the Bible before he had stopped shitting his nappies, who had vested all her emotions and beliefs in him, who, on the evidence of two short articles, was prepared to endow him with future fame and greatness?

And so Arthur, realizing his mother had surrendered her physical self to him, surrendered himself to her dream of their future together and that night dreamed he was in possession of a woman who resembled his mother. When he awakened in the morning, he discovered that his dream was a reality.

CHAPTER

4

NOTHING WAS SAID BY ARTHUR OR SYLVIA. THEIR DAYS AND
nights were divided by a wall of silence. During the day, Arthur continued
as Sylvia's writer-son; at night he was transformed into her husband-lover.
After some time had passed, Arthur concluded that the shock of his father's death, followed by his mother's descent into sordid, dreary poverty
had driven her into a kind of insanity that enabled her to pass as a sad,
courageous widow during the day and a lascivious mistress at night; and
while he understood that what he and Sylvia did was reprehensible, he
also knew that to reveal it would be unthinkable because public knowledge
of their relationship would damn him and crucify his mother.

He obsessively practised his typing skills and within a month was able
to rattle off his weekly articles without looking at the keys. He assembled
a month's supply at a time, and every Monday afternoon selected one,
checked it for typos and other errors, reworked it if necessary, delivered it
on the Tuesday and collected his pound note. He regarded the twelve-mile
walk to and from Ponnewton as a holiday, and before leaving town would
stroll along High Street to one of the shops and purchase a small gift (his
limit was two shillings) for his mother. His weekly walk through town
took him past a ladies' wear shop, and he regretted that he lacked the courage to enter and buy something for Sylvia—stockings or underthings—to
replace the frayed, faded garments she washed each day, then dried on a
clothesline strung above the oven. In such matters, his mother was ultra-
modest; she never pegged her personal garments on the clothesline with
their week's washing because she knew village boys made the round of
back gardens to point grubby fingers at the undergarments billowing in
the wind and to yell obscene comments about the girls and women who
wore them before aiming at each other's fly buttons and scampering off
like over-excited puppies. Still, when Arthur passed the shop each week,
he examined the window display and imagined himself going inside and
buying lingerie for his mother, so that when she removed the new, silken

undergarments that night, magically, she would be transformed from day-mother to night-mistress before joining him in bed. He thought new clothes for her would help, too, to still the voice inside that cried out as he moved over the bed to possess her: "From this I came. Can you blame me if I, the prodigal son, return?"

In the weeks and months following his acquisition of the typewriter, Arthur began composing what at first appeared to be nothing more than inconsequential dialogue and descriptions of village people. After a while, it dawned on him that he had begun to write stories, drawing on all he had observed in the village and its environs. It was fortunate for Arthur that Harry Blythe was receptive to running short fictional pieces, for as time passed, Arthur found himself developing the personalities of his fictional characters and directing them through a series of events toward a specific denouement. In short, Arthur had begun writing a novel, and one after-noon, on his way back from Ponnewton, he had a clear vision of its final pages. This rather frightened him because with it came realization of his youth and inexperience: How could someone like him, whose world was limited to a few square miles of the Ponnewton Royal Forest, successfully narrate a tale of mutual passion between a man and woman that ends in their deaths? The only passion he had personally experienced was his child-hood adoration of the doctor's daughter, and his only love what he felt for his mother. (What happened at night with Sylvia was as far from Arthur's daytime consciousness as the constellation of Andromeda was distanced from the Milky Way.) Though why, he asked himself as he neared home, would ideas for the novel have flooded so easily into his mind if he lacked the ability to formulate them into a complete work? In past ages, restricted environments had not prevented artists from imaginatively encompassing human emotions. The contrary: restriction acted as a stimulant. Why, even the greatest of all writers, Shakespeare, had not travelled further than the distance between London and Stratford, and William Blake in *Auguries of Innocence* had seen a universe in a grain of sand. And youth in and of itself was no handicap. Shelley, for instance, had written and published verse at about the same age Arthur was now. So, if Shelley could do it, why not Arthur Compson? No, there was nothing to prevent him from bringing the novel to a successful conclusion; all that was needed was the discipline to work his way through to the end, difficult and exacting as that might be, for as Arthur had discovered, writing was a painful process. The necessity of living through the experiences of his principal characters he found es-pecially agonizing, then having to type them out, letter by letter, word by word, sentence by sentence left him so drained of energy that it resulted in his having spells, which in turn magnified his exhaustion, so that Sylvia was compelled to deliver his stories for several weeks in order to collect that vital pound note which she then spent on tinned delicacies she claimed would strengthen him and fend off any more spells, though the net result of purchasing the luxurious foods was a substantial reduction in what was left for necessities.

"But darling," Sylvia said, when Arthur protested her extravagance, "I want you to get well. I don't care about myself."

"But I care about you!" he shouted. "Please don't do this again." Of course, Sylvia agreed not to spend any of the vital pound note, then forgot the promise the following week.

"Mr. Blythe is such a nice man," Sylvia told Arthur to divert his attention from the items she was removing from her shopping bag. "He worries about you. He thinks you shouldn't try to do too much. He thinks highly of your forest stories and feels badly he can't afford to pay us more—I mean, pay you more. I had quite a chat with him today. He's from Lancashire. Very well brought up, a real gentleman."

He groaned. "Mother, if you must spend the money, then get something for yourself. You go around in rags!"

She blushed. "Arthur, aren't you forgetting yourself? Really! Everything I do is only to help you." She slumped on a chair and began to cry.

He pushed himself up off his chair and went around the table to hold her and stroke her hair. "Mother, I can't bear that you give things up for me. I don't want this tinned stuff. I care about what happens to you, about the way you look, how you deprive yourself. It's not right for you to wear yourself out."

"Oh, but I'm not. I'm not. I assure you, I quite enjoy the walk and my little chat with Mr. Blythe. Did I tell you how highly he thinks of your work?"

"You did."

"He thinks you're a natural writer." Everything Sylvia said on these occasions confirmed Arthur's opinion that she now lived in a self-created world—an imaginary universe similar to what he, as a writer, might create, except her imagined world was quite real. The displacement frightened Arthur because he remembered the village woman who had one day inexplicably gone quite insane and walked the village lane exposing her genitals and buttocks to anyone she encountered until she was taken away to the county asylum. But that was years ago, when Arthur was still a child, in the days when Heather came to the paddock for a riding lessons in her smart jodhpurs and white shirt.

Sometimes Arthur wondered if the entire village population (himself included) wasn't insane. After all, he had read somewhere how tribes of people, due to deprivation of essential minerals, become deranged and danced wildly until they collapsed and died, or else slaughtered each other, leaving only a few to carry the tribe's genes into the future. To think that his mother might end up running through the village, skirts around her waist, pulling and pushing her faded underwear up and down, screaming, "What d'you think of this, eh?" knotted Arthur's belly, and he thought that he would suffocate his mother rather than allow her to become a spectacle for villagers to laugh at. He resolved, assuming he survived his present torment, he would write a novel in which a group of villagers deliberately drive a woman insane and use her as a scapegoat on whom to expiate their sins before stoning her to death.

"Don't scold me, Arthur," Sylvia would say. "I do my best." When Sylvia said such things, Arthur wanted to scream out the contradictions while knowing it would be pointless; and so he accepted (unwillingly) the way she squandered the pound notes and ate the food she brought home, even though it tasted of wormwood.

Finally he completed the novel, read it, changed words, wrote a short letter of submission, wrapped it in sheets of brown paper that Sylvia had pulled from between the mattress and springs of her bed (Sylvia said the paper was there to prevent floor damp from rising), cross-knotted string around the parcel, addressed it to *Tower & Tower Publishers* in London, then walked to Ponnewton and posted it.

The novel was a simple story (he was too young to handle anything complex) about a man and woman who, separated by class, cannot declare their love for one another until a situation beyond their control forces them to acknowledge it. The story takes place in 1913 when a new vicar arrives to take over a forest parish. He is middle-aged, his wife younger. They appear to be well-suited to each other; he energetically preaches to a bored congregation every Sunday morning, she attempts to infuse the interest of parishioners in the Women's Institute and to persuade village mothers to send their children to Sunday school. For exercise, she walks each afternoon, and during one such walk she encounters a forest labourer with whom she becomes involved, and for whose death she is eventually responsible. (Although Arthur was unaware of it, the man portrayed resembled his father.) At first, the labourer and the vicar's wife do not go beyond eye contact, followed by a polite "Good afternoon" from her and a lifting of his cap from him. Then the labourer disappears, and she learns he has been conscripted and is serving with the army in France.

A year passes, then one day she sees him at an enclosure gate. He wears an army uniform and is using crutches. He opens the gate, she passes through, and these simple gestures break down the reserve and class resistance which had heretofore prevented them from speaking. They end up in a plantation of young firs, where she strips away her clothes and on a bed of dry fir needles welcomes her lover into her innermost bastion with cries of joy. Each afternoon they meet and unite beneath the canopy of dark firs, and as they lie embraced, counting off the last days of his leave, he tells her of his intention to become a deserter. She is torn between the obligations of class (one brother has died in a naval battle, another serves as an army chaplain in France) and the passion she feels for her lover. Passion triumphs. He remains hidden in the fir plantation, and she brings food and whatever else he needs to establish a dry, safe camp. Military police come to the village looking for him. They call at the vicarage to question the vicar and his wife. Due to something the vicar's wife says, they decide to follow her and watch when, like a bird returning to its secret nest, she cautiously enters the fir plantation and embraces her lover. The military police brutally interrupt their love making and kill the deserter when he fails to halt on command. She, half-naked and screaming, runs to fall upon him, and when the military police finally drag her away, she stares blankly at them before running off into the forest. Her body is found a week later in a stream. It was a simple, melodramatic tale, but its intensity coupled with the neo-Biblical prose style, which Arthur had internalized through the years of poring over the Bible, made the novel effective and explains why, when he arrived home after delivering his latest story, he found a stranger sitting at the kitchen table, sipping tea and making polite conversation with his mother.

"Arthur!" his mother cried as he walked in. "It's about your novel."

The woman got up, stood by the chair and looked at him as though she couldn't quite believe he existed. "I'm Laura Dorchester, from *Tower & Tower*. I started to write you, then thought it would be an opportunity to get out of town, so I drove down from London to talk to you about your manuscript." Arthur, who didn't know how to respond, stood there looking at her, holding the bag with the pair of stockings which the shop clerk had assured him would fit his mother perfectly. "I will say at once that *Tower & Tower* will publish it. That's why I've come."

"Arthur usually has a cup of tea when he gets back from Ponnewton," Sylvia interjected. "And a slice of bread and butter. It's quite a walk. I'll make another pot." Sylvia bustled around like a broody hen, acting as if she hadn't a brain in her head. She ran to the back door, then rushed back to the fireplace, all the while jabbering incomprehensible sentences until Arthur said, "Forget the tea, Mother."

"But you always have a cup."

"Later, Mother. I'll have it later."

"I have no objection to waiting," Laura Dorchester said. Arthur glanced at her, then once more told his mother to defer making tea.

"Oh, well," Sylvia said. "Least said, soonest mended." He loved his mother, but knew there existed worlds she could never enter. Not only that, but he also indirectly understood that while Laura Dorchester's status in the literary world was assured by her position at *Tower & Tower,* he, by writing a novel, had also been admitted into that exclusive world. Later, when his relationship with Laura was firmly established, he decided that her acceptance of him into the literary world was demonstrated by her behaviour when he entered the room that day. While not obsequious, it was curiously deferential.

But things eventually settled down, and Arthur and Laura discussed Arthur's manuscript which she had brought with her. She turned the sheets over to indicate where she thought a word or phrase might be changed or deleted. (This was Arthur's first encounter with the word "delete.") She explained that while she personally—he must understand this—had no objections to his realistic descriptions of the lovers' passionate embraces, she thought a few modifications here, a few euphemisms there would take care of the problem she was sure many of his readers would have with his detailed depictions of love-making and other personal—well, actually in-timate—matters. Arthur was outraged that she could contemplate chang-ing a single word of his manuscript. Nonetheless, realizing it would be in his best interest, he agreed with Laura's suggestions, saying he would make the necessary revisions and return a final version to her as soon as possi-ble. She then moved to the matter of royalties and Arthur signed several documents, though later he cursed himself for not having read them more carefully. Finally, Laura Dorchester asked if he was resting or currently at work on another novel.

"Working," he muttered.

"Can you tell me about it?"

"I don't talk about anything I'm working on." At least he had enough sense to be cagy about his new novel.

"Not even to me," Sylvia chirped.

"It's not unusual," Laura Dorchester remarked, which angered Arthur because he wanted her to think he was unique. "Now, about an advance on sales."

It is possible that Arthur would have bargained with Laura Dorchester as he had with Harry Blythe, but the words "one hundred pounds" stopped him cold. "And another seventy-five for your new novel," she added. In a daze, Arthur nodded, then watched while she made out and signed a cheque and placed it in the middle of the kitchen table. She then got up and prepared to leave. She shook Sylvia's hand, then, escorted by Arthur walked along the lane to her car.

"It's so incredibly dark here," she said.

"Isn't darkness the same everywhere?"

"I've never seen such blackness as this. Living in a city makes you think there're degrees of darkness, or at least different shades. But you're quite right, darkness is the same no matter where you are." They halted at her car. "It's been a pleasure meeting you, Mr. Compson, a very great pleasure." He felt her hand being extended and grasped at it while saying he had enjoyed meeting her. "Can we use first names? Please call me Laura."

"I'd prefer that," Arthur said. "Being called Mr. Compson embarrasses me."

He was about to open the car door when she touched his arm and whispered, "Arthur, this is terribly awkward, but I really ought to have used the lavatory. It's the tea, you know."

"Go behind that privet bush. No one'll see you."

"Are you sure?" He waited by the trunk of her car and saw a white flash as she lowered her underclothes and squatted. "It's awful the way our bodies impose their wills on us," she said after returning. "Thank you for being so understanding." She squeezed his hand and got into the car, saying, "I look forward to receiving your revisions."

"Two weeks at the most," he said and watched the car move off. A car was an unusual sight in Hasterley because, apart from Dr. Robertson's Rover, the only other vehicles seen in the village were tradesmen's vans. There was nothing, absolutely nothing, of interest in Hasterley with its two rows of dreary, thatched-roofed cottages that might persuade people out for a Sunday drive to stop for a beer or cup of tea, which explained why the main street remained a combination of gravel and blue clay and why there wasn't even a single light standard to guide the motorist to *The Old Oak*. Arthur, having grown up in the village, liked the dark street and the dim lamplight that shone from small windows inset into the thick clay walls of the cottages. He confidently walked through the darkness and entered the kitchen where his mother sat at the table, staring at Laura Dorchester's cheque.

"I can't believe it! One hundred seventy-five pounds!" she said. "What'll we do with all this money?"

"We'll get out of this hovel, Mother. That's what we'll do. I'll have my cup of tea now, and three pieces of bread and butter."

"We'll be able to buy real butter now."

"You can get new clothes."

They spent the evening basking in the glorious security of having enough money to purchase things: he would buy a whole new outfit, she a frock and new shoes; but once the flurry of imaginary spending passed, they began temporizing: "We'll see how things go. Knowing we have the money when we need it is more important than spending it, isn't it?" Finally, they set the door latch, blew out the lamp and, bearing a candle holder, went to their bedroom where they undressed, got into bed and transformed themselves into a lover and his mistress.

"You love me?" she asked.

"Forever."

"Put out the candle."

"No. I want to look at you." While Sylvia lay with her eyes closed, Arthur pushed back the sheet and blankets and held the candle so that every part of her voluptuous body came into view. Everything Arthur did mirrored paragraphs from the novel he was presently writing. Indeed, everything that happened, his own sensations when he touched and kissed Sylvia's breasts before entering her, feeling his loins gathering momentum as he charged (so Arthur put it to himself) towards the finishing line, all this was recorded for future literary use as were his lover's facial expressions, the movements of her hips, her hand gestures, her pleasurable sighs as his column of flesh hammered her, the quickening heaves and moans she made as she ran the sexual course with him; he even recorded the quiet fart she released after she slumped with victory. Did Sylvia have any idea that her son was impersonally recording her reactions and stringing together words that described, oh so graphically, the different areas of her body at the same time comparing them to what he knew of Dot Perks' body, who, sadly, had died of ovarian cancer within months of being diagnosed? Probably not.

At the time of Dot Perks' demise, being profoundly ignorant of human physiology and the causes and symptoms of disease, Arthur had wondered if his own occasional constipation and stomach aches meant that she had passed her disease to him through his penis. Nor at the time did he know or want to know what caused his own illness, preferring to believe his affliction was the result of some spectacular once-in-a-lifetime event such as his mother being struck by an electronic arrow randomly fired across the universe, something similar to a favourite scene in his illustrated collection of Greek myths, the one of Jupiter splitting mountains with thunderbolts. After all, it was easier to attribute disease to an extra-terrestrial agent than it was to accept the fact that, instead of inheriting money and abundant acres from your progenitors, you receive nothing more than sundry genetic flaws? Besides, why should he have the slightest interest in the passage of food through his stomach, or in his heart pumping blood to his erratic brain, when an event of far greater significance had just happened: HIS FIRST NOVEL HAD BEEN ACCEPTED FOR PUBLICATION. *Dark Passion*—he'd wrestled with that title for weeks before finally deciding to use it—dealt solely with human emotions and had nothing whatsoever to do with what the characters ate, or the clothes they wore, their daily activities or aches and pains. No, for him, the determining factor in every life (except his own) was what people felt and the actions that flowed from their feelings; it seemed that he had always intuitively understood, even as a child, that while people may wish or seek to be governed by thought and reason, in the end, it is their emotions which determine the course their lives would follow.

Arthur went over Laura Dorchester's suggestions for manuscript changes, but refused to alter descriptions of his lovers' sexual encounters, arguing that substituting euphemisms would negate the intensity of the lovers' passion and reduce the man's desertion to cowardice and the woman's betrayal of her marriage vows to sexual opportunism. The furthest he was prepared to go was to remove certain phrases uttered by the man while making love, explaining in a note to Laura Dorchester that the words were common parlance among people in the village. He told her that his readers ought to realize that the language of the English working class was filled with words labelled obscenities by middle- and upper-class people, and that these words reflected the seething resentment of the "lower" classes for those who profited from their poverty. Furthermore, no one would be polite or smell sweet for long, if he or she lived in a village similar to the one described in *Dark Passion:* good manners, polite conversation and clean clothes required an assured income which was the last thing to be found in his village. These words were the first comments Arthur was to make on social disparities in England, a subject he returned to in all his novels, but at twenty-one, his remarks about social conditions were uttered solely in defence of his own work. Furthermore, his vision was limited to the Ponnewton Royal Forest, the village of Hasterley, the town of Ponnewton and, most importantly, circumscribed by his own imaginative powers. Arthur concluded the note to Laura with the following observation: It would be impossible to write truthful dialogue between working-class people without using the words: "shit," "piss," "prick," "arse'ole," "cunt" and "fuck."

The outcome of this correspondence was another visit from Laura Dorchester, who, during a walk through the Hasterley enclosure and across the heath to the clump of Scotch firs, told Arthur that, though she personally would prefer to publish verbatim what he had written, she was afraid his novel would be censored if the scenes were left as they were. Furthermore, she believed a slight modification here and there would not be detrimental to the novel's overall affect on readers. Indeed, restraint in the use of language would heighten the impression his novel would have upon its readership. Of course, he, the author, must make the final decision, although—if he didn't object to her intruding a personal note—she found that some words he used impeded the narrative, which in turn affected her overall appreciation of his work. Her criticism was so artfully crafted that Arthur could actually believe he had made the final decisions as to which revisions would stand and which wouldn't. After settling these thorny questions, they admired the panoramic view, and Arthur insisted on pointing out all the obvious sights. He was proud of his home territory.

"Goodness," Laura trilled, all prepared to be impressed. "What is that tower over there?"

"It's the first building erected in England made of Portland cement."

"Fancy that," Laura cooed. "Have you been at the top?"

"It's rather shaky now. I used to ride up here with my father. Father was a marvellous horseman. He was in Arabia with T.E. Lawrence."

"Goodness me. I'd no idea you had such a distinguished parent." Arthur didn't bother to correct Laura's impression of his father. After all, if he, the son, was on the verge of fame, would not the father also possess those attributes which separate the elite from the common run? Some unique spark must have been present among all the spermatozoa his father had scattered in his mother's womb, which accounted for his son having a novel accepted for publication at the age of twenty-one.

"You realize you are an exceptional young man," she said. "Quite exceptional."

"Am I to reply that it takes an exceptionally perceptive young woman to recognise an exceptional young man?"

"No. But I'm well-educated. Though not especially young."

"I don't think of myself as being young." He watched a cloud edge in from the Channel and hesitate before covering the sun, imagining the cloud a male lover, uncertain if the woman (the sun) would accept his embrace. As he imagined this, it occurred to him that while the Greeks might have conceived of the sun as masculine (Hyperion), he, Arthur Compson, would beg to differ and henceforth, because of the tentative way the cloud had approached, would think of the sun as female. To prove he was thoroughly mature, he said, "When I was a kid I was desperately in love with the daughter of the village doctor. We lived in the forester's house then. It had a fine garden and a paddock for our ponies, Father's Jack and my Mary. Heather, the doctor's daughter, stabled her pony in our paddock, and Father gave her riding lessons. It's amazing how passionately a child can love. When Heather rode with us, she and Father galloped from the Asty gate to here. I'd be way behind on Mary. Dear Mary. I told her everything and was sure she understood. But I could never get her to gallop. The most she'd do was trot. Once I thought I saw Father lean over and kiss Heather. He was a compulsive womanizer." Arthur decided he would shock Laura's complacency and sense of superiority out of her. "He probably fucked every woman in the village. Women are cheap here. Men place greater value on cattle and ponies, pigs too. You can't sell a wife for five quid. I mean, you fuck her once a week and she produces children who have to be fed, and you can't sell them either. And you can't eat them. If you're lucky, they die at birth. Women would rather their husbands get a half-crown fuck at the whore's, but married couples sleep in the same bed, and men get drunk on Saturday nights. If you traced conception back, I bet you'd find most village children were begotten on Saturdays, between half past ten and eleven. My father used girls too. And he may have fucked Heather. Mother told me he fucked Heather's mother." He stopped. Laura, who had been concentrating on cloud patterns over the Channel, glanced at him.

"Did you resent him?" she asked.

"Resent? No. I admired him. So did most people in the village. Father was a marvellous horseman. He went into the cavalry when he was fifteen. He told me about his horse, Sammy. Father had to shoot him when German bullets broke his legs. Father was never upset when he talked of shooting the Turks or the Germans, but he cried when he spoke of Sammy. He loved Sammy like I loved my Mary. I'll never ride again. Father told me that most problems people have come from not using every part of their bodies. He thought that evil came from not allowing young people to fuck, because eventually what they thought about themselves became twisted and they came to loathe their bodies."

Laura hesitantly laughed. "Oh? For some reason I'd assumed country people were simple and uncomplicated." She paused, then continued: "Anyway, I can see you have no shortage of source material."

"A procreative dung heap?"

"Oh no. No, no. I mean all the visible cross-relationships and emotional tensions that would be evident to a sensitive person like you."

"Perhaps. Anyway, when I was thirteen or so, Father arranged for me to fuck the village dressmaker. She handed me over to another whore before she died of cancer. Shall we start back?" She nodded, and they began walking along the track toward the Asty enclosure. "So you must appreciate, I'm not particularly innocent. And maybe you'll understand why I write about certain subjects in a certain way."

"I do understand." She clasped and squeezed his hand. "Believe me, I do." She paused, looked earnestly at him, then suggested they return to the house. On the way back through the enclosure, Arthur pointed out a young, dense plantation of Norway pine and told her it was the model for the setting where the lovers in *Dark Passion* meet. "If you need to—you know—you could go in there. It's nicer than the earth closet at home."

She stared intently at him for a few moments, then said, "Well, when one is in the country . . . You'll wait?"

"Of course. I'll go on the other side of the ride." He watched her push aside the still, green branches, then he turned away to pee on a thick tuft of grass and wait for her to emerge from between the young trees.

As they walked towards the enclosure gate he spoke: "There's a man in the village who earns his living emptying outhouses. I once asked him how he could bear to shovel out mounds of people's droppings, because I thought I'd rather die than do that. First, he'd dig a trench in his own back garden, then put on special oilskins and rubber boots and get out his special wheelbarrow. It had a metal tub mounted on it. When he finished loading it up, he'd take it home, then afterwards, ask his wife to forgive for him for having to do such a stinking job." He abruptly stopped, and leaned on the enclosure gate.

"Go on," she said.

"No. It's just one more instance of the general, ritualized filth around the village. I don't know why I began talking about it. After all, you'll just drive back to London and thank God you don't live in such a place."

"Living here has made you a writer."

They had reached her car. "Don't say that," he said.

"Well, influenced you. I won't go back to the house, but please tell your mother how delighted I was to see her again. I hope the next time I come, I'll have the page proofs for you, and you'll have a manuscript for me." She held out a hand. "Goodbye, Arthur." He took her cool, soft-palmed hand. "Try not to care too much about what goes on around you." She leaned forward and kissed his cheek. "We're friends, aren't we?"

"I hope so," he murmured.

"If I can bring you anything from London, please let me know."

"A house with a proper heating and a bathroom?"

"I wish I could."

They laughed as she got into the car and lowered the window. "Perhaps a wireless set, or a gramophone?"

"No, I'm better off with nothing."

"Well, a few books?" she called as the car moved away.

"Nothing, nothing." He watched the car until it turned onto the main road and disappeared, then walked back to the cottage to drink tea with his mother and give an edited version of his prolonged conversation with Laura Dorchester.

"Such a nice, friendly woman," his mother remarked. "We're so lucky to have found her."

CHAPTER

5

WHILE WRITING HIS FIRST NOVEL AND LATER DISCUSSING IT with Laura Dorchester, Arthur never questioned the validity of its content or style. As he told Laura, he'd developed a style to blend with the content, combining poetical and Biblical styles with down-to-earth references reflecting the vulgarity and coarseness of village life. But now that the novel verged on being published and would be read by people who knew nothing about him or the forest and its people, Arthur began to doubt the very elements he had previously argued were the novel's strengths. He experienced periods of panic in which he wrote letters ordering Laura to withdraw the book because he intended to rewrite it, then tore them up. Finally, he drafted a letter which satisfied him, addressed it and set out for Ponnewton to mail it. Full of self-confidence again, he marched along High Street, halted at the post office entrance, patted the letter in his pocket, told himself he was doing the right thing in asking for a delay in publication and was about to walk up the three steps to the door when it opened and a young woman came out. Arthur looked up at her, and she looked down at him from the doorway.

"Well," she said, "hello there!"

"What're you doing here!" Arthur was so shocked at meeting Heather Robertson he could not think of anything to say and stood there, paralysed. He forgot the letter in his pocket and watched Heather come down the steps to join him in the street.

"You look stunned," she said, and laughed.

"I am. You vanished. And I never knew why."

"We can't talk here." She pointed to a teashop on the other side of the street. "Let's have tea." He nodded, and they crossed the street, entered the shop and sat in squeaky cane chairs at a thin-legged wobbly table. "I've seen your articles in the weekly rag," she said, "and the notice about you getting a novel published." He remembered the letter in his pocket which he now knew he never would mail. "Am I in it?"

"You! No."

"I thought writers included people they know in their first novels."

"That may be true, but I couldn't have included you, since I hardly knew you. Remember? You ignored me. I can't recall you even speaking to me."

"Nonsense. I must've spoken to you when I came to get Billy."

"You ignored me."

"Oh well, that's how girls are. It doesn't mean anything. Are you still living in the same house?"

"After Father died, Mother moved. We had to."

A waitress appeared and Heather ordered tea for two. "With scones and jam," she added.

"What're you doing in Ponnewton?" Arthur asked.

"I live here."

"Live here!"

Heather then explained she worked as a sports and gymnastic teacher at a local girl's school. That, he thought, explained her shabby suit and clipped, authoritarian speech.

"I never imagined you'd become an author," she said. "Do you still have fits?"

Her insensitivity angered Arthur. "I've never had fits."

"That's what Father said."

"Your father's not a particularly brilliant physician."

She laughed. "I agree with that. I only repeat what he said."

"I occasionally faint."

"That's fine with me. At least, you know what you have."

Arthur wished he hadn't agreed to have tea and took out his father's gold hunting watch, opened the lid and glanced at it as though time were important to him, but as he returned the watch to his waistcoat pocket, he noticed Heather twisting her hands together as though unsure what to say next. This puzzled him, since his memories of her were of an arrogant girl unworthy of his devotion.

The waitress came to serve them a small brown teapot, two mismatched cups and saucers and two plates, each bearing one small scone, a tiny pat of butter and a thimble-sized serving of jam. She laid a slip of paper beneath the teapot, tepidly smiled and left.

"Mother always said brown teapots make the best tea," Heather said. "Did your mother say that?"

"My mother's still living."

"Mine is too, but I always speak of her and Daddy in the past tense. I haven't seem them in years." She poured tea into their cups, sliced her scone and buttered it. "I knew you had a crush on me. Girls always know such things."

"Boys know how girls feel, too." Arthur sipped the tea and ignored the scone. He would have preferred a cream cake.

"Did you guess how I felt about your father? Girls at that age are so silly."

"I saw what Father did."

"What d'you mean, saw what he did?"

"I mean, when Father pulled down your jodhpurs."

"Are you crazy? Your father never did anything like that with me."

"But I saw you. And one day I saw him kiss you."

"You may have seen him with a girl, but it wasn't me."

"But I saw you," Arthur repeated, asking himself how it was possible for him to have made such a terrible mistake in identifying the girl he'd seen that day in the enclosure; or had he, close to unconsciousness, created an imaginary scene in which Heather played the role of his father's whore?

"Nothing happened with your father. It was my Mother's favourite brother who made me pregnant."

"I don't understand," Arthur muttered.

Heather let out a self-derisive laugh. "There's nothing complicated about it. If a man tells a silly girl she's beautiful and has a perfect figure, he can be certain she won't slap his hands when he pushes them into her panties. A silly girl doesn't realize that compliments aren't thrown around like dry leaves in the wind. She doesn't realize there's a reason for them. Anyway, writers of novels must know how easily silly girls can get pregnant."

"But I always thought?" Arthur paused, swallowed, then continued. "I thought I'd seen you in the Asty enclosure." He laughed nervously. "So that's why you disappeared?"

"That's the reason. I mean, Mother couldn't allow me to waddle around the village with my tummy sticking out. She'd have killed me first. Actually, she begged Father to scrape it out, but he said I deserved the punishment. Can you believe it!" She laughed again. "But the funny thing was, I didn't understand what my uncle was doing when he got into my bed. That's how stupid I was. Or maybe I didn't want to know. I mean, there're so many things girls don't want to know about themselves. Anyway, I try not to think about it."

"I'm sorry it happened." Arthur couldn't help asking Heather, "What about the . . . ?"

"The baby? I never saw it. It came out and they took it away. Don't ask me any more questions." She pointed to his plate. "Are you going to eat that scone?" When he shook his head, she exchanged plates, buttered the scone and hungrily ate it. "I don't get enough to eat at the school." She ate the rest of the scone. "Do you find being an adult has changed the way you see things? I mean, I look at my girls and see myself as I used to be, a silly chump. But it's not their fault. What's happening to their bodies scares them. Or it did me. That's probably why I behaved badly with you. I mean, I was lonely too. Anyway, what we think now won't matter once the war starts."

"War won't come. There's the Munich Agreement."

"Don't tell me you believe in that scrap of paper?"

"Why not?"

"The war's already started and things're moving fast, like an express train. Once the war gets to England, I'm going to escape into it." She leaned over the table. "Does knowing I made a fool of myself make you feel superior?"

"Of course not."

She smiled mockingly. "But you no longer adore me."

"I've grown up."

"Sometimes I wonder about myself. I mean, most of my girls giggle and chatter away, but there're a few who don't, and I suspect they're the ones who've found out what can happen when you trust someone." She stopped, gave a harsh laugh, then continued. "Well, it's over now. Once the war's here, that'll be the end of net ball and grass hockey for me. Until then, I'll just have to put up with silly girls. Did I ask how your mother's keeping?"

"She's well."

"You know we're remote cousins on our mothers' side, not that it matters. Anyway?" She picked up the bill. "Shall we split this?"

"I'll pay," Arthur said. He took the slip of paper and felt in his pocket to sort through the coins. He was weighted down with money now, though he seldom spent any except on gifts for his mother. He sorted through the coins and left the amount plus a small tip.

Heather fiddled with a teaspoon. "Could we do this again? I mean, meet and talk? I don't have time during the week, but Saturdays and Sundays are fine. Maybe you don't want to, now I've spilled the beans."

"Sure, if you want," Arthur agreed, and followed her into the street where they stood, uncertain how best to end the conversation and separate.

"You don't have a job like mine where you're forced to look at replicas of what you used to be. I'd enjoy spending time with somebody who can talk sensibly." She detained him by grasping his arm. "Have you ever had an impulse to kill yourself? You know, go to a railway station and jump onto the tracks when an express train comes through?" She sarcastically laughed. "Of course, it's easy for me to say that, since Ponnewton's at the end of a line that has no express trains tearing through."

"I'm sure any train would do," Arthur said and hurried on to prevent further talk of suicidal impulses. "Why don't we meet at the post office next Saturday? One o'clock?"

She blushed, then said, "That'd be perfect. Ignore how I carry on. Some of my girls are sweet, much nicer than I ever was, and most are bearable. But they're so ignorant. It makes me want to drum into their heads that the world doesn't spin around them."

"They're at the vortex," he suggested.

She eyed him as if unsure of what he meant, then said, "Until next Saturday at one, outside the post office."

"At one p.m. outside the P.O."

"And thanks for listening. I haven't talked like that in ages." She waved her hand in a gesture of farewell, then ran across the High Street.

Arthur watched her go, then walked along the street, turning over the things Heather had told him about herself. He was pleasantly surprised to find that knowing she'd borne a child didn't shock him. The contrary: his calm acceptance of the fact was proof of his breadth of mind and maturity. But why had he been sure his father had raped her? Was it because he'd always sensed Heather's attraction to his father and also knew that his father was a prodigious womanizer? Had he put two and two together and come up with the wrong answer because he'd been ill that day? Well, never mind, the truly surprising thing about his meeting Heather was that, although he still carried the image of the arrogant girl and of himself as the adoring boy, he now felt nothing except a detached curiosity. He entered a shoe store, looked at several pairs of house slippers and finally selected a pair of fur-lined slippers for Sylvia, then set off for the village.

At home, an excited Sylvia, after putting on the slippers, announced she had some wonderful news. "I've got a house for us." They had been looking for a better place since receiving the two hundred pounds from Laura Dorchester and had concluded they might have to leave the village and rent a place in Ponnewton, and while both were highly critical of the village and its inhabitants, when it came right down to rock bottom, neither wanted to leave, Arthur for work reasons, Sylvia because the idea of living in town among traffic and bustling people frightened her. She enjoyed visiting Ponnewton occasionally, but the enjoyment was based on knowing she could return to the village. "It's the empty house on the far side of the enclosure. You know, there's a lane leading up to it? You used to call it the ghost house when you were little. It's the place the forest commission's been trying to regain for years."

"Yes, yes, I know all that, but how did you . . . ?"

His mother's expression combined cupidity with self-satisfaction. If Arthur hadn't been so impatient to find out how Sylvia had managed all this, he would have laughed at her archness. "From Mr. Joyce."

"You mean Joyce, the butcher?"

"That's who I mean. Mr. Joyce is—"

"For God's sake, Mother! Do you have to go through all the lead-up?"

"Listen to you. Getting angry?"

"I'm not. I just want to know."

"Mr. Joyce is the owner's brother-in-law. It has four bedrooms, a big kitchen, a sitting room and a pantry. The rent's twenty pounds a year."

"Twenty pounds." Arthur rapidly calculated how many years rent they could get for what remained of his two hundred pounds. "Isn't that a lot?"

"Mr. Joyce doesn't think so. Mr. Joyce told me his brother-in-law might even sell it to us. Six hundred pounds."

"Six hundred pounds! For God's sake, Mother, we don't have six hundred pounds, and even if we did—"

"Mr. Joyce said—"

"I don't want to hear what Joyce said."

"Arthur? Mr. Joyce is a businessman. He knows about these things and he said it's a bargain."

"I'll bet it is. You haven't seen it. You haven't been inside."

"Oh yes, I have. Oh yes, I have. Mr Joyce took me there this afternoon while you gallivanted off to Ponnewton."

"I went to post a letter."

"Well, no matter. Mr. Joyce drove me in his van." Sylvia deftly produced a key from her apron pocket. "We can walk over in the morning and you can see what you think." His mother's initiative astonished Arthur. "We'd need to get furniture. But the space in it, Arthur! Compared to this, it's a mansion. The kitchen's enormous. Mr. Joyce said his brother-in-law had planned to retire there, but all the unpleasantness with the commission has soured him, so he's going to retire to Weymouth. That's why he wants to sell it."

"Wait a minute, Mother. How come Joyce has a key to his brother-in-law's house?"

"I knew you'd ask that question." Sylvia was so excited she laughed, something she hadn't done since Compson's death. "He looks after it for his brother-in-law, making sure the village children don't damage it. Just wait 'til you see how big the rooms are."

"But how can Joyce's brother-in-law sell a house that may not belong to him?"

"Belong to him?" Sylvia echoed, and for a few moments panic replaced pleasure. "Of course it belongs to him. It's just that there was a mix-up when the land was enclosed. Mr. Joyce says it's like all land that is enclosed in the forest, only the commission is trying to reclaim this place because nobody has lived there for years. Anyway, Mr. Joyce told me possession is nine-tenths of ownership. And if it was ours, darling, nobody could threaten to put us out for being behind in rent."

"We're not behind now."

Sylvia reached across the table to hold his hands. "It would be wonderful," she whispered. "So wonderful to have our own house."

"I'd have to borrow." The thought of borrowing money to buy a house and worrying about mortgage payments upset Arthur so much he hardly slept that night, and while eating breakfast in the morning, he slipped from the chair onto the floor into a spell of unconsciousness.

Sylvia managed to drag Arthur's mattress into the kitchen, rolled him onto it and put blankets over him. After tidying up the breakfast dishes, she undressed and returned to lie naked on the mattress beside him. From time to time, she sponged his face and pressed her ear against his chest to listen to the steady beat of his heart. "Darling, darling," she whispered. "Don't stay away. Please come back to me." Arthur was dimly aware of his mother's body pressing against his, and perhaps because of his heightened sensitivity as he passed in and out of consciousness throughout the day, he saw for the first time that the woman who was his mother by day and lover by night was beginning to age. Seeing it made him want to cry, since he knew that although he would continue to love his mother, from that moment forward he would have no desire to be her lover. He wanted to tell her that the external world, like an incoming tide, was eating away the insecure castle of their dark, nightly romance, but was unable to speak before slipping into the blackness again.

The next morning, Arthur was still unconscious and, after sponging him and rearranging the covers, Sylvia made herself a cup of tea and sat at the kitchen table, biting her lips, trying to decide if she should seek help. It was into this scene that Laura Dorchester—so Sylvia later claimed—providentially appeared. She punctuated Sylvia's sobbing explanation with periodic "Good God's" and "But surely's," then knelt to look more closely at Arthur's face.

"Shouldn't he be under medical care?" she said when Sylvia rolled back the blankets and invited her to listen to Arthur's heartbeat. "I had no idea."

"Usually he's not away this long," Sylvia said. "Usually, it's an hour or two. He was upset about finding enough money to buy the house from Mr. Joyce's brother-in-law."

"What house?" Laura listened to a detailed reiteration of Sylvia's discussions with Joyce, and how she had accompanied him to the house, been impressed by it and, excited at the prospect of finally living in a decent house again, had told Arthur how it could be rented for twenty pounds a year or purchased for six hundred. Because of the excitement, Arthur had not slept well, which explained his spell at breakfast. "I do wish I'd been here," Laura said. "Arthur doesn't need to worry about money."

Well, that might be fine for Laura Dorchester, Sylvia thought, for it was clear Laura Dorchester had never known what it was like to lack two coppers to rub together and be forced to allow a dirty-minded landlord to look up her skirt in return for being short on the rent. Mind you, she'd never gone further than letting Smithson have a peek, though the filthy swine had told her she could have the place rent free and earn an extra five shillings if she? Well, she'd never done that, and never would. Oh, she knew Mr. Joyce had similar ideas, too, but he was a cut above the landlord and didn't go beyond tipping her a wink and saying she must feel lonely without her husband.

"Six hundred pounds is nothing," Laura said. "We can see to that later, now we must try to bring Arthur around." Those were the words Arthur heard as he regained consciousness.

"Oh, darling, darling," Sylvia cried, then astonished Laura by kneeling, opening her dress and pressing Arthur's face against her bare breasts.

"Water," Arthur murmured.

"Where have you been, where have you been?" Sylvia sobbed, leaving it to Laura to bring Arthur a cup of water. Laura also held the cup while Arthur alternately gulped and dribbled the water, turning her head to avoid looking at Sylvia's nipples splayed out on either side of Arthur's head. She thought it unseemly, although she modified her reaction when Sylvia explained. "Arthur began having spells when he was a toddler, I was so upset. I thought I'd done something wrong, not fed him properly, something like that. It was irrational, but I couldn't help myself from offering to nurse him again. I just couldn't help it. Of course, he never . . . you know? But resting his head here seemed to help."

"I understand," Laura sympathized, while thinking Sylvia was a pathetic example of maternal devotion.

"I know it's ridiculous, but deep down I feel guilty about his spells and don't know how else to express my feeling. I know he does suffer." Laura revised her opinion of Sylvia and decided that after all she was a sensitive woman who condemned herself for failing to bear a healthy child.

While Sylvia prepared tinned salmon sandwiches for Laura and herself and a boiled egg for Arthur, Laura sat on the mattress and reassured Arthur about finding money for the house. "We'll work out something," she said.

"Mother has to get out of this dump," Arthur confided.

"I can understand why." Laura held the cup for him to sip water from it.

"I doubt if you do," he whispered as his mother clattered around the stove and sink. "I'm pretty sure she was pressured by our landlord. You know . . . when we've owed rent."

"How terrible!" Laura expressed synthetic horror. "I'll lend you the money."

"On future book sales?" Arthur asked.

"No, no. As a personal loan."

"I'm not sure . . ." Arthur began.

"I can afford it." She smiled and laid her hand upon his. "I'm quite well off."

"But still . . ."

She leaned forward and Arthur thought for a moment she was going to kiss his lips, but instead she briefly touched her lips to his forehead as though she were a priest bestowing benediction on a worshipper. "I want to help you. It hurts me to see a talented person living in such a . . ."

"Hovel?" Arthur supplied.

"Well, yes, since you use the word. Frankly, I don't know how you've managed to work in these conditions. I couldn't."

"But you weren't raised here, so you wouldn't know there're compensations to living in a pig stye. You learn things you'd never know if you

lived in a decent house. Here, you're looking into the arsehole of society."
Laura was about to say much of what happens in pig sties also occurs
in fine houses, but was prevented by Sylvia bringing Arthur a boiled egg,
a piece of bread and butter and a cup of tea.

"Your sandwich's on the table," she informed Laura.

"Thank you," Laura said and moved her chair to the table. "I think I'll
stay here until Arthur's back on his feet. I'll go into Ponnewton and get a
room at the hotel."

"I'm sorry we haven't an extra room," Sylvia said.

"It's no trouble. And I'm lending Arthur money to buy the house."

Sylvia began sobbing. "It's been so hard. You've no idea how hard it's
been."

"Arthur told me."

"So humiliating . . . tradesmen speaking to me as if I was no better than
village women."

"We'll change things, won't we?" Laura tilted her chin at Sylvia, whom
she thought pitiable, by her gesture letting Sylvia know her life was going
to be radically altered now that the immensely capable Laura Dorchester
was there.

After Laura left, Arthur felt strong enough to get himself off the mattress and go upstairs, and when Sylvia joined him in bed that night and
told him about Laura Dorchester's magnanimity, he said, "I'm not sure I
want it." He did not want to remind Sylvia that debt carries the same burden whether to a landlord or a professional acquaintance. While lying helpless on the mattress, he had looked at Laura and he thought he'd seen a
predatory glint in her eyes. He had no objection to taking advances on
sales of his novel, that being a customary arrangement between authors
and their publishers. It was legitimate payment for something he accomplished. But the six hundred pounds was different. It wasn't a gift, nor was
it a bank loan on which he would pay interest. It could be bait to catch and
make him dependent upon Laura's whims, and he was fearful too that regardless of what he said or did, she would one day turn on him and ver-
bally flay him for some shortcoming.

"She thinks highly of you, dearest."

"I know. What day is it?" Arthur just remembered he had agreed to
meet Heather at one o'clock on the Saturday.

"It's Wednesday. No, Thursday."

"Did you deliver the story to Blythe?"

"Oh darling, no. I couldn't leave you."

"Damn."

"I'm sorry. I'll take it in tomorrow."

"It'll be too late."

"I'm sorry," she said again, and stroked his face. She wanted to forget the two troublesome days and return to their rewarding nights.

"Mother?" Arthur began.

"I'm not your mother." She brushed her lips against his. "I'm your . . ."

"You're my mother. The other has to stop. It has to. We can't go on living in a make-believe world."

Sylvia retreated to the far side of the bed. "Everything I've ever done has been for you," she coldly said.

"I know that."

"Then the least you can do is show appreciation."

"I do appreciate what you've done."

"No. You're like your father. Take. Always take. That Laura Dorchester comes here and makes a big fuss over you, but she doesn't know what I've had to go through to keep a roof over our heads and food on the table. She doesn't know the things I've had to do and the promises I've had to make just to get a week's bread off the baker and scrag ends off the butcher. She doesn't know how those men come here and look at me. All she cares about is you and your books."

"Mother . . ." Although Arthur's head ached badly and moving made him dizzy, he forced himself to cross the bed to hold her. "Mother, listen to me. I've suffered through everything with you. You think I don't know you parted your legs for that bastard Smithson?"

"I never removed my underwear," she cried. "Never." He stroked her face, and though he knew his breath was foul from the after-effects of his spell, he kissed her lips and did what he could to convince her that she meant everything in the world to him and could not conceive of life without her. After a while, she smiled and turned onto her side to embrace and kiss him.

"You're not angry about me forgetting your story?" she asked.

"It doesn't matter so much now."

"Will you be well enough to look at the house tomorrow?"

"Of course." He felt her hand move over his back.

"Miss Dorchester was shocked to see me hold you against my breasts."

"I'm sure she was."

"I doubt if she's ever . . . you know, enjoyed herself."

"How can you know that?" He couldn't prevent his hand from defining the curve of her hip and coming to rest on her thigh close to the mound where Venus dwelt, even though he had just finishing telling her their "romance" must cease.

"It's something I feel. She probably thinks I'm a silly woman." She began sobbing. "When I was sitting with you yesterday, I looked at my hands and realized I'm getting old. I have brown spots on them."

"Not for me," he said, contradicting thoughts he'd had while watching her undress downstairs in the morning light.

"If you hadn't been with me, I'd be dead by now. I know what we do is wrong, but it's all we have." He could not contradict her: Their love had been their refuge from the calamitous poverty and dislocation that had threatened to overwhelm them.

"All we had," he echoed, aware that while he was on the threshold of escape from past deprivations, Sylvia would always would be trapped by them. To divert her attention, he told her about the unexpected meeting with Heather. "She's changed, Mother, but still I recognized her the minute I saw her. She teaches at the girls' school outside Ponnewton."

"Miss High-and-Mighty. Too good to pass the time of day with us"

"She's not like that now."

"Been taken down a peg or two, eh?" Sylvia was glad to be told the doctor's arrogant daughter had experienced humiliation. "Did she tell you where her parents are living?"

"I think in Weymouth. She doesn't see them."

"There was a lot of gossip about her."

"How did you come to hear it?"

"Your father picked it up from the workmen. One story—though I never believed it—was that her father made her pregnant because he hated Belinda for refusing to give him a son. You know how people make up ugly tales."

"Like mine."

"Not like yours, darling. You're a writer. What people here do and say is nasty."

"Like their lives." When his mother didn't respond, Arthur cautiously touched her face and knew she was asleep. He touched her parted lips and felt her exhalations quicken as she descended into ever-deepening sleep, and he remembered standing beside the bed in which he now lay, looking upon his father's calm, dead face, unable to comprehend that he would never awaken again. At the time, he hadn't grasped the nature of death, though he was familiar with dead rabbits and other game his father had killed for his mother to skin or pluck. Once, his father had appeared with a dead fallow deer, carrying it across Jack's neck. It had been hit by a car while crossing the main road, and his father, knowing it couldn't survive, had slit its throat. Upon returning home, he constructed a tripod at the back of the house, suspended the deer, then gutted, skinned and divided it so that a piece went to each cottage in the village. He kept a section of hind leg for them, which his mother roasted, but Arthur did not like the meat and refused to eat it until his father grimly ordered him to do so, while telling him that for hundreds of years only royalty ate venison and men were hanged for taking deer to feed hungry families. So Arthur ate the meat to prove he was the equal of all kings, past and present. His mother had cheered and proclaimed him Prince Arthur, son of King Arthur and Queen Sylvia.

Now he was feeling stronger, he began to feel cheered by the prospect of a change in his life, and he thought that sometime in the future he would be able to find an explanation for his own and his parents' lives and the turgid existence of the villagers. But panic could suddenly flood him and he would question how he would be able to survive after his mother was dead. He would grip her shoulders to awaken her and tell her that she must never leave him, even to sleep. During those seconds of terror, Arthur imagined himself as being so small he could enter his mother's body to live, die and go to the grave with her; or maybe his mother, knowing that he sought refuge inside her, could somehow attain a kind of frozen immortality which would ensure his survival until death claimed both. The thought drove him to the edge of madness where he wavered until the panic retreated and he could release Sylvia and assure himself that really he no longer needed the woman who had borne and cared for him, then reclaimed and transformed him into her lover. He could now support himself with his work, and he had Laura Dorchester to tend to him should a spell occur and leave him as helpless and weak as a baby. And who could say, he might even end up with Heather, for it had been crystal-clear during their meeting that she was extremely lonely. An image of her standing on the post office steps surfaced and he felt the flame of sexual curiosity arise as he remembered how her breasts moved beneath her drab suit as she descended the steps. He had sensed her bitterness when she spoke of her truncated childhood and the humiliation of being seduced by her uncle, and he suspected that she would always zigzag back and forth between gestures of friendship and retreats into hard-eyed hostility. But that she was lonely was as obvious as her physical assets, so why not exploit her loneliness as she had once dug the knife of her arrogance into his boy's heart? Revenge?

Maybe, but he must not be petty. Besides, as a girl, Heather had no obligation to acknowledge his calf-love. She hadn't asked for his adoration, instead had behaved like other girls when they become aware of moon-eyed boys watching them: she pretended he didn't exist. Well, their positions were now reversed, and it was she who had suggested they meet again. He thought: Men expect payment in kind when meetings are arranged by women. He saw Heather and himself in one of the old decaying, litter-filled warehouses on the river, and while she awkwardly prepared herself to make payment, he cleared a spot among the detritus of two centuries where they could copulate. But that embarrassment at least would be avoided, because he was not strong enough to meet her on Saturday and thought, after waiting outside the post office for half an hour or so, she would angrily leave, resolved to snub him if chance brought them together in the future. Exhaustion blurred the image. He sighed and when Sylvia turned and put out her arms, he moved to lie against her and sleep.

"Well, what d'you think, dear?" Sylvia asked.

Sylvia, Arthur and Laura Dorchester were standing in the kitchen of the house Henry Joyce's brother-in-law was prepared to sell, and for which Laura was prepared to loan Arthur six hundred pounds to purchase.

"Do you like it, Arthur?" Laura prompted. "Compared to a house this size in London, it's cheap for the money. It's missing some amenities, but they can be installed later." She smiled at Arthur, who was sitting on a fireplace hob. "Well, what do you think?"

"Suppose we had a disagreement, what then?"

"Disagreement?" Laura asked.

"Yes. For some reason, you didn't like something I did, and we quarrelled. What then?"

"I doubt that will happen."

"I think Arthur means the loan," Sylvia said.

"It'll be like any other mortgage arrangement. I regard it as an investment in your future."

"That's what I mean. Suppose I never write another book?"

"Nonsense. Of course you will. I've been involved with writers all my life and I know a genuine author when I meet one."

"You mean authors are like furniture? Genuines and fakes?"

"There's a similarity. But you do like the house?"

"Of course I like it. It's a mansion compared to what we have now."

"So why don't I buy the house, and you and Sylvia simply live here?"

"That's a wonderful idea," Sylvia said.

"But what if we quarrel?" Arthur persisted. "What then? Or suppose you marry and have children and decide you want the house for a weekend cottage. What then?" He wanted to be certain.

"Don't raise an objection to every suggestion I make," Laura impatiently said.

"Then tell me this: Will my novel earn me six hundred pounds?"

"It'll do well in circulating libraries. I'm not so sure about bookshop sales, but I know it will sell."

"All right. I'll borrow the money and pay it back over ten years."

"Arthur counts every penny," Sylvia said. "He's very cautious about money."

"Having money is more a matter of luck than judgement," Laura informed Sylvia. "My grandfather didn't set out to make money, nor did my father, but still they managed to accumulate a lot. They were in the right places at the right times." She ignored Sylvia and spoke directly to Arthur. "I'll get my solicitor to draw up a simple contract. The loan would be repayable, say, over a ten-year period. Is that agreeable?"

"Can't we draw the contract up ourselves?" Arthur asked. "Why pay a lawyer?"

"All right. We can do it now. I'll get my case." Laura left the house, and they watched her walk to her car.

"Maybe we should think it over," Sylvia cautioned. The idea of being responsible for repayment of money frightened her. She had never possessed more than five pounds in her life at any one time.

"Once I get going, I'll earn double the loan," Arthur said. "You'll see. But I must be careful."

"It's a shame we don't have a bottle of champagne," Laura said as she re-entered the kitchen. "This is quite the occasion: Arthur's novel soon to be released and acquiring a house."

"Only the wherewithal to buy one," he corrected.

"It amounts to the same thing." She pulled out the second hob, sat on it, opened a small, elaborate writing case and removed what Sylvia thought was a gold fountain pen. "So, what shall we say?" She began writing. "We the undersigned hereby agree that Laura Dorchester shall loan Arthur Edward Compson six hundred pounds, which he, by signing this document, agrees to repay within ten years from the date herein. That's good enough. Sign here, Arthur." They scribbled their names and the date, and Sylvia witnessed the signatures, after which Laura made out a cheque, handed it to Arthur and closed the case. "Congratulations," she said, and Arthur, sensing it was expected, embraced her and gave her a kiss which lasted longer than Sylvia thought necessary to celebrate the occasion. Sylvia nervously laughed and discovered she resented Laura Dorchester's intrusion into their lives. She knew Arthur's kiss was a polite pretence, but she did not want the lips of her surrogate night-husband to press on those of any other woman, lest he come to prefer them to her own.

Laura backed away from Arthur, but continued to smile at him. "Now I'm off," she said. "You'll be all right?"

"Yes."

"I'll make sure he doesn't overdo it," Sylvia said, hiding her resentment.

"I'd like to stay, but I must be in London to chat up and sweeten a few book critics. I want to have them licking their lips in anticipation of receiving first editions of your novel."

"I don't care about them!" Arthur flared up.

"I do. Good reviews add up to good sales. Goodbye, Mrs. Compson." She touched Sylvia's hand, then, followed by Arthur, who carried her case, left the house. Sylvia stood at the dust-covered window (she thought: cleaning the house will exhaust me) and watched Laura (what an awful name) put the case in the car, then stand close (too close) to Arthur. Was he going to kiss her again? No. They were shaking hands, though she could see Laura didn't want to release his. Dislike boiled in her. There, thank goodness, she was in the car now and Arthur was raising a farewell hand. They would need more furniture. Perhaps Arthur will agree to hire a couple of village women to scrub the house thoroughly. And it would be wonderful if they could replace the old stove with a cooker that provided them with hot water. But changes would have to come over time, because she knew Arthur's anxiousness about the house had brought on a spell, so he mustn't be worried about such things. Oh yes, she understood Arthur, and she wasn't going to let an uppity woman from London walk in and snare him. Oh, she wouldn't object if he brought Heather Robertson home. She could manage Heather, who was no better than a stray cat looking for someone to give it a saucer of milk. Laura Dorchester was different. She occupied rooms she entered and people deferred to her, especially other women. But Arthur would never kow-tow. There, he was looking at the broken wicket. Better to have a decent carpenter build another than try to mend it. And the garden wall needed fixing. Garden! You couldn't really call that mass of dry grass and thistles a garden. If they had money left over, they could get men from the village to clean the back and front. And a daily cleaning woman. He was coming in. At last she and Arthur would escape the village and she wouldn't have to let those men peep up her skirt any more. When their last day came and that awful Smithson walked in . . . he never bothered to knock . . . she'd spit in his face and tell him to get out. Men. She'd known one good man in her life. The rest were . . . The door opened and Arthur walked in.

"Well," he said as he re-entered the house, "what do you think?"

"Today is the happiest of my life."

"Really?" He looked at her as though he doubted her answer. "We'll offer Joyce's brother-in-law five hundred pounds, take it or leave it. What do you think, Mother, will he take it, or will he leave it?"

"I don't know."

"Maybe we shouldn't offer more than four hundred."

"But we're buying the house, aren't we?" Sylvia's anxiety was so palpable a hug was required to reassure her.

"Of course. Tomorrow I'll deposit the cheque, then we'll begin dealing with Joyce."

"Let me see it." He handed her the cheque and watched her lips move as she silently read it. "I wonder what it's like to make out a cheque like this and think nothing of it." She returned the cheque, which he pocketed. "Let's go around the house again. When the garden's tidied up and the fence repaired, it'll be very attractive."

Arthur kissed her cheek, then together they went around the house and upstairs allotted the rooms in descending order of size: Sylvia's bedroom, his own bedroom and the guest room, should a guest ever materialize. Sylvia, realizing her son was lost to her as a lover, quietly accepted the division of rooms. "Once we move in," Arthur said, "everything'll change for the better. Maybe I'll leave my spells behind in the village. After all, that's where they began."

And on that note of optimism they descended the stairs, left the house and, after standing in the lane looking at it with their heads canted to one side, they turned away, clasped hands and strolled home.

As they walked up the lane to the cottage door, Arthur said, "But in a way I'll regret leaving."

"Don't say that," Sylvia cried.

"But if we hadn't lived here, I might not have become a writer."

"But you would. Mr. Blythe said you were a natural writer. And Miss Dorchester."

"I know, I know, but don't you see? I'm struggling to escape from the village by writing about it. I'm like a buried creature who's fought its way up to the light. No, no. Don't tell me I'd've been the same no matter where I grew up, because I know if we'd lived in Ponnewton in a decent house without having to worry where our next shilling was coming from, I might've been content to drive my MG sports car around town, play tennis and court the bank manager's daughter."

"I'm a bank manager's daughter," Sylvia said.

"But you see what I'm getting at?"

He sounded anxious, so Sylvia said, "Of course I do, dear."

"I wonder if you do," he said. "I really wonder." He opened the door and stepped aside for her to enter, then followed her into the kitchen. "Everything comes from filth. Nothing grows in your garden until you dig in the pig shit. That's the weird part of it, Mother. We need the shit and decay. We need death and destruction. We need crumbling cities. We need men like father who raped girls."

"He never, never did that."

"We need women like you, who sees a father in a son and gets him to fuck her."

"Don't!" she screamed.

"But none of that matters, provided something worthwhile grows out of all the corruption. And that's what happened in me." He held her face between his hands. "You didn't like me kissing Laura."

"I don't trust her. She wants to own you."

"Not quite."

She began to wail and begged him not to abandon her, while frantically opening her coat and trying to expose her breasts, reminding him she had fed him milk from her breasts when he recovered from a spell and was too weak to sit up and drink from a cup. "Will she feed you? No!" she cried. "You'll never get the milk of human kindness from that woman!" Eventually she quieted down, apologized and said she understood their life was changed and hoped he would one day find and marry a sweet-faced girl.

"Someone like you?"

"You could do worse."

"I certainly could do no better."

"Your father thought so." Her eyes focused on something beyond him. "Perhaps she'll have a lovely little girl. I wanted a girl. I could still. I'm not finished."

He looked at her and for a moment was gripped by panic, immediately followed by an enormous sense of relief at realizing that sheer luck had prevented Sylvia from conceiving a child with him. He felt as if he had slipped, overhung a precipice, then somehow managed to drag himself back to safety. Still, the knowledge that he had escaped the penalty of his thoughtlessness made him shake and perspiration beaded his forehead. "I'm not sure I'll be strong enough to walk to Ponnewton tomorrow," he said. "I still feel weak."

"There's no hurry. Mr. Joyce won't be here until next week." She went about putting bread, butter and a piece of yellow cheese on the table.

"I'll be strong enough in a couple of days."

"I'm sure you will." She seemed detached, like a waitress who serves customers while preoccupied with private thoughts.

"The kettle's taking its time to boil," he said.

"No longer than usual."

Arthur went to the stove to glare at the kettle as if questioning its efficiency, then moved to stand behind his mother's chair and finally leaned over to press his face against her hair. "I'm sorry about everything," he whispered.

She did not speak, instead reached up to touch his face. They did not move until steam rattled the kettle lid and Sylvia automatically responded by getting up to make a pot of tea while he went around the table and sat down.

CHAPTER
6

AS THINGS TURNED OUT, ARTHUR DID NOT HAVE AN opportunity to deposit Laura Dorchester's cheque the next day because early in the morning Henry Joyce knocked on the cottage door and, on being told the Compsons were prepared to offer his brother-in-law four hundred pounds for the house, abandoned his round and drove to Ponnewton to convey their offer. "I dunno as 'e'll accept it," he said before leaving. "'E's a 'ard bargainer. I means, e's the sort of chap as charges worms rent fer livin' in apples on 'is tree."

"I'm pretty good at bargaining myself." Arthur thought he had graduated from the school of hard knocks when he'd successfully bargained the price of his articles with Harry Blythe and was affronted when Joyce wagged a doleful finger, pityingly eyed him, got into his van and drove off, still shaking his head.

"Maybe his brother-in-law 'll refuse our offer," Sylvia said, whose own bargaining experience consisted of Smithson deferring rent in return for a peek between parted legs; Williams, the baker, giving her stale currant buns in return for a glimpse of the upper curve of her breasts; Banks, the greengrocer, providing over-ripe Jaffa oranges in return for briefly eyeing her bottom; Green, the oilman, exchanging a month's supply of paraffin for the sight of her lower belly for one minute; Joyce, the butcher, favouring her with scraps of off-colour meat if allowed to stroke her knees with one hand while doing something with the other inside his trousers. In every instance, time spent looking at or touching Sylvia was the reward, not what was seen or touched; and Sylvia didn't hesitate to try and wrangle more out of the tradesmen. She would inform Banks, for example, that if he wanted to look at her bottom while she counted to sixty again, then he'd have to give her a pound of apples in addition to the oranges, but then would adamantly refuse a counter-offer, say, of six bananas to augment the apples and oranges in exchange for raising her skirt one minute. Among the quirks that when taken together added up to Sylvia Compson's personality, a psychologist might discover an inclination in her to find out what would happen if she exhibited herself before male eyes. This urge made its first appearance in childhood and took the form of performing cartwheels and somersaults on the grass in the Tambourne municipal park. The activities were immediately and firmly suppressed by Sylvia's mother, who dragged seven-year-old Sylvia to a park bench and hissed: "You filthy little girl! Every man in the park can see your underwear. Never do that again!" That stern maternal admonition had been sufficient to suppress Sylvia's inclination to exhibit herself before male audiences until years later when necessity in the shape of tradesmen demanding hard coin she didn't have compelled her to bargain for bread, vegetables and meat for her table.

Although Sylvia pretended to hate bargaining, the fact was she quite enjoyed having middle-aged, working class men look at or briefly touch sexually innocuous parts of herself, which she was convinced were far superior in every way to the body parts of their wives. The odd thing was, although Arthur's gratuities from the Ponnewton Weekly and the advance on his novel had banished penury from their lives, Sylvia's relationship with the tradesmen did not change. Things were much the same for Arthur too. He daydreamed of buying new clothes for himself and his mother, but continued to wear his father's cord trousers (not the britches) and riding coats, and the furthest he allowed himself to go, following a suggestion from Laura Dorchester, was to talk vaguely of procuring new clothes "one of these days." To know the money was there, to feel the weight of coins in his pocket and to own a chequebook was of greater importance than splurging money on new clothes. After all, Sylvia rarely ventured beyond the house, and no one questioned his right to stalk around in his dead father's clothes. Later on, he would tell himself, after he was firmly established, he would have suits tailored for himself; but the first step in his long-range plan for a better life was to get himself and Sylvia out of the hovel into a house more in keeping with his mother's social status and his own literary position and aspirations.

"He'll want more than four hundred," Arthur told Sylvia, "but it's best to start out low."

Sylvia nodded, thinking of Smithson who persisted in wanting more from her: "Next time, yer 'ave 'em off, or no deal;" though she had steadfastly refused to concede and thereafter wadded the crotch of her underwear with a dish cloth so that Smithson saw less of her rather than more. Now, as she listened to Arthur boast of his bargaining skills, she experienced a twinge of nostalgia knowing her days of tough bargaining were over, and she would no longer be called upon to struggle (as she thought of it) in order to shelter and feed herself and her son. Victory can be disappointing, especially when no one acknowledges how hard one has fought to survive. Why, in the security of a warm home and a table laden with food, a person might even sigh with regret that the thrills of battle were no longer available to test one's courage and physical stamina.

As predicted, Joyce's brother-in-law proved a hard bargainer. Joyce found brokering the deal exciting, and he abandoned customers to scurry between the two parties, bearing offers and counter-offers until on the Saturday evening, he reappeared at the cottage to solemnly deliver the final word: "Five 'undred's as low as 'e's going."

Arthur frowned, pursed his lips and pretended to consider the offer. "Mother, would you say five's too high?" He twitched his lips with his thumb and forefinger, while Sylvia, apprehensive the deal might fall through, placed a quivering hand at the approximate position of her heart.

"Yer could sleep on it," Joyce suggested.

"I could," Arthur agreed. "But I think . . ." He paused, then continued, ". . . we'll accept it." Joyce gave a loud sigh of relief, while Sylvia clasped her hands and pressed them to her lips before collapsing on the nearest chair.

"Yer done the right thing. "'Ere's me 'and on it." Arthur and Joyce solemnly shook hands.

"Would you care for a cup of tea, Mr. Joyce?" Sylvia asked.

"Nothin' I'd like more, Missus Sylv'a. Yer knows wot time I begun me round? Four o'clock, An' I ain't stopped runnin'."

"Would you like a piece of bread and butter, too?" Sylvia sweetly inquired.

"Ain't she a real lai-dy, Mr. Arthur?" Joyce proclaimed.

"Yes, perfect," Arthur agreed, watching his mother slice a thick piece of bread and liberally cover it with butter. Sylvia was so excited she hardly knew what she was saying or doing. Normally she would never have been so generous with food.

"There ain't many real lai-dys in this world, Mr. Arthur, I can tell yer that. Yer thinks women in big 'ouses is bound ter be lai-dys." He took the bread Sylvia offered. "Bless yer 'eart, Missus Sylv'a. But there ain't more than two or three lai-dys in me entire round. Thank yer, Missus," he said when Sylvia placed another slice of buttered bread beside his cup. "I wors raised real strict. Chapel twice on Sunday. A belt on me bum if I says a word out of place. Every night me dad read 'is Bible ter us kiddies, and I learns about 'eavenly mansions. Thank yer kindly, Missus, I will 'ave another cuppa. An' I gets them 'eavenly mansions mixed up with mansions on earth, so when me dad gets me a stable boy's job shovellin' yer-know-wot outta of stables, I thinks real lai-dys is goin' walk into 'em, but all them lai-dys does when they comes ter the stable is shout: 'Do this, do that.' They doan act nothin' like lai-dys, not like Missus Sylv'a here."

"He's a nice man," Sylvia said after Joyce's departure, conveniently forgetting the tradesman's regular red-faced, puffing antics while stroking her knees and thighs below her garters. Indeed, Sylvia had a strangely intimate relationship with Henry Joyce, because after the knee-stroking was over and he had quieted down, Sylvia would make a pot of tea and listen while he talked about his youth and the terrible confusions in his life as far as women were concerned. He could not accept that the queen was anatomically structured like his wife or the skittish scullery maids and short-tempered cooks he encountered on his daily rounds. It was not possible that the queen . . . well, Missus Sylv'a knew what he meant. It wouldn't be right. There had to be a difference between those who ruled and those who were subservient. His uneasiness after Sylvia told him she and the queen were not made differently was so profound he could hardly finish his cup of tea. Joyce had spent four years in the trenches bayoneting German soldiers in defence of the queen and her relatives, so if there was no difference between her and other women, then why had he spent those terrifying years dodging bullets and risking having his lungs eaten away by poison gas? In order for Henry Joyce to accept a social system that ground him (and millions more) into perpetual poverty, it had to be justifiable on physiological, moral or spiritual grounds; and for Joyce, whose spiritual life didn't go beyond singing *Abide with Me* at the commencement of the soccer cup final match at Wembley and whose moral sense was entirely dependent on opportunity, class separation had to be explainable on physiological grounds. When seen in that light, Joyce's attempts to get Sylvia to reveal more of her body was not simple philandering, but rather a desperate plea to help him shore up his pitiful belief in the British class system.

"He's not doing this out of love, Mother. He'll get a commission. Probably more than he makes in a week peddling meat."

"Oh, well. We must always give each other the benefit of the doubt." Even after experiencing the cruelty of others, Sylvia wanted to believe that people would be motivated by generosity if given the opportunity.

Necessity made people harsh, but behind every mask of crude male importunity existed a gentleman and, in a similar way, behind the screeching, harridan facades women presented to the world were loving feminine souls. Her husband had never shouted at her, and although her parents had contemptuously dismissed him as working class, she herself believed Arthur Compson had been one of nature's gentlemen. She had told her son many times that he must always follow the example of his father and never raise his voice in anger, regardless of provocation, and it says much for Sylvia's teaching that in general her son obeyed this admonition all his life.

"I'll have to get going early tomorrow morning," Arthur said. "The bank closes at twelve on Saturday. I'll need to deposit Laura's cheque, and I'm sure there'll be a big to-do getting the certified cheque for Joyce." He remembered again his agreement to meet Heather on the previous Saturday, but, disregarding any anger she might have felt when he hadn't showed up, he told himself that he'd only lost a chance to add her to the pool of village women he'd known. He likened himself to a cynic who views women as water to satisfy thirst, which at least temporarily could transform even the most polluted of water into a life-saving elixir. The imminent publication of his novel had stimulated the growth of a little pimple of conceit in Arthur, which encouraged him not to waste any time justifying himself to Heather if they should meet again; indeed, he thought, he would never again justify himself to anyone, except of course to his mother.

"Perhaps we should have an early night," Sylvia said.

"Maybe I'll think about getting a bike." He hurriedly continued as though required to justify spending the money. "It'd cut the time getting to and from town in half. I'll waste most of tomorrow walking there and back when I could be working. You know that, Mother. It's half my day."

"But this is a special occasion, isn't it?"

"I know. And I do think about my work as I'm walking, but still I have to get back and make up the time. Look at the time I've wasted with Joyce."

"I know, I know. So, if you think having a bike would help . . ."

"I'm not certain. I'm just considering the possibility. Bikes are expensive."

The next morning, after he had eaten what Sylvia referred to as a "hearty" breakfast, kissed his mother's forehead, and made sure for the umpteenth time that Laura's cheque was in his inner pocket, Arthur set out for Ponnewton. On arriving at the bridge spanning the stream that had its exodus in the Ponnewton marches and on through to the Channel, he reached into his waistcoat pocket for his father's gold hunter watch and realized he had forgotten to bring it. He panicked, began running and did not halt until sweat and exhausted legs compelled him to halt and lean against the Ponnewton parish church wall just as the clock in the church steeple tinnily chimed and clanged eleven times. Arthur swore at himself for foolishly panicking, wiped his face, straightened his coat and strode to the bank where, much to his surprise, he experienced no difficulty whatsoever either in depositing Laura Dorchester's cheque or in having the assistant manager prepare a certified cheque for five hundred pounds, and he was surprised when the assistant manager shook his hand and murmured that he would be pleased to assist Arthur at any time in the future, which Arthur attributed to the advertisement of his novel in the Ponnewton Weekly. Feeling quite exhilarated, he left the bank to see Heather on the other side of the street.

"Heather!" he shouted. She stopped, saw him, then turned and ran. For the second time that morning Arthur began running, this time after Heather who, aware he was behind her, fled along the street, turned a corner into a narrow side street, ran up steps and into a house. Arthur rattled the door knocker and immediately the door was flung open by an overweight elderly woman who coldly asked what he wanted.

"Tell Heather Robertson I want to speak with her," he gasped.

"I don't see why I should tell any young lady in my house nothing from a chap she don't want to see!"

"Tell her I want to explain why I wasn't able to meet her last week." He savagely added: "Do as you're told!"

The woman closed the door and Arthur waited in the narrow street, his back to the door. He didn't hear the door open and jumped when Heather spoke: "All right. Explain." He turned and saw her standing in the open doorway with the woman on guard behind.

"I've been ill, Heather. See here, do I have to plead like a criminal? Damned if I will." Heather looked back at the landlady, nodded at her, then joined him in the street. "It was impossible for me to contact you. I didn't know your address, or the name of your school, though it wouldn't have mattered because I couldn't have come anyway. I've been laid up for over a week."

She nibbled at her lips and stared at the house on the opposite side of the street rather than at him. "I felt like an idiot, waiting on High Street."

"I'm sorry," He added a lie. "I intended to wait for a while today outside the post office, hoping you'd show up. Look, let's not stand here. Can we walk somewhere or go to the tea shop?"

Heather hesitated before agreeing. "All right. I'll be a minute." She leaned forward to whisper, her lips touching his ear: "My landlady used to be cook at the school. She's paid to make sure we don't sneak out at night. You know, get into mischief. I'll tell her you're a distant cousin, which you are." She went into the house, and he moved towards the main street to get beyond the range of nosey Parkers who mightn't have anything better to do than peep from behind lace curtains. "Let's walk by the river," Heather said when she joined him. "It's the only decent place to go around here." They turned into the broad High Street.

"I wonder if Jane Austen came here," Arthur said. "She lived not too far away."

"Why would she? It was probably as boring then as it is now."

"Have you read her novels?"

"No. I'm almost non literate. My girls are required to read one of her books. They hate it. It's tedious."

"What did you read when you were their age?"

"Anything about horses. I saw the advertisement about your novel in the weekly rag."

"I'll give you a copy when it comes out." She expressed no appreciation of his offer, and instead asked if he was writing another. Arthur, who had no intention of talking about his work, simply nodded.

"I suppose once you get going you can't stop. Is that what happens? Is it like boozing? Are you addicted?"

"No."

"But you enjoy doing it?"

"Yes."

"That's more than I can say. I loathe my job." They walked down the long, shallow hill toward the river which, being at high tide, appeared wide and deep enough to accommodate transatlantic liners. "Everything in my life is dull and common," she said. "I'm worse off than a shop girl."

Arthur felt he should protest. "But you're a teacher."

"I'm on staff because I come cheap." At the bottom of the hill they turned into a gravel lane and went towards a reed- filled marsh. "After I've paid room and board—the food is lousy—I have five shillings left. That's how cheap I am. I don't even have enough money for decent stockings and underthings. Everything I have is patched or darned. You're lucky, you know that?"

Arthur didn't know how to tell Heather that his poverty had once matched hers, so he resorted to banality: "Eventually you'll find something better."

"You mean get married? Don't be a fool," she snapped. "You think any self-respecting man'd marry me once he heard I'd had a bastard?"

"I'm not sure what you want me to say."

"Nothing." He obeyed her and looked across the gently swaying reeds where a marsh hawk circled, pestered by shrieking gulls. "Most men are like my father," Heather said. "They pass judgement on other people, especially girls. I've told you what he said. 'You stray off the rails, my girl, you pay for it.' That's men for you—they steal a girl's virginity, then blame her. I hate them."

Arthur, disturbed by the intensity of Heather's wholesale condemnation of men, changed the subject. "Look at the hawk," he said, pointing overhead.

But she was indifferent to the long-winged circling bird. "You talk about getting married, but would you marry me, knowing what I've told you? Come on, be honest."

"I'm not really in a position to marry anyone," he said, "But at one time, I'd have jumped at the opportunity."

"When you were a kid," she scoffed. "I'm talking about what you'd do now."

He wondered why she was bullying him and tried to evade answering her. "A sensible woman wouldn't marry me."

"Who's talking about being sensible? Anyway, I didn't really mean it." She pointed to a launch that was going down the river towards the Channel. "When we lived in the village, we knew people who had a boat like that. I'd forgotten them. He was a solicitor. I stayed with them in the summer holidays."

"Here?"

"No. In Poole. I couldn't stand him. He'd feel under my skirt. You'd be surprised how common that is. My girls talk about it. It's disgusting. I see my childhood being replayed in the girls." Arthur sensed Heather had reached the point where she had little control over what she said. "Their bodies make them feel things they don't understand." She now looked straight at Arthur. "Would you marry me? I mean, if you were desperate?"

"I'm not sure I'd make a suitable husband."

"You're up to doing what other men do, aren't you?"

"Of course."

"It doesn't matter. I don't know why I asked. Do you have friends?"

"None." Until that moment he hadn't realized he was friendless.

"I had friends at school. Other silly girls. We invented love affairs with incredibly handsome men. Sickening, eh?"

"Don't tear yourself apart, Heather. It's not worth it."

"I need somebody who'll just listen."

"Well, I don't care what you did, or how silly you were."

"My father said I was no better than a village slut. He assumed I knew about sex, but I knew nothing. Absolutely nothing. He didn't take that into account." They had reached the end of the lane where a little promontory jutted into the sea. "Let's walk to the point. I often sit there when the weather's decent. It's not far," she quickly added when he hesitated.

They climbed the bank and walked over the rough grass to a spot where they could look down on a pebble-lined beach where little waves briskly crashed and, as though ashamed of their audacity, quickly receded. For some reason, the movement of the water suggested to Arthur an image of parents and teachers showering advice and moral admonitions on the heads of children who, knowing nothing, understanding nothing, inevitably went on to repeat the same mistakes made by their elders. To their left, lay the reed-filled marsh and the estuary; directly ahead the Isle of Wight and The Needles lighthouse; to the right, the English Channel opened like a gullet ready to swallow incoming Atlantic gales and waves.

"Once I saw the *Queen Mary* going out," Arthur said.

"Lucky you. I come here on Sunday afternoons," she said. "Occasionally I'll see a couple down there." She nodded towards the beach. "Always too busy to notice me. Can we sit a while?"

"I can't stay long. I told Mother I'd be home by four."

She pushed up her left sleeve to look at a watch. "You've ample time. It's only twelve-thirty." She sat with her arms around her knees, and Arthur had no choice but to join her. "I've gone swimming here, always hoping I'll drown, but all that happens is I get covered with mud. Sometimes when I watch a stupid woman allowing a man . . . I want to scream. You're clever. You must be to write a novel. So maybe you can tell me why a fourteen-year-old girl's mind could be so blank that she wouldn't know and protest what was happening to her body. And this was a girl who thought she was pretty smart. No flies on her. Well?"

"In my novel, a man is shot and killed. I was in the man, was the man, when that happened. For a few seconds, I experienced excruciating pain and knew I—the man—was dying. But if you ask me if I know much about death—or birth—I have to tell you, I'm an ignoramus. There's a woman in the novel. She loves the man and drowns herself after he is shot."

"My god! High drama!"

"My point is, I knew what she experienced when the man made love to her, because I was her, but as for myself, I don't know anything."

"How could a man be a woman?"

"Because I created her. But when you ask how a fourteen-year-old girl cannot know when a man is having intercourse with her, then all I can say is . . ."

"Don't tell me. I don't really want an explanation. I just want to talk endlessly. Sometimes when I've sat here, I've thought if I repeated the questions enough times, the universe'd become so fed up with me, it would print answers on the clouds. Anyway, it's all quite, quite hateful."

"And you'd still marry me?"

"It wouldn't be the same as marrying another man."

"Why not? I'd expect from you what other men do from their wives."

She shrugged, picked up a rock and hurled it into the waves. "How old are you?" she asked.

"Twenty-two."

"I'd see you at the gate to your paddock and be aware I was three years older. That allowed me to feel superior. That's meaningless now. I don't know what I'd do. I mean, when I see a couple down there on the beach, I wonder if the woman's enjoying herself, or if she's just given in because the man's pestered her. That's what men do, isn't it?"

"I can only speak for myself," he said. "And I've never pestered a woman."

"Sir Galahad, eh? Or lack of opportunity?"

"Must you insult me? I've done nothing to offend you, apart from not showing up last Saturday. And let me point out, I loved you once and you rejected me."

She seemed to shrink into herself and remained silent. After a few moments, she said, "I'm sorry. Things shoot out, like bits of glass flying from a broken window."

"Just as long as you realize I won't be your scapegoat." He got up. "I must go."

She scrambled to her feet and touched his shoulder. "Don't be angry." When Arthur didn't reply, she turned her head to look at the water, and he was suddenly afraid that if he left her alone, she would clamber down to the beach and relentlessly wade into the deep water.

"Heather?" He put his arms around her. "We have to get used to each other. We can't expect things to happen at once." She turned, and because her face was so close, he kissed her and felt the rigidity in her lips and body. He backed away and looked to the west to where a ship was slowly rising on the horizon. He waited a moment, and then said, "Shall we go?"

"When Father asked where I'd got the baby, I said I didn't know. That was true: I didn't know. I didn't connect what had happened with my uncle to what was happening inside me. My uncle said he'd come into my room to chat with me. Chat! Some chat, eh? Was I that simple?"

"Just innocent."

"I'd look in a mirror and see the face of a girl, then get on a stool and look at my belly. There's nothing so monstrous as a young girl with that monstrous bulge."

"Heather, stop it." He held and squeezed her hands.

"I can't. It's what I feel when I talk about it. My belly feels like it's sticking out, and don't tell me it isn't. I know how I look because every night I look at myself and see my fourteen-year-old face and grotesque belly. Forget what I said about us and marriage. That was stupid of me. I'm a mess, and you're probably not much better. Anyway, when the war comes, I'll be the first in line at the recruiting office."

"It won't happen."

"Don't you know what's going in the world?" she cried. "Don't you read the newspapers?"

"There are sensible people in government. They'll put a stop to it."

"What sensible people?"

"Here, and on the continent."

She stared at him in disbelief. "It'll happen and when it does, I'll be gone. I'll escape."

"Is that how you see war? As an escape?"

"For me, it is. I'll escape my childhood, my memory of giving birth to a child I never saw and the shame and embarrassment of people looking at and handling my body. Hateful women and hateful men. God, I hate them!"

"But you asked if I'd consider marrying you!"

She gave a short, harsh laugh. "But you're not the same. You're not like other men."

"But I am."

"You're not. You're the boy who adored me. Remember, I'd saddle Billy and gallop off with your father, leaving you to tag along on—what was your pony's name?"

"Mary."

"Of course. Mary."

"I loved her."

"But that didn't prevent you from selling her to the knackers, did it?"

"I didn't sell Mary. Mother did, after Father died."

Arthur tried to move away, but she held onto the sleeve of his coat. "Don't be angry. Please."

"I'm going." He went towards the lane and she followed him. "Listen Heather, I have enough problems of my own. I don't want to be saddled with yours."

"You needn't worry about that."

"I only meant . . ."

"I know exactly what you mean." They walked down the bank into the lane where a small car was now parked. Inside, a man and woman embraced, indifferent to people passing. Arthur saw the man's hand moving beneath the woman's skirt and tugging at her underwear, then glanced at Heather to note whether she saw what was happening. Momentarily, he envied the man and wished his hand was the one circling the woman's smooth bottom. Heather guessed what he was thinking because she said, "If that's what you want, I'll do it. We can go back to the beach."

"I can get that in the village any day I want."

"Like your father." They reached High Street and walked up the hill in silence and into the side street to the house where Heather boarded. "I'm sorry I told you about myself. I didn't mean to burden you with my life."

"It's not that. But Mother and I went through terrible times too. We almost starved."

She grabbed his hands and pressed them against her jacket. "You should've told me. It might have stopped me moaning on about myself."

"Things are better now. I'm making a little money."

"Why didn't you tell me to shut up?"

"Because? Oh, I don't know. I wanted to hear about you. Look, Heather, I know it seems odd, but if we go on meeting and get to know each other, well, maybe we *could* marry. You know, have an open arrangement, a partnership in past and present misery, and maybe future pleasures."

"Do you mean it?"

"Of course."

She continued to hold his hands and smiled. "I don't know. I'll think about it."

"Shall we meet next Saturday?" She nodded agreement. "Look, Mother and I are moving. Remember the house on the east side of Asty enclosure?"

"Vaguely. My world was very small."

"We're moving into it. You could stay overnight."

"But your mother?"

"She'll enjoy having you. Though the house'll be pretty bare bones."

"Bare bones is my life."

"Well?"

"All right." She blushed. "I'd like that."

"Set a time for us to meet and where."

"No, you set it."

"Let's see. Nine o'clock next Saturday at the little bridge over the stream. Remember it?" She nodded, and suddenly both laughed. "Ridiculous, isn't it, making plans as if I lived in Timbuktu and you at the North Pole."

"But suppose you're not at the bridge?"

"You'll know I was unable to come because I'm ill. But it won't matter because, now you know where I live, you can just keep going." She squeezed his hands, and Arthur thought he could see her eyes water as she leaned forward, kissed his cheek and whispered: "I'll be there," then quickly went up the stairs and entered the house. Arthur, surprised by her show of affection and a little intimidated by the rapidity with which things had developed between himself and Heather, returned to High Street where he stopped at the bakery and bought three currant buns which he ate as he strolled along the road to the village, thinking over his meeting with Heather and the manner in which it had started out with her speaking from the pit of self-detestation and then had ended with vague talk of marriage. Why had he persisted in reiterating the offer of marriage and inviting her to spend the weekend? Was it so she could continue to lacerate her own psyche and scarify his? Or had he extracted perverse pleasure from listening to her regurgitate memories of a sleazy uncle diddling with her unawakened cunt while comparing it to his own adventures in Sylvia's ever-welcoming sheath? Perhaps he wanted to set Heather against the backdrop of their childhood and observe the child in her smile at the child who lingered in him. The snag, however, was that he doubted if he and Heather could ever achieve a simple, easy-going relationship, regardless of Heather's willingness to try and his eagerness to adore her fine, strong body, because in the end her memories would erode her capacity to give and the ensuring abrasiveness would destroy his affection and desire. In other words, he would not be able to rectify past errors by present remediation and would be wise to steer clear of her.

When he entered the cottage, Joyce was already there.

"Arthur!" his mother cried out. "We were beginning to think something had gone wrong."

"I expect 'e's been eyein' the girls," Joyce said. "They likes ter parade up and down the 'igh Street of a Saturday, showin' off what they got to offer." Sylvia grimaced, and Arthur thought how tired she looked.

"You have the agreement?" he asked.

"Course I do," Joyce indignantly replied. "It's ready and waitin' for yer." Joyce tapped a folded document on the table. "Right, Missus?"

"Arthur had to go the bank."

Joyce raised a hand. "I ain't sayin' he didn't, but yer asks if it's ready, and I'm sayin' as it's been waitin' 'ere fer three 'ours. Not that I ain't enjoyed yer company, Missus Sylv'a, I did, but I doan like a chap askin' 'ave I done this or that when I've gone out of me way ter be 'elpful."

"I wasn't complaining," Arthur muttered, now wanting to get the property exchange over and done with. "But I want to make sure the documents are in order, so I can give you a cheque."

Joyce handed Arthur the folded document. Arthur sat at the end of the table and, never having seen a property deed before in his life, tried to interpret the legalese. His only assurance of the document's authenticity was the description of the lot on which the house stood, the year of its erection (1810) and the dates given of its conveyance from one owner to another, until it was purchased in 1921 by Herbert Frederick Tompkins for two hundred pounds and now conveyed to Arthur Edward Compson for the sum of five hundred pounds. Arthur noticed the forest commission's claim that the land on which the house stood was illegally enclosed was not cited in the document, and being anxious to see the last of Joyce, Arthur handed over the certified cheque he had received at the bank hours previously.

"Well, that's that," Joyce said. "When'll yer be movin' in?"

Arthur looked at his mother for her reaction, but she gave him no clue. "Within a few days."

"Tell yer wot," Joyce said. "I'll give yer a 'and. 'Ow about termorrer afternoon? Fer a quid? Me van 'll take all yer things in one load."

The next day at noon, Joyce appeared and within two hours, assisted by Arthur, they had dismantled and crammed their possessions into Joyce's van, driven the half mile, then carried their furniture inside.

As Joyce and Arthur put together Sylvia's bed, Joyce patted it. "Yer can tell by the feel this bed's 'ad good use."

Arthur did not reply, while Sylvia, holding the sheets and blankets, blushed.

"I don't want ever to see that man again," Arthur said, after Joyce had collected his pound note and driven away.

She sighed. "He's no worse than the rest," she said. "Not like your father, or you."

"But why does he think he can say such things?"

"Men think they have that right. Now, let's get a fire going."

As they drank their tea, Arthur told his mother about Heather's coming visit. "We'll manage," she said. "You did explain that we don't have much?"

"She knows we just moved in."

"So long as she doesn't expect too much."

Arthur went around the table, kissed her and said, "Heather knows, Mother. Don't worry. Everything 'll work out. It'll be fine. Just fine."

CHAPTER

7

ARTHUR STOOD BESIDE A FIELD GATE AND WATCHED Heather round a bend on the far side of the little valley. She stopped as if expecting to see him coming towards her or else waiting by the bridge. Knowing she couldn't see him from where she stood, he hung back until she began descending the hill, then, when he appeared on the road, she waved and called out words he couldn't distinguish over the rift of the valley. He reached the bridge first and leaned on the balustrade watching her approach. She had on her usual shabby clothes but was without stockings and wore sandals instead of shoes and carried a rucksack on her shoulder. "You know, I'd forgotten this bridge," she said. "Mother'd always stop the car here so I could try to see a fish, but I never did. I'd forgotten the valley was so pretty." She waved a hand at the pastures lining the valley where cows and two carthorses busily cropped grass. She leaned over the rail and peered into the dark water. "Is that a trout?" she asked.

"Reflected light," Arthur said after peering down into the water. "Very deceptive."

"You don't want me to realize a childhood wish?" she asked.

"I thought you were far too superior to go in for fish-spotting," he remarked. "I used a jam jar to catch minnows."

She laughed. "I paddled here. I did everything children do. You had a perverted view of me." She tucked her arm through his, and he could feel a sigh moving through her. "You know, it's stupid, but at this moment I wish I'd kept my child so I could watch her—I feel sure it was a girl—paddle where I'd paddled. Idiotic, isn't it?"

"But natural," he said. "If I'd known you liked it here, we could have walked from Asty together. But we didn't know, did we? You lived in your small world and I in mine. Shall we go?" They left the bridge but continued to reminisce about childhood afternoons spent beside it. "My minnows died before we got home."

"All Mother cared about was me not getting my frock wet. But I always did—to irritate her."

"Mine sat on the grass and dangled her feet in the water."

They marched in step and halted on the crest of the hill where raw forest heath and gorse bushes were recapturing a pasture that had been arduously carved from the forest over hundreds of years. "England's green and pleasant land," she remarked.

"England's land may be green, but it's not particularly pleasant except for those who own it. The others silently endure in misery."

"We're pessimists," she said. "That's our problem. Can two pessimists produce one optimist?"

"You'd never know until you'd done the sum." They matched their stride and Arthur enjoyed the way she effortlessly paced.

"We're ill-matched," she said. "All we have in common are memories."

"We have poverty."

"That's nothing to be proud of. Do you ever pray?"

"Never."

"Don't you pray your novel 'll be a best seller?"

"That's not the same as praying to a supreme being for assistance."

"It's ineffectual, but I do it anyway. Every day I get down on my knees and pray for another war. That's my hope for the future."

"That's crazy," he said.

"Maybe. But I bet there're thousands of people like me, sick of themselves and their lives, longing to escape dreary rooms and jobs—if they're lucky enough to have work—their shabby clothes, their awful food and boring relationships, women who have to put up with . . ."

He stopped and faced her. ". . . with men like me?"

"Maybe. But I wouldn't be here unless I liked you."

"Then why talk like that?"

"I'm like an overheated boiler. After years of silence, press my lever and out shoot words, words, words. I'll slow down eventually. Shall we go on?"

"No. Wait." He wanted to cover her plump lips with his and dam the stream of self-condemnation that poured from between them. He wanted her mood to reflect the sunny morning; he wanted her to raise her arms and cry out she was happy to be strolling along the narrow path with him; he wanted her to draw his attention to a soaring lark or a hovering kestrel—anything but a continuation of her narrative of misery.

"Well, what it is?" She sounded like an impatient schoolmistress.

"I'd like to kiss you," he said.

"Oh, for heaven's sake!" She returned to plant herself squarely in front of him. "All right. Go on. Kiss me, if that's what you want."

Arthur became angry with himself. He'd been stupid to expect Heather to be magically changed by the sunlight on the pastures or the flickering shadows and bird song everywhere, or the lark rising and dipping, or the blackbird in the hawthorn tree, or the thrush at the top of the oak, because she was incapable of seeing or feeling anything unless it related to her own misery. And now here she was, standing before him, lips puckered, awaiting his kiss. It was rude and insulting! "Damn you!" he shouted. "That's not what I want! What I want is to get you behind a bush and fuck some sense into you!"

"I'm not used to having men say they want to kiss me, but if you want, go ahead. I don't mind."

Arthur put his arms around her and pressed his lips against hers. At first she resisted, but then he felt her lips soften and expand as she slowly returned the kiss. His right hand moved from her head, around her rucksack, down until it reached the curve of her bottom, but as it arrived there, she sprang away from him and began singing the chorus of a popular music hall song: "Oh, you can't do that there 'ere; Anywhere else you can do that there, but you can't do that there 'ere." Then she ran along the path in the direction of the village, leaving Arthur behind. He watched until she was halfway up the hill before he too started running, certain he could overtake her, but she easily increased the gap between them and disappeared in one of the numerous paths made by ponies and cattle among the clump of furze that covered half the village common. He saw the flash of her head behind a clump of stunted birch trees and when he got there found her skipping on a patch of grass, still chanting the chorus. He ran at her, but she easily eluded him, ducking under his outstretched arms until her foot hit a grass-hidden root and Arthur fell upon her.

"What d'you think you're doing?" he gasped.

"Proving I'm not an easy catch."

Their noses were almost touching. "Did I say you were?"

"No, but you were annoyed, weren't you, when I didn't jump up and down and say 'Goody, goody!'"

"Why are you so obstreperous?"

"Why are *you* so conceited?"

Arthur was so surprised by her question that he rolled away to watch pillowy clouds approach the sun, then dissipate and reform once beyond the sun's direct heat. "Did you say 'conceited'?" he finally asked.

She looked at him and smiled. He noticed her teeth were spotted with caries, proof she couldn't afford regular visits to a dentist. In an village where a mouthful of rotting teeth was the norm, Arthur possessed a sound, brilliant white set. He had never brushed them. He had read somewhere of an African tribe that chewed twigs for their teeth, and ever since he had cut and vigorously chomped on willow twigs during his afternoon meanderings. "It's a shock to find other people don't see you as you see yourself," Heather said.

"So you see me as an opinionated snob?"

"Not a snob, just offensively opinionated."

"And what about you, lashing out right and left? What about that?"

"I'm someone who at fourteen believed she was a really important person, and at twenty-five is certain she's heading for the rubbish heap."

"Bosh!" Her fatalistic prediction made Arthur uneasy. "We'd better go," he said, but they continued to lie there, watching clouds form, then dissipate. "Have you ever sunbathed naked?" he asked.

"No. Have you?"

"A few times. It's a strange sensation. I felt fragile, and kept looking around. I was sure someone was watching. And I didn't know what to do with myself. I was embarrassed. After about ten minutes, I bolted back into my clothes, like a rabbit into its burrow. I think we should have a National Nude Day, like a bank holiday." She laughed. "I mean it. It would get rid of pomposity."

"You mean house maids would look better than their mistresses?"

"Maybe. But at least it'd get rid of the social sludge we depend on, all the pretence. People pretending to be this or that. Maybe serious art is the only place left where pretence is impossible. You can't pretend to write a poem or compose a symphony or paint a picture because before you can do any of those things you have to strip away all pretence. If you don't, the attempt to perform will. That's the terrifying thing about being an artist. You can be no more, no less than what you produce." He sat up. "We'd better go, or Mother'll think something's gone wrong."

"I'm happy enough, lying here."

"That's good. Look, don't expect much in the way of furniture. And I'm afraid you'll have to share Mother's bed. Of course, you could say you have to be back in town this evening."

"Don't be silly. Your mother's meals can't be worse than what I get. And I don't mind sharing her bed." She rolled herself over to stare at the cloud-speckled sky. "If I join the air force, I can learn to fly and escape into the clouds."

Arthur turned onto his side to look at her. "I told Mother about our meeting."

"What did she say? Though what does it matter? Do you love your mother? I hate mine."

Arthur didn't immediately answer. He sat up and rested his chin on his knees and finally said: "I've never examined my feelings for Mother, because I've never thought of myself as separate from her. Don't misunderstand me. I'm not a mother's boy. Nothing like that, but I can't imagine how I'd live without her. I mean, I feel the same way about her as I do about my arms and legs, and I'd be pretty useless without *them*. I admired Father, and sometimes I think that when he died his soul passed into me, teamed up with mine, if you see what I mean."

"Did you cry when he died?"

"No. I took his place. I decided what mother and I would do, how we'd manage, you know the kind of thing. We were really strapped for money. I haven't bought anything in years. Everything I wear is my father's. We're in pretty good shape now, compared to what we were. I've had an advance on sales of my novel, and Laura says . . ."

"Laura! Who's Laura?" She sprang to kneel facing him.

"She's with *Tower & Tower*, my publisher."

"Why didn't you tell me about her before?"

"You weren't interested."

"I certainly am."

"But we spend most of our time talking about you—"

"So what about this woman? What's her full name?"

"Laura Dorchester. She drives down from London."

"You mean she has a car?"

"I don't know if it's her car. But she drives it."

"Tell me more."

"Like what?"

"You should find out everything you can about her, where she lives in London, if she owns the car, how much she earns."

"Those things don't interest me. Though I wouldn't mind knowing what makes her tick as a woman. But then, I want to know what goes on inside everybody. It's like opening a clock and trying to figure out how it works, which wheel drives other wheels. I can use myself as a general model for men. I mean, I know how I feel when I look at you."

"And what do you feel?"

"Curiosity. But women aren't easy to decipher. Everything's hidden, you can never be sure what's going on inside them."

"You mean I'm like the walls of a castle you have to batter down?"

"Or find secret doors through the walls." Arthur had never spoken so freely about his work and, after what he had so far revealed, he wondered if he'd said too much, or perhaps had conveyed an impression of a peeping Tom or a sneak thief. "I need to know how men and women feel," he said. "They're my work tools, like a bricklayer's level and trowel, or a carpenter's hammer and chisel. I mean, if I don't know how a woman feels when she's in love, or being loved, then I shouldn't write about her, or how a woman feels in childbirth, or when she's nursing a child."

"What about dying?"

"Since I've never talked with a person who's died, I rely on imagination and what I feel when I have a spell."

"And what do you feel then?"

"I feel as if I'm caught up in a vortex, gazing at the universe which slowly begins to turn, and though I try to stop it spinning, it goes faster and faster until I'm thrown out into pseudo-death. It's unpleasant."

She nodded, then jumped up. "Let's go."

Arthur got up and followed her. "You know, when you write stories, you begin to understand that people's lives aren't single lines going from point A to point B. They're more like mosaics, and your job as a writer is to sort out the bits and pieces. And you can never be sure you've included enough pieces, or the right ones, or if you've left something out that's important in portraying them. I mean, look at you."

"I don't want you to look at me."

"All the complexities, the experiences, the ignorance, all the terrors."

She turned to face him and yelled: "Stop it! Either stop it, or I'll go."

"All right, I'll stop." They continued walking and after a while Arthur said: "You know, we're going in the wrong direction."

"Why didn't you say so!" she snapped. "Am I supposed to know everything?"

"Just ninety percent of what's knowable."

"Hah! I wish I knew *one* percent. The only thing I was good at in school was games. I won every race. They handicapped me, but I still won. So which way do we go?" Arthur pointed in the opposite direction. "You really are an ass, aren't you?" She said. "I believe you'd have just traipsed along behind me, like a pet dog, without saying a word."

"I enjoy watching you walk. Most women shuffle along as if they're carrying a piece of porcelain between their thighs and are scared they'll drop it."

"Or that their slips are showing. Well, come on, lead the way." They returned to the road, crossed it and followed several narrow paths, pushing aside clumps of sweetly scented heather until they reached the broad path that edged the enclosure. "I don't remember riding along this side of the enclosure," she said.

There's nothing here except our house. It was built by a man named Tompkins, who stole a hunk of land out of the forest one hundred twenty years ago, then erected a high wall around the two acres, constructed a brick house and defied the forest commission to take it away from him. I got an advance from my publisher to buy it. Six hundred pounds." They came to the lane and stopped. "There it is. What do you think?"

She was impressed. "It looks wonderful."

Pride of accomplishment drove Arthur to boast how he got the asking price reduced from six hundred pounds to five hundred. "Which means we've got a hundred pounds to spend on furniture. I'll get somebody from the village to clean up the garden and sow grass seed." He could hardly believe he was telling Heather so much about his plans.

"There's your mother. She hasn't changed." Heather waved to Sylvia who had come from house and waited beside the broken wicket. Heather walked quickly down the lane to embrace Sylvia and kiss her cheek. "You haven't changed."

"But you have." Sylvia stepped back, eyed Heather and slowly shook her head. "I wouldn't have recognized you if we'd met in the street in Ponnewton. From a skinny girl into . . . ?"

"A buxom lass?" Heather laughingly prompted.

"A very handsome young woman. Do you agree, Arthur?"

"Definitely."

"I love flattery. It's not something I often get."

"Oh, you'll get plenty from us. Now, come and see our new house. I'm sure Arthur's told you about it. We've not had time to furnish it properly, but we manage, don't we, dear?"

"We do," Arthur agreed. "I've warned Heather not to expect the kind of service she gets when staying at *The Regal* in Tambourne."

The women obligingly laughed at the reference to Tambourne's most expensive hotel, then Sylvia took over, displaying her social graces. She pointed out the fine brickwork in the house, the size of the windows and the three chimneys, then said, "shall we go inside?"

"Certainly," said Heather. "It's wonderful Arthur was able to get an advance on sales of his novel."

"A sound business arrangement," Sylvia said. She could feel the fire of her old dislike of Heather rekindling, but immediately dowsed it and gushed effusive thanks when Heather brought out her gift of scented soap: "Oh, thank you, my dear. How thoughtful of you." Arthur, knowing how little extra cash Heather had, was touched by her thoughtfulness. Sylvia continued in her role as charming hostess: "I suppose this is truly a celebration of sorts, because you are the first guest in our new home, Heather."

Arthur gasped when his mother produced a bottle of sherry and three glasses. "But where . . . ?"

"Ah-ha!" Sylvia held up a forefinger. "There's still a thing or two you don't know, my dear," which let him know that Joyce had procured the wine and glasses for his mother. "Will you open the bottle, dear?" Arthur obliged, but felt annoyed Sylvia had secretly purchased the wine without consulting him. Quite apart from cost, there was the question of mutual trust. "Arthur, will you propose a toast, dear?"

They raised and touched glasses as Arthur said: "After many years of absence, welcome to our home, Heather."

"It's wonderful to be here," Heather responded. "I'm sure you'll be happy."

Pecks on cheeks were exchanged, then Sylvia suggested that Arthur show Heather around the house while she prepared lunch. Together they toured the house and Heather made a surprising number of practical suggestions. "If you eventually turn the small bedroom into a bathroom, I think it will be truly delightful."

They went outside and were standing in the long grass when Arthur said, "You and Mother can furnish the house together."

"She still dislikes me."

"Oh no, she's pleased you're here. She's on edge because we never have visitors. I sprung your visit on her, forgetting we had hardly any furniture in the house, so it's my fault."

"It's nothing to do with the house. She's never liked me. You haven't told her about—you know?"

"Of course not. I said you'd had a rough time with your parents."

Heather pointed to the spring-filled well. "That's why the chap grabbed the land. Water. You can pipe water to the house and install a pump in the kitchen."

Arthur bristled. He wasn't going to allow Heather to think he hadn't considered appropriate alterations to the property. Why, he had even contemplated having a lawn dug and a little pool and fountain installed in the middle of the lawn, surrounded by wisteria and honeysuckle clinging to a trellis with a built-in bench where he and Mother, and Heather too, might sit on the summer evenings.

Sylvia surprised him by the amount and variety of food on the table: cheeses, sliced ham, fancy sausages, sardines, cold salmon, apples and oranges, butter and a large, crusty cottage loaf. "Scrumptious!" Heather cried out when she saw the table. "Heavenly!"

After viewing the spread, Arthur had no doubt left that Sylvia had acted in cahoots with the butcher, greengrocer, fishmonger and the baker. But the cost? Arthur was so shocked he lost his appetite and had to force himself to sample the delicacies on the table. "This is a feast," Heather enthused. "I dream of meals like this."

"I'm glad you're enjoying it," Sylvia purred, "so glad. I know when I was carrying Arthur I could never get enough to eat, but of course that was during the war."

"Well, we're not in a war yet," Heather said, then after a pause, "but it won't be long. Has Arthur has told you, the minute war's declared, I'm enlisting?"

"No, he hasn't. Hm. Well, I suppose nurses will be needed. I worked as a nurse in the Great War, that's how I met Arthur's father, at a tram stop outside the Tambourne hospital. But I don't think you have to worry, my dear. Wise heads will prevail this time." Arthur squirmed hearing his mother use the same facile argument he had used. It seemed so trite, because you immediately wanted to ask which wise heads and what exactly were they doing to prevent war from engulfing Europe.

"Read the dailies. I'm no army general, but it seems clear to me that it is coming like a great tidal wave."

"Mother thinks opposition in Germany will stop Hitler from going any further."

"At school, there's a woman who once taught at a German university. She comes cheap like me, and she's a Jew. She told me opposition in Germany has been stamped out."

"Arthur—my husband, that is—always said the Jews were a nuisance in Palestine," Sylvia said. "They wouldn't co-operate, unlike Arabs."

Heather peeled an orange. "I know absolutely nothing about Palestine. All I know is that one of these days the Germans are going to start shooting at the French or the Belgians and another war will start."

"But if you marry and have children?" Sylvia murmured.

"If I got married, I'd never have children." Heather resumed eating, feeling Sylvia's dislike rise and pulse against her like heat from the summer sun.

Ernest Langford

Still the afternoon was pleasant enough. Heather and Arthur sat on kitchen chairs at the back, chatting about their childhoods. Finally Heather said, "You know, coming here today's been like going back in time. I feel as though I'm ten or eleven years old and should be wearing a gym slip and blue bloomers."

Sylvia came from the house and asked if they wanted another glass of sherry, or tea. Both expressed preference for tea and Sylvia reappeared carrying a large tray with tea paraphernalia and a plate of *petit fours*. These, Arthur concluded, were the baker's contribution to the party.

"Arthur dear, will you get the chair from the kitchen?"

When he returned, Sylvia poured the tea and invited Heather to help herself to cakes. Between bites of cake and gulps of tea, Heather offered advice on how the back yard could be improved: Arthur must hire men from the village to dig and level the ground, then sow good grass seed.

"Grass?" said Sylvia. "Grass?"

"Proper lawn grass. You know, the kind used on golf links and cricket pitches. I'd dig a border all the way around the walls and plant fruit trees which I'd train to grow against the walls, because the house faces directly south, so in the morning one lot of trees would get sun, in the afternoon and evening the sun would hit the rest. You could play croquet and bad-minton here."

"That's a great idea, don't you agree, Mother?" Arthur enthusiastically said. An image of the completed garden appeared before him, with him-self under a sunshade entertaining Laura Dorchester.

"It's not an original idea," Heather said. "When I was a girl, Mother and I visited a place owned by a sixth or seventh cousin." She looked at Sylvia and laughed. "Yours too. Anyway, it had a walled garden where Queen Elizabeth was supposed to have played bowls. Mother hoped the marquis would appear and invite us for tea. She's such a snob. And you know, that cousin's son is at Whitehall now, with the other stupid men who can't understand that a war's hiding around the corner. But what does it matter? War's as good a way as any to reduce unemployment and take care of overpopulation."

"Do you see much of your parents?" Sylvia chose to ignore the un-pleasant subject of war.

"We have nothing in common. It's mutual detestation."

Sylvia stood. "Well, I'll get back to work. Time to start thinking about supper."

"We don't need a big supper, Mother," Arthur protested.

"We're happy with leftovers," agreed Heather. "Please don't go to any trouble."

Sylvia ignored their suggestion and went to the kitchen to peel potatoes, carrots and onions which she then parboiled before arranging them around the loin of pork she had coaxed out of Henry Joyce. A shortage of furniture in the house could be explained away, but she would not allow Heather to think they were short of food. Absolutely not. She, Sylvia, would let Heather know that she and her son were her equals. And something else: she would never forget (or forgive) how Belinda Robertson had snubbed her right at their own paddock gate when Belinda came to pretend she was watching Heather ride. Oh yes, she knew about Arthur and Belinda, but thank goodness, Arthur always ignored her when she leaned on the paddock gate and watched Heather go through her paces. Arthur had been a splendid horseman. She nicked her finger, sucked blood from the little cut, decided it wasn't deep enough to justify a bandage and continued peeling potatoes. She hoped nothing would come of the accidental meeting of Arthur and Heather (she was too loud for Arthur) and besides, there was no reason for Arthur to marry (certainly not the usual reason which drives young men into early marriages), but if some day Arthur *should* consider marrying, then why not Laura Dorchester, who thought so highly of him, always assuming she was free to marry, though Sylvia hadn't spotted a wedding ring on her left hand. Sylvia gazed at her own wedding ring every day, because doing so enabled her to believe that she was still married to Sergeant Arthur Compson and that he had never really died.

After supper, Heather and Arthur sat at the table drinking tea while Sylvia washed and dried the dishes. Heather volunteered help, but Sylvia insisted she relax and chat with Arthur until bedtime. There were a few awkward minutes when Arthur, carrying the lantern, escorted Heather to the earth closet, but apart from that, things worked out, and having Heather in the same bedroom with Sylvia enabled her to look Heather over. She had to admit Heather was well developed—a fine, straight back, strong shoulders, narrow waist, muscular legs. That's all Sylvia could see from the back because Heather hadn't turned to face her until a nightgown flopped around her ankles. Before Sylvia snuffed the candle, Heather said: "You have nothing to worry about, Mrs. Compson. I'm not trying to snag Arthur."

Sylvia propped herself on her elbow to look across the bed at Heather. "Then why?"

"Because I'm bloody lonely, because I need somebody who'll listen to me and won't blame me."

"Blame you about what?"

"For being a bloody fool."

"I don't understand." Heather's savage self-condemnation confused Sylvia. "Why should Arthur blame you? I mean, you never spoke to him when you were a girl, did you?"

"Children don't need to speak to each other. Looks are enough. Anyway, it doesn't matter. I'm not the kind of woman an ambitious author should marry. I'm not literary." Heather groped around to find and squeeze Sylvia's hand. "Don't worry. The minute war's declared I'll be gone. I won't take Arthur away."

"It's not that I'm against his marrying."

"I should hope not. Isn't every dog supposed to have an opportunity to wag its tail?"

"I have no idea how dogs behave." Sylvia was getting lost in the thicket of Heather's innuendoes.

"Anyway, just for the record," Heather said, "I had a school girl crush on Arthur's father."

"It stuck out like a sore thumb."

"I'd been told he went through village girls like a knife through butter."

"That was village gossip. Mostly nonsense."

"Probably it was. Did you love him?"

"Yes." Sylvia lay back on the bed.

"Do you feel whatever women are supposed to feel with their husbands and other men?"

"Always."

"Lucky you. Has Arthur told you what happened to me?"

"He hinted you'd had an unfortunate experience."

"I was at the point where I had to off-load what happened onto somebody, or else blow-up. Arthur happened along and got the brunt of it."

"He's very understanding."

"I suppose." Heather's opinion was that Arthur, by inclination and for professional reasons, vacuumed up people's miseries and recycled them.

The conversation petered out, and Sylvia, after wishing Heather a good night's rest and offering hope that the morrow would be sunny, snuffed the candle and rolled onto her side.

Heather lay in her trough in the mattress, listening as the sound of Sylvia's breathing changed to a quiet snore. She wondered if the side of the bed where she lay had been occupied by Compson. She remembered him as the man she had at first disliked because of his cold criticism of the way she rode Billy. But after she'd heard rumours about him and the village women, she decided she would try to make him fall in love with her, though all she managed to get from him was a pat on the bottom and a paternal kiss on the forehead. Of course she knew now, after finding her mother hysterically sobbing after Compson's death, that he and her mother were lovers. Men were such calculating swine. Of course, she'd been flattered when her uncle paid attention to her. What an idiot she'd been. She hadn't realized she was being seduced. And he would've had plenty of practice among her numerous cousins, watching them develop breasts he would one day fondle. Did he keep a list of names and dates and boast to friends about acquiring another maidenhead? Oh, what swine men were. What swine.

Heather drifted into sleep and dreamed she was being hunted by an army of men: She ducked, swerved and sprang over their heads, but each time she did, she lost a garment. Finally, she was running naked toward a cliff with a pack of men closing in upon her. She could hear Arthur shouting at her to stop, but when she turned, she saw her uncle gaining ground. She hesitated, jumped, fell, saw hands and faces coming up towards her and awoke to see Sylvia leaving the room. Sylvia halted in the doorway and said she wasn't to hurry. "I'll call when breakfast is ready." They nodded their understanding of the protocol, and when Sylvia left the room, Heather slumped under the covers and recalled the day before. In running away from Arthur, she had felt joyously confident she could always outrun him, but if that were so, why had she pretended to stumble and allow him pin her down? Why had she agreed to spend the weekend with him and his silly mother? Why bother with them? War was imminent and on the day hostilities started, she would run from the boarding house and the accumulated humiliations she'd experienced straight into the levelling, vindicating freedom of warfare. So why bother with Arthur and his pretensions about a literary future? Why? She thought again of her dream and understood it as a confused expression of how she wanted to manipulate Arthur and make him suffer for the indifference of his father. She would arouse Arthur—oh yes, she'd noticed him eyeing her—she would tease him, but, when he came to take her, she would run, swerve and dodge until he collapsed from exhaustion, unable to perform sexually, then she'd strip and mock his impotence.

"Did you sleep all right?" She turned to see him in the doorway. "I didn't mean to startle you," he said. She pulled the sheet up onto her shoulders. "How did it go?"

"Very well." She patted the bed. "Are you in a hurry?"

He crossed to the bed. "Mother's cooking a big breakfast."

"I smell bacon. I'm not used to luxuries. Going back to lowly porridge and one sardine on toast won't be easy."

He raised his eyebrows. "Is it that bad?"

"Worse. What's the plan for today?"

"There isn't much to do, except walks. Maybe I could've rounded up a couple of ponies, but it never crossed my mind. Actually, I haven't been on a horse since I lost Mary. What about you? Do you still ride?"

"How could I afford to keep a horse?"

"I believed I could win the Derby on Mary," he said.

"Not if I'd been riding Billy."

"Well, let's say the Grand National."

They politely laughed at their childhood memories, though Arthur's laughter was edged with resentment. He still couldn't think of Mary without experiencing a tug of sentiment, and he privately reaffirmed his commitment to one day write a children's book about a boy and his pony.

"I'll go down," he said and got up.

"This is where your father slept?" she asked.

"Yes, Mother refuses to get another mattress." He thought it impolite of Heather to drag in his father's connection to the bed.

"It seems strange to sleep on the mattress of someone who's dead," she said. "I mean, it's almost as if he's been sleeping here recently."

He looked at the open doorway before replying. "Mother wants to keep things that way. She still won't acknowledge that Father's gone."

"It must be difficult for you."

"It is. Well, I'll see you downstairs."

He left, and she dressed, clattered down the stairs, hurried to the back door and ran to the earth closet where she crouched looking through the broken door at the dark pines beyond the wall. They were like menacing sentinels stationed at a prison wall, watching her, sneering at her performing this private act. In defiance, she poked out her tongue, thumbed her nose and laughed at herself as she heard her faeces soddenly smack the accumulated excrement below. So, down there, was all that was left of a century of eating, sleeping, cursing, beating, screaming, fucking and perhaps even occasional loving by those who lived in this house. And here she was, bare-assed and voiding over God-alone-knew-what secrets that been dumped in this repository during the past hundred years. She saw Arthur standing in the kitchen doorway, cleaned herself with a piece of the Ponnewton Weekly (Arthur's article was on page four), adjusted her clothes and walked to the house.

"I hope you like bacon and eggs," Sylvia said as Heather approached the table. "I've fried some bread in the bacon fat."

"It looks wonderful," Heather said. "Perfect." She sat and began eating the bacon. "I'll probably show up here again."

"You're more than welcome," Sylvia said, untruthfully. "I hope the next time, we'll have more furniture. In the forester's house, all our rooms were furnished."

"I understand," Heather said.

"There was nowhere to store things. Nowhere. I had to sell a lot of furniture for next to nothing."

"Heather understands, Mother," Arthur said. "You needn't explain."

"It looks so bleak."

"To me, it looks wonderful," Heather said. "I'm drinking tea I can actually taste, not coloured water."

Sylvia refilled Heather's cup. "Arthur's father said a hearty breakfast carried you through the day."

"He was absolutely right," Heather enthusiastically agreed.

"Eat this piece of bread, dear. I haven't touched it, and there's bacon too."

Heather held out her plate, and fried bread and bacon were moved from Sylvia's plate to hers. "You're spoiling me, Mrs. Compson," she said. "I'll never want to go back to Ponnewton and that dreary boarding house and boring school."

"Is it that bad, dear?"

"Not really. But it doesn't satisfy me." She scooped up the yoke of the second egg. "I want the world to explode into war so I can rush into all the excitement of it."

"War is Heather's favourite topic," Arthur explained.

"Doesn't anyone understand how terrible wars are?"

"It's a trade-off. You risk horror to escape from day-to-day dreariness, from your year-in, year-out dreary, indescribably boring life," Heather said, finishing her meal. "That was marvellous. Thank you." She returned to her subject. "You met your husband during the last war, so if the war hadn't happened, you might never have married, in which case, Arthur wouldn't be around to write the novels that'll make him rich and famous. Right?"

"Well?" Heather's logic confused Sylvia.

"That's not right, Heather," Arthur said, coming to Sylvia's rescue. "It's like saying if the Normans hadn't invaded England then . . ."

"I'm not talking about the Normans," Heather protested.

"True. But aren't you saying if the Great War hadn't occurred, Mother mightn't have met Father, which is analogous to saying that if the Normans hadn't invaded England, then such and such wouldn't have happened."

"How utterly ridiculous!" Heather cried.

Arthur shook his head. "But it isn't. The Great War's historical fact. As the Norman invasion is fact. Both happened. Therefore, to speculate after the fact is pointless. My father, recovering from a war wound, met Mother, they fell in love, married and she had me."

"But all that doesn't prevent me from saying that if . . ."

"I suppose if you felt like it, you could take yourself back to the beginning of time and rearrange the whole shebang."

"I don't see why you must drag world history into it," Heather replied. "I'm saying that the luck of war brought your parents together. That's all. I'm not trying to rearrange history. But anyway, I think wars are good things because they shake people up, and make them do things they wouldn't have done if they'd stayed in their dreary villages and towns until the undertakers came to dump them in their graves." She glared at Sylvia and Arthur, defending her unpopular position. "Maybe lots of people get killed, but it doesn't take long for the ninnies who're left to fill in the gaps. I'll bet the population of England's greater now than in 1914." She grimaced and shrugged. "Anyway, I'm just one not-too-bright person who's convinced war's the only way she'll ever escape from her prison. Phew!" She smiled apologetically. "It's the breakfast, Mrs. Compson. It's made me feel human for a change. I'm an example of chronic frustration."

"Of course we all get frustrated now and then," Sylvia politely said.

"And I should add that Mother can't imagine a world in which she wouldn't have met Father. Right, Mother?"

"Yes," Sylvia agreed. "People who're meant for each other always meet." She found the conversation quite distasteful and thought it didn't bode well for a friendship between Arthur and Heather. Indeed, Sylvia thought Heather hadn't changed and was as arrogant now as when she was a girl; nonetheless, she would remain the gracious hostess and hope that once Heather turned her back and walked away from the house, neither she or Arthur would ever set eyes on her again.

CHAPTER
8

"I DON'T KNOW WHY, BUT I'VE NEVER LIKED COMING HERE," Arthur said. He and Heather had walked through the home enclosure, crossed the heath, strolled through more woodlands and now were standing at a gate looking across a treeless moor. "The place has always frightened me, though it's just open country, like any other heath. Probably something I made up as a child, maybe I came here once during a thunderstorm and afterwards filled the place with demons and witches, like a Grimm's fairy tale." Heather hadn't said more than ten words during the walk (Arthur had counted them) and he was beginning to wish she hadn't come for the weekend because if she weren't here he could work on his novel, which was approaching a critical point in its development, and he was worried if he stayed away from it the carefully nurtured mood of inevitability would dissipate. Heather's apparent lack of interest in his conversational gambits finally became so noticeable he impatiently asked if anything was wrong.

"No worse than usual."

"You don't seem to be enjoying yourself."

She gave a short, barking self-derisive laugh. "Am I supposed to be deliriously happy?"

"For God's sake!" he said. "I don't expect that!" He expressed his irritation with her by leaving the gate and walking a few paces. "Shall we go back?" he asked.

She ignored the question and said, "I had an odd dream last night."

Arthur waited and when she didn't continue, he returned to lean on the gate. "Well, so you had an odd dream. Everyone does."

"I was running away from you, as I did yesterday, teasing you."

"Hoping you'd see my horn raised and ready for action when you looked back?"

"Must you be so bloody offensive!"

"A woman inviting a man to chase her is the oldest bait in the world. Didn't you used to see the village girls poke out their tongues at the boys, then run away, hoping the boys'd run after them?"

"I never looked at the village brats. You're not interested in my dream?"

"Of course I am."

"I'm running away from you. I know it's you because I hear your voice, but when I look back, it's my uncle."

"That's understandable. After all, he'd harmed you."

"I jumped off a cliff to escape you."

"You mean your uncle."

"Both. Oh God!" She fell to her knees and joined her hands in prayer. "God! Please! Please send a war! Please help me escape! Please God, wipe vile men off the face of the earth!" She looked up at Arthur. "You're detestable too, like the rest."

Arthur couldn't tell if her agony was real or theatrical. He offered his hand and she used it to stand. "What's preventing you from joining up tomorrow? You know the recruiting office's right next door to the post office."

"No, I want the confusion and excitement of war. The recruiters must be delighted to see me when I walk in. And they will be, when they learn I'm an upper-class girl. 'By Jove! Look at her! With a chest like that, she deserves to be a colonel.' The fools! I hate them!" She began to sob. "Oh God, oh God, I'm so miserable."

Having his first novel published had convinced Arthur that his understanding of human emotions was exceptional, perhaps even unique, but when faced with Heather's unhappiness he could do nothing more original than pat her shoulder and say "There, there." He had yet to grasp that there was a vast gap between carefully managed personalities in a story and living people, and that those whom he disliked (like bank clerks) or those whom he genuinely believed were his inferiors (like the villagers) were far more complex than the passion-driven people in his novels. Arthur's early novels demonstrated that he was a curious mixture as a writer: His genuine writing ability and vivid imagination existed beside a set of lower middle-class attitudes inculcated into him by Sylvia, and these permeated his stories with the result that romantic intensity and clever plot lines substituted for emotional truth. Furthermore, while he despised the level of poverty to which he and his mother had been reduced and, in his early novels, indirectly attacked society for allowing this to happen, he did not agitate to alleviate conditions in Hasterley and other places like it. He was no Zola or Gorky. The contrary: he used local misery as stock from which to draw material for his stories. Indeed, although he was not to know this, A. E. Compson, which was the name Arthur went by as an author, was an avid defender of the status quo, which explained why a conservatively-minded person like Laura Dorchester could be so eager to support his work; she knew it would sell. Of the two people leaning on the forest gate that Sunday morning, Heather was the revolutionary, not Arthur, for at least she prayed for human evil to be eliminated by the fires of universal war and destruction.

"Shall we walk on?" he asked.

"No. Let's stay here and talk."

"About what?"

"I dunno. You, me, anything."

Arthur looked down at the tuft of grass near his boots. A stream of ants was passing over his boot to reach the entrance to their nest. "We could discuss what those ants make of my boots," he said.

"They probably don't care about your boots. Arthur, did your mother know about your father?"

"Probably. There are billions of ants in the forest. Billions. There's an enormous nest in the Asty enclosure. I'll show you on the way home. Sometimes I think we're part of a huge farm for insects and bacteria to grow in—and wars are slaughterhouses where we're processed so rats have an available food supply. You have to find an explanation. Any explanation. Otherwise, it's senseless." He kicked the tuft of grass, scattering the ants that ran frantically to gather small white eggs.

"How like a man!" Heather remarked. "You can't leave anything alone." She moved along the gate, shaking ants from her sandal.

"I'll get an article out of it," Arthur said. "Ant co-operation versus human destructiveness."

"You know, for a while after I'd seen your father with Mother, I actually thought he was my father too, but I couldn't decide which half of me was him. Finally, I decided the part of me that wet my bed at night and had diarrhea was your father's half."

"How stupid," Arthur commented. He took out his watch. "We'd better make tracks for home."

They walked back through the enclosure until they came to a plantation of young Norwegian pines. "Is there enough space in there?" she said.

"For what?"

"Idiot!" she said. "Space for you to collect payment from me."

"Do you think I can hardly wait to get my cock into your cunt?" He recoiled when she slapped his face. "Damn you!" he snarled. "Why don't you bugger off, find a nice little war and get yourself killed. It's all you're any good for." The goodwill built up during the past weeks, the partial resurrection of his childhood passion, supplemented by curiosity, vanished. Now all he could think of was getting her out of his life, but when she covered her face with her hands and sank to her knees, sobbing, he was ashamed and knelt beside her to apologise and stroke her hair. "We talk at cross-purposes," he said.

"It's a mess," she sobbed. "A mess." She removed her hands, and he was struck how her tear-glossed visage created an illusion of beauty. The effect was similar to seeing plants or pebbles through a rippling stream. It transformed insignificant items into unique and splendid things.

Arthur found himself saying, "You're lovely." Heather shook her head in denial, saying she was a plain Jane, but managed to smile when he said, "Don't let's argue over that too." He kissed her lips and was surprised by the way she responded.

"I'm so mixed up," she said. "I insult people I like and sweet to those I hate."

"You mean you can actually be sweet?"

"Positively sugary." They laughed, rather shakily as people will when recovering from emotional turmoil and are uncertain how to proceed. "We can't stay here," she said. "Come on, let's go."

They left the broad ride and followed a narrow deer trail through the plantation of conifers beneath towering chestnuts (where Arthur annually gathered plump nuts) to a deer-clipped circle of grass walled by aromatic bracken. It was the setting he had used in his first novel for the meetings of the ill-fated lovers. "It's nice," Heather said. Apparently, she could not allow herself to call the sun-dappled glen beautiful.

"You're so prosaic," Arthur complained. She sat and he stretched beside her on his side.

"Can a person be romantic when the only spare cash she has amounts to less than five shillings?"

"The man and woman who met here in my novel had less," he told her.

"Everything's possible in novels," she scoffed.

"Not in mine. The lovers can either separate or face the consequence of remaining together."

"Well" She hesitated. "At least they had a choice, which is more than most people get. What would you do if you had lots of money?"

"Do? Oh, travel, maybe, though perhaps I'd stay here. I don't know. I may be the kind of author who grows out of a particular place and has to remain in order to write. I can't imagine myself writing in America."

"You wouldn't have to write."

"I can't imagine myself living and not writing. What would you do if you had a fortune?"

"Squander it." She plucked grass and nibbled it. "Do you want to . . . you know?"

"Only if you feel like it."

"Suppose it doesn't work?"

He shrugged. "We'd be no worse off than we are now."

He watched her nibble her lips and wondered if she had become the kind of woman who hated to acknowledge, let alone succumb, to her body's desires. "I don't want you to feel obligated."

"I don't," he said, but quickly added when she looked as though she might spurn him. "I mean, I'll enjoy making love with you, but I don't feel obligated to prove something or other, if you see what I mean."

"I suppose I do. I've never done anything, except . . . you know. Have you?" When he nodded, she seemed angry. "With who?"

"Oh, women in the village."

She surprised him by saying. "They don't count. You don't feel anything for them, do you?"

"Nothing." She looked at him, as though weighing the possibilities. "You know, this isn't compulsory. Not like drill in the army," he said.

"I know that. But I want to find out. And I might as well with you. I mean, I've known you a long time. It won't be so embarrassing. I mean, it can't be worse than having a baby with hateful people staring at me. Well, will it?"

"I hope not, but perhaps it would be better if we just talked," he suggested.

"No. I want to do the other. I have to. Look the other way."

Arthur obeyed, and felt the sultry, late summer air move as Heather removed her clothes. He was puzzled by her behaviour and wondered if she had planned this circumventive way of getting him to have intercourse with her.

"You can turn back," she said.

The effect of seeing Heather naked was galvanic. She lay facing him, her left leg folded over the right as if to hide her vulnerable parts, her left arm along the curve her waist and hip, her right hand spread across her breasts. It was the white totality of her body set against the green grass and dark green bracken that produced in him a hot, ungovernable physical need which compressed itself, then sprang and released to impel him across the space that separated them; but even as he seemed to elude the fear he could see rising in her eyes, he became aware of the band of darkness rushing towards him and cried out: "No! No!" before slumping unconscious over her.

At first Heather did not understand what had happened, but when she finally realized she was stuck in the middle of the woods with an unconscious man, she rolled Arthur away, scrambled to her feet, dressed, then crouched beside him to press different body parts in an attempt to locate a pulse. "Damnation," she said, then, "Bloody hell!" as she walked around him and manoeuvred his body until it lay horizontally across the slope. She then knelt with her left shoulder close, lowered herself and managed to roll him from the grass onto her shoulders, pushed herself upright, and after steadying herself and carefully adjusting him sacklike across her shoulders, plodded back through the woods and across the heath to the house. Anything that might be said about Heather's character would pale in comparison to the feat of her two-and-half mile walk to the house, halting only to open and shut the wide, heavy enclosure gates. "Help!" she called when she reached the back door. "Help!"

The moment Sylvia opened the door she realized what had happened, and together they carried Arthur to his room where they arranged him on the bed while Heather supplied a circumspect description of what had occurred.

"Oh dear, oh dear, I'm so sorry. What a shock for you. And you carried him all that way! How brave of you! You must be exhausted. I'll make you something to eat and a cup of tea."

"I suppose he'll be all right?"

"He'll awaken and be grateful for what you did, dear. I'll undress him later on." They went back to the kitchen where Sylvia plied Heather with the remains of the food she had assembled for the weekend while refilling Heather's tea cup and giving her a history of Arthur's spells, including how none of the doctors and specialists (she quadrupled the number she'd consulted) had ever been able to explain what made Arthur collapse and remain unconscious for hours. "I've always thought," Sylvia concluded, "it's because his brain overworks. You know, making up stories when he was little, and writing novels now, which Miss Dorchester thinks will make him famous."

"How old is she?"

"Oh, thirties, I'd say."

"Nearer forty than thirty?"

"Perhaps. She's always well-dressed. Very expensive suits." Heather had disliked Laura Dorchester from the moment Arthur had uttered her name, for while Heather knew she would probably reject Arthur, she intended to hang onto him at least until war came.

The sun was down and the long twilight fading when Heather announced she must go. "Go?" Sylvia protested. "Surely you're not planning to walk back to Ponnewton now!"

"I have to be at the school by half past eight."

"If you leave at seven, you'll have ample time. Please, you must be exhausted from carrying Arthur all that way. And don't worry, I'm an early bird. I'll make sure you have breakfast and get away in good time."

When Heather agreed to stay the night, Sylvia made a fresh pot of tea, and after going upstairs to look at Arthur, they sat in the kitchen and Sylvia talked about her life with Arthur's father. "He never let me down," she said, fluttering her eyelids and smiling sweetly to make sure Heather understood what she meant.

"I know nothing about men," Heather said. "My experience has been limited to an uncle who seduced me when I was fourteen."

"No! Oh dear," Sylvia clucked. "Well, I'm sure Arthur would never do anything like that. He's very considerate."

"You know a lot about him," Heather commented.

"Well, my dear," Sylvia said, after carefully considering the implication of Heather's remark, "I *am* his mother."

"Of course, of course," Heather agreed. They cautiously eyed each other: Sylvia, worrying she had been too open; Heather, thinking Sylvia was a fool and debating whether to remind her of her husband's philandering. Should she tell Sylvia she'd watched Compson with her mother? But in the end Heather said nothing, deciding Sylvia was just one more silly woman who had created an illusionary picture of a dead husband in order to keep herself from going starkers. "I was a little snob, who thought I was better than anyone else, so I probably deserved what I got."

"Oh no," Sylvia replied. "Girls are silly, but no girl deserves to be hurt, especially by a man she trusts."

That remark softened Heather and she reached across the table to squeeze Sylvia's hand. "You're sweet," she said. "I can see why Arthur thinks the world of you." She was surprised when Sylvia raised her hand and kissed it.

"I worry about him and how he'll manage when I'm gone. I'm always on edge when he's out. Of course, I never say anything to Arthur, but you

saw what happened today, and if you hadn't been there . . ." She began
gathering up plates. "Why don't you go upstairs now? You need to rest.
There's a candle on the shelf. Don't bother with those cups. I'll see to
them."

"I'll go outside for a minute," Heather said.

"Do you need the lantern?"

"Oh no, I'll squat."

"Oh dear, oh dear," Sylvia wagged her head. "The things we're forced
to do. When I was a girl, I was sure I'd have a house with honeysuckle and
roses around the door, a bright fire on the hearth and all the conveniences.
I never thought of outhouses and having to carry buckets of water from a
well. But I tell myself, this is our beautiful, dear old England and we have
a great empire, and there must be millions and millions of people who're
far, far worse off. What do you think, dear?"

"I think our dear old England is a place where a few people own everything and lots own nothing. Worse, those who're poor think they're that
way because they're stupid and don't deserve to be rich. You think England's wonderful? Well, I don't."

"But isn't our countryside lovely?" Sylvia was uncomfortable with
Heather's wholesale denunciation of their country. "Remember, 'Oh, to be
in England, now that April's there'? We learned that poem in school. Doesn't
it say something important?"

"I used to go along with that, but now I think it tells us the man who
wrote those words had a secure income, didn't have to get up at six, eat
bread and margarine for breakfast, then walk out into a dark, bitterly cold
morning and work twelve hours for a starvation wage. That's what I think
all that claptrap about April and buttercups and daffodils really means."

Sylvia, shocked by Heather's condemnation of everything English,
could find no rebuttal. "I suppose things could be improved."

"Improved!" Heather stopped at the door. "I'll tell you what I hope will
happen when war comes. I hope the Parliament buildings, the palaces and
cathedrals, and all the slums where people are forced to live in poverty are
blown off the face of the earth."

Heather went out, leaving Sylvia to open the grate and jab at the smouldering fire while muttering, "Well, really, what's got into her?" She poked
a candle through the grate to light the wick. "Another war?" she said to
herself. "That's impossible. There's the League of Nations, they won't allow war to happen."

"Brrr!" Heather shivered as she returned to the kitchen. "The nights
are beginning to get chilly."

"Yes," Sylvia agreed. "It's almost September. Here's a candle for you."
"Shall I look in on Arthur?"

"If you want. I'll up in a few minutes."

Heather went up the stairs, depressed by the conversation with Sylvia and by her own alienation from everything she had once valued and accepted as the foundation of her life. It frightened, at the same time excited her to realize that the once fixed stars in her childhood world which had shone so brightly could be as easily snuffed out as the candle she carried. She entered Arthur's room and leaned over his bed to find his eyes open.

"You're here?" she whispered. He nodded and she said, "How do you feel?"

"Awful." He licked his lips. She thought it odd that he did not ask how he had been moved from the forest to his bed. His failure to inquire irritated her.

"I carried you. My good deed for the day."

"I missed a golden opportunity. I always do that."

She shrugged. "Better luck next time."

"What time is it?" She told him it was about ten, and added she was staying the night and leaving early in the morning to get to school on time.
"But listen," he said, "why go back? Stay here. We have enough to get by. You don't owe that school anything, do you?"

She hesitated before saying, "I can't do that."

"Why not? You loathe the place."

"The school, yes. But I'm obligated to the girls."

"You told me they're silly."

"They are. But they need me."

"But if war comes?"

"That'll be different. They'll want me to go to war. They'll admire me then. They'll imagine I'm protecting them from enemy soldiers out to rape them. Silly girls: they'll never guess they probably should be more afraid of soldiers who're defending them. But it won't matter, will it?"

"I suppose not." Arthur was angry with himself for collapsing and irritated with Heather for talking about plunging headfirst into the gullet of war as though she wanted him to protest, then turn around and congratulate her for sacrificing herself. He recalled the way she had lain in the glade, how the leaf-filtered sunlight had heightened the whiteness of her skin and the curves of her breasts and belly, and had glittered on the bronze cluster of public hair which, though her left thigh was protectively slung over her right, she had been unable to hide. He wanted to tell her that she was beautiful, but was afraid to speak lest she mock his failure at the crucial moment.

He escaped having to reply when Sylvia entered the room, carrying a glass of water. She took things over, and more or less shuffled Heather out by saying she would help Arthur into his nightclothes. "Heather carried me," he said after Heather had left the room.

"She couldn't very well leave you, could she?"

"Mother! She carried me two miles!"

"I know, I know. I thanked her. I did thank her." And because Sylvia thought her son was reproaching her for not having been present to help him when he lost consciousness, she became defensive, saying Heather was young and twice as strong as herself, but that years ago she had carried him too, perhaps not as far, but nevertheless she had put her arms under his slack body, lifted and carried him to bed. "I know, Mother. You've done everything for me." She took off his outer clothes, then raised his shoulders so he could drink the water. "The jerry's under the bed," she said. "Call me if you need help."

"Oh, Mother," he whispered, "oh, Mother."

Sylvia kissed his forehead and went to her room where Heather lay in the bed. "He'll feel better by morning," she said. She stood at the foot of the bed and pulled the hairpins from her coiled bun to release her hair and allow it to settle upon her sloping shoulders. On the previous evening, Sylvia had undressed in the shadows beyond the candle's pool of light, and Heather wondered now if Sylvia undressing herself where she could be clearly seen was by way of a challenge: a mother-in-law-to-be asking a daughter-in-law-to-be if the unknown body will be an improvement on the known one, and if offspring produced by the union will be superior to either or both. Sylvia draped her clothes over the brass rail. "It's worrisome," she said, "you never know when it will happen. Sometimes when he gets excited . . ."

"We were talking."

Sylvia sighed, slipped on her nightgown, removed her underwear and got into bed. "You must spend another weekend with us, dear."

"Thank you. I'd like to."

Sylvia snuffed the candlewick and settled further into the bed. "I'll try to fix up another room, then you won't have to put up with me."

"I've enjoyed your company."

Sylvia reached over the hump to briefly touch Heather's face. "You don't have to pretend with me, dear," she said. "I'm foolish sometimes, but I've had to make-do, and it won't matter how successful Arthur becomes, I'll still be making-do. It's built into me now. But you'll change. You're young enough to forget."

"I don't think so. I've had the stuffing knocked out of me."

"Oh, you will. Young trees bend in a gale, it's the old ones that get blown down. Anyway, I'm glad you . . ." Sleep intervened before she completed her sentence, and Heather waited until she heard the little snore signalling Sylvia was asleep, before she slipped out of bed and felt her way across the hall into Arthur's room. He sensed her presence before her hand touched his chest.

"I thought you might visit me," he said.

"I won't see you in the morning, so I've come to tell you it's over. I like you, but I'm not going to spend the rest of my life looking after a sick man."

"I understand," Arthur said, "though I'm not a sick person."

"I've made up my mind to give notice at the school and enlist. Why wait? Even if war isn't declared, I can still volunteer to serve oversees. Well? Aren't you going to say something?"

"What's there to say? I'm sorry about what happened today. I understand why you wouldn't want to tie yourself to somebody like me. I wouldn't do it myself. But I could kick myself for missing a golden opportunity."

"I decided it was only fair to tell you."

"I appreciate it." Now that his eyes were adjusted to the darkness he could see the outline of her nightdress and wondered how she would react if he touched her.

"Besides, the idea of our marrying was impossible." Even if she welcomed his hand and invited him to venture further, he doubted he could be of much use to her. "You don't care that much, do you? It was only for old time's sake, because of the way you felt years ago. Well, isn't that true?"

"Perhaps." He was too tired to argue the point. His hand touched the hem of her short gown, then moved to pass over her legs.

"I won't do anything."

"That's all right, because I couldn't, even if my life depended on it." He withdrew his hand. "You know, you looked stunning, lying on the grass. Absolutely stunning! It knocked me for a loop."

"I felt stupid."

"That's not how you looked."

"Talking in the dark is easy, isn't it?"

"Like talking to yourself."

"Yes. Are you up to more talk?" He pushed himself across the bed while she got into it. As she wriggled down, he caught the edge of her gown and felt it rise. Her naked body now rested against his. "Do you think it would've worked between us?"

"It would depend on how much you wanted me."

"Like the woman in your novel?"

"So you *have* read it."

"Standing in the corner of the book shop." Their lips were so close they swallowed rather than heard each other's words. "I can't believe two people could feel that about each other. It's not for me."

"You're abandoning yourself to war."

"It's not the same." His hand moved from her waist to her bottom. "I know what I'm doing."

"It's easy to say that."

"What do you say about sleeping with your mother?"

After a pause. "How did you know?"

"I smelled you on the mattress, and tonight she undressed in front of me."

"Does it disgust you?"

"Not especially."

"She went mad after Father died. I helped her cope."

"That's one way to look at it."

"It's the truth."

"Is that why you wear your father's clothes?"

"I wear them because I've had no money to buy new ones. And, if you visit again, don't say anything to her."

"Oh, I won't. I'll just lie in her bed and listen while she talks about her perfect son."

"Don't be malicious."

"I wish I could hate you." She ground her lips and belly against his. "I want to hate you, because I was prepared to give you everything, but you—with your mother! Why not get up now and crawl into bed with her?"

"I hope a bunch of drunk soldiers rip your knickers off your ass and rape you. It's what you deserve."

He felt her move, manoeuvre over and join herself to him. "Are you satisfied?" she asked. She abruptly stopped when Sylvia loomed over the bed.

"Is anything the matter, Arthur?" Sylvia asked.

"No, no."

Heather sat up and began laughing. "We were talking. That's all. Talking. I explained how much I hate him and all men. That's all. You needn't worry. I haven't deprived you of anything. You can have him for keeps." She left the room, while Sylvia whispered, "Dear me, dear me. Oh well, least said, soonest mended."

Feeling utterly miserable, Arthur turned his face to the wall and refused to speak even when Sylvia leaned over to touch his head and tell him it was all a mistake, that by morning Heather would be gone and he would feel much, much better.

CHAPTER
9

ARTHUR HAD ENVISIONED THE QUICK DEVELOPMENT OF A spacious lawn inside the wall surrounding his house, but after three years there was still little to show. He occasionally employed two elderly men from the village to scythe and rake the thistles and the tall, evil-scented docks in a half-hearted attempt to clear away a century of dead grass and weeds. He hated handing over money in return for the little the men seemed to accomplish. He grumbled to Sylvia about their not having given fair value for what he had paid them. (At the time, Arthur believed the rest of humanity was grossly overpaid, while he, Arthur, did not receive a fair reward for *his* labours. He had calculated the number of hours spent on writing his first novel, divided the sum into the royalties he had so far received and found he was being paid slightly more than a penny an hour for his labours.) Sylvia agreed the men's recompense was too high and told Arthur that after the war and demobilization began there would be no shortage of men looking for work. That's what happened in 1919, and she did not doubt things would be exactly the same once the Allies defeated the Germans.

Once the war got underway Arthur considered volunteering before he was conscripted, but Sylvia, using common sense and tears, persuaded him that once the recruiting office found out about his spells he would be summarily rejected. When Arthur told his mother the recruitment office wouldn't know anything about the spells unless he introduced the topic, Sylvia increased the pressure on him and hinted that she might seek death if he abandoned her, which thoroughly frightened him. Finally, to quell Sylvia's fears and to avoid the possibility of being humiliated at a later date, he agreed to see Dr. Evans, the physician who had taken over Heather's father's practice.

After listening to Arthur's explanation of his predicament, Dr. Evans became suspicious that Arthur was a malingerer, still he shuffled through the patient records until he found a file headed with Arthur's name. "Arthur Edward Compson. That you?" he asked.

"Yes."

"Hm. You had a neurological examination at Tambourne General?"

"I vaguely remember it."

"Hm. Do you take medication?"

"Nobody seemed to know what caused the spells, so no medicine was prescribed."

"Hm. How often do the fits occur? Have you had one recently?"

As always, Arthur wondered why physicians insisted on calling his periods of unconsciousness fits. "Once or twice a year. I don't keep a record."

"Hm. Does *petit mal* occur before a seizure?"

"There's nothing."

"Do you bit your tongue?"

"Look, Dr. Evans, I'm trying to avoid future unpleasantness, not to determine the nature of the spells. If you can't help me in this matter, I see no point in continuing the consultation."

"I want to be sure I'm not assisting a man avoid enlistment."

But eventually Evans penned a "To Whom It May Concern" letter, for which he charged Arthur ten pounds and which guaranteed him exemption from service when he presented it to the medical officer at the Ponnewton recruitment office later that week.

Laura Dorchester had begun visiting two or three times a month and seemed unaffected by the fuel and food rationing which had been in effect now for almost three years. She invariably appeared carrying a box of canned foods, plus a bottle or two of Spanish sherry. She told Sylvia that she could survive the war eating beans on toast, but resolutely refused to surrender her afternoon glass of sherry; Sylvia avidly agreed a glass or two was a wonderful pick-up and she had no trouble matching Laura glass for glass. Arthur never ventured beyond one glass, and even that produced a throbbing headache. However, because he did not want to be outdone by Laura in the matter of hospitality, he visited an off-licence outlet on Ponnewton and, after being shocked by the price of the Spanish wine, came away with a bottle of South African sherry which Laura sampled and immediately condemned: "Pour it down the drain. But don't worry, I'll bring you a case of Amontillado," she said, and true to her word, on her next visit Laura appeared with a case of Spanish sherry. Arthur assumed it was a gift, but in fact she had charged it against his royalty account which had grown through sales of his second novel, *The Mound*. However, Arthur did not follow Laura's advice and pour the South African sherry into the slop pail. After all, he had put out hard-earned money for the bottle, so he kept it in his workroom and occasionally sipped a glass, even though doing so invariably gave him a headache.

While on weekly trips to Ponnewton to deliver his stories to the paper, Arthur had bought and carried home one at a time three fabric lawn chairs; when afternoons were sunny, he and Sylvia sat in them, ignoring the unsightly mess surrounding them by allowing the sun to relax them to the point where they could experience the illusion that world peace prevailed beyond the walls. When Laura came, she and Arthur sat in the chairs and discussed book sales and his latest manuscript, tentatively called *Tempt Us Not.* (Arthur's third novel, *The Hunger,* had been released weeks earlier.) On afternoons when Sylvia sat alone, she would slip off her shoes and stockings, raise her skirts over her thighs and doze. Sometimes she experienced an urge to strip and let the sun's rays still the sharp chest pains she now felt with increasing frequency. Of course, she never mentioned these pains to Arthur, or thought of consulting the village physician about them. She merely hoped, like the war which was blighting the country, that they would eventually cease. She had noticed that the pain worsened at night and she placed several pillows under her head and shoulders to help her sleep. While she accepted that Arthur had acted appropriately when he had tried to replace her with Heather, she didn't understand why he hadn't returned after Heather so cruelly rejected him. Oh, she realized she was aging, but still, she was better-looking and had a firmer body than the women Arthur visited in the village. There wasn't a single varicosed vein in her legs, and she knew that any twenty-year-old would be pleased to own her breasts. Sometimes, when she sat outside alone in the comfortable lawn chair dozing, her skirts raised to where pink ramparts hid and defended her inner vestibule, it seemed as if the warm sunlight had transformed itself into the Greek god, Helios, who gently embraced and aroused her until, seeking consummation, she raised herself, only to awaken and slump into the chair as pain shot through her chest. When that occurred she would tell herself she must say something to Arthur, but once the pains passed, she decided she was being silly and that they were nothing more than an attack of heartburn.

Of course, she played second-fiddle when Laura visited, preparing meals and making sure everything went smoothly. Should the weather not cooperate, Laura and Arthur used the sitting room, perching in the overstuffed chairs Arthur had purchased for sixty pounds from Mr. Joyce's brother-in-law, who also happened to own a furniture store, On those occasions, Sylvia stood by the door listening, and when conversation appeared to lag, she entered with tea, coffee or the save-all, two glasses of Amontillado. She was, Laura once said, the perfect hostess, who anticipated her guests' every need. But Sylvia didn't let them off scot-free; she exacted a toll by interrupting sitting room conversations or collapsing into a lawn chair, then minutes later asking Arthur to help her stand. "I'd love to just sit here," she would say, "but we have to eat, don't we? Give me a hand, dear. These chairs are easy to get into, but difficult to leave, like feather beds. Thank you, dear." And off she would go, leaving Arthur and Laura to pick up the threads of their conversation.

"My father made me sleep on a hard mattress," Laura said, "and once a week on the floor, with one blanket."

"Tell me about him."

"What do you want to know?"

"Everything."

"There speaks the novelist. But I can't supply a complete life, because I don't know everything about him. I know he inherited money, that he admired the Pre-Raphaelites and was influenced by William Morris, though he had no artistic ability himself. He believed the world would eventually evolve into one immense socialist society, so he made investments in companies such as *Tower & Tower*. Originally, the company published books to help the labouring masses educate themselves. The funny thing is, every company my father supported paid off handsomely. Before the first war, he invested money in a small company that made agricultural machinery and wagons. When war came, the company began manufacturing gun carriages and army equipment, and so it went. He was a socialist and pacifist who got trapped in the free-for-all capitalist net. I inherited his money, but it never interested me because I wanted to be a writer. Oh yes, I can write, but I can't create. You have a rare talent, Arthur." She leaned across the space between them and squeezed his arm, and her jacket and blouse opened to reveal her shoulders and the cleft between her breasts. "Is that enough?"

"What about friends?" he asked.

"You mean lovers? Not at the moment. Have I had lovers in the past? Yes. Have my intimate relationships been satisfactory? No. Now you know everything about me. So what about you?"

"Me?"

"Yes. You. The man who hides behind the novels. What about you."

He laughed uneasily. "There's nothing to tell. I work. I walk. I eat regular meals. A couple of times a week I see a village woman. Does that shock you?"

"No. My father did that. And it's no worse than me hunting for lovers, though mine generally don't come up to scratch. I wanted the experiences without the encumbrance of love and marriage."

"I got close to marriage before war broke out. But she ducked out of it into the army." He suddenly found it surprisingly easy to talk about Heather. "She ran away from men. I got one postcard from her saying where she'd been posted, but the destination was blacked out. I suspect it was Singapore. I spent my childhood adoring her. She told me she'd had a child by another man when she was fourteen, but I still wanted to marry her and have a child."

"Write a novel about it."

"I can't."

"Tea time!" Sylvia called from the open back door. They stood and went into the kitchen to eat food neither wanted. Afterwards, Arthur carried Laura's briefcase to her car.

"Why not come up to London for a weekend?" she suggested. "People want to meet you."

"I can't." he replied. "I just can't." He leaned forward and kissed her forehead.

"Thank you," she said. "I feel our friendship has been sealed. Until next week?" She got into the car and drove away.

The morning that followed that particular visit from Laura, Arthur awakened and got up as usual. He went downstairs to find an empty kitchen and, after repeatedly calling his mother's name without receiving her reply, terror-stricken, he ran up the stairs, entered Sylvia's room and saw her still body propped up against two pillows. He reached out to touch cold hands and a cold face. Although he sensed his mother was dead, he managed to convince himself she was merely unconscious and that if he bathed her forehead with warm water he could revive her. He rushed downstairs to the kitchen, started a fire, warmed some water, poured it into a bowl, went to the stairs and was about to ascend when the bowl dropped from his hands and he fell unconscious to the floor and struck his head on the stairs. There he lay until Laura Dorchester entered the house a few days later and found him. After determining that he was alive and Sylvia was dead, she drove to Ponnewton where she commandeered an ambulance to carry Arthur to the Ponnewton Cottage Hospital and his dead mother to the town morgue.

Arthur did not attend the inquest. He remained in the Ponnewton cottage hospital in a private room, solicitously looked after by two nurses, Dr. Leggat, a general practitioner in Ponnewton, Dr. Kingsley, a neurologist from the Tambourne General Hospital, and Laura Dorchester, who mesmerized the hospital staff into believing Arthur was the saviour of English literature, though what actually impressed them was that Laura had persuaded Dr. Kingsley to descend from the heights of Tambourne General Hospital and drive each day in his Rolls-Royce in order to peer into Arthur's eyes, order tests, mutter "Hm-hm," then depart, hurrying past the awed staff who felt a strong inclination to kneel as he exited. Nurses were shocked when they overheard Arthur telling Laura to cancel Dr. Kingsley's visits: "Stop him coming here, or I'll whack him over the head with a bed pan the next time he leans over to examine me. He knows no more than other quacks who've examined me." It was clear to the nurses that Arthur (such a handsome man!) did not appreciate how fortunate he was having Dr. Kingsley treat him, even more amazing was that their medical god would actually halt in the hospital lobby to converse with Laura Dorchester and raise his hat before leaving. One nurse, who as a child had been taken by her mother to watch an aged member of the royal family open a sanatorium for coal miners who had thoughtlessly allowed coal dust to fill their lungs rather than to stop breathing when working in the pits, recalled the deference the top-hatted men had shown in the presence of the royal person and speculated that Miss Dorchester might be royalty-related. It was beyond the nurse's grasp that provincials habitually deferred to Londoners, always had, always would, especially to any encircled by the magical aura of money.

Although Dr. Leggat could find nothing physically wrong with Arthur except for a broken nose and minor bruises, still his patient did not regain strength. He had lost interest in eating, in his work, even in reading the books Laura provided. He lay in bed all day and stared at the ceiling, trying to piece together the day and night preceding Sylvia's death. Had she simply gone to sleep and died? Or had she awakened in the night knowing something was wrong, desperately called for him and he had failed her by not awaking? He vaguely remembered finding her on the bed, running downstairs and filling a bowl with water, then hurrying to the stairs, at which point memory of the event ceased. And it wasn't clear if he had experienced a particularly bad spell, or whether striking his head on the stairs had aggravated his condition and produced a genuine coma. Knowing he had been lying unconsciousness at the bottom of the stairs while upstairs his mother's body stiffened and commenced the process of decaying tortured him, and he wished he had died too. The nurses' kindness and Laura's attentiveness served only to intensify his self-condemnation, and he lay there hour after hour, trying to analyze, never to excuse, the strange relationship which had developed between him and Sylvia. There had been a difference in the way he responded to his parents. He had given them what he felt each needed: his father, respect; his mother, love. His child's insight enabled him to understand his father was as strong as his mother was fragile. He knew that his father dominated other men and that his mother suffered the stigma of women who marry "below" themselves and expected her son to apply balm to heal that wound. When his father died, compelled by love for her and respect for his father, he stepped forward and became her substitute husband. He could not say with any certainty whether his mother understood what had occurred, or if she grasped that people would condemn their relationship as unnatural. But given the appalling degradation of their lives and given that he, Arthur, was introduced to sexual gratification by older women and, further, genuinely believed he was duty-bound to offer his mother the sexual services his dead father had always provided—these factors combined to permit him to cross the barrier which normally separated mother from son. Was it possible that his mother, awakening in the night, had understood their grotesque situation for the first time and her heart had burst at that moment of insight? He knew he would go through life holding fast to memories of his mother: her hair falling over her shoulders when she released it from the confining pins at night; her little social pretensions; her denials concerning her age; how she would never let him see her in full light, but in the darkness would permit anything to intensify pleasure. As he lay in the hospital bed tormenting himself, he concluded that he and his mother had no identity whilst they lay in the dark bedroom; they really hadn't existed during those hours, but were merely shadows on the wall.

Arthur also had time to consider the limitations his illness imposed on him and to be haunted by the ghost of his father's contribution to his country's military victories. He could not escape being reminded of the war when the nurses who made his bed spoke of military setbacks in North Africa, or looked at each other across the bed while whispering news of yet another city bombed during the night or, even more frightening, of the Japanese advances toward the Burma-India border. To be comfortably lying in a hospital bed while men fought and died for their country shamed him, and he resolved to enlist in the RAF and duplicate in the air feats his father had performed in the desert. And he tried. Yes, he did. Weeks after he was finally out of hospital, he took a bus into Tambourne and enlisted in the air force, only to receive a letter the following month which coldly

EXISTENTIALIST

informed him never to waste an enlistment officer's valuable time again by attempting to sneak in where he wasn't wanted. Of course, no one ever accused Arthur of failing his country in its time of greatest need, or gave him the opportunity to say that he had volunteered twice, but his country had rejected him. In fact, the only accusations came from himself and his father's ghost.

He tried to get interested in the sales information Laura provided about his latest novel, but she seemed to be speaking about another writer and an unknown novel. He almost said: "I'm glad he's doing well" and "I hope it sells;" but gradually, as he understood that a part of him had gone into the grave with his mother—that explained his weakness and detachment—and that he was now being forced to exist as an isolated entity without a father who demanded respect or a mother who expected him to replace her dead husband. But was he being too extreme? After all, his father had never demanded respect, and his mother had always poured love upon him, so much so, when a lad—was he eight?—he had pushed her away, deciding he was too old to sit in her lap to be hugged and kissed. As for his father, he had always prefaced any suggestion with the words: "Y'know son, I think as you'd be better off if you did it this way," before showing him, for instance, how to brush Mary, or tie a reef knot, and, by example, inculcating a habit of work and soldierly discipline; as for his mother, in demonstrating her unlimited capacity to love, she had moulded him into a man who would upon request and without question return the love and support she needed. The fact was, when his mother was still alive, he only became himself in those moments when he was creating characters for his novels, because these created worlds were places from which he could exclude his parents. In spite of these torments, Arthur slowly recovered and the day came when he sat up in bed and asked Laura to bring his clothes.

"Clothes!"

"Yes, my clothes. I need them to get out of here."

"You're not fit yet."

"I am."

"I'm not sure the doctor will release you."

"I don't need a doctor to release me."

"You have no clothes here. Remember?"

"Well, get some from the house."

"Arthur." She drew out his name in exasperation.

"For God's sake! You want me to stay in this place forever?"

"I want you to recover."

"Then get my clothes, so I can get out of here."

Laura grasped his hands. "I'll go buy some, but you'll have to wait until I get back. Promise?" He sulkily agreed. Still holding his hands, she said, "There's something I must tell you. I've rented a house in Ponnewton for us to live in for a while."

"Us!"

"You need someone, my dear."

"I don't."

"You need somebody, Arthur," she repeated. "It's dangerous for you to live alone."

He hated Laura for saying he couldn't survive alone. "And what about you? Your work?"

"*Tower & Tower* can survive without me for a week or two." Arthur didn't want to go anywhere with Laura, he wanted to go home by himself, but neither did he want to offend her. After all, she had brought him to the hospital and arranged for his mother's burial. "Now, I'll get some clothes. What size shoe do you wear?"

"Ten or eleven."

"You won't do anything rash while I'm gone?"

"Of course not."

Laura smiled and moved along the bed to hug him. "I've been worried," she said, "very worried." She left, and within minutes two nurses appeared to say he needed a physician's discharge order. "That's the rule," they explained.

"Bugger the rule!" The pretty, virginal-looking nurses were shocked since their commitment to the brutality of their profession was balanced by a propensity to blush at coarse language. Due to his lopsided sexual experiences, Arthur thought all women were sexually active and had lovers, so he went on to ask the nurses how many sweethearts each had. "At least two each?" he suggested, to which the nurses replied what they had was none of his business. He, rather foolishly, persisted by saying, "Don't pretty girls always have lovers?"

"A person doesn't always get what she wants," one nurse haughtily replied, while the other angrily snapped: "I'd like a million pounds, but I'm not likely to get it, am I?" They tugged unnecessarily at the sheets and made it clear that Arthur had no right to pry into their personal lives.

"What's more," one nurse said, "the only decent men are off fighting the war."

"Yes," agreed the other. "And the rest, they only want one thing."

Arthur thought about this for a moment, then said, "But don't all men and women desire that?"

The conversation moved quickly into a danger zone, but was halted by the entry of Dr. Leggat, a middle-aged, overweight man, who gave the impression of having slept in his clothes. On seeing him, the nurses scuttled from the room. "What's this I hear about you leaving?" Leggat asked.

"I'm leaving," Arthur flatly stated.

"Has Dr. Kingsley been in today?"

"I told Laura to keep him away."

The doctor's fleeting smile was partially hidden by his unevenly trimmed mustache. "Give us our due. If you'd had a broken leg, we'd have fixed you up in no time. But diagnosing your particular complaint is much more difficult. So, will you go back to the village?"

"Not for a while. Laura's rented a house here."

"She's a capable woman, and it would be best if you didn't live alone."

"I can manage!" Arthur was furious at Leggat for presuming to tell him what he should and should not do, and with himself for having an affliction which allowed people to make such a recommendation.

"It's only a suggestion. But I'll sign you out."

"Sign me out! What is this, a prison?"

"We're responsible for you while you're here, and we're not supposed to discharge you until we're reasonably assured you're capable of carrying on normally." He took out a prescription pad and scribbled something on it. "You could try this. There's no guarantee it will prevent you losing consciousness, on the other hand it won't harm you." He laid the slip of paper on the bedside cabinet. "Your nose and head have healed nicely. But you still have memory lapses, right?" He posed the question as though he knew Arthur would respond with a lie.

"I forget things I'm not interested in. I remember everything useful to me in my work. I mean, I'll remember your mustache is trimmed on one side only and that you have a slight stutter."

"Oh, that." Leggat brushed a finger against his mustache. "I was in the middle of trimming it when I got an emergency call to deliver a baby. No wonder the nurses 've been giving me the eye! Hah! I thought they'd suddenly discovered I'm attractive." He stepped away from the bed as Laura entered, carrying several boxes. "Taking him away, eh?" he said.

"You approve?"

"Can't wait to see the last of him."

"A decent man," Laura said after the doctor had left. "Let's see now." She opened the boxes and laid out the new clothes, even a handkerchief.

"Nice," Arthur commented as he examined the tweed jacket.

"Shall I leave while you dress?"

He was overcome by a sudden wave of panic. "No. Stay." And so Laura stood at the window with her back to him, while he pushed his legs and arms into the underwear, then put on the white shirt and grey flannels. "They fit," he announced.

She turned and critically examined him. "The flannels 're long," she said, "but they'll do. Try the jacket. If it wasn't for your straggly beard, you'd look normal. Try the shoes. I brought a size ten and an eleven, but I can return one pair. The shopkeeper offered to bring some to the hospital. Which is that?"

"The ten." He walked to the door and back. "They'll do. And I'll keep the beard."

"It'll be fine once it's trimmed."

"This is my first new jacket, you know? I've always worn Father's. Hah! I'm a new man. Do I look like a new man to you?"

She hesitated before saying, "You look recovered."

"Will you take me to the Asty graveyard? I want to see mother's grave."

"She's in the Ponnewton cemetery. You know she was brought here for the autopsy."

"I'd forgotten. She wanted to be buried with Father, but I don't suppose it really matters."

"We can have her moved."

"No, no. It's not that important."

"Whichever you prefer," Laura said. "Are you ready?" As they were leaving the room, Arthur stopped and clutched Laura's hand. "Walk close to me. Make sure I don't stumble as we go out."

"Of course I will." They walked slowly down the hall to a small office where Arthur signed papers, and Laura made out a cheque, which she placed face-down on the desk.

As they re-entered the lobby, the two nurses came over to shake hands. "Forget respectability," he whispered to each as they bade farewell to him, "it doesn't pay off." Each nodded, then waved as he and Laura walked through the entrance doors.

"What was that about?" Laura asked as they walked from the hospital to her car.

"They worry about the shortage of decent men."

"How odd," she remarked. She opened the car door for him. "What is that?" she asked as Arthur tore the prescription into little pieces and dropped them on the ground.

"Nothing of consequence," he replied.

She started the car and drove along High Street. "Would you like to visit your mother's grave first?"

"I suddenly feel quite tired."

"Then why don't we go to the house and rest for a while?"

Since everything was small-scale in Hasterley, Arthur imagined the house Laura had rented would be a cottage in a side street. Instead, she drew up outside a two-storied, bow-windowed house on High Street and led him through rooms packed with furniture and glass-fronted walnut cabinets filled with leather-tooled books, which looked as if they'd never been opened. Landseer-like landscapes of misty crags and tarns covered the walls. There was also a portrait of a man, who, so Laura explained, was a nineteenth-century metaphysical poet who had once lived in the house. The overdone furnishings stifled any creative urge Arthur might have felt on leaving the hospital.

Laura had brought his typewriter and half-finished novel from the house and placed them on a beautiful rosewood table in front of framed pictures of three swan-necked women and two hirsute men whose beards made Arthur's look like a shredded dishrag. Arthur found he was unable to continue his novel (the story of a sister and brother denying their passionate love for each other) with the ridiculous paintings in front of his face. He longed for a blank wall on which to project the scenes he was writing, and even tried to perceive the pictures as though the women were sweating behind whalebone corsets and the men longing to scratch itchy hemorrhoids, but those images only served to increase his longing to go back home and hump Mabel Smith, the village whore he taken up with after Dot Perks died, and did nothing to stimulate his literary imagination. Laura, who had gone to so much trouble to provide this compendium of literary wealth, seemed not to grasp that for Arthur the overall effect was stultifying. For him to insert paper in the typewriter and describe the sweating copulation of an practically illiterate man and woman became a sacrilegious act. Worse, the abundance of pictorial bombast surrounding him made his creation seem puny and meaningless. How could he, Arthur Compson, striving to overcome physical weakness and personal limitations, hope to contend with the accomplishments of other ages? It was hopeless, and during the morning hours when Laura went to excessive lengths to avoid disturbing him, he sat at the rosewood table and helplessly stared at the books and pictures, while telling himself that unless he got out of the house he would either go mad or kill himself.

But he might not have run away had he not heard Laura Dorchester fart. He had left the rosewood table at which he was supposed to be labouring, walked in slippered feet (the lease stipulated the wearing of slippers to protect the floors) and was about to enter the kitchen where Laura was preparing lamb chops for lunch when he heard her break wind. Strange though it may seem, it had never occurred to Arthur that Laura's digestive and intestinal system duplicated his own. He couldn't recall the occasion, nor his age, but he was certain that his mother in one of her ongoing efforts at helping him understand class distinctions had told him that although working class men and women sweated and broke wind, upperclass people, especially women, never perspired or farted, and while it was true that Arthur, the child, had copiously sweated in the heavy clothes his mother insisted he wear and had often amused himself by trying to fart drum rolls, he couldn't remember an occasion when his mother had done either, except for the tiny noise that night in bed, thus confirming Henry Joyce's oft-stated opinion that his mother was indeed a real lai-dy. Somewhere Arthur had read (but didn't entirely believe) that the angelic Wolfgang Amadeus Mozart had engaged in farting contests with his sister and made scatological references to these in letters to female cousins. Arthur was sixteen when he happened upon this fascinating tidbit and at a time of life when he wished he could get rid of his own intestinal tract because it was either suspending operations all together or operating with violent frequency. He thought then that the primeval curse was not expulsion from Eden, but rather being compelled to eat and drink at one end of your body in order to evacuate what remained at the other. He thought a clever individual could easily become the richest person in the world if only he or she could manufacture a substance that, when consumed, enabled people to void perfumed shit. He experimented by eating primroses, wild roses and bluebells, but after suffering severe stomach aches, gave up and returned to his mother's diet of bread and margarine and his first agonizing attempts at writing stories for the Ponnewton Weekly.

He had discovered that fervour was not enough, that after a couple of paragraphs were down on paper, a story could dissipate and leave him flat on his back, gasping for authorial air. Before a story balloon could soar, careful preparations had to be made, and an adequate reserve of hot air carried at all times to keep it aloft. Suspension of belief on the part of those who elected to accompany you on your journey was required, and since your intention was ultimately to reveal territory they had never passed through before, it was necessary to provide fellow travellers with diversions along the way. In composing these distractions, Arthur slowly and painfully developed his craft, though it hadn't been easy to discipline a rampant imagination into a step-by-step approach, projecting sequential images (like a film) onto the empty white wall in front of the little table at which he worked. Oh yes, Arthur laboured. He twisted and turned in his attempt to acquire a suitable form in which to narrate his stories. And while it might seem ridiculous to argue that hearing Laura's plebeian explosion of intestinal gas broke the chain which bound him into a silent acceptance of the shelter she had provided, it remained a fact that when she left the house on a shopping errand, Arthur packed his manuscript, cased his typewriter and left the immaculately furnished house. He was at the bridge, looking into the dark brown water of the little Ponnewton stream when Laura's car stopped. She got out and ran to him. "Where are you going?" she cried.

"Home," he replied.

"But Arthur?"

He wanted to be reasonable, to explain why he couldn't remain in the beautiful house she had provided, but reason deserted him, and what came out was an incoherent heap of words in which his needs as a writer were mixed with his fear of poverty and failure and the requirement that his cock be quieted in the sheath of a village woman. It was a display of total irrationality, and much can be said about Laura Dorchester in that she quietly listened and when he abruptly stopped was able to ask: "Why didn't you tell me this before, Arthur?"

"How could I? You just took over."

"I thought you would enjoy working in the home of a well-known nineteenth century poet."

"But I don't want perfection around me! How can I write about women trapped in misery because no matter how hard they try, they're unable to fight off their bodies' needs? How am I to describe the things they feel when the walls in the room where I work are covered with paintings of never-never land?"

"Stop. You could have told me you weren't happy. I won't say anything about the trouble and expense."

"I'll pay you!" he shouted. "I'll pay you!"

"No. Those are secondary considerations. Your obligation to me as your publisher was to tell me the house was inimical to you. And as for your need to have a woman—well, you could have come to me."

"What!" The word was out before he realized how offensive it might seem. "That isn't what I meant," he mumbled.

"I have a clear idea what you meant, Arthur, although that doesn't alter the fact that I'm as much a woman as your village tarts. But we can talk about that later. What we have to do now is get you back to the house."

"I'm not going back to Ponnewton."

"Where you live is entirely up to you. I'll drive you to the your house if that's what you want."

"You don't have to do that. I can walk."

"You have to accept that you can't live alone. Someone has to be with you. Believe me, Arthur, when I walked into that kitchen and saw you lying at the foot of the stairs, I thought something terrible had happened to you. At the time, I had no idea your mother was dead. I was frantically racing around looking for the nearest telephone to call for an ambulance, but of course there was no telephone. I won't go through that again, Arthur. Someone has to be with you." Her insistence irritated him, but he couldn't deny her right to speak, since but for her chance arrival he might still be on the kitchen floor while his mother crumbled to dust in the bed.

"I'll get someone from the village," he said.

"No. That wouldn't do. I'll work something out. Now, please get into the car and I'll take you home."

Arthur didn't enjoy being bullied by Laura, but he acquiesced and was driven to his house which looked, he thought as they drove down the lane, forlorn and untended in the late afternoon sun. All its imperfections were exposed. The kitchen smelled sour when they entered, and Laura suggested he get a fire going in the stove and open the front and back door to get air circulating. "I'll go back to Ponnewton to pick up groceries. I shouldn't be gone for more than an hour. I'll bring your clothes too."

During the time Laura was gone, Arthur started a fire in the stove, opened the back door, then slowly, very slowly, climbed the stairs to his mother's room. It was strange that losing Sylvia had never made him cry, nor did it now. He lay in the trough in the mattress where he had slept and looked over the top of his new boots at an old pre-WWI picture torn from a calendar of an unbelievably pretty thatched-roof, rose-covered cottage which his mother had pinned to the whitewashed wall. The fantasy image (the reverse of the village's reality) was the only decoration in the house. Why had his mother, knowing it was totally unreal, hung it? Probably it was a reflection of her innate, persistent romanticism. He tried to conjure up an image of her at the foot of the bed, letting down and brushing her hair before joining him on the mattress. Long hair had been fashionable when she was young, and girls aimed for waist-length tresses. His mother's hair must have been so glossy, so prismatic in the sunlight that day at the tram stop that she had reminded Sergeant Compson, so Sylvia had told him, of the portrait of a pretty girl on the top of a box of chocolates. Did that explain the picture on the wall? Had his mother carried the imagined picture of a smiling girl on a chocolate box through the years of relentless poverty, so that no matter what happened, regardless of the coarse trades-men who leered at her and pushed thick-fingered hands beneath her clothes, she had remained true to the image of the laughing Edwardian girl, whose fair-haired lover had obediently enlisted when war was declared and had gone off to die in France? In those days (how far off they now seemed) everyone in Britain, even the working class, believed that fighting for King and country conferred nobility on them, but nowadays, patriotism was passé, and government, face-to-face with years of depression and mass unem-ployment, needed to drum up propaganda that matched in outrageousness anything the Nazis had concocted before it could successfully conscript embittered working class men to go to war on behalf of a country that had done so little for them in a time of need. Arthur had never bothered to crystallize his personal beliefs about his country, about the way it was governed or about the destructive, costly war in which it was now en-gaged. The country had rejected him as unsuitable to die in battle and he, in turn, had isolated himself by writing stories about a tiny rural area of England which, in many ways, was as primitive as a village in the Carpathian Mountains, or some remote pueblo in Central America. There was noth-ing, absolutely nothing of value in the village, nothing was sent out of it, and the little that entered came in the form of meagre wages paid to the few men who laboured in the forest. What he, Arthur, had earned by using the village as the locale for his novels surpassed tenfold the amount of money that flowed into the village each year. Like a sideshow busker, he had urged people to hand over their shillings to enter his dark tent and gape at his exhibition of human passions.

He heard the back door close, then after a while the sound of Laura's shoes on the stairs. He guessed from the way she hesitantly walked that she was afraid she would find him unconsciousness. She crossed to the bed and forced herself to smile. "I have things to eat," she said. "I per-suaded the butcher to give me some ham."

"This is where my father slept. He had his trough, and Mother hers. Separated by the ridge. Being a model husband, he crossed over the ridge to join Mother in her trough. I know that's true, because after his death she told me that a good wife always accepts her husband, even when he's been with other women. I've been lying here thinking about Mother, and about myself and what I've done in my life. I've concluded that I've been consuming my parents, the village and the forest, emotionally and physically, and then shitting them out as novels. What do you think?"

"You're experiencing a reaction to your mother's death and your own illness. Consider that one day people might call this area the A.E. Compson country, much as they refer to Dorset as Hardy country."

"I doubt it." He patted the bed. "See if you can fit into Mother's trough." Laura shook her head. "Scared you'd not be her equal?"

"No. I just don't want to lie there."

"You said I could've come to you instead of a village woman."

"Yes, I did say that."

"It was said to silence me. Right?" Laura did not reply, instead removed her walking shoes and carefully arranged herself in the trough in which Sylvia had slept. "There. It's not so bad, is it? Mother refused to burn this old mattress. She lay there and remembered how Father crossed the ridge to make love with her."

"I can't speculate on your mother's memories."

"But imagine. You're lying here at night, waiting for your husband to cross the ridge and kneel between your spread thighs, waiting to sigh with pleasure as your bodies unite, waiting to feel your hips rising, waiting to gasp as your cunt moistens. Women in this village wait five minutes for men to fill their cunts, then nine months before they push out unwanted children. It's quite senseless. I spend my life waiting for images and words to appear so that I can form them into a novel you'll publish. I have a brain that periodically betrays me and a body that's a shadow of my father's."

"You've accomplished more than your father did in his whole life."

"He fought with T.E. Lawrence in Arabia."

"So did other men."

"I think of Father being alone in the desert, like Jesus wrestling with temptation in the wilderness. You know, I read the Bible as a child. For a while, it was the only book around. Do you know the Book of Job?"

"More or less," which Arthur interpreted to mean she was not familiar with Job's travails.

"I preferred Satan to God. And Job was no worse off than anybody in

Hasterley. Once, when we were living in that awful hovel after Father died, I came into the kitchen and saw Mother bathing herself at the sink, and I remembered reading how David saw Bathsheba bathing. Do girls find it impossible to believe that a part of their father's body entered their mother's and that one day a part of a man's body will enter theirs? Did you look at your parents and wonder about these things?"

"Mother died when I was small, and it would have been sacrilegious for me to speculate about my father."

"But for you to exist, your mother had to allow your father inside her cunt."

"I can't think of my parents like that."

"Did your parents love you?"

"They weren't demonstrative."

"I've imagined other people's lives. I've even imagined you in bed with me."

"That's a possibility." Laura's concession astonished Arthur because it contradicted everything he thought he knew about her. She unfastened the stocking on her right leg and removed it, and was about to start on her left leg when Arthur sat up and said, "Shush!" He leaned over the ridge and whispered, "Somebody's downstairs. Listen."

Laura stopped, sat up, listened, then nodded. "Yes, there is."

"You stay here."

"No."

"No point in both of us going." He looked around for something that could be used as a weapon, saw nothing, shrugged and crept out of the bedroom, followed by Laura. Slowly, with painful care, they descended the stairs into the kitchen where, after Arthur had bellowed: "Who's there?", two dogs raced through the open door and across the lawn to disappear beyond the wicket.

"The bag of groceries!" Laura gasped. "I carried in the groceries and left the door open. Oh no! They took the ham slices. Oh no! I spent so much time inveigling them out of the butcher."

"It doesn't matter." Arthur laughed, pulled out a chair and sat on it.

"Damn dogs!" Laura said. "I could kill them!" She sat on the other side of the table and rearranged the things she had purchased. "This war's made a mess of everything."

"It'll eventually wear out."

"Wear out? What an odd expression."

"I meant, the insanity 'll pass. So, since we're down here, shall we make tea?"

"I suppose." There was a note of regret in her voice. "I'll fetch my stocking and shoes."

"Or we can pick up where we left off?"

"Yes, we could do that," she agreed.

But they did not return to the bedroom. Instead, they sat down to a simple tea, and after finishing it, Laura announced she was returning to London but would come back within the week with a housekeeper who would remain permanently. "It's impossible for me to stay longer," she added.

"As you wish. But I want to make it clear, I won't have anybody living in this house."

"Either you come to London, or have someone with you here. I'm not risking your next novel because you choose to behave stupidly. As it is, I've given—"

"I'll pay back every penny you loaned me."

"I'm not talking about that, Arthur. I'm talking about the time I've spent taking care of your affairs while you were in the hospital."

The afternoon did not end on a pleasant note. It seemed as if the dogs' incursion had opened a breach between them through which now poured the petty dislikes, criticisms and resentments that had accumulated over the almost four years of their relationship. For a few moments, he was overcome by the magnitude of the gap which had opened between them. How was it possible that the woman who had raised shapely legs to unfasten her stockings was now turning away as if she could hardly bear his company? He trailed behind her, then stood by the open door, filled with shame, but also with a desire to renegotiate the terms of their friendship though he was unable to find the appropriate words.

It remained with Laura to provide them. "I'm sure that given time we'll come to a better understanding of each other," she said.

"I hope so," Arthur muttered. "I do hope so."

"But we'll have to arrange things differently." Perhaps she expected him to agree, but when he did not reply, she said nothing further, got in the car and drove away.

CHAPTER
10

ARTHUR'S RETURN HOME AND THE ASTUTE MANNER HE HAD evaded Laura's attempts to organize his life had an invigorating effect on him, and he immediately set to work again.

A theme latent in Arthur's novels was that every significant occurrence in a person's life could be traced back to a incident so small as to be hardly perceptible, such as a chance meeting or even a mere sighting of somebody or something. Arthur's notion of causation might be compared to a very small artificial fly on a fishhook cast across a stream where real flies by the thousand danced above sun-dappled water in which hungry fish wait, ready to leap; no one would ever know why the fish jumped to capture a particular fly from among the thousands hovering there, except to recognize that the act resulted in the fish's death. And no one in Arthur's novels ever explained why individuals became so attached to each other they choose death rather than separation, as in the novel he was presently writing, where a deeply religious brother and sister are so profoundly devoted to each other that, after physically tempting one another in every possible way, they drink poison and die in the hope they can achieve what they have always denied themselves: a uniting of their bodies. Arthur worked through the night until a thrush called from a tree beyond the wall when he went outside to pee, then lit a fire, boiled water, made a pot of tea and thirstily drank cup after cup while eating slices of bread and margarine on which he placed rows of sardines. After eating them, he poured oil from the sardine can over one more slice of bread and smacked his lips when he finished eating it. He was tired, but too restless to sleep, so he decided to walk through the Asty enclosure to the heath, but had to change his plan when, wanting to bank the fire, he found there was no coal in the shed and walked to the general village shop to leave an order for delivery. From there, he went on to a cottage where Mabel Smith sat at a table, drinking tea.

"Early bird, eh?" she said.

"Early?" he echoed.

"It's only nine."

"I didn't realize. I've been working all night."

"With yer 'orn up? Doan that woman as comes to yer 'ouse in a car do it with yer?"

"No."

"Too good fer yer, eh?"

"It's not her style."

"Mine neither. I does it to survive. Here, I'm sorry yer mum died. And sorry to 'ear about yer 'aving a fit and all."

"I didn't have a fit." He wondered if people would ever stop saying he had fits. How he hated being reduced to the same level as the village epileptic, who screamed eerily before his convulsed, contorted body fell to the ground. It was not that villagers ostracized the man, indeed they saw him as possessing special powers and were not above asking advice on all manner of things; but for Arthur, it was a matter of class distinction. Due to Sylvia's social attitudes, he had grown up believing diseases were divided between those that afflicted the poor and those that were suffered by the upper classes, and epilepsy was definitely a lower-class disease.

"Well, whatever it was. I'll finish me tea if yer doan mind."

"I don't mind."

"Like a cup?"

"No thanks." He sat at the table.

"It's a bugger of a life, ain't it?"

"Yes," he agreed, "it is."

"When yer a kid all yer wants is ter grow up, then yer grows up, and if yer a woman yer slaves at washin' floors and cookin' and openin' yer legs ter let brats begin growin' inside yer."

"You never had a child."

"That's the only bit of luck I've 'ad in me life." Although nearing forty, Mabel Smith appeared youthful because her body hadn't thickened from child-bearing. When released from plaits, her lustrous black hair clothed her shoulders and breasts. Among village men she was known as "The Snare," an allusion to the circular wire gins that grabbed, held, then slowly strangled any rabbit that shoved its neck into one. It was a lewd exaggeration of the kind local men commonly made about women, even their wives. Arthur wondered if the men feared their wives because they created new life within themselves after reducing the object the men most valued to a dangling, useless sausage.

Arthur's childhood and adolescence reading had left an indelible impression upon his imagination, and he would never forget that the God of the Old Testament damned women to subservience, nor that Rabelais' Panurge advised Pantagruel the city of Paris could be walled "good and cheap" with female privates, nor that Shakespeare's males happily traded women as chattels. The youthful Arthur had never entirely recovered from the mad King Lear's assessment of women as angels from the waist up but all hell below, nor from the Trojan warrior Trollius's virulent condemnation of women when he discovered his lover Cressida haggling with another man over her body.

Mabel poured herself another cup of tea. "Sure yer doan wan' a cup?" she asked.

"No."

"I needs a pot ter get goin' in the mornin's. I bin thinkin' of settin' meself up in Tambourne. Chaps tell me the Yanks is payin' five quid. Ten quid fer niggers. 'E'eard as a girl bled ter death after a nigger fucked 'er."

"Surely you don't believe that racialist stuff."

"It's because niggers is twice as big as white chaps." She gulped down her tea, stood, stretched, and the not-too-clean dressing gown she habitually wore fell open to reveal her egg-shell white body which, for a pound, he would own for thirty minutes. "Latch the door," she ordered. She removed her dressing gown and lay on the unmade bed. Arthur took off his jacket, shoes, trousers and underpants, but left his shirt on, then lay between her opened thighs, pushed himself into her and lay still, enjoying the warmth and smoothness of her vaginal sheath. He tried, but could not prevent orgasm from commencing and, as he came, he jammed his face into her breasts. "That's fast," she said. "Yer can 'ave another go if it'll go up." He moved his lips over her breasts and felt himself harden again. "Yer know, when I uster see yer mum in the lane, I'd ask meself why she put up with yer dad."

"It didn't matter to her. She knew he loved her."

"She didn't mind 'im fuckin' girls like me?"

Arthur pulled away and began dressing. "I don't want to hear what you did!"

"Me! Yer listen ter me, Mr. Arthur, *I* did bugger all. It was your daddy what did it all. 'E took me and other girls inter the enclosure and pulled down our knickers."

"Shut up! Don't say another word about my parents. My father fought with Lawrence in Arabia, and my mother was . . ." The rage surging through him suddenly melted away, and he looked down at Mabel, ashamed of his behaviour. "I'm sorry," he muttered. "It's just I don't like to talk about my parents. I'm sorry I shouted at you."

"I doan mind what yer does, so long as yer pays and doan punch me jaw or smash me furniture."

"I'll call in tomorrow afternoon," he said.

"Yer do that," she agreed, "and drop the door latch on yer way out."

Arthur walked along the edge of the Common toward the house, puzzling over his outburst at Mabel Smith. After all, why should he care if his father pegged girls who rolled their eyes and bottoms at him? No, it was what Mabel implied about his mother, that she was a silly woman, all but mentally deficient like the woman Bessie, who followed village children around, smiling at everything they said, even taunts and curses; a simple soul easily lured into the furze on the Common to be used like a sow by village youths. He walked through the Asty enclosure and across the heath to the clump of Scotch pines where he sat and looked over the land to the distant Channel, grey, but flecked with white from the wind that drove low black clouds inland from the distant ocean. Some day, he thought, when the war ended, he would stand on the deck of a Trans-Atlantic ocean liner and look back toward the land where as a child he had walked, often with his mother, sometimes with his father, or where he sat alone when he was older and projected images of plots and characters which might eventually bring him fame and, he hoped, fortune. He sighed, then slowly walked back to the house, entered the kitchen and saw Laura sitting at the table with a slender young woman who wore a long-sleeved brown dress, brown cotton stockings and thick-soled black shoes. A small black hat perched on her fluffy, curly dark-brown hair. A raincoat was folded over one forearm and a suitcase stood at her feet. Her cheeks were splashed with scarlet, she had brown eyes, and her full, nicely shaped lips were pursed as though on the verge of challenging the validity of what someone had just said or done. She was, Arthur concluded, a take-it-or-leave-it person.

"Maria's here to keep house for you," Laura said. Arthur stared at the young woman, who briefly smiled. "She's an experienced housekeeper and cook. I've explained your circumstances to her."

"I'm getting along well as I am," Arthur said.

"I'm sure you are," Laura agreed. "Maria also types, so she may be able to help with your work."

"I don't know about that." Arthur felt he must protest before being buried under Laura's efficiency.

"Spelling's my weakness," Maria explained.

"No matter," Laura dismissed the inadequacy. "The main thing is to get you settled in. I've explained to Maria that everything here is very simple."

"It couldn't be worse than the orphanage," Maria said.

"That was a long time ago, Maria. And the orphanage had running hot and cold water," Laura reminded her. "You won't find that here. I'll show you around and give you a general idea of what needs to be done. You don't mind, do you, Arthur?"

"No," Arthur said, understanding he'd been defeated from the moment Laura and Maria entered the kitchen; in fact, he suspected their exchanges had been rehearsed, like a Shaw play where everything you expect to be said *is* said, so that you can be guided to a conclusion predetermined by the playwright. Arthur had been reading G.B. Shaw and had come to dislike the dramatist's mentoring of the audience; Arthur preferred characters to be sufficiently irrational that it would be impossible to know at the beginning of a story or play how it would end. He couldn't stand the sterility of what passed for love with Shaw; he, Arthur, was committed to portraying love in all its emanations, smells and abandonments; *his* women would fling off clothes and expose swollen genitals like bitches in heat, *his* men would strut about with erect penises; not only that, he would also make sure the women and men paid the penalty for their passion in a society where criminal activities were preferred to fulfilled sexual desire.

Arthur soon learned that Maria was breathtakingly competent: She could light and have a fire blazing in half the time it took him; a kettle of water was always sitting on the hob, ready to be moved over and brought to the boil for tea, or in the morning to provide him with shaving water. Maria used the oven his mother had abandoned to bake pies and knobbly hunks of dough containing chopped nuts and raisins she called *rock cakes*. Arthur, whose idea of baked goods was whatever came from the baker, found that he could eat as many as ten of Maria's little cakes at a sitting, and as the weeks passed, he gradually came to realize that although Sylvia had been an ideal mother and surrogate wife, she was a poor housekeeper and terrible cook.

Within days of arriving, Maria had gone to Ponnewton and returned with what Arthur had contemplated purchasing for years: a bicycle. On this she rode to Ponnewton twice a week to buy groceries. Of greater importance, she angrily informed the tradesmen who called at the house that if they didn't offer a better selection of products, they could skip calling at the house.

"You think I'm stupid!" she challenged them.

"Missus Sylv'a never found fault," they whined.

"Don't Missus me," Maria stormed. "You see green in my eyes?" She thrust her nose against theirs. "What happened to the rest of the animal?" she demanded when Henry Joyce offered a scrawny piece of meat. "You call that gristle *lamb?*" It didn't matter that the tradesmen had to cope with shortages and rationing, she still ordered them to produce edible food or else stay away. Food bills rose, but the quality of the meals improved, and every other week Arthur could sharpen his father's knife to carve a roast. "Nothing's so nice as a good cut of meat, done tender," Maria would say and smack her lips after tasting a slice of rare roast beef. She would spoon juices that oozed from the meat and force them onto Arthur. "Your brain needs it," she said, denying that she herself would benefit from the hot, fat-laden juice. "Men's brains aren't fully grown until they're sixty, just before they peg out," she explained. "Women 've got theirs by the time they're twenty. Why else do you suppose men go wacky, regular as clockwork, and go off and kill each other? No brains, that's why." She purchased old hens in the village and made soups which provided meals for several days and ordered loins of pork from every villager who kept a pig in his stye. "We could keep a few hens in the yard," she said as they dipped spoons into the aromatic soup. When Arthur asked who would slaughter them, she pointed her spoon at him: "Killing's natural to chaps," and when he vehemently denied any urge to slaughter, she shrugged and said, "Wait and see."

Maria fascinated Arthur and, although he was unaware of it, he began spending time sitting at the kitchen table, watching her go about daily tasks, listening to her offer judgements on the people of Hasterley and Ponnewton. She talked a lot about her younger sister, Martha, who also worked for Laura Dorchester, explaining she was a flibberty-gibbet who needed someone to watch over her, and how her sister thought of Maria as a mother instead of a sister because, after their mother had died (Martha was two) Maria had taken care of her at the orphanage before Miss Dorchester appeared to take them into service.

The more efficient and effective Maria became the more Arthur wondered how he could afford her wages. He eventually found the courage to ask and gasped when Maria said, "Miss Dorchester's docking your account."

"Docking my account!" he cried. Laura's audacity left Arthur with little to say, except to ask how much.

"A pound a week and board. Miss Dorchester is putting my wages in a Post Office savings. Anyway, you're getting good value for your money. Well, aren't you?" And Arthur couldn't deny what she said. She was a fiend for work, for no sooner had she joined him at the table to pour herself a cup of tea than she would remember an unfinished task and rush from the table, and when he urged her to leave the jobs until morning, she scolded him: "Just like a man," she said, "but what's put off never gets done. Cobwebs in corners and dust under furniture." Lately though, Maria would return to sit at the table when Arthur asked. They seemed to enjoy each other's company.

The matter of Maria's wages, however, was a minor matter compared to the alterations that began to take shape in the house. One afternoon, while Arthur was out walking, two men came to the house, removed the old cast iron stove and installed an Aga cooker.

"But why?" Arthur protested when he returned. "I liked the stove. It worked for you."

"We need hot water," Maria said.

"But there's no water to make hot."

"You'll see," Maria replied.

And he did. A few mornings later he was awakened by male voices, in and outside the house. When he looked through the window, a group of men were digging a trench in the back. He pulled on his clothes, ran to the head of the stairs and yelled: "Maria! Come here!" When she appeared, he pointed to the window with a voice that combined astonishment, anger and trembling disbelief. "Who are those men out there? What's going on? Stop them! At once!"

"They're putting in pipes."

"Pipes? Who said? What pipes?"

"From the well to the cooker." Maria's tone was that of an exasperated teacher explaining elementary arithmetic to a slow pupil.

"But I didn't ask for . . ."

"Miss Dorchester's arranged it. She knows people who get things done. The foreman said they'd have everything in by five. He said, too bad we don't want a bath and a lav too, because they could've done the whole shebang in a few days."

"But who's paying? I counted ten men out there!"

"Miss Dorchester's arranged it. Don't worry, they're working on company time. The Yanks 're building an airfield for bombers near Tambourne. The company chap is a pal of Miss Dorchester. Why don't you give the foreman ten quid to find us a nice lav and bath?"

"But I don't have ten quid on me."

"I'll speak to him. And how about five quid for the chaps to buy a pint when they knock off?"

"Fifteen pounds!" The idea of handing over fifteen pounds to strangers horrified Arthur.

"It's a five hundred quid job."

"But I don't have fifteen pounds here."

"Get it at the bank. I'll tell the foreman. He's an old hand and knows a wink's as good as a nod."

"We could go to prison for stealing government property."

Maria looked at him and shook her head. "Your breakfast's ready," she said and went to discuss the matter with the foreman. Dazed by all the activity, Arthur sat at the kitchen table and, when the foreman came in to sit opposite him, stayed silent as he spoke: "There's no guarantee of colour. If there's a spare green set at the officers' quarters, I'll take it, but white's a sure thing. I'll need to spread a few quid around. Let's say fifty, and that'll include turning the closet into a septic tank. That pit's as pretty a piece of brickwork as I ever did see. And running a field into the forest, the shit 'll make trees grow."

"Watch what you say around Mr. Compson," Maria said.

"A lah-de-dah type, eh?"

"He writes books," Maria said.

"You don't say?" commented the foreman. They spoke of Arthur as though he did not exist.

The outcome of these negotiations was that Arthur rode to the bank in Ponnewton with the foreman, who told him he liked Zane Grey books and asked if he thought Pecos Pete was faster on the draw than Billy the Kid. Arthur, who had never read a Western, said he thought Pecos Pete was the faster. The foreman agreed and regretted that fate had prevented the renowned gunmen from ever meeting. Arthur concurred, then said he might write a Wild West story some day.

"Forget Dodge city. It's wore out," the foreman advised. "Take my advice and head for gold country. California. Have the hero a guy that's wanted for murder in Texas. He disguises himself. Y'know, a beard and what-not."

"The fastest draw in the gold country?"

"That's it. He defends a widow's right to the richest claim in the California diggings."

"And marries her?"

"Well, he could. Mind you, it don't pay women to marry gunmen."

They discussed the intricacies of plot and decided the widow was a Texan and wearing widow's weeds because the hero had shot her husband in a poker game. "Oh, boy! Sounds great. What happens next?"

Arthur looked across the street at the ornate bank entrance and saw a tall, black-suited man emerge from the bank and stroll off. He was the Ponnewton undertaker. Of course, thought Arthur, the hero will do likewise. On the eve of his marriage, the hero writes a farewell letter to the widow, boards a stagecoach and rides off to Frisco to die in a shoot-out with a man faster on the draw than himself. "And," Arthur added, "the great irony is, the widow had known all along that the hero had killed her husband. She was happy about it because it freed her from an unhappy marriage."

"Me and you ought to get together and write that yarn. You do the writing and I'll give you the details about the guns. How about it?"

"Right now I'm pretty busy," Arthur said. "But it's something to bear in mind."

"You bet!" the foreman agreed. "So, I'll wait here while you hop out and get the sixty quid."

"It was fifty."

"No, sixty."

Arthur's parsimonious self protested, but lacking either the courage or experience to defy the foreman, he capitulated and entered the bank with hunched shoulders to withdraw sixty pounds from his account, then, without saying a word, he sullenly handed the foreman six ten-pound notes and watched the lorry trundle off. He began walking along the street, castigating himself for meekly surrendering to a man who viewed the war as a financial opportunity, regardless of the cost of his petty thievery to the country. Arthur wasn't patriotic and he certainly did not object to getting something for nothing. No. What bothered him was the possibility that his acquisition of a bathroom would in some convoluted way have to be paid for by men being maimed or killed on the battlefield because he and the foreman had failed to shoulder their obligations during the years of national emergency. Experience had solidified Arthur's sense of fatalism and strengthened his belief that for everything an individual received, no matter how small, there exists a reciprocal form of payment—somewhere, in some unidentifiable time zone, someone tallied up what each individual received and the amount still owing; and although Arthur would probably have indignantly denied it, his rock-bottom conviction was that a day of reckoning would arrive for every man and woman, and when it did, what

Ernest Langford

the person had already paid would be placed in a balance scale and weighed to find out what was still owed. The more Arthur considered his own dilly-dallying and ineffectual personal behaviour, including his recent fiddle in the black market, the more irritated he became with himself, and he couldn't even foist responsibility for cheating onto Maria because she was simply following Laura's directions, though it was clear she enjoyed the role of supervisor and believed the alterations in the house would benefit everyone.

His progress along High Street was a stop-and-go affair: he purposefully marched forward one minute, then halted the next, when an extension of a previous thought occurred to him. There was no doubt (he now thought) that Maria rode roughshod over him, but still there was something very nice about her. On the other hand, she was his employee, wasn't she, since he was paying her wages. So shouldn't he be the one issuing orders, not Maria? Yes, by rights he should exercise more authority and insist Maria address him as "sir." Yet, the problem was, he didn't think of Maria as his servant, maybe at first he did, but not any more. After their many amiable conversations hadn't she become a friend? And why was it that he became so restless when she wasn't around for him to watch and talk to? "It's all wrong," he said to his reflection in a shop window where he stopped for a moment to repeat to himself, "yes, it's all wrong." He looked up and read the shop sign that jutted out at a right angle: *Jones the Jeweller.* Simultaneously, he realized he would never tell Maria she must say "sir" because, without his knowing it until this moment, he had fallen in love with her and wanted her to remain with him for the rest of his life. He had been puzzled by his reluctance to visit Mabel Smith, and now he understood why. He was in love. Imagine! In love! Yes, he had vested his feelings, emotional and sexual, in Maria without being aware of doing it. But what he felt for her was quite different from the love he had felt for his mother, and was not the same as his childhood adoration of Heather. This was a new feeling! He paced back and forth in front of the jewellery shop thinking he must do something to show Maria how he felt, and it was then that he saw the jewellery arrayed on a velvet cloth in the shop window. A ring! Not an engagement ring of course, it was too soon for that, but a token of friendship. Though why *shouldn't* he get engaged to Maria? Why *shouldn't* they marry? He looked at the rings and spotted the perfect one for Maria: a band studded with three glittering stones. He entered the shop, where a thin, bald man sat at a worktable examining the interior of a watch. He put down his loupe, stood behind the display case and said, "How may I help you?"

"The ring in the window, the one with three stones," Arthur said.

"Ah! That's a lovely ring. Eighteen-carat gold with three small diamonds. A quality item."

"How much?"

"Twenty-five pounds. A good price."

"Can I look at it?"

"You certainly can." The jeweller came from behind the display case to remove the ring from the window. "You'd pay double in London for this."

"You'll take a cheque?"

"Well . . ." the jeweller temporized.

"I'm A. E. Compson, the novelist. I bank at Barclays." Hearing the words thrilled Arthur. He was no longer one of the faceless mass! He was A. E. Compson, novelist, with an account at Barclays!

The jeweller turned the ring and Arthur watched light shatter on the diamond facets. "You live in Ponnewton, Mr. Compson?"

"Hasterley. I own a house there." He could also boast of owning a house!

"Well, in that case, I'll be pleased to take your cheque, sir." As Arthur made out the cheque, using a fountain pen the jeweller offered, he thought his act symbolized his emergence from an existence where pennies were counted into the world of elegant, free-spending people like Laura Dorchester. The jeweller put the ring in a small plush box. "A gift for your wife, Mr. Compson?"

"A token of friendship, for a lady."

"We can fit the ring to the lady's finger if necessary."

"Thank you."

"Good day to you, Mr. Compson. Please call in again."

Arthur left the shop, buoyant, delighted with what he had done. His feet seemed not to touch the pavement stones. But his mood changed when an image of Maria suddenly appeared before him, in which he saw her running from the house. He panicked and bolted like a dog that had been kicked in its ribs until exhaustion forced him to halt at the bridge over the placid stream where he leaned on the rail, panting and saturated with sweat, and stared down into the brown, slowly moving water, asking himself why his response to a momentary image had been so precipitous. As a boy, his favourite summer afternoon jaunt was coming here with his mother to catch minnows in an empty jam jar baited with stale bread, and while Sylvia removed her shoes and stockings and sat on the bank to dangle her feet in the water, he carefully lowered the jar and watched the minnows quivering at the mouth of his trap. The fish were very cautious, and those that ventured inside usually escaped before he was able to lift the jar out of the water; they preferred to cluster around and nibble his mother's toes, which made her to giggle like a school girl on holiday. He recalled that he and Sylvia were wearing wide-brimmed straw hats to protect noses from sunburn—he, in khaki shorts, white shirt and sandals; she in a flower-print summer dress. Emotion flooded him and tears filled his eyes. Those summer afternoons had been idyllic; neither the child nor the mother asked for anything more than to sit beside the little stream for an hour or so before strolling home across the Common, where bees swarmed in thousands around the yellow aromatic gorse flowers and where they sometimes halted to wait while an adder or grass snake sinuously moved across the narrow path in front of them. He thought his mother beautiful on those days, and was enchanted by the way she smiled at him from beneath her hat and asked if he was happy. Of course, he had been happy, wondrously happy. And because it had never occurred to him to ask if *she* were happy too, he would never know what his mother felt on those afternoons.

He climbed down the bank, stripped and slipped into the dark pool beneath the bridge, murmuring, "May all my sins of omission be forgiven," then, as though engaged in a rite of purification, he submerged himself beneath the water until the need for air forced him to surface. He heard a vehicle approach and rumble across the bridge. The image of his mother reappeared: she sat alone on the river bank, stirring the water with her small white feet, and he remembered that when she dried him after his weekly bath, she always kissed his toes and said his feet were like her own, and that slender feet were the hallmark of well-bred people. Her little deceptions still influenced the way he looked at people. His assessments might be shallow, but he had always accepted her social code because it had flattered them. The image of his mother faded as he heard footsteps on the bridge and for one horrifying moment he thought it was his mother's ghost. The footsteps halted and he looked up and saw Maria.

"Is that you down there? Where are you?" she called.

"In the water!"

"Why? What are you doing"

"Cooling off."

"I met the foreman and he said he hadn't seen you. It scared me."

"Sorry. I didn't intend to frighten you."

"Well, you did. Come out where I can see you."

He waded from beneath the bridge and peered up at her. "Satisfied?"

"You've got no right gallivanting around without first telling me."

"I can go where I please. But if I'd known it worried you . . ."

"Get dressed," she ordered and turned away while he left the water, put on his clothes and shoes, and crab-walked up the bank to join her on the bridge. "You're as bad as Martha," she said. "I don't know why I spend my time running after people who can't take care of themselves."

Arthur was insulted. "Let me remind you, I didn't invite you into my home. You were foisted on me by Laura Dorchester. And if you're so fed up with me, you're free to pack up and leave. Anytime!" Maria stared at him, her face ashen, then turned to lean over the rail. After a few hesitant moments, Arthur approached and touched her shoulder. "I'm sorry. I'd no idea you worried about me. Anyway, I don't want you to leave. I admire you. What I mean is, I love you, Maria. Really, I do. I want to be with you all the time. I mean, the time I'm not working."

"All or nothing, is that it?" There was an uncertainty in her voice he had not heard before.

"I just know I don't want you to leave. Ever." He found and held her hand. "Look, could we get engaged? Here, I got this for you." He took out the small box and opened it. "See it?"

"You think I'd fall for a six-penny ring from Woolworth's?" She tried to free her hand. "Don't try to trick me."

"What trick? These are real diamonds."

"I mean the likes of you promising a ring to get into bed with the likes of me."

"You think I'd say I love you just to get you into bed?"

"Men say anything to get a girl into bed."

"I'm a man who loves you."

"You think I don't know about the village tarts? You love them too?"

"Listen, if I'd known you were coming into my life, I'd have taken an oath of celibacy."

"And pigs'll fly."

He laughed, and after a pause she joined him. He raised her hand, kissed it and rubbed it against his cheek. "Let me put it on." He took out the ring and selected the appropriate finger.

"No, I can't." She tried to free her hand. "Miss Dorchester won't like it."

"Come on, Maria, let me put it on. You do like me, don't you?" She nodded, which he took to mean she would accept the ring. "Now we can really talk. You can tell me about your boyfriends."

"I haven't ever had one."

"And I'll tell you about my girlfriends. There's only been one. When I was a boy. Her name is Heather."

Arthur leaned back on the railing, put his arms around Maria and drew her close. "What about Martha?" she said.

"She can live with us."

"Well, I'll see," she said and didn't object when he kissed her, first on the cheek, then her neck and lips.

"You like me?" he asked again, but she avoided answering.

"I'll have to tell Miss Dorchester."

"You don't have to tell her anything. As of right now, you've stopped working for her. Understand? You're with me now. You're part of my life."

"We'll see." Maria wondered if Arthur understood the nature of her relationship with Laura Dorchester. After all, the almighty Miss Dorchester had selected her for service from among the girls at the orphanage and agreed to take Martha too when Maria refused to leave without her. Maria was fourteen then, Martha seven. She remembered Miss Dorchester telling the matron that loyalty was a quality seldom found in the working class, and she was certain the atmosphere of her home would be conducive to the development of decorous habits of thought and behaviour in both girls. So the sisters had remained together in Laura Dorchester's grand London home until Laura persuaded Maria to go to Hasterley, keep house for Arthur and supervise the alterations which Laura had arranged with influential friends. From what Maria had learned in service with Laura Dorchester, she doubted, when it came right down to it, that Arthur would marry her. After all, she was a servant. She even doubted the love he professed. Loneliness was Arthur's problem; she'd seen it in his eyes when he sat at the kitchen table watching her clean up after the evening meal; he was like a stray cat that meows and arches its back when you say a kind word and bend to stroke it. She wouldn't object to him kissing her now and then, it felt quite nice, but she would go no further and feeling his stiff cock against her intensified her determination not to succumb to that fatal weakness that broke down a woman's resistance and left her soiled and despised. Still, after considering everything, she decided that when she next saw Miss Dorchester, she would mention Arthur's proposal, then, if Miss Dorchester didn't object, say she intended to marry him and give as her reason that she wanted a permanent home for herself and Martha. Naturally, she would prefer a bigger house in a nice location, like Southsea or Brighton where she had accompanied Miss Dorchester on pre-war holidays, but beggars can't be choosers, can they? She knew that Miss

Dorchester might fly into one of her rages when she heard. That always happened when she didn't get her way. But the main thing was to provide a home for herself and Martha. And Arthur wasn't a bad sort, though of course she didn't love him. She moved away from him and said they must get back to Asty. "I don't trust those chaps. You have to keep an eye on them."

Arthur smiled, then taking her hand, contentedly strolled with her up the hill and across the broad Common to the house where the workmen were putting the final touches on the alterations. "There," the foreman proudly announced. "The lav's been flushed and there's hot and cold water for the kitchen sink, tub and washbasin. Everything's running as smooth as the Thames under London Bridge. Now you two can fill the tub and have a nice hot bath together."

Maria pursed her lips and glared at the foreman. "Don't tell me what I will do." She then ordered him to make sure the plumbers cleaned up the mess they made in the kitchen.

The foreman gave a mock salute. "Yes, mam!" He ordered his men to collect their tools, but when they began picking up scraps of metal and other debris, he told them to forget it.

When Maria returned to the kitchen she was furious when she found the mess still there for her to clean up. She was muttering recriminations when she heard Arthur shout. After a moment of frozen apprehension, she went back to the bathroom to find Arthur looking into the lavatory pan. "What happened?" she whispered. "What is it?"

"I did it!" he shouted. "I did it! I shit and pissed in the pan and watched it go down the drain."

"That's nothing to feel proud of," Maria coldly said. "Fasten up your trousers and come down and help me tidy up the kitchen." He dutifully obeyed, unaware she had been frightened that his affliction had returned and she might not know how to take care of him.

Chapter

11

"MARIA WAS KILLED IN A BUZZ-BOMB EXPLOSION," LAURA calmly said. "She came here to tell me everything was going well. She was on her way to see Martha when she left."

"That was all?" Arthur asked.

"Was she supposed to say more?" Laura cocked her head to one side.

"No," he mumbled.

"Those horrible buzz-bombs don't give people a chance to get into shelters. The engine stops and it plummets down . . . though I am puzzled why she was in a men's wear shop. Had you asked her to buy socks and handkerchiefs, Arthur?"

"I may have. I don't remember." He would not let Laura know he was bleeding internally with grief, though he could tell by the way Laura watched him that Maria had told her about their relationship and had no intention of revealing what she said; he would not let Laura know when Maria failed to return from London, he, sick with worry, had travelled by train to the city and, dazed by the noise and traffic, and had taken a cab to the *Tower & Tower* offices.

"I buried her in Hampstead," Laura said. "She was a good servant. The police gave me a package of socks and handkerchiefs. Could you use them, Arthur? They're no use to me. Where are you going?" she asked as he turned and moved toward the door.

Arthur had no idea where to go. But what he did know was if Maria had not gone into the shop to buy a gift for him she would still be alive. "Oh, Maria, oh, Maria," his heart silently cried, "because of me, you died." He reached the door, felt tormenting pressure surround him like a dense, black, lightning-pierced thunderhead, grabbed for the door handle and collapsed.

Laura scrambled around her desk, knelt and muttered, "Damnation" as a splinter from the worn, uneven oak floor tore her stockings. The expression on her face suggested she doubted if tending to Arthur justified ruining good stockings. After touching his pulse, she ordered her secretary to call an ambulance and a physician, which set into motion a process that ended with Arthur being placed in a bed in Laura Dorchester's home.

"Mr. Compson has episodes," she told the physician who accompanied the ambulance. "But I understand it's not epilepsy."

"Hm." The physician was noncommittal. He was doing time in a metropolitan hospital and in two years had learned to doubt what patients and relatives said to him about a patient's ailments, even to discredit previous diagnoses by colleagues. He had concluded that medicine was still in the dark ages and what was required was a magical cure-all which could be prescribed for every complaint. The odd thing was that the more he learned about human physiology, the more uncertain he became in the presence of affliction. "I'm no neurologist, but—"

"I'll consult Sir Malcolm Hetherton." (Sir Malcolm was one of the elite group of physicians called upon to apply stethoscopes to Royal chests and whose hands had been sanctified by presence at a Royal birth.) Laura wanted the physician to leave so she could go to her room and change her stockings.

"You know Sir Malcolm?"

"He's our family physician."

"Oh, well . . ." What more could a mere resident say? "Keep him warm," he suggested and escaped to the security of the ambulance where he asked the attendant if he would give medical assistance as conscientiously to an epileptic beggar as to an epileptic prince.

"I dunno," the attendant cautiously replied. "Diseases are the same, no matter who has 'em."

"I wonder," the doctor said. "I really wonder. Hm." He played no further role in Arthur Compson's life, but eventually he quit medicine to become a veterinarian where he discovered animals complained less and no distinction was made between a Duchess's dying Pekinese and a slum child's car-battered cat—each caused the same quantity of tears to be shed by their owners, proof love transcends societal barriers. Besides, it comforted him to know that budgerigars, gold fish and turtles accepted whatever he said about their problems and never asked for consultations with specialists.

Laura removed Arthur's boots and socks and was shocked by their less than immaculate condition. She then left the room to return a few minutes later with Betty, Laura's maid from childhood.

"He's a nice-looking chap," Betty said. "Does he work in your office?"

"We publish his novels. He's the man Maria was looking after."

"Oh, him. Martha's still in a terrible state. Can't stop crying." She rearranged the quilt around Arthur.

"She'll get over it," Laura said.

"It'll take a while."

"Perhaps." They walked towards the door. "I won't go back to the office, Betty. Would you make me a cup of tea? I'm exhausted."

Betty opened the door. "Put your feet up and rest for a while."

"Thank goodness I have no dinner guests tonight," Laura said as the two women left the room. "For a change. I'm sure my friends deliberately angle invitations to save food coupons." As she closed the door, she asked, "You did telephone Sir Malcolm?"

"I left a message with his nurse. I'm sure he'll return your call."

"He'd better," Laura warned, and descended the staircase to enter a small sitting room where she lay on a high-backed couch, but was prevented from enjoying her rest by the sight of her reddened kneecaps beneath the jagged holes in the stocking she had yet to change. When Betty returned with the tea tray, Laura said, "Don't forget the stockings."

"Stockings aren't what they used to be," said Betty. She understood Laura well, having watched her evolve from spoiled girl to bossy woman. Betty had hoped Laura would marry a man who would bully her into subservience, but that had not happened and Betty now believed it never would. Laura had sifted through a lot of men, but hadn't found one she liked enough to marry. She didn't think much of women either, except for a handful of women writers, painters and politicians. The person whom Laura admired most was herself and she made a point of ignoring people who didn't agree with that assessment.

While putting on the stockings Betty brought her, she said, "Check on Mr. Compson. Let me know if he's awake. And call Sir Malcolm again. He doesn't deal with the brain, which is probably just as well, but he should be able to recommend a competent neurologist."

"I'll do that." Betty's position in the household was privileged. She did no housework, polishing or cooking, but spent her time laundering Laura's clothes, providing cups of tea and generally keeping Laura happy.

"You looked in on Mr. Compson?" Laura asked while fastening garters to the second stocking.

"He's the same." Betty hesitated, then asked. "What sort of books does he write?"

"They're earthy. His people are driven by uncontrollable passions."

"Kind of young for that, isn't he?"

"Women who use circulating libraries like his books."

"You don't think they're much good?"

"I'm interested in what A. E. Compson might become, once he's worked through his adolescent phase."

Somewhere outside the room a telephone rang. After a moment, a maid appeared in the open doorway to curtsey and say, "It's Sir Colm, Miss Laura." She began to cry.

"Well, so much for resting. For God's sake, will you ever learn to get names straight? It's Sir *Mal*colm. And stop that crying. It's pointless."

"I'm trying, Miss Laura. Honest, I am."

Betty, following Laura, stopped beside the maid. "Mind your p's and q's, Martha. Remember, there's no shortage of orphanage girls wanting positions."

"I'm trying. But Maria was all I had in the world," she sniffled.

"But this isn't your world, Martha. It's Miss Laura's, so do as she says." Betty moved close to Martha and straightened her cap. "And don't remind Miss Laura about your sister. Maria went to see Miss Laura and told her she was going to marry that chap who's upstairs. You can imagine what Miss Laura thought of that! Between you and me, Miss Laura likes him herself."

"Ooh, Betty! If Maria had of married that chap, would he be my father?" Since losing her mother and never knowing her father, Martha had been seeking parents for herself. She had managed to transform her sister into her mother, but so far had been unable to locate a father. This search was the outcome of her childhood in the orphanage, where her only comfort was to cuddle in her sister's arms as Maria made up stories about happy families in which children knelt beside their mothers and fathers to pray each night and together solved their problems, both moral and financial, through God's assistance. Mythical figures exist in every individual and are carried within from birth to death. Sometimes the figures are ennoblements of the self, wherein the individual desires either to improve or to defend an uncertain psyche, and to these mythic figure people go for reassurance that they haven't been abandoned in a cold, lonely world. So Martha, the frightened child, had entered the shelter of her sister's arms and there internalized the myth of the perfect mother and father.

"If I know anything about men, Martha, he'd be more likely to put his hand into your knickers than be your daddy. Now, stop your snivelling and get back to work." Betty went on into the hall to listen in on the conversation Laura was having with Sir Malcolm. She tried to overhear all such conversations so that she would be prepared to give an appropriate response when Laura commented on the person on the other end of the line.

"Well, it's entirely up to you, Sir Malcolm. I know you're too sensible to tamper with brains, but I'm sure you can recommend a good man. But certainly, if you want to examine him. Oh, are you? I've not heard a performance, though I've never been enthusiastic about Elgar. He incorporated too many dreary German mannerisms into his music. All right. Around seven." Laura put down the phone. "Betty, oh there you are. Good. Sir Malcolm will be here at seven to look at Mr. Compson. Make sure Martha is here to open the door and take his coat and hat. Now, perhaps I can rest for half an hour. If anyone calls, take a message. And check on Mr. Compson again."

Arthur lay in the quiet room where Laura had slept as a child and as an adolescent, and where as a young adult had thought of the men she had sampled and rejected. When her father died, she had his room redecorated and moved to occupy the bed in which her father had more or less raped his bride, the oldest daughter of a purse-pinched Anglican vicar whose wife embarrassed him by producing a child every eighteen months, even though he restricted intercourse with her to once a fortnight and practised onanism. Henry Dorchester had once visited the vicar's parish church to take rubbings of an effigy of a crusader's wife whose husband, unlike Penelope's, never returned, and had been immediately taken with the vicar's eighteen-year-old daughter Juliet, who was arranging flowers on the altar. Within days, Dorchester had presented himself at the vicarage, seeking the hand of the fragile, innocent Juliet, whom Dorchester regarded as a young girl, which explained his attraction to her. Her parents, pleased at the prospect of lightening the family load, willingly surrendered their daughter, though they couldn't know that Dorchester expected to find their daughter's body a match for her girlish face. On their wedding night, when he removed his bride's nightgown in expectation of seeing a girl's body, he became enraged at the sight of breasts and pubic hair and, believing he had been cheated of a virgin bride, revenged himself by raping her orally, anally and vaginally. He never touched her again. Believing she had married a monster, Juliet was horrified to discover she had conceived. In agony, she had borne Laura, then, terrified her husband would attack her again, willed herself into death. Since Laura was four at the time, memories of her mother were vague. She had respected her father, though never loved him, until he died from what his physicians called hardening of the arteries. During adolescence, Laura contemplated being a writer and, in secret, tried her hand at it, but once her father died and she was in charge of things, she put aside literary aspirations and reconciled herself to taking over his business affairs, which included a partnership in *Tower & Tower*. She enjoyed the power she experienced when encouraging new authors and slapping down aging ones who had written themselves out years ago. It was, she found, easier to tell others what to do than for herself to laboriously churn out sentences which would never be satisfactory, no matter how often she reworked them.

At precisely 7:30 PM, Martha opened the front door to Sir Malcolm Hetherton, who entered and was greeted by Laura at the foot of the staircase. Hetherton was a short man whose cadaverous face belied his jovial manner. He wore evening dress and, without looking in Martha's direction, held out an overcoat and top hat which she accepted.

"Ah, Laura. Well now, shall we have a look at your young man?" he said as they went up the stairs.

"He's not my young man, Sir Malcolm. He's a *Tower & Tower* author."

They walked along a passage, entered the bedroom and stood on either side of the bed. Sir Malcolm raised Arthur's right hand and felt his pulse. "Pulse's good." He raised an eyelid and looked into Arthur's eyes. "You said he was upset over something. Ah-ha," he murmured, when Laura explained the circumstances. "Sounds like shock. Not so long ago, women fainted away— 'swooned' was the popular term—when they received bad news. Did he scream?"

"No. He collapsed."

"Rigid?" Sir Malcolm might be pompous, but medically speaking he was no fool.

"No, he sagged."

"It's probably shock, but I'll call Baxter in the morning. I may even run into him tonight, and I'll ask him to call in. You know, your opinion of Elgar almost persuaded me not to attend the concert this evening. But I'll be on my way. Sir Adrian has no patience with late arrivals." He took out and looked at the gold pocket watch given him by a certain lady in gratitude for his delicate repair of her genitalia after the birth of her only child undertaken as a personal favour.

"Thank you," Laura said.

"You've been keeping well? Hm? No problems?"

"Nothing except a tendency to grow out of clothes I bought last month," Laura replied.

"The prescription is a brisk walk every day."

They moved toward the front door where Betty and Martha waited. "The trouble is, what I should do and what I *do* do rarely coincide." Betty held up his coat while Martha proffered his top hat, then opened the door. "Enjoy the concert," she said, "and take a nap in the sections where Elgar runs out of musical ideas and fills in with tepid imitations of Brahms and Wagner."

"Now, now. Don't be too hard on the poor chap," Sir Malcolm said. "He did his best. Don't forget he provided us with *Land of Hope and Glory.*"

"That I'd like to forget." Laura stepped into the doorway as Sir Malcolm passed out onto the broad limestone step. "By the way, have you heard Vaughan Williams's *London Symphony*?"

"No."

"The embodiment of English aspirations."

"I must make the effort." Sir Malcolm made for the door of his Daimler, held open by his chauffeur. He resented Laura Dorchester because no matter what he said about music, a play, book or art exhibition, she had already heard, read or seen it. Above all, Sir Malcolm resented the assurance wealth bestowed upon her. True, he himself enjoyed the appurtenances of wealth, but these were the lures he needed to hook patients. Fundamental uncertainty about his income sometimes caused him to have disturbing dreams from which he awoke in a sweat, convinced he had lost everything and couldn't acquire more. He had no idea where Laura's wealth came from, certainly not from *Tower & Tower*, which was a minor player in the publishing world. No one could live in the style Laura Dorchester affected unless she were floating on top of a deep pool of capital. Even so, what right had she to treat Elgar with such disdain? After all, Elgar'd done more in his life than she would in hers, though her dismissal of him was par for the course for aristocrats, who treated artists and professional, highly skilled persons such as himself with disdain. She had probably picked up that poor bugger lying upstairs in the bedroom and told him he was another Hardy or Galsworthy, and ten-to-one would ditch him when a more attractive man showed up. And while he, Sir Malcolm, knew where he stood with Laura's kind of people, that poor chap on the bed probably had no idea what was in store for him. Sir Malcolm wondered if Laura had ever bedded a man. She seemed to know nothing of coitus, but then wasn't that generally true of upper-class women? They preferred horses and dogs to men, though the men were no better. Many were queers who had grooms and footmen get children on their behalf to ensure heirs. What a sorry state of affairs. Poor old Elgar, man enough to work his way up from a lowly fiddler's job in a lunatic asylum to become master of the King's music, derided by the likes of Laura Dorchester who thought the be-all and end-all of music was some Frenchified piece nobody ever heard of, or that ghastly modern stuff that sounded like the rattle of dust bins. At least Elgar knew how to write a tune. What had the world come to!

He entered the foyer of the concert hall and saw Baxter chatting with Wilkenson, the ear, nose and throat man, and went over to have a word with him word about Laura's young man. That done, he seated himself in the cavernous hall and glanced at the program notes: Oh Lord! Ethel Smyth's *The Boatswains's Mate* overture was first up, then some fiddler scratching out a concerto by a foreigner. Bartok? What a name! Poor Elgar wasn't scheduled until after the intermission. Oh well, if the concerto proved unendurable, he could always escape to the bar and wait it out with a scotch and soda. Sir Malcolm closed his eyes and waited for the concert to begin as the strings tuned instruments, oboes tooted and the flutes slid up and down arpeggios. He then fell asleep and did not awaken until the violinist lowered his instrument and stepped forward to acknowledge the audience's spotty applause.

Arthur was reunited with consciousness at about the same time Sir Malcolm awakened in the concert hall, but Arthur continued to lie motionless beneath the quilt, moving only his eyes, following the lines of an ornately plastered ceiling. At last he heard a door open, and sensed someone approaching the bed, then Laura's face appeared between him and the moulded ceiling.

"You're awake," she whispered. "Can you hear me? Can you speak?"

"Water," he croaked.

"Of course. I'll get it."

He listened to the quick tattoo of her shoes on carpets and floor tiles. He sensed her return and heard the words: "Can you sit up?" He tried, but was too weak. "I'll help you." She sat on the bed, slipped an arm beneath his shoulders, raised him and let his body recline against her. "Poor dear," she said as she held the water glass against his lips, and Arthur, relieved he was conscious again, asked for nothing more than to feel cool water flowing through his dry mouth while he recalled how, recovering from a spell during childhood, he had lain against and been comforted by the soft curves of his mother's breasts. "More?" she asked when the glass was empty. He nodded, and she lowered him, brought more water and raised him again to lie against her. "There, there," she murmured. "You're a baby that's been sick, aren't you? You want your mother to hold and comfort you. I know, I know. Poor boy. Do you know where you are? You're in my home. I brought you here when you collapsed."

"I need to—," Arthur stopped, knowing Laura would draw the correct conclusion. She did, and asked if he could stand. "Poorly." She said the bathroom wasn't far and she would support him. Arthur was grateful for her firm arms as he cautiously stood and felt the room whirl around him. "I've got you, hold onto me, I've got you," she said. Her arms were strong around him, though how embarrassing it was, Arthur thought, to have to be guided like an imbecile or tottering, senile man from bed to lavatory pan, where Laura continued to support him while he emptied his bladder. As he hobbled back to bed she asked if he would be more comfortable if he undressed and got under the sheets.

"Later," he whispered. Now, all he wanted was to escape the storm waves of nausea pounding him and the ignominy of revealing physical weakness before a woman who probably condemned any man or woman that exhibited physical flaws. And yet her eyes seemed to express sympathy and the hand which touched his aching forehead was soft and gentle. "I'm a nuisance," he said.

"No. Just rest."

"I want to die," he whimpered as she lowered him onto the bed and drew the quilt up. "I'm sick of myself."

"Don't say that." She leaned over and kissed his forehead. "Besides, you don't mean it. You're just very weak."

"But it's horrible. And Maria—if she hadn't gone—"

She touched his lips "Sh! Sleep. Sleep. You know the line: 'Music that gentler on the spirit lies, Than tir'd eyelids upon tir'd eyes'? I think it's Tennyson."

"I know nothing. I am an empty failure."

"Oh dear, what an admission," she mocked. "But what nonsense."

At the door, she switched off the lights and he was left with a bar of light coming from the bathroom. But of course it was true that he was ignorant, for only an ignorant person could believe he could write novels and have them published. It was the equivalent of a man making wings from feathers, then, in the belief he is capable of flying, jumping off a cliff. Who but an ignorant person like himself would dare imagine that the poverty-driven grubbing and copulating carried on in the sordid, stinking little village he called home could be compared with life in cities like London, Paris or New York? Oh no, standards of people residing in those places were high, and people living there were intelligent and knowledgeable. If they happened upon what he had churned out, they would read it for the same reason well-informed people glance through magazine articles about New Guinea Stone Age tribes where men used their fathers' skulls as pillows. He was finished. He would write no more. He would return to Asty and rot. Why try to hang on when, without Maria's presence, nothing would have value? Tears welled up over his eyelids and he cried for a while, from weakness, from general physical discomfort and from thinking that, for women, he was comparable to a scourge which, once contracted, killed. He thought of Heather and saw her striding down the hill to where he waited at the bridge. Had he been afraid of her that afternoon when she lay naked on the grassy knoll? Afraid she would dismiss his performance as contemptible? Sylvia had always praised his sexual skills, though she had been mad and used him as women use fingers while their imaginations create perfect lovers. Strange that he should think of Heather now, strange that he saw an image of her as a child side by side with an image of her as a woman, each showing an expression of disdain, that slight definitive curl of the lips. Could she already be dead? And would the contemptuous look she carried from child to woman have remained on her face when she came face-to-face with her own annihilation? Yes, he felt it would be so. Not like him, not like the men Heather had known, who hung onto life no matter how miserable, no matter how desperate their tenure might be. Yes, it was true—he was afraid of Heather, had been since childhood. He preferred accommodating whores, who for an extra shilling or two, allowed him to investigate (and later document) their secret parts. And now he would never know what Maria could have offered him. Never. Her high clear voice, her chatter, her capable mind, all gone into a common grave along with her shattered body.

He slept, awakening when Laura entered the room, though he pretended to be asleep when she leaned over to look at his face. He smelled bath oil and wondered if she had come into the room wearing a dressing gown. He wanted to open his eyes to find out if wearing that feminine garment might have softened the sharp edges of her personality. He slept again and when he opened his eyes, she was still in the room, sitting on the bed, watching him. "How are you feeling?" she asked.

"Thirsty. What's the time?"

"Around seven."

"Which day?"

"Thursday." Her answer meant little to Arthur. He couldn't recall which day, panicking over Maria's failure to return, he had made his way to Laura's London office. "I'll get water." He watched her cross the room and saw her dressing gown briefly outlined by light from the bathroom. "Can you sit up yourself?"

"I'll try," He tried, failed and welcomed her supporting arm. "Sorry," he said. "It takes a while."

"There's no hurry. You'll stay here and rest, though I do think you'd sleep better if you undressed and got into bed."

"I will, later." For Arthur, one of the oddest things about returning from unconsciousness was that blood raced around his body, filling every pore, like tidal water surging across flats into every nook and hollow. When he was a boy, his mother, seeing him fleshed out (so to speak) would say: "There, you're back. All's well again." Arthur thought the phenomenon had a physiological explanation, similar to his bowels reacting to a dose of Epsom salts. He sensed Laura's embarrassment as she pulled off his trousers and underpants and saw his erect penis. Perhaps she thought he was malingering. "It happens," he mumbled. "I've heard it happens to hanged men and there's nothing *they* can to about it either."

"Shh," she said, "you don't have to apologize." She crossed the room, and for a moment Arthur thought she was leaving, but instead she locked the door, returned to the bed, dropped her dressing gown on the floor, climbed onto the bed, raised her gown and straddled him, moving on top of him until his penis was inserted in her. "Don't move," she ordered.

Arthur would always maintain that everything he wrote, regardless of how crude or rough it might be, had certain hallmarks which allowed a reader to identify him as the author. His preference was to have people acknowledge his power to communicate passion rather than admire his skill in manipulating plots and language. But which words, and how many, were required to describe sexual union between a man and woman? Arthur had found it impossible to find combinations of words that adequately conveyed the sensations he had experienced with Sylvia and what, at this moment, he was experiencing with Laura. So, which words ought he to select to convey a sensation that overrode his nausea and worry over his costive bowels and increased each time Laura rose to the tip of his member before, with a sigh of ineffable pleasure, she slowly sank to embrace every inch of his pulsing red column? Perhaps its nature defied description. At best, you could narrate what was said and what was done, but you couldn't capture the sensation itself. But being young and ambitious, he sought to accomplish what wiser hands at the game had carefully avoided or been shrewd enough to know that attempting it was the equivalent of walking on water. Perhaps loving the person with whom you were having intercourse enhanced sensations, although if he were honest, he would have to admit there was little difference between what he felt with Sylvia and what he felt with Laura, who was now surging toward the culmination of panting completion as he observed and documented the expression on her face and the way she shuddered, then cried "Oh" three times before slumping forward upon him. He heard her whisper: "It was wonderful. Just wonderful." She kissed him and, after leaving the bed to put on her dressing gown, said: "Dr. Baxter will be in later to examine you."

"Tell him to stay away. He'll be no more use than Kingsley."

"Please, dear." She sat on the bed and stroked his hands. "Please. He may be able to suggest something to help."

"I won't have another ignorant, pompous—"

"Don't get worked up."

"You have no right to impose charlatans on me."

"They aren't charlatans, Arthur. I know they're full of self-importance, but they do know more than we do about what goes on in our bodies. I can't stand them, but when I'm sick, I suffer them."

"I'm not sick."

"Something is wrong, dear."

"I leave my body for a while, that's all."

Even as he offered this unlikely explanation, he knew Laura wouldn't be able to understand what he meant (who could?) though apparently she believed she did. "I know, dearest, I know." She looked down at her hands. "I feel I took advantage of you."

"Don't be silly."

"I came to find out how you were. I had no intention of . . . You mustn't think I make a habit of preying on men. What I feel for you is special."

"Of course."

"Believe me, I've never done anything like this before."

Arthur couldn't refrain from asking: "You mean, you've never had a man before?"

"Oh no, I've had men. I meant—oh lord, why are things that're the most important so impossible to express?"

"For that very reason, I suppose."

"Then I needn't try to say it, need I?"

"Not unless you want to."

"I went with men because—well, I suppose, from curiosity. I never felt anything until now. You must know what I mean." She pressed her teeth into her upper lip. "I'd better go. Could you eat breakfast? An egg and toast?"

"I'd like some tea."

"I'll have a tray sent up." She assisted him to get beneath the bed covers, kissed him and left the room. There was, Arthur thought as he watched her go, a lightness in her step, a youthful bounce he hadn't noticed before. He dozed and dreamt Laura came to him and became infuriated because she saw that the tides of his blood were ebbing. Her strength was manic. She snatched up large pieces of furniture to hurl at him, though the chairs, couches and cabinets seemed miraculously to vanish before they reached him. He awoke to find Laura, dressed, standing beside the bed with a man whose hollow, parchment-coloured cheeks made him resemble Lazarus emerging from his tomb.

"This is Dr. Baxter. Remember I told you he was coming?"

"Yes, I remember."

"You remember the moments leading up to your fit?" Dr Baxter asked.

"I do not have fits."

"Whatever they are. Do you remember what you felt?"

"I've no intention of engaging in conversation with you if you talk about having fits. Do I make myself clear?"

"I take your point, Mr. Compson, but since I have no idea what your problem may be, I use common terminology. However, if you find it offensive . . ."

"It's not a matter of *me* being offended," Arthur said. "It's a matter of a bunch of asses assuming fish is fowl. Do you see what I mean?"

"I think so. But isn't there a possibility you're mistaken?"

"Certainly," Arthur agreed. "But one thing I never do is expose my ignorance by changing feathers into fish scales, or the reverse."

"I trust I've never denied there's a limit to what I and my colleagues know about the brain. We could use that as a starting point."

"We could—if I were interested in running a neurological race," Arthur replied, "but I'm not."

"That's a pity," Dr. Baxter said. "I would've enjoyed continuing the conversation."

"I have better things to do." Arthur was annoyed he had allowed himself to be engaged in a verbal sparring match.

"As you wish," the doctor said. "Miss Dorchester informs me you have a headache. I'll leave a prescription with her. You may or may not choose to have it filled. Good day."

Arthur knew Laura was angry by the tone of her voice when she told him his breakfast tray was being readied. His impulse was to find his clothes, dress and make his way back home as best he could. He wondered how the house would feel without Maria's presence. Maybe the silence would prove unbearable. For months, he had lived each day in expectation of hearing her voice, and its absence what had sent him running to Ponnewton and the buses, trains and taxis that had finally taken him to Laura's office where, with such casual brutality, she had informed him of Maria's death. How could she have been so callous? Assuming Maria had told Laura about the ring, she must have known the agony he was experiencing. How then could she expect him to feel anything for her? Of course, he would play the sexual game: after all, it cost him nothing to have her satisfy herself on him, though he did think it was odd that a person who was so indifferent to what other people felt should suddenly expect consideration for what *she* felt; but maybe that was par for the course, for the truth was, most people really don't really give a damn for what others feel, all they care about is satisfying themselves and reducing others to helplessness, compelling them to listen to endless chatter about their trivial lives. He had to get away from Laura. For him, she was like a purgative that must be taken in small doses. He wouldn't object to having sex with her, would even enjoy exploiting her sexual dependence. In fact, now that he stopped to think about it, sexual addiction would make an excellent theme for a novel: the story of an overbearing, middle-aged woman, dragged into the gutter by a handsome younger man who mercilessly exploits her. It would work well if the theme were carefully developed. The woman, married but sexually unawakened; the man, a house painter who comes to work on the house; his lackadaisical attitude angers the woman to such an extent that she confronts him, but instead of cringing in the face of her reprimands and promising to mend his ways, he splashes paint on her; she protests his action and he grabs and kisses her; she breaks away and tries to escape, but he pushes her onto her knees, throws up her skirt, wrenches down her underclothes and has her as she wildly thinks "like a bull on a cow." In the midst of her revulsion, she experiences sexual pleasure and henceforth becomes his supplicant. He could make the story work, it would be a break from his novels of village life, but he needed to be back in his work room, alone, hunched over his typewriter. And he must remember to buy a couple of ribbons at the Ponnewton stationer's.

He heard the door handle squeak; the door opened and a maid carrying a tray approached the bed. Her nose was red, her eyes inflamed and dribbling water. Arthur thought she had a severe head cold and censoriously told her she ought not to be breathing and sneezing over food other people were going to eat.

She indignantly dumped the tray on his chest and informed him she didn't have a cold, but was filled with sorrow because she had lost her sister in a bombing raid. She sat at the end of the bed and rubbed her eyes with the back of her hand.

"Oh!" Arthur cried. "You're Martha?" He unsuccessfully tried to move the tray. "Take this away, please." Martha leaned forward and dragged the tray to his feet while Arthur propped himself against the headboard. "Maria talked about you. She said you were a scatterbrain."

"I'm not!"

"Well, she worried about you."

"She was a mum to me."

"I know. We planned to have you live with us after we married."

"Miss Dorchester said all they could find was pieces of her. Isn't that horrible? She said we couldn't be sure the right pieces was in the coffin. Oh, I'll never laugh again. You know that? Never. Ever."

"Please yourself. Anyway, you can still come and live with me."

"I dunno about that."

"Why not?"

"Maria wouldn't be there."

"That shouldn't make any difference. I promised Maria . . ."

"But Miss Dorchester . . ."

"Laura Dorchester doesn't own my life."

"But Betty told me . . ."

"Betty? Who's she?"

"She's the one who knows what Miss Dorchester's going to do, and she said—"

"I don't care what she, or Laura, or anybody else in this house said. As soon as I can get my clothes, I'm going home. And you can come with me."

"I'm not. Maria told me not to believe anything any chap said. What's more Betty told me Miss Dorchester fancies you."

"That's ridiculous. Where are my clothes? Get me my clothes!" he shouted as Martha stood and made for the door. "Martha, please. Come here a minute. Please." She halted and moved to stand at some distance from the bed. "I fell in love with Maria. She said she liked me and she took my ring. I think she came to London to ask you to come back to Hasterley with her. That's where I live. You can believe whatever I say, Martha. You must believe I loved Maria."

"Okay," Martha said. "I'll try."

"I want to look after you."

"Like a father?"

"Something like that."

"And you don't like Miss Dorchester?"

"Of course I like her. She's my publisher. But not the way you mean." She stared intently at him without speaking, and Arthur thought he could see behind her misery and adolescent gawkiness a resemblance to Maria. "You know, you look a lot like Maria."

"Honest? Do I?" A smile flickered on her lips. "But I'm bigger and taller than her."

"Yes, you are, but just as pretty. And something else: Maria and I lived in the same house, but we respected each other. You understand what I mean?" He felt he shouldn't directly say he had never pushed a questing hand into Maria's knickers.

"You mean you didn't do what Betty says all chaps do?"

Arthur untangled that, then said, "No, I didn't."

"Well, I'll see. But I'm not sure." She turned and left the room, and though Arthur wanted her to remain and listen to him narrate in detail how he had grown to love and admire Maria, he let her go. He realized her acceptance of him would take time and would entail battling her fear of everything she'd been warned against by Maria and the other women in the house. He eased the tray over the rumpled bed linen, poured cold tea into a cup, tasted it, then pushed the tray away and, filled with a misery that matched Martha's, lay down and pulled up the bedsheet so that it covered his head.

CHAPTER
12

"YOU MUSTN'T THINK I'M TRYING TO MANAGE YOUR LIFE," Laura said.

They were sitting in the spacious drawing room (even the lavatories in Laura's house were roomy) beside windows that allowed them to look out onto a large cedar-hedged garden where borders of purple Michaelmas daisies and multi-coloured chrysanthemums richly bloomed. Laura sat in one armchair, Arthur in another. Between them was a low table on which rested a tea tray.

"More tea, dear?" Laura asked. Since that first morning when, astride Arthur, she had raced and won the sexual contest, she had started calling Arthur "dear" or "dearest." ("Darling" was yet to come.) Arthur thought there was something pathetic about the way she appeased him during the day in order to experience a few moments of late-night and early-morning ecstasy.

"Please."

As Laura levered herself forward in the soft-cushioned chair, Arthur glimpsed inner white thighs beyond the upper edges of her stockings and idly wondered how she would respond if he suddenly knelt on the carpet and pushed his face between her legs.

Six days in Laura's house had passed and Arthur was stronger and increasingly restless. Laura had provided him with paper and pencils and offered to fetch his typewriter from the house or to provide another. "One Royal portable's much like another," she said, but quickly added: "I know, dear, typewriters often do take on a life of their own, especially if they've slaved away for an author in the midst of a novel."

Arthur nodded. He didn't want her to provide him with typewriter or paper. He wanted his own work room with his own machine, because when there and he placed his fingers over the keys it seemed as if the words and sentences magically appeared on the paper. Besides, he longed for the quiet of his house where the only sounds were those of trees conversing with the wind and birds celebrating the rising and setting of the sun. There was so much noise at Laura's:

doors opening and people walking along passages and beyond, the sounds of the great, external city permeated the walls to fill rooms and halls twenty-four hours a day. You might think the house was quiet until you carefully listened, and then you heard distant anti-aircraft fire, bombs exploding, air-raid warnings and all-clears, train whistles, clicking of steel wheels and lines, bus and car engines and horns, plus human chatter that carried on every minute of the day. He would lie in bed and feel the accumulated sound rolling toward the house like waves in an angry sea. He wondered where sounds generated on earth went. Maybe they rose into the stratosphere where they were sorted out by wave-length, then amalgamated with other wave-lengths into clusters that streamed across the universe. You are mistaken if you think sound conveniently dies because you can no longer hear it. For the fact was, every sound that has ever been made, every new-born whimper and dying moan, every shriek of protest, every cry of lust was still circulating out there in infinity, and if you only had ears that could truly hear, you would be able to gather and decipher the voices that were borne on that great invisible stream that had neither beginning nor end. There were several wireless sets in the house, and everyone listened to the BBC morning and evening news. Laura listened to symphony concerts and recitals and took it upon herself to enhance Arthur's cultural awareness by explaining musical forms to him, but both the music and her explanations bored him. Her attempts to educate him were finally squelched when Arthur told Laura he preferred listening to a blackbird give a morning performance of its own themes and variations to Brahms's variations on a theme by Haydn. Privately, Laura thought Arthur's musical preferences absurd but told herself that talented people often revealed blind spots in unexpected areas. It was as if the energy required to deploy special skills resulted in unbalanced individuals.

Arthur also noticed that Laura hadn't yet spent a night with him, although you would have thought as mistress she could do whatever she pleased. She sneaked into his room after household activity was halted, did her thing, sneaked away and reappeared in the morning for a quickie before Martha arrived with his tea. She now removed her nightgown so that he could fondle her breasts and she told him she wished they could go away somewhere together, while he lay still, silent, wondering how she would react if she came to his room one morning and found him with one of the household staff, not that he had any intention of seducing Betty or Cook or Suzie who mopped, dusted and polished, or Martha, who ran errands and helped Cook. According to Martha, Betty had been with the Dorchester family since Kingdom Come and Cook had told her that Betty was Laura's half-sister from the wrong side of the sheets. This chitchat between Arthur and Martha took place during the three days Arthur stayed in bed. During a talk with Martha she told him Laura's house was located in Hampstead where, so Martha said, only the rich lived.

"How far is it to Waterloo station from here?"

"A long way." Martha had an inexact sense of size and distance as evidenced by her telling Arthur she had walked on Hampstead Heath with Betty. "It's ever so big!"

"Wait 'til you see the forest," Arthur told her. "It's enormous."

"I'm not going there," Martha replied.

"Maria wanted you to live with us."

Martha's lips vibrated and tears spilled from her eyes onto her cheeks. "I don't want to hear about her. It hurts my heart too much." She laid a hand over the bib of her uniform.

"You'll like walking through woods and hearing the thrushes and blackbirds singing."

"I won't." Martha was obstinate. "I'll bet girls go into those woods and never come out again." Martha's favourite reading were magazines that featured lurid stories of young women who innocently accepted invitations to enter houses and became victims of white-slave traders who drugged them, then shipped them to far-off barbaric countries where they were put into stinking rodent-filled cellars and told they must work as prostitutes, or be eaten alive by the rats. Martha believed the stories were true because when she was younger Maria used similar neo-Gothic examples of fiction to scare her sister into never talking to, or accepting an invitation from anyone to enter an unknown house, even from kindly old women. Maria's *Never! Never! Never!* reverberated in Martha's head to the present with the result that Arthur's assurances about village life fell on deaf ears. Martha was convinced threats to her person waited behind every tree and in every shadow.

"You'll have Maria's room," Arthur explained.

"Is there a key?" Martha had read that girls, desperate to preserve chastity, turned large keys in locks conveniently left on the bedroom side of doors.

"Key?" Arthur repeated. "Why would you want a key?"

"To lock my door."

Arthur, shocked by the realization that Martha apparently thought he was inveigling her into his home in order to have sex with her, protested: "Really, Martha, you have a cock-eyed view of my intentions. All Maria and I ever did was kiss."

"You can never tell!"

Arthur was annoyed. "If Maria hadn't worried so much about your harum-scarum ways, she probably wouldn't have come to London and got blown up."

Arthur stopped, realizing he had no right to suggest Martha was responsible for Maria's death. Besides, wasn't it also true that if he, Arthur, hadn't purchased the ring for Maria, she wouldn't have entered the shop to buy a gift for him seconds before a buzz-bomb appeared and fell onto the building? If you once started looking at cause and effect, you could shove blame for Maria's death onto Laura for having brought Maria into his home; or why not go back even further and blame his mother-lover for dying and himself for having a spell at the bottom of the stairs where Laura found him, and on and on back into an infinity of people shucking-off responsibility. There was no end to the chain of men and women saying: "Not me," so why drag in Martha, whose knowledge of the world did not extend much further than Laura Dorchester's house and whose common sense had been corroded by her sister's admonitions and further weakened by reading sensational fiction which began by terrifying her, but which she now read for thrills.

"Well, at least you can tell me how to get to Waterloo station. That's where I'm headed as soon as I'm strong enough to travel."

"I'm not too sure where it is." Martha was uneasy. On the one hand, she didn't want to offend Miss Dorchester; on the other, she thought Arthur wasn't quite right in the head and couldn't understand why Miss Dorchester thought so highly of him. She had also overheard Betty and Cook talking about Arthur and Miss Dorchester doing things together, but Martha had chosen not to speculate what those things might be, since she couldn't bring herself to believe that the grand lady who had taken her and Maria from the orphanage could engage in such activities.

"Think over what I've said," Arthur said. "Do you want to spend the rest of your life as a servant? I could adopt you. Or legally make you my sister."

"Sister!" Martha echoed. "You're nutty!" She grabbed the tray, ran from the room and almost collided with Betty, who knowing from experience that there was only one reason for young maids to run from bedrooms, held Martha's arm and asked what had been going on. "He's talking about me being his sister."

"Is that all?" Betty scoffed. "Listen to me, my girl. Don't believe a word he says."

The conversation was reported to Laura who nodded and remarked it proved Arthur was extremely lonely. "He always has been. Totally isolated in that vile village. You wouldn't believe the conditions he and his mother lived in when I first met them. Mind you, the place I bought for him wasn't much better before I had renovations done. It's habitable now. Eventually, after I've got the grounds landscaped, it'll be quite pleasant. But it's no place for a silly girl like Martha. Tell her not to listen to Arthur. Adopt her! What nonsense!"

"Well, in a pinch I could go," Betty said.

"No, no. I can't spare you. Besides, you've forgotten how to cook and clean," Laura cruelly reminded her. "You're good for nothing but hand-laundry and gossip."

Betty, who acknowledged she had never had to cook or sweep or polish silver, shrugged and suggested Laura accompany Arthur back to his house. "After all . . ." Betty paused and smiled before saying, ". . . you're spending time with Mr. Compson." Experience had taught her how to dig below her half-sister's armour.

"I don't want to jeopardize our professional relationship," Laura said.

"I see," Betty commented.

"Don't smirk at me like a dirty-minded house maid, Betty."

"You mean you don't want me to say that everybody in the house knows you spend time in Mr. Compson's bed?"

"What I do . . ." Laura began. She was angry with Betty. "For God's sake, can't you keep those women from tattling!"

"Oh, they don't care . . . but they don't understand why you don't spend the whole night with him."

"Because . . ." Laura chewed on the left side of her upper lip, which Betty knew signified indecision. "I'm not sure what to do. He's dependent on me in many ways. But I'm not sure how he feels about me."

"And what do you feel about him?"

Laura and Betty were seated at a table in the breakfast room. "I'm not sure about that either. He gives me something I've never had before. But I don't know, Betty. He's a strange man. I'm not sure he's capable of love."

"What about Maria?"

"Oh, that. Maria told me he was willing to provide her and Martha a home, so she thought she would marry him."

"Had he and Maria . . . ?"

"Oh no. Maria wasn't that kind of woman. She explained what happened."

"And you actually believed her?"

"Of course. She was incapable of lying to me. What she wanted was the security of her own home, and having Martha with her. Of course I was angry at first, when she told me she was going to marry Arthur . . ." Betty, who had frequently been the object of Laura's anger, could easily guess at the fury let loose on Maria. In Betty's case, when Laura had been younger, her fury culminated in slaps, punches and kicks, but had always been followed by a profusion of tears, apologies and gifts of clothes and perfume. Laura tended toward the lavish in everything she did. Once, she ordered Betty to leave the house and did not revoke the order until Betty threatened to find a newspaper reporter and tell him the story of her father, the sanctimonious Fabian who, when he wasn't preaching socialism and universal love, was impregnating young house maids. After that, Laura and Betty handled each other with care.

"What we must not forget is that Martha's a big girl," Laura said. "I mean, she is fully developed."

"Not upstairs, where girls need to be." Betty poured more coffee into their cups. "Will you marry him?" she asked and was pleased to see Laura's teeth appear to nibble her left upper lip.

"I can't decide."

"Are you trying to have a child?"

"Well . . ."

Betty smiled and thought that only bastards could fully appreciate the dangers of reckless, thoughtless copulation. "Maybe you should use something."

"No, no, I couldn't do that. I mean, what I feel is so . . . spontaneous."

Betty shrugged. "Another bastard in the family won't make much difference, will it? Mother always said . . ."

"Yes, yes," Laura interrupted. She didn't want to hear again about Betty's mother being young and foolish enough to believe a stiff dick signified love. After Laura's father had impregnated Betty's mother, he had shuffled her off to a nearby house where she was transformed into the widow of a railway worker conveniently (for Henry Dorchester) beheaded by a careless locomotive. Fortunately, things turned out for the best in the end, which sometimes *does* happen in the haphazard course of human affairs: After Laura's mother died, Betty, three years older than Laura, was brought into the house as a companion for Laura, and later became her personal maid, while Betty's mother occasionally dropped in for tea with Betty, and Laura, too, when she was home. In a house run by females, cross-class relationships didn't seem out of order, since women, far more than men, understand that whereas class is an artificially imposed system, physical needs of both female and male are basic to the human condition, therefore it was no surprise that an upper-class male would be as likely to be tempted by a house maid's springy buttocks by the decorous swaying of his wealthy fiancée's hips. Moreover, it could be argued that Laura's father had chosen well, biologically speaking, when he grabbed Betty's mother, for when Laura and her half-sister stood side by side, the bastard was not only superior in looks, but in conversation revealed she was brighter. Laura and Betty got along well: Betty made sure of that; and it helped that Laura had promised to provide Betty with a substantial dowry should she find a man liked; but Betty, having observed at first hand what happens when young women were trapped by irrational urges, decided to remain celibate. And why not? Laura was demanding and had a sharp temper, but she was not a petty person and after flare-ups always apologized. Betty didn't know with absolute certainty where the money Laura spent so freely came from, but she suspected most was income from rental properties in London, some in the worst slums, which, so Betty concluded, may have explained why Laura had taken in Maria and her sister, unless of course, unknown to everyone, their father had also sown germinal seed in slum soil; which wasn't all that impossible when you recalled that during his Fabian years, their father had occasionally sat shoulder-to-shoulder with other believers in damp halls where the Fabians on the stage outnumbered the audience of slum dwellers. During one such evening he could easily have spotted a slum madonna and gone to work on her. After all, London was a vast city, so why should residents of Hampstead know anything about a widow in Maida Vale, or a young woman in Pimlico whose two daughters were placed in an orphanage when she died of tuberculosis? So Laura may have had good reason to be generous with her money. Furthermore, when you stopped to think about the similarities, you could detect likenesses between Laura and Maria, even between Laura and Martha.

Laura was prepared to be generous with Arthur too. "Dearest," she said, as she lay upon him, weighted down with a surfeit of pleasure, "there are quiet streets in Hampstead. I'd be happy to lease a little house for you. We could use the forest house for weekends. Will you think about it? I mean, seriously."

He nodded, looked over her right shoulder at the mounds of her buttocks and remembered the beef roasts his mother had cooked on Sundays before his father had died. After his father had sharpened the knife, carved the meat and given two slices to Arthur, he would always say, "Eat up, son. These'll build muscles. And stiffen your dickie." He remembered his mother had always smiled and nodded when Compson said this. Arthur was not sure how old he was when his father took him to the stable and ordered him to lower his trousers. First, his father examined his testicles, then massaged his penis until it thickened and stood at a sixty-degree angle from his groin. He looked pleased, then said, "I doubt it'll grow bigger. But you needn't worry. It's bigger than most. All Compson men have large cocks. And once women hear about it, they'll be after you. Don't be afraid to ask women for it, son. Some will say no, but you'll be surprised how many'll say yes. Now, pull up your trousers." At the time, Arthur had understood little of what his father spoke of and had been too embarrassed to ask questions, though his father had said, "Any questions, son?" Arthur couldn't be sure, but he thought that soon after that conversation he had been introduced to Dot Perks. He remembered his father telling him that love and sex were different. "Cocks and cunts don't give a damn about feelings, son. Love has nothing to do with them. The cock just wants to go into the cunt, and all the cunt wants is to feel the cock there. Sometimes love's involved, but mostly the two Cs go their own way. We mix the two things up, like we mix up everything else and generally make a mess of it." But Arthur, apprehensive about what was happening to his own cock, was incapable of assimilating what his father said. It certainly did not register with him that his father had gone on to observe that *where* women got their children was not as important as how the children they bore were fed, clothed and what they were taught; nor did Arthur have any memory of his father telling him that women would be better off if there were places they could go, like men did, when they wanted to fuck. "So they'd know a thing or two before they married," he had said. "You get trained to be a soldier, or a bricklayer or carpenter, but nobody gets trained for marriage. I was lucky, son. I hit on a fine woman. And always remember, that no matter what happens, your mother is a good woman. You must always respect her."

"What are you thinking about, dearest?" Laura asked.

"Oh, nothing much. Things my father said."

"He was important in your life?"

"He told me some useful things."

"Mine told me nothing." Laura waited a few minutes, then said, "I don't want to be a nuisance, dearest, but I do worry about you being alone in your house. I know you'll be careful, but thinking of you alone there frightens me. I want to come with you, but it's impossible. I have to be in town. I've thought of sending Betty with you, but perhaps you two wouldn't get along."

"I don't need anyone."

"Not even me?" She sounded hurt.

"You're different." That seemed to satisfy her, especially when he emphasized his point by passing his hands over her bottom, then back and forth along her thighs. "I don't mind being alone."

"But suppose something happened? Suppose you fell down the stairs?"

"I don't know. Maybe that'd be the end of it."

Laura, unable to comprehend such fatalism, mutely shook her head. Like others of similar upbringing, Laura believed she determined her own destiny and found it impossible to accept that each time Arthur stood at the top of some stairs he risked death. She had to admit, though, there'd been times in her own life when she thought fate had decreed she would never find a man with whom she could satisfy her needs. She had been seventeen when, full of hope, she accepted her first lover only to be devastated when she experienced nothing. Nothing. She had closed her eyes, felt the man labouring on her (he was a friend of the family) and that was all. When he later returned for an encore performance, she coldly rejected him. And so it went: she tried men and rejected them, and until Arthur had appeared, she had concluded she was one of those women described in books illustrating the inadequacies of female sexuality. She did not understand how it had come about that Arthur, apparently without any special effort on his part, had touched a hidden spring in her, and she vaguely speculated that it might have something to do with his physical vulnerability, which in turn created a response in her that allowed emotions to build up and overflow, rather like a jug fills and overflows when held beneath a flowing spigot, or as a woman's breasts overflow with milk when she leans over the cot where her child sleeps. That had to be the explanation, because what she did with Arthur was much the same as with former lovers. Or was it possible that while in Arthur's arms, she experienced the sensation of being embraced by death? Her reactions puzzled her.

"I have to go," she whispered. "There's so much to do. But listen, dearest, at the weekend, if you're strong enough, we'll drive to the house and pick up your typewriter. We'll stay the night. Would you like that?"

"Of course," he said, while hardening his determination to get away as quickly as possible.

"Please yourself," Arthur later told Martha. "I'm offering to take you out of this rut, but whatever you decide, I'm going."

"I need more time," Martha protested. "I got to think about it."

"Think!" jeered Arthur. "You don't have to think. You need to act."

"It's easy for you," Martha complained. "You're set up, but I don't have nothing."

"You won't have anything if you stay here."

"That's not true. Miss Dorchester's been good to me."

"Miss Dorchester's good to Miss Dorchester. Get me a cab."

"How am I supposed to do that?"

"Look in the phone book!" They glared at each other, until Arthur, who had been knotting a broken bootlace, tied a bow with the shortened lace, got up and made for the bedroom door.

"Where're you going?" Martha asked.

"Home," Arthur replied.

"What about me?"

"You turned down my offer."

"I didn't turn it down. I said I needed time to think."

"You've had three weeks to think about it."

"So how was I to know you'd suddenly get up and leave?"

"Stay then. It doesn't matter to me."

"That's not fair. You know what you're getting. I don't."

"I've told you enough times."

Martha took several deep breaths and shivered like someone about to dive into cold water. "I'll get me coat and bag."

"I'll wait for you at the side gate. Bring any money you have. I don't have much."

To decide to return home was easy, but getting there proved difficult. Although Arthur would never acknowledge it then or later, he had commandeered Martha because he mistakenly thought she would know how to go about getting to Waterloo station, but it turned out her ignorance of London matched his. Cabbies ignored them, and those that did stop became suspicious of what they saw—an untidy man and shabbily dressed girl—and demanded what Arthur thought was an outrageous amount of money to deliver them to Waterloo station. They ended up riding buses, which were cheap but slow, and involved numerous transfers. By the time they reached the station, the day was almost gone and to make matters worse, a train was about to leave, which meant running to get on board before having something to eat. The train was packed with service men who sat in the corridor and resented having to move when Arthur tried to find seats for them. By the time they reached the Ponnewton junction, they were exhausted. The station was dark, the only sign of life was the coach and tanker locomotive that chugged each day between the junction and Ponnewton. Their bladders were overfull, and after Arthur had walked back and forth on the platform looking for, but not finding a lavatory, they went out into the station yard where Martha squatted in the shadows and Arthur peed against the wheel of a freight car in the siding.

Martha complained about being hungry when they returned to the platform and sat on a bench. Arthur said nothing. He was exhausted and worried whether he could manage the walk from Ponnewton to the house. Eventually, the coach, pushed by the aging tanker engine, moved from the siding into the station, and without saying a word Arthur and Martha and scrambled into a compartment. They slept uncomfortably, lying against each other while the coach swayed and jolted the few miles from the junction to Ponnewton, where the station clock registered 3:00 AM, which was incorrect. The clock had stopped when a bomb exploded during a raid and no one had bothered to set and rewind it.

"Where are we?" Martha mumbled.

"Ponnewton."

"What happens now?"

"We walk home. It's not far."

"I'm so hungry I could eat a cat."

"They'll be making bread at the bakery. We'll go there. They'll give us a loaf." They trudged to the hill and along High Street to the bakery shop where the scent of bread assaulted them. Arthur shook and rattled the door, but no one came to open it, so he finally took Martha's arm and they walked on. Years later, recalling that night, he was not quite sure how he managed to get Martha to the house, but knew he had used a mixture of threats of abandonment, promises, cajoling and slaps on her bottom. The one memory he had was that just as they turned into the lane, the predawn light revealed the house and the nearby line of trees. "There it is," Arthur said. "Home."

"It looks scary," Martha whimpered. Arthur ignored her. She had whimpered during the entire six-mile walk from Ponnewton. "I'll bet it's haunted."

He hurried her down the lane and into the kitchen where he struck a match and got the lamp going. "There, that's better."

Martha looked around and said, "You don't have electric lights!"

"There's nothing wrong with paraffin lamps. The oil man calls every two weeks to fill our can and make sure we have enough candles. That reminds me." Arthur went to the stove peered into the fire pit, then stirred what appeared to be dead coals. "It's still smouldering." He hunted through a box holding old editions of the *Ponnewton Weekly,* found some splinters of wood, laid them around the smouldering coals, opened the draught control. "We'll have a cup of tea," he told Martha as he filled the kettle, felt the hot water tank and told her she could bathe while the kettle was heating. "There's a bit of hot water. I'll show you where the bathroom is." He lit a candle, "Come on." But Martha, not wanting to be alone in the kitchen trailed behind him. "At bedtime, did your mother say, "It's time to go up the wooden hills"?"

"I didn't have a real mum. Only Maria."

"Of course, I forgot. Well, here it is." He put the candle holder on the edge of the wash basin. "Tea'll be ready when you come down. There could be some cheese and eggs in the larder. I'll see."

"Are you going to leave me here?"

"Certainly. I'll be in the kitchen."

But Martha had read one too many stories of what happened to young women left alone in strange houses. "I don't want a bath," she said.

"Don't be silly," he said.

"You don't know what might happen."

"Happen! Nothing can happen. You'll take a bath while I make some tea, then you'll put on your nightgown and come down to the kitchen. Flush that spider down the drain before you start. I don't know why spiders don't have sufficient sense to stay out of the tub."

"I'm not staying by myself."

"But Martha . . ."

"It's scary."

"Are you saying you'll never use the bathtub if you're alone?"

"You can stand outside the door and make sure nobody comes in."

Arthur stared at Martha's obstinately compressed lips and realized he was dealing with a fear not amenable to reason. "All right," he said. "I'll check the kettle, then come back and wait outside the door. Run the water. I'll be back in a couple of minutes." He clattered down the stairs, deliberately increasing the noise his boots made, looked at the fire, added coal to it, looked into the kettle and went back up the stairs to stand by the doorway. "Are you in yet?" he asked.

"No. The water's dirty," Martha said.

"That's nothing." He went inside to find Martha standing in baggy knickers and vest, looking down at the brownish, steaming water. "For God's sake, Martha," he said, "that's the natural colour of water around here. It's not dirty."

"You sure?"

"Absolutely." He was surprised at what happened next, for Martha being reassured, took off her undergarments, got into the bathtub and, after cringing as her bottom encountered the water, lay down in the water. "Oooh!" she said. "That feels nice."

"Wash your hair," he said. "It's covered in train soot." She rolled over, ducked her head under the water, rolled back, sat up with eyes closed and said, "There's no soap."

"I'll get some." He clattered down the stairs to the kitchen, grabbed the coarse dish soap from the sink and a towel from its hanger, ran back to the bathroom and placed the soap in Martha's extended hand.

"Smells awful," she complained as she rubbed the soap into her hair.

"I'll hunt around later for something with a nicer scent."

Martha dropped the soap onto the floor and Arthur picked it up and placed it on the tub flange. Martha rolled over and ducked her head several times. "How's that?" she asked. "Good enough?"

"It's fine."

Arthur looked down at her egg-white, square-shouldered body and wondered if it resembled Maria's. He experienced no sexual response at the sight, nothing except a tired curiosity akin to the jaded determination that compels people to continue drifting around a museum or art gallery long after their capacity to intelligently absorb anything has departed. "The kettle'll be boiling. So you'd better get out. Did you bring a nightdress?"

"'Course I did."

"I'll get it while you dry yourself." It suddenly occurred to Arthur that everything Maria had brought must still be in the room where she slept. He clattered downstairs to get a candle holder, lit the candle, climbed the stairs, opened the door and entered the room where Maria slept during the months she had lived with him. Her nightdress and dressing gown were hanging on a nail behind the door, and Arthur held them against his face and breathed the fading scent of Maria's skin before he carried them to the bathroom, where Martha, sitting on the lavatory, was drying her feet.

"This towel's no good," she pronounced.

"I'll get new ones. These are Maria's."

"I need a comb."

"There's one in the kitchen. One of Mother's. Ivory. Father brought it from Egypt."

"You ought to have towel racks in here."

"Eventually I will." Light from the candle shimmered on her body and bronzed her bobbed hair and body down. "Put those things on. The kettle's boiling."

She slipped the nightgown on, then said. "You really think I look like Maria? I want to be just like her."

"In general, you do. But you're larger."

"Miss Dorchester says the orphanage food made Maria thin, and *her* food filled me out."

"Bring the candle with you."

"You don't have a wireless?" Martha asked after sitting at the kitchen table, watching him inspect half a dozen eggs.

"No. Do you know how to cook?"

"I washed veggies for Cook."

Arthur had no intention of allowing Martha to sit around while he prepared their meal. "You can grate that." He indicated a piece of rock-hard cheddar cheese. "I'll mix it with the eggs and scramble them. Mother used to scramble eggs with bacon and lamb's kidneys and serve them on toast. That's the one drawback with this cooker, you can't make toast with it. Not like the old fashioned grate."

"Miss Dorchester has electric toasters."

"The best way to make toast is to take a thick slice of fresh bread, put it on a long fork—Mother's fork is around somewhere—and hold it against hot coals."

"I don't see how it can be any different to toast made in a toaster."

"Well it is. It's—" Arthur halted, because when he thought about it, he couldn't differentiate between the toast his mother had made and the toast he'd eaten at Laura's. "The grater's in the drawer."

"What'll I grate the cheese on?"

"Plates 're in the dresser."

"Miss Dorchester has a gold service."

"That's enough cheese. The frying pan's in that drawer below the cooker. Maria was a good cook."

"She could do everything."

Arthur stirred the egg and cheese mixture in the pan. "This looks good. Cutlery's in the table drawer."

"Miss Dorchester has sterling silver."

"Don't tell me what Laura has. I'm not interested." He drew a line through the cooked egg mixture with a spatula and scraped two-thirds onto Martha's plate and the rest onto his. "We'll eat this, then get some sleep."

But Martha resolutely refused to enter Maria's bedroom, even after Arthur had explained how Maria had enjoyed months of quiet rest there. "I'm not going in there," she repeated. In the end, Arthur had no alternative but to allot her one side of his bed.

"For God's sake, don't wake me up every time a bird calls," he said as he took off his trousers and got into bed.

"Don't you have pyjamas?" Martha asked.

"My underpants are fine." The sun had risen above the dark wall of trees and light from it came through the uncurtained window to fill the room.

"What if I have to go?"

"Use the bathroom."

"But what if there's a ghost there?"

"There won't be."

"You don't know."

"I know what'll happen if you don't shut up!"

"You've got no respect," she complained, turned her back on him and immediately went to sleep, while Arthur lay awake chewing his cud of memories until he too slept.

Those first hours were the prelude to what happened on the following days. Martha willingly worked around the house, provided Arthur was present, but refused to sleep in Maria's bedroom, and during the morning hours when Arthur worked, crept into the work room and sat on the floor with her back to the wall. At first, Arthur ordered her to leave, which she did, to sit on the floor outside the door, whimpering. "Damn you!" he shouted. "What a fool I was to bring you here!" But after a few days, he found he could ignore her presence while he tapped away at the typewriter keys.

She slept soundly and on her back like a child, and more often than not kicked away the covers, so that on awakening Arthur was offered a clear view of her down-covered, wide-lipped privates. But she seemed always, like some wild animal, to know she was being watched and would awaken, snatch up the covers and angrily say he had no right to look at her, to which he invariably replied she had no right to occupy half his bed and apparently didn't realize he was treating her like a gentleman because of the promise he had made to Maria. "If you weren't Maria's little sister, I'd be doing more than look," he said, which made her blush and drag the covers over her head, while Arthur, like a censorious parent, delivered a short lecture on "proper behaviour," for the fact was he had begun to think of Martha as his adopted child; he had discovered that while the constant presence of a child can be an irritant, it could also produce affection in an adult who likes knowing the child is dependent upon him and wants to do everything possible to please. With a rapidity that astonished him, he found himself correcting Martha's table manner, her habit of wiping her nose with a forefinger, the way she sat, walked and talked, and little things about personal hygiene, which he ignored in himself, but found conspicuous in her, but which Martha, due to Betty and Maria's tutelage, quietly obeyed. And Arthur liked lecturing her; he enjoyed hearing himself drone on about cleanliness. He ordered her to open her mouth so he could see her teeth (they were exemplary). He would lean an elbow on the table, point a finger at her and say, "You think when you're grown-up, a man— and I'm talking about a decent man—will ask you to marry him if you haven't taken care of yourself? Hm? Well?" Years later he would remember those days with Martha and be amazed how, like a chameleon, he had changed the colour of his nature from that of a somewhat misanthropic author to a worrying, talkative parent in order to accommodate Martha's presence in his life.

For three day, regardless of weather, they walked in the afternoons through the Asty enclosure and across the heath to the clump of pines where they stood to look out over the Channel to the Isle of Wight and the Needles. "Before the war," he told her, "you could see ocean liners coming in and going out. Once I saw the Queen Mary. She towered above the lighthouse. There's a cliff on the island that's made of different coloured rocks and sand. People put them in glass containers and sell them." Martha asked if they could visit there one day.

"We'll see," Arthur replied. He spoke like a parent, not firmly committing himself. He behaved like a parent, too, when after questioning her about the dark circles under her eyes and learning she was menstruating and using a folded towel to catch the blood, he became angry with her for failing to tell him what she needed. "I have a right to know," he said. He forced her to lie on the sitting-room couch while he walked to Mabel Smith's to find out what she needed.

"'Ow old is she? Fourteen? Then it'll be light," Mabel said. "I'll give yer a packet. Yer can pay me next time yer visits. When're yer comin', anyways? Yer ain't doin' it wi' the girl, are yer?" Arthur assured her he was not, explained he had not been well and promised to visit soon. "I 'ope so," Mabel said. "I miss yer. 'Ow about right now?" But Arthur said no and hurried home with the package of sanitary napkins, pleased that he, the one formerly ill and requiring attention, was successfully playing the role of physician-nurse-parent.

"Not feeling well?" Henry Joyce asked when he came that afternoon to palm off meat scraps. Since Arthur's house was his last call and Maria was gone, Joyce had no qualms about offering whatever was left.

"An upset stomach," Arthur answered for Martha.

Joyce pursed his lips and wisely nodded. He thought Arthur was making out with Martha and that what was in her stomach could eventually turn out to be a thorough-going headache. "That's 'ow it is," he said. "If yer puts a loaf inter the oven it's bound ter rise. I kept these chops and this 'ere nice little roast fer yer. Me other customers bin after 'em, but I says them chops and that there roast is ear-marked fer Mr. Arthur. I served the Sarge and Missus Sylv'a, and she were as fine a lai-dy as any yer'll find in the land, so I feels 'onour bound ter provide Mr. Arthur with the best I 'ave." Joyce then produced a bill for several week's meat which Arthur, being absent from the house, had never received; but, as Joyce pointed out, the meat had been saved for him and he'd have to pay for it. "Like I says, I can't get me meat if I don't turn in me coupons."

"What did you do with it?" Arthur asked.

Joyce, who had sold the meat to another customer, replied, "I give it to the Salvation Army, which is wot I knows yer'd want. Thank yer kindly, Mr. Arthur. I'll be on me way now. And I 'opes yer tummy settles down, Miss. I'm sure as it will. Me missus could 'ardly touch a bite fer three months, but after that she'd all but eat us into the poor 'ouse. See yer next week."

"Sometimes I hardly know what Joyce's talking about," Arthur said after the rattling of Joyce's van had faded.

"He thinks I'm in the family way," Martha said. From listening to kitchen gossip in Laura's home, she was familiar with the effects of pregnancy.

"Good God!" Arthur was so surprised he sat down. "How dare he think such a thing?"

"He thinks what he pleases," Martha said. "You can't stop him doing that."

"No, but I can set him to rights next week."

But Henry Joyce would never see Martha again, for the next afternoon when they returned from their afternoon walk, two middle-aged men in grey suits waited at the front door. One wore spectacles and did all the talking: "Miss Dorchester doesn't want you charged with abduction, or criminal interference with a minor. She appreciates you acted hastily and the girl being easily influenced."

"Are you policemen?"

"No, but we have some authority, Mr. Compson." He told Martha to fetch her belongings. Later, in recalling the incident, Arthur decided the worst of it was the speed at which it happened. He and Martha had spent an entire day escaping from Laura Dorchester's house, but in less than ten minutes Martha was gone. She had kissed his cheek and said she would tell Miss Dorchester he had treated her like the father she'd never had, which served to increase Arthur's indignation at being treated like a criminal by men who in all likelihood lounged around on Sundays, drinking beer and reading *News of the World*. It was insulting.

Before the day was over, Arthur discovered how much he missed Martha's presence—missed her in the kitchen preparing a concoction of cheese and ketchup she called Welshies, missed hearing her chatter away about life at the orphanage and how Maria defended her from the bully-girls. Arthur discovered that what he had formerly resented as impositions were now empty spots in the day, and regretted not having to stand outside the partially closed bathroom door while Martha used the lavatory. He even missed sharing his bed and asked himself why he hadn't used the opportunity afforded him to have sex with Martha, which his father would certainly have done. He supposed it proved he was less of a man than his father. To reassure himself, he visited Mabel Smith and, while copulating, imagined he was punishing Martha for imposing continence on him. He, who had previously felt proud of his restraint with Martha, now felt ashamed he hadn't poked his risen cock into her warm, dew-laden slit. To be sure, he knew it was not unusual for men to pluck their daughters' maidenheads. Having her father spread her legs had been Mabel Smith's introduction to sex, and his visits to her bed in preference to his wife's had resulted in Mabel being driven out of the cottage to live for a while in a ramshackle stable where she was visited on Saturday afternoons by her father and, later, by other men loathe to see her smooth, pert-breasted girl's body going to waste. Yet, though it seemed ridiculous to him now, he had been unable to violate the trust Martha had placed in him. For the brief time Martha was with him, he had experienced the problems and pleasures of parenthood. That Martha had formed such a relationship with him, he thought, said so much about the nature of small creatures. It explained why goslings and pig-lets and any other animals you might think of would, when given opportunity, become deeply attached to the hands which nurtured them. He thought per-haps that fact might even serve as an explanation of why great masses of underpaid factory workers passively accepted the working conditions imposed on them by factory owners. Still, for all that he missed Martha, he did not alter the pattern of his life. He ate, slept, worked and walked as usual.

His anger surged one afternoon when he entered the lane on his way back home from an afternoon walk and saw Laura's car parked by the gate. Inside, Laura stood beside the kitchen table on which sat a large wicker picnic basket, and if Arthur hadn't been so filled with self-righteous anger, he might have observed how nervous she was. "Hello, Arthur," she began.

His reaction was to lean over the table and shout, "Get out of my house!" he shouted. "And something else. I'm changing publishers."

That flat statement steadied Laura. "Don't be silly," she said.

"I mean it."

"Well, if you're foolish enough to do that, you'll find other publishers won't treat you as generously as *Tower & Tower*. In fact, they may very well reject your manuscripts for faults we've attempted to correct or have over-looked. However, if you think our house has treated you badly . . ." Laura was experienced at handling complaining authors.

"You bloody well know it's not the house! It's the way you butt into my life!"

"That isn't true, Arthur. I've done my best to help you."

"You can't let me go my own way. You can't understand that I'm not afraid of falling down those stairs and breaking my neck." Arthur emphasized the point by dramatically pointing to the stairs. "I've been at risk all my life."

"I understand that. But it doesn't change how I feel."

"I need to be left alone."

"Even if you abduct an under-age girl?"

"I didn't abduct Martha."

"I've heard from Martha about you being the father she never had. You should know, I've punished her for disobedience. She shouldn't have run off."

"You think I brought Martha here to fuck her, don't you? And you couldn't bear to think that, could you? So you hired men to come here and threaten me."

"No, Arthur. They came to remind you it was wrong to let Martha come with you."

"You want to keep me around so's you can get yourself off on me."

Laura's tongue briefly touched her trembling lips, and she turned her head aside to prevent him seeing her face. "At least there's affection in what I did."

"Like my affection for village whores?" Although Arthur couldn't see her face, he knew she was sobbing. It was then that he realized he mustn't push her too far; that it was to his own advantage to have her emotionally malleable, and for himself to play an apologetic role. "I'm sorry," he muttered. "I get worked up and say things I don't mean."

"It doesn't matter," she sniffed. "We're both at fault." Arthur knelt and rested his head in Laura's lap, a gesture which allowed her to stroke his head. "You need a haircut," she said.

"Mother used to trim it."

"I'll see what I can do." She passed her hand over his face. "You've lost weight. Have you been eating properly?"

"Enough."

"I've brought a few things. Martha told Betty that you slept together."

"Martha was afraid to sleep alone."

"I jumped to the wrong conclusion and got very angry. Now I realize it must have been very difficult for you. I'm ashamed of myself."

"Oh, I wanted to follow in my father's footsteps. I was always an obedient son. I knew father would have wanted me to take over where he left off with Mother." He heard Laura gasp and looked up at her. "Didn't you guess what was going on? Mother was quite mad. Yes. And I should have taken Martha too. Father would've. But the fact is, I'm something of a coward. Women have to push themselves onto me."

"No, you're mistaken about yourself. You . . ." Laura hesitated as she tried to find the words to reassure him and blot out his memories of his early life. "You were placed in an impossible position and did the best you could. You aren't a coward. Anything but. You're a courageous man. Believe me, it takes real courage to isolate yourself from the world and compose novels." Laura embraced him, and he inhaled the aroma of her perfume and beyond that, the scent of her flesh. "Don't worry," she whispered, "don't worry. We'll work things out. We will, dearest. You'll see. We will." Arthur accepted her reassurances and remained there, kneeling, with his head resting in her lap while she continued to stroke it.

Chapter

13

IN THE LATE AFTERNOON OF THE FOLLOWING FRIDAY, AFTER LAURA removed packages and cans from a large wicker picnic hamper and put some items on the shelves and others on the kitchen table for their meal, they sat to eat a variety of tinned foods which made Arthur wonder how Laura had managed to procure them in wartime when other people in Britain felt fortunate to possess a single tin of ham. The table was isolated in a pool of lamplight and beyond the warm circle of light, the room seemed to fade into an impenetrable darkness.

"We lost so much when we changed over to gas and electricity," Laura said. "Oil light intensifies everything we feel and say. No wonder most great works of art were created in the centuries before electricity. Look, dearest, this circle of light is our universe, anything and everything can happen here. Does that excite you?"

"Not especially." Arthur resisted Laura's attempts to build weekend pyramids of romance, perceiving their artificiality, knowing on Sunday evening or Monday morning, she would be off to London, leaving him to reassemble the envelope of isolation he needed to work. Moreover, he resented the fact that ordinary male and female coupling was insufficient for Laura, that for her there had to be a special something that touched their souls and created a spiritual connection that bound them together and transformed them into more than two groaning, sweating animals. Laura wanted to believe what existed between her and Arthur was akin to the passion which Arthur, the author, was so adept at conjuring up in novels. Indeed, she had no true sense that Arthur's response to her was based on cupidity combined with a young male's abundant sexual energy. In fact, after Arthur watched Laura drive away at the end of a weekend, he went to Mabel Smith to fuck her, free from the emotional embroidery Laura tried to infuse into the act. Afterwards, he listened to Mabel spin village gossip, including speculation about Laura which Arthur didn't bother to contradict beyond saying she came from London on the weekends to discuss the publication of his latest novel. Mabel thought this was funny—she could not imagine a woman driving from London to spend an entire weekend with a man merely to talk about a book.

"There're people in the world who talk of nothing else," Arthur told her.

"Yer jokin'," Mabel said. "If yer ain't doin' nothin' more, yer can get off me. I ain't yer bed."

Visiting Mabel always helped and for a few days Arthur would forget Laura and work intensively. Then, late on a Friday afternoon, she would return for the weekend with smiles, kisses and another hamper of food and wine.

"Dearest," she said as she prepared their evening meal, "did you remember the wine glasses?" On previous weekends, they had used teacups, and although these were remnants of Sylvia's precious Worcester set, Laura had instructed Arthur to buy wine glasses because, so she said, civilized people could not appreciate good wine when sipped from cups. "You promised. Remember?" She tried but couldn't prevent anger from edging the reproach. She was used to having her requests fulfilled.

"I've been busy," Arthur replied, allowing irritation to edge his reply. "I'll get some tomorrow."

"No, no," she said. "It doesn't matter. It's not that important."

Still, acid had been dropped, and while the meal and the evening were pleasant, they were aware that the rich flavour of their relationship had turned a little vinegary. Of course they went to bed and made love as usual, but each, especially Laura, felt something vital was missing from their union and blamed herself because, aside from Arthur's failure to get the wine glasses, he had consistently lived up to her expectations. Yet, for some reason, she felt he had withdrawn from her, spiritually and emotionally. This frightened her because she had managed to convince herself a true marriage of body and soul between her and Arthur had been attained.

On the Saturday morning, Laura rather desperately tried to rekindle the flame of passion and to reinforce her belief in the uniqueness of their relationship and when unsuccessful, she told herself it was due to the morning being grey and wet, bringing with it an overall depression to the house and the couple within. In the afternoon, they drove to Ponnewton and hunted through shops until they found wine glasses. As they drove along High Street, Arthur was silent, mulling over bits of dialogue from his novel.

"What's wrong, dearest?" Laura asked.

"Oh, nothing, nothing. I'm going over something in the novel."

"Is that why you've been so withdrawn?"

"Probably. It's at a difficult stretch. Has to do with the development of a particular character."

"I understand." She smiled and pressed his hand. "Perhaps I should have stayed in London."

"No, I'm glad you came. It's just that things intrude. You know how it is."

"I certainly do. But you mustn't keep things from me. Promise?"

"A promise. Maybe I'll redo my description of the woman. When something like that nags at me, I know I've gone down the wrong path."

"How would you describe me?" she asked as they left town.

"Mature. Very feminine." Arthur had known sooner or later Laura would ask that question. "Just right for me," he added. His mother had posed similar questions and been satisfied with his carefully crafted responses, though he'd always thought it odd for a woman to think that the shape of her nose or the colour of her eyes would be a decisive factor in explaining why a man was attracted to her. Arthur's answer was clearly what Laura wanted, because she smiled and hummed a popular love song as she steered the car off the highway, across the Common and down the lane to the house.

"There's something I want to tell you, dearest." Her hands grasped the wheel, and she looked straight ahead at the tall trees beyond the house. "I've not told you my age. Maybe I was afraid to. . . but I must be . . . well . . . ten years older than you. Maybe more."

"It doesn't matter," he quickly said.

"I knew you'd say that. But there's something else. I've never thought before of having a child, but I must tell you, darling, I've done nothing to prevent myself from conceiving one. Quite honestly, I want to feel a child growing in my womb. I've never wanted anything so utterly and so fiercely. So, now you know how I feel."

Arthur allowed a few minutes to elapse before answering. "Well, I have to say I've not thought of our relationship ending in a child, but that's probably because I have trouble imagining myself as a parent."

"So you won't object if I . . . ?"

"Why would I?" he rhetorically asked.

"Oh, I don't know." She paused. "People in our circles who have children are usually married." She hurried on. "But of course that doesn't mean we'd have to." She sighed. "I suppose I want to anchor you to my life. The fact is, knowing another woman might wander in and scoop you up frightens me. I'm jealous." She looked at him and managed a strained smile. "There, I've admitted it. I'm terribly possessive. Am I overloading you with my feelings? I don't mean to. I only want to share everything I am, but if you think I'm making a fool of myself, just tell me to shut up."

"I consider myself fortunate having a person who understands my needs. That I need to be alone to work."

"Yes, yes, of course."

"Then shall we leave things the way they are for the time being?"

"Yes, yes, we can do that." It was clear she was disappointed by his response to her revelations about herself. She pressed his hands, and he obliged by kissing her, and when he was sufficiently aroused, he half-pulled, half-eased her from the car, bent her over the hood, hoisted her skirt, pulled down her white underclothes and fucked her from the rear, grunting like a village boar on a squealing sow. It must have worked because he heard her give a prolonged hissing squeak just before he orgasmed. He promised himself that before she returned to London, he would get her to crawl around the grass in the walled garden while he sniffed and licked her cunt before mounting her. He would reduce her to the elemental in life. He would force her to experience, albeit briefly, the level at which the village women existed where they were little more than reproductive organs, no more than grubs that continued to duplicate themselves until they shrivelled up and waited for Death to reap them during its yearly winter visit to the village. And most welcomed death as a relief from the burden of life and did not question Death's right to harvest them. Their attitude toward life was as removed from Laura's as the distance of the planet Neptune was from the sun. They had no beliefs and religion as preached by the curate was alien to them. All they could do was engage in grub-like reproduction and accept their lives on those terms. Sometimes, in a fanciful mood, Arthur would envision the villagers as worshippers of a faceless god, and women like Dot Perks and Mabel Smith were its temple vestibules where men deposited their tribute to the unseen, implacable god. He imagined that when Mabel Smith died another woman would be selected by village consensus to replace her. Arthur asked himself by what process this group of people subjugated themselves to a god that imposed on them such a torturous burden of grub-like reproduction; but at this point his speculations would falter and he would laugh at himself for attributing profound beliefs to the Hasterley villagers when, in his experience, the men were ignorant and crude, the women sullen, heedless sluts who, year after year, continued to bear children neither they nor anybody else wanted.

But Arthur never had an opportunity to teach Laura that particular lesson because rain fell throughout the Sunday, and they spent most of the day in bed, sleeping, talking and doing their best to make and express love. When Sunday evening came, Laura delayed departure. "I'll leave in the morning, darling." In the morning, she still exhibited reluctance to leave, but then remembered an important engagement. "No, I can't stay. I mustn't. Force me to stay, darling. Hold me down. Compel me." Finally, she put her suitcase into the car and drove away across the Common, watched by Arthur, who diligently waved until the car disappeared from sight, then walked to the village and reoriented himself downward from Laura's romantic heights to the village earth in which his work was rooted by expending what little sexual energy he had left upon Mabel Smith, after which he returned to work.

Arthur never thought of himself as being lonely or unhappy. The contrary. He sat at his typewriter, day after day moulding the lives of his people, observing and recording. What could be of greater interest? The morning's work, which consisted of the last chapter of his story about the ill-fated brother and sister, drained him of energy, but two bowls of canned beef stew and three thick pieces of bread soon restored him, and he left for his afternoon walk satisfied with the way he had brought his novel to a conclusion. He walked through the enclosure and across the heath to the pines where he stood a few minutes and watched ragged clouds wrenching themselves from the Channel horizon to run like escaping prisoners who are unsure in which direction to bolt.

He knew by the open gate that somebody other than a villager had been to the house, because everyone in the forest understood an open gate was an invitation to forest ponies and cattle to invade gardens, consequently no one ever left one open. He went around the corner of the house and saw Martha sitting on the kitchen doorstep.

"What're you doing here?" he barked as he approached her.

"Miss Dorchester's been mean to me. Really mean," she said. "You should hear what she says."

"I don't care what she says. You can't stay here. I don't want somebody coming here and accusing me of kidnapping."

"You said you'd be my dad. You said you'd take care of me."

"Maybe I did, but you still can't stay. That's final."

"I'm not going back," Martha defiantly muttered.

Arthur sat beside her. "Martha, you know you shouldn't have come here. Well, don't you?" Her answer was to shrug her shoulders. "You said you admired Miss Dorchester."

"She wasn't nasty then. She didn't call me names. Now it's just work, work, work."

"We all have to work, Martha, you know that." Arthur was disgusted with himself for resorting to such feeble, middle-class, moralizing. He should simply order Martha to return to Hampstead. "Miss Dorchester works hard every day."

"She don't scrub floors, she don't run up and down stairs. Oh, no. She don't peel spuds. Oh no, she drives away in her car. Besides, she don't like me now. She acts like I've done something horrible."

"Maybe. But what do you think you'd be doing if Miss Dorchester hadn't taken you from the orphanage and provided you with a home?"

She glanced at him from the corner of her eyes. "Once you promised to be my dad. Now, you want to get rid of me."

"That's not true, Martha. I'm prepared to help you, but not here. I can't have you following me around. I can't have you sneaking into my bed. Surely you can understand that. Are you certain you're not imagining things about Miss Dorchester?"

"She hates me."

"Nonsense." Arthur put his hand around her shoulders and she wriggled closer. He wondered how it had happened that a man who asked for nothing more than to be left alone to work should become entangled with a succession of demanding women. Perhaps in the future (assuming he had one) he would write a novel about the freedom of childhood and the bondage of maturity. "You're like a stray kitten, Martha. No matter what you do, the kitten comes back to meow at your door, so you're left with either keeping it, or drowning it." She laid her face against his and he kissed her cheek, then her lips. They were greasy. "You've been eating fish and chips," he said.

"Only chips," she said. "I had to have something to eat."

"They'll give you pimples. And where did you get the money for the train ticket?"

She hesitated. "From Betty's purse."

"Oh, Christ." His hand rested on her legs where tight garters held up her lisle stockings. "Garters are bad for your circulation," he said. "They'll give you varicose veins. How much did you steal?"

"A pound, and some silver."

"You'll have to pay it back."

She nodded. "Did you miss me?"

"I may have," he cautiously said. "Come on, let's go inside."

They went into the kitchen where Martha made herself at home by brewing a pot of tea. "What will you do when Laura comes next weekend? Or suppose she sends those men after you? Surely, you realize you can't stay here."

"Do you want bread and butter?"

"No. I want to know what you'll do when Laura comes. Or the men."

"I'll hide."

"Where? In the enclosure?"

"No. I'll just hide. Or you can tell them you're my father."

"Oh, for God's sake, Martha! Forget that nonsense!"

"It's not nonsense," she said, while Arthur, who couldn't think of any further arguments to discourage her from staying, cupped his chin in his hand and stared glumly at the back door as if he expected it to be flung open by Laura and the two men. "I love you," she whispered. "I really do."

"I know," he bleakly acknowledged. "I know you do, but it doesn't solve anything."

"I dreamt about you."

Arthur thought no experienced woman would ever make so dangerous a confession. During their long nights together, Sylvia had narrated the history of her dreams and their significance in her life. She dreamed she would meet her future husband at the entrance to a railway carriage and, like other not-overly intelligent people, took coincidence as proof that her course through life had been predetermined, though she never ventured beyond that point to speculate on who might have plotted the path that she and presumably everyone in the world was destined to follow. As he made clear in his novels, Arthur believed men and women were governed by degrees of desire ranging from passions that are easily accommodated within community mores to more uncontrollable ones that break all bounds and generally destroy those they possess. He conceived of desire as a disease which no medication could suppress or cure, but no doubt Sylvia's obsessive sexual demands, which he now attributed to madness, had profoundly influenced the way he viewed human relationships. His view of women was probably askew; maybe even his love for Maria had not been genuine, but rather based on her apparent asexuality, which allowed him to feel confident she would never demand anything from him. Had there been a religious bent in Arthur, he might have found Maria's double in a church saint and worshipped her accordingly. Perhaps Maria's death was a stroke of luck for Arthur, for had she married him, he might have uncovered an aspect of her personality that would prove she was another Sylvia or Laura or Heather, but as it was, he would always remember her as the neatly dressed, highly efficient organizer, mother/sister of the harum-scarum girl seated across from him at the kitchen table. In taking on Martha, he thought, he was like a man who hungrily gobbles up undercooked pork without knowing it is contaminated and ends with a tapeworm in his guts. The worst part, he thought, was that Martha now believed everything he'd told her about him and Maria getting married and having Martha live with them, because she couldn't believe her beloved sister would agree to marry a man who indulged in self-deception, or engaged in outright lying when it suited his purpose.

Martha came around the table to stand beside him. "I don't mind if you hug me," she said.

"I don't think I will."

"Did you hug Maria?"

"Yes," he said, although he had not done so.

"Then you can hug me too." She sat on his knees.

Arthur felt trapped. He wasn't sure what to do next. He thought of himself as being sophisticated sexually, but the only thing he could think of doing was to pat Martha's back gently, as he would have a child's. He thought of his father pulling down girls' underwear to mercilessly deflower them and images appeared of their faces as his father's sexual horn ripped apart their downy genital lips, and of himself pounding Laura's doughy ass. But nothing happened. "Get up, will you? My left leg is asleep." He rubbed his leg and allowed her to sit again. "Laura stocked the kitchen with soup. Let's have some. With toast. You like making toast, don't you?" It was odd, but actually he felt pleased Martha was back. Odd that he should prefer her company to Laura's. He supposed it was because she had allotted him the role of a major player in her life and was prepared to accept whatever he said and did, a little like his beloved Mary. As he sat with one arm around Martha's waist, her warm breath tickling his ear and hunks of her long, tangled hair brushing against his neck, he momentarily felt he was holding his own child. It was a strange, illuminating experience for him, for until that moment he had never thought of children except in the context of the village: puny babies, grubby, foul-mouth boys, cheeky girls—sickening to behold and proving beyond all reasonable doubt that only the upper classes could produce attractive progeny, and that the inability of the lower class to propagate decent children justified keeping them at the bottom to carry out all society's dirty work for a pittance and bolster army ranks during wars and offer themselves to wholesale slaughter without protest. He wondered why he, who knew what it was like to live in the detritus of England, had not seized Laura's offer of marriage.

When they finished the soup, they ate a small jar of brandied cherries, then washed up. As they stood together at the sink, Arthur said, "We'll talk more tomorrow about getting you back to London. I hope you're not planning to make a fuss about the bathroom and sleeping in Maria's room."

"You'll stand by the door?" she asked.

"For God's sake, Martha, must we go through that again?" Later, he stood on guard outside the half-closed door to the candle-lit bathroom as Martha used the lavatory while running water into the tub, and because she refused to wear Maria's nightgown, he was forced to dig through his own meagre collection of clothing to come up with one of his father's long-tailed shirts, while sympathizing with parents all over the world, who, like himself, feel they must, from parental obligation, not only feed and clothe their offspring, but also accede to their most irrational demands. He even insisted that Martha give her hair the traditional one hundred strokes before getting into bed where he lay with his hands behind his head.

"You don't brush yours," Martha protested.

"Mine doesn't need brushing."

"It's as long as mine."

"What I do with my hair is none of your business. So do as you're told."

Martha counted and stroked to one hundred, joined him in the bed. "You still like me, don't you?"

"Of course. Go to sleep." He blew the candle out and turned on his left side, then felt her hand touch his shoulder.

"Hold me," she begged. "I'm scared. I really am. I haven't got anybody now Maria's gone. Miss Dorchester hates me. She called me awful names. Please hold me." Arthur turned and put his arms around her. She lay with her head on his shoulder and her legs intertwined with his. "You're all I've got now," she whispered. "You won't let nothing bad happen to me, will you?"

Aware that the pressure of her smooth legs was arousing lust, he sighed and said, "You expect too much from me, Maria," he said.

He heard her gasp before she said. "But I'm *Martha*."

"Oh yes, of course. I forgot."

"Did Maria . . . ?" There was an overtone of resentment in her voice.

"No. Now, for heaven's sake, get onto your side of the bed and go to sleep."

"But you'd rather I was Maria?"

"For God's sake, Martha, don't make things worse than they are. Do as you're told." She tensed, then obeyed and moved across the bed. "We have to make other arrangements," he said. "We simply have to do that."

At some point, after falling asleep, Arthur was awakened. The bedroom was filled with yells of rage and screams of terror. In the dim light, he saw Laura standing beside the bed thrashing Martha with the heavy leather belt she often wore. Each time she brought the belt down on Martha, she shrieked: "Bitch! Whore! Bitch!", while Martha writhed and screamed and tried to escape the lashing belt and the slapping buckle that was ripping the shirt and bruising her back.

"Laura! Stop!" Arthur shouted. "Stop!" Martha scrambled over him, careened around the bed and past Laura, who followed her from the room, still shrieking. Arthur stumbled from the bedroom and saw Laura pursuing Martha into his work room. "Laura!" he screamed. "Stop it! Stop it!" As he entered the room, he saw Martha backed against his work table, mouth gaping, eyes blank with terror, watching Laura as she advanced, the belt raised ready to strike again; but as Laura swung the heavy buckle up, Martha screamed, reached behind to snatch up Arthur's typewriter, then leaped forward and brought it down on Laura's head. How long had it taken? A minute? Two minutes? Afterwards, when Arthur recalled the scene, he thought of it as having been played out in an eternity of time: Martha slowly moving backwards to the work table; he, with infinite slowness, approaching and kneeling beside Laura, touching her and with the same incredible slowness coming to realize she was dead. He looked up at Martha who was attempting to cover herself with the torn shirt. "She's dead," he said, then looked around the small, bare, low-ceilinged room and repeated: "She's dead." He stared at the typewriter from which the ribbon spools had flown and slowly grasped the magnitude of the drama in which he and Martha had played starring roles; he saw himself in one vivid image, hanging from a scaffold, Martha swinging beside him. He could think of nothing except they must get away. "Put on your clothes," he ordered. "Go on!" he shouted, when Martha continued to stand by the table, shivering. He grabbed her and pulled her from the work room to the bedroom, where he more or less dressed her as he would have a child, while telling her she must get away to London and hide. "Whatever you do, don't go to Hampstead! You hear me? Don't go back to Hampstead. Do anything, but not that. You know the way. Catch the London train at the junction. Don't talk to anybody. Maybe if I cut your hair and gave you some of my clothes, you'd look like a boy. Take off those things!"

When Arthur turned back from rummaging among his clothes and saw Martha still sitting on the edge of the bed, he yelled at her: "Damn you! Take off your things!"

"I don't want to do anything," she whimpered.

"You want the hangman's rope around your neck? Because that's what'll happen, if you don't get out of here."

"I'll go with you." She began removing the clothes.

"No."

"You put my knickers on backwards," she said.

"Oh, my God, what does it matter?" As he moved towards her holding Sylvia's sewing scissors, he could not prevent himself from thinking his chances of escape would be greater without having to worry about Martha. What if, instead of using the scissors to cut Martha's hair, he thrust the points under her pointed, pink-tipped left breast? If he did that, if he killed her, he wouldn't have to hang around the Ponnewton railway station to make sure she boarded the train. In the time he spent there, he could be miles away from the house and Laura's body. Martha looked at him trustingly. "If you're dressed as a boy, people'll think you got that bruise on your cheek in a fight." He began cutting her hair. "That's more like it," he said and backed to eye her critically. "It's rough, but it'll do. Put the shirt on. I'd take you for a boy anywhere." He brushed the heavy clumps of hair from her shoulders. "You can make up a name and volunteer for the army. Tell them your birth certificate's gone missing in the bombing. No! Even better! You can be Maria, and if they check up, which they probably won't, you'll be in the registry. That's good. Say that you had a sister Martha, who was killed in a buzz-bomb raid. But you must get away from here, Martha. God! Laura's car! We'll have to hide it. We'll push it into the trees. No one'll see it there. Come on, put your shoes on."

"I want to stay with you. I'm scared," she whimpered.

"You can't. Listen, Martha . . ." He held her face and compelled her to look at him. "This is a matter of your life and mine. Understand?" She nodded. "You're going to disappear. You *must* disappear, because when Laura's body is found, the police'll start looking for me, and you too, and we have to make sure no one ever finds us. Ever."

"I didn't mean to do it!" she wailed. "I was scared!"

"But who'll believe you? No one'll understand you were so frightened you didn't know what you were doing. That's why you have to hide." She clung to Arthur. He put his lips against her forehead. "You must be brave."

She continued to cling to him. "No, Martha, no," he said. For one maddened moment, he wondered if she, like some wild creature, wanted to celebrate the destruction of her enemy by mating with him. "Martha, listen to me. Come on. We have to go. Come on. We have to get the car."

At first, he didn't know what to do with Laura's car. Finally he got into it, released the brake and, because it was on a slope, Martha had no trouble pushing it, while he steered it along the wall and into the trees. Then they ran across the Common to the road, then along it in the half-light of dawn through Ponnewton and down the hill to the unpretentious railway station where Martha, still in shock, obediently entered a compartment, took the five pounds Arthur held out, then watched him walk away. In some ways, she was lucky. At the junction, she simply boarded the packed London express and was standing in the corridor when she was spotted by an army officer on leave who, presuming she was a plump-bottomed youth, picked her up, took her to a hotel, and upon discovering the boy was actually a girl, good-humouredly cut his losses, laughed uproariously when she told him she was dressed in men's clothes in order to join the army, gave her with a decent meal, then escorted her to a recruiting office where he facilitated her rapid entry into the WACs under the name of Maggie Bottomly. There, she met and married a staff sergeant, became pregnant, was honourably discharged and settled down in Pimlico to bear and raise three children.

Arthur, at first, thought of his escape as miraculous, but later he realized that because the country was packed with troops and in such a state of organizational ferment that no one was really in a position to be too concerned about a quiet, well-spoken young man who told strangers he was taking a well-earned holiday from a strenuous spell of work in—well, a certain ministry—and was wandering around the counties on local trains and buses. It was quite touching, strangers thought, when Arthur told them: "I'm really seeing England, my England, for the first time." What patriot could possibly quibble with a man who voiced such sentiments?

Eventually Arthur reached Liverpool, where he circulated from district to district, spiralling ever closer to the docks and public houses where ships' crews drank weak beer to ease the turmoil of their dangerous North Atlantic crossings. Arthur couldn't be sure what or who he was looking for among the men he observed in the pubs. The British were unapproachable: weeks and months of continual danger had knitted them closely together and they eyed outsiders suspiciously. It was this chauvinism which eventually saved him, because, one night, it resulted in a lone American speaking to him in a pub.

"Those guys sure hang together, don't they?" he said.

"Understandable I suppose," Arthur replied.

"But how far d'you take it?" the American asked. "They fight together, they die together. Does that mean they have to drink together and piss and fuck together? Hell! My crew can't wait to see the last of each other once they get ashore."

"You're off a ship?"

"Hell! You think I swum the Atlantic?"

"You could've flown."

"And if I'd had any goddamn sense, I would've joined the air force. Except, knowin' my luck, I'd've probably ended up in some goddamn hole in the Pacific, shot down by the Japs. You want another glass of this piss?" Arthur drank with the American, went outside with him to pee against a wall and returned to drink again. He man turned out to be the first officer on a U.S. freighter. "What d'you do, pal?" he asked.

Arthur had a ready answer for that. "I write propaganda," he said, then went on to hint that he was looking for a change, finally admitting he wanted to get out of the country.

"I thought so," the American said. "You look like a guy that wants to move on. We'll be casting off in a couple of days. Maybe I can fix you up . . . for a consideration. How much dough you got?"

"Enough," replied Arthur. After leaving Martha, Arthur had gone back through the town to the churchyard where he sat until Barclay's opened when he walked in and brashly emptied his account. He had two hundred pounds left.

"Hm . . ." The American looked him over. "Ever crewed on a ship?" Arthur shook his head. "I wouldn't recommend it, even to a dog I hate, but sometimes a guy don't mind landing in the fire if he's escaping the frying pan. Right, pal?"

"Perhaps," Arthur agreed.

"Being a cook's helper aboard my ship is pretty close to being in hell."

"What's involved?" Arthur asked.

"Nothing except getting your ass worked off."

"How do I get on board?"

"Pal, you must be running from something awful."

"A terrible accident. Two women—one my wife—the other her lover . . . both killed."

"Okay, okay. I get it. We leave at 2:00 AM, high tide, tomorrow. Meet me here at 7:00 PM sharp. And get used to being called Mike Steele because that's the name on the ship's papers you're paying for. And after tomorrow, start calling me 'Mister.' Got that?"

"Okay, Mister," Arthur said. "Do I salute too?"

"Hell no! This is a merchant ship, not the fucking navy. All you do is work your ass off."

That briefly summarized how Arthur escaped from England and assumed a new identity. That he was ignored by the ship's captain, stared through by officers, sneered at by the polyglot crew and bullied by the cook can be accepted as fact, as it was fact that after two days at sea, Arthur thought he would die from sea-sickness, but fortunately he recovered and was able to spend what little free time he had standing below the transom outside the galley, scanning the shore as the ship ploughed through panoramic Chesapeake Bay to dock in Baltimore. He went ashore at Baltimore with the Negro cook and made his first acquaintance with racial segregation when he was ordered to go to the front of a street car after boarding it and automatically following the cook to the rear.

"Do what the guy says, Mike," the cook advised. "Get off when Ah do." Ashore, the cook was a changed man. He volunteered to take Arthur to the front door of a white brothel, but Arthur, in the role of randy sailor fresh from sea, dug the cook in his ribs and replied that tightness was what mattered in cunts, not colour, a comment that pleased the cook, and resulted in Arthur discovering, after handing over part of his limited shore-leave money to a plump-bellied young prostitute, that, in the essentials, Negro prostitutes were no different from the whores in Hasterley on the other side of the Atlantic.

"So whadda'ya think, Mike?" the cook queried as they walked along the dock back to the ship.

"Fine and dandy," Arthur said.

The crew had never questioned how or why Arthur had suddenly appeared on board. All they were concerned with was getting ashore and into the nearest bar. If crew members had families in America, none was mentioned, and the only men who truly knew anything about the ship and the oceans over which it wallowed were those on the bridge, or those who worked the engine room. The chief and second engineer had their own table in the officers' mess, where an irascible steward served the food and cursed the cook and his helper. It seemed to Arthur that every man on the ship complained about the food, the ship itself, the officer, the crew. That they did so was due in part to the ship's being old and leaky, though Arthur, knowing nothing of ships, simply accepted that what went on was the same for all merchant ships. His concern was finding out if the ship's next passage would be to England, and if so, he planned to leave the ship and disappear into the vastness of America. He ventured to approach a second officer, who, after eyeing him as though he was a scrap of offal, said they were shipping to Los Angeles via the Panama Canal, and from there to an unnamed Pacific island.

Due to their shore excursions together and because Arthur exhibited none of the prejudice the cook had experienced in his life in North Carolina and on board ship, the two men became friendly. Arthur utilized the friendship to get the cook to talk about the southern states and gather information he thought might come in handy when he finally disembarked. He also persuaded the cook to teach him how to make simple dishes, and within a week Arthur, supervised by the cook, was able to prepare meals. Although his corn bread tended to be soggy and his chili lacked the cook's zip, he nonetheless learned to produce adequate meals. He paid careful attention to the way he spoke and punctuated his conversations with the American slang he picked up from the cook and crew. He enjoyed the passage through the Panama Canal, even though the temperature was oppressively high, especially in the galley, where he combined mixing ingredients for meals with strings of American obscenities that even impressed the cook. They tied up in San Pedro for twenty-four hours to take on cargo that consisted primarily of coffins. And Arthur, who had planned to see Los Angeles and Hollywood, saw nothing of California except the wharf, a littered road and a bar filled with smoke and off-duty U.S. Navy personnel. As they were walking back to the wharf, the cook told Arthur he was quitting.

"Just like that?" Arthur asked.

"Jes like that," the cook replied. "Ah dunno why Ah didn't before now. I guess Ah jes nevah had me a helper that wanted to learn how to cook. The galley's all yours, man." He shook Arthur's hand and walked away.

Back on board, Arthur submitted a written request to the first officer for a cook's helper, but it was returned with the words "Forget it, buddy" scribbled across the page. This Arthur did, and discovered that by reorganizing the galley and menus, he was not only able to cook the food and clean up the utensils, but treat himself to additional time standing below the transom, looking out over the ship's wake, watching sea birds career over the ship's wash. At their base in the Marianas—Arthur never learned which island it was—their cargo was unloaded onto lighters, and after the ship was reloaded—this time with broken-down army vehicles—they sailed for the Panama Canal and Baltimore. Halfway across the Pacific, somewhere in the vicinity of Easter Island, they lost power, and from there proceeded at half-speed (three knots) to Baltimore where the crew was paid off and the ship tied up for repairs. Arthur received his pay packet from the second officer, was informed that repairs would take several weeks and was told where to make inquiries about shipping out again. He then walked along the dock, looked back at the ship's rusted hull, turned and strolled ahead while toying with possible new names for himself. Earlier he had decided to discard the name Mike Steele since he wouldn't need that man's ships' papers any longer. He would keep the initials, though, to preserve the luck that had enabled him to survive so far. He tried "Matthew Steele," then "Matthew Shield," because, after all the new name would be his shield against adversity, but then thought it might be too obvious. He rearranged and added letters to come up with "Sheiler," to which he decided to add a "c" and make it "Scheiler." Matthew Scheiler. Matt Scheiler. How many Americans would have this surname? Probably not many. It was even possible the name was unique. And it would be a good name to use should he ever decide to write again. Thus, Arthur Compson having completed the first phase of his metamorphosis into a new being, shouldered his kit bag and briskly marched forward into an unpredictable American future.

CHAPTER

14

HE HAD WALKED INTO AMERICA AT BALTIMORE WITH A MAP OF the country in his swag, but with no real idea where he might go from there. His assets were the clothes he wore and the dollars in his wallet. He wanted to sample each state, but was uncertain how to go about it. In the end, after walking the streets of Baltimore for a day and returning to the brothel he had previously visited with the cook and wasting (he afterwards decided) five dollars for fifteen minutes with an unenthusiastic whore, he boarded a Greyhound bus and set off on a course that would take him through the Virginias, then diagonally across North Carolina and Tennessee to the Mississippi state line, where, by now revolted by the blatant prejudice he observed, he turned north, hoping to find evidence of America's greatness of mind and spirit in the northern and mid-western states on the other side of the great river that split America in half. So far, it seemed to Arthur that, aside from the evil of prejudice, there was little difference between the people in America's small towns and those in Hasterley and Ponnewton. All were narrow minded, full of gossip about their neighbours and intensely suspicious of strangers. He could not fathom the contradictions in America and concluded the Americans had built their political house on moral quicksand. They had composed a grandiloquent constitution and then had gone ahead and assembled a society that bore a close resemblance to the English class system with Negroes at the bottom. Freedom! Arthur concluded Americans in the southern states did not know what the word meant. Originally, his intention was to ascend the Mississippi on a river boat, but after a few days in northern Mississippi and glimpsing what went on there (he saw a black man hanging on a roadside tree) he decided to turned north and continue his journey in that direction.

It might seem that Arthur did nothing more than board a bus heading north, but, metaphorically speaking, he was running from something that chilled his soul and made his skin creep. He was running from the gun-toting men who were always present, even in small towns, when tired passengers climbed down the two or three steps off the bus; men who scanned him, his clothes and his duffle bag, which he would later discard for a small lockable case. In the deep South, these men apparently had the right to approach and question him: identity? job? profession? length of stay? destination? There were moments in Mississippi when he could believe he had landed in a fascist state, not in a nation whose constitution supposedly guaranteed freedom for all. But still he kept travelling on buses until one day when the bus he was riding pulled into the small depot of a mid-Illinois town where, for no apparent reason, he decided to get off and stay awhile.

"Take it easy," the driver said.

"You too," said Arthur.

"Main Street's not far," the driver added.

"I'll find it." He gestured as the door closed and the bus changed gears and moved on. He picked up his cases and walked into the town, which was nestled behind a levee that protected it from being inundated and swept away by the great, swirling, muddy Mississippi River.

No matter where Arthur had gone in the southern states, no matter where he stopped for a night or where he boarded another bus, somebody always asked: "How did a healthy young fella like you serve his country?" And Arthur had a ready answer for the question, and the further he advanced into the continent, the more he elaborated on it: He had been a crew member on a merchant ship torpedoed in the North Atlantic. Part of the ship's cargo was ammunition, so when the torpedo struck, the ammunition exploded, literally blowing the ship to pieces. He, standing on the stern below the transom (explaining the transom's function took several minutes) was thrown upward and out into the water. Oh yes, he was wearing a life jacket—that was mandatory—but it was of little use in the bitterly cold North Atlantic water. Had his listeners ever seen such waves, or heard such winds raging over them? Debris was floating everywhere, but fortunately for him, he bumped into a life raft and clambered onto it, though he knew his chances of rescue were one in a million. He pretended a certain reluctance in narrating his story, but once he started he became quickly caught up in it and supplied an authenticity convincing to listeners. When people asked why he was riding a bus around the country, he explained he was reassuring himself he was alive, because when he was spotted quite by chance and picked from the raft by a crew from a vessel in another convoy, he had been in the water for three days. Nobody ever asked how he had managed to remain alive for three days and nights in the icy North Atlantic, which was just as well, for his story might have become unravelled at that point. But was Arthur telling lies when he narrated his story? Maybe, in the strictest sense of the word, but in another sense, he was moulding and shaping fiction which he would later bang out on a little second-hand portable typewriter he picked up in a store in Tennessee. Using the name Matt Scheiler, he mailed the stories to a national magazine published out of Philadelphia which accepted them for publication. But that came later.

At first, the "rescue" story served as a convenient excuse for travelling around the states. When he got off a bus, he might tell the driver he was going for a stroll along the main street in order to gulp down the sweet air of America, thereby ridding his body of any salt remaining in his lungs. The buses often stopped at state capitals and, if he liked the look of the place, he would hunt up decent accommodation and stay a few days. The capitols and other public buildings such as high schools with their columned facades fascinated him because they seemed at odds with the townspeople's down-to-earth, blue overalls way of life. It was as though the buildings were imported from elsewhere and symbolized alien political beliefs. Later, much later, after he had seen elaborate churches in Mexico, he revised his opinion and decided that the churches in Mexico had nothing to do with religion, nor the U.S. state capitols with democracy, but rather both symbolized the defeat, subjection and, in many some instances, the obliteration of the aboriginal people who occupied the land first. In one story he wrote, he compared America to ancient Rome, likening the mutilation and hanging of a black man to a Roman crucifixion; but while he gave full rein to his misgivings about the status of Negroes in America within the parameters of fiction, he was careful not to give offense to anybody he met because he sensed an propensity in Americans, especially men, to react violently to any implied criticism of themselves or their country. American men seemed to spend a lot of time poised and waiting for someone to say the wrong thing. At first, Arthur had compared them to cockerels high-stepping around hens, but later he decided the reason for their defensiveness was that they suspected the underbelly of their society was rotten and therefore defied strangers to speak ill of it. Still, everyone sympathized with Arthur after hearing his story of rescue at sea and invariably told him he had come to the right place to clear his lungs of salt and his brain of memories. "Just passing through, admiring your lovely city," Arthur always murmured when anyone asked why he was in town and where he was headed. He found that it paid to describe every village and town as lovely, even when the place was jumble of squalid false-fronted shacks.

The day after he got off the bus in Illinois, Arthur went for a walk around town and reached a milestone in his journey when he stood on the wide dyke looking out across the Mississippi at the home state of the President of the United States. He thought of going back to the depot and boarding a bus that would take him across the river, but felt a surprising reluctance to take that step, somehow feeling he had to remain in the town beside the river for a while in order to absorb and appreciate fully what the crossing meant for him and his future. Thus far, he had carried himself over the Atlantic and Pacific Oceans, meandered through the southern states of America and had gradually come to the belief that his crossing of the Mississippi would sever him (symbolically) from his past and that the Arthur-Compson tail he was dragging behind would then fall off and vanish forever. Then, and only then, would he finally be free to become Matt Scheiler, and becoming Matt Scheiler would enable him to review the notes he had taken during his travels and, after discarding the intense, romantic prose he had successfully used in the past, coldly, yet graphically, lay out stories and novels about the people and places he'd seen in the new (to him) world. It was strange, but as he looked at the swiftly moving water that day, Arthur became convinced he had been destined to arrive at this particular point in his wanderings. Surely that must be the explanation, otherwise his rutting father and half-crazed mother and the other people heretofore in his life: Heather, Laura, Maria and Martha, were nothing more than punctuation marks in an incomplete, pointless saga. What remained was for his spiritual, creative being to catch up with the body that stood on the dyke beside the muddy river.

He turned away and returned to the bus depot and left his suitcase and typewriter there in a locker. He walked around the town until he saw a notice in a window advertising a room for rent. It was curious that he also felt he had been destined to see that sign and to meet the middle-aged woman who showed him the room, all the while explaining her husband worked on the railroad and was often away weeks at a time and that she rented the room to have company while he was gone. Her motives were so candidly offered that Arthur couldn't believe she ever thought anyone could possibly misread them.

"You know, how it is," she said. "Mr. Svendsen is so attached to his locomotive, he can't stand other men driving it. I swear to goodness he dreams about it. Now, Mr. Scheiler, what about meals?"

It was amazing, Arthur thought, how such bland innocence could be carried through a lifetime, how a woman with a husband who buckled himself to her, at least every once in a while, could retain trust in a complete stranger. It compelled him to give more information than he usually offered: he explained that he was looking for a quiet place where he could do some writing, though he planned to seek part-time work to supplement his limited income.

"You won't have trouble finding work," she said, "what with so many men still overseas." When he told her he was a cook, she promptly advised: "Go see Trina. I'm sure she can use a cook. Her husband served his country and got a real bad wound. Tom's in hospital now. Poor Trina, such a lovely girl." In his travels, Arthur had observed that American women, regardless of age, were referred to as girls. "A hard worker. She carried on with the diner, which was a good thing because it prevented her from stewing about Tom. Anyways, let's settle about your meals, Mr. Scheiler. Either way, it don't make that much difference to me." On and on she talked, describing in detail the food she prepared for herself, how more often than not she cooked too much and had to eat it the following day or throw it away, which she hated doing because her mother had raised her to believe that to waste food was a sin against God and nature. Arthur had no sooner told her he would take his meals with her, than she raised the matter of his laundry. She was quite prepared to do it, she told him, provided he didn't get a job that got his clothes filthy.

"That's unlikely," Arthur assured her. "I prefer clean work."

"You'd be surprised," she told him, and proceeded to give him a detailed account of one lodger who, after obtaining work at one of the town's two gas stations, habitually returned from work smelling like an oil sump. "I did my best," she said, "but it was impossible to get out the stains, and when he complained his work pants wasn't clean, I told him he could take his clothes to the chink's, which he did and paid double what I charged."

"Perhaps I should do the same if it's too much work for you."

"I've worked hard all my life," she remonstrated. "That's how I was raised, as I'm sure you were. As was Mr. Svendsen. That's the American way. Don't you agree? My brothers still work the farm. My sisters married farmers. I was the only one that married outside, and that's only because I met Mr. Svendsen by accident at the railway depot coming back from State Fair. He was a fireman then, and I went to look at the locomotive where he was oiling the wheels, and he looked at me and said: "Hi there, pretty missy." I was only twelve, but the next year coming home from the Fair, he leaned out of the locomotive cab—he'd got promoted—and said hello, but my parents said I wasn't old enough to marry, especially a railroad man who'd be away from home half the time. So the next year coming home from State Fair, he leaned out of his locomotive cab and says, 'Hi there, pretty missy. So what's it to be? You marrying me, or a farm boy?' I said I didn't know any farm boys I felt like marrying, and he said that meant I'd prefer marrying him. I was fourteen. My parents said I'd live to regret it."

When she didn't go on, Arthur asked: "And did you?"

"All I regret is knowing Mr. Svendsen has a wife in Chicago and one in St. Louis. He says he needs a bed to sleep in when he's away from home. Those girls've got babies, not that I wasn't willing to do my duty by him, but God was against me having one."

"That must be tough, God denying you a family," Arthur said.

"He moves in mysterious ways," she told him. "Now, let's have a look at your room. So, about coming in late . . . One lodger took to coming home any ole time, and when I told him I didn't allow that, he reared up on his hind legs and told me I was an old fuss-budget, packed his belongings and left."

"I'll tell you if I plan to be late," Arthur promised. "Generally I'm in bed by eleven."

"That's when I'm in bed too. Come on."

The room was small and the furniture consisted of an iron-framed single bed, a chest of drawers and a chair. "Do you have a small table I could use, Mrs. Svendsen?" Arthur asked.

"I don't have no spare furniture."

"For my typewriter. Well, perhaps I can buy one at a furniture store."

"There's no furniture store. People order what they need from the Sears 'n Roebuck catalogue. I have one. You can look through it. Now, about keeping your room tidy."

"Neatness is necessary on a ship. That's where I used to work. You can count on me always to be tidy."

"Hm. Well . . ." She peered around, as though looking for another rule to lay down. "I'll get the catalogue," she said and left the room.

Arthur sat on the bed, pulled the chair over, placed the typewriter on it and decided he wouldn't need a table after all. "This will do," he said when Mrs. Svendsen returned with the massive catalogue.

"Hm. Is that thing noisy? I sleep next door."

"I'll show you." He set the margins, took a piece of paper from his suitcase and typed the words: "Now is the time for all good men to come to the aid of their native country," while Mrs. Svendsen stood at the foot of the bed watching the keys flick up and down as the carriage moved from left to right. "Quiet, isn't it?"

"Do it again. I'll go and lie on my bed." She left the room, and he heard her voice from beyond the head of his bed. "All right. Can you hear me? I'm on the bed."

"Yes," he called back, wondering what he might hear when Mr. Svendsen appeared. Would he hear Mrs. Svendsen telling her husband she saw no point in doing what he proposed because so far it hadn't produced a child, and doing it just for the sake of doing was a waste of time and energy. Or maybe she would pester Svendsen for it, while he tried to avoid complying with his connubial obligation by pleading exhaustion. You could never safely predict how women and men behaved in bed. That was what fascinated, frustrated and puzzled Arthur, who had begun his authorial life by deluding himself into believing he intuitively understood what made other people tick, in bed and anywhere else. Experience had stripped away most of his conceit, but the tendency reappeared now and then, especially when he encountered a fresh face, as with Mrs. Svendsen, whose masks he was now in the process of removing in order that he could, so he imagined, better probe her inner life. He thought his landlady might well be one of those puritan-faced American women who, beneath a veneer of Christian modesty, long to dance with devils, the kind of woman who pretends the sole reason she reluctantly hoists her nightgown and opens her legs for her husband is because she's taken an oath of obedience before her Christian god, though in truth she can hardly wait to get her husband into her slot, hates it when he quickly leaves and has a compulsive urge to invite hired help and every other man who visits the house to perform between her spread legs.

"I couldn't hear anything," she said as she entered the room, startling Arthur out of his bout of prurient speculation.

"Then I have nothing to worry about."

"That's right. Now, Mr. Scheiler, you can sleep, eat and have your laundry done here for fifteen dollars a week."

"Well . . . it's a bit high."

"Mine is high-class lodging, Mr. Scheiler. And there is one other thing: I must tell you, there are a few low-class women in town. Some men, even the Christians, associate with them."

"I can assure you . . . "

"I know how men are. Still, I won't allow any man who associates with those women to remain in my house and give it a bad name. I know men promise one thing and do another, so I want you to know, if you ever think of visiting one of those women, you are to come to me first, because I won't have people saying this is not a respectable house."

Arthur hardly knew how to respond to her astonishing offer and wondered if it was motivated by her need to maintain respectability or if, as seemed more likely, it veiled a need which couldn't otherwise be expressed. "Thank you, Mrs. Svendsen," he said. "I'll bear that in mind."

"I'd appreciate having your first week's rent now," she said, and Arthur took out his scuffed wallet, selected three five dollar bills from the diminishing number and handed them to her. "Supper is at six sharp," she said and left him.

Arthur transferred his few belongings from his suitcase into the chest of drawers, sat on the bed and typed out what he could recall of the conversation between himself and his landlady. (In fact, Arthur would never use the conversation, but Mrs. Svendsen's remarks about respectability were eventually transformed into themes for three short stories in which explicit reasons given for the characters' actions masked their real motives.) When he finished, he went downstairs to the kitchen where his landlady sat at the table, reading a weekly newspaper and listening to music from the local radio station. He asked for directions to Trina's diner, got them and left the house, although not before Mrs. Svendsen reminded him that supper was at six sharp.

It was a typical highway diner, built during the dirty thirties when hundreds of men filled the CCC camp just outside town in order to implant four concrete towers (sadly, with some loss of life) in the swirling, protesting Mississippi before stringing a two-lane highway onto them. Some people in town, especially those who ran the ferry, swore such a bridge could not be safely built and that the river would sweep it away; and for a while, townspeople rose each morning fully expecting to find the bridge had vanished during the night; some even resented the bridge's failure to do what was expected of it and some never ventured onto the bridge, swearing they wouldn't risk their own and their children's lives driving across it, even though enormous trucks roared across it every day, and once, half a dozen thirty-ton army tanks had rattled across the bridge during manoeuvres designed to simulate the shoot-up of a building (Trina's diner was used for the exercise) where a simulated German general and his staff sat around a table, formulating plans for simulated attacks. The simulation ended successfully, so the story went, and everything in the vicinity was blown up, including the diner, by a cool Yankee tank commander who, deploying typical American initiative, drove directly to the diner, surprised the thick-headed krauts and theoretically blew them away.

The diner consisted of a long room with cubicles on the window side facing the highway. The kitchen, storage space, service counter and rest rooms were at the back. Directly in front of the entry and exit was the cash register, where Trina sat in the days before her husband Tom, lit by fires of patriotism, enlisted in the Marines and was wounded on Iwo Jima. Tom had jumped from a landing craft onto a beach of white coral sand only to be knocked down in a storm of Japanese machine-gun bullets set to fire at the height of an average American soldier's hips.

"Bastards, sons of bitches," Tom weakly sobbed when Trina visited him in the hospital. Trina didn't want to know the specifics about her husband's wounds, but she had guessed from the way he wept they were serious. She was also shocked by Tom's language, because she had never known him to venture beyond a "darn it" before serving overseas.

Arthur sat himself in one of the cubicles and watched Trina emerge from the kitchen area and hurry to his table. She looked tired, and Arthur understood how she felt, for he too had often been exhausted and at the end of his tether trying to prepare a meal for the crew as the cumbersome ship lurched over Pacific rollers. "What can I get you?" she asked. She jerked the menu from behind the serviette container and thrust it at him.

"Mrs. Svendsen told me you might need help," he said.

"Did she?"

"I'll be lodging at her place for a while."

"I'm frying hamburgers for the guys over there. I'll be back." She hurried back to the kitchen, while being surreptitiously ogled by customers (all men), who appreciated the movement of her fine, strong legs and broad buttocks. Arthur thought Trina could be an end product of successive waves of polyglot immigrants: Irish in her blue eyes, Balkan in her black hair, German in her waistless torso. Her chin was small and her plump lower lip protruded beyond the upper as it the lip had been sullenly jutted out so often it had permanently altered the shape of her mouth. While none of her features was particularly beautiful in and of itself, nonetheless the composite resulted in an attractive young woman. She addressed customers by their first names and carried on conversations with them while preparing dishes in the kitchen. She appeared with two plates holding hamburgers, french fries and coleslaw, which she placed before two men sitting in a booth near Arthur's while saying she was sorry to have kept them waiting. "You know how things are these days," she said. They nodded, then one said: "How's Tom?"

"Oh, much the same."

"Tell him hello from me, will you, Trina?"

"I'll do that, Hank. And thanks." She moved on to Arthur's booth. "You were saying?"

"Only that Mrs. Svendsen said you were shorthanded."

"Maybe I am, maybe I'm not. But if I am, I need somebody that knows how to cook, not some Joe who'll make a mess of things."

"I know how to cook anything you'll ever need here," Arthur asserted. "I cooked for a freighter crew until the ship was torpedoed."

"So, what're you doing in town?"

"Reestablishing my identity with the earth." This ambiguous statement seemed to impress Trina. Visiting her husband at the hospital had convinced her that men who experience battle trauma need extra time for their new identities to be created.

"You know the quantities to cook, things like that?"

"Sure thing." Arthur had picked up the expression and said it so often that it rolled off his tongue as if he had been using it all his life. "You want pies, bread, rolls, cakes, I can do all of it. Sauces, too."

"I don't want a high-class chef. Only someone to give me a hand in rush hours."

Nothing was said about wages until two weeks had passed and Trina, who had become increasingly uneasy about the subject, broke down and said, "Look Matt, I need to know how much you expect me to pay." The diner had been exceptionally busy that Saturday, and they were sitting in one of the booths drinking mugs of coffee before going home.

"Whatever the business'll bear," Arthur said.

"That's no answer!" she snapped. "You ought to have some idea of what you're worth."

"I'm worth fifteen bucks a week to Mrs. Svendsen."

"Jeez, that's a rip-off!"

"You don't like Mrs. Svendsen?"

Trina shrugged. "All I know, she claims she's got a husband."

"A railroad engineer. She told me."

"Everybody's heard about the guy. Nobody's ever seen him."

"You mean he doesn't exist?"

"I don't know. That's the rumour. About your pay: what about ten dollars a day? And Matt, could you manage on your own if I took off a day to visit Tom?"

"Sure. How is he?"

Trina chewed her lips before answering. Arthur had discovered Trina was the sort of person who needed to bring other people into the circle of her activities and feelings. "I'm real worried about him. I still don't know how bad he's been hurt."

"Ask the doctor, or his nurses."

"I'm scared to." Then the dam burst. "We put off having a family until we got the diner going, but now I'm scared something's happened. Tom doesn't say anything, it's something I feel. He used to be real happy. Full of beans, singing all the time. He could cook anything, like you. But now . . ."

"Ask him, Trina."

"I can't. I want a family. So does Tom. Guys come in here and think they can . . . just because Tom's not here. It's awful."

"They're opportunists," Arthur said.

"They're detestable. They don't respect a woman who's faithful to her husband."

It had taken Arthur only a couple of days of working at the diner to observe that, while Trina's conscience dictated she remain faithful to her wounded husband, the manner in which she moved between the booths, the serving counter and the cash register clearly indicated that at least some parts of Trina were at odds with her moral code.

The situation was perfect for Arthur. In the mornings, he tapped away on his typewriter, turning out a page or two of manuscript which, not trusting Mrs. Svendsen, he locked in his suitcase, then walked to the diner to take over the cooking from Trina: frying beef patties and onions, ladling out bowls of soup, stacking BLTs and grilling cheese sandwiches. Most of the patrons were truck divers or elderly widowers, who came more for company than for the food. One fellow showed up every day for two meals. Trina explained why to Arthur.

"There's some guys in town who think they've got to keep an eye on women whose husbands've gone off to war. He's one of 'em. Y'know what I'm going to do one of these days, Matt? I'm going to parade around with a cushion stuffed inside my shirt. That'll make his eyes pop out." She laughed. "He sits in his car across the street from my house at night and watches me go in."

"Complain to the cops."

"You're joking. He's in cahoots with them *and* the ministers. Has Mrs. Svendsen been after you yet, to go to church?"

"She's mentioned it. I don't see much of her."

"Laid eyes on her husband yet?"

"Not yet." Trina went off to wash the mugs, while he followed her into the kitchen to check everything was in place for opening the diner the next morning. "Look Trina, I want to ask you a question. It's because of something Mrs. Svendsen said to me the day I rented the room . . . but it's kind of awkward."

"I'm used to awkward questions," she said as she hung up the towel.

"She told me she was a respectable woman, living in a respectable house. Then she talked about some women in town she called low-class. She said men visited them."

"They live across the river, not in town."

"Whatever. But then, and this is what floored me, she said if ever I was tempted, I was to go to her." Trina began laughing. "What's so funny?" he demanded.

"You'd only get a reading from the Bible, and you'd have to kneel and pray with her."

"The hell I would."

"Did y'think she was inviting you into her bed? You don't understand the people in this town, Matt. That woman's always sniffing around other women to see if she can't smell men's stuff on them."

They went out into the cool fall night and walked down the hill to the intersection where Arthur turned to go to his lodgings. Leaving Trina to go home alone always made Arthur uneasy because she was carrying the day's takings in her shoulder bag. "You sure you don't want me to walk you home?" he asked.

"Listen Matt, I was born and raised in this town and I know every man, woman and kid in it. People here do a lot of stupid things, but nobody'd dream of stealing money a person's earned working like a dog all day. Besides, there's that guy sitting in the car making sure I go in, remember?" Still, Arthur waited at the intersection, listening for the sound of Trina's shoes crunching on the gravel, wanting to know for sure that she turned into the path to her front door before he walked on to his lodgings, all the while working up resentment of Mrs. Svendsen for inviting him to her room under false pretences. He thought of walking across the bridge in the morning for good. No, that wouldn't do: when he finally made his decision to cross the Mississippi River, he wanted to do it in such a way that he would be able to shuck off the past and emerge as a new being. Yes, that was what he wanted. That was his destiny. But not tonight or tomorrow morning, for whichever day he finally did it—it won't be long now, he thought—he wanted to be sure that the shell of his old self was ready to split the moment he stepped onto the western side of the mighty river. Then, from the cracked carapace, would burst forth a fully formed Matt Scheiler.

Before entering the house, he urinated against a utility pole, then stood in the hall to remove his shoes, crept up the stairs to his room where he undressed, went to bed and dreamed he was making love with Sylvia and Laura in the cab of a locomotive where a devil dressed in an engineer's coveralls and cap was trying to push them into the roaring firebox. He awakened to the sound of Mrs. Svendsen vacuuming the passage outside his bedroom door. It was seven in the morning.

When, later that day, Arthur explained why he was yawning, Trina said, "Why didn't you tell her to cut it out?"

"It wasn't worth the effort. I'll be going on in a couple of weeks anyway."

"Do you have to? What's the rush? Is your mom's house burning down or something? Listen, Matt, you don't want to spend a winter in Nebraska or the Dakotas. Honest to God, it's so cold there, guys don't know whether they're coming or going. Look, stay here through the winter and start off in the spring when everything's green and looks pretty."

And so, against his inclinations Arthur stayed, though he felt sure there was little difference between the ice-impregnated winds that rushed down the Mississippi to assail the little Illinois town and those that blasted over the western plains. He stayed because he was finishing several short stories and also because he liked and admired Trina and the way she presented a cheerful persona to her customers, even though she was shot through with anxiety about her husband's condition.

"Look, Trina. Shall I go and ask Tom what's wrong?"

Panic rushed across her face. "No, no. You mustn't!"

"I'd just talk to him, that's all." He made the offer, although he couldn't see himself engaging in a buddy-to-buddy conversation. He was, he thought, more likely to exchange intimate information with a woman than with a man.

"What'll I do if we can't have a baby, Matt? I mean, we planned to have a family. We talked about it even when we were in grade school." She was so anxious to prove her faithfulness to Tom she reached out to touch Arthur's hand. "I never dated another boy. Never. Oh, some asked me, but I wouldn't. And Tom never dated other girls, though a bunch of girls once ganged up and tried to get him away from me. You'd be surprised how nasty girls can be over boyfriends. In high school, Tom and I talked it over. You know, how we'd get married, start our business and have our family."

"Why didn't you have the family first?" Arthur enjoyed teasing her. She took everything he said so seriously. "I've been told starting a baby's not difficult."

Trina blushed and looked away from him. "That's none of your business," she said. When all Arthur did was shrug, she continued, "Tom and me agreed we wouldn't do anything until we were married. And then when the bridge got built, Tom said this would be a perfect spot for the diner. So we put off having a family."

"You mean, you never—?"

"Eddie—that's Tom's brother, he's a pharmacist—he told Tom what to do."

Arthur, who had carelessly spilled generative fluid into each woman he had known, could only say, "I've never been married, Trina, so I don't know much."

"I'm surprised you haven't been caught by now. You're an attractive guy."

"No money," Arthur said.

"People think girls have their eye on a guy's wallet. But that's not true. Girls look for guys who'll give them beautiful babies. Tom's handsome."

"You deserve a handsome guy, Trina."

"I just want him to get well and come home. That'll be the happiest day of my life."

"Even happier than the day you married Tom?" Arthur knew he ought not to tease, but he couldn't prevent himself, In a way, he envied Trina because she was packed with proper emotions, while he seemed devoid of all feeling.

She tried to answer without being too explicit. After all, she was a modest woman. "That was different. It was like a birthday party when you get excited, though you know everything that's going to happen. I knew Tom and I could move one step ahead. I mean, by the way we loved each other. And everything did happen the way we planned, except we decided to put off having a family until the diner was up and running good. And then the war came, and Tom felt he had to volunteer."

And so it went. Each night after the diner closed, they drank coffee and talked, usually about things that dominated Trina's life: her wounded husband, her longing to have him back and her desire to have a child with him. What did Matt think: should she have said no when Tom wanted to postpone having a family? Arthur would look at Trina and imagine her on her wedding night, throbbing with the desire imprisoned during the years of their courtship, waiting for his embrace, waiting to receive the man she loved, then feeling her passion slip away when Tom followed his pharmacist brother's advice and shrouded his living member which by rights ought to unite her to him. One night, when she asked Arthur if she had done the right thing, he replied that he didn't know, but was certain that to live by hindsight was pointless.

"I suppose." She got up and went into the kitchen to wash the mug, and he followed with his. "But suppose you're scared you've missed your only chance? What do you do then?" He couldn't answer the question; instead, he gestured as if to say asking him was futile. He put his arms around her, patted her shoulders and stroked her hair. After a while, they found themselves on the floor, she with her underclothes around her knees, he kneeling at the back of her, pushing against her firm, ample bottom. It didn't take long, and when it was over she stared at him in horror and ran to the ladies' room where he supposed she tried to ream out his semen with wads of toilet paper.

"It was an accident, Trina," Arthur said as they walked down the hill into town. "I'd better clear out." They reached the intersection where the road turned to Trina's house. So far, she hadn't said one word, and he expected her to go on walking while he stood and listened to her shoes crunching the gravel. It wasn't far to her house because the town was small, so small, so it was said, that women too lazy or too busy to walk stood on their doorsteps and carried on shouted conversations with friends on the other side of town. That other people could hear what they said didn't much matter because everybody knew everybody else's business down to which wife was expecting because her husband forgot himself at the last moment, whose kids had pin worms (everybody's), whose elderly husband was expected to pass away because his bowels had ceased functioning, which school girl had fainted in the school washroom when she pulled down her panties and saw they were covered with blood and on and inconsequentially on.

As she opened her front door, ignoring the man who sat in his car across the street, Trina would often call out: "I'm home, Matt." But that night she didn't call, so he moved along the street, urinated in the shadow of a juniper tree, entered the house, removed his shoes and crept up to his room, where he lay on the bed without bothering to undress. It was easy to see why it had happened: Emotional intimacy had been established and confidences exchanged, followed by expressions of physical need that could go nowhere except to the linoleum-covered floor and the mindless embrace. But that wouldn't have mattered and could've been passed off as a single lapse of common sense, except that Trina had a wounded husband stuck in a hospital where he lay in bed and sobbed whenever she visited, and where, so she implied, there was a conspiracy of silence among hospital staff about the nature of his wounds. Apart from admiring Trina's determination and stamina, Arthur liked her as much as he had once liked Maria. But while the sex was happening, nothing had mattered except breaking down the barrier that prevented him from spilling his seed and escaping from himself and his past. He tried to recall if she had uttered any sound which he associated with female expressions of sexual pleasure, but there had been nothing comparable to Sylvia's cries or Laura's pulsating moans of culminating triumph. And yet Trina must have pulled down her own underclothes, for he had no memory of his hands moving from her shoulders and head to her thighs and bottom. Therefore, she must have initiated their coupling by kneeling and offering him access, but he couldn't remember the sequence. All he could remember was his own gasp as he escaped from bondage and Trina's terror-filled eyes before she bolted to the bathroom.

But why should he regret what had happened when he had only to look into the eyes of men who haunted the diner and know that behind polite interest (even the old men) lay images of Trina naked and of themselves squeezing her breasts and pushing urgent cocks between her nether lips. And he'd be willing to bet a hundred bucks that the man in the car whose job was to make sure Trina didn't fall into the slough of fornication wouldn't recoil in horror if Trina walked across the road one night and invited him to share her bed. And why was that? Because, when Jehovah moulded Adam from Eden's dust he had installed in every Adam that would ever live a need that would defeat all dogma and social restriction devised by man, that is to say, an instinctive male response to swaying hips and rotating buttocks.

He asked himself if the time hadn't now arrived for him to cross the bridge and commence the next phase of his life. For a while before he slept, determination was strong; but when morning came he was not able to get up, pack his few possessions and leave. Instead, he tapped out an account of what had happened between him and Trina, shaping it into a short story in which a single man and married woman are trapped by love and circumstance. Writing the two thousand words enabled him to walk to the diner and go to work as though nothing unusual had occurred the previous evening. And so things continued for a week, until Trina, while picking up an order from the counter, whispered, "Everything's okay." When he looked blank, she hissed, "I've started my monthly." Later, when they were drinking their after-work coffee, she asked Arthur if he would take over the next day so she could visit Tom. It meant opening the diner for breakfast, but she would pay him for the extra work and try to get back in time for the supper rush.

"Ask him what's wrong," Arthur said as they left the diner and started down the hill.

"I'll see." When they reached the intersection she said, "I'll try to get back in time to help at supper."

"I can manage," he said and walked on.

She called out: "It depends on the buses. If I get an early bus, I'll be home in time."

"Forget it," he called. "Just get the truth from him."

"I'll try."

But Arthur was doubtful she would and wasn't surprised when Trina appeared just before closing time the following day and glumly shook her head when he looked the question at her. Several days passed before Trina told him that Tom was being transferred to a hospital back east for further treatment, and that the government would pay her expenses when she visited Tom every third month. Arthur's only comment was a nod.

Winter arrived and stayed on like an unwelcome guest. Arthur continued tapping out short stories, some with definite themes, others that were little more than character sketches. It was good practice, he told himself, for the time when he began writing a novel. Most of his free hours were spent thinking about future stories and reflecting on those he had already written. Now, what he had formerly written seemed immature, the characters' passions artificial and forced, and though he told himself he couldn't have written them any other way, he experienced a little quiver of shame, knowing he had exposed his limitations to the world. His early novels, he had concluded, were trite. And therein lay Arthur's literary problem. Some writers create their novels from the commonplaces of life, but for Arthur, whose creative foundation was the Bible and Shakespeare's plays, fictional life was tempestuous, conflicted and passionate. He observed Trina closely and made notes of the contradictory things she said about herself and her relationship with her husband, thinking that some day he would write a novel about a woman whose life would illustrate the conflict between her impulse to fulfil natural desires and her need to conform with the religious and social strictures of her community. He would have her end an embittered woman, unable to explain the resentment she feels, or shrug off her helplessness and enjoy life. He wrote, rewrote, cobbled paragraphs together, recobbled them, and when he was sick and tired of what he had written and knew he was incapable of improving it, he sent the stories off to the magazine editor in Philadelphia and forgot them.

Sometimes in the mornings when he had written himself out and was feeling depressed over the damnably cold weather, he walked up onto the dyke to stare at the ice that cracked and rumbled and reformed again. He decided he had reached his limit, that he should go back to his room, pack his few possessions and get out; but he never went that far. The warmth of the house and the diner and his allegiance to Trina, all worked to defeat him. There was something sad about Trina, he thought, the way she held onto her fragmented beliefs. He felt like holding and comforting her, but he knew such a gesture would be seen as another dangerous advance, though she, quite unknowingly, inclined her body towards him and invited his embraces, or leaned over in such a way that her short skirt was raised to the edge of her lace-trimmed panties. He wanted to warn her that he was not invulnerable to temptation and to tell her that each night he dreamed of her white, luscious half-moons and the half-crazed delight he had experienced between them.

In the days preceding Christmas, she dug out boxes of lights and dusty paper chains which he played out while she, standing on a stepladder, suspended them on cup hooks left in place from former years. "Hold my ankles," she said as she climbed to the uppermost step to reach the highest cup hook.

"Let me do it? I'm taller," he said.

"Just steady me. That's all you have to do." Aware what he would see if he looked up, Arthur concentrated on the lowering grey sky and the ridges of ploughed, dirty snow along the highway. Once, as she climbed down, she misjudged her step and might have injured herself had he not grabbed and lifted her off the stepladder. "Thanks," she said. "I thought my foot was on the step."

Arthur, unsure whether she had tripped or was playing tricks on him, angrily told her to stay off the highest rung. "Who cares about the stupid paper chains, anyway?" he said.

"I do." She sounded hurt. "Tom and I made them together the first year we opened the diner. Anyway, that's it, except for the mistletoe." She held up a bunch of artificial mistletoe which she then suspended over the cash register where customers were allowed to kiss her briefly after making a cash donation to a charitable organization. Trina's regulars were familiar with the ritual and solemnly dropped dimes and quarters into the slotted box before making the most of the moments when Trina's pursed lips touched theirs.

"What'll I get if I put in five bucks?" jokers would ask. "Five smacks you know where?" That comeback always produced prolonged laughter, and Arthur could barely look at Trina as she posed under the mistletoe with her lips pursed and eyes rolled heavenward.

"You're a spoil-sport, Matt," she said, "At Christmas everybody around here acts friendly."

"It's all pretence." But his comment changed nothing. Trina had been raised to believe peace and goodwill reigned in December, though when Arthur asked if the Japanese soldier who had sprayed machine gun bullets at Tom had believed in Christmas and good will, she refused to answer.

He had not thought to give Trina a gift and was taken aback when, on Christmas morning, he received a carefully wrapped gift and a card on which she had written "Much love, Athena." He could do no more than look up from the card and say, "Is that your real name? I had no idea." Inside the box was a black and red lumberman's shirt. "To go with your boots," she explained. As always, Arthur refused to spend money on new clothes, and when something needed replacement, he shopped at secondhand stores or at the Sally Ann. Boots were the one exception. His present pair were high-laced and broad fitting, which allowed him to wear two pairs of socks, and while the upper parts of his body might shiver from cold and icicles would form on his eyebrows and around his nostrils, his feet remained warm. Trina often teased him about his boots, saying that if only he had an ox and carried an axe, he'd be taken for Paul Bunyan. She was the kind of person who enjoyed gently teasing people she especially liked.

Trina's gift compounded an earlier embarrassment. Arthur had told Mrs. Svendsen he would be working at the diner the whole of Christmas day, and hardly knew what to say when, as he sat on the bottom stairs lacing up his boots, Mrs. Svendsen appeared, holding out a small package. Her hair was braided, but not coiled and pinned to her scalp as usual; this, combined with her long dressing gown that touched the edge of her nightgown and slippers, gave her the appearance of an adolescent girl. Knowing these two women had gone out of their way to buy him gifts touched him. He mumbled, "I never dreamt," which he thought might please them, since it suggested women were ten times more thoughtful than men when it came to gestures of friendship.

"I appreciate your company," Mrs. Svendsen had said, while Trina's gift had been accompanied by the words: "I told Tom about you, and he said to wish you all the best." It was almost too much for a memory-ridden man to bear.

"I just wish he was recovered and back here with you," Arthur replied. "Athena. Hm . . . I always thought your name was Christina."

"I hated my name when I was a kid and when anyone asked my name, I said 'Trina' and it stuck." Arthur had been about to say she was the namesake of a classical goddess while his was of a mythical English king, but caught himself in time. Trina walked to the counter to stand under the mistletoe.

"I'd better not, Athena," he said.

"I don't know why, but I keep thinking somehow it'll help Tom get better. Just once, then we'll put the turkey on."

Against Arthur's better judgement, he put his arm around her waist, dabbed a quick kiss on her expectant lips, withdrew and said, "You know Trina, if I allowed myself, I could easily fall in love with you. But I'm not going to do that, and I'm telling you right now, as soon as decent weather arrives, I'll be shoving off."

CHAPTER

15

HAD TRINA THOUGHT HE WOULD REALLY LEAVE? WHILE RIDING on buses, moving through landscapes that seemed to duplicate endlessly what he had seen during previous days, Arthur rummaged through his memories of her, replaying the final weeks and days of his interval on the east side of the Mississippi River, eventually concluding neither Trina nor Mrs. Svendsen thought he would actually pack up and leave the town which was the pivot of their world. And yes, there was a Mr. Svendsen.

A spurt of laughter rose in his gut as he remembered the mid-December night when, after listening to the crunch of Trina's boots in the snow filled path, he walked to his lodgings where he removed his boots at the bottom of the stairs, silently undressed and got into bed. He yawned, rolled onto his side, then sat up and felt hair rise on his neck when bed-creaking sounds punctuated by loud grunts and quickening huffs and puffs came through the wall close to his left ear. The noises ended with a very loud gasp, followed by more bed creaks, mumblings, and what sounded like pre-sleep snorts.

The next morning when Arthur went down for his coffee, corn flakes and toast, his landlady introduced him to a long-faced, bald, stout-gutted man who sat at the table with her. "This here is Mr. Svendsen." She said to Arthur, then to her husband, "and this here is Mr. Scheiler, the lodger."

"Glad to meet you," said Mr. Svendsen, who reached across the table to shake Arthur's hand. "Took her in to get her tubes cleaned out and thought I'd step on down an' see how Ruthie was gettin' along."

"He means his locomotive," Mrs. Svendsen explained.

"The guy knows what I mean. You don't have to explain every goddamn thing I say."

"I heard you're a railroad engineer," Arthur said.

"Bet your life I am. So you're keepin' Ruthie company?"

"When I can," Arthur said.

"But no further than her bedroom door, right?"

"Walter!" Mrs. Svendsen yapped.

"What the hell. The guy can take a joke. Well, can't you?"

"Of course," Arthur politely agreed, thinking that for a man with three wives, Mr. Svendsen seemed mighty possessive, but then maybe polygamists were that way inclined. Perhaps the more wives a man had, the less he felt inclined to share with the unfortunates hovering around the perimeter of his harem.

"Anyways, Ruthie here's a bit long in the tooth for a young guy like you." Mrs. Svendsen blushed and turned away from the table. "Ruthie tells me you was a cook on a freighter."

"I was," Arthur said.

"Got blowed up, eh?"

"Torpedoed," Arthur explained. "It's something I'd as soon forget."

"I'll bet you would."

At that point Arthur excused himself, went back to his room and recorded his observations of Mr. Svendsen, who remained two more days, then disappeared. Curiously, his incursion into his wife's body, which for some reason occurred each of the three nights shortly after Arthur returned from work, seemed to strengthen ties between Arthur and his landlady.

She indirectly apologized for her husband's behaviour by saying he was so accustomed to having his locomotive do exactly as he pleased he had a tendency to deal with people the same way.

"I'm sure you know more about his locomotive than anyone," Arthur agreed. "What about his other wives? Are they as well-informed?"

"I suppose they know about it too." In one of their breakfast chats, Mrs. Svendsen informed Arthur she was born in 1904, which meant she was still on the lee side of forty-five. She also spoke of her inability to have children, explaining it was the principal reason for Svendsen taking other wives. "He's one of twelve," she said. "Seven boys and five girls, all big and energetic, like him."

"Heavens!" Arthur exclaimed. "Are they all locomotive engineers?" An image formed of seven Svendsen boys and five Svendsen girls dementedly driving locomotives back and forth on American rails. The idea for a story came to him in which a father in one locomotive crashes head-on with another driven by his son. At the last moment, each recognizes the number plate on the other locomotive and both father and son realize they are on the verge of destroying each other. Arthur asked Mrs. Svendsen if she'd ever considered the possibility that her barrenness was caused by her husband. The suggestion riled her, and matters didn't improve when Arthur hinted that Mr. Svendsen's other wives might have had children by other men.

"They're good women," she said. "They wouldn't do anything like that."

There's no way to know," Arthur pointed out. "After all, being 'sinful' takes a mere five minutes of the entire time they spend being 'good.'" He wasn't sure if the blush that appeared on Ruth Svendsen's cheeks came from embarrassment or anger. "And the children your husband thinks are his could just as easily been fathered by other men. And something else: what does your husband think you're doing when he's not around? He has no way of knowing if you have relationships with other men."

"I never thought I'd live to see the day when a person thought himself free to say such a rude thing to me," she said. But she did not order him to leave her house, nor to leave the kitchen. Instead, she remained at the table, staring so fixedly at him that Arthur thought he could actually see the wheels of cognition slowly turning in her head. "Mr. Svendsen says the children look like him," she said.

"All kids look like everybody else's kids." Arthur shrugged and got up to leave. "Anyway, it's not important."

"What d'you mean, not important?" she demanded.

"I mean, it was just a thought." He went toward the kitchen archway.

"Just a minute," she ordered. He halted. "You're real free with your thoughts, aren't you? First off, you say Mr. Svendsen's wives is off-loading other men's children onto him. Now, you say I go with other men."

"That's not what I meant."

"That's what I took in, Mr. Scheiler. That's what I heard." Fortunately for Arthur, she then branched off from her original point to accuse him of being exactly like the ministers in her church who condemn the congregation for what they themselves do every day. This left Arthur with no alternative but to edge toward the kitchen door, apologizing and lamely trying to explain he thought it wasn't fair that Mr. Svendsen blamed her for not having children. He left the house angry with himself for having needled his landlady with those quite unnecessary comments. Was he hoping she would present him with an opportunity to embarrass her by saying that he'd heard Mr. Svendsen's thumping away at her? Or had that been intentional? Was Mr. Svendsen purposefully letting his lodger know that he, Mr. Svendsen, was the only cock bird allowed in his wife's roost?

He was still angry when he got to the diner and could barely speak to Trina, who wanted to talk about New Year's Eve: Should she serve breakfast, then close up until evening when friends and customers would join her to party and welcome in the new year?

"I don't have any friends," Arthur sourly said.

"You *are* in a lousy mood, aren't you?" Trina sniffed, and for the rest of the day addressed him as Mr. Grump, aggravating his mood by provocatively rolling her bottom each time she left the kitchen. It was a childish gesture that reminded him of the village girls in Hasterley wagging their rear ends at boys. But later, after they had closed the diner and were tidying up, Trina leaned on he counter and said, "Come on, Matt. Tell me what's wrong." When he rebuffed her by shaking his head, she urged, "Come on, that's not fair. After all, I've told you what's wrong in my life. Friends tell each other when something's not right."

"I'm depressed about my work. I'm not getting anywhere." Trina knew Arthur wrote stories and was impressed.

"Then why didn't you tell me, instead of letting me imagine worse things. That's not fair, Matt."

"I agree. It's not fair."

She walked around the counter to stand beside him. "We are friends, aren't we?"

"Trina, we are *not* friends, we're celibate lovers." He remembered every word of the exchange, including how Trina had momentarily averted her eyes before responding.

"That can't be helped, can it?" she said.

"No, it can't."

"I have to be faithful to Tom. That's what I promised." In a way, the very hopelessness of their relationship allowed Arthur to feel love for Trina; he could even experience perverse pleasure in knowing his phantom-like love could never be tested or questioned. "I broke down that one time, Matt, but I'll never do it again and I'll always be ashamed of myself for it."

He held and raised her hand to kiss it. "You're a sweet girl. Listen, if you want to hold a New Year's Eve party, then go ahead. After all, it's your diner."

"But I couldn't manage without your help." The conversation withered, there being nothing left to say.

In the days following the New Year's Eve party, Arthur had simply waited for the ice and snow to melt, and while Trina might not have believed he would finally leave, she seemed intuitively to know he had emotionally and spiritually removed himself from her life, for she didn't attempt to change his mind. Indeed, there came a time when she, and Mrs. Svendsen too, became so distant it seemed as if they could hardly wait to get rid of him, as women at full-term resent the foetus which occupies their bodies that once were nimble enough to run and dance about whenever the spirit moved them. Trina had lined up a cook to replace him, and Mrs. Svendsen had obliquely let him know another lodger was in the offing and she was politely waiting for him to vacate the room. Before he left, he received another cheque from the magazine to which he had been regularly contributing his short stories. This time the cheque was accompanied by a note from the editor suggesting they meet to discuss publication of a collection of his stories. At the bottom of the note was printed RSVP followed by several exclamation marks. The note he ignored, but he deposited the cheque in the bank, except for five hundred dollars which he calculated would be enough to last him for a while. He informed the friendly bank manager that he would henceforth be travelling to the west and, while he intended to be self-sustaining, still he might have to withdraw funds from his account. The manager assured him this would be no problem, all he need do was to call in at any bank branch, have the manager phone collect, and money could be speedily transferred. The banks were there, the manager assured Arthur, for no other reason than to serve their customers.

And so, supported by assurances from the bank manager, Arthur was free to wander middle-America. The bus zigzagged into Missouri and on into southern Iowa, and Arthur had the impression that, although the land looked much the same as what he'd seen heretofore, the people living west of the Mississippi seemed to possess greater freedom than those on the east. It was, he thought as he rode along, as though only adventuresome folk had crossed the river, leaving the timid behind on the east bank. This was evident in the way people viewed the river. In the little town east of the Mississippi, people spoke of the great river with awe, but those on the west bank simply put their backs to it and turned their attention to the land. When Arthur (now sealed in the armour of Matt Scheiler's identity) spoke of possible destinations to agents in bus depots, they would say, "Take your pick, pal. There ain't nothing but land between here and the Rocky Mountains." It was difficult for Arthur, a man who had grown up in a few square miles of English woodland, to grasp that no matter in what direction he looked, there were millions of acres of undulating land such as he'd seen when he got off the bus for the day in a small town somewhere in Missouri and had walked to the edge of town and looked westward where a few clouds gathered on the horizon around the sun, so it seemed to him, for an evening gossip. To the north, the plains extended beyond the U.S.-Canada border as far as the Hudson Bay, even beyond; to the south, they reached all the way to the Gulf of Mexico. And as he travelled further north, he found that the more he looked in any one direction, the less he was able to comprehend of the vastness of the plains. He felt his own insignificance and asked himself if similar thoughts affected the people who settled the plains. His map told him that the settlers had seen the emptiness of the plains as an enemy and tried to defeat it by laying latitudinal and longitudinal rail and road lines over it. From his study of the map, it seemed as though Americans sought to reduce the overwhelming magnitude of the land by somewhat arbitrarily chopping it up into states, whereas Canadians had divided only the southern plain into entities (provinces), but beyond sixty degrees north latitude had surrendered themselves to its immensity and simply designated the aggregate as the Northwest Territories. He thought that to survive in such a land, an individual would first have to gather every fragile asset of egoism, then hide all of them in a secure place deep within; for unless a person did that, the unending vista of impersonal land and sky would destroy him or her.

One day, as he stood outside a store somewhere in Iowa, which served as post office and bus depot, a long truck stopped, a window was lowered and a man leaned out to ask where he was heading.

"Anywhere. Where're you heading?"

"Packing plant outside the capital," the man replied. "Taking my steers to be slaughtered."

"Fine with me." Arthur opened the door, swung his suitcase and type-writer case into the cab and climbed in.

"Just outta the service?" the driver asked. Arthur laid out his story and the man clucked sympathy. "Jeez," he said, "and I used to think this here was the worst place a guy could be stuck in. Funny, ain't it? You drive around this state in winter sure things can't be no worse, then you meets up with a guy that makes what you got seem just fine, just fine."

"It was hell," Arthur emphasized.

"I was took to church every Sunday as a kid, and I heard about hell fires and sin, but you know, I never believed a word of it, because I know'd the preacher'd laid half the girls in the front row, and my old man done the other half." He laughed and slapped the steering wheel. "And why not? It's what women wants."

"I guess they do," Arthur agreed. On board ship, men had thrown around their opinions of women, telling each other what they'd do with them if they had a chance. As a rule, the men ended up in the head, using their hands to pump out what they'd boasted they were reserving for harems of faceless, nameless women.

"You aiming to find work?" the driver asked.

"Enough to keep my belly full and my feet decently shod."

"There's jobs for the picking. The plant my steers are headed for's begging for workers. Hells bells! There ain't much difference between killing a Jap and killing a steer, except a steer's worth more. Lots of bucks back there." He poked a thumb over his shoulder at the trailer in which cattle sadly lowed. "The war's been a blessing. Funny how things work out, eh? Ten years ago, a guy could hardly turn a buck on his section. My dad come up here from Kansas, got hisself a section, but he never ploughed no land. He was a cattle man. What the hell. You get a decent bull, a few dozen cows for breeding stock and you're all set. They ain't going to cost you nothing. You divvy up your section and move your steers around to fatten 'em up and sell 'em in the fall. You ain't gonna make a million, but you ain't gonna starve either, or watch your soil blow away, like them poor bastards in Oklahoma and Kansas. Me and my sister split the section when Dad passed on." He thumbed the trailer again. "Half is hers. Jeez, packing plants'll take anything nowadays. I got my eye on a section across the highway from mine. I figure I'll need it 'cause I got a couple of boys coming home from Germany. Got a couple of girls, too. They'll be grabbing themselves husbands when the soldier boys come marching home. They ain't beauties, but I figure them boys'll be happy to get a healthy American girl. Right?" Arthur agreed that health is an important factor in marriage. "You bet it is. You married?"

"No."

"Our preacher used to tell us it was better to marry than burn up with lust. I guess he was right. He sure burned enough. Funny how girls go for them preachers, eh? Maybe they think it bring them closer to the Lord."

"Hm. Could be."

And so it went, as the steer-filled trailer roared along the straight, undeviating highway. The cattleman talked in snatches about himself, his own and other men's land, his parents, his wife and children. (Arthur had discovered Americans had an unrestrained capacity to spill details about their lives.) From there, he went on to talk about life and death. "Just remember, a guy comes out of a hole when he gets born and he goes back into one when he dies. And every goddamn thing you do when you're alive is putting somethin' into a hole at one end and spewin' stuff out of t'other. There ain't no difference between you and me and a worm that eats its way through the soil. Every spring my dad'd go round each parcel of land in his section and dig holes, then spread out the soil and turf and count the worms. The bigger and the juicier the worms, the better the soil. He kept a worm record. Funny, eh? I told the wife I don't want to buried in no graveyard. Hell, no. She can dig a hole right in my own land and drop me into it. I'll do the same for her if she goes first. What the hell, I figure I owe that much to my land. Mind you, she ain't so enthusiastic about being put bare-assed into the ground, but I figure she'll come around eventually. Look, I'll drop you off in the middle of town. There's a hotel there where guys that get themselves voted into the state assembly hangs out and puffs out their chests. I've even thought of runnin' for governor myself, the one we've got now's a jerk. Can't make up his mind over nothin'. There's a couple of guys in the state pen that's headed for the chair. The sonsofbitches kidnapped a little girl, raped her, then slit her throat and dumped her in a ditch. But our sittin'-on-the-fence governor's chewing his nails over whether to pardon 'em. If it was me, I'd cut off their balls and stuff 'em in their mouths. A little ten-year-old kid that probably don't even know she's got a twat. It makes a guy sick to think on it." He turned the trailer into a square and stopped beside a park in which sat the copula-crowned capitol. "Ain't much goes on in there," he remarked, "but it looks kind of impressive."

"It does. Well, thanks for the lift and the conversation."

Arthur stood on the sidewalk and raised a hand as the trailer slowly moved off before turning into a street that presumably would take it to the outskirts of town and the packing plant.

The four-storey brick hotel that Arthur stood in front of looked as though it had been built at the same time as the capitol. The lobby was small, the reception counter a single slab of mahogany and the elevator an open box edged with a folding door. When the middle-aged woman behind the counter looked at the typewriter case Arthur held, she concluded he was a newspaper reporter, which Arthur did not bother to contradict. He had discovered that it was easier to go along with people's assumptions than to correct them.

"There's not much going on at the moment," she said, "but you could interview the Governor. He can't decide whether to pardon two murderers."

"He may prefer to be alone with his thoughts," Arthur suggested.

"Oh no, he enjoys being interviewed. I'll just call his office." Before Arthur could protest, she had taken up the phone, dialled a number and explained to somebody at the other end that Mr. Scheiler, a reporter, would like to see the Governor if he was available. She covered the mouthpiece while saying: "He's a nice man. Soft-hearted. That's why he can't make up his mind about those two killers. I know what I'd do."

"Oh, thanks Sally," she said into the receiver. "I'll send him right over. Bye." Then to Arthur: "Sally's a lovely girl. So helpful. The Governor's wife's niece. Why don't you tell the Governor any guy that kills a little girl deserves to die. Don't you agree?"

As the receptionist looked across the counter at Arthur, he couldn't help but compare her countenance to that of an English woman. Whereas faces of English women seemed to him generally vacuous, the expression he had encountered so far on the faces of American women was that of earnest attention. They wanted to know what you thought and felt and what had happened to you so far in your life, which might explain, too, why they so pitilessly rejected men who didn't match their expectations. No wonder American men circled and eyed their women as they would dangerous snakes! While a President of the United States might imagine he could determine the destiny of his country, in fact, women, like Trina and the earnest-faced receptionist and the cattleman's wife were the ones who controlled the country because they selected the men who would bear their children, which meant the mothers of George Washington and Abraham Lincoln were perhaps of greater importance than the sons they bore: The veneration those two American presidents inspired ought properly to go to their mothers.

"Leave your things with me," the receptionist said. "They'll be as safe as in a bank." He handed over his suitcase and typewriter. "These sure look like they've gone places," she said. "They've been around."

"I notice everything about a person. You have to when you're on reception. I knew, as soon as you came in the door, that you were a travelling man."

"Actually, I'm gathering material for magazine articles describing how American families have come through the war years. At first, I thought it would be simple, but I'm realizing the subject's very complex." Arthur proceeded to give the receptionist an outline of his conversation with the cattleman and ended by saying, "You see what I mean about the complexity—his relationship to the land and with his family is truly profound." Arthur leaned on the counter. "But he doesn't know that. For him, life is a series of everyday tasks. You could pass the guy in the street and think there goes a untroubled, simple guy, whereas in fact he is the pivot on which a complex miniature world spins."

The receptionist was impressed. "You know, I've never thought of it like that. But I guess you're right."

"Mind you, everybody has a little world they're spinning around in. You have this hotel."

"You better believe it, especially when our law-makers are in session. It's a circus. Things are quiet now. You'll be able to see the Governor with no trouble, just ask the guard in the rotunda."

Where else but in America could a stranger walk into a capital city and be met by the state governor? In England, you wouldn't be able to walk into the office of an insignificant town clerk without first producing a list of credentials. But here he was, being greeted by the Governor, who shook his hand and asked how he could oblige him. True, he was a shade more persistent than the hotel receptionist, wanting to know the name of the magazine in which Arthur's articles would be published, but the inquiries were superficial and, within minutes, he was urging Arthur's participation in solving his dilemma: Should he allow the executions of the two men to go ahead, or revoke the death sentences?

"I would consider whether the offence was severe enough to let the court verdict stand," Arthur said, as he walked beside the Governor along a broad hallway where the walls were crowded with enlarged photographs of state bigwigs.

"The men claim they're innocent, and there's evidence suggesting they were nowhere near the scene of the crime."

"I'll assume that evidence came before the court."

"It did. But the trial was coloured by public revulsion of the crime. You must understand, Mr. Scheiler, that such incidents are exceptionally rare in our fair state, so outrage was immediate and, as you know, initial reactions tend to stick. Let me put it this way: If the men are guilty of the heinous crime, I believe they should die. I weep inside when I think of what that poor child she must have suffered. In fact, neither of us can conceive of her terror. Even as I walk along these halls, I have an impulse to rush home to make sure my little girl is safe. When I ran for elected office, I knew what could be involved; I knew I might face a situation similar to this, but I never understood how difficult it would be to actually play the role of God and decide one way or the other if men ought to die."

"We all die," Arthur pointed out.

"But in our own good time."

"I rode into town in a truck packed with steers going to slaughter."

The Governor raised his hand. "I've heard that argument before, but it doesn't sway me. Steers don't reason, or distinguish right from wrong. We do." He stopped a moment, then said, "I'm on my way home, Mr. Scheiler. Would you care to walk with me? It's not far."

"I'd like to," Arthur said. They walked across the rotunda, where the Governor greeted people he recognized and introduced himself to strangers. The very model of a successful politician, he covered every base to ensure that, while chance would inevitably play a role in his electoral performance, the Governor would do his best to ensure its part was reduced that of a bit player.

They left the building and walked across the park that surrounded the building on three sides. "When I entered politics I never thought I'd end in the Governor's Mansion," he revealed. "The house came by its title for no reason other than that an incumbent governor in the last century occupied it. Actually, it's no mansion. However, getting back to the question we were discussing. That of moral responsibility. I come from a long line of church ministers."

"Are you suggesting churches have the sole prerogative of exercising moral responsibility?"

"No, I'm simply describing my background. I had to take a daily dose of individual morality responsibility, much as my children get a daily spoonful of cod liver oil. I'm not sure what effect the cod liver oil will have upon my children, but I know my daily dose of morality left me with an acute awareness of right and wrong." Once again he raised a silencing hand. "And don't use the argument that what's wrong for me could be right for other people in other circumstances. That's the thief's argument. I should add that my father assumed I'd follow him into the church, but I became a lawyer instead; and if my father knew how to deal—*manipulate* might be the better word—cards in the theological deck, I've used every trick in the legal pack. While I practised, I assisted men guilty of chicanery in evading punishment, but as a lawyer and as a private individual, there exists a line that divides what I may do from what I may not do. It's the same for the everybody. And should we choose to transgress it then each of us, as individuals, must accept the consequences. Would you agree with that, Mr. Scheiler?"

"As a principle, yes. As long as it's applied fairly." Arthur was thinking of the treatment of Negroes he had witnessed in the South.

They had reached the road which encircled the capitol where Arthur could see a veranda-enclosed house. "The mansion," the Governor announced. "When I look at it I have the impression that those who built it favoured bachelors or widowers as governors. So, before we cross the street, tell me, do you believe the two men who the courts have found guilty deserve to die?" He grasped Arthur's arm. "Tell me what you'd do. Don't try to weasel out. Yes or no."

"Yes," Arthur said and heard the other man sigh, as though relieved of a terrible burden.

"Let's go in," he said. "I expect my wife'll be sitting on the back porch. Often she and the children walk across the park to meet me. She knows I enjoy watching the kids, especially our daughter, run over the grass toward me as soon they spot me coming. There is something inexplicably wonderful about seeing them. You become acutely aware they are your future. Do you have children, Mr. Scheiler?"

"No."

"The experience is wonderful and nerve-racking."

"You seem to find most things nerve-racking."

The Governor gently laughed and said, "Remember my childhood doses of morality? It tempers everything I say and do."

They crossed the road and walked along the side of the house to a wide lawn presumably laid out to accommodate gubernatorial receptions. Two boys and a girl played on the lawn, engaged in a game which probably only children comprehended, beyond the ken of any adult. On seeing her father, the girl abandoned the game and rushed toward him, arms wide, shrieking, "Daddy! Daddy!" After glancing triumphantly at Arthur, her father reached forward to swing her up, turn her head over heels, while saying, "Little Patsy here's five, going on six." Arthur sensed that the Governor was reminding him that only a few years separated his child from the one brutally murdered and cast into a roadside ditch.

"Mr. Scheiler's a reporter," the Governor told the plain-faced woman sitting on the broad porch steps. "He kindly agreed to accompany me home."

"How do you do, ma'am," Arthur said.

"A reporter?" she asked.

"I write short stories too. I'm presently gathering material."

"Would you like a glass of lemonade, Mr. Scheiler?" The Governor's wife asked. She moved to stand beside her husband who had settled the girl upon his right forearm. Arthur noticed how she hunched her shoulders to match her husband's height. As always, whenever Arthur observed a woman, he could not resist imagining how she might react to the hands, lips and loins of any man who pressed his body down on her. He didn't get very far with his thoughts because the boys on the lawn, after being called by their father, ran up to be introduced to his guest.

"How d'you do, sir," they piped and proffered their hands to be shaken.

"They know the rules," the Governor said.

"A tribute to you," Arthur replied, wondering if a ruler or strap had been used on the children's bottoms to inculcate good manners. He would wager coercion was used somewhere along the way. Impoliteness generally characterized childhood behaviour, and only pain, or memory of pain, brought them to heel. Observing the children and sensing their mother's body beneath her decorous skirt and blouse reminded Arthur of what was lacking in his own life: sex. Except for his brief frenzied coupling with Trina, Arthur had been as celibate as a Carthusian monk from the day he had climbed the gangway of the freighter and entered it hot, stinking entrails. Throughout that time, he had done no more than eye his erect cock, ignoring its urgent demands. He discounted the paid-for fuck with the bored, Baltimore whore, which now seemed an event so far away in time that it had become part of another, earlier age. Even his months working at Trina's seemed to have happened long, long ago, and he could not even manage to conjure up an image of Trina's face or of her swaying hips swishing around the diner: all that remained in his memory was the spot of still, cadaver-whiteness into which he had sought to instil a moment of life. He hated to acknowledge it, but even now, far from England in the middle of the United States of America, every minute of each day continued to be regulated by his fear of exposure, which in his own mind, explained his kow-towing behaviour with the Governor, who probably faked concern about the seriousness of the execution simply in order to bolster his own sense of self-importance. Great God, who cared whether two such criminals were eliminated from the face of the earth? Get rid of them. Scrub them out.

The Governor's wife repeated the offer of lemonade.

"No thank you. I really must go," Arthur said. "It's been a pleasure meeting you, Sir, and you too, ma'am."

"Well, deal kindly with us. We do our best," the Governor said.

"I certainly will. So long, kids." Arthur had learned that everyone in America said "so long" and everyone referred to young people "kids." You could safely ask a father of grown children how his 'kids' were, even though a daughter might have married, suffered birth pains and borne a 'kid' of her own, she still remained her father's 'kid.' It was as though parents, especially fathers, were uncomfortable acknowledging their own mortality. Perhaps people emigrating to America from the agricultural and industrial slums of Europe had imbued their vision of the ideal American with immortality; perhaps, in their dreams, they transformed America into an Elysium; and even though the decades that had flown by proved otherwise, the myth remained and resulted in the curious notion that poverty in America was somehow superior to destitution in a country like England. England! The word produced a kaleidoscope of images of a life that Arthur believed he had shucked the day he crossed the Mississippi, but now, as he crouched in the middle of the park, staring at the capitol dome, he fought the devils of memory that threatened to tear away the flimsy defensive walls he had erected to protect his new life.

A voice asked: "You okay?" He looked up and into the face of a Negro who wore a grey uniform and soft-peaked cap.

"Yes, yes. I'm okay."

"You kinda staggered, like you was having a heart attack."

"I've had a bout of flu. Get weak in the knees now and then. You work here?"

"Groundsman. Ain't seen you around before."

"I've just arrived . . . been talking to the Governor about the guys slated for the chair."

"Best place for them."

"The Governor's of two minds."

"That's because one of 'em's a nigra, see? The Governor wants us nigras to know he ain't like them governors in the South, who'd burn or string up every nigra in America if they could. No sir. The Governor wants me and every other nigra in this state to know he's wrung his hands and prayed to the Lord for guidance."

"Has he asked you for guidance?"

"Me? No sir. I'm nobody. But he asks newspaper reporters who he figures will write stories about him. He's one smart cookie. Well, go easy on them shaky legs."

They parted, the groundsman moving toward the capitol, Arthur to an intersection where he passed a woman standing idly at the corner. He passed her, then stopped and went back, guessing she was in the trade. "How much?" he asked.

She looked him over, then said, "Five bucks."

When he nodded, she walked him to a small house that faced the backside of the capitol. In the room they entered, a girl sat at a table, writing in a lined notebook. "Pay her no mind," the woman said. Arthur followed her into a bedroom where she turned and held out her hand. When Arthur found he had nothing but a ten dollar bill, she said he could either take a rain check or do a double. He gave her ten dollars, then asked her to lean over and quickly had her twice from the rear. Before leaving, he asked if she was always available. "Afternoons and evenings," she said. "Mornings I clean floors in the capitol."

Arthur said he might visit her again and left, wondering if he could get a short story out of the girl, busily doing her homework while her mother entertained a man on the bed where she and her mother slept at night. He sketched a mental outline on his way back to the hotel where the receptionist beckoned him over and informed him the coffee shop was closed for meals because the cook had run off.

Arthur, buoyed with a sense of self-confidence conferred by his sexual adventure, told her if the hotel would provide the materials he would be happy to cook his own meals.

"I don't see how we can allow that," she responded.

"Why not? I've probably cooked more burgers, flipped more flapjacks, and scrambled more eggs than you've ever served in your hotel," he said.

"Oh no," she sniffed. "You should see the dining room and coffee shop when the house's in session."

"You should've seen the ship's galley I worked in. Or the diner where I cooked, every night of the week."

"I'll check with the manager," she conceded and went into a room beyond the reception desk, closing the door behind her. Several minutes passed before she returned with another woman who looked remarkably like her. This woman examined the hotel register, looked at Arthur and said, "You're registered as a journalist. So what's all this about being a cook? Aren't you the guy that interviewed the Governor?" When Arthur nodded his reply, she went on to explain that she was the sister of the receptionist and that their grandfather had built the hotel and her son managed it, but had gone off to war and wasn't back yet, though was expected any day. They were running things until he returned. Unfortunately, the hotel cook was given to falling madly in love with younger men and ran off with them to cheap motels across the state line. Of course, she always came back, weepy and remorseful, swearing she would never love another man as long as she lived. From experience, the sisters knew otherwise, but since she was an excellent cook and help was hard to find, they tolerated her "eccentricity," as they referred to it.

Arthur then narrated his story, and the upshot of that was that the sisters, whose names were Miss Jean and Miss Joyce, escorted him to the kitchen, where, after looking over the available food, he selected a tenderloin steak and a hunk of iceberg lettuce. They watched as he whisked up a French dressing, turned on the broiler, peppered the steak and slapped it onto the grill.

"He seems to know what he's doing," Miss Joyce remarked to her sister as Arthur expertly flipped the steak, put a plate near the broiler to warm, poured the French dressing over the lettuce, turned off the broiler, placed the steak in the middle of the plate, sat at a small table and sliced a piece of juicy red meat into his mouth which he placed in his mouth and started chewing on. "Delicious," he pronounced. "A-one. Done rare."

The women became quite fluttery as they earnestly informed him that the coffee shop was famous for its beef. "President Theodore Roosevelt once ate here. *And* President Harding." They looked at each other and nodded, before Miss Jean said, "Of course you won't be charged for meals you prepare yourself."

"Nonsense," said Arthur, secretly delighted at the prospect of saving money.

"We wouldn't dream of it," they protested, and afterwards joined him at the table to talk about themselves and the hotel. In the course of the conversation, it was revealed that Miss Jean was unmarried, which led Arthur to wonder if she had long ago surrendered her maidenhead to some travelling man. He rather hoped she had. They told Arthur that their grandfather had operated the hotel with an all-male staff because, as they explained, "You know how men are." They eyed him askew, chins tilted to let him know they too knew how men were; and when Arthur replied he had no idea what they were talking about, they pointed fingers and said, "That's because you are one! Men never know! They just are!"

When Arthur offered to make breakfast for hotel guests, the sisters told him the problem was not breakfast, but the other two meals. He asked to see the coffee shop menu, scanned it and gave a response he had frequently heard at Trina's: "No sweat."

"You sure?" Miss Joyce asked.

"The cook never stays away more than seven days," Miss Jean said. "Usually it's all over in three or four." An image of an overheated cook, satiating herself with booze and a pulsing male body flew into Arthur's head.

"It's your decision," he said and was amused how the sisters chewed their lips and communicated to each other without words. Finally, Miss Joyce told Arthur they would think over his suggestion and give him their decision in the morning.

Arthur came to think of the sisters as representative of middle-America women: honourable, dependable souls who, though they preferred an asexual life, could always be relied upon to produce their quota of patriotic sons and daughters. They believed the sole purpose of the Supreme Being was to look down from the Heavens and bless America; they believed the depression of the Thirties had been sent by God to punish them for the flippancy of the twenties; they believed that Hitler's Germany and Hirohito's Japan had been created in order that America might demonstrate its might; they believed that everyone in America, without exception, received his or her just due, because America was a land that offered equal opportunity for wealth and happiness to everybody who dwelt within its confines. In fact, the sisters believed that the Supreme Being made millionaires to let people know what they could achieve if they would only get off their backsides and put their noses to the grindstone. Arthur learned all this by chatting with Miss Jean as he prepared meals in the kitchen four days running. On the fifth day, he entered the kitchen only to find an overweight woman whose age could have been anywhere between fifty and sixty-five.

"Who the hell are you?" she demanded. "Get outta here!"

"It's all yours," he said, and went to sit in the still dark coffee shop where Miss Jean arrived a few minutes later to take his order and to apologize for not letting him know the cook had returned the previous night.

"She's always bad-tempered the first day," she whispered. "Thank you for helping us out. But that's the American way, isn't it, helping one another?" It surely was, Arthur agreed and ordered two eggs, cooked three and one-eighth minutes each. He was delighted when he heard the cook yell: "One-eighth!

Who the hell heard of eggs boiled three and one-eighth minutes! Tell the jerk he's getting his eggs done in three-and-a-half."

The cook's return did not worry Arthur, although he could have used the money he saved cooking his own meals for afternoon visits to Rebecca, the prostitute, who had agreed to a reduced rate of, as she phrased it, two fucks for seven and fifty. So, every fourth day in the early afternoon, when his organ would invariably rise and remain erect to remind him there was more to life than just tapping out words, he would visit her. In between, he amused himself by surreptitiously watching Miss Jean's thighs move beneath her modest black skirt and lace-edged apron as she served him his mid-day meal. "Once the war started, we couldn't get waiters, but our food's as good as the old days, just not as much variety as before. Father employed three chefs when the assembly was in session." She went on about the hotel's past glory, while Arthur, eyes waist-high, couldn't help imagining how Miss Jean would look naked. Sometimes he wondered if she knew what he was thinking because she always stood squarely in front of him, as though to direct his eyes to that particular part of her body, but in the end he decided he was mistaken, that neither she nor her sister would ever dream of any stance that didn't place them foursquare in front of the world. Still, Arthur allowed licentious thoughts to spill over Miss Jean before finishing off his meal and dashing off to visit Rebecca. Afterwards, he would return to the hotel and, cleansed of prurient thoughts, spend a few minutes chatting with Miss Jean or Miss Joyce.

One afternoon, on returning to the hotel, a woman came out from the shadows near the stairs and approached him. "Are you Mr. Matt Scheiler?" she asked.

"Yes." He looked at her and thought she might be from the police or the immigration bureau.

"I'm Phyllis Ackroyd. Fiction editor at *Showcase*."

He stared at her and for a whirling second he thought he was about to have a spell. During this nanosecond, he saw himself lying on the kitchen floor of Trina's cafe, surrounded by trousered legs and muddy boots and Trina kneeling beside him and looking down at him with wide, sorrow-filled eyes. There was also a man in a chequered suit, who turned out to be the town physician, and who, after asking if he was epileptic which Arthur vehemently denied, gave him a superficial examination, wrote out a prescription which Arthur later threw away, then departed. But during these minutes, as he lay on the floor with his head cushioned on Trina's winter coat and as she continued to kneel beside him, uttering comforting words, unaware of herself and concerned only with his well-being, he knew that he loved her and that were it not for the image of her war mutilated husband who stood between them, he would've been content to remain with her for the rest of his life.

Of course, he made light of the incident, telling Trina that such a thing had never happened to him before and that it was probably a delayed reaction to his experiences in the North Atlantic. She nodded but he doubted whether she fully accepted his explanation, and afterwards when he sometimes glanced at her face, the expression in her eyes reflected her belief that she had been unlucky with the men in her life.

"I'm Phyllis Ackroyd," the woman repeated. "We've been corresponding."

"Please go away." He walked past her to the elevator.

She followed him into it. "I only want to get to know you."

"But I don't want to know you." He left the elevator and walked to the stairs. "Go away."

"No, I won't." He halted at the fourth stair and looked down at her. "I've done nothing inappropriate," she said. "It's normal for editors and authors to meet."

"But I do not want to get together with you, or with anybody. So go away."

"I won't."

"Please yourself."

He went up the stairs, leaving Phyllis Ackroyd at the bottom, where she was joined by Miss Jean. "Mr. Scheiler's such a nice man," Miss Jean said. "Very obliging. He took over our kitchen while our cook was . . . ill." She moved closer. "What sort of things does Mr. Scheiler write?"

"Short stories. They're very good. Reminiscent of de Maupassant and the Russians at their best."

"Fancy that," Miss Jean said. "The Russians, eh? So, will you be staying."

"Yes," Phyllis Ackroyd said. "I'll be here for a few more days."

CHAPTER
16

"YOUR STORY ABOUT THE MAN WHO GETS DRUNK TO AVOID responsibility for making a critical decision reminded me of Chekhov," Phyllis Ackroyd remarked. They were walking the perimeter road around the park.

"I'm not interested in writing like Chekhov," Arthur said. He either ignored or flatly contradicted her attempts to start conversations.

"Your stories aren't imitation Chekhov. I simply meant you have the same ability to reveal character in a few sentences, whereas some writers take pages to describe people without ever succeeding in revealing what's hidden in their hearts and minds. It's a rare ability," she added, perhaps hoping flattery would modify Arthur's attitude toward her.

"Maybe they don't understand what motivates people."

"But you do?"

"I have some understanding."

Phyllis Ackroyd's intrusion into his life annoyed Arthur, and he alternated between insulting and ignoring her, while at the same time trying to hold at bay his stultifying fear that if he said more than ten consecutive words she'd realize he was a sham. A day or two passed before Arthur grasped that Phyllis was so preoccupied with appeasing him that she had no time to be suspicious. She swallowed his insults and earnestly repeated that she just wanted to make his acquaintance in order to discuss his work.

When she asked about his antecedents, he replied: "What's it matter where I come from? I'm the result of a man fucking a woman. What matters is where I am now and where I'll be tomorrow." Oddly enough, this statement appeared to satisfy her, perhaps because it was in keeping with the stark reality of his stories.

He got used to her presence at the hotel and having her approach him in the coffee shop at meal times to politely ask, "May I join you?", though he continued vehemently to refuse to discuss future plans or say anything about himself. When she raised the subject of his writing style, he responded: "Look, I'm a dropout who manages to string ten-word sentences together that make sense." But from the way Phyllis smiled, it was clear she didn't agree with his self-deprecating remarks.

He continued to reserve each morning for work and each afternoon for a walk. Phyllis would wait in the hotel lobby and join him as he passed through the hotel entrance. So what if he ignored her? She was determined to carry through with her attempt to get acquainted with him, filling the silences with literary chit-chat and running commentaries on the state capitals of middle America, making comparisons between them and eastern cities, such as New York where she grew up, Boston where she attended university and Philadelphia where she now lived and worked. She assumed that Arthur, like a hen on its eggs, was brooding over work he had laid during the morning and she even contemplated writing an article herself about the tortured life of the creative artist, but gave up the idea when she found she had nothing to say.

Arthur's behaviour was petty and vindictive, and he knew it, but he believed that his only option, short of telling Phyllis the truth, was to maintain a defensive wall around himself, flimsy as it might be. But then shame appeared in the equation when it became apparent that Phyllis was a thoroughly decent woman, anxious to do her best by him and unable to understand why he treated her so shabbily. During fleeting moments, when he was able to free himself of his need to ensure safe anonymity, he would glance at her face and acknowledge she was passably handsome, probably with a Jewish background. As a child, Arthur became well acquainted with Hebrew women through his exposure to Biblical stories and pictures, and he thought Phyllis resembled depictions of Naomi, or perhaps Ruth, though not beautiful Bathsheba or calm, faithful Esther who, after marrying King Ahasuerus, not only saved *his* life, but also thousands of Hebrews by exposing a plot to assassinate Ahasuerus. In his pre-pubescent years, Arthur spent hours poring over Biblical pictures and transporting himself back in time to participate romantically in the lives of the women portrayed. He would never be sure to what degree those pictures influenced his portrayal of female characters in his early novels, and now in his short stories. As he tried to frustrate Phyllis's desire to get to know him, he came to the realization that if he wanted to protect his new persona of Matt Scheiler, he should pack his belongings, sneak out of the hotel and disappear into the vastness of America, because if he didn't do that, he would eventually capitulate to Phyllis Ackroyd's determined siege. His impulse to run was strong, but was held in check by another, equally strong impulse to shift the burden of his past onto Phyllis's shoulders, although he realized that would be impossible until some sort of intimacy was established between them; and as things stood, he could not imagine *that* happening.

A few mornings after her arrival, Phyllis and Arthur sat in the coffee shop, waiting to be served breakfast. After bidding them good morning, Miss Jean said, "Well, Mr. Scheiler, those two swine are gone. Last night. I say, good riddance."

"What was that about?" Phyllis asked when they were alone.

"Two men were executed last night for—," Arthur was unable to go on, for the flickering image of a man (himself) strapped to a vibrating metal chair with a vast current of electricity snaking through it had appeared before him. He slumped in his chair.

Phyllis raised a hand as though to reach across the table and touch his. "You all right?"

"Yes," he answered. "I'm all right." But he wasn't. The vision of himself face-to-face with death had shaken him and he was forced to the realization that he couldn't remain silent much longer, that he must somehow find a way to tell Phyllis about himself. He felt an overwhelming compulsion to empty his conscience of its memories of the past, and was afraid that unless he did so he would lose control of his new life. Unless his memories were eliminated, his past, despite his best efforts, would seep through the barricades he had erected around it and contaminate his present and future life. Guilt might be metaphoric, the metal chair of his own making, but both were real enough to him; and his belief that crossing the Mississippi was the equivalent of rebirth was now revealed as illusionary. The shell of the man he was might bear the moniker Matthew Scheiler, but the inner core remained Arthur Compson. "Let's go for a walk. I'll skip work," he said.

Phyllis immediately agreed. They began walking and to fill the void between them, she began to criticize the city, calling it Dullsville. "Places like this must be deadly for creative minds."

"The contrary," Arthur murmured. "Emptiness stimulates imagination."

"But isn't it a weird mixture? Everything's been brought from the east and dumped here. Nothing's indigenous."

"That's true no matter where you go." He wanted her to be quiet so he could devise a way to tell her about himself.

"New England churches and houses look as if they emerged from the land," she said.

"So do slums." He remembered the village of his childhood where cottages on foggy days resembled heaps of rotting vegetation. "Don't talk to me about white churches with Gothic spires and neat little cottages with boxes of geraniums outside the windows. It's the stinking, fermenting slums that matter. Slaves are always more important than masters."

Delighted Arthur was speaking so freely and desiring to stimulate further discussion, she went on: "Aren't you being overly judgemental? New England settlers utilized rock and lumber from the forests." They were now walking along the wide, pivotal avenue and approached an intersection.

"People who settled here used sod for shelters. But no matter. See that woman?"

"What about her?"

"She's a whore from a mining town in West Virginia. I know her." He waved and Rebecca, on the way home from cleaning capitol floors, smiled and waved back, while Phyllis acted as if she was accustomed to men telling her about their visits to prostitutes.

"Why tell me about her?"

"To prepare you for something far more important than me paying for a ten-minute fuck." They turned at another intersection, and as they walked towards the park the capitol came into sight. "No matter where you go in this town, you see that pretentious dome," he said. Then he plunged: "Listen Phyllis, before I say anything, you must put your hands between mine and swear you'll never repeat what I tell you."

"You mean like an oath in court?"

"More than that. I mean that if it were a choice between your life or revealing what I tell you, you'd choose death."

"Does this have something to do with our country? Atomic secrets, that sort of thing?"

"It's to do with me personally."

They reached the perimeter road, crossed it and stood on the immaculate lawn. They were so intent on the exchange they didn't notice the Governor walking across the park towards them. "All right, I promise," Phyllis answered. She thought Arthur's behaviour might be symptomatic of persecution mania, and if that were so, she could legitimately agree to his request for an oath of silence. She had read psychology and felt certain a competent psychiatrist would use similar tactics.

"Put your hands in mine." She raised her hands as though in prayer and was about to place them between his when the Governor spoke: "Hello there, Mr. Scheiler." Their hands fell as they spun to face him. Arthur, thinking the man looked like someone recovering from a serious illness, introduced Phyllis, after which the Governor, thinking he had interrupted a lovers' tryst, said, "A pleasure, Miss Ackroyd. I hope you're enjoying our beautiful city?"

"It's delightful," she dutifully responded. "Actually I'm here on business. I'm the fiction editor of *Showcase*. I'm here to discuss the trade publication of a collection of Matt's stories." She paused and glanced at Arthur before continuing. "And also to discuss the making of a movie of one of them."

"How interesting," the Governor said. "I had no idea Mr. Scheiler was a well-known writer."

"Very well-known," Phyllis gravely told him.

The Governor hesitated. "Well, I'll be on my way. Nice meeting you, Miss Ackroyd." He moved away, stopped, then said, "You heard the news, Mr. Scheiler?"

"Yes." Arthur said.

"So, it's over," the Governor said.

"Over and done with," Arthur agreed.

"Well . . . one can hope." The Governor nodded at Arthur and walked on, wondering if his moral dilemma had indeed come to an end.

"Was that about the execution of those two men?" Phyllis asked, and when Arthur explained his conversation with the Governor, she said, "He shouldn't be in politics if he can't stand the heat. Now, you were about to tell me something of importance."

"It can wait."

"All right. Can we talk about the book and the movie? That's why I'm here."

"Do whatever you think's best. I can't plan beyond tomorrow morning's work."

"Does my being here interfere with your work schedule?"

"No. Only from seeing Rebecca."

She grimaced and turned away. As they approached the hotel entrance, she said, "You could've told me you preferred to walk alone."

"I was being rude. Besides, I saved money not seeing Rebecca. I'm a real skinflint."

"I wouldn't mind a drink. It's odd the hotel doesn't serve liquor."

"I survive nicely without it. I have other vices," he said as they entered the hotel lobby. "I'll bet Miss Jean has some liquor stashed away (Arthur took pride in his usage of that particular American colloquialism). She's the sort who hides money under floorboards for rainy days."

"It doesn't matter. We could have coffee."

"No." He raised a finger and spoke solemnly: "Ask and thou shalt be given."

When she responded by saying, "There *is* something Biblical about your stories," Arthur wondered if she was one of those nincompoops who transform nonsense spouted by artists into the wisdom of the ages. Laura Dorchester had been so inclined, so maybe both women were the type who hunted through swarms of fawning men before finally offering their sacred vaginas to some up-and-coming writer, prepared to suffer three minutes of sweaty fucking provided they were compensated by hours of discussion about their feelings, or perhaps lines of obscure blank verse. Arthur, whose sexual knowledge was a compound of Sylvia's obsession, Laura's needs and the mechanical accommodation of prostitutes had nothing but contempt for women who regarded copulation as a bridge over which the sexes passed into a unreal world where they could talk endlessly about themselves and magnify their insignificant lives into something grand and glorious. At rock bottom, he was disgusted with the way sex was traded in the human commodity market and judged those who speculated in the merchandise of "feelings" the worst offenders of all—they deserved to lose everything. Though unaware of it at the time, Arthur was in the process of eliminating from his stories all the romantic clutter and provocative nonsense written about sex and replacing it with a world in which women and men were honest with each other about their bodily needs. Since he was an interloper in America, ghosting as it were across the land, it sometimes seemed to him that he was passing through a country where men mercilessly hunted down and destroyed everything around them, including their women. He had tentatively decided that American society was based on a form of social cannibalism in which successive generations consumed everything in sight, leaving nothing for their progeny.

"Perhaps most writers exist in a perpetual Day of Judgement," he acknowledged. Before Phyllis had time to think of another author who might have had a similar thought, he walked to the reception desk, leaned over it and spoke to Miss Jean. "I've just discovered today is Miss Ackroyd's birthday. I thought you might have a bottle of whisky handy, which we could use to celebrate it."

Miss Jean frowned. "As you know, we stopped serving liquor when our men went off to war, though in grandfather's day, full liquor service was provided. I'll ask my sister. She'll know if there's a bottle around somewhere. She keeps the keys." Miss Jean entered the manager's office and closed the door. When she returned, she carried a small canvas bag. "Here you are, Mr Scheiler," she said passing it across the counter to him.

"Thank you," he said.

"You'll be careful, won't you?" she hissed. "One of the other guests might see the bottle."

"Of course," he hissed back. Back in his room, he opened the bag and took out a bottle of Old Granddad.

"Boy, oh boy!" Phyllis exclaimed, taking the bottle from him. "This is quality stuff!" She uncapped it and poured the bourbon into toothbrush glasses.

"Do you really want me to make publishing decisions about your work?" she asked as she gave him a glass.

"I'll do the spade work, you market the fruits of my labour."

They touched glasses, sipped the whisky, and while Phyllis said "Lovely" and smacked her lips, Arthur, unfamiliar with the bite of bourbon, shivered, then gulped it down as people do a evil-tasting dose of medication. She laughed at his obvious reaction and poured more into her own glass. "You know, eventually you'll have to accept notoriety. It's unavoidable. And what were you going to tell me that required an oath of silence?"

"Nothing. A temporary weakness." Arthur examined her carefully arranged hair, neat black skirt and jacket, white blouse and remembered that Laura Dorchester had worn similar business attire. "You want to get to know me, is that right?"

"That's why I'm here."

"Then why don't we have a drink, then get into bed?"

"I'm not sure I want to do that."

"You want to find out what makes me tick, don't you?"

"What's wrong with that?"

"Everything, since I want to be left alone."

"I came to meet an author whose work I admire. I'd hoped to establish a congenial relationship. Obviously, you don't want that. I don't understand why you're so opposed, but I accept your decision." Arthur put down his glass, stepped up to her, took the glass from her hand and motioned her towards the bed. "You won't have to rape me," she said. "I'll undress."

"For Christ's sake!" he said. "I'm just trying to make a point!" He handed the glass back to her, poured more bourbon into his own and sat on the bed. "It's a pity you came," he said. "I thought I'd made it clear I preferred to handle everything at a distance. You've introduced a wild card into the pack."

"I wasn't to know that."

"You know now."

"But why do you object to me? I'm not running around talking about you. Besides, what's there to tell? Are you guilty of some major crime? I've merely read your stories, admired the craft in them and thought it would be advantageous to meet you and discuss publication of a trade book and the phone call I had from a Hollywood guy, trying to get the name of your agent. Right off the bat, I told him that I was acting on your behalf, though now I don't know why I said it. It's clear you don't want any truck with me."

"I've said you can act for me."

"No. That's impossible. How can I represent a person who won't even talk to me?"

"Take your clothes off," he said.

"But why? There's nothing between us."

"Look, either we go through with this, or I call it quits." She stared at him much as a blind person would trying to determine the physiognomy of an individual from the sounds of his voice, before she put the glass on a bedside table, licked her lips, swallowed, then methodically removed her clothes: low-heeled black pumps, jacket and calf-length skirt, blouse, slip, gartered stockings and underpants, from which she voluptuously emerged, ivory-skinned, pear-breasted and black-muffed.

"You're like a nineteenth-century nude waiting to be crucified on a French photographic plate," he remarked.

"You must mean like the Thanksgiving turkey waiting to be served on the family platter? I'm not sure if I'm up to this."

He quickly stripped, went to her, put his hands around her breasts, and licked first one nipple, then the other. "Sylvia loved that," he said. "I'll tell you about her presently." He eased her onto the bed, knelt between her thighs, found the pathway and after a few minutes, obeying her plea not to leave anything in her, managed to drag himself out to spew his stuff onto her pubes, then lay like a milk-satiated child between her thighs with his face against her breasts and narrated his story.

"Oh, my God," she said when he stopped talking. "Oh, my God." After a bit, she asked. "What happened to the girl? What was her name?"

"Martha. I don't know what happened to her"

"And you don't know if the woman's body was ever found, or if police searched for you?"

"I know nothing."

"What will you do? I mean, eventually?"

"Go on as I am now. Maybe one day I'll write a novel about my crazed mother."

"It would be a best-seller. Was she really mad?"

"Not lunatic mad, just crazy. My father drove her crazy with his fucking around, and she avenged herself by trying to destroy his son. Though what choice did she have? She could've bedded the butcher and the baker and the rest who came after her, but since father wasn't there to watch, it would have been pointless. So she used me."

"But her son . . ."

"During the day she loved me as a son. At night, I became my father."

"But didn't you understand?"

"I knew I had to match Father to satisfy her expectations. That's all I cared about."

"But surely . . ."

"Don't say 'surely' this or that. At this minute, do you have any idea of the consequences might be of what *you're* doing?"

"I guess not."

"Well, neither did I. You don't understand anything when experience is exploding around you."

"Go on," she said.

"That's all there is," he said. "Isn't it enough?"

"I wouldn't mind another shot of bourbon," she said. He slipped from between her legs, went to get her another drink and returned with her half-filled glass and a few drops in his own. "I needed that!" she said, as she downed it.

"I'll never acquire a taste for whisky." He wrinkled his nose.

"You need to be raised with it to appreciate it." She pushed herself up and leaned against the headboard. "I'll stay a couple more days," she said, "but only if you agree to talk about the future." She still had to sort through the information Arthur Compson/Matthew Scheiler had confided in her, and because she hadn't yet fully digested its implications, she wasn't sure if she should fully believe him. After all, he could be stringing together a bunch of lies.

"We'll see," he said. He sat beside her and put his hand on her belly. "I think Eve must have looked like you," he said.

"A typical Jewish woman."

"Perhaps. Biblical women fascinate me. I always pictured Eve with the serpent coiled around her waist and imagined that while Adam slept she had fooled around with the animals in Eden. That's what kids did in the village where I lived. Little girls got dogs to mount them, boys pushed erections into bitches and sows."

"It sounds vile."

"No worse than in any other foetid slum. Where did you grow up?"

"In a very sedate upper middle-class New York apartment."

"No neighbourhood boy sat on your tummy and pushed his fingers into your panties?"

"Absolutely not."

"You didn't even have a pet dog that got excited and humped you when you crawled around on your hands and knees?"

"My parents would never have tolerated a dog in our apartment."

"They deprived you of feeling what Eve experienced before eating fruit from the tree of knowledge and being barred forever from having the serpent's tongue nudge her nipples and glide between her thighs." He drained his glass. "Why am I talking like this?"

"Because you've never had anybody to listen to you before. But is it all true? I mean, no kidding?"

"It's a film I can't halt. I thought I could stop it by becoming another man. But it goes on and on and on. I merely add more to it."

"You said something about spells? What were they like?"

"I collapse and remain unconscious for a while. I don't want to talk about them."

"Have you consulted a neurologist?" When he didn't reply she continued: "There's some good ones in Philly. I'll ask around."

"You'll do nothing of the kind!" He gripped her jaw in his hands. "You hear me?" He released her, but days afterward his finger marks remained on her skin, showing as faint bruises.

"Sorry. I'm trying to understand . . . to get the bigger picture. Pour me more bourbon."

"Shall we fuck again?"

"Why not say 'make love'?"

"Because there's no love gained or lost here."

"But the other sounds offensive."

"You don't object to crudeness, provided it's fictional, right?"

"Perhaps," she admitted. "On the other hand, I don't want to risk an abortion." That stopped him, and he muttered something about men ceasing rational thought while inside women. "You don't have to tell me. The family doctor behaved as if I'd . . ."

"Messed your underpants?"

"Something like that." She tried to laugh. "I was nineteen, and quite dumb. I'm tougher now. And it's not that I wouldn't enjoy doing it again, but I don't want the risk. You do understand?"

"Yes." His hand followed the curve of her belly from her pubis to her navel, and he thought that at some distant point in human history, a potter, or perhaps a silversmith, had, while similarly caressing a woman, imagined creating a chalice or grail, so shaped that it would symbolize the eternal resurrection of life rising from the dead. "I want us to clearly understand each other."

"Of course. But I have to rethink you." She handed him the glass. "I'm slightly tipsy. I'm not used to drinking so much."

"You've disappointed me. I've been operating on the assumption that you chug-a-lugged a bottle a day with the finest of America's literati."

"Oh, anything but. I wade through heaps of rubbish." She slid down and rolled onto her side, facing him. "It's funny how things work out. I'd pictured you as a Hemingway sort of guy, but you're nothing like that. I'll have to rearrange everything. Did you go to college?"

"I never went to any school."

"You're joking. You must have gone to grade school."

"I had Mother Goose, the Bible and a copy of Shakespeare's plays." He waited for her to be express astonishment that a child's entire education could consist of those three books. When she said nothing, he saw that she was asleep. He examined her calm face and wondered if he'd been a fool to trust her. Suppose, sometime in the future, while in bed with another man, she forfeited the trust he had placed in her? What if she made the mistake of equating an exchange of sexual pleasure with mutual, enduring trust and spilled the beans to a coercive blackmailer? What then? Some people killed others to preserve their secrets. Why, no more than twenty-four hours ago two men were electrocuted for trying to preserve their secret. So why had he invested so much in a woman he hardly knew beyond the fact she liked his stories well enough to pay for them and allowed him to enjoy her warm, avid body? Maybe he should say that he'd invented his story to test her loyalty, or something equally farfetched. He lay beside her, warning himself not to sleep, for sleep increased vulnerability, but realized he had dozed off in spite of his fear when Phyllis's voice awakened him.

"Matt, I've thought of something. Your English publisher must have an American affiliate. Every respectable house has one, which means your books are read here, and in Canada." She was lying on her stomach, head turned to observe him.

"If you so much as ask . . ."

"Oh, I won't. I promised. I just wondered if you'd seen them in book-stores."

"I've never gone into a bookstore."

"Honestly? Never?" The admission surprised her so much she rolled onto her back to stare at him, mouth ajar. He used the opportunity to get inside her again; he felt her flesh pulse around him and, remembering the quickening spasms that preceded Sylvia's final releasing convulsion, he lengthened and timed his thrusts while watching a vivid blush travel from Phyllis's face onto her neck and breasts (a detail he would use in a story) to vanish beneath his belly, like the sun behind a range of hills, before she shuddered, sighed, turned her face away from his and lay quite still under him.

"Okay?" he asked.

"Yes." There was a pause before she asked, "Did you leave stuff in me?"

"I hadn't got that far."

She digested that, then said, "It probably doesn't matter. I wonder who said, 'All's fair in love and war'?"

"Undoubtedly a man."

She sighed. "Can we talk just a little about my reason for coming here?"

"No. It's been decided. How old are you?"

"Early thirties. I can see the capital dome from here."

"Does it look like this?" He cupped one of her breasts. "Years ago, I imagined America as a place where capitalists stood at windows at the top of skyscrapers masturbating as they conjured up money-making schemes, and where politicians erected temples with teats so that voters could suck civic security at their convenience."

She laughed. "No, it's nothing like that. Everybody in America tries for the gold ring. It's all hit-or-miss. A never-ending gold rush."

"What's struck me about America is that it puts into practice the worst characteristics of the Old World while pretending everything is new."

"We don't hide our defects, that's all."

"It's a land of lost opportunities. I walked through the Baltimore slums and couldn't see any difference between them and slums in England."

"Blame the men who signed the Declaration of Independence. They're the guys who invented equality. Have you been south?"

"Far enough to see a Negro hanging from a tree outside a small town. I was afraid I'd come across some men trying to hang a Negro woman and knew I'd not have the courage to intervene. I'm a coward. Tell me, what's the difference between Germans gassing Jews and Americans hanging Negroes?"

"I'm not sure there is one." She swung her legs around and sat on the bedside. "I'll shower, then meet you in the coffee shop for dinner."

He moved across the bed to sniff at the cleft in her buttocks, recalling the summer nights he walked though woodlands and smelt the intoxicating odours of damp bracken mixed with strange, hot, subterranean fungal smells emanating from the mold-covered path. Sometimes it had excited him so much, especially after a summer rain shower, he would spill his seed in a moment of creative ecstasy onto the procreative fungus. "You smell like a forest," he said.

"Deciduous or coniferous?" She stood and put on her skirt and blouse.

"Both. You could shower here."

"No. I have to do my hair, and other things." She pulled on her stockings, put on her shoes, collected the rest of her clothes, took the key to her door from her bag, then said: "We now have a relationship, don't we?"

"We have something," Arthur agreed.

She went to the door and stopped. "If I can get a reservation, maybe I'll fly out tomorrow," she said.

"Do whatever suits you best," Arthur replied.

"But you don't have to worry. I'll keep my word."

"I'm sure you will."

She opened the door and looked into the passage, then turned and whispered, "I'll see you in a while" and left.

Arthur looked over his chest and belly at his now quiescent male organ and, after wondering if telling Phyllis the truth would function to ease his conscience and give him a better chance of settling into his Matt Scheiler identity, he left the bed, capped the bottle of bourbon, rinsed the glasses, showered and dressed, then went down to sit in the coffee shop to chat with Miss Jean and wait for Phyllis.

"So you're going back to your fancy office," Arthur said as they rode in a taxi to the airport the next day.

"My office is a crummy hole-in-the-wall. Will you stay on here?" she asked.

"I don't know," he replied. She mustn't be allowed to think she had a proprietary right to organize his life. Women never let well enough alone—they allowed you into their secret places, then wanted to know your medical history and if your bowels moved every day. He told himself he was being unfair. After all, Phyllis had tried to be a real pal. She had agreed to share the weight of his obnoxious past; and although she'd probably been shocked when he described how he rutted with his mother, she accepted his jerry-rigged explanation that Sylvia was half-crazed, which was an out-and-out lie. His mother was an average woman driven to despair by the sudden death of her husband and the sickening poverty which followed and reduced her to bartering a quick feel of her legs for bits of tough meat, stale bread and tired vegetables. There was a limit to the indignities a woman could suffer before she became so crazed that she escaped into night-shrouded fantasies that featured her adolescent son as the star player. He knew Phyllis was returning to Philadelphia because she needed to regularize (her term) the information he had sprung on her, but her life was irrevocably tied to his now, no doubt about that. After their evening meal as on the previous night, they strolled around the park and, later, she came to his room where they coupled, then slept until dawn when she got up and returned to her own room.

Arthur understood he couldn't simply shrug Phyllis Ackroyd off as one more experience. She was ground into his psyche, and he would carry her through life as he carried Sylvia, Heather, Laura, Maria, Martha and Trina with him wherever he went: These were not women with whom he had been casually intimate; they had become necessary structural components of his being; and so now, as he stood on the apron outside the small airport building and watched Phyllis enter the twin-engine plane, he understood that she had left part of herself with him. He watched the plane take off, then walked the three miles back to town, going straight to Rebecca's where he watched her iron her daughter's clothes, even her socks.

"Nobody can say my girl ain't dressed decent," she said "That lady you was with the other day, she your wife?"

"Business acquaintance."

"I'll just finish these few things. You ain't in no hurry, are you?"

"I thought I'd stop and say goodbye before I left town." He got up, took out his wallet and put a five dollar bill on the ironing board.

"Don't you want to—?" she asked.

"No thanks."

"Well, if you come this way again, stop by and see me."

"I'll do that." He left, as pleased by his generosity as a millionaire after donating five grand (another Americanism Arthur had picked up) to charity, though it didn't last. As with most parsimonious people, once the self-congratulatory glow of giving has faded, he condemned himself for his generosity and, but for his cowardice, would have gone back to reclaim the five dollars.

That same day he paid his hotel bill and, after shaking hands with Miss Jean and Miss Joyce and assuring them he would always think well of them and their hotel, he walked to the bus depot and, after safely stowing his typewriter and suitcase in the guts of the bus, resumed his journey across America.

CHAPTER
17

ARTHUR WAS SITTING BEHIND THE BUS DRIVER WHEN HE FIRST became aware of the mountains. They had crept up with the dawn and now, with the sun rising behind the lumbering bus, the golden equilateral triangles jutted above the western horizon. He leaned over the driver's seat and asked, "What are those?"

"I dunno about the near ones," the driver said, "but the ones at the back is *The Tetons*. French for women's tits, though I ain't never seen tits like those on a woman. Pretty, eh?"

"Lovely," Arthur said.

"My old lady's sag." Then, with the American frankness about intimate matters which never ceased to astonish Arthur, the bus driver proceeded to describe his wife and the disappointment he experienced when he first saw her naked. "For crissake, she wore a corset to hold in her guts and push up her tits. Jeez, I hardly recognized her. But what's a guy to do? Hell, if I ever get another life . . . You believe in reincarnation? Anyways, I'll make sure I sees the dame bare-naked before I goes to the altar. You married?"

"No."

"It ain't that so bad. I mean, it's like the guy says, you can't tell one quackin' duck from another, and dames is the same. Let me tell you somethin': I thought my daughter was goin' to have a pair like them peaks; and believe you me, when she was twelve they was real pretty. Yeah, real pretty. So what happens? She marries, has a couple of kids, and now they're damn near knockin' her knees. So, you're not married?"

"No."

"Maybe it's just as well. I mean, you turn your back, you don't know what the hell she's up to. Maybe layin' every guy in the neighbourhood. That's a fact, Mac. Is it ever. Hell, when I was growin' up, there was a dame on the block that'd kiss her husband goodbye at the front door, then let a guy in at the back. Jeez, what a dame!"

"Were you one of the guys?"

"Hell no. I was just a kid. But my older brother laid her, so he said. So, how do you turn a buck?"

Arthur now related his dolorous story, while the bus driver "hmhm-ed" and chorused "you don't say" throughout the telling. Arthur wound up by telling the driver he was riding around the country and doing a bit of writing.

"Good for you," the driver said. "If I could—which I couldn't, even if I tried my best—I'd sit myself down and write a book about the specimens that rides buses. Name it, and I've carried 'em: bank robbers, murderers, hustlers. I've had dames offer me tail in return for tickets; I've had 'em work passengers on the back seat, even had preachers yellin' hellfire sermons. Brother, what ain't I had! Y'know, when guys gets on a bus, it's like they've went to another planet, know what I mean?"

"I believe I do," Arthur said.

"It's crazy," the driver said. "I stand at the door and punch the ticket of some quiet guy or dame, then look in the mirror and see him standin' in the aisle stark naked and her suckin' a guy off three seats back. Most guys is plain nuts. Plain and simple nuts. Look at me: I sit behind this here wheel, hour after hour, five days a week, then I get into me old wreck and drive to me two-bit shack and get into a bed with a dame who tells me she's my missus, though she's so goddamn fat I wouldn't know her if I seen her backside somewheres in the street, What a life. Think of all the things that guys did in the olden days just to get here in the first place, like wipin' out the buffalo and the Indians, and you wonder why the hell they did it."

"People survive on illusions," Arthur replied.

"I dunno what them things is," the driver said, "but I know there's a lot of disappointed guys in the U.S. of A., and there'll be a whole lot more once all the GIs gets back." He gloomily shook his head. "Wouldn't surprise me if there ain't another depression. I grew up on the Kansas-Oklahoma border and back then you could of bought the whole damn county for a few thousand bucks. Where did you say you was from?"

"New England." Arthur had come to understand that extended conversations demanded reciprocity and he'd decided New England would be Matt Scheiler's birthplace. This wouldn't have been too difficult to deal with, except that in America a person couldn't ever never be certain of any other person's birthplace. People floated from one side of the country to the other, like bits of wrack on a flood tide. Not that those Arthur met were particularly curious about him; most were preoccupied with their own little existences, but occasionally he encountered someone who would ask him to pinpoint his place of birth in the New England states. After checking to find out if the person came from Maine, he would then say he had been born in Vermont or Massachusetts, hopping from one New England state to another, depending where his questioner had been born. After all, a man who earns his living concocting stories should be able to produce a halfway credible autobiography, and Arthur was above all else inventive. He was the kind of writer who had only to look at people in the street to utilize their facial expressions and physical configurations to concoct a life story. With no trouble, he could transform the facial expression of a man fretting about his bowels into the lineaments of high tragedy, or the lip-nibbling of a woman undecided about which cereal to eat for breakfast into speculation about where her lover was at that particular moment. But while Arthur knew of the danger of reading too much into facial expressions, he still spent a goodly portion of his professional life injecting *his* mind's concoctions into the heads of other people; and while this might not matter in fiction, where it was easy enough to mould the minds and bodies to fit the narrative, in real life, it tended to have a warping effect on social interactions. Since he was capable of attributing all manner of motives to individuals, especially women, he was apt to jump to conclusions about people he met based on the flimsiest of evidence; and although he pictured himself as a open-faced, jovial hail-well-met kind of fellow, he was actually incredibly reserved in his behaviour. His manoeuvres in the social arena were similar to those of a savage creeping though a hostile tropical jungle, or a mole burrowing through the soil and popping up here and there to survey the scene and identify its position relative to the rest of the universe. Since Arthur viewed himself as eminently sane (though afflicted with a mysterious illness nobody understood), it followed that he judged the behaviour of other people to range from the simply unpredictable to the slightly insane, and he was unable to grasp that he, operating at the periphery of society, was himself in danger of becoming insane. Furthermore, since he was highly persuasive and could readily justify his behaviour to himself and to others, as for example to Phyllis Ackroyd, he could think of no reason why he should alter anything about himself or his mode of life.

Thus, the further Arthur withdrew in time and space from the horrible event that had occurred in his former home, the more he magnified the event and the ensuing danger to himself. He sweated profusely whenever he recalled his weakness the day he lay between Phyllis's strong thighs and told his story. Then, he had thought he would never write again, that his energy would be devoted entirely to finding a deep, safe hole into which he could disappear; and although the drive to find a haven remained, the need to create fictitious lives for the people he saw on buses or in streets of small towns was greater than his impulse to go to ground. The creative turmoil which resulted affected the style and content of Arthur's work and started him on the path which ultimately transformed him from a concocter of melodramatic tales into a narrator of simple, but moving stories of everyday life in America. There was an immediacy in the stories, since most were written in gales of creative fury after leaving a bus and were built on an amalgam of voices, faces and bodies of men and women on the buses. These he would mail off to Phyllis without bothering to rework them, all he wanted was to rid himself of the images that pounded in his skull. The hastily written stories shocked Phyllis because they conveyed less about the characters than about Arthur's feelings of desperation. Some stories she was able to edit and publish, but many were set aside because she found them teeming with savagery and disregard for individual dignity. It was as though the author wanted to strip away every illusion people had about themselves and their lives, much as a pathologist disembowels a cadaver, and, though it wasn't explicitly stated, the message communicated to readers was one of contempt and hatred of humanity. This puzzled Phyllis. She had lain in Arthur's arms and had felt certain he was not wanting in human kindness. With her, he had been a considerate, gentle lover and had done everything to satisfy her, which was more than could be said for other men she had bedded. Almost without exception, they had quickly shot their bolts, then run from her as quickly as possible. She supposed that Arthur's mother (what a vampire she must have been!) had taught him how to satisfy a woman, and if that were so, you would think that when he came to write stories, he would be tolerant of people's limitations and not focus on, even exaggerate, their weaknesses. Of course, people *were* mean and stupid and, yes, men took every opportunity to look up a woman's skirts and women took every opportunity to lean forward to tempt men with glimpses of their breasts, and of course everybody told off-colour jokes and used coarse language, but when you stepped back and looked at what the average person actually said and did, it was all pretty harmless, no more than extensions of social customs, such as the young women who worked at the magazine hanging onto their virginity, indulging their dreams of waiting for the right man to come along, because they believed they were destined to meet, marry and have children by the one man who was just "right" for them. But Arthur's stories suggested that "rightness" didn't exist, that there was nothing in human life but a turgid concoction of lust and hatred and writhing, sweaty, grub-like, stinking corruption. It was all very disquieting for Phyllis, since she had been raised to believe in the importance of personal and civic dignity and responsibility, which in turn meant the ultimate purpose of fiction was to elevate the moral tone of a community. It wasn't a question of censoring, but of authors understanding that they were in a very real sense the keepers of public morality. No one denied that awful, terrible things happened in life, but describing them in detail served no useful purpose. On the contrary, the task of an author was to guide readers from the mundane to higher planes of thought. Her governess had vaccinated her with injections of Ralph Waldo Emerson, Nathaniel Hawthorne and Oliver Wendell Holmes in order to forestall any inclination she may have had in childhood to be enthusiastic about Nancy Drew or the Hardy boys; nor had she ever toddled around woodlands with Pooh bear. Her introduction to literature was *Little Women*, followed by *Treasure Island* and *The Last of the Mohicans*. She had been taught that proof of maturity was to think and act coolly, so she had taken lovers coolly and given and taken limited pleasure in order to enjoy cool, intellectually literary conversations. But what she had experienced with Arthur changed her, and she was astonished, rather ashamed, at the way her body swelled with desire and her limbs writhed when she thought of him. She wrote letters to him, but had no mailing address, so she couldn't mail them. Instead, she wrote more and more unmailed letters describing in detail how she felt. She blushed when she later reread them. They were so personal, so intimate; but they also allowed her to gain the insight that the difference between herself and Arthur Compson/Matt Scheiler was one of perspective. He objectively recorded what he saw, whereas she was trapped by emotion and education. He did not care for anyone or anything, only the practising of his art. She had beliefs in things provided by others; he had nothing except a belief in himself. She had been (and continued to be) moulded by others, whereas he had formed himself, by himself.

Phyllis intended to let Arthur know that while she would continue to publish his stories in *Showcase*, she wanted him, in exchange, to exercise restraint with subject matter and language. But it turned out she never had to caution Arthur, because his stories changed in style and content, and the harsh realism replaced by a dreamy, speculative idealism. The change bewildered Phyllis, though the explanation for it was simple enough: Arthur had encountered America's vast continental mountain ranges, and on beholding them had asked for nothing more than to sit and contemplate them as he had once gazed at the Mississippi. Of course he knew he must eventually pass through the mountains, and he also recognized that his present reluctance had nothing to do with their magnitude, but rather was the outcome of a psychological barrier within himself. He realized that before he could enter the mountains he must reach an accord with them, as he had done with the Mississippi before it had allowed him to cross it. He actually addressed the distant giants: "I'm willing to make peace with you," which sounded silly and childish, but for the man, Arthur Compson, who so desperately longed to integrate himself wholly into the skin of Matt Scheiler, it was an intensely serious business. There were days when he turned away from the peaks, even thought of journeying back to Trina's diner and the comfort of her friendly smile and casual chatter. He imagined he was holding her and making love, giving in to momentary weakness, longing for her presence because he knew she would be there to hold him when his spells occurred. He rode in buses that took him backwards and forwards along the perimeter of the mountains, through landscapes where the rounded hills reminded him of the breasts of adolescent girls, and where a town consisted of a junction in the road that ran north-south and east-west around which were gathered a store, a gas station, a church. Arthur left the bus at one such town, entered the store and asked about available accommodation.

"There ain't nothin' for the next two hundred miles."

"Why're you here then?"

"Big reservation's a ways up north. That's why the minister's here. Lots of souls up there to be hooked, provided he can dig up the right bait. Hey, you could mosey over to his place and see if his missus's gotta extra bed. You a peddlar?"

"Just travelling through."

"Most guys don't stop."

"There's a fine view of the mountains from here."

"Oh, them things. Damn nuisance. They get in the way."

"You been on the other side?"

"Why the hell would I do that? This is as far as I'm going."

"But how can you make a living?"

"Come back next week and you'll see why." He waved a hand at the rear of the store where bottles of rum and whisky lined the shelves. "See that? Guys come from fifty miles around to get their bottles. At the end of the weekend, them shelves 'll be empty."

"I see. So, the minister's house is right over there?"

"It was this morning."

"Can I leave my cases with you?"

"You bet." Arthur put the cases behind the counter and walked to the minister's house which sat four-square on the highway intersection. As he walked, he observed the landforms that had been so beautifully contoured by delicate winds and in which the roads were sabre slashes and the few buildings ugly encrustations over deep wounds.

A pre-war Ford sedan bearing outdated Massachusetts plates was parked in front of the house, and before Arthur could knock on the door, it was opened by a small, thin-faced woman. Her grey-streaked hair was tied back with a piece of frayed blue ribbon, and her face and clothes streaked with soot. When Arthur explained why he was there, she turned her head and called: "He wants a room."

"For a day or two," Arthur said.

"A couple of days," she called.

"What's his name?" a man's voice said.

"Matt Scheiler," Arthur told her.

"Matt Scheiler," she called.

The man's voice said, "Matthew, eh? Bring him in."

"You can come in." The woman stepped back and Arthur entered a room which held a table and two chairs, a coal stove and four apple boxes. Opposite the house door were two smaller doors which Arthur assumed opened onto bedrooms. Everything was cramped and dingy. A middle-aged, thin, bald man sat at the table.

"Why are you here?" he asked.

"I'm travelling to the coast. Los Angeles," Arthur replied.

"But why have you stopped here? Why have you come to this house?"

"To get a room for the night."

"My name is Abram Drummond. She is Sarah, my wife."

"A pleasure meeting you, Mr. and Mr. Drummond."

"Show him the room, Sarah." The tiny room held nothing but an iron-frame bed and a couple of folded blankets.

"How much?" he asked Mrs. Drummond.

"Four dollars," she said.

"Does that include meals?"

"Just the bed. Four dollars more for meals."

Although Mrs. Drummond had what all capitalists long for: a monopoly, Arthur still tried to bargain. "Six for the bed and meals," he offered.

"Four and four," she replied. "Eight."

"Make it seven," he suggested.

"Take it or leave it," she told him.

"Get the fire going and make coffee," Drummond ordered, then to Arthur, "Sit!", pointing to the chair across from him. "Are you prepared to believe I'm a graduate of Harvard Theological School?"

"I'll swallow anything you have to say about yourself," Arthur said.

"Where I was bitten by the missionary bug."

"Like a fool," Mrs. Drummond said from the stove she was lighting.

"I could have sucked on the teats of a prosperous congregation. I could have gone to China, or Africa, to preach and rescue lost souls, but instead I came here."

"Have you succeeded in rescuing any souls?" Arthur asked. He thought the two were mad.

"No." Drummond looked directly at Arthur and asked, "Do you know who you are?"

Arthur was unnerved by the question and paused before answering in as firm a voice as he could muster. "Of course I do."

"No one can say who he truly is."

"Well, I have a fairly clear idea."

"You may think so. Actually, you're a messenger from God."

"I'm flattered you should think so."

"You were sent here for a reason." He pointed to his wife who was adding coals to the kindling. "Sarah drove Hagar and her son out."

"She was cheeky," said Sarah Drummond.

"No. You envied her because she proved you barren by bearing my son."

"Cheeky bitch!"

"No!" Mr. Drummond shouted. "You blamed me. You said the fault was mine. That my seed was dead. You laughed at me. You picked Hagar from the flock. You told me to go to her and prove my seed would grow. And when it did, you told her to take herself and the bastard child back to the reserve, then God would sent a messenger to open your womb. Am I right? Isn't that what you said?" Arthur had the impression that Mr. and Mrs. Drummond knew these lines perfectly, like actors who have performed a play a hundred times.

"Why shouldn't God have mercy on me?" Sarah Drummond cried. "Why should he allow a no-good Indian to have what I'd give an arm and a leg for?"

"Because you're a sinful woman, that's why, wanting me to stay in Massachusetts and suck at capitalism's teats."

"What's wrong with wanting a decent life? If we had a decent life, I'd've had children. I know I would."

"But your womb shrivelled up with envy and hatred. I say, here is the messenger God has sent to open your womb." He pointed a shaky finger at Arthur. "Thou shalt go unto her and behold, she shall bear a son. And I shall name him—"

"Isaac," Arthur said. He then stood. "I'll get my things from the store." Before Mr. and Mrs. Drummond could protest or move to detain him, he was out of the house and running toward the store. A bus was turning at the intersection to head south, and when Arthur saw it, he yelled and jumped up and down, waving his arms to catch the driver's attention. After the bus turned, it drew into the roadside and stopped. When the driver opened the door, Arthur asked where he was going.

"South. Where're you heading?"

"Eventually to Los Angeles."

"You've got a way to go yet," the driver said, "but it can be arranged."

"I'll get my cases from the store. Won't be a minute."

Once he was safely ensconced in the seat behind the driver, he was able to think about, even regret, not having remained to participate in the little Biblical drama being played out in the Drummond's miserable shack. He did not question that the circumstances of isolation and poverty had driven the couple insane, and he was certain that they replayed over and over the scene he had witnessed, much as he and Sylvia had played their nightly scene. That was the nature of insanity: it held you in one place and forced you endlessly to repeat a word or action. It was the breaking of a cog in the complex mechanism of an individual's being that held him in a position from which he would never escape because whatever had been broken was irreplaceable. As he half-listened to the driver talk about himself and the land through which they were passing, he began to sketch the outline of a story in which the minister and his wife and a wanderer like himself engage in an emotional tug of war.

Arthur's admiration for bus drivers continued to grow. Their knowledge of human foibles seemed far greater than his own. Furthermore, in a land that spanned a continent, a bus driver commanding a great machine was responsible for the safety of several dozen passengers. Later, Arthur realized that bus drivers, like truckers and railroad engineers, had created their own mythology, which eventually all drivers came to accept and passed on to passengers such as himself, gullible enough to believe whatever was good and evil and crazy in America could be found on a bus.

At the depots, he was passed from one driver to another like a piece of fragile china. They pointed out motels where he could lodge and diners where he could get decent, cheap meals. Their runs were timed, but their "Knights of the Road" ethic demanded they assist anyone stranded on the highway. "You gotta do what's right," one driver solemnly told Arthur, "even when it goes against company rules. A guy's got to live with hisself for the rest of his life. Right?" Some drivers wondered if Arthur was a company stoolie checking on them, otherwise why would he ride around in the byways of Utah, Colorado, New Mexico and Arizona when he could go direct to Los Angeles? But other drivers accepted Arthur's story that floating around in the middle of the Atlantic in a life jacket for two days was enough to make a man seek the security of a bus for the rest of his life.

One driver insisted on introducing him to his wife and putting him up for the night. His wife, Carla, was of Mexican origin which, the driver explained, made her a good wife because she was raised not to expect much. She already had one toddler and was thick-waisted with another child. Her younger sister, Inez, lived with them. The driver suggested that Arthur take Inez to the local movie house. "Give her a break," he said. When Arthur protested he knew no Spanish and Inez little English, the driver responded, "So what? Sex is an international language."

Arthur ended up escorting Inez to the movie after weighing it against the disadvantages of losing bus-driver assistance for the remainder of his journey. Inez clearly thought the movie was wonderful, while he thought it was nonsense. "Bueno, bueno," she said, clutching his arm as they were pushed through the exiting crowd. He guided her into a nearby diner and ordered a banana split for her and coffee for himself, then became irritated when she and the waitress giggled together and spoke Spanish. Inez ate like a child, licking the spoon after each mouthful and Arthur thought she might be no more than eleven or twelve, though the bus driver had told him she was sixteen, which for Mexicans, so he told Arthur, was the same as being a woman. Realizing an underage girl had been fobbed off on him, he became offended and before Inez had finished eating, he stood, put some coins on the table and said, "Let's go." She hurried after him, upset because she didn't understand his behaviour. She grasped his hand raised and kissed it. He swung her around and was about to kiss her and move his hands around her slender, attractive body when he saw the expression in her eyes. She was frightened. Of what? Of the unknown? Or that he was getting ready to repeat something already done to her? "It's okay," he said. "Don't worry. I'm not going to do anything." He took her hand and led her back to the house.

Later, before bedding down on the couch, he told the driver he hadn't touched Inez. Then asked, "Have you?"

"For crissake, what d'you take me for!" the driver blustered.

"I'd take you for a guy that'd take any cunt that came his way."

"I don't go after kids."

"I'll bet."

"What the hell, a little feel don't hurt them. Mex girls expect it. They ain't like American girls who scream blue murder if a guy touches them. Mex girls think they ain't got what it takes unless a guy tries to make out. Don't get me wrong, Mex women're real straight-laced. But like I say, they don't want a guy to be disappointed when they strip down. No sir. You marry a Mex girl and that's it. You don't bugger around with no other women, or kid sisters."

Ernest Langford

"Like you."

"Hell, Carla knows I got another gal at the end of my run. I give her what she wants and she knows I ain't playing the field. Sure, she knows I pat Inez's ass and squeeze her tits once in a while, but like I said, she knows I do it for Inez's good. Yes sir. I do it so's Inez'll know what she'll get when she goes out with a guy like you."

Arthur nodded, and felt the lumpy couch.

"It ain't as bad as it looks," the driver said. "And another thing: The worst thing a guy can do is ignore a gal's assets. That's what I've learned. Maybe they don't look like goddamn movie stars, but they're all made the same. Yes sir."

The next morning, after a night of trying to accommodate himself to the couch, Arthur shook hands with Carla and palmed Inez a dollar bill while whispering she should buy herself a little gift, walked to the bus depot, climbed aboard another bus and continued his circuitous journey to the Pacific coast and Los Angeles.

Eventually one of the many buses Arthur rode halted for a ten-minute rest stop at a place where, on dismounting the bus and looking westward, he was confronted by a mass of bleak, triangular mountains so close and overpowering that his impulse was to turn back and make for the open plains; but after his moment of panic subsided, he decided to follow the highway to the point where it curved around a ridge. There he saw assembled a gas station, a general store, a few houses irregularly placed along the highway and a shabby, rundown motel on the other side of the highway. He decided he would remain there for a while in order to familiarize himself with the spiky barren peaks before making his final crossing into California. He told himself he had successfully bluffed his way across the continent so far and could feel confident he had securely embedded himself in the landscapes of the vast country. But he needed more time to shuck the final layer of old psychic skin before, with eyes clear and a mind emptied of confusing memories, he would board the bus that would take him through the great continental barrier into a new life. In his memory, waiting to be utilized, were all his American experiences. Oh yes, they were all there, ready to be transformed into stories with which he would recover the literary position he had lost when he fled England. He had sent more stories to Phyllis Ackroyd, requesting her to withhold payment for any accepted manuscripts until he reached Los Angeles.

Arthur went into the motel office where a tall, black-haired, severe-faced woman curtly informed him that yes, she had a unit he could occupy for five bucks a day. He reserved it, walked over to the store and asked if it had general delivery service, and when the proprietor said, "You betcha," Arthur returned to the bus to collect his cases. "Jeez!" the driver commented. "Why here? This place ain't even a town. It's damn near the end of the world."

"That's what I like about it."

"There ain't a goddamn thing to do here, except kill flies and watch vultures." Arthur smiled, picked up his luggage and crossed the highway to the motel, watched by the passengers in the bus who, like the driver, thought Arthur must be out of his mind to leave the security of the vehicle for such desolation. The passengers were on their way to Los Angeles, determined to forget what they had left behind, believing nothing else could ever match their California dreams.

"Number Eight," the woman said. "You can pay now, or when you leave, but I'd as soon you paid now." Arthur handed over two twenties and said they would settle up if he stayed longer. When he asked if she could feed him. "I could," she said, "but it won't be no la-de-dah meals."

"As long as the food's edible," he said

"My old man likes his chow." She examined the register. "Scheiler. That a Kraut name?"

"Dutch." Arthur said. "Matthew, usually called Matt."

"Suits me. I'm Lillian, but I don't allow nobody to call me Lil. Seems like every hustler in the country is a Lil, for crissake."

"Okay, Lillian. Could you fix me up with a sandwich and a cup of coffee?"

"Half an hour suit you?"

"That'll be fine and dandy." (Arthur tended to over-do American colloquialisms.) He strolled by the row of shabby units to Number Eight, opened the door and halted when he saw a man on the bed humped over the naked buttocks of a kneeling woman. He closed the door, put down his cases and went back to the office. "Number Eight's occupied. Must be honeymooners."

She exploded. "The bastard! He's got Dolores in there again. I'll fix her." She rushed from the office and entered the room, leaving the door open. Arthur could hear her yelling at the woman to get off her property and take her filthy carcass to the nearest whorehouse.

A woman, naked below the waist, backed from the room onto the cracked blacktop, crouching, knees pressed together, begging for her clothes. Arthur dispassionately eyed her, noting tooth marks on her buttocks and fluid on her thighs. A pair of sandals was thrown from the room, followed by fluttering underwear and skirt. "Stinking bitch!" Lillian yelled.

While the woman dressed herself, Lillian shrieked at the man who retaliated by saying, "If you didn't lock up your tail like it was Fort Knox, I wouldn't need to look no place else." He emerged from the room, nodded at Arthur and strolled across the highway to the store. He was a tall man and would have been uniformly thin but for the pot belly sagging over his belt.

In the evening, Lillian's husband came to his room and introduced himself. "The name's Herb," he said. A portentous pause followed as he shook Arthur's hand and cleared his throat. "Biggest mistake (pause) a guy can make (pause) is to think (pause) his missus (pause) had got his interests (pause) at heart." Arthur nodded while wondering what the connection was between a man's best interests and shagging the domestic help. But the long and short of it was that Herb apparently did not object to Lillian yelling at him, provided she didn't do it in the presence of strangers. It was a question of male dignity, and Herb hoped Arthur would forgive Lillian for her breach of good manners. He shook Arthur's hand again and departed.

The next day, while Arthur was in his room typing up his notes, the woman he'd seen with Herb arrived to make the bed and sweep the floor. "I'm Dolores," she explained. She swirled a broom around half-heartedly. "You can't do nothing about the sand around here," she said. "It's scorpions you have to look out for. Don't leave your shoes on the floor at night." She leaned far over the bed to tug at the sheets and her skirt rose to reveal fine thighs and the edge of blue underpanties. "Lillian don't mean half what she says," she said over her shoulder, but when she saw Arthur was looking at a column of ants on the wall, she quickly completed her cleaning and left. She was not accustomed to men ignoring her.

"Has Dolores pushed her ass in your face yet?" Lillian asked when he next saw her.

"Well . . ." Arthur wasn't sure what to say.

"She can't help it. It's the way she was raised."

"Is she Mexican?"

"Part. God knows what the other parts are."

"I guess it's the unknown parts that count in most of us."

"That's about the cut of it," Lillian agreed. "You like doughnuts?" She explained that she scorned commercial food products and always made her own doughnuts. "There ain't nothin' better than doughnuts if they're made proper."

Arthur agreed to coffee and doughnuts, and it became clear Lillian was thrilled to have an audience for her grievances, generally about Herb, whose infidelities and laziness, so she said, marked the course of their marriage and eroded the affection she had once felt for him.

"Basically Herb ain't a bad guy," she said, "but he thinks the world owes him a living on account of his havin' got born. He's one of them guys that thinks what other guys got is better'n what he's got, know what I mean? I may not be much to look at now, but I had the same equipment as every woman, still do. This motel belongs to me. Herb don't own one goddamn thing, not even the pants he pulls down to hop onto that bitch Dolores. No sir. It's mine. My daddy come here in 1930, and he seen guys comin' outta the mountains lookin' for a place to stay. When all them Okies was comin' along the highway makin' their way to California, he let 'em park their broke-down cars and trucks out in front, cuz they didn't have money for nothin' else. That's when Herb showed up. I should of know'd better, I should of guessed he was lookin' for a sucker. My daddy said Herb wasn't no good, and he was right. When you got a man like Herb, you're stuck with him, because he don't do nothin' that'll let you to go to the law and get rid of him. He plays around with the help, that's all, and that ain't good enough for a judge 'cuz most of them guys do the same, only more so. Besides, you gotta have a man around the place, even if he's an imitation like Herb. He told Daddy he come out here to develop a gold claim up in the mountains. Mark my words, he'll try and palm it off on you, and when he does, tell him to go fly a kite. Well, that's enough gab for one day. Anytime you feel like having a doughnut and coffee, stop by. You like it here, eh? Quiet most of the time. But Saturdays is busy as hell. Workers from the dam site comes into town, and a joker rents units for his girls."

"I'll take that into account." Lillian followed Arthur from her small living area, decorated with knickknacks, into the office and from there to the shallow porch. Now that the conversational barrier was down, she couldn't stop talking—everything flowed out, like water from behind a breached dam. They saw Dolores emerge from Number Eight. "She's a good worker, but any brains she has is in her rear end."

"Maybe that's because she knows where men store theirs." Lillian managed a thin smile and head bob to signify agreement. "That's about the cut of it," she said. Arthur had learned this was Lillian's standard response to comments made by other people.

Each afternoon Arthur walked along the road and climbed onto a ridge to look at the highway where it curled into the mountains, much as he had once stood on the dyke to look at the bridge spanning the Mississippi. His reluctance to move on now had less to do with lack of confidence in his new identity than with his need to feel he had totally assimilated his American experiences. In a sense, he was like a child who, though knowing the water beneath the diving board is commodious, nevertheless hesitates in order to appreciate fully the significance of a first dive, which can never be repeated, for once the act is done, the thrill of its newness fades and that which was once marvellous and astounding becomes a commonplace.

So Arthur remained at the motel, each morning organizing his memories, writing descriptions of the people and places he'd encountered and outlining plots for future stories. In the afternoon, he chatted with Lillian or gossiped with Herb and fended off Herb's efforts to sell him a mining claim. When that topic wore out, Herb offered to procure Arthur anything he might want from a used car to a succulent girl with an intact hymen. Herb was the eternal panderer, slinking around the edges of unspoken, unfulfilled desires, whispering promises into ears, offering to provide a heart's desire for an unstated price.

On Saturday afternoons, Herb and Arthur sat on the porch and watched construction workers from a dam site in the mountains come into town and hand over their hard-earned dollars to a pimp sitting in a car parked on the highway. Herb claimed he could gauge the sexual state of each man by the way he walked toward the units. "Take that guy," he said. "He'll shoot off before he gets in there. Yes sir. He's trigger-happy." Arthur wondered how the money was divided between the pimp and the two whores who serviced a man every fifteen minutes from noon to midnight. Herb said the split was 75/25. At precisely five minutes past midnight, when Arthur and Herb reconvened on the porch, the pimp drove his car close to the units where, unseen by Herb and Arthur, the women slipped into the back seat, and the car drove away.

"He's a smooth operator," Herb said. "Been at it for years. I've told guys I'll get Dolores for 'em, cheaper." Herb looked around to make sure no one could hear. "You tried her? Give her a five-spot. That'll help her out with her kids. Her husband ain't worth a hog's foot." Arthur thought Herb's assessment of Dolores's husband out of order, since it came from a man whose wife considered *him* a useless encumbrance. Still, Arthur tried to bear in mind that the way people see themselves is often in direct contradiction to the way others appraise them, and naturally it was understood by everyone that unflattering judgements of one's character made by others were always mistaken.

One morning, it had to be a Sunday because of the wholesale rutting which had gone on the previous afternoon and evening in the units adjacent to his, Arthur knew the time had come for him to pass through the mountains. He packed his things, took them across the highway to the general store, bought a ticket to Los Angeles, then went back to the motel to settle his account and eat a doughnut with Lillian and Herb. They were sorry to see him leave. Lillian said she would miss their afternoon chats, and Herb wagged his head while telling Arthur he had missed the opportunity of a lifetime by not taking up the mining claim. They stood on the office porch and waved as the bus pulled away from the store, and after acknowledging their farewells, Arthur got down to the business of observing and recording his impressions of a landscape that changed imperceptibly from barren mountain to desert and from desert into the lush, unbelievably varied shades of green that were southern California. He was astonished by what he saw beyond the bus windows. Could land be that fertile? Could there really and truly be such a place in the world where mile upon mile of fields and orchards filled with vegetables or fruiting trees blanketed the air with delicious aromas? The sight assailed his senses and cowed his capacity to ask what sins might have been committed in order that the land could become so abundantly fertile. Quite by accident he had found a battered copy of Richard Henry Dana's *Two Years Before The Mast* in a bus depot and had absorbed the account of the months Dana had spent on the deserted beaches near the mission of Los Angeles, gathering stinking steer hides to ferry out to a ship waiting miles offshore. Arthur found it difficult to believe that land could be so utterly transformed within the period of a hundred years and that everything he beheld was the product of imported water. The elegant palms, the scented orange groves, the grapefruit, the walnut, the pecan and every other fruit and vegetable he could name—all were there because precious water had been transported from a source unknown to him. That miraculous, magical substance: clean, pure water had converted the arid land of the original settlement into a grid of streets where pink houses vied with gaudy flowers to attract eyes glazed with light and reflected colour. Nothing in his journey across the continent (it had taken Arthur three years to cross America from Baltimore to Los Angeles) had prepared him for this profusion, which, for him, symbolized every hope, every ideal, every dream ever conjured up by Americans. It was the ultimate: The re-creation of Eden on earth. Little wonder then, when he left the bus at the Los Angeles terminal, that he failed to recognize Phyllis Ackroyd standing in the depot waiting for him.

Chapter

18

"I WAS CERTAIN YOU WOULDN'T FLY," PHYLLIS SAID AS SHE greeted him, "and pretty sure you'd go as far south as the Mexican border, then back to L.A. through the Imperial valley. So I got myself a bus timetable and waited for your arrival."

"Long?" he asked.

"Not really." She refrained from saying she'd been going to the depot off and on for months.

"It's unbelievable you're here. Did you get the stories?"

"Yes." They walked from the depot to a parking lot. "Put your cases in the back."

"Is this yours?" He waved a hand at the white convertible coupe.

"I'll teach you how to drive. A car's essential in Los Angeles. I've rented a house in Beverly Hills. It's reasonably quiet. Not like here." She lifted her hand from the steering wheel and gestured. "That's the University of California, L.A. campus." He stared blindly at buildings beyond walls of elongated palm trees, unable to grasp fully what Phyllis was telling him.

The light, space and quantity of trees and flowers reduced him to silence. He wanted to question her, but couldn't articulate words beyond yes and no. He nodded when at some point she told him they were passing through Hollywood and would soon turn into Beverly Hills. She explained how she had convinced the owners of *Showcase* to open an office in Los Angeles because so many of America's finest writers worked in Hollywood. "Like you," she said. They left the wide boulevard edged in palm trees, climbed a narrow, steep hill to a mid-sized pink-plastered, pan-tiled house. "A certain movie mogul kept his girlfriends here," she said. "You can see the ocean from the front windows. There's an orange and fig tree in the back."

"Eden," Arthur said. "A serpent too?"

Phyllis laughed. "Oh no, they were killed off years ago, when the developers arrived."

They stood at the windows and looked out over roofs to an enormous, uninterrupted blue patch seemingly a continuation of the sky. "We can sit here and watch the sun set. It falls into the ocean." She tentatively put her arm around Arthur's waist and he did likewise, then he turned to kiss her. He couldn't recall them embracing like this before. "I missed you," she said. "I wanted to chase after you, but I knew you wouldn't want that." They went into the small bedroom, stripped and made love on the unmade bed. She cried out at her climax, and Arthur recalled how, when they lay together in that distant hotel, he had wondered if guests in other rooms had heard her cries. By contrast, *his* copulation was always so quietly managed it seemed as if nothing eventful was happening. They repeated love-making, then he showered and went to look at ripening oranges and figs while Phyllis concocted a supper for them. Later, they stood at the window, hands clasped, watching the sun hesitate a moment before sliding below the horizon.

"Isn't it a sight?" she asked.

"Everything's amazing in this place," he replied, "but the most amazing of all is that I'm actually here, on the Pacific coast of America. I see myself as a rat that has crept out of some fire-consumed building and swum across an ocean to restart life as a domestic cat."

Phyllis laughed and hugged him. "You're not a rat. You're a survivor." They didn't discuss what they felt for each other, but Arthur knew what Phyllis felt for him was deeper and more intense than what he felt for her, maybe her feeling was akin to love, while his was not much more than self-preservation combined with sexual appetite, although he did respect her. He valued her intelligence and literary skills and because he was emotionally neutral toward her, he could objectively observe how emotion flooded her and how, during intercourse, a rosy blush covered her body as she trembled and panted during orgasm. He took pleasure sniffing her skin and told her the odour of musk was strongest around her knees and dark-rose nipples. She said he was worse than a pet dog, but she never objected when he put his face along her inner thighs and parted her labial lips with his tongue to sniff and probe there. She thought she was lucky to have him and she wondered how many, if any, women had attained similar heights of physical pleasure.

She enjoyed parading naked before him, stretching her arms high, confiding that all her life she had longed to walk naked before a man and watch desire rising in him. One evening, in the twilight, she ran naked from the house to snatch a handful of ripe figs from the tree and race back, breathless and triumphant. "I don't care who saw me!" she cried. "I don't care!" They ate the sun-blackened figs, and afterwards, giggling, played what they called the Eden game, wherein each investigated the other's body parts, identifying them as being different from each other's, yet capable of joining together in a marvellous union of pleasure. It was childish, but their closeness enabled Phyllis to speak about her childhood and the physical and moral do's and don't's her parents had imposed upon her. "You have no idea what it's like to grow up in middle-class America where you must always think and do the right things. You're squeezed between the working class who—so you thought—can say and do anything they please, and the rich, who don't give a damn about anything and escape to Europe, or at least they did before the war. Mother put me in dainty dresses and was horrified when I wet my underpants. I knew nothing until I began reading French and English novels and discovered the women in them weren't bound by my strictures. I'm like the child who wants to pull down her panties and show the boy next door what's between her legs. I mean, I never had anyone admire me for what I was—only people telling me what I was supposed to *become.* So now, I want you to look at and admire every part of me. Arthur watched and listened closely, and because Phyllis was important to what would happen to him in the future, he pulled the cords in her which he knew would release the strings of her long-suppressed desires. He made notes of what she revealed about herself and later incorporated parts of it into women he portrayed in his short stories and novels. In general, his cold, analytic intent was to have Phyllis appreciate their interdependence and realize that, like bee and flower, they couldn't survive without each other.

Of course they discussed his work and Arthur asked if the short story collection was still going forward. "You bet," she said and told him she had widened the publication of his stories to other periodicals and was reviewing final selections for the trade book. "The more you publish, the more impressed critics'll be. They'll realize you're not a creative-writing teacher who's wrung a few skimpy tales out of himself. They'll recognize you as a genuine writer of clear, lucid prose, like Hemingway."

"I don't see myself like Hemingway."

"You're not, but you write lucid prose. That's a characteristic of good writers. You never get lost in wishy-washy prose, or write down to your readers."

Phyllis kept to her nine-to-five office hours, while Arthur began the arduous (to him) job of transforming his optioned short story into a movie scenario. He quickly discovered that the task which had appeared simple on the surface was in fact extremely difficult. The first script conveyed to the director by Phyllis came back with the words: "What's this shit?" scrawled across the title page. He was so enraged he refused to speak to Phyllis for two days; however, by the third day, his confidence returned and he began another version, cautioning himself that he must learn to visualize his story through the camera lens. Thus, the lens would trace the movements of his main character from the moment he awakened beside his still-sleeping wife to the final shot of him awakening from a drunken sleep to face responsibility for the deaths of two innocent men. The early shots of the man watching his sleeping wife must reveal his complacency, they must show how well-satisfied the man is with the way things are going in his life; he would reinforce the self-satisfaction in a scene with his ten-year-old daughter, who has absolute trust in him. Let the camera tell the story, he told himself. But problems with execution remained, and he found it difficult to set aside his learned craft to write and revise until he produced what was needed for the screen. The labour left him exhausted and irritable, which he took out on Phyllis by refusing to make love. After all, she was responsible for dragging him into this alien world. After several weeks, late one night, he crawled into their bed while muttering "finished," then became more annoyed with her when he discovered she was wearing a menstrual pad.

When the script came back with the words "It'll do" on it, Arthur told Phyllis, "That's it. No more screenplays. From now on, I stay with what I know."

"Too bad," Phyllis said. "Scripts pay well." They were standing at a viewpoint outside the Mount Wilson Observatory looking across the San Fernando Valley towards Los Angeles.

"I guess so," Arthur agreed, "but it's too constrictive for me."

"We'll see," she said, then added, "We should get around more. There's so much to see in California. We could spend a weekend in Palm Springs, or drive north to Muir Woods. You must see the sequoias."

"I'd like to see Death Valley."

She dabbed a kiss on his cheek. "Okay, next weekend we'll visit Death Valley. The weekend after that, we'll fly to Mexico City."

But while they talked about getting away, something always came up which prevented them from going. More often than not it was Arthur—a story he was intent on finishing or a new chapter in the novel he had started. The furthest they got that summer was to Laguna Beach, where Phyllis body-surfed on the breakers while Arthur sweated in the hot sun and timidly waded into the foaming backwash.

"Come on in," Phyllis called, as she floated over a rising heap of water. "There's nothing to it." Afterwards, they lay face-down on beach towels, listening to the breakers crash, then slowly nudge the shore, and without being aware of it, they allowed the sun to redden their backs and the wind-driven spray encrust their hair with salt. Phyllis had worn herself out body-surfing and was too tired to make love when they returned to their motel. "Tomorrow morning," she said, but when morning came, they were good for nothing but to yawn and complain of the fog which had descended during the night and made driving the winding road from Laguna Beach to the state highway hazardous. It seemed as if their relationship couldn't be sustained in the rough and tumble of the external world, and they eagerly returned to the house in Beverly Hills where, after plastering soothing ointment on each other's back, they got into bed, slept for the remainder of the day, then woke up and made love.

"I wonder if I'll ever get pregnant," Phyllis said. "I ought to. We're not using anything."

"I wouldn't object to having a girl," he said.

"Why not a boy?"

"I'd prefer a girl. Do you have any pictures of yourself as girl?"

"My parents have dozens. I was plump and serious."

"I imagine you being like Heather."

"You mean the woman who joined the army to get herself killed?"

"When I was a boy, more than anything in the world, I wanted to see Heather naked. That's how boys are."

"I doubt if any other boy resembled you."

"Maybe."

"You should feel pleased I want to have your child."

"Is that why you cry out when you come?"

"Maybe you're the only man who's ever got that from me."

"Completely calculated."

She turned away, and he guessed she was crying. "Sometimes you can be brutally insensitive."

He moved over her hips into the valley of her thighs. "Listen, Phyllis, you're my friend. You saved me from disaster. You rescued me from the loneliness eating away my life. It's true, I may not love you, but that's not because of you. I'm not capable of love. But I admire you more than any woman I've ever known. Is that understood? If I say or do stupid things, please ignore them."

She clutched and rocked him, then pleasurably sighed as his risen shaft breached her again. "Oh God!" she cried. "Don't let us be separated, don't let anything come between us."

"Amen to that," he whispered. "Let anything and everything that's happened to us float off and vanish into an infinity of forgetfulness. Let's start from the here-and-now and never look back."

They lay entwined as one, in a mute, still moment of consummate certainty, believing nothing would change, that from that moment onward the direction of their lives was as irrevocably fixed as the pole star above their heads. And they honestly believed that their pledges, uttered in a moment of passion, would somehow (magically?) be transmuted into a golden indivisible future. Moreover, they fully intended to keep their vows and, while the question of marriage was avoided, they reinforced the foundations of their relationship by first talking about, then actively looking for a larger house that would provide Arthur with a separate room for writing. They spoke of renting, but by increments slid into a discussion of the advantages of owning a house. Phyllis argued that renting was pouring money into a pit from which it could never be retrieved, whereas if they owned a house, they'd have something real in the end. Of course, interest payments on the mortgage would be a nuisance, and they would need to assemble a down payment, but they mustn't forget that the principal would decrease with every monthly payment. Phyllis's arguments appealed to Arthur's parsimonious instincts and while he never directly agreed to the purchase of a house, he did not protest when she laid out information about available properties on the supper table. The house prices made Arthur's working-class soul tremble; his bank balance might have risen, but he continued to operate financially at the level of a labourer. Still, the urge to own a place where he could safely hide from the rest of the world finally overcame his miserliness, and then a day or so later an unforeseen event intensified it.

Arthur was in the midst of writing a story about a man who loses a beloved wife and tries to create images of her by arranging on the bed clothes she has worn. He wanted to "live" the man's experience, so he removed Phyllis's scanty underwear from her dresser drawer and lifted them to his lips and nose. He had expected that handling the panties and bras would conjure memories of love-making, but instead he was embarrassed and felt like a thief violating the privacy of a woman he doesn't know. At some point, hands still in the drawer, his fingers touched paper and when he moved the underwear aside he saw the garish cover of a magazine called *True Crimes*. He picked it up, opened it and saw a photograph of himself as he had once been in an article headed with bold letters: **WHERE IS THIS MURDERER NOW?** That was all Arthur remembered until he returned to consciousness and saw Phyllis standing beside their bed. He remembered the magazine and whispered, "Why did you hide it? Why did you betray me?"

"I was afraid to tell you."

"It's a bunch of lies."

"I know, I know. I'll destroy it."

"I didn't kill Laura Dorchester. It was Martha. She was terrified Laura was about to kill her. What else have you done that I don't know about?"

"Nothing. I've not broken my word. I never will, my darling." Endearments rarely passed between them. At most, after lovemaking, Phyllis might call him "dear." She now lay on the bed, uncovered her breasts and pressed his face against her smooth skin as Sylvia had once soothed him as a child when he'd had a spell. She agreed the article was libellous, but obviously there was no option to sue, and she made the point that Arthur was as safe in Beverly Hills as anywhere else in the world, though she now thought it would be a good idea to acquire a birth certificate in the name of Matthew Scheiler. She then undertook to procure one and any other papers required to prove his American citizenship.

"Everything can be bought and sold in L.A.," she assured him.

Arthur was sceptical: Hadn't he successfully embedded Matt Scheiler into his psyche? Hadn't he installed himself into America's literary and movie world as Matt Scheiler? Why do more? And since only he and Phyllis knew of his previous identity, why let someone else in on the secret? It was too risky.

"But you might need back-up some day," Phyllis argued. "It's like insurance." But that was as far as the discussion went because Arthur fell into a profound sleep, and Phyllis, after undressing Arthur, removed her own clothes and joined him.

Arthur's lassitude continued for more than a week. During the day, he sat outside on a lounge chair, staring at the distant ocean where colour and pattern was determined by the clouds and the texture of the sky. He likened the ocean to a huge chameleon engulfing whatever threatened to oppose it, begetting and spawning storms and rain, then eating its offspring. Of all things it had created, it alone endured. Odd, thought Arthur, that this particular image had not occurred to him while he was slaving as cook's mate in the stinking guts of the rust-diseased freighter. He supposed he was too busy then just surviving, preoccupied with polishing his sea-going wherewithal, constantly glancing over his shoulder expecting to see someone coming from behind to arrest him for involvement in the death of Laura Dorchester. Now that he had successfully entrenched himself in America and become a new person, he had a tendency to forget he had once been Arthur Compson and had known a woman named Laura Dorchester. It was difficult for him, as he sat gazing at the sea, to recall the contours of Laura's face or the sound of her voice, which had conveyed in every syllable she uttered her inviolable sense of superiority. He must have appeared uncouth to her, unsuited to enter the haunts of published and hope-to-be-published writers. But he could still remember the aroma of expensive soaps and perfumes which emanated from her as she rhythmically churned on his poker-stiff cock, and during the bus trip through southern California, when he had first seen the heavy rocking motion of oil well pumps, he was reminded of her. It was amazing, he had thought at the time, but nobody in California or anywhere else seemed to object to the smell of crude oil that hung over beaches and parts of Los Angeles, or the presence of pumps beside highways, even in gardens. The pumps were so pervasive that after a while he began to think of them as biological realities, giant ducks or immense beetles. For him, their ugliness symbolized the ruthlessness of American society and the contempt Americans felt for their landscape. Of course, the rest of humanity was no better, but somehow human deprecation of the land seemed more gross when carried out by Americans. Yet if what Dana wrote could be relied on, all of what was now southern California had once been desert, where a square mile was required to support one lean cow and where a few aboriginal people wandered, digging roots and gathering acorns.

Now, as he gazed down the hill, he could see children playing in a swimming pool where later in the day he watched a man and woman sitting beside the pool, drinking from tall, ice-packed glasses and picking at food the man had prepared on a brick-faced grill. For Arthur, the scene was a window through which he could peer into the life of what he imagined was the perfect American family: Four healthy, golden-limbed children; the mother, commodiously hipped, heavy-breasted, casually managerial; the man accepted in the role of provider and boss. Arthur used Phyllis's opera glasses to look more closely at the boys' flat stomachs and immature testicular protrusions and the girls' supple torsos with hints of budding bosoms and at their cloven, pubic deltas pressed against tight swim suits. Phyllis rectified his concept of the American family: Arthur might wish to think the people he observed were the ideal American family, but in fact the woman was a divorcee with one child and the man a bit player down on his luck, and Phyllis didn't know where the other three children had come from.

The restoration of Arthur's self-confidence paralleled his physical recovery to the point where he nodded and smiled when Phyllis told him the shooting of the movie was completed and he had been invited to a studio party to celebrate the occasion. "It'll be low key," she said. "Bill Knight, the director, only drinks soda pop and refuses to waste money on booze for any one else. And I've got more good news. I've found the perfect house for us." This meant Arthur would now have to round up the deposits he had made in banks across middle-America to contribute to the down payment and for furnishing the house.

"You'll love it," she said. "It's secluded, has a pool and a marvellous view of the ocean, better than the one here." She then opened her handbag, took out a brown envelope and from it pulled an official document which stated that a male child, Matthew Edward, had been delivered to Louise Margaret Scheiler, nee Schultz, of East Shaylerville, New Hampshire, by midwife Anne Doffler, on the fifteenth day of October 1919.

"Is this real?"

"Of course. That child was actually born on that day."

"Then he must still be floating around somewhere."

"He died four days later."

"How do you know this?"

"Because the person who prepared the certificate is paid to check out every detail. No one will question its authenticity."

An image of two women appeared on the paper in front of Arthur's eyes: one woman was lying on a kitchen table, the other standing between spread legs, supporting the head of a baby oozing from the body of the woman on the table. The second woman catches the baby, slaps its bottom, points to its tiny male organ, lays him on the mother's belly, ties the umbilical cord, then severs it with a pair of sheep shears. "My God!" he said. "It's a wonder I survived."

"You're tough."

"I'm a night creature. A rat."

"What utter nonsense!" she cried.

"It's not. I hang out in dark corners, watching, waiting to eat pieces of people's lives. I'm driven by the desire to know everything about men and women, though I realize that's impossible. Isn't every child curious to know about its mother?"

"If I was curious, I never allowed it to show. Any personal questions I might've asked were quashed forever when Mother got mad at me once when I asked her why I didn't have a baby sister like my friends. I've always blamed her for that."

"I blamed my mother for prostituting me and preventing me from having youthful romances. Sometimes I wonder if my parents didn't see me for what I was—or rather, what I was going to become—and without realizing it went about trying to provide me with experiences of life so that I'd have something to write about when I set up as an author. You know, in order to write my early novels I had to split my parents' lives open, because I nothing inside myself to use. Nothing."

"I've read your English novels," Phyllis said. "*Tower & Tower* has a U.S. affiliate." She rushed on. "I checked the catalogue and there they were. I agree they're emotionally overwrought, but apart from that, I can see in them the germs of the stories you write now. I mean, in the tensions you develop between your characters. Don't be angry, Matt. You must have known I'd end up reading them. Tell me you're not angry."

"Are they terrible?"

"Anything but. In the one about the soldier and the woman, you retell the story of your father and mother. You dextrously shift the guilt you felt about your mother onto the army deserter and make sure he's hunted down and shot like an animal."

"Perhaps. But could anyone read my early novels and my stuff now and know they're written by the same author?"

"I don't think so."

"That's good. Now, tell me more about the house."

"Jesus H. Christ!" the director exclaimed when Phyllis introduced Arthur. "So Matt Scheiler actually exists! I thought maybe Phyl was churning out the script herself, but all the time there you were, a honest-to-God pissing, shitting, fucking guy pounding away on a typewriter somewhere. Well, we finally got a halfways decent script out of you. Everybody thinks it'll do okay at the box office. Hey, Joey! Get this guy a drink, then introduce him around."

Arthur never understood how or why he fell in love with Joey Gambarasi. All he knew was that it was instantaneous. Nor could he, at the end of his life, explain why he had remained in love with her. It annoyed him, because a major portion of his working life had been given over to detailing the nature of love and other complex human emotions and relationships, and if he couldn't explain his own love for someone, what right had he to claim authenticity for his fictional characters? Joey, whose full name was Josephina, was pleasingly plump (she eventually became fat), had indifferently blonde hair and a face which was almost a perfect sphere and in which were set a pair of wide, questioning blue eyes and two pouting pink lips. Her usual expression reflected the questions she'd never been allowed to ask and the resulting confusion from the answers she'd never revieved. She was the third child and only daughter of a Guiseppi Gambarasi, whose criminal ancestors had emigrated from Italy and settled in New York around 1890 to labour diligently at their trades of extortion, theft, murder and prostitution until, during Prohibition and by uniting forces with the Mafia, the family acquired more wealth, which they immediately buried in legitimate enterprises. Joey's father, considered 'clean,' was a studio executive. His role was to acquire the financial wherewithal from external 'angels' to produce the studio's movies, which involved assembling stables of cute, big-breasted young women who, driven by their ambition to appear in the movies, agreed to be fucked by the men who would provide the cash needed for the films in which they aspired to play a role, but in which they were fated never to appear, even in crowd scenes. In many ways, Joey was no better off than the aspiring girls in her father's sex stable, because everybody in the industry knew that although Joey actively publicized her ambition to become a movie director the likelihood of it happening was about one in a zillion. Why? Because Sophia wanted Joey to marry, have children and stay at home with them; and Joey's father, realist to the core, thought Joey was deficient in the brains required to grasp the complexities of directing movies, and he let it be known that under no circumstance was anybody in the industry to offer Joey a job of more importance than continuity girl. The inability to advance in her chosen profession contributed to the puzzled expression on Joey's face; it seemed that no matter how hard she applied herself, regardless of how much time she spent studying film techniques, no one was prepared to offer her a directing job. When she asked why, people patted her on the shoulders and said, "Better luck next time, Joey." She lived at home with her parents, and always wore white, as though to let the world know she was still a virgin. which in itself was something to be wondered at in Hollywood.

Arthur, expecting decadence, did not appreciate the degree of Joey's innocence. Thus, when she introduced him to the male star of the cast who jovially exclaimed, "Hey, why do you think of our Joey?", Arthur assumed she'd been around. The female star ignored Joey, which Arthur interpreted to mean she was jealous of Joey, which couldn't have been further from the truth. "She's awful," Joey confided. "I won't cast her in my movies."

"Will you direct one soon?"

"Yes. Pretty soon." She attempted an optimistic outlook, but didn't quite bring it off.

Arthur, already smitten by love, made a promise Joey never allowed him to forget. "I'll write the script for you," he said.

"Gee, thanks!" She expressed gratitude by kissing his cheek. "A person has a better chance with a good screenplay," she explained. "You can go to the studio with exactly what you plan to do."

"It's an advantage."

"You bet it is."

Arthur wanted Joey to kiss him again but couldn't think of how to get her to do it. All he could manage was to say, "It'll take time. I'll have to dream up a theme."

"That's okay. I need to line up my financial backing."

"Hi, Joey," Phyllis interrupted. "Give me a call tomorrow, will you? I want to discuss something with you."

"You bet." Joey smiled affectionately at Phyllis, who said, "Joey and I've known each other for years."

"We're cousins," Joey amplified.

Their actual relationship was explained by Phyllis while driving home from the studio. "There's no family connection, but that's how Joey thinks of it because my father kept her grandfather out of prison on charges of extortion and income tax evasion. After that, our families visited back and forth. I once thought of marrying her eldest brother. Thank God, I didn't. He's a car dealer. Luxury models. That's where I got this coupe. At cost . . . Matt, you're awfully quiet."

"How old is Joey?"

"Twenty. She wants to direct movies, but Joe's warned the studios off her. He's scared she'll make a fool of herself and him a laughing stock."

"And would she?"

"Hard to say. She's more like her mother, not obviously on the ball. I watched you with her. You've fallen for her, haven't you?"

"Temporarily."

"The only way you'll get Joey into bed is to make out you want to marry her, and for that you'll need Joe and Sophia's approval. Sophia's a bit of a nut case. It wouldn't surprise me if she doesn't examine Joey's panties before they go into the wash. Joey's a bit of an odd bird herself. She's not interested in men, not like the rest of us, who try to guess the size of every man's income—and other things."

"Really? She kissed my cheek."

"That's because you said you'd write a script for her. Silly of you." Phyllis parked the car, and turned off the motor.

"It popped out."

Once inside, Phyllis embraced him. "I'll get Joey for you if you really want her, provided you promise not to leave me out in the cold." Arthur lifted her skirt and pushed his hand beneath her underwear to feel the substance of her heavily muscled bottom before slipping fingers under it to touch her vaginal crease. "Once upon a time I wondered what I would do if ever a man touched me there," she said.

"Now you know."

"Yes. Listen, I'm serious about Joey. I'm fond of her, and would prefer knowing she was sleeping with you than with some Hollywood scumbag. And believe you me, most men in the industry are sleazy. Like Joey's father, who treats girls like cattle. As long as his pals put their money into the kitty, he doesn't care what happens to the girls. Kitty box litter, he calls them. The only reason Joey hasn't been screwed to death is because guys are scared of Joe."

"Are you warning me?"

"Not if you told Sophia you had marriage in mind. Now, what did you think of the house?"

"It's fine."

"Gary Cooper's supposed to have lived there before he became rich and famous."

"Doesn't fame precede wealth in the entertainment business?"

"I guess. Listen Matt, are you serious about providing Joey with a script? You said you'd never write another."

He shrugged. "I could do an outline."

"Something simple."

"Is she that dumb?"

"Relative to the people she works with, yes."

"You mean people in the industry are intellectual giants?"

"No. But they're quick to spot advantages. They have pan-shot minds, but could no more create stories than fly. They just know when a story's good box-office."

Arthur's hand moved around Phyllis's hip to rest on the curve of her belly. "How well do you know Joey?"

"I probably know more about her than she knows about me. And why not? I was a teenager when she was still a kid. Sophia always liked me because I was, quote, *serious.* Joey's good-natured, but obstinate and single-minded. When you meet Sophia, you'll see how Joey'll look at fifty. But I'm very fond of her, Matt, and wouldn't object to incorporating her into our lives. I think I can manage things. Though I'm not sure she's capable of handling you. She doesn't know much about men, much less about someone like you."

"You flatter me. Now, shall we have something to eat, or shall we lie on the bed and tell each other home-truths about ourselves?" They went into the bed-room, stripped and lay side by side on the bed.

"You begin," she said.

"Having to take my cock out to piss told me I was a boy."

"Having to squat on the toilet told me I was a girl."

"I admired my cock."

"I could never make up my mind about what I had."

"I rubbed mine to make it stand up."

"I can't admit what I did."

"You ought to."

"I pushed things inside it."

"I pushed my cock into a bar of soap."

"I pushed a bar of soap into my hole."

"I was scared when I made mine bleed."

"I was terrified when I couldn't get the soap out."

"There. Now we know how each of us figured out we were girl or boy." He put a hand on her breast and said, "What did you feel when you grew these?"

"Terror."

"I envied girls their breasts. I wanted to duplicate them."

"I showed mine to my brother as a trade for him showing me his erect thing."

"I picked shit off my asshole and ate it."

"I licked menstrual blood off my fingers. Now, let's stop this talk, I feel like I'm acting in a porno movie."

"Maybe pornography's the stinking rectum of our personalities, what's leftover after whatever's of value in our minds and emotions has been used up."

"Perhaps. So what're the worst things about you?"

"My overall pettiness, my readiness to use other people's limitations for my own ends, my inclination to peep up female skirts, regardless of the woman's age, and the sexual thrill I get whenever I see a girl sprawled out on a chair. If I had the guts, I'd collect pictures of women's genitals. So there you have my grotesque personality: a blend of Peeping Tom, repressed child molester and genuine mother-fucker. And you can add physical cowardice to the list."

Phyllis turned and looked closely at Arthur's face. "You've read *Macbeth*?"

"Of course I've read it . . . 'is this a dagger I see before me?' I've read everything Shakespeare wrote. Sometimes when I'm in the thrall of my characters, I wonder if I'm only reiterating lukewarm Shakespeare. Damn him. Is there nothing he didn't put his finger on?"

"Remember the scene where Malcolm tells Macduff that putting Macbeth on Scotland's throne might be replacing an evil he knows with a far greater one? I remember it well, because it says something about the impossibility of knowing what people think and feel—and what they will do—simply by looking at their faces."

"'There's no art/To find the mind's construction in the face'?"

"Yes. And so maybe you can't tell what *I'm* thinking when you look at my face."

"I think you're completely trustworthy, regardless of the expression on your face, which is more than I can say of myself."

"But there are things I haven't told you."

"I know."

"But I ought to. Hold my hand." He obeyed the request and she began. "I'm one of those people who seethes with envy. I envy beautiful women. I envy people with talent. I used to envy prostitutes, even ugly ones. I know I'm ten times smarter than any movie star, but that doesn't help, I still envy them. When I was around fifteen, I had a kind of emotional breakdown and my parents put me in a private clinic. And you know what cured me? I found myself feeling envious of the women there who were *really* insane. I finally understood there was no point in trying to escape my limitations, so one day I told the doctor I was all better and wanted to go home. I've never quite forgiven myself for acting so stupidly."

"I would say what you did as an act of desperation, like most things I've done in my life."

"You agree with Henry David Thoreau that most people live lives of quiet desperation?"

"I believe people are driven to action to escape despair. That's the division between apes and human beings. Apes shiver and submit to cold rain, human beings build shelters and strike flints to make fires. Most actions human beings've taken since time began were in revolt against the conditions that produced despair in them. You think shivering monkeys or dogs imagine heaven? You say that you envy others. You're not alone. I envy too. I envy Shakespeare and the men who compiled the Bible and those who later translated it. I view envy as a spur to the human soul." He laughed. "Look at us, lying here. We began by listing our unsavoury quirks and end by talking about our souls."

"I'm not. You are."

"It was implied in what you told me about yourself. What you really wanted was to have someone fuck you, maybe your father, just as I wanted to fuck my mother and actually did it when my father conveniently died." He sat up and leaned back against the wall chewing his lower lip and looking down at her. "You know, the more my work forces me to think about how we human beings behave, the more clearly I see just how neatly we rationalize and justify everything in our memories. I know for certain I'm an unpleasant man who also happens to be a writer and you're . . ."

"Well . . . what am I?"

"You're a shrewd, intelligent, beautiful-bodied woman who masks her envy behind a mask of polite smiling interest. I know I've altered my own history, and I imagine you have yours. I hated what was written about me in that cheap magazine, but some part of me wishes I'd stayed in England and lived though the experience of being tried for the murder of Laura Dorchester. If I'd been convicted, I'd have pissed and shit in terror when they came to take me to the gallows. I might even have screamed and begged for mercy, which would have increased society's contempt for me. Have you ever imagined yourself being raped?"

"I've tried not to, but yes, I've imagined it happening." Phyllis got up and sat on the bedside. "Let's make supper. We've done enough talking."

"Let's make love first."

"No." She stood and put on a bathrobe. She glanced at him. "I think . . . oh, I don't know . . . I think we've begun to substitute talk for . . . it's not good." She left the bedroom, and after a while Arthur joined her in the kitchen to tear up a head of lettuce and slice cucumber and tomato for salad, while Phyllis scrambled eggs. Later, lying in the dark bedroom after forcing themselves to make love without really wanting to, Phyllis turned to him and said, "Don't let's ever talk like that again. Let's agree to have a few secrets from each other."

"All right." Arthur rolled onto his side and kissed her neck and shoulders. "Everything's safe with me."

"I know that. But we don't have to strip ourselves down to the bone. There has to be something unknown left."

"I'm inquisitive."

"That's what scares me. Perhaps when you know everything there is to know about me, you'll discard me. Well?"

His reply was to dab kisses on her face and breasts until she went to sleep and he was able to roll away and think about the personal revelations they had exchanged. Was there anything left inside themselves now, for the other to explore? Maybe nothing was left except the phoenix of sex, though their sexual encounters were like summer squalls, furious but brief. He thought: the consequences of sexual encounters was what mattered, because if sexual desire was an appetite like hunger for food, then the consequences of satisfying desire must be of greater importance than the desire itself because the consequences remained long after appetite was satiated. To satisfy physical hunger was simple. He'd done that with Sylvia night after night without taking into account the manner in which he satisfied his hunger, which might poison him psychologically, even emotionally warp him for life. Lying the darkness listening to Phyllis's breathing, he wondered if he was fated to spend his life looking for Sylvia in every woman he encountered. Was he caught on the rack of consequence? Had he, from the time he was a boy and adored Heather, who ignored him to give love to his father, begun the process of eliminating the capacity to feel spontaneous affection for any one? Was it possible that when he thought of his mother, it was only to see himself as a small child basking in the warmth of the maternal love she poured onto him as she would honey onto scones. There had been no signs of weakness in Sylvia in those far-off days, whatever she did then revealed only her strength. But, after his father's death, her weaknesses were revealed, and she forced him to enter into their strange relationship to which he submitted like a prisoner entering solitary confinement and where she stripped him of his ability to feel other than through his imagination, where everything was possible, even love. He could admire and desire Phyllis, but he couldn't love her. He wasn't sure about his feelings for Joey. If he was incapable of love, how could he love her? After all, it had happened suddenly and might not mean anything. He had better be careful. Especially about the marriage part, though he did want her, which was odd, since Phyllis satisfied him sexually. But he couldn't imagine himself married to Joey Gambarasi, or indeed to anyone else. He wasn't the marrying sort.

In sleep, Phyllis sighed as though aware of his thoughts. He rolled toward her to place his hand on her breast. He must have slept then, because being kissed by Phyllis awakened him in the morning when they made love again. Afterwards they got up, showered, dressed and ate breakfast together. Agreeing she would return in the early afternoon when they would re-inspect the proposed new house, Phyllis departed for the office. Arthur went into the bedroom, and after roughly remaking the bed, sat down at his work table, inserted a sheet of paper into the typewriter and began tapping out the story of a man whose actions as an adult consist of sequential attempts to eliminate a single founding event from the record of his life.

CHAPTER
19

THE IMMEDIATE EFFECT OF JOEY GAMBARASI'S ENTRY INTO Arthur's life was to have Phyllis put their house purchasing project on hold. She had asked herself where she would she fit into Arthur's life if he became seriously entangled with Joey. When he assured her that loving Joey wouldn't change his relationship with her, she told him he was imagining things if he thought getting mixed up with the Gambarasi family wouldn't turn his world topsy-turvy. But when he told her (untruthfully) he wasn't serious about Joey, but only wanted to find out what lay behind her guileless manner and that he was only reacting like a boy denied a toy or candy bar his heart was set on, Phyllis went along with it. That is, until Joey told her that Arthur came every day to the movie studio were she was preparing the set for a new shoot. When Phyllis confronted Arthur with this, he said he was interested in learning more about the production of movies so that he could cut corners if he ever decided to write another movie script. After that, Phyllis got the picture, and she drove Arthur to the studio, watching glumly while he engaged Joey in conversations about production techniques. Naturally, Joey was delighted to have someone who was prepared to listen to her talk about producing and directing movies, and if Arthur stared fixedly at her while she talked, it meant he was absorbing every word. She said as much to Phyllis when they met for lunch (at Phyllis's suggestion).

"But Joey," Phyllis said, "Matt doesn't give a damn about producing movies. He's in love with you."

"Me?" Joey squeaked.

"For God's sake, Joey. All you have to do is look at his face. So, what're you going to do about it?"

"I don't see why I need to do anything. I thought he was yours."

"He is, but he's fallen for you. It happened at the studio party. We have to work it out, Joey, because instead of working on his novel, he's spending time trailing around after you on movie sets. It won't do, Joey. It has to stop."

Being told Arthur wasn't interested in her movie-making expertise upset

Joey. "I don't like Matt doing that. It's almost as bad as Daddy using his girls."

"Don't be silly, Joey. Matt's nothing like your dad. Matt's a serious person. I'm quite sure he didn't want to fall for you." Phyllis watched Joey closely, gauging how far she could manipulate her. Being so much older, she had always been the dominant of the two, but she knew from experience that if pushed too far, Joey would stick out her lower lip and refuse to be agreeable. "Did I tell you Matt and I are thinking of buying a house? Look, Joey . . . why don't you come in with us?"

"Me? But why?"

"It would get you away from your parents. Give you independence." Phyllis began to improvise. "You know how everyone in the studio thinks of you as being a kid. They don't see you as an independent adult."

"You think it would help my career? Really? No kidding, Phyl?"

"I don't see why not." Phyllis normal discretion flew from her, like leaf skeletons on a February wind.

"Could I see the house?"

"Of course."

The upshot was that Joey accompanied Phyllis to the realtor to get the keys, drove to the house and inspected it. They stood in the empty living room while Joey explained to Phyllis that while the Gambarasi family might be rich collectively, as an individual, she had nothing except her studio salary and a monthly allowance from her father. After much discussion, Phyllis provided a solution.

"Here's what you can do, Joey. Your mother's having your place redecorated and refurnished. Angela Marcusi's doing the job. Right?" For as long as Phyllis had known Joey she had tacked the word "Right?" onto sentences addressed to Joey, since she, and other people too, had always assumed Joey was something of a slow learner. "Well, Angela can give us Sophia's old furniture. And we'll have her people repaint this house and add it to your mother's bill. Right? And remember all the stuff your mom has stored away? It won't cost you anything to furnish this place. And the furniture'll cover your obligation in the deal. Right?"

"But why?" Sophia asked Joey when she informed her parents she was leaving home.

Arthur's response was the same when Phyllis gave him the news. "But why?" The idea of Joey moving in with them was equivalent to putting a bowl of food just outside the reach of a chained, hungry dog.

Joey checked with Angela and got back to Phyllis with the information that her mother had enough furniture and linen and cutlery and china to fill the house, though not everything would be perfectly matched. She also said that her mother wanted to meet Matt first.

"But why?" Phyllis asked.

"She says she wants to look him over."

"Doesn't she trust our judgement?"

"I dunno. But Mom wants to meet him. There's nothing wrong with that, is there, Phyl?"

Of course there was nothing wrong with having Arthur meet Joey's mother, except that each came to the meeting with false expectations: Sophia was convinced Arthur was up to no good; Arthur was sure Sophia would be a bossy hag.

Phyllis drove Arthur to the house and left him at the imposing double wrought-iron gates. Before driving off she called, "be brief and stick to generalities."

After hesitating a moment, Arthur told the security guard on the other side of the gate that Mrs. Gambarasi was expecting him.

"That's what you say," the guard said, "but I'm not so sure Mrs. Gee wants to see you."

"Give her my name."

It worked. The massive gates opened, and Arthur passed through and walked up the palm tree-lined, circular driveway to the front door where a neatly dressed maid of indeterminate racial origin waited to take him to the living room where Sophia stood in front of French doors, coldly assessing him as he advanced. She wore a caramel-coloured silk dress that hung loosely from her shoulders to mid-calf. Rings were wedged on her plump fingers and multiple strands of pearls rested on her bosom. On the other side of the French doors lay a vista that summarized everything the mind and heart associated with southern California: shimmering blue swimming pool set in a patio of red tiles and surrounded by arrays of flowers, annuals and perennials, beyond which stood flowering trees reminding the viewer of a Persian carpet, and at the back, a wall of Junipers crowned by a row of majestic palm trees. It was so dazzling Arthur had no trouble imagining he was seeing a re-creation of Eden.

Joey's mother's voice brought him to earth. "So you're Phyllis's friend, eh?"

"Phyllis is my agent."

"And you live with her?"

"We share a house."

"And a bed?"

"What Phyllis and I share is our private business."

"That's as may be, as long as you don't drag my Joey into it."

"I don't intend to drag your daughter into anything."

Sophia had been storing up questions she intended to ask Arthur, but now that he was standing in the middle of the carpet (Angela Marcuse had assured her it was a genuine Persian) and looking her straight in the eye, she was at a loss for words. Neither had she expected him to be so good-looking. She hid her confusion behind combative armour. "Well? What do you have to say for yourself? You earn a good income?"

"What I earn's my business, Mrs. Gambarasi."

"You say everything is your private business. Well, that isn't so. If you're going to live in the same house as my Joey, then some of your business is *my* business." After prolonged discussion, Sophia and Joe had decided they could safely leave the interview with Phyllis's friend to Sophia, although Sophia was worried she might lose control and threaten to geld him if he so much as thought of placing a finger on her Joey.

"Frankly, Mrs. Gambarasi, I am against involving Joey in the deal. It's Phyllis that wants Joey in."

"Oh . . . I know what I wanted to ask you. Do you drink alcoholic beverages?" Sophia knew that men lost control of themselves when drinking hard liquor and afterwards hit women when their sexual machinery didn't function properly.

"I rarely drink. And I don't smoke."

Sophia thought that was too good to be true. Every man she had known from childhood smoked and drank. "You're a recovered alcoholic?"

"Of course not. I do not drink. I never have."

"You're religious?"

"I am an atheist."

"Is that why you're against Joey moving in?"

"No. I have the misfortune to be in love with Joey. Her being in the house could distract me from my work."

"In love with our Joey? Does she know? Have you told her?"

"I think Phyllis has. We're hoping familiarity will erode my feelings for Joey. You know, alter love to indifference."

Sophia was unsure what to say. "But what are your intentions toward our Joey?"

"My intention is to protect myself. I'm not a marrying kind of man. To be honest, I fell in love with Joey the minute I saw her, but I don't think she feels anything for me. In any case, as I've said, I'm not the marrying sort."

"Are you . . . you know . . . a homo?"

"No. I am not homosexual."

"There's no shortage in Hollywood. If you're a pervert, I won't allow Joey to live in the same house with you."

"I'm not."

"Then why . . . ? It's natural for a man to want to marry the girl he loves."

"It's natural for a man to want to have sex with a woman he loves."

"So that's the reason you're luring Joey into your house!" Sophia moved her body in such a manner that it reminded Arthur of a boxer preparing to attack, left hand forward, right at the ready to deliver the knockout blow.

"It was you who said it was natural for a man to want to marry a woman he loves. I merely pointed out that men marry women they imagine they love in order to have sex with them. And I should also point out that what applies to men equally applies to women. I'll go so far as to assume that's why you married Joey's father. Now, is there anything else you wish to discuss?"

"Discuss! We haven't discussed anything yet. I want to know something about you. And so does Joey's father."

"You can tell Mr. Gambarasi that I'm a temperate man, a hard worker, and under no circumstances would I ever inflict myself on Joey. Is that what you want to hear?"

"It sounds okay. How old are you?"

"Thirty-two. But my age is not relevant to what we're discussing."

"You look older. But beards do that. You're going grey early. Where were you born? Where'd your parents come from?"

Smouldering panic flared in Arthur and he pressed an elbow against the inside pocket which held his fraudulent birth certificate. "New England," he tersely replied.

"If you hadn't told me you're a genuine American, I'd have taken you for one of those smart-alec English actors who come to Hollywood looking to make a bundle. My husband can't stand them."

"Neither can I, Mrs. Gambarasi, neither can I."

The interview was not going as Sophia planned. She and Joe had intended that the combination of her authority and their imposing residence would rip away any defenses Phyllis's friend would erect and expose him to be what Joe called a "flake," one of those men who arrive in Los Angeles in old automobiles and latch onto women with nine-to-five jobs. "Joey says you're a script writer."

"I'm not a script writer. I am an author. The movie rights for one of my stories was purchased by the studio where Joey works. I agreed to write the screenplay. That's how I met Joey."

"You have family in Boston?"

"I have no one in Boston."

"You said you were born in New England."

"That covers a number of states." He dowsed flaring panic. "Do I have to pinpoint the precise hospital, in the precise town?"

"There's no crime in asking, is there? I know where I was born. And which month and which day. As does my husband. You didn't come out of nowhere, did you? Well?" Sophia went on the attack. "For all I know, you could've spent the last ten years in jail."

"Oh, no. I spent years in a place far worse than any jail. I spent the war years in the guts of a freighter." He thought of embroidering the tale, but decided against it. "Then three years crossing the country by bus." He almost slipped up and said he'd done it to regain his sanity. "To renew my contract with America." That stopped Sophia's advance. She retired to her position in front of the French doors.

"I'm not accusing you of not doing your bit in the war effort," she said. "But I want to know something of your background. You're not ashamed of it, are you?"

The direct question left Arthur with no choice but to say, "I come from an obscure village in New Hampshire." There it was, floating in the air between them. "I may or may not have any living relatives there, but what I do know is that I've worked hard all my life." He could not stop himself from adding because (for a change) it was the truth, "And have earned my living as a writer since I was seventeen." He would not allow her to impugn his authorial dignity. "I am a master of my craft, Mrs. Gambarasi. And before I leave, let me repeat that I have no intention of harming your daughter." He turned to go while Sophia, motivated by the need to have more to report to Joe blended with an onrush of respect for what Phyllis's friend had said about himself, trotted across the room to prevent him from walking out.

"You don't have to leave, do you? Would you care for a drink? Ginger ale? A cup of coffee or tea?" She stood between Arthur and the entrance to the living room. "I didn't intend to offend you, but my husband and I want to make sure that our Joey will be happy living with you and Phyllis." In the management of household affairs, even in business matters, Sophia was relentlessly practical—her one vulnerable spot was Joey. On the one hand, she wanted Joey to marry and provide her with grandchildren she could spoil, but on the other, she feared Joey would end up in a series of loveless, childless marriages. She'd seen many like that in Hollywood. But if it turned out that Joey did marry this man, she would certainly have lovely children, because Joey was beautiful and Phyllis's friend as handsome as any movie star.

Although she would never have admitted it, least of all to herself, Sophia wanted to relive her life through Joey. It has often been said that fathers strive to fulfil ambition through sons, but it is not so often recognized that mothers seek to fulfil their dreams of love through their daughters. Sophia loved Joey for what Joey had been, but even more for what Joey, if properly managed, could become: the perfect mate and mother. When Arthur tried to walk around her, she grabbed his arm and held it. "We're both trying to make Joey happy, aren't we?" she appealed.

"No," he said. "If Joey being happy coincided with what I want, so well and good, but I won't go out of my way to make her happy. Phyllis wants Joey to live with us and, since I respect Phyllis, I've agreed. If I'd known I was going to be grilled by her mother about my past life, I wouldn't have come." It was a bravado performance, but it had no effect on Sophia who had grown up in a family where men had customarily bellowed and pounded tables and had married a man who did the same.

"Maybe you could call in again," she said.

"There wouldn't be any point."

"We could get to know each other better. You could tell me about your family. Did anybody go crazy or have fits, or anything like that."

"My family's full of crazies. Every second one's a lunatic." Arthur pulled his arm from her grip and forced himself to stroll, not run from the house. Once beyond the gates he wandered along the roads, uncertain which to take to get back to the house. Eventually he reached Santa Monica Drive where he halted a cab that delivered him safely to the little pink house in Beverly Hills where he sat at the kitchen table to have supper with Phyllis and give her a detailed account of his encounter with Joey's mother. "You know," he concluded, "for a minute there, I thought she was going to ask for proof I could do it with Joey."

"What!" Phyllis leaned over the tray, coughing and spluttering as she laughed while swallowing bits of sour dough bread. "Oh, my God! That's the funniest thing I've heard in ages. Listen, Matt: Sophia won't even put on a swimsuit and get into their pool if a man's around, and she refused to have a single man and an unmarried woman attend her dinner parties together, which means half the stars at the studio have never been inside Sophia's house. They wouldn't like the dinners anyway, she never serves anything to drink but ginger ale."

"Where's Joey's mother from?"

"Monterey. Her father and grandfather operated a cannery there. Now the family owns hunks of land in the Carmel valley. That's why Joe married her.

Ernest Langford

There's more behind Joey than her pretty face: there's fields of artichokes, tomatoes, lettuce, broccoli, asparagus, onions—hundreds and hundreds of acres."

"Why didn't you tell me before?"

"You might have fallen for Joey for the wrong reasons. You do like getting and hanging onto money, don't you?"

This was the wrong thing to say. "Listen, Phyllis, while you were flaunting your ass at an elite girls' school in New York, I existed in absolute poverty, knowing my mother let every tradesman who came to the house stick his filthy hands on her body in return for stale bread, rotten meat and spoiled vegetables." Arthur radiated anger. He stood and leaned on the table. "So don't you ever lecture me on what I might do to get a few measly bucks." Phyllis's side of the table rose, Arthur's collapsed, and both watched helplessly as plates and uneaten food slid onto the floor. "Sorry," he finally said, "I didn't mean that to happen."

In silence, they straightened the table, gathered up the spilled food and coffee mugs, mopped the floor and attempted to restore some order to the meal.

"I'm sorry," Phyllis said.

"It doesn't matter." They stood on either side of the table, uncertain how to deal with the spectre that had unexpectedly arisen between them.

"But I feel I should apologize," she said.

"For what? You're not responsible for what happened to me and my mother. It's just that I go a little wacky when I'm reminded."

"I understand. Or maybe I should say I do my best to understand. Maybe I'm envious . . . jealous."

"Jealous? Of what? To have lived in poverty?"

"Perhaps the experience . . ." she murmured.

"The experience! Let me tell you something about poverty. It stunts the body and cripples the mind. It rots teeth and gives children rickets." They sat at the table and began picking large, shiny black grapes from a bunch lying across a bowl of oranges they had picked from their tree. "You can't imagine eating grapes like these, or picking oranges and figs from trees in your garden. Those are beyond your comprehension. You never look up. You nose is always to the ground, like a pig shuffling in leaves for acorns."

"But it's given you insights I'll never have."

"It gave me a hatred of poverty. And of the people who create and deliberately exploit it."

"Still you don't write about social problems."

"I write about problems that arise from social problems. I write about women who marry men they don't love because they had no opportunity to go out and look over available men. And so they're stuck with men who'll never satisfy them. And the men they marry are ground down by menial work and consumed by the hatred they feel for the women who hate them, and a loathing for the children that result when tipsy men with beer-proud cocks force the women to fuck on Saturday nights. There's no love squandered in poverty. It's a lost world."

"Some day," Phyllis said, "you'll write a very great novel about that world."

"I wonder." He shook his head, then held out his hand to her. "But nothing's changed between us?"

Phyllis managed a bleak smile. "I hope not, but I'm not counting on it," she said.

That same night Arthur had a strange, disturbing dream. He awakened in the same bed where he slept and saw Joey leave the bed and get into another bed with a stranger. He called her, but she ignored him and began caressing the stranger. He then left his bed, pulled the faceless man away from Joey, drove him from the room and began beating Joey, first with a cloth belt, then with one made of thick leather, while she coiled in a fetal position in the middle of the bed. While beating her, he noticed that the room was a narrow, low-ceilinged attic, filled with tattered clothes and assorted clutter. He stopped the beating, then moved around the room, urinating into its dark crannies, like a dog staking out territory. The dream was so real that when he awakened, he expected to find Joey lying beside him. Instead, Phyllis was there, lying on her back, lips parted, rhythmically breathing. To reassure himself, Arthur turned and passed a hand over Phyllis's belly and onto her breasts, but preferring sleep to sex, she rolled onto her side. He curled against her bottom and pushed his penis between her thighs and lay there, trying to make sense of the dream, asking himself if it could be related to the unsatisfactory conversation he'd had with Phyllis. It wasn't his fault he'd fallen in love with Joey, he hadn't planned it, it had just happened. Maybe he would've forgotten all about her if Phyllis hadn't proposed that Joey share the house with them. Why had Phyllis done that? Wasn't it an invitation to calamity? After all, it wasn't as though he was an inexperienced adolescent, sick with first love, and he certainly wasn't sexually deprived. If anything, he would be willing to reduce his sexual activity with Phyllis and use the saved energy for work. Of course he was up to it, he was up to anything sexually, but now that he'd begun to write a novel in addition to the short stories, perhaps he ought to think more about conserving his energy. It was a heavy load. The novel was set it a small midwest town located alongside a major river (the Mississippi wasn't specified). A stranger comes to town and gets a job in a restaurant. The novel concludes with a devastating flood that sweeps the restaurant away. He was at the point in the manuscript where he had to decide if the stranger or the restaurant owner's wife—they had become lovers—should be drowned. His inclination was that the woman should die, the stranger survive and wander on into the sunset. He saw the novel as a meeting of the static and the seeking, where the static loses out. Arthur thought the novel was pretty good and was holding it back to surprise Phyllis. He had chosen an episodic structure because he had not yet freed himself from his early single-theme novels and the short story formulae which had worked so well for him. He hoped the intensity of the passions revealed in the characters would bridge any structural defects in the novel.

When not actually writing the manuscript, he would spend time reflecting on his work and had concluded that his major weakness was in structuring his stories. He reread a recent short story and was horrified to notice places where he blithely leaped across structural crevasses, trusting the emotional thrust of his characters to transport readers across the voids. He made notes about stylistic problems and tacked them to the wall above his typewriter, which Phyllis then read. She disagreed with his opinion about structure, arguing that too close attention to it would detract from the emotional impact of his work, which was its strength. Besides, she thought while ideally a story or novel should be balanced between structure and content, in practice, it seldom worked out, and most novels, being imitations of life, ended up necessarily reflecting life's weaknesses. In any case, she believed content should always take precedence over structure, for wasn't structure the servant, which had been abundantly proved by the fact that whenever structure dominated, a story or novel was usually a failure. Arthur took Phyllis's comments seriously. After all, he not only respected her judgement, but was also dependent upon her to market his work. Besides those considerations, he didn't feel he could openly disagree with her literary views since she was so much better read than he.

He remembered his unsettling dream about Joey and pressed his naked loins against Phyllis's warm, naked rump, hoping the movement might shake her from the cocoon of sleep, and when she didn't respond, he moved away to watch the morning light slowly slither around the edges of the curtains. His absence succeeded where its presence had failed. Phyllis moved, then he heard her sleep-heavy voice ask if anything was amiss.

"A lousy dream," he said, and narrated it in detail.

"Joey'd never do that."

"She did in the dream." He nuzzled his bearded chin against her breasts to console himself, then copulated with her, though she had asked him to wait until she went to the bathroom and emptied her bladder. When it was over, he rolled away from her to fall asleep, leaving Phyllis to yawn her way to the toilet, then back to bed where she remained sleepless. She thought highly of Arthur, perhaps even loved him, but he was a demanding person to be with. Oh, she was lucky having a man who satisfied her sexually. It must be rare, since every second magazine she read had articles about women who didn't experience pleasure with their husbands. Imagine! Old women, married fifty years, who'd never known what she had with Arthur. Women put up with a lot if they had that, though maybe everything she felt was in herself, not in him. She didn't know. Maybe sex meant more to women than it did to men, although men did most of the talking about it, maybe because they could easily throw off the sensations they felt, whereas women had to catch and experience mutual ones. It was strange how a man's member going into your vagina could make even the tips of your fingers and toes tremble, though she mustn't forget that, unlike Arthur, she'd had limited experience before him. What kind of father would take his son, little more than a child, to a prostitute? And then his mother! She must have been insane. She had to have been, or she couldn't have let him play the role of lover in the same cavity from which he'd emerged only a few years earlier. Of course, Arthur's early novels weren't very good, though it was easy to see why middle-aged, emotionally repressed women might be attracted to them. He'd always need a good editor, someone not afraid to demand rewrites . . . She felt him awaken and said, "Hold me, Matt."

"What's wrong?" he asked. He pushed aside her nightgown and mouthed her breasts.

"Listen, Matt. You mustn't marry Joey."

"You suggested it."

"That was before I realized how dangerous it could be for you. No, don't," she said as fingers slipped between thighs. "Matt, please, it's important."

"I'll stop if you'll explain my dream."

"No. Listen to me, Matt. You mustn't marry Joey. In fact, I don't think she ought to live with us in the new house. I don't know what came over me."

"You'll tell Joey?"

"I'll have to come up with a reason. I'll think of something. I'll say the house is too small."

That might have worked had not Joey, pleading with her parents for weeks, become excited at the prospect of escaping the parental home. She flatly refused to accept Phyllis's reason. "But we agreed, Phyl," she said. Phyllis, watching Joey clamp her lower lip against her upper, knew she was determined to move into the house with her and Matt. It was futile to say more.

"So: you've dislodged the rock," Arthur said when Phyllis told of Joey's reaction. "Now, no matter how fast you run down the hill, you'll never be fast enough to catch the rock and prevent an avalanche."

"Don't be so damn philosophical!" Phyllis snapped. "Remember, it's your skin I'm protecting. You're the one who's liable to end up in the doodoo." Phyllis rarely used such expressions.

And so a few weeks later Joey arrived at the new house in her white Cadillac convertible accompanied by Angela Marcuse, who came to supervise the arrangement of the furniture brought in separate vans. A single bed went into each bedroom with other pieces made from matching woods: Joey had walnut, Phyllis redwood and Arthur mahogany. In the dining room stood a rosewood table and six chairs with a sideboard (unmatched) for storing Wedgwood china (place settings for twelve), silverware and crystal glassware. A slightly worn Persian carpet was laid in the centre of the oak hardwood floor in the living room and around it deep, cushioned couches, armchairs and side tables. Three walls were adorned with prints of French Impressionist paintings, the fourth taken up by windows and a sliding glass door to the patio and swimming pool. A massive butcher's block, surrounded by an armoury of knives, sat in the middle of the kitchen. Suspended above it was a galaxy of copper-bottomed cooking pots and frying pans. Cupboards were filled with an assortment of bowls, whisks, appliances, canisters of flour and sugar and a selection of spices in little metal containers. In the refrigerator stood a bottle of sparkling white wine with a silver cord around its neck, a house-warming gift from Angela. Hanging from the cord was an envelope addressed to Joey. Inside was an invoice for six thousand one hundred twenty-five dollars and forty-nine cents.

Joey stared at the bill, then said. "Why forty-nine cents, Phyl?"

"God knows," Phyllis replied. "Anyway, I thought Angela was using your mother's old furniture."

"She said she needed to get a few new things."

"A few!"

"I'll get a cheque from Daddy."

"You could get Angela to take away her furniture," Phyllis advised.

"Don't you like it?" Joey sounded distressed.

"Of course. I'm not used to it, that's all. But it's fine, Joey, just fine."

That evening, after they had drunk the wine and eaten dinner, Phyllis took Joey aside. "Look Joey, I need a double bed."

"Why didn't you tell me?"

"Didn't you know the third upstairs room was Matt's work room?"

"I'll get the bed changed. But you should have told me, Phyl. I wish I'd known. I mean, I'm sort of the odd guy out."

"No, no. We want you to live with us."

"Mom said Matt was in love with me. That's what you said too, but I don't see how it can be true if he sleeps with you."

"It is true though. But Matt and I have an arrangement. He fell in love with you the minute he saw you."

"I don't know about that, Phyl, I really don't."

"Don't worry, Joey. Things'll sort themselves out, once we've settled in."

Excessive optimism on Phyllis's part? Probably. But why not? After all, the single bed in Phyllis's room was exchanged for a double, and the one in Arthur's room replaced by an ornate writing table Arthur couldn't use because it was too high for his typewriter, though he stored paper and typewriter ribbons in the drawers. No one commented when he took a side table with a kneehole from the living room and used it for his typewriter. Externally, the threesome appeared to have settled in, though flies of discontent buzzed around the periphery of their apparent harmony, one being the restraint Joey's presence exercised on Phyllis's behaviour during intercourse. Another was Joey's apparent inability to grasp that she ought not to turn on radios when Arthur worked. He complained to Phyllis who spoke to Joey, who, so Phyllis reported back to Arthur, agreed to lower the volume. But nothing happened. The radio in Joey's bedroom came on automatically at 8:00 AM, and she didn't bother to turn it off when she went down to the kitchen to make coffee and toast, eat a bowl of cereal and switch on the radio perched on the counter. So, while Arthur could withstand external sounds—cars, airplanes, busses and so on—every other sound within the house had been declared verboten because it interfered with the wavelengths on to which his creative vision was tuned. By rights, Arthur should have directly ordered Joey to turn her radios down, or turned them off himself. But he did neither. Instead, he fumed and complained to Phyllis, who spoke to Joey once more, though when she saw Joey's lower lip rise, she stopped and later told Arthur she thought Joey might be deliberately provoking him.

"She wants you talk to her. You're supposed to be in love with her. Remember? She's got the idea we leave her out of things. I'm sure that's behind her turning the radios up so loud."

"She was told I worked in the mornings before she moved in."

"Joey didn't know we sleep together. She feels we deceived her. I've told her—and Sophia did too—that you love her. But she doesn't understand our situation."

Ernest Langford

A couple of days passed with no change in the volume of the radios until Arthur could no longer stand it. He left his work room cursing, tore into Joey's room, disconnected the radio, then rushed to the kitchen where Joey sat in the breakfast nook, drinking coffee and presumably listening to the radio. "Turn that goddamn thing off!" he shouted.

Joey stood and said, "Don't shout at me."

"Shouting's the only way to get something into your thick head. Turn off that radio!"

Arthur was horrified when Joey, instead of defiantly screaming back as he had expected, began to sob like a small, lost child. Her resemblance to a child was reinforced by her ankle-length, flannelette nightgown. Her aura of helplessness impelled Arthur to put his arms around her and croon, "Don't cry, sweetheart. I didn't mean it. It's just the noise, that's all. Don't cry. I love you." He kissed her eyes and brushed the tears from her cheeks. He kissed her lips again, then, strength matching sexual desire, he carried her upstairs to her bed where he removed her nightgown and, after stripping off his clothes, made love to her in a delirium. Afterwards, when he regained a degree of normality, he stroked her face and high, pointed breasts and said, "We'll get married, sweetheart. We'll live happily—" But he gagged at the words "ever after" and left the sentence dangling. He was confused, he didn't understand why he was making promises, he didn't understand the feelings that overcame him. Was this how a man felt when he was in love? He looked at her and thought there was nothing special about her. And she didn't seem to realize that he had just demolished the sacred membrane her mother had jealously guarded for so many years. He began kissing her again, but she pushed him away.

"We can't do this again. It wouldn't be right," she told him. "I only let you, because you were so unhappy."

"Darling," he said, "I was unhappy because you were crying. I couldn't bear it."

"I'll tell Mom what you did."

"But my dearest, I did it because I felt that's what you wanted. You did, didn't you?"

"It's all right. I don't mind once, but you can't just go on any old how. We have to be married first."

"I know, dearest. And we will be." He wanted to make love again, and although Joey allowed him to kiss her lips and eyes, she firmly crossed her legs and put her arms over her breasts, denying him access to the rest of her.

"I'll shower, then drive over and tell Mom what happened. I'll say she and Daddy needn't worry because we'll get married."

At that moment an explanation for his weird dream came to Arthur. As people often do in dreams, he had turned the sequence inside out. It was not Joey who had slipped from their bed to copulate with an unknown man in another bed; it was he, Arthur, who had got up, leaving the warmth and security of Phyllis's arms, to take virginal Joey, thereby risking (remember the still body on the bed?) himself to being attacked and savagely beaten, perhaps to death, by minions of Joey's father. As he lay beside her with his nose in her left arm pit, he silently cursed her for setting a trap to catch him, and himself for blindly walking into it. He saw it clearly now: Joey was another Martha: smooth, white, delectable bait, waiting for a fool like him to rise to the temptation and set in motion the machinery that would either hook, behead or crush him. Images of village women, images of Heather, Sylvia, Laura, Maria, Martha, Trina and Phyllis passed in slow motion before him, interspersed with brief shots of the prostitutes he had used, the knickerless village girls he watched as they turned cartwheels on the Common, the glossy, mature female thighs he had sighted in streets beneath wind-risen, thin summer skirts. Perhaps his father had been fated to die that day as he fucked a village woman; if so, then he, Arthur, his father's true and faithful son, was also destined to die for the sin of weaseling into the wrong coney burrow. He raised his head to look at Joey's face and saw nothing there except placid satisfaction.

"I have to get back to work," he said. Joey removed her arms from their resting place on her breasts. "Your breasts are exquisite," he said as he leaned over and kissed her small pink nipples before getting up and dressing himself. "So you're going to tell your mother? Do you think that's wise?"

"I'll tell her everything. How you carried me upstairs, took off my nightgown and did it with me, but made up for it by saying we'd get married."

"That about summarizes it," Arthur agreed. "You'll tell her you didn't protest?"

"I won't add anything that didn't really happen."

"Of course not." Arthur sat on the bed and held Joey's hand. "I don't know why, Joey, but I do really and truly love you. I know quite a lot about people, and about love. It's what I write about. Yet I don't understand *why* I love you." He gazed down at her: her round face, her dimpled stomach, down-covered pubis, plump thighs, tapered calves and small feet and thought he had never seen anything so beautiful, but at the same time so monstrously primitive and impersonally evil. "Do you feel anything for me?" he asked.

"I like you. I'll probably like you more after we're married."

"I see."

Once, while on his bus journey through middle-America, waiting between buses, Arthur had sat in a dark movie house and watched a short movie about life forms in the Great Barrier Reef. It showed static organisms opening themselves to sweep in food from the water that passed over them. He had immediately noticed the similarity of these organisms to human reproductive organs, and thought, as he sat in the dark, frowzy auditorium, that there was an awful sameness in every aspect of life. For instance, if he, or if any man, ejaculated semen while swimming in reef waters, the sperm would have entered and fertilized the ova of the grotesque creatures adhering to the coral below. And now, while he knew it was wrong to think so, he couldn't escape the thought that there was something mindless and vegetative about Joey, that she did not exist independently, that she was nothing more than a large white-skinned organism (a sea cucumber?) lying in wait to commence the reproductive process. He hated himself for thinking such derogatory thoughts and for viewing her lovely breasts, even momentarily, as nothing more than mere protuberances. He must call a halt to this train of thought, he must stop digging up ugly comparisons from the pit of his loathsome imagination. But the problem was, he didn't know how to carry on a conversation with Joey and, having at last declared his love for her, he felt he had nothing more to say.

"You'll come back after you've spoken to your mother?" he asked.

"I expect so. Shall I tell her you're sorry for what you did?"

"You can tell her that, although . . ."

"Only if you mean it."

"I do." The conversation with Joey was similar to exchanges he had once had with Martha: jumbles of accusatory "you saids" and retaliatory "I didn'ts," phrases denoting nothing except dumb obstinacy.

Finally, after she reiterated her intention to talk to her mother, she left the bed and the room, while he sat down on its edge, scared and despondent.

She returned. "You're still here," she said.

"I was just about to leave," he replied. She began dressing, while he watched, fascinated by her indifference to him. As she pulled her white dress over her head, he stood and said, "Well, I'll get to work," to which she replied, "Okay." And that was that.

He heard Joey's car leave, sat at the little table and, though he tried to work, nothing happened. An image of himself talking to Sophia Gambarasi appeared before him on the wall and refused to leave. He heard Sophia's voice saying that she knew how men were, and his own voice assuring her that he was an exception to the rule. He saw Joey describing what he had done, and Sophia rushing to the telephone to pass on the terrible news to Joe, who after saying "Leave it to me" removed an outsized razor from his desk drawer and ordered his thugs to pick up Arthur, take him to a deserted movie set and cut off his balls. He told himself that such a thing could not possibly happen, that Joey would return to announce that her parents had blessed their prospective marriage. He told himself he would be a faithful husband to Joey and within a year they would have a child. But panic churned in his gut. He paced the room; he ran down to the front door and out in the street to see if Joey's car was returning. He ran back to the house into the living room and outside to stand beside the pool where Phyllis and Joey vigorously swam lengths every evening and he dog-paddled across the shallow end every afternoon after finishing work. He ran back to his work room, looked at the typewriter, turned and ran into the bedroom where he brought out and stuffed a few clothes into his battered suitcase, returned to the work room, latched the typewriter into its case, stacked the pages of his almost finished manuscript on the desk and scribbled on the top page: 'Only five pages to go. I'll forward them to you. Needs a title.' Then he telephoned for a cab, rode in it to the bus depot, purchased a ticket for a bus, which the ticket agent said would eventually take him to Fairbanks, Alaska.

Feeling utterly depressed, Arthur joined a line of passengers moving along a ramp to the place where the bus driver stood waiting to examine tickets before allowing them to climb the steps into the bus. As Arthur handed over his ticket, the driver said, "Going home?"

"No," Arthur said, looking past the driver at the approximate spot Phyllis had welcomed him to Los Angeles. "Change of scenery." He boarded the bus, stowed his two cases in the overhead rack and seated himself in the first seat across from the driver, waiting for his exodus from California to commence.

CHAPTER

20

"WHAT'S HAPPENED? COME ON, JOEY, SPILL THE BEANS. WE'VE been telling each other secrets for years."

Phyllis had returned to an empty house, Arthur's manuscript and his note, and hadn't known what to make of them until Joey came back and explained. They sat on Phyllis's bed, Phyllis with Arthur's manuscript in front of her, Joey holding crushed kleenex which she used to dab away the occasional tear that spilled from her eyelids onto her cheeks.

"But Mom said Matt raped me," Joey reiterated.

"Joey, what your mom says isn't important. She's always been paranoid about you and sex. Now, exactly what did Matt do?"

"I've told you. He shouted at me to turn off the radios."

"I'd already spoken to you about that. Then what?"

"He came over and began kissing me and saying he loved me."

Phyllis pointed a finger at Joey. "I told you he'd fallen for you."

"Then he carried me to my room."

"You mean he actually carried you up the stairs?"

"That's what I said."

"Go on."

"Then he pushed my nightie up to my shoulders."

"For God's sake, Joey, why must you spend half the day running around the house in your nightclothes? Well?"

"Then he took off his clothes."

"But what were *you* doing, Joey? That's what I want to know."

"I was lying on my bed."

"Waiting for Matt to get on top of you. Right?"

"He didn't at first. He kissed parts of me and said he loved me and that I was beautiful. I don't want to talk about it any more, Phyl."

"But you *are* going to talk about it, Joey. And something else too. You're going to telephone your mother and tell her you provoked Matt into having sex with you."

"I didn't."

"Yes, you did, Miss Josephina. I know how you go about getting your way. I watched you conning your parents when you were little. But don't try to con me. And if you don't tell Sophia what really happened, I'll never speak to you again. Never."

"You're jealous, that's why."

"I'm not. I don't mind sharing Matt. But don't try to fool me, Joey, I know what you did, because when you were a kid I saw you holding your breath, making your mother run around in a panic."

"I helped furnish this house."

"So you did, Joey. But if anything happens to Matt as result of what you've told your mother, I'll throw you and every stick of furniture out of the house. Now, finish telling me what happened this morning."

"I've told you. He did it."

"Did you tell him you didn't want to? Did you, Joey? Did you push him away?" Phyllis was now shouting.

"No."

"You're a sneaky little bitch, Joey. You just lay there on the bed and didn't do one thing, though inside yourself you crowed because you'd got Matt into bed and set him up to feel guilty."

"That's not true."

"Oh yes, it is. You told him you were going to tell Sophia."

"Only because years ago I promised Mom I'd tell her if anything happened."

"For God's sake, what does a promise made by a silly, ignorant girl matter? So what happened next?"

Joey sketched figures on the blanket. "I told you. He said we'd get married."

"And you agreed?"

"Yes, and I told him he couldn't do it again until after we were married."

"What a hypocritical bitch you are! What a scheming little tart! You play your goddamn radios to prevent Matt from working, then bugger up his life by blackmailing him after getting him to screw you."

"I didn't blackmail him."

"You make me sick, Joey. I don't why I ever thought of you as a friend."

"That's because you wanted Matt for yourself."

They continued to sit on the bed, Phyllis against the headboard, Joey at the foot—Phyllis consumed by anxiety, Joey by a blend of defiance and pleasure because Phyllis was thoroughly rattled.

"Maybe's he gone to the airport and taken a flight somewhere." Phyllis spoke more to herself than to Joey. "Or a train, but probably he's on a bus because that's what he's done before. So which direction would he go? Not south. That would mean crossing into Mexico. He can't go west and he came *from* the east, that leaves the north. But where would he go up north?"

"Anywhere?" Joey suggested.

Phyllis ignored her. "He could go along the coast or through the Central Valley." She chewed the nail of her left thumb. "If he goes along the coast into Oregon, he'll eventually end up in Ashland or Coos Bay."

"I was in Coos Bay once, with a movie crew. Horrible place. Fog and rain all the time"

"The crew should've drowned you."

Joey began bawling like a child. "How could you wish I was dead!" she wailed.

"It's what you deserve. Oh, forget it. I didn't mean it. I'm upset."

"I was being honest with Matt. That's all."

"I know all about your wacky version of honesty. Stop bawling. So, let's assume he wants to get as far away from us as possible. He's not going to get off the bus in some hick town to chat with the locals. No. He'll go straight through to San Francisco or Oakland, change buses and keep going north. God! He might even go to Alaska! We'll drive north. You and I, in your car."

"But what about my job?"

"They won't even notice your absence, Joey."

"I didn't try to take Matt away from you, Phyl," she said. "I never thought of it."

"You never think, Joey, that's your problem. Now, pick up that phone and set Sophia straight about what happened. Go on."

"She won't believe me."

"You make her believe it, or—," Phyllis stopped when the bedside phone rang. She hoped it was Arthur calling to reassure her. She snatched it up. "Oh . . . it's you, Sophia," she said and handed the receiver to Joey. "Go on, tell her," Phyllis hissed. While Joey said "Yes, yes" in response to whatever Sophia was saying, Phyllis printed on the back of the last page of Arthur's manuscript a message for Sophia: 'I invited Matt to have sex with me. What happened was my fault. I'll never forgive you if you and Daddy make trouble for Matt.' She thrust the paper under Joey's nose and Joey dutifully read it. She sounded like an inexperienced actress reciting from an audition script. When Joey finished, Phyllis grabbed the receiver from Joey and began speaking.

"Are you listening, Sophia? This is Phyllis . . . Will you shut up and listen! Are you listening? Matt Scheiler did not rape Joey. Repeat. Matt did not rape Joey. She invited him to screw her."

"I didn't," Joey protested.

"I repeat, Sophia. Joey invited him to have sex. So you and Joe lay off the heavy stuff. Yes, he'll marry her. God knows why, because she's nothing more than an empty-headed, spoiled brat." Phyllis slammed down the receiver and told Joey to leave because she was going to bed.

"Let me sleep with you, Phyl. I'm upset."

"All right, provided you don't talk." Phyllis put the manuscript into her briefcase, began undressing, then stopped. "Maybe I should go to the bus depot now. He might still be there. No. He wouldn't hang around. He'd get the first bus out. But we'll have to start early." She continued undressing. "We'll get on the 99 and pray he's going that way."

"I wish I had a figure like yours, Phyl," Joey said.

"Forget it," Phyllis said. "Anyway, there's nothing wrong with yours."

"I'll be like Mom some day."

"Stay away from French fries and ice cream." Phyllis went into the bathroom.

When she returned, Joey said, "Remember how we'd plan what we'd do when we grew up? You were going to write books."

"Now I read other people's."

"I planned to direct movies. Remember?"

"We're failures, Joey, you better get used to it." Phyllis got into bed.

"I'm not a failure. One day I'll have my own crew. You'll see."

"Okay, I'll see. Now go to sleep." Phyllis turned off the bedside lamps.

Joey spoke into the darkness. "I wouldn't do a anything to hurt you. You know that, Phyl. Honest. Apart from Mom and Daddy, you're the one person I love. My brothers don't count."

"I know." Joey wriggled across the bed and Phyllis, sighing, embraced her. "You should start loving Matt."

"I don't want to take him away from you. Honest."

"We'll share him."

"Remember how you used to hold me when I woke up from a bad dream? I hated it when you had to go back east. I used to wish you were a boy so we could marry and have children when I grew up."

"You can have a baby with Matt."

"Why don't you?"

"I guess there's no reason why not. But I'm not sure I'd be a good mother."

"If we both had one."

"Don't be silly. And for God's sake, get onto the other side of the bed and go to sleep."

But, though Phyllis wanted to sleep, sleep danced just beyond her ken, mocking her. Much of the night was spent in desultory give-and-take with Joey, who dug up memories of the summers they'd spent together, then both dozed until they were jolted awake when the alarm rattled at seven. They got up, hurriedly showered and dressed, bolted down orange juice and cornflakes, packed overnight cases and drove across the city to the coast highway.

The landscape slowly changed before Arthur's red-lidded eyes from elegant palms to scrub-covered hills and salt-battered conifers. With much changing of gears, the bus ground its way along the narrow highway cut into hill and cliff side with the ocean always visible through dusty windows on the left side of the bus.

"This ain't the fastest way to go no place," one driver told Arthur. "When the road was first cut, guys thought they had all the time in the world to get from L.A. to Frisco. Now, guys in a hurry go overnight on the train, or drive like hell through the San Joaquin Valley. And flying's getting big now. You on vacation?"

"Sort of."

"Looking for work?"

"Not exactly."

The driver shifted into high gear. "You ever thought how roads start out? I'll bet Indians had a trail around here, maybe right where this road is, then the Spaniards make a mule track, then we come along, grade it with steam graders and build bridges, and now we want to bring in the 'dozers. But people say: 'Wait a bit now, 99's historic. We can't chop it up.' Hell, you should see how they chopped up the rest of the state. Know what I think? They kept it like this is because William Randolph Hearst didn't want no four-lane highway in front of his castle."

"That could be," said Arthur, who knew nothing of Hearst and San Simeon. "Guys who own castles are particular where roads go, unless they also happen to own the roads."

"That's a fact," the driver nodded. "For all I know, Hearst could own this here highway, like he owns one hell of a lot of real estate in this country. Hey, wouldn't you think a guy'd get fed up with having to worry about all that property and dough? Jeez, I got a house mortgage and that's enough for me."

"You know the old saying: 'The more you have . . .'"

"Is that ever a fact. Like movie actors that collects wives."

"What about movie actresses who collect husbands?" Arthur countered.

"You bet. So what're them dames looking for anyways?" The driver glanced over his shoulder to make sure no female passengers were listening. "A guy with a bigger one than the one they just ditched? Beats me. It's like my old man used to say about his axe: it ain't size, kid, it's how you uses it."

"That is so true," Arthur agreed.

"My old man seen a lot of this country. I tell you. He helped cut down them forests in Michigan and northern Wisconsin, then high-tails for California and starts on the redwoods. Hey, you seen that picture of half a dozen guys standing in a redwood undercut?"

"Not that I recollect."

"My old man's one of them guys." Arthur's opinion that Americans were the most loquacious people on earth was confirmed once again. In every town in America where he had stayed or strolled around, people had talked about themselves, their husbands, wives, girlfriends, boyfriends, cousins, aunts, uncles, relatives to the fourth degree, the President, Henry Ford, movie stars, the church they attended on Sundays, whether people living in other parts of the world had any right to use America's God without paying for Him, whether an east-west line should be drawn to keep the coloureds from going north, the condition of their hearts, intestines, bowels and bladder and the colour of their piss and the texture of their shit, whether the U.S. ought to kill off the Russkies with atom bombs and maybe do the same to any other country that's a pain in the ass and no goddamn use to America, Oh yes, Arthur thought, Americans talked, they had to talk, couldn't stop talking, because once they did, they'd see the flaws in their country, so they kept on talking and while they talked they persuaded themselves into the belief that if they stayed around long enough and worked hard enough they'd achieve perfection. The thing was, Arthur thought: America was a land of social illusions; a country where people accepted mirror images as truth and where pseudo-slavery continued in many states and millions of low-paid workers lived in grinding poverty in urban slums everywhere in the country.

Arthur gazed through the bus window, impressed with Big Sur, got off in Monterey, nauseated from the twists and turns of the highway, ate breakfast in a restaurant adjacent to the depot, and turned his back to the signs that beckoned him to visit the fisherman's wharf made famous in a Steinbeck novel and to tour Pebble Beach in an open coach to view estates of the rich and famous and the fabled golf course by the sea. He paid for his meal and went into the men's washroom where he sat on a lavatory seat feeling sorry for himself and where, after much straining and grunting, he managed to excrete a lot of gas and few lumps of faecal matter. He then walked around the bus depot, unaware that four eyes were observing him from the car park.

"Let's hope he bypasses San Francisco," Phyllis said. "If he goes to Oakland, we'll know he's going through Sacramento, then all we have to do is go on ahead and wait."

"He looks kind of sick," Joey remarked.

"Bus travel does that."

"So what do we do now?"

"We'll wait to find out which bus he takes. If it goes through Salinas, we'll know it's heading north via the Central Valley."

"Maybe he'll go past Uncle Eugene's farms."

"We could count the artichokes."

"That's not funny, Phyl."

"It's not meant to be. Your uncle's artichokes are like the stars—uncountable."

Joey yawned. "Why don't we speak to Matt now," she said. "Why wait?"

"Because Matt's desire to eat a decent meal and sleep in a decent bed has to be greater than his panic. That's why. Don't worry. I understand Matt, Joey."

"I could go back to Los Angeles."

"You have to be here. It all happened because of what you did. There, the bus is getting set to leave. There's Matt. The bus'll exit on the other side of the depot. Drive around so we face it."

"He might see us. Couldn't we go in and ask where it's going?"

"No. Do as I say. We'll drive ahead and look for a decent roadhouse and have something to eat."

"We could stop and see Uncle Eugene."

"No. Move, Joey, move. The bus is pulling out." Joey obediently drove around the building to a point where they faced the bus and could see where it was bound on its destination slot. They crouched in their seats and bowed their heads as the bus growled past them, and when it was gone, Phyllis punched Joey's arm and said, "We guessed right, Joey. Sacramento via Stockton."

Funnily enough, Arthur saw the car and glimpsed the women's bowed, scarf-covered heads, but, preoccupied with his physical state and the indefinable sense that he had made a terrible mistake by surrendering to panic and bolting, he didn't recognize them. The psychic, physical and emotional components he had gathered together in the course of his three-year journey across America in an attempt to forge a new identity for himself had all but vanished. Once again, he was the old panic-stricken Arthur Compson blindly groping his way from village to village through England's northwest counties. He recalled the day he went to the Baltimore brothel with the cook from the freighter, for that was the day he had begun (or so he believed) the real transformation of

Arthur Compson into Matt Scheiler. External changes had been easy: changing his name, getting a crew cut, growing a short nautical beard, buying new clothes, these had sufficed for a while, but the inner person and the psychological and creative drives that had made up the man Arthur Compson were not so easily expunged or remoulded. This explained his periodic hesitancy, his stopping and starting as he gathered sufficient psychic strength to tackle the Mississippi River and the Rocky Mountains. These two geographic barriers had functioned as symbols against which he could measure the growth of his Matt Scheiler identity. He had erected the barriers to test himself, mistakenly believing that by breaking through them and reaching the Pacific coast, his transformation into a new individual would be confirmed once and for all. Discovering the magazine in Phyllis's dresser drawer and the spell of unconsciousness which followed should have warned him that Arthur Compson still thrived within the shell of Matt Scheiler, but he had ignored the signal because, due to Phyllis's support and influence, he believed his present and future as a writer was assured. So he had pushed back the dread and fear he first felt when he saw the photograph and read the article. The panic which had driven him from Los Angles could be likened, he thought, to a deep, subterranean force which volcanically explodes when least expected. As Phyllis had explained to Joey, though Arthur was not to know that, his panic had to run its course in order to burn itself out.

Joey and Phyllis journeyed, sometimes behind, sometimes ahead of Arthur, always unbeknownst to him, through California's prolific Central Valley, through the Klamath Mountains into Oregon, where, at the bus station in Ashland, they greeted his arrival as he stepped from the bus with a cardboard sign on which they had printed in large capitals: OREGON WELCOMES MATT SCHEILER, GREAT AMERICAN WRITER.

"Oh, Christ," Arthur said when he saw it and quietly wept, thankful he had been rescued from the foundering vessel of his former, tortured self.

With suitcase and typewriter in hand, Arthur got into the back seat of Joey's white Cadillac and was driven to a motel on the outskirts of town where Phyllis had rented a unit with a kitchenette, two double beds and a bathroom. Arthur was treated like royalty, even Joey, reared to believe what she wanted took precedence over everybody else's desires, smiled agreement and didn't mention the real or imagined discomforts she had experienced while trailing Arthur around California, nor did she speak of her parents, or the incident which had precipitated Arthur's flight. While Arthur lay on the bed and tried to relax, Joey and Phyllis sat in the kitchenette and played gin rummy. That evening they had dinner at a nearby restaurant, strolled around the downtown, then returned to the motel where Arthur retired to one bed and Phyllis and Joey to the other.

During the night Arthur was awakened by Phyllis whispering in his ear. "Everything is settled," she murmured as she got into the bed. "You can return to Los Angeles and marry Joey, or you can marry her before going back." Keeping his voice low, Arthur told Phyllis that he wasn't going back. He could not go back, he said. The panic he had experienced had bitten into his psyche and had ripped away the self-confidence which three years of wandering across America had built up in him. He was now seriously wounded and would need time so that scars could form over the cuts and bruises. His lips against Phyllis's ear, he whispered that more than anything else he regretted falling in love with Joey because she was not a woman who could come anywhere near matching Phyllis. He said he wished he could reverse time and decide not to attend the studio party where he met Joey. He told Phyllis that she would continue to be the most important person in his life and acknowledged his contradictory feelings and asked her to forgive him. He couldn't see her face, but he knew she was silently crying. When he felt her tears drench his cheeks, he turned and lapped them up, feeling an uncomfortable blend of sadism and genuine sorrow. He told her they need not end their relationship and tried to move between her thighs, but she shook her head and denied him access. Phyllis was prepared to accept friendship—personal and professional—but she couldn't bring herself to allow casual sex with Arthur. She had given too much in the past and would rather forfeit everything than to hope and pretend that one day he might return to her.

"What about Joey? What should I do?" Arthur whispered.

Phyllis advised him that Joey ought to be rewarded for setting the record straight with Sophia and for patiently following him from one end of California to the other. At least, he ought to give her a hug. Arthur, aware he was being pushed out of Phyllis's intimate life, went to the other bed to awaken Joey and put his lips to her ear to whisper that he couldn't stop thinking about her during the day and that she haunted his dreams at night. He moved his lips from her ear to her mouth and found her lips eagerly puckered. From there, his lips touched her chin, her neck, then her nipples that also agreeably puckered before he removed her the bottoms of her Baby Jane's, then moved to guide his erect penis into her. He could not be sure if the sounds Joey made were the spontaneous result of pleasure or deliberately manufactured to let Phyllis know that she, Joey, was now the boss. Indeed, Arthur would never know, because he wasn't able to muster the courage to ask, complicated by the fact that during all the years of his marriage to Joey, her responses to their physical union were so varied that Arthur was never sure from one love-making to the next how she would respond. She remained an enigma, which partly explained why Arthur continued to be fascinated by her and wove her personality into characters which appeared in the novels he later wrote, where she was often likened to those spring days when it is impossible to forecast what the afternoon would be like by observing the glorious morning sunrise.

The next day the threesome made the round of the town's churches until they found an elderly minister who agreed to marry Joey and Arthur "shortshrift" (as the minister put it). The most peculiar part of the ceremony came during the confused minutes when the minister requested Arthur to place a ring on Joey's finger. Of course, Arthur had no ring. Joey looked at Phyllis who, after sighing deeply, removed a gold band from a finger and gave it to Arthur. Afterwards, Arthur wanted to return the ring but Joey refused to take it off. Before Phyllis left for Los Angeles, Joey purchased another of greater value, but Phyllis wouldn't accept it, which Arthur took to mean that while Joey might have him in the flesh, Phyllis preferred to believe she possessed everything else.

After seeing Phyllis off, Joey asked, "What do we do now?"

"Get to know each other," Arthur replied. "We can drive around Oregon and Washington."

After seeing the local sights, they decided to spent the winter in a small town on the Olympic peninsula at the northern end of Puget Sound in a rented house a stone's throw from a ferry slip where trucks, cars and foot passengers were disgorged four times a day. On clear days, they could see the mainland peaks: Baker, Rainier and St. Helens, rose-tinted at dawn and in the evening resembling, Arthur said, Joey's beautiful, round, white bottom. Other days, dense fog covered the Sound, and they would walk hesitantly past the ferry slip, hearing fog-bound ships calling out like lost children wailing for mothers. Arthur hated the dark winter days when rain fell unimpeded, but when Joey suggested returning to southern California, he wouldn't hear of it. Phyllis flew from Los Angeles to spend Christmas with them, bringing the final proofs of Arthur's novel. She didn't like the ending and thought it would be improved if one of the lovers, perhaps both, drowned in the flood instead of the woman returning to her husband. Arthur rejected the idea, saying extra-marital affairs were often products of boredom or lack of an interesting occupation, therefore his ending reflected a truth about life. It was right and proper, then, for the woman to return to her husband and help rebuild the couple's home and business premises after the devastation caused by the flood waters. Phyllis shook her head and sniffed disapproval, but allowed her author the prerogative to end the novel as he saw fit. Joey talked of flying to Los Angeles to visit her parents, but after a private talk with Phyllis decided against it. Phyllis had warned Joey against leaving Arthur, lest she return to an empty house. On the whole, Joey didn't regret marrying Arthur, though on dull, wet days she wished she could be back at work in the studio. Still, Matt was slowly putting together a movie scenario for her, and once it was completed, she could start making her movie. It did not have to be made in Hollywood. Any location would do.

They saw in the New Year together, sipping champagne, which no one really enjoyed. Joey, usually very temperate, got tipsy on two glasses, fell asleep and was carried to bed by Arthur, after which he tried to talk Phyllis into making love for old time's sake. Phyllis, unaffected by the wine, shook her head to indicate refusal, then started to quiz Arthur about his plans for the future. Arthur shrugged and asked if Joey had indicated she was discontented. No, Phyllis replied, only that she wanted to have a baby and expected him to produce a movie script for her. "Are you using anything?"

"Certainly not!" Arthur was wine-indignant. "If she wants a baby, she can have one."

"You still love her?"

"Of course." He then went on to tell Phyllis that by rights he should've fallen in love with her because they operated at the same intellectual and emotional level. When Phyllis objected to the word "operated" (which suggested they were mechanical and deficient in emotion), Arthur took her hand and swore he still valued her more than any man or woman he had ever known. Phyllis asked if he had suffered any spells since marrying Joey and was pleased when he told her, that apart from a head cold, his health had been good. By then, Joey had awakened from her nap and was descending the stairs, blinking and yawning. She wanted to know why Arthur and Phyllis were holding hands and why Arthur hadn't come to bed.

"We're holding hands because we're talking about you," Arthur said. "Come on, Joey, I'll take you to bed." After Joey and Arthur left the room, Phyllis went through the kitchen into a small, cold room that an earlier owner had altered from a store room into a guest bedroom. There she spent a chilly, rather miserable night regretting she had come to visit a couple who clearly didn't need company to infuse change or excitement into their lives.

"Why were you holding Phyl's hand?" Joey asked again when they were settled under the down quilt.

"I was thanking her for bringing me to the studio party where I met you. Just think, sweetheart, if I'd not known Phyllis, we wouldn't be lying here together. I held Phyllis's hand because she was part of the coincidences that led me to you."

"You've made that up. You make things up to avoid the truth."

Joey's perspicacity amazed Arthur, and he levered himself onto an elbow to examine her face. He was beginning to understand that while Joey's intellect might be limited, there were certain things she saw very clearly. "Okay. I held Phyllis's hand because I'm tipsy and because she's the second most important person in my life. That's the truth."

"I'm the most important?"

"Number one."

"Would you . . . you know, with Phyllis . . . if I wasn't here?"

After a pause, Arthur said, "Maybe, but I'd miss you."

Joey yawned and her champagne-soured breath flooded into his nostrils. He took her into his arms and told her she had the prettiest mouth and teeth in the world. He put his lips on hers and said he wished he could go down her throat and explore every part of her body on the inside. She smiled satisfaction, told him not to be crazy, then made him promise never to hold hands with Phyllis again, even for sentimental reasons. After extracting the promise, she encouraged him to make love and gave a loud prolonged cry when she climaxed. Arthur wondered if she'd done that on purpose, hoping Phyllis would hear. He realized, too, that Joey had indirectly told him that if he expected her to give up things for him, he must reciprocate by sacrificing his sexual relationship with Phyllis. He thought he had underestimated (perhaps Phyllis had too) Joey's ability to sort through information and reach conclusions, which caused him (ever proud of his own insight into human minds and emotions) to feel put down by her ability to dupe him. He wondered if he had been indulging in gross self-deception. They spent the next day driving Phyllis to a hotel near the Seattle airport where they all spent the night, Phyllis in a separate room, which Arthur thought symbolized the degree to which the relationship among the three had deteriorated since his marriage. He was forced to acknowledge that their tripartite relationship, formerly managed by Phyllis, was now controlled by Joey. The next morning they had an early breakfast, drove Phyllis to the airport where she insisted they not wait to watch her depart, then ferried back across the Sound and along the winding highway to their house which somehow didn't appear as attractive as when they first inspected and leased it for a six-month period.

"We could leave any time," Arthur suggested.

"But shouldn't we see the lease out?" Joey had surprised Arthur by being a penny-pincher who, although she had never shopped for groceries in her life before, was genuinely outraged at the price of food when she and Arthur walked around the market. Arthur's preference in meat was lamb chops and beef steaks, whereas Joey preferred fish, though she always complained about the odour in the kitchen when Arthur cooked it. At first, she hadn't believed Arthur had once cooked for a living. Both liked Chinese food and frequently ordered it in, and they had also discovered one or two good Japanese restaurants. Before the war, Joey's parents had employed a Japanese cook, but he, and their gardener too, had been interred after the Japanese bombed Pearl Harbour. Joey, echoing her parents, never forgave the Japanese for the surprise bombing, although she told Arthur that their invasion of Korea and China didn't bother her at all. Arthur was uncomfortable with Joey's political views and tried to avoid discussing politics because she talked like a fascist. When weather discouraged them from leaving the house, they usually went to bed in the afternoons, got up to fix an evening meal, then returned to bed. They preferred this arrangement to sitting around because when they did that they invariably bickered, though there was never much substance to their quarrels; that is, nothing except Joey's obstinacy and Arthur's tendency to make snide comments. Those occasions ended with Joey sobbing and saying she wanted to go home and Arthur apologizing for everything said and unsaid, pleading she mustn't leave because he couldn't live without her. It was much, much easier to turn up the thermostat, go to bed, make love, sleep, awaken and kiss again, and when the glum afternoon finally faded into night, get up and sauté a steak or a fish fillet, prepare a salad and scoop out ice cream from a container for dessert. They might play a few games of gin rummy, which Joey had taught Arthur. She always won. At nine, they returned to the unmade, still warm bed to cuddle and make love.

Joey had begun to say such things as, "I suppose one of these days I'll stop menstruating" and "Why do you think it's still happening?"

Arthur said he didn't know, but in fact was beginning to feel uneasy that she hadn't conceived and wondered if the continuation of Joey's menstrual periods had anything to do with him. However, he said nothing, there being no evidence one way or the other.

Every month Phyllis sent Arthur a cheque drawn on his royalty account and also forwarded a larger cheque from Joey's parents, who were determined to protect Joey from sinking into poverty, which would have been humiliating for them and degrading for her. Every day Joey faithfully made a call to Los Angles (collect) and mother and daughter talked for an hour. Sophia said Joey must be miserable living in the boondocks, and Joey replied she was having the time of her life. "I'm happy, Mom," Joey would say, "I'm telling you, Mom, I'm happy." Once, Arthur wrote 'Ask her to visit us' on the gin rummy pad and passed it to Joey, who shook her head, crumbled up the paper and dropped it on the floor. A conversational variation occurred when Joey began saying, "No, not yet, Mom." The following month, another variation: "No, I'm not. No, he doesn't," which Arthur took to mean Sophia was asking if he used a contraceptive, which irritated him. He told Joey he didn't want her mother poking her nose into their business.

"She can't help it," Joey said. "Besides, she has a right to know how I'm doing. All she does is ask if I'm pregnant. That's all."

"And says it's my fault you're not."

"No. She says it often takes time for a woman's body to get used to the idea of having a baby."

"Hm . . ." Arthur murmured. He was of the opinion that a female's reproductive organs were indifferent to what the rest of her body felt, but he went along with Sophia's explanation. He liked the idea of having a child, especially a girl, but was opposed to having anybody or anything in the house that would interfere with his morning work routine, though he had to admit when he and Joey saw a heavily pregnant woman in the street or in a store, he wished he could have the experience of watching Joey's belly slowly expand until in the ninth month she and her womb-enclosed infant would be suspended in time, like perfectly ripened fruit on a tree, waiting to drop to earth.

They didn't regret leaving, even though spring flowers profusely glowed beside front doors and crimson disks opened on tall camellia bushes and neighbours appeared in front gardens to express curiosity about the young couple who had occupied the house during the winter, and whom they had not, until now, had an opportunity to meet. A writer. Oh, how interesting. Had he met so-and-so who lived at the end of the street? Was he aware of the writers' club that met monthly to discuss, criticize and offer advice on each other's work-in-progress? Arthur was annoyed when Joey blurted out that his novel, *Waters of Babylon,* had just been published. Her revelation capped his determination to leave the place. But Joey saw things differently: Why didn't Matt want people to know about his novel and his wonderful collection of short stories? And what about the movie? Was he ashamed of his work? When she, Joey, got around to directing *her* movie, she'd boast about it and promote it everywhere. Still, in the end, she did what Arthur wanted. She packed the suitcases and sulkily drove with him the next morning onto the ferry which they had so often watched approaching and departing from the slip.

That evening, Joey telephoned Phyllis from the office of the motel where they were staying. "Matt behaved like a mad man when I mentioned his novel," she said. "You'd have thought he had something to hide from the way he dashed back to the house and began packing."

"He's a recluse, Joey. Remember that. It not so unusual in writers. There are blabbermouths like Norman Mailer and Truman Capote and a few others, but most writers prefer being left alone. And they certainly wouldn't want to get mixed up with writers' clubs. Think about it, Joey. Would any respected Hollywood director let himself get mixed up with a small town photography club? Matt's a professional, and it's up to you to keep people like those away from him."

"Well, maybe, but all the woman said was—"

"I know what she said, Joey. I deal with readers and book clubs every day. Now, this is the way to handle it: Say that Matt never gives interviews. Understand, Joey? Never. So, any idea where you're heading?"

"To Vancouver. That's in Canada. I don't know where we'll go after that."

"Hm. Did Matt get the novel?"

"Yes. He only looked at the title page. He's into another. He calls it the 'David novel'."

"Oh, that one." While lying with Phyllis in the dark hotel room and revealing his past, Arthur had told her he planned one day to write the story of David in a contemporary setting. And he continued to be fascinated by the appalling consequences of David's lust for Bathsheba and his betrayal of Uriah, her husband. When Phyllis remarked the story had probably been told many times, Arthur grimly replied he didn't care, he was going to tell it again. "Keep in touch, Joey. One of these days you'll find a place where Matt wants to settle down. Remember, you're not the first wife to tag along behind her writer husband. You're in good company."

"That's easy for you to say, Phyl. But what happens when I get pregnant?"

"You'll manage. Are you okay for money?"

"We have plenty. But I've been having trouble with the car."

"Trade it in."

"But I love my Caddy."

"Cars are like shoes, Joey. They wear out. Trade it, before you get stuck on the side of a road somewhere in the Canadian wilderness." Although Phyllis had received extensive formal education and considered herself one of America's literary elite, when she thought of Canada (which was rare) it was to produce fleeting images of endless ice and snow-covered tundra where two Americans had once quarrelled over the exact location of the North Pole and who had reached it first. To her, Canada was a northern appendage of America, and of little value except to supply fresh water to the great American lake system which served to flush American-produced pollutants into the Atlantic Ocean via the St. Lawrence River. That Canada was the second largest country in the world and might well have a greater reserve of fresh water than any other nation didn't interest her, for Phyllis, along with millions of other Americans, innocently believed in the endless enormity of America and its inexhaustible resources. There was nothing America could not produce, or could not do if it put its mind to it. It may seem strange that an intelligent, highly educated person would actually believe such chauvinist nonsense, but nevertheless Phyllis assumed that whatever Americans thought, said and did was superior to whatever the rest of the world thought, said and did. And she could hardly be blamed for sharing a view of America also held by the rest of the world, where people gazed with awe and admiration at American gangsters so infinitely superior to their own home-grown thugs, and whose young people aped American styles and jargon brought down to earth by glamorous angels from Hollywood's heaven.

"Phyl thinks I should get a new car," Joey told Arthur, whose parsimonious soul trembled at the idea of laying out money for an automobile.

"Can't it be fixed?" he asked.

"Phyl said I wouldn't want to risk it breaking down in the middle of the Canadian wilderness."

"What wilderness? Canada's a settled country."

"Phyl said . . ." What ensued next was one of their little quarrels which ended, as they usually did, when Arthur saw Joey's lower lip rise and clamp over her upper. The next morning, instead of continuing their journey north to the border, they drove from car lot to car lot, where Arthur fretted and Joey expertly bartered with sales staff between calls to her father soliciting his opinion on the trade-in for the Cadillac offered by dealers relative to the price of a new car. Joe advised his daughter to hang tight because the Cadillac still had a lot of value. Eventually, Joey's father talked with a salesman who offered a trade of six hundred fifty dollars accompanied by a down payment of one thousand for a new Chevy Malibu.

"You'll never own a better auto than this beauty," the salesman assured a tearful Joey.

"Mom and Dad gave me the Caddy when I was sixteen," she wept.

"Safety before sentiment," commented Arthur, then asked, "you been to British Columbia?"

"Oh sure," the salesman replied. "It's no different to here, except the liquor laws're blue. Canadians're nice folks. Lots of 'em own property here. And they come down to shop in droves."

"Rains a lot, eh?"

"Depends where you are. The interior's dry as Utah or Nevada, but the winters are colder. Y'know, it'll take a day to register the Malibu and get plates, but what's a day when you've got a new car? Your father sounds like he's a big shot."

"He's vice-president, finance, at Galaxy Studios."

"We'll leave the dealer plates on your Malibu," the salesman told her, thereby buying time for the dealership to find out if Joey had more than ten dollars to her name and if the California automobile licensing authority had in fact issued a valid driver's licence to her. He was surprised to learn that Joey not only had a clean driving record, but also had more than enough cash to purchase three or four Malibu's had she wished to do so. As a footnote, it can be said that the car dealer replaced the sparkplugs in the Cadillac, adjusted the timing, rolled back the odometer, washed and polished the body, then sold it for more than Joey had paid for the new Malibu, though of course none of this mattered to Arthur and Joey. They were enthralled with their new vehicle, which, so Arthur remarked, seemed to gobble up the miles between the town where they had purchased it and the U.S.-Canada border.

The Canadian border officials politely smiled, asked who they were and why they were entering Canada; Joey and Arthur politely smiled back and identified themselves as Mr. and Mrs. Scheiler of Beverly Hills, California, entering Canada to tour British Columbia and enjoy its spectacular scenery. The border official wanted to know why they were driving a car with Washington state licence plates.

"Oh . . . I never thought. Well, you see, my other car acted up, so we traded it in for this one."

"Do you have a California driver's licence, Mrs. Scheiler?" The officer remained polite, but his voice was now flat with suspicion. Car thieves were common at the border crossing.

"Of course." Joey sorted through her handbag and handed over her driver's licence, proudly remarking she had never been in an accident.

"What is your destination in B.C.?" the official asked as he handed the licence back to Joey.

"Vancouver, then into the interior," Arthur explained. "Generally smooching around."

"Into the Okanagan, sir?"

"That's right. The Okanagan," Arthur agreed, rolling his tongue around the word.

As they drove away from the border station, Arthur repeated the word. "Okanagan. Okanagan. What a delightful word. O-kan-aa-gan. Let's go there first. Where's the map? Look, there's a lake there, a really big lake. If you have a baby girl, we'll name her Okanagan. It's probably an Indian word."

"I'd like to have twins," Joey said. "A boy and girl."

"No. Just have a girl, a duplication of you. Okanagan . . . Okanagan. I feel at home already, as though I've been here before."

"Maybe in another life." Joey believed in reincarnation, although the exact process was hazy to her as were time and location of the phenomenon.

"Perhaps," Arthur agreed. He examined the map. "We take the Number One highway. It goes though a place called Hope. That's an auspicious name, isn't it? We can name our girl Okanagan Hope."

"We'd need a home."

"We have one, Joey. Remember, you and I and Phyllis own a house together."

"I don't feel as if I have anything to do with that house. It's Phyl's."

"We'll have another house by the time Okanagan Hope arrives."

"Where do we get onto the highway?"

"It's not far. The car salesman was wrong. Everything *is* different in Canada. Don't you notice the difference in the air, Joey? There, ahead, there's the sign. Number One."

"Why are you happy all of a sudden?"

"It's the name, Joey, the name. O-kan-aa-gan. Hope. Everything's in a name, yours and mine. *Matthew!* I'm a gospel—a long, tendentious, moralizing gospel. It weighs me down. If we had other names, we'd be different people."

"I wouldn't." Joey slowed down, bore to the right and edged the car into the highway traffic. "Where does the highway eventually end?"

Arthur spread the map over his knees and traced the red line across it. "Alberta," he said, "but we turn off long before that. Do you love me, Joey?"

"I guess so. This isn't much of a highway, is it?"

"But it'll do. You already know I fell in love with you the moment I saw you. Think about that, Joey. It was an incredible happening. I mean, how is it possible to know just by looking at a person for ten seconds that that person is the one you want?"

"Maybe you knew the person in another life. Maybe you carry what you want and feel into another life."

"That's very perceptive, sweetheart. Because of your ancestors, the person you end up loving likely falls within a specific range of possibilities. Look at those mountains, Joey. You know, when I was on the east side of the Rockies, before I got to L.A., I had to gird my psychic loins before I could tackle them."

"Don't be silly. *Gird your psychic loins,*" she repeated and laughed.

"It's true. I needed to defy them. I had to stand on little hills and tell the peaks they couldn't defeat me."

"You could've flown over them."

"That would've been an admission of defeat. Why don't we find a place where we can eat and spend the night?"

"Okay," Joey agreed.

"Maybe tonight we'll start our little girl."

"You never can tell," Joey agreed. "Though I've never been able to tell what was going to happen from one day to the next. All I know is, I have to get up, eat, sleep and go to the bathroom."

"And make love, Joey, don't forget that."

"Oh yes, I mustn't forget that."

She steered the Malibu into a driveway and stopped before a motel office. "You know the first thing I'm going to do when we get to the Okanagan?"

"No. What?"

"Teach you to how to drive. That's what. I don't want to ferry you around for the rest of my life. Now, let's reserve a room."

Arthur leaned over kissed her. "To think of all I went through before I found you, Joey, it passes understanding. And yet I did it. I did it. I crossed oceans and continents to find you. Think of that, Joey. Think of it. Maybe our meeting was determined by a conjunction of stars so far away that millenniums had to pass before light and energy flowing from that cosmic union could reach me and make me walk into that garish movie set where I found you waiting for me."

"But I wasn't waiting for anyone. Certainly not you."

He kissed her again and drew her lips between his before saying, "That's the point, Joey. That's the very point. You couldn't know. Neither could I. But if we *could* see it, if we *could* understand what really happened, then we'd realize that our being here together, kissing, is nothing short of miraculous."

Joey wiped her damp lips with a paper tissue. "I suppose that's one way to look at it, but I don't know if getting mixed up with you was good or bad luck for me. Now, please stop talking and get us a room."

CHAPTER
21

AT FIRST THEY FOLLOWED THEIR USUAL HABIT OF STAYING in motels on noisy highways, but after a couple of days they went to a small hotel and rented a room from which they could look out over a park and across the lake to the curvaceous hills on the other side. The hotel was quiet and once they were settled in, Arthur set up his typewriter and picked up where he had left off in the David novel. The city was a comfortable size, which meant that within days they were meeting the same people in the afternoons when they walked through the parks that bordered the lake and halted to turn back at a spot where an insignificant looking stream signalled the point at which the lake drained. It looked so puny when compared to the lake itself which stretched almost a hundred miles to the north.

"This lake doesn't like giving away its water," Arthur said. "It's a miser."

"It's just rain," Joey said.

"Rain! There's more to a lake than raindrops. There's memory and determination." He looked across the lake. "When I was younger, I thought rivers and lakes the most mysterious creatures on earth."

"But they're not alive."

"I thought they were. Then, I believed everything was sentient. I still do, more or less." Since starting the David novel, he had become preoccupied and moody, given to fixedly staring into empty space, or at a tree, or at a part of Joey. When she asked about the novel, he wouldn't say much, only drew her attention to the apple orchards in full bloom across the lake, or the lake itself and how beautiful it was.

Joey thought Arthur's reaction to the lake excessive. True, its setting in an orchard-filled valley was lovely but, in her unspoken opinion, other lakes, other orchard-filled valleys were just as pretty. Moreover, that her husband was intoxicated with a place so far from southern California, her parents and the movie industry made her uneasy. He reminded her of a puppy she'd had as a child, whose idea of playfulness didn't coincide with hers. He preferred to yap, run around aimlessly and dig up her mother's flowers. The dog was a pure-bred fox terrier, unsuited as a small child's pet, and eventually, after nipping Joey's arm one day when she grabbed hold of its stubby tail, it disappeared forever from her life. Obviously, Matt wasn't a puppy, only excited and, like a puppy, chasing after something, not knowing exactly what it was.

Each morning, Joey awakened to find Arthur standing at the windows, watching as the sun rose in the sky and the shadows retreated from the lake and the distant brown hills that enclosed it. He often invited her to come and watch, and she, yawning and rubbing her eyes, would leave the bed to join him at the window and agree it was beautiful, though in her heart of hearts she didn't think the sight anything special. Joey was a realist, and she put the scene beyond the window in the same category as Matt telling her she was beautiful. Well, perhaps she was, to him, but it was a love-endowed beauty, for she thought of herself as being no different from dozens of other women. Still, it was pleasant having Arthur slip an arm around her waist and tell her she and the morning sunshine were a perfect match.

One morning, standing at the window, Arthur told Joey there were times when he regretted not being a painter, for then he would have been able to paint pictures of her in this place, standing nude, communing with the flowering trees.

"And having mosquitoes and bees sting my bum," Joey said.

"No . . . pollinating you. There's a lot to be said for paintings versus novels. A picture's immediate. You don't have to write half a million words to get the message across."

"I skip pages. I can't stand seeing all those words on a page. I always read the end first."

"You're an insult to a serious author. It's what comes of being raised on movie scenarios."

"Oh no. If you read the end of a novel first, you'll know if the author had known at the beginning what the end would be, or just tacked on. Movie directors do that."

"And there'd be a danger that novels would be written to formula. Also, now I think of it, that's the limitation of painting, the image once fixed, never changes. Whereas we know people change, sometimes a lot. When you were a girl, did you ever imagine you'd marry a writer and stand here, looking out over a beautiful valley filled with flowering fruit trees? Of course not." He hurried on to prevent Joey making an ill-considered reply. "Did I foresee myself standing at this window with you? No. If I went back into my childhood, I'd be incapable of imagining what in fact has happened to me and the degree to which I've changed. In a way, I've become another person. I mean," he quickly added, "I used to be more opinionated than I am now. I thought I knew everything."

"You're still like that."

"No. Now, I listen to what people say. Have you changed much?"

"I suppose I have. But I don't know how or why."

"Learning to read changed me. I started with the Bible, though I'm not sure how I learned to read it because I never attended school. Where I lived in New England, lots of children never went to school."

"Honestly? Really and truly never? Not even for one day?"

"Really and truly. Instead, I read Bible stories: I wandered around Sinai and Palestine with the Hebrews, I sat with them beside the waters of Babylon, I was there when David stood on the roof of his palace and saw Bathsheba bathing, I watched Solomon build his temple and followed him when he slept with one of his eight hundred wives and concubines. I even watched Mary bear her baby and after he grew up I played marbles with him. I fell in love with Mary Magdalene and became a peeping Tom when I watched her entertain her customers. But I got out of the habit of reading the Bible after I became impatient with Mary's son for not escaping when given the chance. It was years before I understood he was a devoted masochist. I switched to Shakespeare, though it took a while before I understood what was really going on in his plays. I finally grasped that Shakespeare listened in on the thoughts of the characters he created. They spoke through him, he was simply the medium. By means of his art, he transformed his characters from the petty individuals they started out as into everything noble, romantic, comic or evil possible in humankind. Do you think Shakespeare's mind could have created Hamlet? I don't think so. Hamlet, and everything Hamlet thought and did, came to Shakespeare the same way the ghost of his father came to Hamlet. I don't compare myself to Shakespeare, of course, but I do know when I write without listening to voices, what I write is flat, without life. But when I listen quietly and allow people to reveal their inner selves, I occasionally produce something that's quite decent. A writer is like a musician in this regard. You have to train yourself to listen, but because you think you know a lot, you try to butt in and interrupt. That's the biggest mistake a writer can make. It's one I make because, sometimes, the voices are faint. I don't know why. Like someone on the telephone from the other side of the world, or calling from some Antarctica of the mind. I know the people are real, usually I see them clearly, but if I don't listen carefully I can't hear their voices. I think that's why I misrepresent them sometimes. For a writer, misrepresentation is a sin—a capital crime, from an artistic point of view . . ." He abruptly stopped, coughed and said, "Why am I talking like this at this time of the day? I embarrass myself." He patted Joey's bottom. "If I were a swarm of bees, I'd make straight for this."

Joey leaned against him, hesitated, then said, "I should have started my period yesterday."

A man bird-watching in a boat on the lake moved his binoculars to observe a group of newly-arrived violet-green swallows. As his binoculars passed over the hotel facade, he spied a man behind a window kneel, raise a woman's nightgown and kiss her belly and golden pubic down. The bird-watcher was so embarrassed at having unintentionally intruded into their privacy that he hurriedly turned and missed spotting a pair of white-throated swifts examining the hotel facade to gauge its suitability as a nesting site. Of course, the flustered bird-watcher could not have heard Arthur murmuring to whatever he imagined was inside Joey's womb: "Hi there, Okanagan. How's it going? Lucky you, I wish I was in there too." Neither would he have heard Joey say: "It's not certain yet. Put down my nightie, Matt. There's a man on the lake looking in this direction with a binoculars;" or Arthur's reply: "He's a harmless bird-watcher." Joey turned from the window, Arthur resumed looking out the window and the bird-watcher continued to scan the water and sky.

Later, while Joey and Arthur were having breakfast in the hotel coffee shop, the bird-watcher entered. When the hostess asked if he'd seen anything special, the man replied that the sighting of rare species occurred only once in a blue moon and he had been content to spot a pair of wood ducks and some violet-green swallows. The hostess, who referred to avian species as "birdies," smiled blandly and led him to a booth where he sat and began to write in a notebook.

Arthur spent the morning working, then after lunch he and Joey drove into the hills and along a rough gravel road on the east side of the lake. Arthur thought the panoramic view was sensational, even Joey was enthused, saying how fresh and aromatic the air was with its scent of sage brush. "I should've kept my convertible," she said.

"I'll buy you another," Arthur said, At that moment, he was prepared to give Joey anything.

"It doesn't matter that much," she said. "It's just nice to wish for something you don't happen to have at the moment."

"Stop! Stop the car!" Arthur suddenly ordered. Joey, responding, pressed her foot so heavily on the brake that the Malibu skewed in the gravel creating and created a dust cloud.

"What is it?" she asked and, trembling, lay back on the seat. "What on earth's the matter?" Arthur did not reply, but left the car and walked through the dust to the side of the road where a narrow track wound down the steep hillside.

"Come and look," he called. Joey left the car and crossed the road to stand beside him. "Look," he said, "just look at that!" At the bottom of the steep incline, beyond a clump of pine trees and an orchard of what looked like cherry and apple trees, they could see a cove enclosed by two small promontories and a beach where blue water rested on red-gold sand. Beside the track, partially hidden among the sagebrush, was a small plywood sign: *For Sale by Owner. No agents.*

"Haven," Arthur whispered. "It's Haven."

"There's nothing there," Joey said.

"There's a shack. See, to the left, behind the bushes? Let's go down."

"I'm not driving down there."

"We'll walk. It's not that far. Come on."

"I don't know why I should," Joey said, but she followed Arthur down the track, which looked as if it was seldom used.

"Smell the pines, Joey," he said as they passed beneath the Ponderosas. "Intoxicating, eh?"

"You couldn't get a car down here," Joey said. "Never."

"Look at the bees, Joey. Walk close to me, so they won't make a bee line for your bottom."

They reached a grassy patch, then circled a spreading lilac bush and a small house trailer, propped on concrete blocks, came into view. "It's a haven," Arthur repeated.

"You mean heaven?"

"No, I mean a haven, a refuge, a sanctuary. It's perfect." They walked over the crackling sand to the lake edge and Joey slipped off her sandals to stand calf-deep in the water.

"It's surprisingly warm," she said. "Someone's coming, Matt."

Arthur turned and saw an elderly man emerge from the trailer. "We're just looking at the beach," he shouted as he began to walk toward the man. "You lived here long?"

The old man looked at Arthur, tapped at his ear with his forefinger, returned to the trailer, then came back, fumbling with a hearing aid and said, "You were saying?"

"Just that we were passing and saw this place. We're Joey and Matt Scheiler." The old man nodded, told them his name was Don MacPherson and that he was pleased to meet them. "We noticed the *For Sale* sign." Arthur's voice trembled as he spoke.

"Don't want to stay on, now the missus's gone. She was the one as liked it here. She'd get up in the morning and go for a swim. Every day. Fine swimmer. Won races when she was young."

Arthur tried to prevent interest from showing. "So it's up for sale?"

"That's the idea. Twenty acres." A sly expression appeared on the old man's face. "Good land."

"Pretty steep," Arthur countered.

"Protected from frost," MacPherson said. "Faces south."

"What're you asking?"

The old man paused and eyed Arthur, gauging his degree of enthusiasm for the property. He twisted his lips, then shot out: "Five thousand an acre."

"Five thousand," Arthur repeated.

"Let's go, Matt," said Joey.

"I could have a realter look at it," Arthur suggested.

"I wouldn't do that," MacPherson warned. "Those guys'll screw you right and left."

"Like you're trying to," Joey said from a distance.

The old man waved a reproving finger. "This is prime land. Look at the waterfront. You could build a fancy hotel here."

"We don't want an hotel," Arthur said. "Just a quiet place to live."

"What you've got here's a bit of rough land with an old trailer stuck on it," Joey piped in.

"That's a good trailer," MacPherson defiantly claimed. "You won't get a better trailer than that."

"I'm not interested in owning a trailer," Joey countered. Arthur knew she wasn't interested in the property, but had to admire the way she persistently pushed down its value. "There's no sanitation, not even a septic system." Arthur wondered how Joey could possibly know about septic tank systems.

"Yes, there is," the old man angrily said. "You think I'd expect my missus to go outside and squat? I got a proper outhouse in them lilacs. Go on, take a look."

"Let's go, Matt, there's no point in talking to someone that thinks what he's got is perfect."

"Look, there's five acres of Lamberts and five of Red Delicious," MacPherson said. "Look at the flower on them trees."

"Hah! Flowers! My Uncle Eugene has 400 acres of all kinds of fruits, and his trees don't look like these overgrown, unpruned stumps in the ground!" Joey's attack was devastating. And relentless. "The lake water doesn't look any too healthy. It's probably polluted. Five thousand an acre?" She waved a disdainful hand at the slopes. "Five thousand an acre for that? You must be crazy!" Having delivered that broadside, she grabbed Arthur's arm and forced him to leave. MacPherson watched them climb the slope, then disappeared into his trailer.

"You're a wonder, Joey," Arthur said as they plodded up the slope. "I'd no idea you knew anything about fruit trees."

"I don't," she said, "but I've heard my uncles talking about their orchards."

"Really? Then it's even more amazing."

"I won't let anybody take me for a ride. No, sir. Besides, do you know how much the property would cost at five thousand an acre? One hundred thousand! And we don't have that kind of money. You don't make enough."

"I make enough to keep us on easy street, Joey."

"It's peanuts compared to what Daddy makes. And my uncles."

Arthur halted beneath the pine trees. "If having money means so goddamn much to you, why don't you get in the car and bugger off to California?"

Joey, surprised by his anger and unsure what caused it, looked back and tried to smile appeasement. "What's the matter?" she finally said.

"I'll tell you what's the matter. You dared compare my work with your uncles' crops and with that crap your father's studio churns out."

"I didn't mean it like that."

"Then what *did* you mean when you called what I do peanuts?"

"I meant . . ." She began to cry. "I don't know why you're so angry when I'm doing my best to help you buy this place, though it doesn't really appeal to me. I'm not saying you ought to make more money." She turned and stumbled on toward the road, while Arthur, horrified by the effect of his angry outburst, scrambled after her.

He reached her as she was about to open the car door. "Joey, darling Joey, I didn't mean a word I said. We'll forget this place. I don't want it. It's not important, a flash-in-the-pan. Sweetheart, don't cry."

He held her, and she, having released several jumbo sighs, stopped sobbing. "But you *do* want it, I can tell."

"At different times in my life, I've wanted things, but I always gave them up when I realized I couldn't have them. But the one thing I'm not going to lose is you, Joey."

"I'm not a thing."

"Whatever you are, I'm not losing you. You're quite right. There are carbon copies of this place everywhere."

"I didn't say it isn't pretty, but it's so far away. What if one of us got hurt?"

"We won't."

"But Matt, you don't know. Maybe the old man's wife had a heart attack and died before he could get help."

"Don't speculate further, Joey. My fever's gone. Now, let's get back to the hotel and tomorrow morning we'll pack up and go back to L.A." At the time, Arthur meant what he said and immediately became as determined to abandon the idea of purchasing the property as Joey grew resolute in buying it. "Look Joey, I was carried away with the idea that I'd found the perfect spot for us. I was mistaken. So we'll forget it."

"But I know you want it."

Variations of this exchange continued for the remainder of the day and escorted them to their room and into their bed. "Well, for the sake of argument, let's assume I still want it," Arthur said. He lay with his hands folded beneath his head, a position taken by people who imagine reason directs their lives, a sort of recumbent rationality, while Joey lay on her left side in a foetal curve with her hands folded beneath her chin. "What will the repercussions be if I don't get it?"

"You'll blame me," Joey suggested.

"I might. On the other hand, I might shrug and add it to my long list of lost opportunities."

"Maybe we should offer him two thousand an acre."

"As little as that?"

"We'd have to bring in electricity."

"It's not worth it, Joey. Too much hassle."

"If we put a row of quick-growing trees at the edge of the grassy patch, the beach would be hidden from the road."

"That's true. But let's not speculate about what might be, because I've given up the idea."

"Honestly?" Joey had moved until her face touched his. "Honestly?"

"I don't want you to be unhappy, Joey." He turned his head, kissed her forehead, then resumed his position. "Y'know, something occurred to me while we were standing on the beach. The property would make a fine setting for a movie."

"A movie?"

"Yes." He began concocting a script. "Let's say, a young woman's crippled by polio. You know, there's been a lot of that around, practically an epidemic. There'd be shots of her limping into the water, swimming around for therapeutic reasons. Nudity, but not going too far."

"But what happens?"

"Someone comes to the cove in a boat. A sports fisherman."

"Hm."

"The isolation and purity of the setting can be exploited by the camera. Then the man arrives, sets up camp, makes a fire, fries trout, drinks beer from bottle, which he throws into the lake. You know, suggestive of despoiling it."

"But wouldn't he know the woman was there?"

"No. She has a shack that's hidden behind the bushes and trees. You'd emphasize the man's crudeness by showing him peeing in the lake." Arthur was spinning the scenario partly to divert himself, partly to offer Joey a carrot to munch on, but as the jigsaw bits of the plot fell into place, he could visualize its potential. "Of course they meet. That's essential, but they're immediate antagonists. He sees her as a malformed woman, she sees him as a wilderness despoiler."

"Ah!" Joey cried. "I know what happens! He can't swim, so she upsets his boat and then—"

"He drowns, or she rescues him, or he drags her down and they both drown. Something dramatic."

"If I had the right equipment, I could do some wonderful underwater shots. Maybe at the last moment they realize they love each other and die embracing." Joey was so excited she pushed herself up and sat beside Arthur, arms around her knees. "Brando'd be perfect, but he's out of my price range."

"You never know. But I've thought of something, Joey. Small towns usually have theatre groups. You could take a few people and train them. Combine the making of the film with teaching."

"I could. But what about the camera work?"

"I agree you'd need a good cameraman, because half of it'd be good camera work."

In the excitement of their discussion, they forgot they had yet to acquire the property. Joey went to sleep on top of the covers, and Arthur, hands still behind his head, lay awake and embroidered the movie plot before he slept. It may have been the excitement, or perhaps the position in which he was lying, which was unusual for him, or a combination of these and other unknowable causes, but in the middle of the night Joey was awakened by the violent shaking of Arthur's body followed by his collapse into unconsciousness. Joey, terrified, sprang from the bed, bolted from the room and was half way down the stairs to the hotel lobby before she remembered Phyllis telling her that she must never panic if Matt had a spell because he would soon regain consciousness. She ran back to the room, found she had locked herself out and was forced to go down to the main lobby where, in her flimsy nightdress, she invented a cock-and-bull story about sleep-walking in the hall and finding herself locked out. The clerk accompanied her back to her room and opened the door, extracting payment for his services by ensuring she walked ahead and between him and any light fixtures. Joey spent the rest of the night awake beside Arthur, praying to a god she hadn't believed in since her first communion, to bring Matt back to her, and even went so far as to say, "Thank you, God" when she felt his fingers twitch and saw his tongue touch his dry lips.

"You okay? You okay?" she whispered. Apart from normal childhood afflictions, Joey had never been ill or come into contact with sickness. Good sense and policy dictated that while drunkenness was tolerated (to a point) in movie stars, sickness was anathema. In fact, Hollywood was practically a duplicate of Erehwon in deeming sickness as well as lack of physical attractiveness as crimes for which the only appropriate punishment was excommunication.

"Drink," Arthur hoarsely pleaded. Joey ran to the bathroom, brought a glass of water, clumsily raised his head and spilled most of the water over him and the sheet. "Sorry," she said, "I'll get more."

"No, it's okay. It's the dryness." She put the glass on the table, lay beside him and held him in her arms. "When did it happen?" he asked.

"In the night. I don't know the time. You should see a doctor."

"No." The inside of his mouth felt vile and his head ached. "Don't be scared when it happens. It's nothing."

"Maybe you were over-excited," she said.

"Perhaps." That was as good a reason as any he could think of. After having a spell, he always regretted he'd never been able to utilize the event to further his spiritual development. It seemed that all he was ever able to do (his mother might be responsible for this) was attempt to regain his physical strength as rapidly as possible, and afterwards deny anything untoward had happened. Of course, he had learned from his reading that in past ages individuals suffering from various complaints similar to his had somehow been able to use their affliction as a springboard that brought them closer to whatever supreme being was part of their mythology. But the problem for Arthur was that he experienced nothing—a void—during the actual spell and afterwards, only physical discomfort and exhaustion. Moreover, his inbred scepticism caused him to think that those who had claimed unification with their supreme being were deluding themselves. He had tried to interpret his own experiences of nothingness as being alliances with a god (he didn't believe in God) by equating them with what he thought of as his "little deaths," although he didn't find that comparison particularly exciting or helpful. Dying for a short period of time really had nothing to do with elevating the soul or venturing into and exploring unknown spiritual realms. It was a pity, and all rather depressing, but he had to admit that the sum total of his spells were headaches and prolonged physical lassitude. He compared himself to a man who imagines that having sex with a woman will magically expand his understanding of life, but discovers all he has achieved is a bout of incapacitating venereal disease. He had never gained anything from whatever possessed him in his spells, and now it seemed ridiculous to think he had once believed that whatever physical, emotional or intellectual defects caused his spells would be balanced by corresponding gains. It was merely the gambler's consolation, or the naive tenet of the Christian believer that a merciful God would not withhold compensation for suffering. He thought about his mother: Would she have so desperately denied his condition had he suffered from some other illness, say tuberculosis? No. That indeed was a scourge, but on a scale of one to ten, it would only register around six, especially if it were a poet who died from it. You could languish for years before you coughed out your bloody lungs and died, all to the good of your literary reputation. Oh no, you don't quibble when superior folk agree to board and feed a disease, provided they don't engage in embarrassing (to you) behaviour such as screaming or shouting or gibbering in the streets, as in Hasterley where the village idiot masturbated in public and the sole epileptic regularly fell rigid to the ground with a fearful cry. Perhaps his mother, fearing he too might be seen in the street, mouth agape, jiggling his penis in his hand, in her unique way had provided the coolant she believed was necessary to dampen the raging fires of his adolescence. Odd, but that explanation for his mother's conduct had never occurred to him before, though maybe he was going too far, for, after all, his mother did know his father had introduced him to Dot Perks so that he could empty his spunk into her. His ignorance of his mother's feelings (and his father's too) about his unusual physical ailment astounded him. How dare he, who knew so little of himself and his own parents, set himself up as some kind of authority on the lives of others? How could he think that he knew how men ambitiously planned conquest, or how women, on assurances from men ruled by unappeasable lust, opened their arms and allowed access to their sweet loins? No. He would never be able to transcend what had been moulded into him in his mother's womb. He was a mass of contradictions; his mind, emotions and body were at war, each striving to dominate the others. To be as he was, to be forced to experience the terror of merely existing overwhelmed him. He panted like a dog and begged Joey for more water. She suggested analgesics, and he swallowed several tablets when she offered them, but as he gulped down the water, he shivered and thought he would have just as readily swallowed poison had it been offered. He lay back, felt the pain recede and thanked Joey for her kindness.

"That's okay," Joey said. "You're supposed to take the bad with the good."

"I guess," he agreed. Joey then hung the *Do Not Disturb* sign on the door and went back to bed to make up the hours of sleep she had lost. Arthur slept too, due to a sleeping pill which Joey had slipped in with the analgesic tablets. It was one of a number she had garnered from her mother's large collection of pills and potions. Joey belonged to the 'you-never-can-tell' school and would go nowhere without her pill boxes, hidden cash and list of addresses and telephone numbers. She slept through the morning, showered, dressed, then called the main desk, informed the receptionist her husband was indisposed, ordered room service and met the waiter at the door with a finger pressed to lips. She had him place the serving cart by the window, gave him five U.S. dollars, shushed him from the room, sat down and ate a substantial meal: half a grapefruit, scrambled eggs, ham, toast and coffee, then sat at the open window, watching people strolling through the lake side park. She risked disturbing Arthur by telephoning Phyllis's office.

"Oh, Phyl," she whispered, "I just *had* to call you. I had a terrible night. Matt had one of his spells. He's sleeping now. It was awful. I panicked."

"There's nothing to be scared of Joey."

"Well, I was. I ran out of the room and was halfway down to the lobby before I remembered what you'd said. But that's not the worst of it, Phyl. I'd locked myself out and I had to go into the lobby in my nightie. Oh, I'm sure he'll be okay, but listen, Phyl, there's something I have to tell you."

"You're pregnant."

"I wish I was. For a few days, I actually thought it had happened. No. Matt's set his mind on buying property here. It's sort of a cove on Okanagan Lake. It's nice, but we'd have to build a house. And the locality kind of scares me, Phyl, it's so isolated."

"I'd better come up. Can I fly there from Vancouver?"

"I think so. I think Matt's awake. I'll call later."

Joey played nurse and helped Arthur walk to the bathroom and supported him while he emptied his bladder. She went further by undressing and helping him step into the bathtub, holding him as best she could while he groggily turned beneath the shower head.

"That feels good," he said as water cascaded over him. "You're my angel of mercy, only much lovelier."

"No. I'm me," Joey insisted.

Arthur lay against her while she leaned on the tiled walls to support their weight. "Were you ever in love with anybody before you met me, Joey?"

"I'm not really sure I love you."

"You must, or you wouldn't suffer me."

Once again Joey surprised him with her response. "Is love nothing more than willingness to put up with another person's irritating little habits?"

"Do I have annoying habits, Joey?"

"I guess no more than anybody else." It was an unsatisfactory answer, Arthur thought, but he accepted it since she offered nothing more. He stepped unsteadily from the tub and more or less collapsed onto the toilet seat and glumly sat there, eyes closed, refusing to look at Joey's body while she sketchily dried him. He insisted on dressing, and as soon as he had clothes on and was seated at the small table by the window, Joey called the front desk and ordered their room cleaned and the bed made. She then transferred to room service where she ordered a small tenderloin steak, cooked rare, and hearts of lettuce for herself (her father's usual room-service order) and for Arthur, orange juice (make sure it's fresh) two poached eggs with whole wheat toast and coffee for two.

"Phew," said the waiter who took the order. "There's a virago in Room 210."

"You should've seen her last night, tearing around in her nightgown," said the night desk clerk, now sitting in the kitchen on his coffee break. "She said she'd locked herself out of her room. I didn't ask how she managed that, I just enjoyed the scenery. Hope she does it again."

"Some guys have all the luck," the cook's helper complained.

"They're from the States," the room service waiter said, as though that explained everything. "She gave me a five-spot. The guy was lying in bed. He sure looked wore out." The men's conversation became increasingly salacious as they waited for Joey's order to be prepared, then finally fizzled out when the room service waiter pushed the delivery cart into the service elevator.

Joey opened the bedroom door and directed the waiter to lay out the food on the table where Arthur sat. "On your way down, I want you to stop at reception and get them to ring me. I need to reserve an adjoining room for a friend who'll be arriving tomorrow, probably late in day." Joey dismissed the waiter, then explained. "I called Phyllis last night while you were sleeping, to let her know you were okay."

"She wouldn't have known I was unwell if you hadn't called her."

"I know that. We talked about a couple of other things too." Someone knocked on the door. "I hope that's the chamber maid, the sheets need changing." Joey opened the door and a maid entered pushing a cleaning cart. "Be sure to change the sheets," Joey ordered.

"They're changed daily," the maid replied.

"You never can tell," Joey said to Arthur as she sat opposite him. "At home, Mother inspects the rooms, though the maids have been with us since before the war."

"I can't face more than one egg, Joey. I'll have to leave the rest."

"Would you care to inspect the room, madam?" the maid asked. She had a pronounced Scots accent.

"That won't be necessary as long as you've done your job. And in future don't listen to conversations of hotel guests." Joey was normally the soul of politeness, even to busboys, but she had surmised that every member of the hotel staff now knew she had been seen running around the hotel in a skimpy nightdress. Being rude to the hotel staff was her way of fighting back. When she first went to work at the movie studio, it hadn't taken her long to become aware how cruelly staff gossiped when someone got involved in an embarrassing situation, even the stars didn't escape magnification of little mishaps. That was one of the nice things about Matt: he never gossiped about people. When he spoke of them, it was always at a generic level, though he wasn't high-minded or simon-pure or anything like that. Maybe he wrote novels where people did terrible, awful things, but he didn't pick on niggling details, like a pimple on a person's chin (not that she, Joey, had ever had a pimple) and transform it into a erupting rash of skin-scarring boils. No. What Matt wrote about were emotional entanglements that raised people to intoxicating heights or precipitated them into black hells, and of course she knew that one day he would be recognized as one of America's great writers, that's what Phyl said, and of course, Phyl was always correct in whatever she said about literature. Maybe she, Joey, didn't fully understand Matt's reasons for tearing around the countryside, and the little cove he thought so wonderful, in her humble opinion, was no different then tens of thousands of other coves in the world. Still, if he was prepared to settle down, then she'd agree to purchasing the property, because she had to acknowledge to herself she did love Matt in an odd kind of way, though she'd never admit it to anyone except herself. Maybe it had to do with his telling her that she personified everything that was good and glorious in women. In the beginning, she had thought he was teasing her when he talked like that, but she'd come to understand he meant every word. And that was difficult for her, because she couldn't see anything special about herself and of course, compared to what Hollywood had to offer, she was pathetic. Apart from that, she was grateful that Matt had got rid of her virginity, which her mother insisted she retain and had practically made her neurotic. It was so ridiculous. Poof! It was gone, just like that, and it was sort of funny the way Matt had collapsed onto her tummy as though he had just run five miles, and then the expression on his face when she told him they couldn't do it again until they got married! That was even funnier, for although their marriage was delayed, due to Matt's flying the coop, she had become increasingly impatient at having to wait, because she'd discovered she wanted to re-experience what they had done that morning in the bedroom. There were only two things she really wanted to get out of life: one was to direct a movie; the other, to have a baby. She hoped and continued to believe Matt would provide the wherewithal for both, and it looked like buying the lakeside property was going to be part of the deal.

"I can see why Matt likes the place," Phyllis said as she stood with Joey on the road, looking at the cove. Arthur had pleaded weakness as his excuse to remain at the hotel so that Joey could be alone with Phyllis and talk freely. "Would you object to living in Canada?"

"There's not much difference from home, except this place's so far from anywhere. I'm not used to that."

"If you're going to live here, you should think about getting a passport. And Matt too."

"He'd need a photograph. And you know how nutty he is about having any picture of himself taken."

"I think I can talk him into it. We'll do everything through the office. You'll just have to sign the forms."

"Okay, fine with me. Shall we go down to the cove?"

"Sure. The fruit trees are lovely," Phyllis commented as they walked down the trail.

"They need pruning."

"That's nothing. Oh, the beach is spectacular!"

"Matt thinks I can use it as a setting for my movie." Don MacPherson came out of the trailer and walked over to be introduced and stand with them.

"Pretty place, isn't it?" he said to Phyllis. "Me and the missus was on holiday one summer. We rented a boat, come up the lake and into the beach for a picnic. And the missus just strips and goes for a swim. Me, I hadn't ever seen a bare-naked lady walk into a lake. Come to that, I hadn't seen my missus bare-naked all that much neither. Y'know what she said when she come out? 'That's how this place makes me feel, Don. Free.' Course, we didn't have much money, nothing except what I made deliverin' mail in Vancouver, even less when the war come along and I joined up. But Irene got a job in a shipyard, worked her way up to welding. Anyway, she hunted down the guy that owned most of the land between here and town and talked him into selling twenty acres. Down payment was a hundred bucks, so when I got my discharge papers, we come here by boat. The road's new, something to do with connecting Highway Six and the Number One at Revelstoke."

"Does the lake freeze in the winter?" Phyllis was under the impression everything in Canada was frozen solid in the winter.

"The cove freezes about once in ten years."

"How did you get into town before the road?"

"I got a Peterborough canoe behind the trailer. One and a half horsepower outboard. Half-hour down the lake, tie up at the government wharf, do our bit of shopping, half-hour back. Cheaper and easier than a car." He looked at Joey. "Made up your mind yet?"

"Is the property staked?"

"You bet. I had a guy survey and restake it before I put up the *For Sale* sign."

"How much beach is there?" Phyllis asked.

"I never measured it. I know it was plenty for Irene and me."

"And the property includes the headlands and acreage on each side?"

"Sure does. Them headland's why Irene liked it so much. She said it was like living in our own world."

"I can see why she would say that," Phyllis said. She left them to pace across the beach.

"She from Vancouver?" MacPherson asked.

"Los Angeles."

He looked impressed. "Bound to be in the movie business, eh?"

"She's my husband's agent." Joey could not resist a little boasting: "My father's a VIP in the movie business. I'm a movie director." On the strength of Matt's script-to-be, Joey felt she could lay honest claim to the lofty position. "My uncles have farms and orchards near Salinas. I used to holiday there, that's how I know about fruit trees." She smiled at him, feeling slightly ashamed of boasting, because in fact she had been touched by his story and sentimentally connected it to how Matt felt about the cove. "You miss your wife," she said.

"Nothing's the same," he said. "I got to leave because whenever I come out of the trailer, I expect to see Irene out here."

"It must be hard for you. You'll take the trailer?"

"It's all I got to live in. There's a trailer park in town. It's not that I want to go, but I can't stay here and not have her with me."

"You have children?"

"That's somethin' we didn't have."

"I intend to have a couple," Joey said. "A girl first, then a boy."

"There's worse places to raise kids," he said as Phyllis returned from inspecting the beach and promontories. She inclined her head toward Joey, indicating she wished to speak privately.

"I'd offer him twenty-four fifty an acre and be prepared to go a little higher if he doesn't accept. Have you checked land prices around here?"

"No, but I figured he was asking double what people are paying for lake frontage. I don't think I should pressure him any more. I have the feeling he might get upset."

"Since the property extends past the headlands, there's probably more than a thousand feet of frontage. He was probably thinking of that when he quoted his price."

"Perhaps."

Phyllis turned to look up the hill. "There's no power, no water, no sewage. I know next to nothing about these things, but by the time you've built a house and taken care of all that, you'll probably've spent more than a hundred thousand." She looked at her wristwatch, then at the sun. "It's almost noon," she said, "and the sun's high, so that means the beach faces southwest," She was practical. "You know, Joey," she said as she left the beach and moved up the hill, "if you dug all this out, built your house curving around the beach and put dirt and rocks on the roof, no one would know a house was here. They couldn't even see the beach from the road, only the headlands and a bunch of rocks between them. Think about it, because you have to ask yourself if it's worthwhile to lay out big bucks for acreage you're not going to use and a small beach that's visible from the road."

"I suggested we could plant trees at the roadside," Joey said.

"Trees take years to grow."

"Matt's already made up his mind. It's this, or more rushing from pillar to post. I'm fed up with that, Phyl. I don't like living in a hotel. We've been in there almost a year now. I want a house where I can do things as I please. And have a baby."

"You're sure how Matt feels?"

"You should have seen him. He was trembling, like a kid with a new bike. I'm sure that's what brought on the spell."

"All right," Phyllis said. "We'll make an offer and see what happens."

Of course it wasn't quite *that* simple. Land titles had to be searched to find out who had bought and sold what. Thus, they learned that by mid-nineteenth century all the land in that particular area had been claimed and presumed owned by that most vague and powerful of political entities, the Crown, after which parcels were leased to sheep herders, then cattle ranchers who, after years of occupation and "improvements" (a variety of fencing and gates), now claimed ownership. The land grants were generally a square mile, but as time passed, land adjacent to the lake was split up, first into half sections, then quarters, then eighths, and so on down to the thirty-second part of an original six hundred forty-acre section, which in turn could be and was divided, then ended in the hands of companies and individuals, until one individual who had purchased an eighty-acre parcel sold a quarter of it to Donald MacPherson for the sum of one thousand three hundred dollars, who then transferred title on June 27, 1951, in return for the sum of fifty-five thousand dollars, to Phyllis Ackroyd, Josephine Scheiler and Matthew Scheiler, who found themselves in the possession of a thirty-second part of a square mile of land.

A few weeks later the trailer was taken away, but the Peterborough canoe remained, neatly sitting on a pair of saw horses. Joey had purchased three collapsible lawn chairs, which now sat on the beach with Joey, Phyllis and Arthur in them, their faces radiating proprietary satisfaction. A bottle of champagne was cooling in the lake and three glasses rested on the sand.

"Okay, Joey and Phyllis, the lake's all yours." Arthur gestured at the still water. "Take possession."

Phyllis laughed and said, "Why not?" She stood and began undressing.

"Matt wanted this place so he could gloat when we lower our bums into the water," Joey said, as she too began taking off her clothes.

"No," Arthur said. "I just want to feel content and secure."

"We should have thought of towels," Phyllis said.

"We couldn't think of everything," said Joey. "I could go back to town and get some."

"Too far. It's not worth the trouble."

Arthur watched as they walked down the beach and hesitated before entering the water. He had noticed that women, unlike men, don't careen down beaches to plunge helter-skelter into unknown waters; they don't seem to enjoy flaunting their athletic prowess. Instead, they usually approach water cautiously and test it, much as they would a prospective lover. Phyllis's body appeared dark beside china-white Joey, and Arthur noticed, although Phyllis's hips had a fine womanly flare, her back and shoulders were held with military stiffness, as if she'd been cautioned as a child never to slouch, whereas Joey hunched her shoulders as she advanced into the water so that, from the rear, she looked like Durer's humiliated Eve being expelled from Eden. Phyllis dived, resurfaced and stroked powerfully out to the headland on the east, while Joey slowly sank and allowed the water to embrace her, then swam out to join Phyllis who had pulled herself out of the lake to sit on a boulder. Arthur, watching from the beach, thought they looked glorious, like women in a Renoir painting. He experienced a momentary glow of satisfaction thinking the woman were there to serve him (in the best sense of the word), though his chauvinism was squashed when Joey called, "Don't be such a coward, Matt! Come on in!", reminding him that his relationship with Joey and Phyllis was based on his dependence on them, not on his masculine superiority.

Shamed by the women's readiness to surrender themselves, he undressed and made a big show of splashing into the water and falling waist-deep, where he remained on his back, undecided whether to make a complete fool of himself by trying to swim, or pretend he didn't feel well enough yet to race around in the water.

"Come on," Joey called.

Phyllis, who knew so much more about Arthur than Joey, backstroked inshore to crouch beside him. "Did you ever learn to ride a bike?" she asked.

"Of course. Everybody in Engl . . ." He stopped.

Phyllis ignored the slip. "Pretend you're riding a bike out to Joey." When he hesitated, she said, "Go on. I'll ride with you." Driven by shame, Arthur lurched forward into deep water, frantically pedalled, beat the water with his hands and gulped mouthfuls as his head bobbed below the surface. Joey was now beside him, and he felt both women's supportive arms beneath his. "Slow down," Phyllis said. "You won't sink."

He fought panic, followed Phyllis's instructions and felt the water buoy him. "I'm all right," he gasped. "Haven't swum in years." The women smiled, allowing him to save face.

After a while, they came inshore, sat in waist-high water, facing the beach and discussed the kind of house they wanted to build. Arthur finally got out of the water to fetch the glasses and bottle of wine, and while Joey held the glasses, he opened the wine and poured each a full glass. When he finished pouring, he threw the cap and cork to where their clothes lay, stood the bottle in the sand, retrieved his wine from Joey, sat down, held up his glass and said: "To Haven! Long may we remain here!" Phyllis and Joey repeated the words, sighed and sipped the wine, while each, gazing at the beach and the hill beyond it, perceived a building perfectly suited to their own personalities and needs: Arthur, an army bunker with a retractable Spanish facade and patio; Joey, a miniature of her family's house in Los Angles; Phyllis, always the most practical of the three, a beach house similar to the one her parents rented each summer at Cape Cod when she was a girl.

"Now, all we have to do is get it built," Arthur said. He poured the last of the wine into their glasses. "And that shouldn't be too difficult."

CHAPTER

22

DREAMING THE PERFECT HOUSE HAD BEEN EASY. BUT REALIZING the collective dream came so close to failure that by the end of the summer, Joey and Arthur were asking each other if they should forget about the house and install a house trailer on the site. Sure, it would be unattractive, but they could dolly it up with flowering creepers on the outside walls. They mulled over types and sizes of house trailers and collected numerous brochures which increased their depression when they looked at pictures of people with white hair and glittering false teeth sitting in front of trailer doors. They simply couldn't bring themselves to accept that ending to their dream of Haven House.

"I'd rather live in a tent," Arthur said, "I'm not going to desecrate Haven with one of those coffins." He was exhausted from working on the David novel, which was proving to be extremely long and so complicated that characters disappeared and reappeared, were named and renamed, married the wrong people, even produced children without having gone through the begetting process. It was a mess and, because he didn't want to acknowledge the problem was largely due to his failure to have sketched out a rough timeline before beginning to write, he laid the blame on his preoccupation with getting Haven underway. And his general overall irritation was aggravated by Joey's activities: Acting on his suggestion, she had contacted a local group of players and, using his rough script and a shoulder camera provided through the good offices of her father, was enthusiastically training a young woman named Margaret and a sullen Marlon Brando look-alike called Ian in the elements of movie acting. Through a combination of Hollywood connections and her own youthful charm, Joey had persuaded the proprietor of a local movie house to run the try-out shots on the big screen. They certainly were rough, but Joey seemed indifferent to the poor acting, which she attributed to the fact Arthur had written the script so hurriedly. All she cared about was that at last she was in control, and she happily froze shot after shot, patiently instructing the actors how to improve. Thus, Joey explained to Margaret, where the heroine is on the beach in the first scene, she should behave as if she were alone in her bedroom, moving naturally around on her crutches, relying on the camera to reveal every nuance. She assured Margaret that she could count on the camera to convey that the heroine is imagining she is gliding around a dance floor with a handsome male partner—the more awkward her movements, the greater the perfection of the imagined dance. (Joey planned to superimpose shots of ballerinas performing Swan Lake.) She had instructed Margaret that the heroine was to misplace a crutch as she danced, then fall, shattering the imagined perfection of her dance. Afterwards, the heroine was to drag herself into the water, intent on drowning herself, only to retreat when she hears the sound of an outboard motor. Joey had spent an hour in a helicopter, taking shots of the lake and the hills, finishing with a gradual, descending approach to Haven cove, but afterwards, when she saw the rushes, she was dissatisfied and planned to reshoot. To add to the confusion, Ian had got a crush on Joey and, progressing from comradely, casual, theatrical kisses, suggested they spend time together in bed. Joey, who had never been to bed with any man except Arthur, was surprised by the invitation and told him she would seriously consider it. What, he asked, was there to consider? You either did it or you didn't. To that, Joey replied she guessed she wouldn't. She wasn't shocked or offended by Ian's offer, but it had simply never occurred to her any other man than Matt would want to have sex with her. She enjoyed making love, but seldom thought about sex and never speculated about other people's sexual lives. Some people might argue her sexual curiosity had been repressed by a domineering mother, but it would be probably closer to the truth to say that Joey was naturally modest, the kind of woman who would never step beyond the line that defined conventionally correct behaviour, so that any man who confused her ambition to direct a movie that involved scenes of nudity with her code of personal behaviour seriously misjudged her. Arthur now wished he hadn't provided the scenario and was irritated when she dragged him along to see the rushes. However, after seeing them, he sensed she might be on the edge of something significant, some truth about human beings, and he was momentarily stabbed with envy. Here he was, stuck in the morass of his panoramic novel, while Joey was getting near to the truth of things in her little amateurish movie. She had no right to do that. Identifying truths about people's emotions was *his* prerogative. Still, after they had left the movie house and walked arm in arm back to the hotel, he was careful to offer only encouraging words.

"You'll get it right in the end," he said, "It takes time, though. You have to make every mistake in the book before you get what you want." He could have been talking about himself and his own frantic efforts to dislodge himself from his creative quagmire.

Joey ignored what he said. "But I think it'd be a mistake to sleep with Ian. A director should keep everyone in the cast at arm's length."

"He propositioned you! I'll break his goddamn nose!" That a two-bit amateur actor would try something on with his Joey enraged Arthur. He then began to wonder if perhaps she hadn't already swallowed the bait and was telling him after the fact in order to disarm him and forestall future gossip and accusations. He looked at her sideways, trying to gauge her capacity for deception. When she smiled sweetly at him and pressed her arm tighter against his, it occurred to him that men might interpret Joey's smile as come-hither, and maybe Ian had. Yet it wasn't so. Actually, Joey's greatest asset was her quirky moral integrity, though it was the last characteristic you would expect to find in a person raised in the phoney environment of Hollywood. Arthur continued to rehearse in his head all the things he would do to Ian, knowing he'd never actually carry them through. Yet, he felt aggrieved. After all, no one except he, Matt Scheiler alias Arthur Compson, had the right to make love to Joey. "Don't let that happen, Joey," he muttered. "I couldn't bear it."

"I wouldn't. But you do it with Phyl," Joey pointed out.

"That's different. Phyllis is part of us . . . part of our lives. Anyway, it hasn't happened for a long time."

"Since she last visited?"

"Listen, Joey: I'm obligated to Phyllis. She and I planned to be together, but I met you and fell in love. I mean, I'm happy I have you, but I hadn't planned it."

"I don't mind sharing you with Phyllis. I expect I feel more for her than for you. So why shouldn't I share?"

"You can't mean that, Joey."

"If I didn't, I'd either have walked out or refused to let her stay with us." Arthur should have been pleased he had uncovered another, deeper layer in Joey's personality, but learning that she thought more of Phyllis than of him depressed him. "I've known Phyl nearly all my life. She's the big sister I never had. Sharing you with her is like—well, like giving her some of my candy. I don't mind, because I know I have a whole bag full."

"Let's walk through the park," Arthur said. They crossed the road and walked through the park to a viewpoint where they sat on a bench holding hands. "It's not too bad here, is it, Joey?"

"I like it better now."

"At the moment, things are at sixes and sevens, but once we're in our house things'll settle down."

"I suppose." She turned his hand and rubbed it as though to stimulate circulation. "I'm thinking of going to a doctor for a check up, to see if there's a reason I'm not getting pregnant."

"Let's wait a bit, until we're in the house."

"Did you and Phyl try to have a baby?" The question was so unexpected that Arthur didn't know how to reply. Finally he said, "I don't know if we did, or we didn't."

"I'll ask her the next time she's here."

Arthur uneasily remembered Phyllis lying on the bed in the dark hotel bedroom, saying she hoped their bouts of sex wouldn't result in her getting pregnant since she hadn't used anything to prevent conception. Was it coincidence Joey hadn't conceived either? He was a virile lover and amply supplied Joey with the condiment required for conception. *Amply.* He reassuringly repeated the word to himself, then hugged Joey. "Don't worry," he said. "It'll happen one of these days. Don't bother Phyllis about it. Besides, you know I don't skimp when it comes to giving you the stuff you need." Arthur hoped that Joey would smile at his feeble joke, but he didn't get a response. Phyllis had told him that the only kind of humour the Gambarasi family responded to was the slip-on-a-banana-peel kind. Arthur had noticed, too, that while Joey often made comments that were funny, her delivery was so deadpan the humour passed unnoticed. Once she had told Arthur she didn't understand why people were so keen to get to the moon when everybody knew the world was oversupplied with cheese. It took him a few minutes to get the joke and when he laughed, Joey became offended because by that time she was in the midst of describing three drunk men she had seen on the town's main street that morning. "It's not funny," she indignantly said; and it took Arthur a while to convince her he was not laughing at the town drunks, but at her remark about people wanting to travel to the moon. Later, he wondered if the joke wasn't on him, since it was common knowledge that Americans would go anywhere in order to prevent competitors from a staking claim first. He, himself, hoped that human beings would continue to remain earthbound, being a person who preferred a mysterious and unknowable universe than one mapped out to the nth degree, which was not too surprising in an author who made his literary debut with tales of men and women fated to destroy themselves by leaping off emotional precipices.

As the summer wore on, Joey and Arthur drove to Haven each afternoon to swim, sunbathe, picnic, and of course talk about the house, which hadn't progressed far. They purchased a large garden umbrella, table and matching chairs and retired to the umbrella's shade when the fierce afternoon sun threaten to overpower them. They also bought a camera, and Arthur took pictures of

Joey in the buff, but none of the film was ever developed because Joey said she couldn't tolerate the idea of strangers seeing the photos and making unflattering or licentious comments. They picked and ate handfuls of ripe cherries, although they had contracted out harvesting the crop.

One afternoon, early in the summer, Arthur had spotted two men on the road getting out of an old truck to inspect the cherry crop, then watched as they strolled down the track to where Arthur and Joey sat. Afterwards, Arthur and Joey told themselves they had practically given their cherries away, although the men assured them the price they offered was the same as what all growers in the valley received. It wasn't that Arthur and Joey wanted an excessive amount for the crop; they merely wanted to feel they hadn't been cheated. When the men sensed reluctance, they told Arthur and Joey they could pick and market the fruit themselves, which would involve either shipping the fruit to a packing plant, or hauling it to Vancouver to peddle on street corners. That was enough for Arthur, He accepted their bid, reserving one tree for personal use.

When Joey and Arthur arrived at Haven a few weeks later, several battered cars with Quebec licence plates were parked on the road and two trucks in the orchard. Young men and women swarmed among the trees, some picking, some packing the cherries, then loading them on the trucks.

"Now I really know we're in another country," Arthur said, when he heard the young people speaking French.

"France?" Joey said. "We'll go there one day."

"We can think about it." Arthur was not enthusiastic about going anywhere that required a passport.

In the late afternoon, the pickers walked to the beach and asked if they could bathe in the cove. "Go ahead," Arthur said. He and Joey watched as the group stripped to underclothes and ran into the water where they happily swam and splashed around. Their employers joined Arthur and Joey at the umbrella and brought up the subject of the apple crop, but held back with a specific offer until the size and quality of the crop was more evident.

The man gestured toward the pickers. "Cheerful bunch, eh? Good workers, though." The men continued to stand there, and Arthur supposed they wanted to observe the pickers as they emerged from the water in order to ogle the dark, triangular patches beneath the women's thin underpants and the outline of pointed nipples against wet brassieres. Even Arthur found himself responding. The group ran out of the water and took up their clothes while calling: "Merci, monsieur et madam." They waved, then ran up the hill, followed by their employers who eyed the women's buttocks churning as they ran.

On their way back to the car, Arthur and Joey stopped at the cherry tree they had reserved and picked pick a bowl of fruit, but their pleasure evaporated when they saw several heaps of human faeces on one side of the tree. They threw away what they had picked in disgust and went on up to the Malibu.

Before he got into the car, standing at the roadside looking down on the cove, Arthur said, "The trouble is, we condemn people for doing what nature forces them to do. A child is born, and we call it a bastard or deem it legitimate. We make artificial rules and punish people when necessity forces them to break them. What do we say to people who have nowhere to go?"

"They could have brought a bucket," Joey said. "No worker'd do that in my uncle's orchards. They did it to show contempt for us."

"I hadn't thought of it like that," Arthur admitted.

"It's the first thing I thought of. Thieves in Los Angeles do that, especially the niggers." Arthur was surprised by the derogatory term. In childhood, he had heard his father speak of eye-ties, of frogs and of gypos. He'd not associated those epithets with racism, but had interpreted them as expressions of his father's own national pride. It was similar to boasting, as when his father claimed English beef and English beer were the best in the world, which was undoubtedly true if you ate prime rib roasts and drank Worthington ale. But even though a man or a woman might eat only beef scrag-ends and drink weak flat beer, it still didn't prevent them from acclaiming their native land's superiority, especially when it had been tested in times of national emergency, as England's had, many times. However, Joey's comment brought to light yet another facet of her personality, though Arthur didn't take offense, rather he excused her, telling himself prejudice against Negroes had been drummed into her by her parents, therefore she couldn't be blamed for it, any more than he, Arthur, could be blamed for experiencing lust when he saw the black shadows under the pickers' wet underpants. Of course his was a natural physical reaction, but it was possible that Joey experienced something similar: a physical antipathy to black people, a shuddering inability to get close them, as some people apparently experience with snakes and spiders.

The next day, before they drove to Haven, Arthur went to a hardware store and purchased a shovel. Joey didn't ask why or express surprise when he left her on the way down to the beach, entered the orchard, removed and buried the offending clumps, then returned to the tree where he picked two handfuls of large, perfectly ripe cherries which he washed in the lake before offering them to Joey.

"Luscious." she pronounced. "Better than Uncle Eugene's." She lay face down, head on her crossed arms, popped cherry after cherry into her mouth and spit out the pits. "Pick more," she ordered. Before he left to gather more fruit, he bit a cherry in half and used the purple juice to write "I love you" across her bottom.

The still summer days, the scent of ripening fruits mingled with sagebrush from the surrounding hills and the clicking of insects in the dried grass combined to dull their interest in finalizing plans for the house. In the mornings, Arthur would arouse himself to write more pages of his David novel at the hotel, but by the end of the day, after practising his embryo breast-stroke and boasting he could now swim to the headlands and back, he was too water and sun sodden to bother with anything except eating and making love. Joey's movie-making was on hold, and she was content to eat, swim, sunbathe and sigh with pleasure when she felt Arthur's lips pass over her neck and shoulders to settle on breasts. One afternoon, while making love under the umbrella tilted to prevent anyone who chanced to be passing along the road seeing them, a family with two small children paddled their canoe into the cove, realized what was going on, grimaced, then hurriedly swung the canoe around and paddled away.

"Did you hear voices?" Arthur asked, but didn't mention the voices he'd heard were children's. Their somnambulant days had apparently diminished Joey's desire to conceive and he didn't want to arouse it.

Then the weather changed: One night at the hotel they were awakened by thunder claps that vibrated the entire structure; they watched at the window as lightning zigzagged across the lake to scorch earth and forests and start fires which, fortunately, were immediately dowsed by the torrential rain that followed, filling creeks, gullies, drains and streets, beating fruit from trees, grapes from vines, and sweeping acres of ripe tomatoes, peppers and melons into irrigation ditches. The air seemed almost visibly to change from that of hot, languid summer to cool, unpredictable fall.

"We must get on with the house, Matt," Joey said, indicating the blueprint laid out on the table. "I think we should go with this one. It's not perfect, but it's more or less what we want. Well, isn't it?"

"All right, Arthur agreed, "but we'll need to confirm with Phyllis."

And so began construction of Haven. It went on through the fall and most of the winter. Arthur's mornings were spent on tedious page-by-page revisions of the David manuscript. In the afternoons, Joey, who had decided to postpone filming movie until the following summer, drove with Arthur to Haven to inspect progress on the house. Construction seemed pathetically slow; they couldn't understand why, after the long concrete box had finally been inserted into the hillside, tradesmen did not immediately appear and rapidly complete everything, dismissing the architect's caution about needing time for the concrete to cure as an excuse, and offended when he pointed out that they had been the ones who dilly-dallied through the summer months, which would have been the perfect time to install the concrete frame and roof. There was also the problem of power supply, which the power company said they could provide if Arthur and Joey were prepared to pay for the installation of miles of poles and lines. As an alternative, the company suggested an oil-burning motor and electrical generator that would require a separate building. The architect had already informed them that the house involved a radical design in unsympathetic terrain, but had said not to be too concerned because he was investigating the practicality of solar panels as an energy source, a radical new idea, which he had discussed with colleagues in Arizona and New Mexico, who had advised him, as a first step, to gather and collate data regarding annual hours of sunshine. Arthur and Joey blindly nodded agreement with this. "Sounds fine to us. No shortage of sunshine here."

Joey and Arthur stood in various areas of the partially constructed building and unsuccessfully tried to envisage panelled walls, tiled floors, floor-to-ceiling windows and doors opening onto a red-tiled patio. After unenthusiastically eyeing the dusty walls, they would climb to the road, get into the car and return to the hotel, not speaking, only shaking their heads and wondering why they had started the project in the first place.

It took a full year, but finally one day when Joey and Arthur arrived at Haven, they saw trucks parked on the roof of the house, and after they'd gone down the steps, could hardly believe that windows were being installed, floors tiled, plumbers were at work, an electrician was affixing wiring to the end of tubing embedded in concrete walls, carpenters were installing grey cedar panels and door frames and doors. In the midst of the noise: drilling, slapping and hammering, stood the architect and the contractor.

"It's beginning to take shape," said the architect. "The solar panels and storage batteries should be here in a few days, so if all goes well, we should have everything up and running within a month."

A few weeks later, Joey was able to drive the Malibu down the lane with its newly graded double S bend, although achieving the esses had meant sacrificing four smaller pines and several fruit trees. The moving vans, though, couldn't negotiate them, but fortunately the movers were able to use dollies to transport the furniture to the front of the house and then carry it inside through the patio doors. There were a few snafus before the solar panels were able to provide power comparable to that which would have flowed through utility lines. Eventually, Arthur and Joey were able to drive from the road, park the

Malibu in the garage, descend the steps, unlock the door and enter Haven. When Phyllis arrived a month later to celebrate the house warming, she walked through it, then pronounced: "Terrific! Just terrific."

"The patio will be laid out in a month or so. We'll start when the weather warms up a bit," Joey explained.

Arthur brought out three chilled glasses and poured champagne. "To Haven!" he toasted, and the women repeated, "Here's to Haven!"

The next day, Joey gave Phyllis a lengthy description of the tribulations she was experiencing with her movie. Phyllis, however, was more interested in Arthur's manuscript, and when she asked if it was finished, Arthur nodded. "But I'm not sure I've got it just right," he said.

"You're too close to it," Phyllis suggested. "Perhaps you think it reveals too much about the author?"

"I don't think so. It has something to do with what the novel says about people. There were things about the characters I didn't particularly want to reveal. But I was forced to, because that's the way the people were. You can take it with you."

"I could read it while I'm here," Phyllis offered. "I plan to stay a few days."

"No, no. I couldn't stand that. I'd feel like a person about to have his leg amputated without anaesthetic. No. Condemn or praise it from a distance."

"I'm sure it will be praise," Joey said.

Phyllis noticed that Joey had gained weight and that the contours of middle age were already revealing themselves. She wondered if Arthur had noticed the changes. Probably not. He appeared to be as enamoured with her as ever. As for Joey's movie. Really! It was a joke. Surely Arthur didn't take it seriously!

Arthur, sensing what Phyllis was thinking, said, "Joey's on to something, you know. I've seen the rushes. There are problems, bad angles and so on. But she's captured something special."

"Seeds of truth germinating in the midst of chaos?" Phyllis asked.

Arthur looked at her, suspecting irony. "Perhaps," he agreed. "Arguably, seeds of truth are always present in chaos, or perhaps we deceive ourselves and only see what we wish to see, though I don't think that's the case with Joey's takes. It had to do with a sense of longing that was communicated. The young woman who's playing the lead role seemed to capture the character's desire to transform herself into something whole. At first, I couldn't identify the emotion. I should of, because longing is present in everybody: Joey wants to transform herself into a movie director; I suppose I want to become a great writer. And what about you Phyllis?"

"Great editor, agent and friend will do."

The three friends talked together the rest of the afternoon and over a late dinner. Afterwards, they bade each other sleep well and went to bed. In the night, when Joey was asleep, emitting puffing snores, Arthur walked through the house, entered the guest room and sat on the bed.

"Should you do this?" Phyllis asked.

"Probably not, though Joey's told me she doesn't mind sharing me with you."

"She does mind," Phyllis said. "Maybe you don't feel it, but I can. She radiates dislike of me."

"That can't be true. You're her oldest friend. She thinks of you as an older sister."

"It's not unknown for one sister to hate another. I'll leave tomorrow."

"Stay a while. I need to talk over a few things."

"Common sense tells me to leave." In the darkness, Arthur touched her face, then moved his hand to her shoulder and breasts. "Don't," she said, and he withdrew his hand.

"Joey's going to ask if you took precautions when we made love. Please tell her you did."

"But I didn't."

"She hasn't conceived."

"Have her see a gynaecologist. You're afraid it's your fault?"

After a pause, he said, "Yes. I don't know why, but yes, I do think I'm responsible."

"Have you thought it might be connected to your illness? You ought to consult a neurologist, Matt. Things have changed a lot in recent years. Physicians know more."

"I daresay." He touched her face again. "I'm afraid Joey'll leave me if she finds out I'm incapable of giving her a baby."

She sighed. "Lying's always dangerous."

"I don't want to lose her."

"She may not ask."

"She will. She's persistent. She's dead-set on making a movie and having a baby."

"I'll do what I can."

"Thank you. You know, I miss you." He leaned forward and kissed her cheek before leaving the room. He walked through the house, stopping to look through the living room windows at the outline of the headlands and the still lake. It was hard to believe all this was his. Yet, though he had been successful at burying himself like a gopher in the hillside, he still felt threatened by things unknown, things unforeseen and unrecognized. He watched flakes of snow drift by the window as if uncertain where they were heading before returning to the bedroom and slipping into bed. He was surprised when Joey asked where he had been.

"In the living room, looking at the snow falling."

"Why?"

"I couldn't sleep." To avoid having to say more, he embraced her and began the preliminaries of love-making, but Joey resisted, saying she'd didn't feel like doing it and was tired of pointless love-making. There was an edge to her voice, and Arthur felt as though a lump of ice had been thrust into his gut; this was replaced by anger when Joey said she would, if he really wanted to. When he muttered "No," she rolled onto her side and went to sleep. After a while, he left the bed and went back to the living room where he spent the remainder of the night watching snow quietly descend and accumulate. He did not review his life, he did not speculate why Joey's love for Phyllis had been transformed into animosity, nor he did not reflect on the fate of his completed novel, what it might mean financially, or how it might affect his standing in the literary world. There was nothing but an animal numbness. He reminded himself of a dog lying outside a store, ears down, eyes anxiously watching a door, waiting, because there was nothing else it could do. It waits for someone to emerge from the door and lead it away, but should no one appear, it would still remain there, waiting, emptied of all impulse and will, nothing left except the need to wait.

In the morning, cold white light filled the room. Joey, still in her dressing gown, came to stand at the windows and ask how long he had been there. When he shrugged and said he didn't know, she said, "What's the matter, Matt? Are you wishing we'd never built Haven? Aren't you glad to see Phyllis?"

"Of course."

"What's the matter then?"

He improvised. "I'm worrying about the novel. Realizing too late I should have taken out certain things and put in others."

"There'll be time to revise when you read through the proofs. Anyway, I don't think that's what's bothering you. It's to do with me and Phyl. I felt it in you last night. Did you creep into her bed and do it?"

"Maybe I should've after you pushed me away."

"I didn't. I was sleepy. But now I'm awake." Part of him wanted to scream at her, part of him wanted to say he wished he'd never met her, but other parts wanted her and so he allowed her to lead him to their bedroom, where he clung to her and sobbed like an overwrought child restored to its mother. He knew Joey was digging her proprietary claws into him and realized that this might be the last time he and Phyllis met and that there was nothing he could do about it. Regardless of what Joey had said about sharing with Phyllis, Joey's actions made it clear she was determined to eliminate Phyllis from their lives, even though she was his agent and owned one-third of the house and the property in Beverly Hills.

Fortunately, the sun blazed and the snow evaporated, so that two days later, at dawn, Joey and Arthur were able to drive Phyllis to the airport for an early flight to Vancouver. They waved vigorously when she boarded the small regional plane to begin her journey back to Los Angeles. Before ducking to enter the plane, she turned toward Arthur and Joey who were standing in the waiting room, raised her briefcase holding the manuscript, made a vee for victory sign, then lifted her fingers to her lips and blew them a kiss.

"Well," Joey said as they drove home, "it could've been worse." She steered the car around a cowboy herding cattle along the road. "She's not happy about losing you." He refused to look at Joey, but instead stared across the lake where patches of snow remained on slopes beyond the warming eye of the early spring sun. He heard the mixture of resentment, jealousy and envy in Joey's voice, and for a moment he wanted to say he'd returned to Phyllis's room and done it with her, then compare Phyllis's sexual performance with Joey's and find hers wanting. But the moment passed when Joey spoke: "I followed you when you went to her room," she said.

"Nothing happened."

"She saw me in the doorway, that's why."

"I didn't know you were such a sneaky bitch!" he said.

"I didn't know you were such a goddamn liar! You were feeling her tits."

"You can leave any time," he said, unable to believe their relationship had deteriorated so quickly. "I don't understand. What's happened? Why are we talking like this?"

"Because you and Phyl mocked me. That's why. And something else: I told her I didn't want her here again."

"Goddamn you! Phyllis is my friend. S-s-s-he's done everything to help me." Arthur was so upset he stuttered.

Joey turned off the road, deftly steered the car down the double S into the garage and turned off the motor. "She's still your be-all and end-all. Too bad, because I won't have her in this house." Arthur trailed after her down the steps and into the hall where they removed coats and snow boots.

"I'm supposed to jump when you crack the whip, eh?" he finally said. "Is that it?"

"You could put it like that. But I'm not going to sit around and feel I'm an appendage while you and Phyllis chat over my head."

"But we don't!"

"You think I didn't hear you criticizing my rushes?"

"You're mistaken. What I said was that you'd hit on something valuable."

"That's not what I heard. I heard two people, who think they're intellectually superior, mocking a person who's trying to make a decent, honest movie."

Arthur was stunned, aghast at the degree to which Joey had misunderstood his and Phyllis's comments. Hadn't he made it clear that he had detected a grain of truth among the chaff, which she must encourage to flower? Joey was badly in error if she had concluded he and Phyllis were snobbish about her work. "If that's what you heard, if you think I've mocked what you've done, then I apologize, because as an artist myself, I admire any one who can see and hold onto a truth in the great heap of trash that's everywhere we look."

"You really and truly mean that?" Joey asked the question without looking at him. "You're not putting me on?"

"Listen, Joey. I may sometimes bend the facts to suit myself, but I never lie about anything to do with art. Never." He saw her lips compress as she turned away, then he heard her sobs. He followed her from the hall, through the living room to their bedroom, where she lay with her face in a pillow, shoulders trembling. Arthur sat beside her and after a while began to stroke her hair, saying he would always love her.

"What'll Phyl think of me!" she eventually whimpered. "I must've hurt her so much."

"She'll understand." He turned her head to kiss her tear saturated face and trembling lips and watched himself become aroused by her soft vulnerability while debating if she would later despise him if he exploited her present weakness. In the end, he repressed desire and limited himself to offering reassurances, which in general were sincere, because he did love her and wanted her love in return.

"I've been a silly fool," she said when she finally stopped crying.

"Overly sensitive."

"You do understand, Matt? I don't mind if you and Phyllis make love, but I can't bear it when you treat me like an idiot."

"Dearest Joey, what can I say except that I love you? Anything else'd sound banal, because all the words of love have already been said a million-million times. There're only a few words available to a man when he wants to express his love."

"Even a writer?"

"Even a writer . . . I will always admire and respect Phyllis, and I daresay I'd have no trouble going to bed with her. But I happen to love you, Joey. Don't ask me why or how, but I love every part of you. I've told myself you're exactly like millions of other women—you've said so too. Yet even as I say it, I know it can't be true, otherwise I would be in love with every woman I see."

"Maybe you are."

Arthur ignored those deep, unruly waters. "So I must love you, Joey. For me, you're unique."

Joey gave him a kiss, but she wasn't convinced Arthur's words meant anything. All her life, Joey had carried around a rag-bag of opinions about men which her mother had systematically stuffed into her. Even before Joey was an adolescent, Sophia had tapped her daughter's flat chest and said: "Never believe anything a man tells you." Sophia had also packed a myriad of superstitions into Joey's bag. Joey still touched wood a dozen times a day, and when the real stuff wasn't available, she would tap her head and say, "This'll do for the time being." A friend of her mother's had once told her that people residing in the southern hemisphere put glue on their shoes to keep from falling off the earth, and when working at the studio, even though by then she had learned in school something about the force of gravity, she automatically examined actors from the antipodes for any residue of glue on their shoes. Arthur, who carried around a sack of superstitions himself, was amused by Joey's collection, especially those relating to sex. Joey, who had gone to parochial schools, attended Sunday mass and whispered invented sins in the confessional box, believed that couples should not make love on Fridays or Sundays, that a husband who saw his wife's bloodied menstrual pad would be rendered impotent, and that a wife who engages in sex by straddling her husband would eventually change gender. In addition to the superstitions, there was Joey's deeply-felt belief that the sole purpose of making love was to conceive a child. And while she was able to hold her belief temporarily in suspension and extract considerable pleasure from the sexual act itself, once the trembling had ceased and she had calmed down, she became uneasy, afraid that on some far-distant judgement day, she would be condemned for failing to beget. But quite apart from the religious obligation to bear a child, Joey really and truly wanted one, in fact wanted a child so badly that when she saw pregnant women or women with babies, her breasts and groin ached with the pain of emptiness, and once or twice she had to smother an impulse to snatch a baby from its mother and claim it as her own. But still she believed (as her mother did) that one day it would happen, one day her period would not arrive, and when it failed to appear in the second month, she would need to wait only seven more months before her baby would be placed in her arms. Only then would she feel assured that all her preliminary sighs and culminating trembles, and all Matt's kissing her everywhere and the lurching and pushing of his thing into her as far as it would go, had finally paid off. Some day. Some day. And she must never forget that the most beautiful babies were made by the wife who delights in embracing her husband, who himself adores his wife and asks for nothing more than to be able to lie beside her and do it.

"Shall we make coffee?" she asked. "We never did have any this morning."

"And something to eat?"

"Okay." Arthur noticed a certain deference in the way Joey treated him now her feelings about Phyllis had been aired, perhaps because, having disclosed so much, she needed assurance he wouldn't exploit her fragile hidden, quivering self, which he wouldn't ever do, since the more he knew about Joey, the greater became his love. That was true: He wanted to kiss and caress her odd, unseen quirks; he wanted to nibble further to uncover more layers of her personality. Joey had sensed this and had already told him that their self-exposure sessions were too one-sided, that he ought to reveal more about himself; but so far he had evaded her challenge, claiming he had no personality, that he was merely a mechanism that churned out stories about more interesting people than himself, such as Joey. Of course, Joey didn't entirely believe him, but there wasn't much she could do because he had deftly enclosed her in a cocoon of love that bordered on adoration. How could any woman escape those bonds?

Joey wrote a long, explanatory letter to Phyllis and received an affectionate reply which arrived in a package that also included a sealed envelope containing Phyllis's comments on Arthur's manuscript. Joey ventured to ask what Phyllis had to say about the novel. "Oh, she says it'll sell. Though she thinks it might've been better if I'd split the story into two novels because the length might put people off. On the other hand, she says, some readers like books that're a two-or-three-week read." Once he had turned over the David manuscript to Phyllis, he had immediately started writing another novel. It would have a few autobiographical elements, since Arthur had told himself that every writer should be permitted to use his or her own life at least once in a literary lifetime, though it was true some writers become so fascinated with themselves they told the same story over and over. Arthur believed that the mark of a good writer lay in the capacity to divorce the self from the work, but since this merely confirmed the care he personally took to avoid references to himself in his work, perhaps it wasn't a fair judgement from a literary point of view. At times, Arthur experienced bouts of uneasiness about his stories and novels, wondering how they fit into the vast accumulation of world literature. He thought books which survived their author's own lifetime were few and far between and probably had managed to survive mainly because teachers of literature required them as fodder for their students.

A month or so later, Arthur received a letter from Phyllis advising him that an interested publisher wanted biographical material and photographs. He turned the letter over, printed "NO" on the back and mailed it back to Phyllis.

A few weeks went by, when Joey, responding to a knock on the door, opened it to find Phyllis standing in the dim stairwell. "You should get a doorbell installed, Joey," Phyllis said as she walked into the entry hall and on into the living room where Arthur was sitting. "Sorry I didn't phone first, but I knew I'd have to see you face-to-face."

"I've given you my answer, Phyllis. It's NO," said Arthur.

"The publishing house is prepared to make a big splash, novel of the year, and all that. But they want you in New York, Arthur. And I get the impression they might renege on their offer if you won't help promote it. They can't publish a novel of that magnitude and not have it sell."

"No," Arthur repeated.

"You have anything to drink, Joey?" Phyllis said.

"I'll see."

Phyllis spoke quietly even though Joey had left the room. "You have nothing to worry about, Matt. Nothing. Nobody's going to question your name or your appearance."

"The point is, Phyllis, not every book that's published has the author's face splashed all over it. Just the author's name and a list of other titles. I'd prefer that, even if I didn't have plenty to hide."

"What do you have to hide, Matt?" Joey asked as she came back with a tray on which sat a bottle of rye whisky and a bottle of B.C screw-capped red wine.

"I'm hiding you from the world," Arthur smoothly replied, "because I know if I let you out, you'll grabbed by some other man."

"He flatters me like this, Phyl. If I say, what a gorgeous day, he says not half as gorgeous as you. Silly things, like that."

"Lucky you," Phyllis said. "Most wives are plastered with complaints."

"Sometimes I wonder if Matt's not conning me. So, what'll you have, Phyl, rye or B.C. red?"

"I don't think writers should make exhibitions of themselves," Arthur said. "In a few years' time, publishers'll want to put a male author's penis and a female's breasts—or more—on the cover. That's why I refuse to be dragged into the publicity game. One thing leads to another. If the publisher you've got lined up doesn't like it, find another."

"It's a respected house, Matt."

"Oh sure."

"Matt," Joey interjected, "you don't know anything about these things. What the publisher asks isn't unreasonable."

"You know even less than I do about publishing," Arthur said.

"I know about the movie business. And I can tell you, publicity is everything."

Phyllis emptied her glass and poured herself more rye. "That's right," she said. "Look here, Matt, I'll manufacture a bio for you, okay? I'll say you're a compulsive recluse who resides in a modified rabbit's hole in the middle of nowhere."

"Do as you see fit," Arthur said.

"Wouldn't groundhog be better?" Joey suggested.

"Perfect," Phyllis agreed. "A groundhog who pokes his nose out in February, sniffs the air and retires into his den. The marketing staff'll go to town on you being a hermit. They could design a shadowy cave for the cover. Matt, you have to learn to appreciate that publicity, publicity and more publicity is what is needed to sell a book these days, the country's awash with them. Years ago, a bookstore could be nice and quiet and ooze cultural superiority, but not any more. They're all big chains. And the next thing you know, they'll just be open warehouses filled with stacks of books. Book supermarkets. It scares me, but it's going to happen. Books'll be nothing more than products, like everything else. Maybe it's being snobbish, but I can't help but think whatever is cheaply made is easily discarded." The whisky was affecting her. She slouched in the chair and became argumentative, waving her right arm to the emphasize points. "Newspaper and magazine publishers are terrified readers'll switch to television once more of them are around. People like me'll become superfluous. No more short-story magazines, instead thirty-minute TV shows. You should consider that market, Matt. You'd have no difficulty adapting your stories. Shall I ask around?"

"I'll leave it to you."

"You dump everything into my lap, don't you? No, I didn't mean to say that. Forget it. I'm tired. I've been up since dawn. Is the bed made up, Joey?"

"Of course." Joey left her chair and crossed to take the glass from Phyllis. "You look exhausted." That Phyllis was tired and near the breaking point made Joey feel good. She was seldom able to play the dominant role in their relationship. She helped Phyllis up from the low, deeply upholstered chair, supported her by holding her elbow, much as hospital nurses support the elderly and infirm, and guided her from the room.

Arthur could hear the woman talking, the sound of doors closing, then the hum of the pump which automatically functioned to lift sewage from the house to the septic tank system in the orchard where, so the architect explained, effluent from the tank could provide appropriate nutrients for the trees. The pump was the latest in efficiency and effectiveness, but like everything else in Haven had been very expensive, and Arthur had cringed as he signed the cheques that paid for it all. He poured himself a dollop of red wine and waited for Joey to return. The wine was rather sweet, but that didn't bother Arthur, who seldom drank anything alcoholic and preferred something on the sweet side when he did.

"She's upset," Joey announced when she returned. "I've never seen Phyl like that before. Why don't you go in and tell her everything's fine?"

"What d'you mean, fine?"

"About the novel. You know."

He shrugged, then walked along the hall, knocked on the bedroom door and entered it. Phyllis was propped on pillows, leafing through a magazine. Arthur sat at the foot of the bed saying, "I suppose you think I've exploited you?" He didn't wait for her to respond. "Maybe I have, unintentionally. But remember, I'm a prisoner, maybe of my own making but nonetheless a prisoner. And I've depended on you to supply me with what I've needed to survive. You even pushed Joey at me."

"I had no idea it'd end like this."

"Me neither. I probably should've told Joey the truth about myself long ago, but I don't trust her as I do you. Not even now. Odd, isn't it? How is it possible not to trust the person you love?"

"Or don't love, but trust. Your story's a burden to me too, Matt. I could be charged with aiding and abetting a crime, or with complicity in hiding it. The publishing house is number three in the U.S., maybe in the world. And the novel'll be published by an affiliated house in England. It's a good deal for both of us."

"All the more reason to keep information about me off the cover. Anyway, if the story ever did come out, I'd flatly deny you knew anything. Besides, it's not illegal for an author to use a pseudonym. And don't forget, Matt Scheiler's the name that's on everything I've published in the U.S. There's no inconsistency, and I haven't defrauded anyone."

"Then why am I suddenly so afraid?"

"Irrational panic. I should know, I'm an old hand at it."

"But I've always been so confident nothing untoward could happen." As she reached forward to take his hand, her nightgown fell away from her dark-nippled breasts.

"Nothing will happen," he said at the same moment Joey tapped on the door, opened it, looked in and asked if everything was all right.

Phyllis arranged the bed covers while Arthur retreated to the door to stand beside Joey. "Everything's fine," he told Joey, though he knew everything wasn't fine with Phyllis, because while he could conveniently forget who he had once been, his past was now a dominant factor in Phyllis's life.

When they returned to their bedroom and Joey asked what he and Phyllis were talking about, Arthur replied they had spoken in generalities and he couldn't recall specific words. "Did you notice," Joey asked while putting on pyjamas, "that Phyl's nightgown was open at the top?" Yes, Arthur replied, he *had* noticed it, but how could he be expected to ask her to close the gown to relieve him of the embarrassment of looking at her exposed breasts. That was impossible. He added: "But they're not as attractive as yours."

"Sort of gross," Joey said.

"Sort of," he agreed.

They got into bed, turned out the lights, agreed that Phyllis would unquestionably feel better in the morning, after which Joey rolled onto her left side while Arthur lay in the dark, reviewing his conversation with Phyllis, trying not to dredge up images of past disasters and stir them into imagined scenes of one gigantic, future catastrophe.

CHAPTER

23

EACH TIME ARTHUR RECEIVED A COPY OF A NEWLY PUBLISHED novel, Joey would hold it up and say, "It looks good. Aren't you pleased?" She never understood why he did little more than look at the title page before he, so Joey thought, discarded it. Once he had tried to explain how he felt about his work: If a person travelling around becomes enamoured with a particular place because it seems to contain everything he has ever sought and remains there, he can never know whether the perfection he seeks may lie just beyond the next hill or bend in the road. When Arthur looked at a finished book, he was looking at his past. At the time his massive David book was published, he told Joey the novel drained him of everything he would ever know about men and women; and since he believed he must never repeat what had already been said by himself or others, there was nothing left for him but to spin out the rest of his life, idling in Haven. But (metaphorically speaking) he *had* walked forward, around other bends and beyond other hills which had opened up new vistas and perspectives in the human landscape that he had not formerly dreamed. He supposed that eventually he would quit his mind-wanderings, in which case he would probably die, because he could not envisage a time when he would be content to drag out the heel-end of life vegetating. He glared at Joey and said. "I either work or I am nothing."

When the David novel had been released, Phyllis sent along the reviews, which Joey read to Arthur. "Listen to this one, Matt, The reviewer says you've joined the ranks of major North American authors. And Phyllis says the book is selling well, even without author photos."

"Of course."

"Phew!" She held the book in both hands, as though weighing it. "It's heavy. Like an over-sized baby. That reminds me, I'll have to make an appointment to see Dr. Biggstern. I'm keeping my fingers crossed that everything's okay. Are your fingers crossed, Matt?"

"Certainly."

Crossed fingers or not, it turned out Joey had no problem, but Arthur did.

Weeks after Joey's visit to Biggstern, Arthur visited the one urologist who practised in town. The physician examined him, said he appeared to be in excellent health and took a sample of his ejaculate. When Arthur returned to the office a week or so later, the urologist informed him his semen carried so few sperm that for all practical purposes he was infertile. "Though we physicians don't always have the right answers to fertility problems." Of course, Arthur was obliged to convey this information to Joey, though it took a while before she fully grasped that Arthur would never father a child.

"Listen, Joey, why don't we adopt a child?"

"No. I want my own child."

"Okay. Then have one by another man. You and I can raise it as our own."

But Joey obstinately held to the position that she had married Arthur for better or for worse. Further, she had no intention of running around the countryside looking for some Tom, Dick or Harry to make her pregnant. It was a disgusting idea. They concluded the discussion melodramatically, when Arthur knelt before Joey and begged her to fulfil her maternal role, while Joey shook her head and said, "Never! Never!" And the funny thing was (if you could call such a situation funny) Joey meant every word she said, though later, she had to admit she sometimes resented Arthur because he couldn't give her what she wanted and expected from marriage.

Over the years Arthur had become more reclusive than ever, though he did accompany Joey to town on weekly shopping expeditions where he took advantage of being among people again to study every individual who passed by. Joey thought Arthur was slowly but surely heading into a state of craziness, because from somewhere she had picked up the notion that crazy people watch the world through slitted eyes and observe those who watch them from the corners of their eyes, which is exactly what Arthur did when he came to town with her. He even made comments about the people they passed on sidewalks or in grocery store aisles. He would say something about an eye-catching feature: the person's big nose, protruding eyes, floppy breasts, bowlegs— anything that separated the person from the average run.

One afternoon, an elderly woman overhearing Arthur's comment about her protuberant breasts and rear-end, turned and grabbed him, shook him, slapped his face and told Joey to zip up her husband's mouth before she stormed off, bust and hips indignantly rolling. The confrontation embarrassed Joey. Arthur had gone too far. He didn't seem to realize that people could hear his comments. Surely that was a sign of being a crazy person. His behaviour embarrassed her because she had established a casual, friendly relationship with people in town. Most knew her as the movie gal from California who lived somewhere on the lake and gave a course in film history at the college. They assumed the scrawny guy with her was her husband, but little was known about him except that he was a writer. However, most thought he couldn't possibly be any good. If he was, he would be teaching at the college, instructing young people in creative writing courses. Few had seen his novels in the town library and bookstore, fewer still borrowed or purchased and read one. Joey told Arthur he had no one to blame but himself if no one in town knew about his books. She, Joey, had been her own publicity agent and had let everybody know about her movie, thereby gaining status as a local celebrity, whereas the only status Arthur had in the valley was as a "the gopher guy" who buried himself in his "bunker" all day.

It had taken Joey three years to make her movie, using notes for a screenplay supplied by Arthur. Arthur disliked thinking about Joey's movie because, although he never admitted it, he envied the cinematographic skills that had enabled her to take his dry outline and turn it into a sixty-minute feature that continued to make the circuit of film festivals, where it was screened as a prologue to imported French or Italian movies. Ian and Margaret, the young actors Joey had trained, had gone to Hollywood, hoping the film would serve as a stepping-stone to careers in the motion pictures, but Margaret received nothing more than expressions of interest from porno directors, and Ian found himself duplicated by the dozen in the agents' offices and studios he visited. They were back in the valley within a year, Margaret teaching in an elementary school, Ian driving a delivery van for an express mail company. Over time, both came to resent Joey's limited notoriety. Margaret believed her young virginal body had been prostituted by Joey, and Ian came to feel that because of Joey's movie, every woman in town viewed him as an untrustworthy, uncouth, potential rapist. Arthur once remarked to Joey that her movie was like a Greek play where the audience knows from the beginning what will happen but accepts that, because whatever happens, must happen. There was an inevitability in Joey's movie, a knowledge that paradise would be destroyed and from it arise sexual enmity between the sexes, which always made Arthur think of a line from a metaphysical poem by Herman Melville, where he asks "What Cosmic jest or Anarch blunder/The human integral clove asunder." And if so fine a thinker and writer as Melville had asked the question and failed to find an answer, then how could he, Arthur, who did not consider himself Melville's equal, expect to provide a solution to the universal problem? Or Joey in her little movie?

So, whenever Joey asked if the publication of a new novel pleased him, he shrugged because he knew the book had not provided any definitive answers to the questions posed in it. He always tried to escape the necessity of supplying answers by dextrously cheating and replacing an expected answer with more questions. To himself, he acknowledged the deception, but rationalized it away by telling himself that an apparent solution was tantamount to an admission of failure, for you could never solve that for which no solution existed. At best, you could identify the problem, but never the explanation. The unanswerable questions bruised his rational mind and imagination, so it was always a relief to drive with Joey into town and stroll along the main street, idly speculating about people who approached to pass the time of day with Joey. He eyed the women and ordered his private devil to sneak beneath their clothes and explore their thighs and up around their smooth-fleshed bellies to encircle their breasts. He looked at big-bellied men and wondered how women supported them during copulation. Would any cock be long enough to project beyond such bellies? Why, some male stomach were so large they aped women at full term. Maybe women deliberately stuffed men's guts until, like bullocks, they were rendered impotent, thus freeing themselves from an act they found repugnant. Speculation was limitless. He enjoyed watching children, and imagined the boys stroking their cocks as he once done, and the girls touching their rising breasts and awakening pudenda. The children in the playing fields were well fed and well dressed, but apart from that they behaved as children did in the village where he had spent his childhood. It was both consoling and depressing to know little or nothing was changed from one generation to the next. For some reason, you imagined that all the human striving, beliefs and expressed ideals would result in changes in people and societies; but it never happened and although the vocabulary was different, the thoughts had been uttered a thousand times before. Fifteen years ago, during the year he and Joey lived in the hotel, they had often halted at the playground to watch children on teeter-totters and swings, but now Joey avoided driving past elementary schools and walking in the city park. Nothing was ever said, but Arthur knew that seeing small children was a painful reminder of something she did not have, and probably never would have: a child.

By now, Joey had traded in the Malibu for a Chevrolet station wagon which never carried anything except Joey and Arthur and their groceries. Arthur felt rather ashamed at pulling so much empty space behind him. He never got accustomed to the off-hand way people in North America regarded automobiles. That a personal possession, which in his childhood, had sharply divided upper and lower classes could be seen by the dozen in the high-school parking lot amazed him. Whenever they passed the school, Arthur would say, "Imagine, all those kids owning cars!" There was a note of resentment in his voice.

"Why not?" Joey would retort. "They've got as much right as us."

Joey was a typical American, Arthur thought, an advocate of the right to own whatever the heart desired, which had always struck him as the feature which most distinguished North America from European countries, where ownership rights were heavily dependent on class and social and political affiliations. But in this lake-haunted valley, even adolescents didn't question their right to own a car. When Joey asked, as she did from time to time, why he didn't learn to drive, Arthur usually put her off with some excuse, but now he said, "Think about that for a minute, Joey. It's not just putting my life at risk if I were to . . . you know. But what if something happened and there was a kid on the road?"

Joey was not sympathetic. "That's why you should see a doctor. Phyllis tells me there's something around now called an EEG. The doctors could pinpoint what's wrong with you. Maybe give you medicine. Your refusal to deal with your spells makes me cross. What if I get sick or die? Who would transport you around? At least, you should let me give you a few lessons."

"I'll deal with that problem when I have to," he bravely replied, while inwardly quaking at the thought that something might happen to Joey. He could not, would not, envisage Joey ill or in death's grip, and ordered her never to speak again of such a possibility.

Joey thought Matt's refusal to see a doctor fitted in well with his refusal to leave Haven when she suggested they spend a few weeks of the winter months in Southern California. "Phyllis would be delighted to have us, or we could stay at Daddy's place in Palm Springs."

"Heaven forbid!" was Arthur's response.

"Then what about Hawaii? We don't have to stay at Mom and Dad's place. We could go to a hotel." Having seen a decimated Pearl Harbour while standing at the rail of the rusty freighter, Arthur said he never wanted to see Wakiki again. "What!" Joey cried: "Again! Why, you've never even *been* there!"

After this slip, Arthur reached out for Joey's hand, squeezed it and told her he loved her. Joey, who had taken to wearing voluminous Mother Hubbard dresses to camouflage her thickening waist, didn't answer. Through the years, she'd continued to be uncertain exactly what it was she felt for Arthur. She wasn't sure it was love. For her, the mode of life Arthur had imposed on them wasn't particularly congenial. It contradicted everything she had known and expected from life. He had become a total recluse, suspicious of strangers and, except for herself and Phyllis, indifferent to other people. When Phyllis told her that Arthur had once crossed the continent by bus, staying in small towns for days, weeks, and once, for an entire winter, Joey found it difficult to believe he could have undertaken the socializing required for the trip. During a long telephone conversation with Phyllis about their horribly restricted life, Phyllis had explained that Arthur was chameleon-like, in that he could modify his behaviour to blend into the background of wherever he happened to be. About this, Joey was doubtful, but while she might grumble to Phyllis about their life together, she didn't really object to living at Haven, which she now habitually referred to as "the bunker."

The road to town had by this time been paved, and power and telephone lines strung along the road, which allowed Joey to run up even larger bills for daily long distance calls to Sophia (though these had finally stopped when Sophia suddenly died) and to Phyllis twice a week. Arthur was shocked at the monthly amounts, but was afraid to censure Joey's overuse of the phone. He was adamant, however, in his refusal to have electric power lines brought in, saying their solar generator had never failed them and they should stick with the tried and true. Joey complied with his wishes, although she told him he was becoming an "old pill" in middle-age.

"You're beginning to look old, you know," she said. "You never go out, never do anything. Just stay inside and tap at that old typewriter."

"I bought my typewriter new, last year. And you've no right to talk about me getting old when I can still make love every day. If you want, we'll do it twice a day."

"Well, your hair's grey and you're getting skinny. And look at all the lines on your face."

"Lines? What lines?" He ran to the bathroom to look at his face and returned to say: "Don't exaggerate, Joey. My skin's still youthful. I'm in pretty good shape for my age."

During the winter months, they spent time bickering. At least once a week Arthur would say, "I am nothing if not consistent in my work habits and in loving you." And Joey would retaliate: "I'm nothing if not consistent in suffering you," which angered Arthur because he knew Joey enjoyed making love and would often use her small plump hand to stiffen him when, after slogging all day at the typewriter, he would've preferred to sleep. Joey refused to talk about their love-making. Even after almost twenty years of marriage, she still did not want to admit that Matt opened her genital lips to kiss whatever he found there. It was too intimate. She weighted his invasion of her privacy against the pleasure of having him there, and although afterwards she censored herself for having licensed him, she had found she could not resist the temptation to "sin" when his lips moved from her breasts down over the tummy to rest upon her thighs, like a cat that patiently waits to pounce upon a bird or mouse. Arthur thought Joey's continued refusal to admit liking sex was attributable to Sophia whose influence extended beyond her death. No doubt, her mother had told Joey that a state of suspended warfare permanently existed between the sexes and during brief armistice periods, wives must ration sex and reduce contact to brief sightings and skirmishes in the night: a yell, a splattering, ineffectual shot fired, then silence.

But once the sun had passed over the meridian, they ceased niggling at each other. Then, even though snow still lay on the upper reaches of far-off hills, they sat on the patio. Joey might even bring out a blanket to lie on and, one piece at a time, discard items of clothing until her winter-whitened tires of protective fat lay exposed to the impersonal sun.

"You're looking marvellous, Joey," Arthur said, because of course he loved all of Joey, even accretions of fat on her body. The original Joey was still there under it, the Joey he had seen in the movie studio and had loved from that first moment.

On one such occasion, while looking along the lines of her barrelling stomach, she told him how, as a child, she had once run into her parents' bathroom and been terrified by the sight of her mother's body with its bulging, sagging wads of fat. "In a way, I'm glad I've never had a baby," she said, "because I wouldn't have wanted it to see me like this." Joey rarely spoke of the children she had never borne, but when she did, Arthur's lips tightened and twisted as though he were suppressing an arrow of pain ripping through his heart, because he did feel genuine sorrow that Joey had no children. Yet, he also thought that since she'd rejected the idea of adopting a child or having one by another man, she really hadn't a right to raise the subject, even in passing.

After a couple of weeks of lying in the sun, Joey's skin would bake to a gorgeous amber. When that happened, Arthur compared her to a Polynesian queen of old, freshly plumped before adding yet another virile youth to her retinue. Arthur's first woman had been overweight (he could still see Dot Perks sprawled on her cot), a circumstance which might have indelibly imprinted itself upon his immature mind, so that forever after he associated bodily copiousness in females with the provision of sexual pleasure and the maintenance of potency. This may explain why Arthur could love a fat Joey at the same time adore the lissom youthful Joey he still perceived within the barricade of her increasing corpulence.

As the years passed, the number of Arthur's published novels increased and his characters and settings more and more reflected his new life in Canada. However, during this period, his excursions into the outside world sharply decreased. It seemed as if an increase in age was accompanied by a corresponding heightening of his fear that his identity as Matt Scheiler was threatened and that his past (somehow) was on the verge of being revealed. At most, he left the house for a short walk among the pines, then moved into the orchard which, so a fruit-tree expert had told him, ought to be replaced with young stock, but which Arthur preferred to keep as it was, because each year when the trees were in blossom, he was reminded of the afternoon they had stopped on the road and first seen Haven. But when a car or truck passed on the highway, he turned and hurried back to the house, or got behind a tree.

Joey claimed that Arthur was becoming "absolutely paranoid," an accusation he denied. He was merely guarding his privacy. There was a considerable increase in boat traffic on the lake, resulting in watercraft entering the cove, obviously ignoring the two Private Property signs Joey had placed on the lake side of the headlands. Somebody, Joey suspected drunk youths, had clambered up the cliffs and painted "Fuck You" on the signs, then strewn broken beer bottles and garbage everywhere. Joey was furious and, without telling Arthur, telephoned the local RCMP station and demanded that an officer come to Haven immediately. Arthur was sitting on the patio when the officer arrived and for a moment he was filled with an intense panic that made him want to leap from his chair and bolt into the house and hide himself behind dresses and skirts in Joey's closet. He heard Joey say, "Well, at least you showed up" before she led the officer away to the headlands. The officer, who was trying to figure out how he'd missed the buried house below the massive gates on his rounds, nodded glumly when he saw the mess and told Joey he would pass the information to the lake patrol. When he mildly suggested that putting up the large signs amounted to waving a red flag before a bull, Joey indignantly asked, "Are you telling me we're supposed to let people do as they please on our property?"

"I'm only suggesting the reason why kids racing around on the lake came onto your property might be the signs." He eyed Joey from beneath his peaked cap, surprised she was unable to see what was obvious to him, but perhaps it was understandable. After all, he spent a great deal of his time dealing with teenagers who regarded every sign they saw as a deliberate provocation. "You know, Mrs. Scheiler, I've seen your husband's books in the library. It'd sure be nice to meet him."

But when they returned to the house, Arthur was nowhere to be found. He emerged from the orchard later in the afternoon and helped Joey gather and bag the debris, and after some debate, they followed the police officer's advice and removed the signs. Because Joey was so angry about the trespass, they discussed hiring a man to patrol the property, but in the end decided it was impractical. They did, however, arrange for a fieldstone wall to be built on the highway side of the property and a ranch-style fence erected to clearly define the east-west boundaries of their twenty acres. Growth in the town's population and the slow but steady encroachment of developed land on either side of Haven had forced them, they told each other, into staking out the boundaries, and so they were doubly outraged when one day a man suddenly appeared at the roof edge to look down on Joey and Arthur sitting in the patio. The stranger tried to engage a sunbathing Joey, who grabbed a towel to cover herself, and a partially-hidden Arthur beneath an umbrella in conversation about selling some of their acreage.

"How dare you trespass on our land! Get off at once!" Joey shouted.

"But Ma'am, I did try the door first."

"Get off! At once!" Joey yelled at the man, while Arthur retreated further under the umbrella. The man shrugged and left. Later, meeting a colleague, he remarked, "That Haven place seems to be a nudist colony."

"Bunch of nuts, eh?" the colleague replied.

"Yeah, but do they ever have a spectacular location. Boy, oh boy! A guy could build exclusive housing there. Think of it: marina, California-style houses dotted around, a small golf course. Jeez! There's real potential for big bucks."

"So what's there now?"

"Christ only knows. I go down some steps, knock on a door. No answer, so I walk around some bushes and look down on patio and see this naked fat dame stretched out on a lounge and a guy hiding under an umbrella. I introduce myself, and she jumps up and screams at me to get out. Jeez! People don't have any manners these days!"

The intrusion caused Arthur and Joey to discuss having automatic, house-controlled locks installed on the gates, but they finally decided it would be ineffectual in keeping people off the property. While the locks might serve as a psychological barrier, they wouldn't prevent determined individuals from vaulting over the walls or the fences. Joey raised the question of buying another place, but Arthur had become thoroughly habituated to Haven and refused even to contemplate moving. "After all," he said, "trespassing is rare and occurs mainly in the summer when vacationers boat on the lake."

Of course, every year the fruit harvesters (one had died and was replaced by his nephew) returned with their pickers to strip the trees. The two men would shake their heads, telling Arthur that the deteriorating quality of the fruit meant a lower price, but Arthur and Joey no longer had any interest in bargaining and accepted whatever was offered, insisting only that the men set up a portable toilet at the site. Arthur and Joey still sat on the patio, however, and watched the pickers come down the slope to swim in the cove. They no longer swam in their underwear, but stripped to the buff. "A sign of the times," Arthur said. "That's what the 60s have done. And I wouldn't mind betting the new generation is superior to ours."

"Maybe, but I'll bet the guys still lead the women around by their noses," Joey said. "Like you did me."

"I didn't lead you anywhere, Joey. You wanted me as much as I wanted you."

"Phooey! Anyway, I saw you eyeing those girls."

"They wanted me to. They'd be disappointed if I didn't. The point is, biologically speaking, females know that the more males see of them, the greater their chances of getting a suitable mate. Walk along any public beach, Joey, and you'll see what I mean."

"Matt! You've never been near a public beach in your life."

"I had a life before I met you, Joey. Maybe it was limited, maybe not perfect, but a life."

"For God's sake, who cares about what went on in your life before me?"

Arthur laughed, then said, "You're probably right. No one really cares. I suppose most of the women'll end up with kids, though not necessarily with the fathers of them. And the men'll fade into non-entity middle age, lose their muscles, acquire beer bellies and end up yakking (Arthur had picked up this word on his rare trips into town with Joey.) about hockey players: Who's best, Guy Lefleur or Bobby Hull?"

"There's another thing you don't know anything about—hockey."

"Maybe so, but I've got a pretty good idea of what men talk about when they get together: Sports, cars, women and work, in that order. And sometimes they resort to fist-fights over which hockey player is the greatest, because they mistake admiration for athletic prowess with religious beliefs and patriotism. And they think politicians are self-serving liars and the truth is, they aren't far off the mark."

"How you go on," Joey said.

"I'm bored with myself."

"Why don't you walk up and get the mail?"

"Come with me. And bring a bowl. We'll pick some cherries on the way down."

"Hand me my dress. And my sandals," Joey ordered. Arthur retrieved, passed them to her and watched her pull a billowy, white dress over her head, thinking how little her face had changed over the years, her skin, especially, was still as clear and unlined as when she was twenty.

They went through the house, picked up a bowl, then strolled up the ser-
pentine drive to the gates where from the mailbox just inside, Arthur took out
their mail. There was one large envelope from Phyllis's office, and as Arthur
turned it over in his hands, he asked Joey if she and Phyllis had spoken on the
phone recently.

"Not for a while," Joey said.

"Hm. That's odd."

"She's probably away. Maybe in New York."

"Doesn't she always tell you when she's going away?"

"Perhaps there was a family emergency."

They walked back to the orchard, located their tree and gathered a bowl of
cherries. "There's nothing wrong with this crop," Arthur said. "I don't know
what those guys have to complain about."

"They want us to lower our price, that's all."

"But look at the price of cherries in stores."

"What do you know about prices? You hardly ever go into the store any
more."

"Cherry prices were mentioned yesterday on the morning radio." Arthur's
contact with local and national affairs was dependent on the CBC regional
station located in town. Someone at the station had once tried to interview
him, but had got no further than Joey, who said "No" and hung up the phone.
But both Joey and Arthur listened faithfully to the eight AM and five PM
newscasts, and Joey, with the sound turned low so as not to bother Arthur,
listened to the local stations which broke the tedium of commercials with
spots of country music and local news.

The contents of the envelope from Phyllis's office contained shocking news
for Arthur and Joey and eventually altered their lives. A note from Phyllis's
secretary revealed that Phyllis had collapsed in her office and been taken to a
hospital where she had undergone exploratory surgery. The secretary apologized for not telephoning, but she had been run off her feet contacting Phyllis's
clients.

"We must call Phyllis's office right away," Arthur said as they hurried back
to the house.

"This is terrible. Oh, terrible. I wonder if Bernard knows. You know, her
brother. Maybe I should call him."

"Call the office first. Hurry."

"Poor Phyl, Yes, long distance. Los Angeles. The number is . . ." Joey read
off the office number, waited until she was connected, then said, "It's Joey
Scheiler here, Matt Scheiler's wife. I'm calling to inquire how Phyllis is." An

expression of horror appeared on Joey's face. Arthur would remember for the rest of his life seeing tears literally spurting from Joey's eyes. "Oh no . . . oh no . . ." Joey dropped the receiver where it dangled on the cord. "She's dead, Matt, Phyllis's dead."

They immediately made arrangements to fly to Vancouver and on to Los Angeles. Arthur was rigid from shock and from the claustrophobia that hit him as soon as he was belted into his seat. (The first time in his life he had flown was to Mexico City some years earlier with Joey and Phyllis. It was then he learned he dreaded being enclosed in small, narrow spaces.) By the time they reached Los Angeles, Phyllis had been buried by her brother Bernard, his wife and a cousin who had flown in from New York. Bernard told a shaken Joey and a shrunken Arthur that Phyllis had been taken to the hospital where an emergency operation revealed inoperable bowel cancer. She had died a few days later. Joey was distraught, Arthur tight-lipped. "Why didn't Phyl tell us something was wrong?" Joey whimpered. "Why didn't she tell me? I was her best friend."

"She told no one. She didn't want anyone to know," Bernard said.

"But I loved her. She should have told me." Bernard shook his head and turned to look through the window of Phyllis's apartment. He had known little about his sister, though her sudden death had disrupted the daily round of his placid life. He hadn't seen Joey for years, and although he'd heard of Matt Scheiler, knew nothing of his novels and suspected it would be a waste of time to inquire now, because the man crouched in the living room chair was be-numbed with shock. Still, Bernard thought, he should offer them the use of the apartment for their overnight stay. He and his wife were staying at the Beverly Hills Hotel.

At first, Joey couldn't bring herself to sleep in Phyllis's bed, but Arthur convinced her Phyllis would have wanted it. Joey's abundant tears saturated the pillow, and she clung to Arthur, narrating stories of her and Phyllis's child-hood friendship. Eventually, Arthur's sympathy and Joey's grief were tempo-rarily expunged by love-making. Before he finally fell asleep, Arthur won-dered at the ease with which he and Joey had undertaken the sexual act. Had grief functioned as an aphrodisiac? Or, in their own unique way, had they aped the centuries-old rite in which a grieving mother, after burying a child, seeks to be immediately impregnated? Later, when Arthur thought about this, he concluded it had been nothing more than a temporary displacement of one set of feelings by another, because while loving had momentarily quelled Joey's tears, their overwhelming sense of loss remained and would never leave them.

"I'll never feel the same again," Joey said as she rearranged her nightgown before going to sleep.

But something occurred that night which neither Joey nor Arthur could have foreseen. Joey conceived a child. Of course, Arthur and Joey had no idea this had happened until after they returned to Haven, some eight or ten weeks later, when Joey, feeling off-colour and slightly nauseous, made an appointment to see Dr. Biggstern.

"No, I can't be," she told Biggstern when he told her she was pregnant. "It's impossible. Matt's sperm isn't any good. Besides, I'm forty."

"All that may be so. Mrs. Scheiler," Biggstern said. "But nevertheless you *are* pregnant."

"I thought my periods had stopped. Early menopause, or something."

"You're in your third month, Mrs. Scheiler." He leaned back in his chair and looked at the ceiling. "You know, there are people who can help you . . . terminate . . ."

"You mean . . . ?" Joey asked.

"Yes," he replied.

"No. I'm having it. I've always wanted a child."

"Take a few days to think it over."

"I'm having it," Joey repeated. She then stood, walked from the office and out the building to race back along the highway, down the driveway and into Haven, yelling at the top of her voice: "Matt! Matt! It's a miracle! We're going to have a baby! We're going to have a baby!"

CHAPTER

24

JOEY'S PREGNANCY PROVED EASY-GOING. SHE TRIED TO LOSE weight while at the same time was determined to provide appropriate nutrients for the foetus in her womb. She did a few of the exercises (not all) illustrated in the pamphlets she received from Dr. Mackenzie, the obstetrician, whom she had engaged because, as she told Arthur, her mother would have wanted that. Still, regardless of what the doctor advised and what Joey did, her legs swelled and she needed to be hospitalized in the final week of her pregnancy, her body elevated from the waist down. She patiently bore being heaved around like sack of potatoes, but was worried her elevated legs might adversely affect the baby, though the nurses reassured her the position wouldn't have any ill effect.

Arthur moved into town and into the hotel room where he and Joey had waited for Haven to be built. As usual, he worked each morning and in the afternoons walked to the hospital where, hunched in a chair beside Joey's bed, he would listen to Joey recapitulate the saga of how the child within her womb had been conceived because of Phyllis's miraculous intervention. Arthur, resigned to Joey believing what she pleased about the event, nodded in agreement with everything she said, but had doubts. He missed Joey's presence, watching her dress and undress, puttering around the house, hearing her high-pitched voice on the telephone with her older brother Tommy with whom she had long conversations now that her mother and Phyllis were gone; but most of all, Arthur yearned to feel the warmth of Joey's body in bed at night, then watch her awaken and say she simply must empty her bladder. Arthur equated Joey's need to relieve herself with a finance minister's need to eliminate a budgetary deficit. It was the incongruity of the contrast that drove Arthur to uncover the similarity, which he summarized in one simple word: CALAMITY. Why calamity? Because Joey had told Arthur about peeing her panties and bed as a three-year-old, and how her mother had predicted future moral delinquency and physical decay because of her inability to control the outflow of her urine. In short, her mother had viewed her daughter's wetting her pants as a calamity. In a similar way, Arthur mused, finance ministers also view a deficit as a dire prediction that a nation is heading for bankruptcy as a calamity. In fact, when a person stopped to think about it, it didn't take much in the way of brains to figure out that the entire world was fuelled by calamity, natural and human-made. Consider the effect of little Joey's wetting herself on the local economy and compare it with the effect of a deficit on the income and spending habits of individuals. Very similar! Why, before Joey grew out of her bed and panty-wetting phase, her mother had spent enough money on replacement mattresses, bed linen, rubber sheets, rubber pants and cotton underwear to provide several people with several days' work. Seen from an economic point of view, Sophia's attempt to break Joey's wetting habit was downright anti-social because weren't wet-bottomed babies and children actually benefactors of society, happily contributing to increase in the GNP? Arthur leapt from that thought to reasoning that every nation, corporation, corner store and individual owed something to someone. A lender cannot exist without a borrower, thus it followed that every person to some degree balanced lending with borrowing. This was true, he thought, even with individuals who, on the surface, appeared destitute. They put their lives in hock in order to provide awareness of prosperity for those who have enough food and rest easy at night in warm beds. Every gain and every loss is made at someone else's expense. Someone laboured to drop the tree from which was cut the lumber that the carpenter used to make the cross on which Christ was crucified; someone shaped the planks that transported heavy-hearted men and women across oceans into slavery; someone designed and built the gas chambers and furnaces in which thousands were gassed and burned to ashes. Yes, he thought, calamity has ruled the roost from the moment the earth trembled and something wiggled in the primeval slime. But it was better, and much wiser too, to forget the past and stick with what was to come. Better by far to "Phew!" in admiration as Joey's great belly preceded her from the bathroom and across the room to rejoin him in bed, where the most she allowed now was for him to press an ear against her taut skin and listen while the creature inside kicked. No, he wasn't permitted to touch the place from which the Phyllis-blessed infant would emerge, lest Joey's interior quivers would cause the baby to get the idea the time had come for it to commence its journey to the outside world. At best, he could share in the contentment which Joey experienced with each expansion of her body and always fervently agreed when she looked at herself in the bedroom mirror and said, "Isn't it incredible, Matt?" And he supposed that for Joey it was truly incredible. She had been determined to make a movie, which she'd done, and as equally determined to make a baby, which she was now doing. No wonder she felt contented. In the early months of the pregnancy, he had wondered for a moment if she might have gone elsewhere to procure the necessary ingredient for conception, but now he had come to accept his role in the manufacture of the baby, however inexplicable it might be.

In the evening, after visiting hours, he usually wandered around town before going into the hotel lounge to stare at the glass of beer he ordered but never finished. He noticed the women who haunted the night streets, and if one raised a questioning eyebrow in his direction, he felt he had betrayed Joey when he was momentarily tempted. After a while, the women stopped eyeing him. After all, this guy was merely filling in time, while they were working gals with a living to make. At night, since the town centre was relatively quiet, the streets were not strictly policed, and as a rule the women bargained with men in cars, then drove away with them to one of the darker spots in the lakeside parking lot, which made Arthur wonder how a woman could summon up sufficient trust to drive off with an unknown man into the night. Occasionally, he spotted a man and woman coupling in a dark building entry, and he saw himself mirrored there, and wondered if he, too, had used women in the past as thoughtlessly as the men he observed with prostitutes in shadowed doorways, though as he remembered it, no village woman he had gone with had accused him of exploitation, rather they appeared to take pride in his precocious virility. Or was he mistaken about that? In any case, the woman he had most desired, Maria, he had never possessed, though, now, the simple resurrection of her name intensified his regret. Yet, from his desire for Maria and the agony of losing her, there had sprung the coiled, warped tree of succession that had brought him to Martha, to Trina, then to Phyllis and Joey, and finally to their lakeside haven in British Columbia. Phyllis . . . He missed her, missed the security of knowing she would always be there for him, a firm, unshakeable wall against which he could rest and be supported. He has been surprised when he learned she had divided her estate between him and her brother Bernard, also named executor, except for her personal collection of jewellery which she bequeathed to Joey. He appreciated Phyllis's generosity, but would have preferred she was alive. Then there was the unpleasant disagreement between him and Bernard about the disposition of Phyllis's agency, which she had expanded into an successful enterprise. For Arthur, it was a question of survival, since he had no idea what records Phyllis kept on him, whereas for Bernard the agency represented nothing more than selling a business that was highly dependent upon personal contact, therefore having little commercial value. Eventually, they agreed to transfer the agency to Phyllis's long-time secretary, Betty Arnold, for a nominal amount. The agency was re-named *Ackroyd and Arnold.*

Joey took great pleasure in her legacy from Phyllis. Each day, she carefully chose which items of jewellery she would wear: the pearl necklace, the diamond broach, the silver bangles, or the gold rings. The platinum and diamond watch, which Phyllis inherited from her mother, was the only piece Joey never wore because the band was too small to fit her plump wrist, but she kept it on her bedside table at home and in the hospital where she could easily consult it. Joey had arranged for a private room, and everybody who entered was treated to the story of her baby's conception, which caused some staff to wonder if she wasn't slightly mad, since it was one thing for Mary miraculously to conceive Jesus as the result of divine intervention by God Himself, but quite another for an ordinary woman to conceive a child as the result of the untimely death of a dear friend.

"I'm not saying Phyllis actually came and put the baby inside me," Joey would say. "No, not that. I'm not that big a fool. What I think happened is, because Matt and I both loved Phyllis very, very much and were so terribly upset at her passing on, something inside Matt sprung loose and allowed one— just one—" At this point in the narration, Joey would pause, raise a portentous finger and fix her listener with her large, vivid blue eyes before continuing, "—one teeny tiny sperm to leave his body and meet up with one of my ovum (Joey had picked up this word from Dr. Mackenzie). And if you think of how long Matt and I've been married, and all the times we tried to have a baby, the only possible explanation for the pregnancy is that our friend Phyllis helped us while we were . . . well . . . you know, sleeping in her bed. Don't you agree?" Most people did. What grounds had they to disagree?

This went on for several days, until one afternoon Arthur arrived at the hospital and found Joey lying curled up on her side, happily smiling.

"What happened?" Arthur asked. "What's going on?"

Joey didn't say anything, instead, she waved him around to the other side of the bed. He obeyed, and there beheld a high bassinet on rollers inside which he saw a baby wrapped in a pink receiving blanket. "I've already named her," Joey said. "Miracle."

"But when?" Arthur, in shock, whispered.

"This morning. I told Mackenzie not to call you because you'd be working and coming in the afternoon. Anyway, there weren't any problems. Everybody was surprised at how she just popped out."

"Is everything all right? Are you okay?"

"Yes. And Miracle's beautiful. Perfect."

Arthur leaned over to examine the baby's face. "She looks like you," he said. "I'd have brought flowers if I'd known." From his hospital visits he had discovered that husbands customarily offer bouquets of flowers to exhausted wives after they emerged triumphant from their nine-month ordeal. Arthur had never felt so unwanted and unnecessary.

"So what do you think of your daughter?" said a nurse who had entered the room. "Is she what you ordered?"

"I'm speechless."

"So you should be. We are all pleased. Mrs. Scheiler did a wonderful job." (Arthur remembered his mother words: "Did you do your job today, dear?" For a few awful seconds he had an urge to lean over expecting to see steam rising from the "job" he had just deposited in the outhouse pit. He shook himself, returned to the present and saw two dark-blue eyes focused on him.)

"She looked at me," he said and backed away.

"You're just a blob to her," the nurse said. "It's Mom she'll want."

"Give her to me now," Joey said. "I have to hold her, I just have to."

The nurse laughed. "After months of getting up at night to feed her, you'll be glad when she sleeps."

"No, never."

"Don't expect her to feed, Mrs. Scheiler," the nurse cautioned. "Your milk's not in yet."

Arthur's eyes widened in shock at the sight of Joey's swollen nipple pushed against the baby's twitching lips and practically ran from the room. He needed time to adjust to a changed Joey and to the new presence in his life. He needed something to tide him over the shock, and it came to him they would need money to provide things for the baby, because Joey had done little in the way of preparation. Without a word to Joey, he left.

At the bank, he was forced to spend fifteen minutes convincing the manager and tellers who he was, since prior to this visit, they had never seen him before. It wasn't until he finally lost patience and began shouting that he got some action. "Look, must I go to the hospital and drag my wife and baby in here in order to convince you I'm Matt Scheiler?" But it wasn't Arthur's shouting that did the trick, it was the word "baby." Everyone in the bank knew of Joey's miracle pregnancy and had already planned to club together to buy "a little something" to celebrate the miracle when it finally occurred.

"You mean Mrs. Scheiler's had her baby?" a teller asked.

"Why else would I be here?"

"What is it?"

"A girl."

The teller turned and called out: "Listen! Joey's had her miracle baby. It's a girl." Other female employees (not including the manager, who was male and apparently disinterested in childbirth) abandoned their posts to swarm around Arthur. "How wonderful!" they cried. "A little girl! Does she have Joey's blue eyes? How much did she weigh?" The women varied in age: one looked nubile, another's white hair proclaimed she verged on retirement, but all asked Arthur to give Joey their love and a kiss for baby. As he looked at their faces, he understood that beyond the realms of caste, class, ambitious politicians and warring armies there existed a world-encircling domain which transcended national borders, government edicts and even assaults of brutal, mindless male armies. This was the domain of women who shared knowledge of the pleasure of conception, the pain of labour and the joy of cradling a new born child. It was something no man could experience, yet awareness of it was in the faces of all the women there, even the youngest, who asked him to congratulate Joey. He noticed that their best wishes did not extend to him.

Still, the encounter with the excited bank employees went a long way to restore Arthur's shattered ego, and he decided he wouldn't emulate the male spider about to be consumed by his mate after all, but would allow himself to feel he had achieved something of importance for which he should receive some credit. Thus Arthur was transformed into a proud father. He then went to the flower shop and bought two dozen red roses, next came a visit to the jewellery store, where he purchased a gold necklace with four diamonds to symbolize the formation of their new family. The fourth diamond represented Phyllis. Finally, he entered a food store where he bought fresh fruit and two packets of licorice allsorts, Joey's favourite candy. He then returned to the hospital room.

Joey demanded to know why he had left so suddenly, but instead of answering, he simply handed over the gifts. She ooh-ed over the flowers and aah-ed over the necklace, which she immediately put on, then ordered him to peel an orange, of which she gave him one section, ate the rest, after which she pulled a handful of allsorts from a packet, popped them one at a time into her mouth and began chewing. She gave instructions about everything Arthur must do to prepare for her own and Miracle's homecoming. Arthur remembered the bank tellers' request he give the baby a kiss, and moving to the high bassinet, he pressed his lips against the forefinger of his right hand, then touched the baby's cheek.

"What are you doing?" Joey cried, looking as though she were about to spring from the bed and attack him. "Oh, did they?" she said, after he told her about his visit to the bank. "That was nice. Okay. You can kiss Miracle. She won't mind."

"It might wake her."

"It won't, but be careful you don't jab your nose into her face." Arthur leaned over, kissed the air above the baby's cheek, then sat on the bed and told Joey how much he missed her and wanted her back home.

"It'll be a while before I can do anything," Joey warned him. "My breasts are sore. The nurse said they'll be fine, once my milk begins to flow." She opened her gown for him to see her maternal breasts. "That's colostrum," she informed Arthur when saw the fluid that oozed from them. "The nurse thinks I'll have plenty of milk. Now, don't forget anything on the list. You want a licorice before you go? And don't forget the bassinet will be in our room for a while. You may prefer sleeping in the guest room."

"I don't think so."

"We'll see."

"Oh, there's something I forgot to tell you. What with the baby . . ."

"Miracle," Joey firmly said. "Call her Miracle. So what did you forget to tell me?"

"There was a letter from Betty Arnold about a literary award. It's for authors who write about the 'common people.' A left-of-centre foundation sponsors it." Arthur halted, reluctant to say more.

Joey said, "Well, go on."

"It would mean going to England."

"Its easy to fly now."

"I'm not sure I want to fly anywhere. I get claustrophobic."

"Don't be silly, Matt. Sooner or later you'll have to get over it."

"You could collect it for me."

"Rubbish. What's the award?"

"Twenty-five thousand dollars. I could write a thank-you letter and you'd give it to the committee."

"Matt, I have absolutely no intention of going halfway around the world to collect an award for you. There's nothing wrong with you going. It'd be good for you. Get you out of your shell."

"We'll talk about it later."

"When is this happening?"

"Later in the spring. The end of April."

"I'll be nursing Miracle." An image flickered before Arthur's eyes of Joey suckling Miracle in the midst of a circle of literary types.

"Maybe I'll turn it down," he muttered.

"Don't be ridiculous," Joey said. "We can use the money to set up a trust fund for Miracle. After all, you never can tell what'll happen in the future. And we want to be sure we've got enough money to raise Miracle properly. You know, singing and dancing lessons cost money."

"Joey, what's come over you? What's all this about needing money? You inherited more than enough from your parents."

"I've got a baby now, that's what. We've got to think of Miracle's future, that's what. And you have to do your share, Matt. That's all I'm saying."

"It *isn't* all. Listen Joey, I fell in love with a lovely young woman, which you still are, but you're starting to sound like your mother and I didn't fall in love with her."

"I've got my baby now. I want to make sure nothing goes wrong." Overwrought and stressed from childbirth, Joey leaned on Arthur's shoulder and sobbed as she had not done since Phyllis's death. "I wish Phyl could see her," she sobbed. "It breaks my heart knowing she died so I could have Miracle."

Arthur said nothing, but hoped Joey would eventually regain objectivity and drop the idea that Phyllis's ghost had unravelled his testicular coils, rounded up his sperm and herded them to the top of Joey's sheath while simultaneously jolting her ovarian ducts into releasing an egg that flew along her tube to embrace the first, strongest, most adventurous spermatozoon it encountered. He was prepared to accept the possibility of chance, even that Phyllis's death had somehow been a precondition of allowing his and Joey's germinal cells to meet, fuse and appear nine months later as Miracle; but he didn't relish the thought of raising the point with Joey because the outcome would be a search through the garbage dump of history looking for The Prime Cause. And he had enough of Prime Causes in his novels. He must stop the intrusion of Phyllis into his life and concentrate on getting Joey back to Haven and in bed with him again. He would start his campaign by a visit to Baby World where he would buy everything Joey and Miracle would possibly need when they got home.

The shopkeeper was overjoyed to assist Arthur in outfitting the nursery: bassinet, crib, change table, blankets, clothes, rattles, dozens of diapers and numerous other infant accoutrements (cost: three thousand dollars). It took him days to arrange for the transport of his purchases via taxi to Haven (cost: a hundred dollars).

After Joey and Miracle got home, Joey appeared to think one of his fatherly duties consisted of flushing the contents of diapers down the toilet, then when the diaper pail got full (every third day) to commence the cycle of washing, drying and folding the rectangles of white cloth. Joey, still resting much of the day, showed him how to fold the diapers, but then took over the task herself because Arthur seemed incapable of doing the job properly. "It's simple," Joey instructed him. "Look: this, this, then this. Get it?" But Arthur sensibly never did.

During the early months of their daughter's life, his sole pleasure was watching Miracle hungrily gulp down the milk she pumped from Joey's breasts, and, standing beside the change table, watching Joey bathe the baby after he delivered a pail of water from the kitchen to the nursery at just-the-right-temperature. When he casually remarked it might be easier to bathe the child in the kitchen sink, he received a pointed rebuke.

Miracle's first smile occurred while she was in her bath. Joey gasped: "Did you see that?"

"What?" asked. He was watching Miracle's feet kicking the water.

"She smiled."

"She did?" Arthur leaned over to look at his daughter's face, whose expressions he had trouble identifying, though Joey claimed she could see evidence of every imaginable things from bliss (after nursing) to speculative thought on seeing a new mobile hanging above her crib, or a shudder when her father's face appeared in her angle of vision.

"I saw it. She looked straight at me and smiled. She knows I'm her mom."

It wasn't that Joey entirely expelled Arthur from her life. No. She said it was pleasant to have him back inside her, but did he notice any difference? It was Joey's preference for Miracle that hurt him, and while he understood it was probably within the natural order of things, still her preoccupation with the baby affected his vanity and ultimately brought him around to softening his resistance to visiting England. After all, he told himself, why shouldn't Matt Scheiler expose himself to a group of people prepared to admire him and his work? Surely there was no danger in that. He was imagining things if he thought otherwise.

"But why don't you want to go?" Joey had asked.

"Because I don't like the place."

When Joey pointed out he wasn't in a position to say anything about England since he'd never been there, he unwisely retorted he had been, then was forced to invent a tale, which didn't even convince himself, about wandering around wartime-shrouded Liverpool with shipmates and getting involved in a fight with English navy personnel, during which an English sailor might have, just might have, mind you, been stabbed and killed.

"Was it you who stabbed the guy?" Joey asked.

Arthur turned his ahead away as an image appeared of Martha bringing the typewriter down on Laura's head. "Certainly not."

"Were you questioned by the police?"

"No, nothing like that. Just a fight among drunk crews."

"Then you have nothing to worry about. For God's sake Matt, get on the ball."

But Arthur found excuses to dilly-dally about his decision: he had a head cold, his stomach was upset, his back was sore. "Everything was okay with your back last night in bed," Joey pointed out. He offered another excuse: he was reluctant to leave Joey and Miracle alone in the house. "For God's sake, it'll only take two days to get there, a day to accept the award, two days to get back. A week at the outside. Or do you plan staying ten years? If you are, tell me and I'll sell Haven and move back to southern California."

A few days following this unsatisfactory conversation, Betty Arnold called from the agency to say she was frantic and would Arthur please let her know as soon as possible if he was prepared to go to London to accept the award. She was thinking of increased sales of Arthur's titles.

Arthur sat in his workroom and strung together long lists of wishes: he wished he had never laid eyes on Joey; he wished the events of the past thirty years could be wiped out as though not a single one had happened; he wished he had never put pen to paper and fingertips to typewriter keys; he wished he had never known any village women; he wished that Heather, Maria, Martha and Laura had never entered his life; he wished he had remained east of the Mississippi, instead of continuing his rite of bus passage across America; he wished he had stayed in the cafe with Trina and grilled hamburgers and hot dogs and made love with her until his death; he wished his desire to possess all women sexually had not been overridden by his love for Joey; he wished his fear would vanish and leave him in peace, though, as with his other wishes, he knew this wish too was unattainable; he wished he might rise to great heights as a writer and wished he could regret past failures, but couldn't bring himself to this, because those very failures had brought him Joey and financial success; he wished he might be a child again and not have to suffer the affliction that had so profoundly influenced his life; he wished, at the same time he recognized the wish was an expression of failure and folly, that his mother had remained his mother only and his father had not destroyed his innocence by introducing him to whores, at the same time he wished, though condemning himself for it, that he was more like his father and could arbitrarily take any woman he fancied at the moment; he wished he could once again be the child who had stroked his beloved Mary's neck and felt her affectionately press against him; he wished —oh God, how he wished—that he had not stood by and silently watched her being led into the knacker's van, knowing on the morrow she would be dead; and finally, at the end of the wish list, he wished he had remained in perpetual childhood, or better yet, been born into an imbecilic unawareness that would free him from present temptation and memories of a life riddled with unfulfilled desires; because what he truly he desired was to reach a void of desire, where no wish needed to be expressed, where he would find himself standing alone on the torturous precipice of his own existence, from which he had no alternative but to plunge.

Although there was no objective evidence he would be in danger if he returned to England, nonetheless he was uneasy about going. He believed that somehow or other the inexorable mill of societal vengeance would grind him as punishment for a crime he had not committed, although he had run as if he were guilty, hadn't he? And surely his running was a crime too? And what about Joey if he was found out? Why hadn't he been as truthful with her as he had with Phyllis about his past? For days, he vacillated between going and not going, then one evening, sitting in the living room with Joey, he announced: "I'll go."

"Of course you will," Joey replied, moving Miracle from her left breast to her right. "I don't know why you make such a fuss about it. It's no big deal." The latter phrase was a favourite of Joey's, and whenever she used it Arthur wondered if it originated with people whose financial bottom lines were in the millions, whereas if he, Arthur, were to divide the dollar amount of the award being offered him by the years of labour it would be seen as a pittance. So maybe Joey was right after all: it was no big deal. He'd fly in, stay at a decent hotel, everything arranged by Betty, accept the award, maybe stay an extra half-day to rest, fly home, all within a week. And he could take steps to minimize the risk of being recognized as his former self. For instance, he could get the barber to crop his hair short as it had been when he crewed on the freighter and bussed across middle America. Maybe not quite so short, because some people associated crew cuts with convicts, and he didn't want to risk that. Before his "troubles," he had worn his hair at what he imagined was "Shelleyian" length, mistakenly believing (like Samson?) that hair-length determined the strength of his literary imagination, and that a shearing would drain him of creative force. And back then, in the period when he moved stealthily northward from Ponnewton to Liverpool, when he had first shorn his hair, there were days when the bitter north winds nipped his exposed ears and he actually believed he had been permanently depleted of authorial energy. And something else he could do: Acquire a brand new wardrobe to reflect his notoriety as the author of novels about the ordinary people living in small-town America and western Canada. It would be fitting for him to receive the award in blue jeans, lumberjack shirt, windbreaker and work boots.

"Nonsense," Joey said when Arthur told her about buying his new outfit. "You'll wear a navy blue blazer, grey flannels, blue shirt, striped tie and black shoes. We'll go to town this afternoon and buy them. We'll get your hair trimmed too."

"I'm having a crew cut."

"For God's sake, Matt, do you have to show up at the ceremony looking like a guy from a construction site? Or a convict?"

"What's wrong with construction sites?"

"Nothing if you're a construction worker. But you have to look like a distinguished author."

"I don't feel distinguished."

·"Practice. That's what movie stars do. They can't afford to disappoint fans. Besides, I'm not having you trotting around England looking dishevelled."

"I won't be trotting anywhere. Besides, clothes do not make the man."

"Of course they do," Joey said, "You should know that by now."

"I do know it, but I don't want to be seen as that kind of person."

"You've got to be recognized as somebody who matters. That's all." Joey put a diaper over her shoulder, placed Miracle on it and patted her back until she burped. Arthur looked at Joey's damp, milky breasts and wondered why she continued to deny him access to her breasts, because he knew from past love-making sessions that having his lips and tongue touch her nipples intensified her pleasure; but he couldn't bring himself to ask because he sensed the reason for her refusal was that she was afraid she would experience shame if she used the essence of maternal love to satisfy the needs of her grosser, sexual self. Shame . . . Arthur remembered a long-ago incident, when he was a boy, which had started out with his idly opening and closing the drawers of his mother's dresser. Within, he found a box of chocolates, from which he took and ate one. In the days following, he became consumed by guilt and shame, and also by the fear of what his mother would say or do when she discovered his theft. But nothing happened and, compelled by desire to re-experience the delicious sensation of chocolate melting in his mouth, he returned to the bedroom to take another chocolate, then another and another, until only one remained. When he returned two days later, the box was gone. Many years afterwards, when Arthur understood more about his mother, he concluded that the box of chocolates had come from one of his mother's admirers, possibly as an expression of hope, even as part-payment for rendered services. By that time, Arthur had come to understand that with his father gone all day, and he, Arthur, frequently absent for entire afternoons, his mother was alone many hours during the day. Indeed, until his father's death and their move from the forester's house to the damp cottage where he began writing his forest articles, he had always exercised his masculine prerogative to walk out of the house as he pleased, so it wasn't beyond the realm of possibility that, even before his father's death, his mother had welcomed lovers into her bed during his own and his father's absences. He remembered the afternoon when he sat beneath the kitchen table, watching the hand of the man sitting opposite his mother move to rest on her knees, and he now realized he would never know with certainty if his mother, after putting a finger to her lips, had shaken her head while pointing downward to indicate his presence under the table. Until his father's death and his mother's transformation of himself into his father and herself from his mother into Sylvia, Arthur had thought his mother was unapproachable, but now he wasn't so sure. People hid so much about themselves. Joey was a good example of this, for while Arthur had believed at one time that his physical intimacy with her would open a window through which he could discover her innermost thoughts and feelings, that had not happened, and he had realized he would know only as much of Joey as she was prepared to reveal. And as for himself, well, he had built his relationship with Joey upon a foundation of lies.

As his departure day came closer, so too became Arthur's need to uncover more of what lay in Joey's heart and mind. "Joey," he asked as they lay together in bed, "do you tell me everything about yourself?"

"What's to tell?" Joey asked.

"Oh, I don't know. This and that."

"If you don't know me by now, you never will."

"But aren't there things about yourself you've hidden away? Little things in secret cabinets of your mind?"

"You know what your trouble is, Matt? You think everybody has secrets. You think everybody's like you."

That stopped Arthur, and he moved against her until their faces touched and he could feel her expelled breath on his cheek. "You mean like me, specifically?"

"Of course. You think people hide things they don't want the rest of the world to know."

"Such as?"

"How would I know? Maybe dishonest things, or sex things. Anyway, you think the worst of people."

"That allows me to be agreeably surprised when I discover I'm mistaken."

"I sometimes wonder what you really think about me."

"I think you're wonderful."

"I'll bet. And that's something else, you're not honest. You're not open, you don't always tell the truth."

"But what each of us thinks is the truth may be different, Joey."

"There. That's what I mean. I say you don't tell the truth, and you say there're different truths."

"Are you truthful?"

"I try to be. Why're you asking me these questions?"

"I want to know everything about you, every thought, every feeling, so I can carry a complete image of you in my mind while I'm away." What Arthur didn't say was that he was desperately probing to find something that would assure him that, should anything untoward happen in England, he could feel confident Joey would not abandon him.

"Why should I tell you everything about myself, when you hardly tell me anything about yourself? Sometimes I think you're only interested in the people you write about."

"At least I create characters that aren't as bad as some people really are." Arthur paused, then continued, "Such as my parents. My father chased women, and I think my mother may have had other men, though I'm not positive about it. But everyone knew about my father."

"You see? That's what I mean. You've told me dozens of times that your parents were respectable people, but now you want me to believe some cock-and-bull story about your father. That's what I mean when I say you're not honest."

"Would you accept the truth if you learned it?"

Momentarily, Arthur was tempted to spill out everything, but the impulse passed as Joey said, "I don't suppose I would. It might be just another story you concocted."

"Listen to me, Joey . . . I have a premonition if I go away, I'll not be able to get back."

"You're being silly. There's nothing to prevent you getting on a plane and coming back."

"I know, I know. But it's like one of those dreams where you're in a room, and no matter how hard you try to escape from it, you can't, because wherever you go, you carry the room with you."

"Silly," Joey said again. She turned her head and dabbed a kiss on his nose, which was unusual, because in their relationship Arthur did most of the kissing. Arthur clung to her and asked her to kiss him again. She did, then said, "That's enough."

"Always remember I love you, Joey. You'll remember that, won't you?"

"Of course," she replied, and rolled away from him. "Go to sleep," she said. "We need to make an early start in the morning."

Arthur lay awake, conjuring up scenes of himself being greeted at Heathrow airport. Heaven forbid anyone would have a camera! But no one would. The award ceremony was going to be low-key. That's what Betty said. And she knew how he felt about photos. Ever since the time he laid down the law with Phyllis over the David book, no one had the nerve to ask him for any information except what Phyllis, and now Betty, manufactured out of thin air. And there've never been any photographs! Phyllis had seen to that. Only the passport photo. And he'd never let Joey take any pictures of him, even one of him holding Miracle, which made her quite angry. She had begun to assemble an album of snapshots of Miracle and spent hours sorting through them as though she needed them to prove that the sleeping child actually existed.

A few days before Arthur was to leave, Joey had thrust a photo of Miracle at him. "Take this with you when you, Matt. Go on. Put it in your wallet now. Otherwise you'll forget. And look at this one, Matt. See, she's in the bath. I put the shutter on time-release, remember? You can take this one too." Arthur shook his head. "Anybody'd think you didn't want pictures of your daughter."

"The one in the bath is mostly of her genitals, Joey, though I suppose in the end they summarize her existence."

"Give it here. I'm not having you talking like that about Miracle." She angrily snatched the picture from him.

"But Joey, that's the place where we carry the aggregate of our lives."

"I don't care. You have no right to say that about your daughter."

He smiled in an attempt to appease her. "I'm sorry," he said, "but people's bodies do make a big difference in their lives. Right now, Miracle's digestive and intestinal systems is where all the action takes place."

"That's all you see, Matt, because you have hardly anything to do with her." Joey moved Miracle to the other breast.

"How can I when she spends most of the day sleeping?"

"You don't see how she's growing because you hardly look at her."

"You know that's not true, Joey. I hold her every evening and I watch you bathing and feeding her."

"You don't love her."

"You mustn't say that!"

"I've seen the way you look at her."

"She's a baby, Joey. I'm looking forward to the day when I can play with her."

"Honestly? You're not kidding?" Joey was suspicious. She thought Matt was too "intellectual" to play with a child.

"Absolutely not. I think she's fascinating. I like children, especially girls."

"What do you mean, like them? You mean you're a creep who sneaks around looking up little girls' skirts?"

"That's absurd, Joey. I like girls because they're smarter than boys."

"I never heard you say that before."

"I never had a daughter before. And she is mine, isn't she, Joey?"

"What do you mean?"

"Well, you know . . ."

"You're the limit, Matt. You think I shopped around for other guys?"

"It's just that . . . well . . . she's such a surprise. That's all."

"Half the time I don't know whether to believe what you say. You're such an out-and-out liar."

"Me, a liar? I never lie to you, Joey. Never."

Joey eyed him over Miracle's head. "Men lie all the time. Mom used to say the first thing a girl has to know about men is that they lie in their teeth."

"I hope you won't inculcate such nonsense into Miracle."

"She'll have to learn a truth or two. Sometimes I think the only reason you watch her feeding is so's you can look at my breasts."

"That's ridiculous . . . I enjoy watching you nurse. In a way, I envy you. I wish I could feed her and hold her, but and since the time I accidentally stuck a pin in her, you won't even let me change her diaper."

"You could have hurt her."

"Don't exaggerate, Joey. It was tiny prick. And you won't let me bathe her because you're scared I'll drop her."

"You almost did, once. And I'll bet you wouldn't't've said that about her picture if she was a boy."

"No, no, that's not true. Anyway, I'll miss her, miss seeing her nursing like a little calf or piglet."

"So, that's what you think! That I'm no better than a cow or a pig!" Joey was now furious.

"I'm only saying that all young animals behave the same way with their mothers. That's all. She butts you like a calf or foal." But his explanation didn't help.

The night before he left Arthur told Joey how much he loved her, but for some reason that seemed to increase the irritation which had been simmering during the previous days. She pushed him away when he tried to make love, then suddenly dragged him between her thighs and clamped her legs around him so tightly he couldn't move and a moment later just as suddenly thrust him away again. When he asked what was wrong, she admitted she didn't want him to leave.

"But you were the one who said I had to go!"

"What's that got to do with it?" she snapped. She then began crying. "I'm afraid to be left alone."

"I won't go," he said.

"No. You have to." And so it went, with Arthur saying he wouldn't go and Joey insisting he must at the same time telling him she didn't want to be left alone. Yet she was annoyed when he suggested that Betty book passage for her and Miracle, then angry when he reiterated that he wouldn't go. "If you don't go, I'll leave you. You've got to go! You've got to do something besides sitting at that damn typewriter 365 days a year!"

But at daybreak she welcomed him. She sighed with pleasure when he sucked her breasts and she climaxed quickly before he was securely within her. He rubbed his body against hers, squeezing her breasts so that her milk was smeared onto his torso, saying he wouldn't shower until he got home. He indicated he wanted to make love again, but she rebuffed him, telling him Miracle had to be fed and changed before they left for the airport. They were cool with each other on the drive and neither said much in the waiting room.

Joey stood at the window and watched as he crossed the tarmac to board the aircraft, thinking he looked far more distinguished in his habitual corduroys, tee shirt and desert boots than in the grey flannels, navy blue blazer, blue shirt and striped tie he now wore. She lifted Miracle from the carry-all and waved her dangling arm. "Wave goodbye to Daddy, sweetheart," she said. She watched the plane taxi along the runway and whispered in Miracle's ear, "Now there's just the two of us, darling baby. Just the two of us. But we'll manage nicely, won't we?" She didn't remain to see the plane take off, but quickly walked through the airport, got in the car and drove back to Haven.

CHAPTER
25

"TRAVELLING TO TORONTO?" THE ELDERLY WOMAN SITTING across the aisle asked.

"No," Arthur curtly replied.

"Then where?" she asked.

"London, England." How was it that old age apparently licensed some people to ask impertinent questions? Maybe because they didn't have to worry sexual innuendo might be detected in their overtures. The woman was sixty-something, maybe seventy-something, with greying hair, worry lines between plucked eyebrows, unobtrusively rouged cheeks, pink-painted lips and a well-defined chin which supported two subsidiary chins beneath it. Arthur's attitude toward double chins had changed after Joey developed hers. Now he found them attractive, especially on women over thirty, because their presence suggested that the women had made peace with their bodies' irrational demands, replacing them with a cosy, though still sensual, appreciation of what life had to offer. And the woman across the aisle certainly looked as though she were extracting the best out of life. She had preceded him onto the plane into the first-class section, and he had noticed then the breadth of her hips and the fullness of her substantial bosom when she removed her coat and the jacket of her navy blue suit and handed them to the waiting attendant. She was probably somebody's grandmother, and the fullness of her blouse-hidden breasts suggested that once upon a time she had provided voluminous quantities of maternal milk for hungry babies. He sighed. He would miss watching Miracle gorge at Joey's spigots. The woman confirmed his deduction when she leaned across the aisle and confided that she had been visiting a daughter and three grandchildren in Victoria and was on her way home to Toronto. "Enjoyable, but tiring," she told Arthur, then asked if he lived in Vancouver. When Arthur explained where he lived, she remarked she had never visited the interior of B.C. but had heard it was beautiful, especially the Okanagan valley. Of course, Canada itself was so huge a person was lucky to see even a small part of it. She was Ontario born and raised, but there were parts of her province she had never seen and, now, at her time of life, probably never would. Had he travelled much? To reinforce his self-created myth of Matt Scheiler, he told her about freighting across the Atlantic and Pacific oceans and busing from coast to coast through small towns in the U.S.A. She was politely and suitably impressed, confiding that when she was young she had planned to be adventurous, but marriage and three children in a hurry (she coyly lowered her eyelids to suggest youth's voluptuous abandonment) had put a stop to all thought of travelling the world. "When we're young, we think time will wait for us, don't we?" Ah well, we were lucky if we ended our lives with a fraction of what we had once hoped to extract from it. But we ought not to grumble. Would he think her too terribly inquisitive if she inquired about his line of work. The law perhaps, or teaching, at the college level of course.

Arthur had hoped to avoid questions about himself, and now here he was, imprisoned in a metal cigar, hurtling through the sky, being submitted to a cross-examination by a friendly, but impertinent old dame. How could he *not* answer? Should he reply with lies? But why do that? Was he ashamed of his profession? So, out with it.

"A writer, eh?" He ought to have known, he told himself, when she assumed he was a journalist. "Oh, a novelist!" Might she ask his name? She went on to say she couldn't be sure, but she thought perhaps she'd read one of his books. Arthur felt like telling her she was a poor liar, but refrained, realizing that her ignorance of his work penalized her more than him. No, he wasn't going to London to persuade a publisher to issue a book, he explained. He was collecting an award for his work. "Wonderful!" she enthused, while Arthur supposed, somewhat maliciously, that his inquisitor had been raised in a social milieu where wives enthusiastically agreed everything their men did was wonderful. No doubt she was a woman who, following her mother's advice, sought and permitted regular sexual intercourse with her husband, so that he would not be tempted to chase after other women, or worse yet, find solace in his daughter or niece's bed, for as every good woman knows, the world is overrun with predatory males for whom any female cavity will serve the purpose. Arthur remembered Trina telling him about a friend who had stabbed her drunk husband as he was trying to prise open his ten-year-old daughter's legs. He tended to remember stories which confirmed his low opinion of men, at the same time reinforced his elevated opinion of women. Besides, snippets of information about human foulness were grist for his novelist mill.

The woman chattered on: She had read—was it Mclean's?—that nowadays writers were compelled to peddle their books, like patent medicine hustlers did years ago. "Yes, I'll have a drink," she told the attendant who appeared with an order pad. "Scotch on the rocks." Arthur ordered tonic water and took a moment to feel grateful he hadn't experienced any claustrophobia since getting on the plane. It must be the spacious first-class cabin. When the attendant departed to fill their orders, the woman across the aisle continued: "There's no dignity nowadays days in the professions." Her father had been a lawyer and everybody knew him and tipped their hats. One of her sons—she paused to accept her drink with an inclination of her dowager's head—was a lawyer too, but his secretary—can you imagine?—called him by his Christian name. Everything was so degraded these days. Perhaps it was because practically everybody had a television now. What did he think?

Arthur received the tonic water and, as he lifted his glass to his lips, half-wished the dozing man sitting beside him would wake up so that he could turn his attention away from the woman across the aisle, who now went on to say she always felt a little guilty drinking alcohol so early in the day. Her husband had been a famous drinker in his day—rye and water—not that he'd ever shown any evidence of alcoholism, no, nothing like that. He drank rye as some people drink coffee or tea. He'd been in advertising, where men always must be one step ahead of competitors. Such a stressful job, wasn't it?

Arthur regretted he hadn't purchased a book he could read to discourage "HER," as he now thought of the passenger. The attendant passed and smiled benignly at him. She was, he thought, stunningly beautiful, a smooth-skinned black-eyed beauty of Asian origin, too lovely, in his opinion, to be doling out booze to people who apparently had nothing better to do during the five-hour flight than force fellow passengers to listen to their life stories. Everyone in the first-class compartment (except his seat-mate) seemed intent on eating and drinking, which reminded Arthur of a village wake he had once attended with his father (his mother said such gatherings were "morbid" and had refused to go) where the mourners copiously ate and drank, presumably in an attempt to escape awareness of their own mortality and past offenses. He had never forgotten the wake, because, lured by his desire to see what a dead man looked like (the deceased was a forest labourer, killed by a misdirected falling tree), he slipped into the room where the man lay and was shocked when he saw the dead man's wife lean over to kiss her husband's cold lips, while another man, drunkenly grinning at Arthur, stood behind her doing her defunct husband's duty against her naked bottom. "That's how it is, son," his father had said when Arthur described the scene. "Half the time people don't know what they're doing nor why they're doing it. Like Mrs. Tomson. She used Bert Tomson's death to do with Harry Wilson what she hated doing with her husband. So there you have it in a nutshell, son." Years passed before Arthur fully understood what his father had been talking about. His lack of insight was a built-in flaw of his early novels. He'd had to experience terror and remake himself into another man before he truly understood the depth and extent of the struggle between "ought to" and "want to" in every individual. For Arthur, it had been a process of taking his old self apart, then painfully remoulding and remaking a new individual.

"Yes, please," the woman across the aisle said to the attendant. "I'll have another scotch." When the attendant left, the woman leaned across and said, "Isn't it unusual for a Canadian writer to receive a British award?" When Arthur explained it was an international award, she said, "I see," and continued talking. Yes indeed, America was a fascinating country. When her husband had retired, they decided to spend winter months in Florida, that is, before he died, which was four years ago. Such a change from Toronto, though she had to admit she missed the snow. When her kids were young, she had carried on her own family's tradition of winter outings, bundling everyone up in warm clothes, skiing, playing in the snow, skating, hockey games. She had vivid memories of herself flying over the ice towards a toque-marked goal. Yes, winter was a wonderful time for Canadian kids. But was she monopolizing the conversation? Did Arthur have children? One! A little girl after so many years of marriage! Oh yes, it did happen. An old friend of hers had gone through many years of marriage before she got pregnant, which sparked the usual gossip, though her friend's conduct of conduct was absolutely impeccable. She's one of those women who question the propriety of a mistletoe kiss at Christmas. In her opinion, it was just one of those mysterious, inexplicable things that sometimes occur in life. And her friend had given birth to an absolutely beautiful little girl.

"Like Joey," Arthur said, ready to match their Miracle against any woman's baby.

"Joey?"

His wife, Josephina, known as Joey all her life, Arthur explained. Ah, wasn't it shocking how parents bless their children with lovely names like Josephina, then use a diminutive. She had a friend who named her daughter Natasha, such a lovely name, but the poor girl ended up being called Nutty Natty by her brothers. Miracle. How unusual. Her own babies had come so rapidly she'd snatched the first names that came along: John and Jean and Jill. "Shockingly ordinary, wasn't I?"

The attendant leaned solicitously over Arthur to ask which *entrée* he would prefer, salmon or filet of beef. "The salmon will do," Arthur replied and could hardly refrain from telling the attendant she was the most beautiful woman he'd ever seen (except Joey) while she assessed her passenger as an average Joe only travelling first-class because he'd been lucky enough to win a raffle where the prize was a first-class return flight to Toronto, a weekend at the Royal York Hotel and a ticket to a Maple Leaf's game. She pitied him for having become the target of a woman who had the energy to talk the head off a donkey all the way to Toronto. Clearly, the woman had money, you could tell from her clothes, but Mr. Scheiler looked as if he'd purchased his blazer and slacks especially for the trip, though he wasn't a bad-looking man, quite good-looking in fact, just somewhat out of place in first-class.

"Where are we?" Arthur asked the attendant.

"Where are we? . . . Oh, I see what you mean. Depending on the route our captain has chosen, dinner will be served either over northern Manitoba, or the Dakotas." She would ask the captain to pinpoint their exact position if Mr. Scheiler needed to know it, but Arthur declined, saying it wouldn't be necessary. Knowing he was dining five miles above the ground in Manitoba or North Dakota was sufficiently awe-inspiring in and of itself. She gently smiled at her passenger's lack of flight experience and retired, as she did when paying respects to her maternal grandparents in Vancouver, who seemed so terribly old and not particularly wise, only bewildered when she told them about her days spent flying miles above the earth between Toronto and Vancouver.

"Beautiful girl," the woman across the aisle remarked. "She probably thinks I'm nattering away too much."

"Not at all, not at all," Arthur muttered. "It helps pass the time." Still, if he wanted to read or sleep, he must tell her, to which Arthur murmured, "Of course."

A tray, over which the attendant's face hovered, now appeared before him, and he was reminded of pictures seen in childhood of angels' faces peering down from Heaven's void at Christ's nativity. He remembered that every year, on Christmas day, he showed the contents of his Christmas stocking to Mary when he went outside to wish her a Merry Christmas and give her a piece of the Christmas pudding and also a slice of Christmas cake he had helped his mother mix, stir and bake. Before his father had died, brandy was poured over the pudding and a match applied which produced ghost-like blue flames. That ritual went by the board, along with Mary and Jack, and other things too, when his father died.

He nibbled the salmon cutlet and waved away the opened bottle of Bordeaux white the attendant expectantly tilted over the glass on his tray. The woman across the way busily sliced and chewed her beef filet and, between chews, explained to Arthur that the reason she flew first-class was because of the food. It was much better than in tourist. She had always enjoyed eating, even the awful meals she'd made when she was first married and learning how to cook. Now she thought meal preparation should be a compulsory part of the school curriculum, along with teaching young people about marriage. The only things she'd learned at school were the names of the Canadian provinces and a few French words, which she had forgotten the minute she left school, but she'd no idea how to prepare meals, or of the consequences of a young husband and wife going to bed together. No wonder she'd had three babies in three and a half years, though she doubted if she was any sillier than her contemporaries. Did Arthur have any views on the best kind of education for his daughter? Arthur laid down his knife and fork and said, "I've gone no further than to imagine her scampering around on our beach."

"Private beach?" she queried, and when he nodded, she immediately upped him a social class. Arthur then admitted he had never thought of himself as being a father, especially of a girl, it was a big responsibility, to which the woman responded by saying she knew exactly what he meant because her husband had been the same. He knew what to do with their son, but was stymied when it came to the girls, In the end, he spoiled them rotten, though he really and truly adored them. Arthur thought it inadvisable to reveal *his* conflicting emotions about Miracle, especially his tendency to look at her waving arms and legs and see the woman in the child. (It shamed him to think that one or twice when he'd looked at Miracle, he'd seen a woman waiting to receive a lover.)

He added, "I haven't managed to get past my expectations for her childhood."

"Oh, expectations!" she cried. Well, she knew something about that, which was that parents must learn not to expect too much from their children. To give him a for-instance: her daughter Jean had recently told her that she'd been oppressive and demanding as a mother. Of course, she'd had no idea what on earth Jean was talking about, maybe it was just different generational perspectives. Arthur nodded agreement, wishing she would shut up for a few minutes. He moved his fork in the congealed serving of rice on his plate and remembered how his mother filled a pan with rice and sugared milk and baked the mixture until a brown crust formed on the surface. He had loved the crust, but not the pudding and always dawdled his way through the rice, while his father told him how Bedouin tribesmen threw handfuls of rice into boiling camel's milk, then ate it with hunks of roasted camel or goat meat, using their fingers, which his mother said was crude and something young Arthur must never do. Eventually, Arthur would come to understand that his father's contribution to the Palestinian campaign had been minimal, but his mother had died believing no battle could have been fought or won there without her husband's active involvement; Arthur had also concluded that, though it might be slightly delusional for wives and sons to believe their husbands and fathers were heroes, nonetheless it was beneficial because it sustained faith. After all, how can a man believe himself worthy if he damns his progenitor as a drunkard and liar, or a woman honour herself if she knows her mother is a whore?

The woman across the aisle talked on. It was strange, she said, how your children turn out. Jill, who always thought politics a huge bore, had suddenly become a left-winger. Arthur interjected by commenting how often children discard one toy for another. Oh yes, she agreed, what an astute observation; she remembered her own childhood enthusiasms which now seemed so ridiculous, and how, in adolescence, she gathered and discarded boyfriends as she'd once picked up and dropped toys. How clever of him. And we aren't much better as adults either, are we? We think we have found the man or woman we want, then once passion is appeased we regret the bondage, but by then it's too late, we're trapped by the house and the kids, and from that point onward, whatever games we play must be carried on in secret. Shocking, isn't it, to imagine we can never escape the impulses of childhood. We merely revise and extend our horizons. Oh, what an interesting conversation! But, of course, as a writer, Mr. Scheiler would know all about such things. He would know so much more about human behaviour than most people, wouldn't he, much as physicians eye people they meet and automatically diagnose complaints? Oh lord, Arthur thought, was the woman going to spill the beans and tell him she'd taken off her panties for men other than her husband? But no, her entire past consisted of monotonous feeding, bathing, clothing and scolding three noisy, inconsiderate children, and by the time they had broken their toys and sulked their way through adolescence, any inclination she might once have had to sample relationships outside marriage had been totally eroded. Dull, so dull. Since the death of her husband the big excitement in her life was flying between Toronto and Vancouver. Meeting someone like him made her realize how tedious her own life was.

No worse than his, Arthur protested. He was a typewriter's slave, chained much like a child to its loom in Bukhara, only he tapped out people-patterned novels, while the child at the loom wove intricate patterns into carpets. He wasn't sure which would endure, carpets or novels. Oh, but you're an artist! she exclaimed. "So is the child," said Arthur, "so is anyone who transforms raw materials into products that didn't previously exist." He had successfully turned the conversation away from the dangerous area of personal revelations, and was even grateful when she took up the topic of an exhibition of Australian aboriginal art a friend had dragged her to. Yes, she would have coffee and a tiny bottle of Khalua. Just coffee, Arthur said, only half-listening to the woman across the aisle now saying she saw absolutely no difference between the drawings of Australian aboriginals and the scribbles of her own grandchildren; nevertheless, going had been worthwhile because she had met a very interesting person: a woman, who had been a prisoner in a Japanese army camp in Singapore. (Arthur wondered if the attendant was of Japanese origin and if her body was as lovely as her face. He tried to guess how many lovers she had.) And she told me she had been forced to watch another prisoner being beheaded for saying something insulting to the camp commander. Arthur turned to look at the woman across the aisle. He hadn't been really listening. What was it that she'd just said about a Japanese war camp? Imagine, the woman across the aisle said, just imagine! Watching someone being beheaded! Oh, my God, he thought, could the woman have been Heather? "Was the woman's name given?" he asked.

"Who? Oh, that woman. Her name was, let me see . . . I've forgotten."

Arthur felt the nose of the big aircraft tilt and heard the attendant's reassuring voice state that the plane was commencing its long descent into Toronto. "What? What did you say?" he asked.

Oh yes, the woman's description of what went on in the camp was frightening. And the execution! Simply terrible! Everyone had to watch. And the prisoner shouted obscenities at the camp commander. That's what the woman told me. The prisoner shouted obscenities, and then they made her kneel on the ground.

Oh God, oh God, Arthur thought, was it possible that the executed woman might have been Heather? It was so like her. She would have defied her executioner, wouldn't she? Yes, she would. She would have spit in his face and screamed out how much she despised him. Yes, that woman could easily have been Heather. In fact, it must have been. It had to have been. Arthur closed his eyes and imagined the captured woman, knees in the dirt, in front of a Japanese officer and an assembly of gaunt female prisoners. Had the women turned their heads away? Had they closed their eyes as the officer's sword hissed down onto the kneeling woman's neck? Had Heather felt pain? relief? as the weapon sliced her head from her shoulders. Was a final thought frozen in her flesh? The images ushered a torrent of weakness into his body, and he clutched the seat arms, afraid he was on the threshold of a spell. He saw concern flash across the attendant's face and heard her say any slight dizziness he might be experiencing was due to the change in the plane's altitude.

"It's nothing," Arthur assured her. "I'm fine, just fine." And he did feel better because the attendant's voice had made the images of Heather disappear, so that when the woman across the aisle started talking again he felt everything was going to be all right.

Which airline was he flying to London? Oh, really. Friends had travelled to England on BOAC. They said the service was excellent, and of course there'll be an airport lounge for first-class passengers, but you know, she'd been really and truly offended the first time she'd walked into an airplane and seen how passengers were divided between first-class and the rest, it reminded her of Sunday school where as a child she learned that on Judgement Day some souls were bound for heaven, others to hell.

An image of Heather returned and Arthur felt a sense of urgency. He leaned across the aisle. "The woman you met. Did she give the name of . . ."

What nonsense that was! Yet she had no doubt today's children were being taught similar rubbish. The plane thudded as the undercarriage was being lowered and locked into place. The woman across the aisle droned on: Usually when she flew, she never spoke to anybody, but he'd looked so anxious, as if he needed company, as though he regretted leaving his wife, with that hangdog look that women find so irresistible.

Good God, did I look that bad, thought Arthur, although Phyllis once told him that he looked like a lost dog. But that was different; Phyllis had known what made him tick, why he was always sniffing at the facades of people until he found a door which enabled him to slip into the tunnels of their minds and emotions where they hid, trembling with hates and desires. God! To think of Heather's head rolling like a soccer ball in the dust. God! He must try to get that woman's name. He leaned over. "Would you do something for me?"

A voice interjected, requesting passengers to prepare for landing. After fastening her seat belt, the woman across the way told Arthur the first thing she did after flying anywhere was to dash home or to her hotel and take a shower to wash off all the bad bugs she'd picked up on the aircraft. How foolish people were, Arthur thought, to believe that practically every affliction can be washed away, including sins. He remembered that his father had never washed himself below the waist. There . . . there was the image: his father standing at the stone sink in the kitchen, shirt and vest off, braces hanging to the knees of his britches while his mother soaped, sponged and dried his muscular back. They enjoyed the once-a-month ritual. His mother would poke his father's ribs and he would twitch like a horse trying to shoo away a persistent fly. Arthur's weekly bath was taken standing in the galvanized washtub placed on the kitchen floor in front of the stove. He hated having his hair washed, which came first, but enjoyed his mother's soapy hands moving on his bottom and around his testicles. He watched himself clench his fists and fold each arm to the shoulder to bunch his puny biceps and saw a mother kneeling before a son whom she transformed into a husband after death and poverty had driven her mad.

"I've heard," confided the woman, leaning across the aisle, "that the most dangerous part of flying is taking off and landing." The image of his mother and father dissipated, and now he wondered what Joey would do if the plane crashed. Probably she'd cry for day or two, bury him, go back to the important job of raising Miracle, and within a year marry again. Why not? She might be overweight, but she was a prize financial sugar plum, and hungry male flies'd be encircling her within weeks of his demise. A thud announced the airplane's wheels had contacted the runway. The engines reversed, roaring protests as they raced toward the far end of the runway. The plane slowed and gently rolled towards its assigned docking gate. "Well, that's that," the woman said. Ignoring the attendant's request to remain seated, she stood to retrieve her jacket and coat and quickly moved to occupy a position of advantage near the exit as the other passengers, whom Arthur had only glimpsed on their way to and from the washroom, now emerged from their seats to stretch and prepare to leave the aircraft. Even his seat-mate came to life.

Arthur started forward, but was prevented from continuing by a square-shouldered man who blocked his passage, so that he had to call out his question over the man's head: "The woman at the arts show! What was her name?" The woman turned to look blankly at him as if she'd never seen him before, then turned and hurried through the opened doorway and up the drab passage. Impeded by other passengers also eager to escape the confines of the plane, Arthur ran along the chute to tap the woman's shoulder. "The woman. You know, the woman you met at the art exhibition, the one imprisoned by the Japanese. Did she give you her name?" But the once-garrulous woman eager to get home shook her head and hurried away.

Arthur would have followed, but someone called his name and he turned to see the flight attendant hurrying towards him with his raincoat and battered suitcase. Being halted in his pursuit of the once-talkative woman frustrated him, and the attendant was bewildered when he snatched the coat and case from her without a word and hurried on. But the woman was nowhere to be seen near the baggage-recovery wheel, or among the people who swarmed in the concourse.

Arthur knew he had to give up, so he slowly made his way to the departure level and the BOAC counter, where he waited for the agent to process his ticket, and nodded when he was informed of the guest lounge where he could comfortably pass the hours until departure. As he stood there, he realized how disoriented he felt among the mass of people swirling around him. He seemed to have no ability to break up sounds into distinguishable tones, instead they rushed at him like an ocean wave, leaving him breathless and struggling to maintain his balance. It wasn't until that moment in his journey that he understood how far he had gone over the past twenty years in isolating himself from any social environment. He checked his raincoat and suitcase, which the agent had scornfully eyed as though it were a relict of an earlier age no reputable contemporary person would be found dead with, and following the directions, entered a large room filled with pleasant odours, soft chairs, small tables and racks of magazine and newspapers. A steward brought him a cup of coffee and a newspaper. He tried to read the paper, but after scanning the headlines, found he was too disoriented to continue. Fear that he might have a spell and be thrown into the maw of some nameless institution overpowered him. He tore off an edge of the newspaper, took out a pen and printed the following words on the paper in large letters: SHOULD I BE FOUND UNCONSCIOUS, PLACE ME ON A BED. WITHIN AN HOUR I WILL RECOVER. I HAVE NOT HAD A STROKE, HEART ATTACK OR EPILEPTIC SEIZURE. I AM MERELY EXPERIENCING A PERIODIC CESSATION OF CONSCIOUS-NESS FROM WHICH I WILL FULLY RECOVER. He added Joey's name, address and telephone number, signed the paper, then folded it and put it in the breast pocket of his jacket where it could easily be found. Writing the note relieved the tension, and he fell asleep and dreamed he had gone back in time and was walking with Heather along the edge of the village Common. They had been to the house where they would live with his mother after their marriage, and he wanted Heather to say she liked it. The bright, warm afternoon with its scents of flowers and sounds of insects voluptuously feeding on the aromatic yellow gorse flowers aroused in him an overwhelming desire to push Heather up against a tree, pull off her clothes, then do what he knew his father would have done. But it didn't happen that way: Heather stripped herself and when he advanced to take her, he realized her head was off and rolling across the Common. He wanted to scream, but instead he awakened to the steward's voice saying passengers were now boarding the flight to London. "No hurry, sir," the steward said. "But take-off's in fifteen minutes. Your boarding pass, sir. Mustn't forget that. Nice to have you fly with us, sir. Have a good flight."

The head steward welcomed Arthur as he stepped onto the plane and accompanied him to his seat in the first row. The space in front of him and the roominess of the compartment comforted Arthur, and he knew he would be free of his claustrophobia a second time. What luck! The steward solicitously inquired which beverages Arthur preferred, offering a selection of French and German wines selected to please the tastes of passengers rich enough to fly first-class. His eyebrows went up when Arthur confessed he seldom drank anything except on celebratory occasions, though, on a very hot day, he might have a beer. When the steward heard that, he asked if Arthur would care for a German lager once they were "up in the air with the angels." Having taken care of Arthur, the steward moved on to the woman sitting behind him, who ordered a double martini, easy on the vermouth. "Will do," promised the steward before strapping himself into his tip-up seat facing Arthur as the plane turned into the runway and halted to test its engines and poise itself for take-off. The engine sound increased and the heavily loaded plane slowly rose and moved away from the ground lights to penetrate and slip through layer upon layer of ragged cloud. An authoritative voice announced the height and speed at which they would be cruising and their expected arrival time at Heathrow.

The steward returned to Arthur with an elegantly shaped, long-necked bottle and glass, which he carefully tilted to avoid the formation of foam, then asked Arthur if he would like hors d'oeuvres to accompany his drink. The plane shuddered as it broke through turbulent air, and Arthur's fear and apprehensiveness must have been revealed on his face, because the steward uttered reassuring words which to Arthur's ears sounded contrived, as if they had been rehearsed too many times. After the steward left, Arthur spent a few minutes speculating what might really be going on in the man's mind, behind his mask of bland smiles and polite conversation. He remembered, as a boy, believing every face he saw revealed the mind hidden behind it, except perhaps for oriental people, who, so his father had told him, were inscrutable, though Arthur had never been able to confirm this because he'd never once seen an oriental person in Hasterley or Ponnewton. And his mother had been just as bad. She claimed she could see from a nose that such and such a person was honest, or tell by looking at another's eyes that he was a shifty character and up to no good. He eventually discarded such stereotypes, and now believed pre-judgement of individuals by external signs was a mistake no good novelist dare make. He himself made every effort to ensure this sort of misjudgment was never reflected in his work, though sometimes he had an uneasy feeling that because of creative exhaustion, or through simple carelessness, bias sneaked into his prose. He also strove to attain a bleak simplicity of style, and each day told himself that anything which couldn't be expressed simply wasn't worth writing. Moreover, he reminded himself that the book from which he had learned to read, the most enduring of all books, the Bible, was written in clear, everyday language. He had come to believe the biggest mistake a writer could make was to assume that great ideas require complexity of language. "In the beginning was the word and the word was God." No profound thought had ever been so simply stated, and though he himself might not attain that level of profundity and simplicity, still he must strive for it. As he sat quietly in his seat, again thankful his claustrophobia wasn't acting up, he wondered if he hadn't, over the years, like the stylite-of-old living atop a pillar in the desert, exiled himself within a self-created wilderness, hoping isolation would clarify his vision and, now, returning from the desert to the city, he discovered that neither he nor the world was changed. He got up and went to the toilet.

As he approached his seat on the way back, the woman sitting behind him glanced up from the book she was reading, frowned, compressed her plucked eyebrows, then said: "You look familiar. Have we met before?" Arthur, anxious to avoid the experience of the flight from Vancouver to Toronto replied, "It's unlikely."

The woman leaned forward to peer intently at him. She was a small-boned person, coarsely handsome, with a mop of henna-streaked black hair. Arthur put her down as being in her early forties. "I have a memory for faces," she said. "It was in Hollywood, years ago. Back then, when I believed I had the makings of a star. You were . . . let me see . . . directing? No . . . wait . . . I've got it now . . . doing a screenplay. That's it. You were talking to Phyllis Ackroyd."

Images of the studio party flooded back. He heard the brusque director shouting: "Joey, for God's sake, get the guy a drink!" And he saw Joey turning to face him, while at that same moment, he fell in love with her, even as Phyllis, with whom he had planned to spend the remainder of his life, stood beside him, aware he was about to abandon her for Joey. "I don't recall seeing you," he said.

"Why should you? I was a bit player. But I'm irritated because I can't remember your name. In my business, remembering names is vital."

"Scheiler," he said.

"That's it. Of course, Matt Scheiler. You dropped out. Wait. Somebody told me you married the continuity girl."

"Joey."

"That's right. Litter-Box Joe Gambarasi's daughter. And don't look at me as if you think I was one of Joe's. My boobs were too small. Besides, I was too bright for him. So here we meet again, over the Atlantic Ocean. If it goes on like this, pretty soon we won't have to go anywhere, because everybody that counts'll be in one place. I'm Peggy Lewis." She wanted to know why he was flying to London and said "Bully for you" when supplied the reason, then asked who his agent was. She was surprised when he gave Phyllis's name.

"Her secretary took over when Phyllis died," he explained. "You know, *Ackroyd and Arnold*. There's never been any reason to switch."

"Fair enough," she agreed, "but you never know." She dug into her handbag and produced an engraved business card. "*Peggy Lewis & Associates.* Actually I'm the whole shebang, but it reassures people when they think there's more than just me, if you know what I mean. Will you be in London long?"

"A few days."

"I'm at the Ritz. I stay there when I'm in London. So if you have time, maybe you'll look me up."

"Sure. If I have time, I'll do that. Nice meeting you again, Peggy."

"You bet."

She returned to her book and he to his seat where panic suddenly streamed through his body, for if Peggy Lewis could recognize him as a man she'd seen years ago at a Hollywood studio party, wasn't it possible there were people in England who would spot him and know him for someone other than Matt Scheiler? But wait, wait. He had nothing to worry about. Wasn't he carrying an authentic American passport that proved beyond all doubt he was Matt Scheiler? All right, all right. So they wanted to see his birth certificate. Look. Here it is. Born in New Hampshire. The birth certificate and the passport were irrefutable evidence that he was Matt Scheiler. And what about Arthur Edward Compson, son of Sylvia and Arthur James Compson? Never heard of them. And Laura Dorchester? Didn't ring a bell. Maria and Martha, servants employed by Laura Dorchester, did he know them? The names meant nothing. No indeed, *his* memory was filled with images of freighters, of the river that split America geographically and spiritually, of southern California, of Phyllis Ackroyd and his wife Joey, of British Columbia, Canada. And anyone who thought that he, Matt Scheiler, knew anybody in England was way off-base, or slightly cuckoo. In fact, he knew nothing about English women, although he supposed they used their boobs and behinds to hook a guy, same as American and Canadian gals. Yes sir, it don't matter where a guy goes, he's goin' find old Eve there, twitching her hot little tail to let him know what's available—for a price. Could be, he'd try a couple of Brits while he was in London and compare 'em to the gals in Iowa. Stodgy, you say? Hell no! Obviously you ain't never seen no Iowa gals . . . No, playing the fool was alien to him. He could only outstare people and hope they would ignore him.

He ate a little from each dish placed before him: a spoonful of leek soup, a slice of Welsh lamb, which resurrected memories of being at the kitchen table with his mother and father, eating a Sunday dinner of roast lamb and blackberry pie. Listen, he told himself as he tamped down the memory, he mustn't allow his Arthur Compson memories to surface; it won't do, they must be relegated to a distant file box in his brain. He listened to the steward chatting with Peggy Lewis, and it reminded him that no harm had come to him from acknowledging he had once lived and worked in Hollywood. He must remember to tell Joey that he'd run across Peggy Lewis. She'd have a clearer memory of the people involved in the film industry. Funny how directing that one movie seemed to satisfy Joey. Apparently it was all she needed as proof she could co-ordinate all the disparate parts that went into the making of a movie. What a contrast to him. He had stumbled around and made so many mistakes before he'd learned how to write a good short story (he had long ago discounted his "English" novels as being overwritten and emotionally facile). And what trepidation he had felt when he set out on the voyage through his first novel! A good novel was as much a voyage of discovery for the author as for the reader. Characters must surprise you, for if they didn't, the novel would become no more than a trip over the same flat country traversed many times before. That was why his characters sometimes had to think and do things that embarrassed and shamed him on their behalf, and the only way he, as a writer, could make sense of that was to conclude that God created the monstrous in order for people to be able to recognize and appreciate the beautiful, which meant that he, Matt Scheiler, novelist, was simply following along in God's footsteps. Or was that fallacious reasoning?

He dozed, and when the steward offered him a blanket, he lowered the seat and slept until he heard the steward telling Peggy Lewis the plane was now over the Irish sea and would soon pass over north Wales, though not much could be seen through the cabin windows because Britain was blanketed by cloud, which was not unusual.

When the steward saw Arthur had awakened, he took the blanket and asked if he wanted coffee before the service closed down. Arthur nodded and drank the hot, bitter coffee, then made use of the washroom to splash water on his face, careful not to look at himself in the mirror, fearful he might see a shred of his old self. As he returned to his seat, he nodded at Peggy Lewis, who was repairing her make-up, then seated himself and previewed what he would do once he was in the airport: how he would negotiate hostile passageways before setting his feet on alien soil. He touched the passport and felt assured: It was his protective shield, certain proof he was Matt Scheiler. He heard and felt the jolt of the wheel carriages being lowered and locked into place and wondered what counterforce was used to prevent the wheels from collapsing when they hit the runway. Some day, if an opportunity arose, he would ask an engineer how the carriages and wheels were secured. Wasn't it true that everyone, and everything, in life had a device to protect itself? He was protected by the invisible armour of his passport, it was the shield that would defend him against those who might doubt his identity and attempt to dig up his past. He must never forget that he was now Matt Scheiler, American citizen, born in New Hampshire, resident of British Columbia, Canada, where his loving wife Josephina and daughter Miracle awaited his return to Haven, his hidden castle, his hearth-and-home beside the loveliest lake in all of North America. Yes, he was Matt Scheiler, he *was* Matt Scheiler. Yes, he was. He was. He was. Was he? He was. He irrefutably was. Was. Was. He suspended himself in time until, raincoat and suitcase in hand, he left the baggage area and approached the passageway that would take him to customs and immigration. He paused a moment, then resolutely walked toward the officials who examined his credentials, gave them their approval and welcomed him to the great island nation on which he had never before set foot.

CHAPTER
26

"YOU COULD BE MISTAKEN, MR. JONES," SAID THE DRIVER OF the parked car to the elderly man sitting in the back seat, peering through the car window at two men standing on the opposite side of a street in London, one of whom was gazing at a statute of Admiral Horatio Nelson. The other man was Arthur Compson, who stood with his hands in his raincoat pocket, looking at the pavement and occasionally nodding as his companion gestured and talked.

"Don't forget, Mr. Jones, you're talking about a man you say entered your shop more than twenty-five years ago and purchased a ring," said the driver whose name was Percy Donaldson. He was an inspector, CID, London. "Let's place your memory of that incident against what we know about the man across the street: He's an American, resident of Canada, carrying an American passport, which means he had to show a birth certificate—passports aren't given out *carte blanche*. On top of all that, he's a well-known author here to receive an award."

"Compson wrote books too, and people said he'd be famous one day." Jones held up two of Arthur's early novels. "See?"

"I've seen them. Consider it like this, sir. Suppose someone's been murdered and police suspect a man and a woman he's diddling on the side, but both vanish into thin air. No trace of them. Then, twenty-five years later, a shopkeeper sees a photo of a man in the newspaper and says he looks like the murder suspect. That's like you, sir, only you went to the Ponnewton constabulary who got in touch with us, and now we're driving around London, following a man named Matt Scheiler who's being taken on a sight-seeing tour. Except you're convinced the man's not who he says he is. You say he's Arthur Compson, a suspect in a twenty-five-year-old unsolved murder case."

"That's right. And I'll tell you something else I remember about Arthur Compson. He never looked a person in the eye, same as that chap across the street. He's looking everywhere but at the bloke who's talking to him."

"So would I, if the bloke was reeling off details of Nelson's death at Trafalgar. I wonder where they're going now?" The two men had turned and were walking, heads lowered against the driving rain. "Back to the hotel, I'd say, or the nearest pub. Had enough, Mr. Jones?"

"I wouldn't mind getting a closer look. I suppose you think I'm an old crackpot?"

"Of course not, sir," responded Donaldson, thinking the retired jeweller had described himself accurately. "You're a citizen who believes he must act in the public interest to bring a suspect to justice."

"They're going into a tea shop."

"Can't say I blame them, it'll be warm in there. We'll do likewise. Look, assuming this man is who you think, is it likely he'll recognize you?"

"I don't know. I remember him because I trained myself to look at faces and remember them: shapes, eye colour, hair style, and so on. In my business, you never knew if a customer was on the up-and-up. Nowadays, shops have surveillance cameras, but in my day you had to depend on yourself."

"All right, let's take a close-up peek at him." Donaldson parked the car, placed a clearly visible police reserve sign on the dashboard, got out, and strolled across the street, halting traffic with a raised hand, trailed by Mr. Jones. They entered the tea shop and sat at an empty table not far from the other men. The officer indicated that Mr. Jones take the chair facing Matt Scheiler. After tea was ordered, Donaldson leaned over the table and asked, "So, what d'you think?"

"It's him."

"You understand what the outcome might be, Mr. Jones?"

"He'll be arrested."

"I wish it was that simple. We've already checked a few things out. We know that Scheiler is booked to leave for Toronto tomorrow afternoon, which means if the man sitting over there is who you say he is, we've got twenty-four hours to establish his identity. Let me remind you, he carries a valid U.S. passport. Thank-you," he said to the waitress who had placed two cups and a teapot on the table. "We've no right to detain a citizen of another country unless we can show he has been engaged in something illegal. And I should tell you, sir, as a rule, we urge such people to leave England, rather than detain them. We have enough problems with our own citizens."

"That man was born in England. He committed a terrible crime here."

"I've got to wonder, Mr. Jones, if you're not engaged in a personal vendetta. I mean, what reason do you have for wanting to prove the man is Arthur Compson?"

"Because I've always been law-biding."

"So are most people, sir. That's a given."

"I follow unsolved crimes. It's a sort of hobby. And that man bashed in the head of an innocent woman with a typewriter."

"Let's suppose for a minute that on the night Laura Dorchester was murdered she was alone in Compson's house, heard something going on in another room, went to investigate and was hit by an intruder who picked up the most convenient weapon at hand, which happened to be Compson's typewriter. Could you prove me wrong? Suppose the reason Compson was never found was because the intruder killed him too and buried his body. Could you prove me wrong? And consider motive, sir. Evidence gathered at the time of Dorchester's death tells us that not only was Miss Dorchester Compson's publisher, but according to statements taken from Dorchester's housekeeper, she and Compson were lovers. The only fly in the ointment was that a servant girl disappeared around the same time, though according to Dorchester's housekeeper, the girl was a scatterbrain and no one was surprised when she just up and ran away, possibly with a soldier. It's all circumstantial, Mr. Jones. There's no direct proof Arthur Compson killed Laura Dorchester, nor were the investigating officers able to connect her death with Compson's disappearance since there was no clear motive. All we know is that Compson's bank account was emptied shortly after Dorchester's death."

"He emptied it."

"Can you be sure? The initials scribbled on the bank withdrawal slip were indecipherable. I've seen them."

"The bank teller'd remember Compson withdrawing it."

"The teller had no memory of a man resembling Compson in the bank. You see how difficult it is, Mr. Jones? And of course, the police looked everywhere for him. Some thought he might've died in an air raid. At any rate, he never returned to the village, or to his house."

"Are you saying I shouldn't have come forward?"

"No. I'm saying that what may seem straight-forward on the surface won't be that simple."

"You've already told me that."

"I'll say it again and again, sir." Donaldson's expression hardened. "And for very good reason. I have the job of proving Matt Scheiler is Arthur Compson and that he murdered Laura Dorchester. Even if you confirm the man two tables away from us is who you think he is, I know from experience how unreliable a witness can be. And you're not even that, sir, you've only got a vague memory of a man's face."

"All right, all right." Jones pushed his cup away and prepared to rise. "I get the point. You think I'm some old fool who doesn't know what he's talking about."

"Sit down, sir." Jones made a show of reluctance, then complied with the officer's request. "I point out the very real problems in this case. Compson was in your shop for a total of how long? Fifteen, twenty minutes?"

"Something like that."

"Compson was then in his early twenties. You're now looking at a man in his mid-fifties, yet from a single memory of attending a customer all those years ago, you're sure this is the same man. I'm stretched to believe it, but we have a duty to follow through. Walk past him on the way to the lav, sir, but don't be too obvious, just glance. I'll pay the bill." Donaldson got up, went to the front counter and grimaced when he saw Jones pointedly turn and look directly at the man as he passed the table.

After, when Jones had returned from the washroom and whispered, "It's him," and the two men had crossed the street and got in the car, Jones asked, "What happens next?"

"Hard to say. I'll probably call at the hotel where Mr. Scheiler is staying and go from there. I'll take you to Waterloo station."

"You'll let me know?"

"Of course. If anything comes of it, Ponnewton will be informed."

"They're not exactly an aggressive bunch."

"They're the way police officers should be—unobtrusive, but vigilant."

"They're neither."

Donaldson responded with a sour smile. "The easiest way to find out if police are doing their job is to break the law. You could try that."

"I've told you, I'm a law-abiding person."

The car pulled up and stopped in a no-parking zone. "Thanks for trying to help us out, sir," Donaldson said as Jones left the car, slammed the door and angrily strode into the massive terminal. Donaldson shrugged and drove off.

Arthur, standing in Trafalgar Square, was aware of water seeping down his neck and of the hem of his raincoat slapping soddenly against his pants. He glumly nodded as his companion explained why a grateful country had erected the monument to commemorate the achievements of Horatio Nelson, but the fact was, the sights of London bored him. He didn't want to visit churches, galleries, museums and the Parliament Buildings. All he wanted was to board an airplane and fly home to Joey, Miracle and Haven. Granted, the reception hadn't gone too badly, though there was a general lack of enthusiasm in the audience and he had observed no hands bruised from clapping when the se-

lection chair introduced him and afterwards shepherded him around to meet a
few better known English authors, who could hardly drag themselves away
from enthralling conversations with acolytes to shake his hand and murmur,
"Nice to meet you. Good show." But none of that mattered because he had the
medal and the prize money in hand as well as reassurance that everyone accepted him as Matt Scheiler, American author and resident of Canada, whose
novels about the lives of small-town people in the mid-western U.S. and southern British Columbia were finally being acknowledged. Hog farmers, bus drivers, who served as links binding the chains of circumstance together, sallow-
skinned ministers, despairing wives, used-car dealers who waited in incon-
spicuous huts on the edges of car lots, like spiders at the perimeter of their
webs, elderly male and young female teachers, cafe proprietors, workers and
customers, thieves and whores, convicted murderers and their executioners,
people who ran from such places, those who fled to them as places of refuge,
all were present in his novels. One English reviewer remarked that there was
some similarity between Matt Scheiler's work and Thomas Hardy's: a perception of high tragedy in the commonplace, but, unlike Hardy, so the reviewer
wrote, Scheiler never ventured beyond scratching the surface of life because
he skipped from incident to incident, thereby reducing major themes to transi-
tory events and substituting action for perception, which rendered much of the
work ephemeral. But what other people said or wrote about his novels had
never affected Arthur, and now, literary award in hand, he felt he could totally
ignore the literary opinions of others. He rarely spoke about his writing or
other writers, but had once remarked to Joey that if a writer were also a book
reviewer, then that person would never be able to defecate more than one or
two novels from his constipated imagination in an entire lifetime. As for critics, since their imaginations were totally costive, they were reduced to criticizing other writers, like himself, blessed with prolific imaginations. To hell
with all of them; he would only acknowledge their right to assess him when
their work matched his in volume and breadth. The reception, the people, the
weather and the narrow streets jammed with traffic, all confirmed the rightness of Arthur's long-held resistance to returning to England. He listened to
his companion describe the implacably determined heroism of Nelson's life,
while privately reviewing his own subterranean existence, and while acknowledging that he, Arthur, had done nothing heroic enough to deserve a statue,
nonetheless he thought he hadn't done too badly, albeit in a sneaky, secretive
way, like the gopher that pops out of its maze of tunnels to squeak defiance at
the afternoon sun. He felt like interrupting his host to say: "Listen, Nelson got
what he wanted, from a taste of Lady Hamilton's muff to a statue of himself on

top of an oversized prick. You may think getting yourself killed at an opportune time's an heroic act, but let me tell you, staying alive and at large when thousands search for you with the intent of nailing you for a crime you didn't commit demands ten times more courage than getting yourself knocked off in battle. What's more, metamorphosing yourself from a hunted creature into a respected author is the equivalent of transforming a monstrously shaped pupa into a gorgeously patterned butterfly." But of course Arthur said none of this. Instead, he dutifully listened, nodded his head and gaped at buildings and statues and pavements where literary, artistic and musical immortals had paced, and when his companion finally noticed that Arthur's eyes were glazed and his step faltering, he bought him a cup of tea, then put him into a cab that shuttled him back to his hotel, where on entering the lobby he encountered Peggy Lewis.

"For God's sake," she cried when she saw him, "you look as if you've had a dose of Buckingham Palace, Nelson's Column and the British Museum."

"Up to the neck," he said. "What're you doing here?"

She told him she'd been having a lunch meeting with an English director. "God Almighty! You'd think I was trying to steal the shirt off his back. I need a drink."

Arthur agreed to accompany her to hotel lounge, though what he really wanted was to go to his room, remove his shoes, lie down and rest. Still, meeting up with Peggy was probably a good thing. Listening to her chatter would keep at bay panic that surfaced whenever he remembered he wasn't home yet and still had almost twenty-four hours to go.

So, he was leaving the next day, she asked. Lucky guy. She'd be stuck in gloomy London for another week. Did she ever miss the California sun! Didn't Arthur, living so far north? Arthur pursed his lips before saying it was possible that the valley where he lived received as much sunshine as Los Angeles, except that the winters were colder. She nodded and informed him that when she was down, she drank champagne and, before Arthur could say he would prefer something non-alcoholic, ordered two champagne cocktails.

They touched glasses and wished each other future success, then she began talking about herself. Of course she knew *his* future was assured, but she wasn't so sure about her own, though in the entertainment business, optimism *was* a matter of faith, comparable to a committed Catholic's belief in the Virgin Mary. She was Jewish herself. Her father's name was Lewesky. The big break was always just around the corner. Next week, next month, next year, you'd look up and you'd see success come a-galloping over the plains towards you, like the U.S. cavalry in an old-time oater. Oh yes, you had to have faith to be in the movie business. You had to continue to believe something would happen, even when nothing did, and for most folks in the business, nothing *ever* did, certainly not a big, humdinger success, and it was worse for women. Far worse, because for women looks were everything. Had he ever seen an ugly movie queen? Of course not. Sometimes having to break bad news to her girls near broke her heart—they were so vulnerable, just like she'd been. She ought to be tougher, tell them to smarten up, but she never could, because she couldn't bear to see hope fade from their eyes. They were much prettier than she'd been at their age, but just as vulnerable. Really she ought to advise them to look for husbands and have a couple of cute kids. She wished *she'd* done that, because she'd had opportunities and rejected them until it was too late, and sometimes she thought her unexploited maternal instincts got mixed up with her business interests because she carried a lot of dead wood she couldn't bring herself to dump. They were like children. So what if they were over twenty-one, they still wanted to hear good things from a parent. While regaling Arthur with the problems she had navigating the treacherous oceans of movie land, she drank two more champagne cocktails. (Arthur pretended to sip his first.) She knew totally merciless agents, who, when their clients didn't deliver the expected percentages, immediately dropped them, but she couldn't do that. Did authors dump characters in their novels as cruelly when they didn't come up to scratch? Did Arthur permit his male characters to think licentious thoughts about his female characters? Did he license men to think and do whatever they pleased with women and use obscenities when they described their bodies?

Arthur had been prepared to sit quietly throughout, but now Peggy posed a question that interested him, one he could not readily answer. Finally he said that so far as he was aware he didn't censor thoughts of characters in his novels, but he couldn't speak for other authors. That, Peggy agreed, was understood. "But why do so many writers have their male characters speculate about a woman's performance in bed, while the female characters only think about a man's take-home pay? Is it because the men who write novels know next to nothing about women?" Arthur replied he wasn't sure, only that he himself strove to have his characters' thoughts and actions consistent with their personalities, more *or* less as shoes conform to the shape of a person's feet. He realized his metaphor was not apt when Peggy responded that women's feet were forced into crippling shoes designed, produced and sold by men. He repeated he could only speak for himself, while wondering if Peggy's ingestion of alcohol was causing an icy sliver of antagonism to edge its way into their conversation. He decided to move away from the topic of male versus female characters and went on to speak of other problems facing the modern novelist, pointing out that so much more was expected of them now than in the past, that simple tales of young love marred by parental interference no longer sufficed, that novelists had been forced to recast themselves into new roles, including those of teacher, historian and preacher. Retelling old stories was no longer enough, which resulted in the novel being viewed not as a story, but as a "work of art," thus being crucified on a form from which it could not now free itself. Contemporary novelists, he concluded, ironically smiling, live in the best and worst of times. He stopped when he saw Peggy Lewis yawning, looking into her empty glass, then standing to pick up her Gucci briefcase and mink coat. She smiled down at him, saying that while she always enjoyed a highfalutin conversation about art, she really must leave because she had an horrendous evening coming up. A publisher's party. *Tower & Tower.* (Arthur's heart lurched.) Ever heard of them? (Arthur shook his head.) Would Arthur be kind enough to order a cab while she went the powder room? The abrupt change from convivial fellow drinker to disinterested business woman puzzled Arthur, and he could only assume his talk of the novel as an art form bored Peggy so much she couldn't tolerate hearing more, which, Arthur thought, wasn't too surprising. Even he, a practitioner, found any abstract discussion about the art of writing tedious, though he was never unaware of how he'd had to struggle to perfect his craft.

Arthur went into the lobby and asked the desk clerk to hail a cab. While he waited for Peggy to return, he noticed a man sitting in an armchair reading a newspaper. Arthur thought he'd seen the man somewhere before, perhaps at the award ceremony. Thinking of the ceremony reminded Arthur he mustn't forget to collect the medal and cheque he had deposited in the hotel's safety box before he left. He watched Peggy Lewis swish across the lobby, then helped her into her coat, walked her to the cab, touched her lips with his when she tilted her head and expectantly puckered her lips after saying, "Give me a tinkle if you're ever in L.A." He made the promise, watched the cab leave and returned to the lobby to be intercepted by the man he had noticed reading the newspaper.

"I wonder if I might speak to you for a few minutes, Mr. is it . . . Scheiler?"

"Why?"

"A small problem has come up."

"Problem? I have no idea what you're talking about. Anyway, who are you? What's your name?" Arthur had not been part of a polyglot freighter crew for two years and bused across America without learning how to tackle people who came on heavy. He'd been involved in several unsought fights on the freighter, and though he would undoubtedly have lost them had they not been broken up by the second officer, still he had bloodied an opponent's nose in one fight.

The man, closely observing Arthur's reaction, produced and held out a badge for Arthur to inspect. "Inspector Donaldson."

"So what do you want?"

"Could we go somewhere private, Mr. . . . Scheiler?"

"Look, I don't like your attitude. I'm an American writer visiting in London to accept a literary award. I can't think of a reason why I should go anywhere with you."

"How about a pub or cafe for more privacy? But it's your choice, Mr. Scheiler. Whatever you choose is fine with me."

"We aren't going anywhere. I'm staying here and you're leaving. That's my choice. And perhaps I should inform you, I carry a U.S. passport."

"I know you do, Mr. Scheiler." Donaldson smiled. "It's really very straightforward. I'll explain. A man spotted a photograph of you in the newspaper and swears he knows you, but under another name. See?" He handed Arthur a folded newspaper.

Arthur's heart pounded as he looked at the photo. He couldn't remember any pictures being taken at the ceremony. And Betty had made everything clear with the event organizers. No photos!

"What's this? A joke? What name?"

"That's immaterial."

"If it's immaterial, why are you here?"

"You're sure you wouldn't prefer to go somewhere and sit, Mr. Scheiler?"

"No, I would not. I repeat, why you are here?"

"Some years ago a woman was found dead in a house in the village of Hasterley, not far from the town of Ponnewton. The owner of the house disappeared and was never found. The man who saw your photograph says you're the owner."

Arthur frowned, then laughed. "The guy must be nuts, and so are you to believe him. For Christ's sake, what kind of cops do you have in this country?"

"I agree it seems far-fetched, but the gentleman was very insistent. Look, I know this may seem like asking a lot, but would you consider delaying your return to Canada for a day or two?"

"Certainly not. The sooner I'm back home the better. I don't like London. And I certainly don't like the way you cops treat visitors to your country."

"I do apologise, Mr. Scheiler, but I promised the old gentleman I'd speak to you, and now I've done so. The last thing I want is for you to leave England with a poor impression of the police, but unfortunately it is sometimes necessary to approach well-known people like yourself and ask a few questions. Not so long ago I had to have a little talk with a celebrity pop singer about importing narcotics into the country. Very awkward, it was." Arthur moved towards the elevators and Donaldson moved with him. "You've been a writer all your life, sir?" he asked.

"Not always. When I first left home, I crewed on freighters."

"You mentioned your birthplace, sir. Where might that be?"

"Where the hell d'you think? You ever heard of a place called America, Inspector?"

"I vaguely know of it, but I was wondering where exactly in the United States you came from."

"Northern New Hampshire, near the Canadian border. Cold winters when the warmest place is bed, and since people can't sleep all the time, most children are got in the winter and born late summer or early autumn. Pretty good system, eh? Eighteen months to fatten and wean the baby, then all ready to go for another one. That's what it was like for my great-great-grandparents."

"So you go back a long way in New Hampshire, Mr. Scheiler? Your people farmers?"

"Bit of everything, Inspector, a bit of everything: farmer, lumberman, carpenter, stone mason, preacher, undertaker. Name a trade and someone in my family'll hold up a hand and say: 'That's me.'" Arthur knew he was talking too much, but couldn't stop.

"You left home as a young man, eh?"

"You bet I did." Arthur had carefully memorized the names and shipping routes of half a dozen freighters, knowing the lines would be long gone by now and the ships either sunk during the war or scrapped afterwards. He spun out a few names, then added, "And I'd wager crews are housed and fed today no better than back then. Get the crew away from land, feed 'em muck a self-respecting dog wouldn't touch and bunk 'em with the rats."

"Sounds awful." Donaldson stepped into the e1evator. "You don't mind if I ride up with you, do you? Something you should know: the gentleman had a close look at you and swears you're a man named Arthur Compson. Are you familiar with that name, Mr. Sch- ee -ler?"

"Stop playing dice with my name. It's a good American name that goes back a long way. Get it? And don't leave the elevator with me. I've had enough of your company."

"It's just that I want to make sure . . ." Donaldson held the elevator door to prevent it from closing. "Give me five minutes and I'm gone."

"No." Arthur walked from the elevator and down the hall, aware Donaldson was trailing him. "If you weren't a cop, I'd take a swing at you," Arthur said, now at his room door. "But as it is, I'll simply ask you to leave, because if you don't, I'm going into my room and call the U.S. Embassy and ask them to do something about it."

"By all means do that If you think it'll help, but frankly, I think you're getting unnecessarily upset over something that's a routine matter. I've made it clear that I think the old chap is mistaken. But he was very insistent."

"So what! Some people insist the world's flat, but it doesn't follow the rest of us're going to stop travelling north, south, east or west out of fear we'll fall off the edge of it. For crissake, if I walked along a street in London and spotted you, I'd as easily think you once crewed with me as you were a cop. So don't talk to me about an old geezer imagining I'm somebody he saw a thousand years ago."

"Well, it would't matter so much, Mr. Scheiler, except that a woman was killed in the house."

"Wait a minute, Inspector." Arthur raised a hand. "You find a dead woman in a house. The owner's missing, and when you can't find him, you assume he killed her."

"I don't assume anything. But just so you know, Mr. Scheiler, the owner's name was Arthur Compson. Does the name strike a bell with you?"

"Not a tinkle."

"Compson was a writer, like yourself."

Arthur managed to smile. "You should've told the old guy to get lost."

"That was my initial reaction, because I know how faulty memory can be. But some years ago I got stuck with an identity case. Very interesting. A young mother took her toddler son to a park to play where she chatted with another mum. When she looked around for her boy, he was gone. He was never found. Twenty years passed and one day while walking along the high street, she saw a woman about her age with a young man. She recognized him as her son. It all came down to a matter of identification. Each woman claimed the young man was hers."

"I see no similarity between the cases," Arthur said, as he inserted the key into the lock.

"Except the truth hinged on memory."

"And what was the truth?"

"Oh, the mother was right. The other woman had stolen the little boy and kept him using forged adoption papers. But that part of the case isn't important. What's important is that the birth mother saw her child's face in the young man. Keep in mind, Mr. Scheiler, that during all her years of walking along the high street, she would've seen hundreds of boys, youths and young men. That's the important point, that's why I persisted when the woman's file landed on my desk. And that's why I'm standing here with you. Why, I ask myself, out of all the men Mr. Jones must 've seen during all those years, did he recognize you. Can you explain that?"

"Because he's nuts?"

"No. He's a spry old gent with all his wits about him. And here's another question for you. How come you've never allowed publicity photos of yourself to be taken?"

"I value my privacy."

"There could be another reason."

"There is. I happen to believe that the business of authors is to write books, not to look good on dust covers."

"But there could be another reason too, Mr. Scheiler. Maybe you're afraid a photo would identify you as the man British police want to question about the death of a woman named Laura Dorchester."

Arthur slowly opened the door, stepped into the room and turned to face Donaldson. "You amaze me, Inspector. You're in the wrong trade. You would make an excellent novelist, spinning tales out of thin air." He tried to close the door, but found Donaldson's shoe in the way. "Move," he ordered and rammed the door against the officer's shoe.

"No. We need to come to an understanding, Mr. Scheiler."

"I don't know what understanding you're referring to. But I do know I intend to board a plane tomorrow and get out of this inhospitable country."

"I want to understand why you're so anxious to get away. I'd also like you to understand there's no personal animosity involved here. Only a few things that need to be cleared up." Arthur slowly opened the door and Donaldson entered the room.

"Sit," Arthur pointed to a chair as he sat on the bed. "Okay. Begin."

"Well, first, I acknowledge I'm dealing with an intelligent man. Secondly, I'm certain any documents you produce will show you are an American citizen, born in New Hampshire, but then, I've come across numerous people with documented proof they were born in England when I knew for a fact they were born elsewhere. I suspect you are Arthur Compson, but I have no proof, because the police didn't fingerprint the room where Dorchester's body was found. I've gone through the files, and there's nothing much there except a medical report on the deceased and a note summarizing the unsuccessful search for Arthur Compson and a fifteen-year-old servant of Dorchester's by the name of Martha Sowerton. She and her older sister Maria both worked for Dorchester, but the sister was killed in a bombing raid around the same time, and no one on the staff at Dorchester's residence was able to tell us anything more about her, except that Martha and her sister had come from an orphanage. The Sowerton girl was never found, though by today's standards, it wasn't much of a search, but then a war was going on, remember? Masses of people coming and going, up and down the country, in and out of it. So the significant question is: What happened to Martha Sowerton and Arthur Compson? As to Compson, he probably got out of England as fast as he could. Likely on a ship. That must have been tough on you. I mean him, Mr. Scheiler."

"I have no idea. My talk of ships is based on personal experience."

"Tell me something. Why is a full-blooded American like you living in Canada?"

"Accidental. My wife and I were on holiday, driving from southern California, specifically from our home in Beverly Hills, through Oregon and Washington, then into British Columbia. A beautiful province. We happened upon a lakeside property for sale, fell in love with it, bought it, built a house on the property and stayed. An idyllic spot. I can hardly wait to get back."

"I'll do everything I can to ensure your speedy departure, Mr. Scheiler. Any idea how Compson got out?"

"How should I know? Your guess is as good as mine. In any case, where's proof Compson was responsible for the woman's death?"

"None, except he couldn't be found."

"He's probably dead."

"Maybe. But somebody tried to hide Dorchester's car by rolling it down a hill into the woods. Who would do that except Compson, possibly with the aid of an accomplice?"

"Accomplice!"

"A ticket collector at Ponnewton station remembered seeing Compson with a young woman."

"Young woman!"

"Rumour had it that Compson was . . . well, pretty loose. Get what I mean? So the assumption was, he and a female accomplice murdered the Dorchester woman, then bolted the country. And it's logical, because if Dorchester's death was an accident, surely Compson would have contacted a doctor and the local police. You agree, Mr. Scheiler?"

"That could be. Although as a novelist, I can easily imagine other ways the woman might have died."

"Such as?"

"Well, if, as you suggest, Compson had a reputation as a womanizer, then the murdered woman could've been killed by another woman. You know, in a fight over his affections. I once saw one woman kill another. It was in a bar, in San Pedro. She picked up a bar stool and brought it down on the other woman's head."

"Was it over a man?"

"No. A fifteen-buck debt." It was true: Arthur had witnessed such a skirmish between two women, and afterwards had used it in one of his more successful short stories.

"So what happened to the woman?"

"I don't know. I was due back on my ship. Could be she ran. Could be she was tried and executed. I can't say."

"But you can imagine the Dorchester woman dying in such a fight?"

"Why not?"

"A fight between two women?"

"Or an accident where one woman grabbed whatever was handy and chucked it at the other. Sure, why not? Am I supposed to give you a blow-by-blow account?"

"You could, if you had been there when it happened."

"But I wasn't. Now, will you have the courtesy to leave?"

Donaldson stood and went to the door. "The file contained another piece of interesting information. The Dorchester woman was well-off. Some weeks prior to her death, she had revised her will and left a substantial sum of money to her publishing house, *Tower & Tower*—ever heard of it, Mr. Scheiler? They're still in business—with explicit instructions the money be used for the preservation of the A.E. Compson country, which was where Compson lived and the setting for his novels. Another interesting fact: Dorchester's solicitor informed investigators she had told him she was carrying Compson's child and that she and Compson were soon to be married. Even more interesting, the autopsy did not confirm her pregnancy. No mistake about that. And just the sort of contradiction, Mr. Scheiler, that's right up your alley as a novelist." For a moment, the two men silently stared at each other, then Donaldson said, "Well, I suppose that's it. I appreciate you going over things with me. Perhaps I can now clear things up."

"This is the last I'll see of you?"

"I can hope so. Good night, Mr. Scheiler."

Donaldson opened the door and was about to leave the room when Arthur spoke: "Just a minute."

Donaldson closed the door and leaned against it. "Yes?"

"You say maybe you can clear things up. Well, let me tell you, Inspector, you'd better clear things up. You are not to badger me any more. I won't stand for it, understood?"

"I understand you don't want me here again, but it doesn't follow I won't come, because I believe you are Arthur Compson. And I have every intention of getting you to tell me what happened the night Laura Dorchester died. You may think your credentials are solid, but I've not been a police detective for twenty-five years for nothing. And I'd say that Arthur Compson, this very moment, is trembling with fear beneath his guise of Matthew Scheiler."

"I intend to call the embassy and lodge a complaint. I let you into my room only because you said you were obliged to follow up the old chap's story. I told myself: let him in, we'll clear things up in a few minutes, then I can get a good night's sleep, go to the airport tomorrow and fly home. But no, that wasn't good enough for you."

Donaldson walked back to the chair and sat again. "In my line of work, I deal with a lot of people, usually men who're not particularly intelligent, not like you, Mr. Scheiler. You're a clever fellow. Of course you are. And you're a writer. Who knows, maybe you've created a scene like this one before. Why not? So how does your character behave? What does he say? First, he'll be puzzled by what the copper wants, then he'll act indignant, then he'll say to himself: well, the guy's only doing his job, so why not suffer him for a few minutes. At the same time, you'll have your character caution the copper that there's a limit to his patience, that behind him looms the U.S. Embassy, and behind that, the President of the United States and the crushing weight of the entire American nation."

"Get out!" Arthur shouted.

"Come now, Mr. Scheiler, why not give me a few more minutes? I rather enjoy listening to your lies. And take it from me, I know they are lies. Lies're my daily bread and butter. Get It? As soon as you opened your mouth, I knew Jones was on to something. You can deny it until you're blue in the face, but he spotted you for who you really are. So what're you going to do now? Go on denying everything? I'm ready to deal, Mr. Scheiler. I get the truth, you get to go home. But only on the condition you convince me you're not a murderer. If you don't, the deal's off."

Arthur stared at the dark green patterned carpet, licked his lips and said, "I'm Matt Scheiler, not Arthur Compson, so I will tell the story in the third person. Agreed?"

"Yes."

Arthur swallowed and began. "You appreciate this is not easy. I have to resurrect people and emotions Compson has put aside for many years."

"I appreciate that."

Arthur began: "Arthur Compson was a young writer who became profoundly upset, emotionally and physically, when he found his mother lying dead in her room. He was so disturbed that he lost consciousness. Days later, he was found by Laura Dorchester, his friend and publisher. He was lying at the bottom of the stairs in the house he had recently purchased with Dorchester's help. His publisher took charge of burying his mother, getting him to the hospital and hiring a couple of know-nothing physicians to examine him and prescribe medications. She then rented a house in Ponnewton once owned by a Victorian poet so that she could watch over him. She intended that she and the young writer would live there together. It was Dorchester's kind of house: highly polished furniture, pictures of the poet on the walls, knickknacks everywhere, but the house stifled the young writer's creativity and he hated it. So, he up and left. But Dorchester followed him back to his house and, though she didn't like it, agreed he could stay there on his own. Later, Compson and Dorchester became lovers, and even slept in the same bed in the house that the young writer's mother had once slept in. But I'm getting ahead of myself. I could tell you much about the young writer's mother, but I won't pause on that subject, since it's not strictly relevant to what eventually happened.

While Dorchester was deferential toward young Compson because she believed he was talented, it's important to understand she didn't want to leave her protege on his own because she was afraid something untoward would happen to him. The physicians at the hospital and, later, following another episode of unconsciousness in Dorchester's office, her family consultant in London, had informed her that Compson suffered from an epileptic-type illness. She had known about his spells of unconsciousness almost from the beginning because the young writer had been ill one day when she visited him and his mother. But while Dorchester didn't want Compson to live alone, she was not prepared to move into his house in the forest. In fact, she disliked the house because it had few amenities, and of course she had her work in London. So she returned to town, but came back a few days later with a young woman, an employee at her Hampstead residence named Maria, whose job it would be to look after Compson and keep house for him. Maria was an efficient housekeeper and attractive, too, though at first the young writer ignored her because he was caught up in writing the final chapters of a novel. But as time passed, he began to spend more time with Maria. (Are you wondering what she looked like, Donaldson?) Well, she was tall and slender and held herself very erect, which the young writer later learned was the result of daily drills in the orphanage where she was raised and trained to be a domestic. She not only ran the house, but also coordinated renovations to it, such as running water and central heating as Dorchester had instructed her to do, presumably with the thought that Dorchester would then be more comfortable at the house and could spend more time there with Compson. Maria was the opposite of the young writer: She was meticulously tidy, he untidy; she was talkative, he rarely spoke. His habit was to work from eight in the morning until just past noon when he had lunch, then afterwards he went for a walk unless inclement weather kept him in the house. But after Maria's arrival, especially after the kitchen became a warm, pleasant place to sit, the young writer began to dawdle away afternoons drinking cups of tea in order to stay and listen to Maria talk about her life In the orphanage, what it was like to work in a grand Hampstead residence, and her favourite topic, her younger sister Martha, whom she had protected during their years in the orphanage and who looked upon Maria as more of a mother than an older sister, though there were only seven years between them.

Maria worried about her sister because she was such a scatterbrain that Maria was afraid she'd be taken in by some sweet-talking roan. During their discussions after lunch and in the evenings, when the young writer and Maria sat together in the renovated parlour, he found himself falling in love with her. Because he believed he was as happy as he was ever likely to be, he suggested Maria marry him and bring her sister to live with them in his house. And so it was arranged, although oddly enough, the young writer did not look upon Maria as a woman with whom it would be appropriate to have sex. Oh no, that would've been improper because, for him, she was emblematic of the ideal woman and therefore untouchable, at least for the time being. He even bought Maria a ring (But Donaldson would already know that, wouldn't her?) though they agreed it was to be a token of their friendship, not necessarily an engagement ring, since Maria wanted to get Laura Dorchester's permission first. The day Maria returned to London to finalize their plans, the young writer accompanied her to the railway station in Ponnewton, chastely kissed her before she got onto the train that would take her to the junction where she would catch the London express, then returned to work on the final pages of his novel. He never saw Maria again because she was killed later that day in a German buzzbomb explosion, which Compson learned about after he went to Dorchester's office in London demanding to know Maria's whereabouts. The shock of her death, so close to his mother's passing, caused him to fall into a deep state of unconsciousness which lasted several days. (Remember, I've mentioned the episode of unconsciousness in Dorchester's office?)

Dorchester took the young writer to her home in Hampstead where he remained until he regained consciousness and, afterwards, for a period of recuperation. It was during that period that Dorchester made the young writer her lover. (Was Inspector Donaldson getting bored with the details? No?)

Dorchester was more enthusiastic about this arrangement than Compson, but he had no real objection to having sex with Dorchester because, though she was much older than he, she had an attractive Rubenesque figure. You know, the kind of body that energetic young men enjoy fucking. At this point, Maria's sister entered the young writer's life. She had come into the bedroom where he rested, carrying a breakfast tray, and he surmised she was Maria's sister. Their mutual love of Maria drew the two together, and it wasn't long before Martha thought of the young writer as her father, as she had once thought of Maria as her mother. They conspired to escape from Dorchester's house, though they knew it wasn't going to be easy. The young writer hadn't fully recovered, and Martha, while technically a Londoner—she knew of no other place—had no idea of how to get around in the city. Neither had any money—his had been sequestered by Laura Dorchester, and Martha had only her wages and the half a crown per month the housekeeper paid into a Post Office stamp book which was accessible only if Martha remained in service for twenty years. (Was Inspector Donaldson still interested?) But finally they got enough cash together for cab fare to Waterloo station and two one-way train tickets from there to Ponnewton. The young writer believed he was keeping the faith with Maria by bringing her sister to Hasterley to take care of her as Maria would have done had she not been killed. This proved to be a serious error, because the silent, isolated house in the forest without the everyday London sounds Martha was used to frightened her, and she wouldn't leave the young writer's side. Even at night she refused to sleep in the room Maria had used and insisted on sleeping with him, as a daughter would with a parent. Before long, two men appeared and took Martha back to London. After this, Dorchester visited her author-lover on the weekends, which she viewed as romantic, passionate interludes, whereas the young writer was slightly bored with her attentions. But within weeks, Martha reappeared and pleaded with the young writer to allow her to stay because, so she said, Laura Dorchester had turned on her and she could no longer bear to remain her servant. Although the young writer had secured Martha's agreement to sleep alone before he agreed she could stay the night, when it was time for bed, she refused to go into her sister's old room. Unable to budge her from his bed, the two of them then went to sleep, and the next thing the young writer knew was that Dorchester had appeared in the bedroom and was pointing a flashlight at Martha and beating her with a heavily buckled belt. Everything happened quickly: Martha slid from the bed and ran from the room, followed by a belt-swinging Laura Dorchester. The young writer wasn't exactly sure what transpired next, but as he entered his workroom, he could see his typewriter in Martha's hands, which then rose and smashed down onto

Laura Dorchester's head. When he realized Martha had killed Dorchester, he panicked, though he was able to recognize Martha was in shock and could be persuaded to do anything he asked. They pushed the car down an incline into the forest enclosure, then walked into Ponnewton where the young writer put Martha on the train for London, which was the last he ever saw of her. Finally, Compson became a fugitive, even though he knew he hadn't committed any crime except the covering up of an accidental death which was the product of a ghastly, jealousy-driven mistake, for had Laura Dorchester stopped and asked a few questions she would have discovered that her servant and her young lover existed in a state of sexual continence." Arthur sighed. "And that is the truth," he concluded, looking at Donaldson for the first time since starting the narrative.

"It was very stupid of you, I mean of Compson, to have behaved like that."

"Of course it was. But all Compson could see was an image of poor, terrified Martha being tried and hanged."

"Now, now. English justice isn't that cruel."

"Is that so? Compson's father used to tell him of the days when women were flogged with a cat-o-nine-tails and hungry kids strung up for pinching a rabbit."

"Times have changed."

"But not that much, Inspector, not that much. Tell me how much mercy an upper-class judge would have shown a servant girl who killed her mistress?"

"It would depend on circumstances."

"No. It depends on class. And I'm telling you, whatever Compson did on that morning was done because he wanted to protect a harebrained girl who accidentally killed a woman in the course of defending herself against a brutal beating. Make no mistake about that, Inspector, when Laura Dorchester attacked Martha with the heavy belt buckle, she was mad with rage."

"Why didn't Compson restrain Dorchester?"

"It happened too fast. When Compson entered the room, Martha was backed up against the work table and raising the typewriter. She was an innocent girl. And I repeat, she was in Compson's bed because of her little-girl fear of the dark. She trusted Compson as a child does a parent, as she had trusted her sister. Compson's feelings for Martha were a mixture of affection and irritation. Not unlike what most parents feel about their children. Think a minute, Inspector, about the nature of trust. It's a word that's used very loosely; it's a word with frightening implications. A child trusts its parent with its body, with its life. Martha saw Compson as a proxy father. You say that's ridiculous, and I suppose it was. But it happened. It happened because Martha, though mature enough to menstruate, was a child who desperately wanted and needed the security of being loved and protected by a parent. Maria had taken on the role of Martha's mother, and Martha had forced Compson into the role of father, though it took him a while to grasp this. And if Laura Dorchester had not been so certain Compson was fucking Martha, the terrible accident would never have occurred. I suppose it proves we ought not ever feel certain of anything."

"I happen to believe there are a few certainties in this world," Donaldson said. He chewed his lips, then said, "So Arthur Compson never saw Martha Sowerton again?"

"How could he? He had no idea where she was. He didn't even know her surname."

"I suppose that could be the explanation."

"You won't hear better."

"I don't want a better explanation. I want to be convinced of the truth."

"You've heard it."

Donaldson rubbed his nose, eyed Arthur, grimaced, stood, then walked to the door where he halted. "It may be. It may be. Perhaps I won't have to see you again. Good night, Mr. Scheiler."

After Donaldson closed the door, Arthur, slowly shaking his head and compressing his lips to keep them from trembling, removed his clothes, performed his usual nightly ablutions, got into bed, switched off the light and lay in the darkness, stripped of all emotion, numb, like a corpse awaiting its coffin and eventual entombment.

CHAPTER

27

SO FAR SO GOOD, BUT HE WASN'T OUT OF THE WOODS YET. HE wouldn't feel completely secure until the airplane rose from the runway and disappeared into the clouds that adored England so much they remained there like a man covering a woman's body after loving her. For years, he been like that with Joey, even slept on her, then awakened ready to start again, and if only Joey were beside him now, she'd accept him and they'd pulse together to the beat of copulation; but sleep was what he needed now in order to cope with tomorrow. Except he was already in the morrow. His wrist watch, a seldom worn Christmas gift from Joey, told him it was twenty-three minutes after one, and he added ten minutes because he'd noticed the watch was losing time. But could time really be lost? It was a universal constant and therefore couldn't be lost or stolen or wasted, though people spoke of it as sentient. People had invented all kinds of ingenious contraptions to measure time because it was reassuring to believe they had control of it. He remembered as a two-year-old learning to count to ten by slowly winding the knob on his father's hunter watch ten times as his father counted the beat, like an army band master. When he and Martha had run away that night, he had pocketed the watch, but later, after deciding to purge himself of his old identity, he knew he had to dispose of it and threw it overboard on the journey eastward through the Panama Canal.

He wondered if the entire fandango of the literary prize, the invitation to come to England, even the "legacy lure" Donaldson had let drop, were all pieces of bait set out to trap him into revealing himself as Arthur Compson. Even the newspaper photograph after Betty made it clear there was to be no publicity; even that, in light of the way things had developed, seemed suspicious; and then to hear from Donaldson about Laura's ridiculous trust fund for preserving A.E. Compson country. Well, he had been surprised, but he hadn't let on, so Donaldson had got nothing out of him. But he must stop this line of reasoning. He must use common sense, he must refuse to allow his overheated imagination to forge an impossible chain of identification, circumstance and co-ordination, all deliberately deployed to trap him. He must stop. Donaldson hadn't even known that he, Matt Scheiler, existed. It was all chance and the carelessness of the event organizers, who had allowed a photographer to slip in, take a snapshot and leave. Chance, too, that the retired jeweller, Jones the busybody, on seeing the photo, had rushed off to the constabulary in Ponnewton.

But no matter what Donaldson might suspect, never mind what he, Arthur, had said in his third-party account of how Laura Dorchester met her death, still, Donaldson had no power to detain him because he was protected by his passport which identified him as Matthew Scheiler, American citizen, born in the State of New Hampshire. And he could prove it. Yes sir. He left the bed, went to the chair on which his jacket hung and took his passport from the right hand inner pocket, and in the light which permeated into the room from the street lamps, he examined his photograph and the vital information Phyllis had provided for him. "See that? he whispered. "Bless you, Phyllis." An image of her appeared as she introduced herself to him that day in the cock-eyed hotel in the state capital. So persistent, so determined to establish a relationship with him, even after he'd insulted her and told her the only way they could get to know each other was if she allowed him to fuck her. She was the most loyal person he had ever known. What could he say about Joey's loyalty? He didn't know, because so far nothing had appeared to test it. But Phyllis had remained loyal, even though he had betrayed her trust by abandoning her for Joey. As he returned the passport to his jacket, he noticed a corner of paper jutting from the breast pocket. He pulled it out and saw it was the note had written in the BOAC lounge in Toronto describing his spells. He read it, grimaced and condemning himself for surrendering to momentary weakness, tore it up, dropped the scraps into a wastepaper basket and returned to bed.

Still, the painful confrontation with Donaldson and the explanation he provided of Laura's death had served as a useful pseudo-catharsis, though it left him exhausted, physically and emotionally, as if he'd experienced a bone-racking fever. Rationally, he knew nobody would be at the airport to prevent him from boarding the plane, but irrational fears still continued to assail him during the early morning hours as he lay in his hotel bed, time he knew would be better spent getting needed rest to strengthen himself for the journey ahead. Yet he couldn't sleep. He reviewed the events of his life and, like others before him, condemned youthful excesses and his mature self for his sins of omission. By the time daylight crept into the room, he had finally died once and for all as Arthur Compson and had resuscitated himself even more solidly, more firmly as Matt Scheiler, award-winning author, American citizen and resident of Canada.

He now asked for nothing more than to be with his wife and daughter and could hardly wait for the moment when he stepped from the commuter plane and saw Joey waiting with Miracle. Oh yes, he knew he hadn't taken as good care of Joey as he should have, that he shouldn't have been so anti-social and preoccupied with his work, but from this moment onward, he would make up for his past failures. Remembrance of a monstrous storm he had experienced when crossing the north Atlantic flowed into his memory: Certain the freighter would founder, he had knelt in the water-filled galley and prayed for mercy; but when the storm finally subsided and all was well again, he was ashamed at having knelt in prayer and swore he would never do it again. Nonetheless, feeling solid and secure in his guise as Matt Scheiler, he now dropped to his knees beside the hotel bed, though once there he had no idea to whom to pray or what to say. When no words came, he hoped the simple unadorned act of supplication to a higher power would be sufficient acknowledgement of past sins, and even though he had done everything possible to protect himself since that terrible night when Laura died, still he must recognize, as with the storm at sea, he could well be helpless in determining his fate. Anyway, no one person among the billions of human beings now sleeping or awaking, being born or dying, lying alone, or sweatily mating with someone of his own or the opposite sex, knew of him, or had the slightest interest in his twisted life of deception. His survival depended on vacillating courage and the thin paper shield he carried in his jacket. And so, still kneeling, he covered his face with his hands and finally found a few words: He asked all those whom he had used, brushed aside or victimized to forgive him, for he hadn't understood what he was doing, though even now, as he prayed, he knew he couldn't in all honesty promise not to injure someone in the future. Still, when he got up, he felt better for having indulged in this short ritual of penitence.

He showered and dressed and was surprised to find he felt rested, even energetic. He hummed a sentimental tune he had heard played over and over again on the juke box in Trina's cafe as he crossed the lobby to reserve a cab to take him to the airport with ample time to spare, then went into the coffee shop and ate breakfast, afterwards returning to the lobby to the desk clerk to suggest a store where he could purchase gifts for his wife and daughter. When the clerk suggested a nearby jeweller's, Arthur, thinking he'd had enough of jewellers to last a lifetime, inquired about the location of the world-famous London store where everything a person might need, even a live animal, could be purchased. Arthur followed the directions given him and entered the store to wander aimlessly until he spotted a display of leather handbags. He picked one up and was examining it when a familiar voice said, "Don't buy that. It's too expensive."

And there she was, middle-aged but looking much as she had at fifteen. "It'll come apart," Martha said. "Poor stitching."

Arthur put the handbag down. "How did you find me?"

"I saw the photo in the paper," she said as Arthur looked nervously around. "And the name of the hotel where the presentation was. I guessed you might be staying there. So I waited across the street until I saw you come out."

"You shouldn't be seen with me, Martha."

"I wanted to see you again. I knew it was you, but with a different name. Like authors use. You know, a pen name."

"Yes, something like that, Martha. But you shouldn't be seen with me."

"But I wanted to find out how you're getting along."

"Yes, yes, I know, but it's dangerous. Look, I must buy a gift for my daughter. Go to the children's wear aisles and pretend you're getting something for a little girl. Go on. I'll follow."

"I wouldn't shop here. It's too expensive."

"Go on, do as I say," he said, and selected and purchased the handbag Martha had condemned.

Martha went through the store while Arthur covertly followed. When she stopped to browse through a rack of girls' dresses, he approached her. "How old's your daughter?" she asked.

"A few months. Just a baby."

"Then she'll grow into anything you buy. This here's a pretty one. Pretty price tag, too."

"What happened to you, Martha?"

"I joined the army."

"You did!" Arthur was impressed.

"I ended up in transport and learned to drive. Look, here's a nice frock. Then a chap, a sergeant, said he fancied me and wanted to marry me."

"What do you think of this one?" Arthur held up a dress.

"Too many doo-dads. I wasn't sure if I should. Anyway, I did. It was all right, I suppose, but I could've done better if things had been different."

"What about this dress?"

"You must have plenty of money to think of buying these frocks!"

"We're comfortably off. You have children?"

"Three. But my husband's dead now. Last year. Cancer."

"Your children are grown?"

"Hm-hm. Two girls and a boy. Much smarter than me."

"Give me your address. I'll write you, or phone."

"Here. I come prepared." She took a piece of paper from her handbag and gave it to Arthur, who folded it and put it in his wallet.

"You should go now, Martha. Someone might see us together."

"I still remember how nice you were to me. When I look back, I think of the few days with you as the happiest of my life, except for when Maria was still here. I mean, you were good to me, didn't take advantage. I was a silly girl who didn't know up from down."

"You weren't silly, Martha. Just innocent."

"Maybe, but it don't pay to be like that. I gave my girls a good talking-to."

"I'm sure you did. I still remember how you tried to make me your dad."

A blush covered her face. "I was a dope. I thought having a mum and dad was the most important thing a girl could have."

"Listen, Martha, we can't talk any more. It's too risky. But I'm glad things've worked out well for you."

"This one's pretty. What's your girl's name?"

"Miracle. We'd thought we'd never have children."

"Most girls thinks it's a miracle when they don't have one."

"I'm sure they do. But you must go, Martha. The police don't know anything about you."

"Police? What about them? I don't know nothing about any bobbies." There was a quiver in her voice and he thought it was possible she had managed to block out memories of Laura Dorchester's death, perhaps by romanticizing her bizarre relationship with him. "Of course you don't," he said, "and that's why we mustn't be seen talking like together here."

"But I'd like to have a cup of tea and a real nice chat."

"We will, Martha. We will. I promise. But not now. Off you go before the sales clerk comes over."

Martha looked puzzled but, as in the past, was prepared to do as he said. "Promise you'll write? I've put my phone number down, too. On the paper."

"I promise," he repeated, as she turned and went off. He selected and paid for two dresses and arranged for them to be boxed securely with the handbag and put into a large shopping bag. He strolled out of the store and along the street as though he hadn't a care in the world. He idly peered into shop windows and in passing a bookshop was tempted to enter to see if his books were on the shelves, but instead, looked at his wristwatch, noted the morning was almost gone and strolled back to the hotel, impatient to get to the airport to board the plane and leave forever a country where he felt himself to be totally alien.

But as he walked into the hotel lobby, he saw Donaldson waiting for him. "Correct me if I'm wrong," Arthur began when Donaldson approached him, "but I was under the impression I'd seen the last of you."

"I thought we should have another little chat."

"My plane leaves at two-thirty."

"If all goes well, you'll be on it. I have a car waiting." Arthur left the boxes at the reception desk, and he and Donaldson drove in silence along streets Arthur had never seen before to a building near the Thames. There they entered an elevator, rose to an upper- floor office where a black-suited man sat at a desk. Arthur thought he would do well officiating at a funeral home.

Without giving his name, the man in the black suit asked Arthur if he would like a cup of tea, which Arthur declined and he repeated was due to leave London at two-thirty. The man smiled and said, "In that case, we'd better get down to business. Did you murder Laura Dorchester?"

"Explain to me how I could kill a woman I've never seen, in a country I've never been to. Go on, tell me."

"Then who did?"

"I have no idea."

"Yesterday you gave Inspector Donaldson an explanation of sorts. Hm?"

"He badgered me into inventing an imaginary explanation for an accidental death. I'm planning on using it as a theme in a novel."

"But if it was accidental, why did you run?"

"How could I run if I wasn't there? I was probably in the middle of the Pacific Ocean when the woman died. Explain that to me."

"You seemed to know a lot about the woman's death."

"I'm a writer. My job is concocting stories that convince readers certain events have taken place."

"But Donaldson here seems to think you were actually in the house with Laura Dorchester and another person when the murder was committed."

"How many times must I state that I know absolutely nothing about the woman's death? I'm in London to receive a literary award, not to be hounded by the police."

"Are we hounding you, Mr. Scheiler?"

"Yes."

"I have the impression Donaldson is prepared to accept your fictional solution to this very nasty business. Ever been fingerprinted, Mr. Scheiler?"

"No." Remembering Donaldson telling him that no fingerprints had ever been taken, Arthur was about to say he had no objection to being fingerprinted when he realized Donaldson might have been lying to him about the absence of fingerprints in order to inculpate him.

"I have not," Arthur said. "And I won't."

"Yes, well . . . Do you recollect now what you said to Donaldson last night?"

"The actual words, no, but I recall the gist." Arthur glanced at his watch and stood. "I have to be the airport an hour before take-off."

"Airlines tell everybody that, as we tell people whatever they say may be taken down and used in evidence against them." The man smiled, turned away, then swung back. "One other thing, Mr. Scheiler. Did Donaldson tell you about the legacy to preserve A.E. Compson country?"

"He mentioned it."

"What d'you think Compson would do if he knew about the bequest? How would you handle it in a story?"

"I have no idea."

"You mean, you can't think of a scheme whereby Compson would derive benefit from it?"

"No."

"But you had no difficulty giving Donaldson some ideas about how Laura Dorchester died."

"That was relatively simple. People bicker, they quarrel, they hit each other, but to know how a man might behave when he has been left a bequest is another kettle of fish entirely, especially if the man knew the cops were looking for him."

"Have a go at it anyway, just to impress me with your ability to make up stories."

After a pause, Arthur spoke. "If—and it's a big if—*if* the man were still living and doing reasonably well and knew the cops were looking for him, he'd forget it. Look, I understand this is an old case, but I'd advise you to do the same: Forget it."

"We're doing our job, Mr. Scheiler. Trying to catch a murderer." The man in the black suit cut the interview off by swivelling his chair to look out a window. Donaldson led Arthur out of the office and down to his car. The two men didn't speak until they reached the hotel when Donaldson said, "I'll drive you to the airport."

"Thanks, but no thanks."

"It'd save cab fare. Besides, you're home free, Mr. Scheiler."

Arthur looked at the car clock, then glanced at his watch to confirm he had about two hours to spare. "I'll get my stuff," he said. "There's not much. A small case and a shopping bag with presents for my wife and daughter."

"I'm used to waiting." Donaldson turned off the engine. "In police work, periods of activity are short—waiting and preparing for action long. It's a bit like courtship and sex. Know what I mean?" Arthur ignored the question, went into the hotel, collected his bags and the contents of the safety deposit box, turned over his room key, decided he might as well accept Donaldson's offer, cancelled his taxi reservation and left the hotel. "So you've never been here before?" Donaldson asked as they passed through the suburbs.

"You've already asked me that question. Ask something different."

"In police work you repeat questions. I mean, if you think a man murdered a woman, you ask the same questions about the event in different ways. So tell me again in which state you were born."

"New Hampshire. Lots of mountains. But mostly forest. Lakes everywhere. Few big ones like Winnipesaukee."

"And the capital city?"

"Concord. We have our very own state assembly, a governor and our very own police force. We're much like every other state in the Union."

"You know a lot about America."

"I should. I was born and raised there."

"But you spent years at sea, isn't that so?"

"Quite right."

"Have you written about life at sea, Mr. Scheiler?"

"Short stories. Not about life on the bridge, though, but about what goes on in a ship's guts. I was on a freighter disabled in the middle of the Pacific. Talk about the ancient mariner drifting around! The engineers jury-rigged an engine that gave us two knots. Two knots! Forty-eight knots a day! Going nowhere in a hurry."

"Quite an experience."

"It was."

"So then you left the merchant navy."

"That's right. I told myself I really knew nothing about my own country, just New Hampshire, so I hopped onto a bus to have look around, and ended up in Los Angeles."

"It's a convincing tale."

"It had better be."

"But there's one thing I've noticed, you never speak of your childhood, or about your parents, brothers, sisters or grandparents."

Arthur had a ready explanation. "I don't talk about my childhood because I'd as soon forget it. I'd as soon not remember my father knocking Mom around after a few drinks; I'd as soon forget the place we lived in was as filthy as a cow barn. So don't tell me what I ought to remember, because I can tell you when I was fourteen, I had a choice between slugging it out with my father, or getting the hell out. And since I knew he was bigger'n me and could beat the be-Jesus out of me, I left. I don't talk about my childhood, because life for me began the day I shipped out as cook's help. Sure, I got kicked around, but I was fed and paid a few bucks and had a warm bunk, which was more'n I'd had before."

"I give you credit for taking every angle into account, but then you're a very smart man, and a smart person would do precisely what you've done. You know I won't be able to discredit your story. All I've got is the file of an unsolved murder, a newspaper photograph and intuition backed by experience. I could get a warrant and arrest you, but if the case were ever to come to court and couldn't be proved, it could wreck my career." Donaldson stopped the car in front of the airline terminal and put his police authorization card on the dashboard. "So, given all that, I'd like you to tell me more. I want to close the file."

Arthur rolled down the car window, got out of the car, removed his case and parcels from the rear seat, slammed the door and leaned into the car through the open window. "You're out of luck, pal. And let me tell you something else: I don't give a fuck about your career. I've paid my dues in this shitting world. I've paid a helluva lot, which means I don't owe you or anybody else one goddamn thing. Maybe I acted like a fool in the past, but not any more. I'm heading out of here on an airplane into the future. So, Inspector Donaldson, you can take your file and shove it up your ass." He picked up the case and shopping bag and walked towards the terminal entrance, and once inside, made his way through the crowds. He felt as though he had slipped from the space he had occupied when he entered the terminal into another space and time, where no one moved, but stood in twos and threes, like trees in a forest, through which he passed, blindly groping, knowing he had a destination, but uncertain of where it was.

"You're going the wrong way, Mr. Scheiler." Donaldson had come to stand beside him.

"So many people milling around," he grumbled. "I'm not sure where I'm heading."

"It's a crowded country. Some say, over-crowded." He guided Arthur through the crowds to a counter where Arthur presented his ticket, handed over his case, shopping bag and raincoat, told the agent to make sure the shopping bag wasn't crushed, nodded when the agent said he was free to relax in the lounge, then turned to Donaldson. "You needn't wait around," he said.

"I was hoping we could have a cup of tea, maybe lunch," Donaldson said, pointing ahead. "I'm told the restaurant serves a decent mixed grill."

"You paying?"

"Of course."

Arthur smiled. "I've never turned down a free meal." He thought Donaldson was giving him a final chance to put his case. He'd have to be convincing, which might not be easy. He was feeling disoriented and could hardly focus on anything except his desire to get back to Haven. But if he wanted that, he'd have to outsmart Donaldson, wouldn't he?

A waitress led them to a table, raised her pad and asked if they wanted a drink. Arthur ordered a large glass of iced water, Donaldson a scotch and soda. "You don't drink?" Donaldson asked after he had ordered a mixed grill for himself and Arthur.

"Rarely. It doesn't agree with me. I try to avoid things that don't agree with my system, like police officers."

"I can't close the file without knowing more. Sure you wouldn't like a drink?" Arthur shook his head. "I started out in police work believing an orderly mind would be useful, but I've discovered it's actually an impediment."

"But you like to tie up loose ends?"

"Yes that, but the thing I've learned is that there's no real order to criminal acts. Very occasionally you come across a carefully planned poisoning, but that's rare, and most crimes, especially murders, are products of manic rage or blind retaliation. I'm sure, as a writer, you must know that."

"When I was busing around America, I met a woman who later became my editor. She was the most intelligent person I've ever known. I told her a few things about myself, my miserable childhood, and what came after, but none of it especially bothered her. She only cared about how I used my experiences in my work. But the point is, I've never utilized my own experiences. I use other people's. I think the reason is that my own experiences scared me too much."

"Too traumatic?"

"No. I simply lacked the ability to make sense of them."

"Thank you," Donaldson said to the waitress, who placed a tumbler before him and a glass of water before Arthur.

"The point is, Donaldson, we're enemies."

"I think you misunderstand my role. My job is to find people who've broken the law."

"Precisely. And it wouldn't matter to you if a thief was rapped on the knuckles or hanged."

"Are you suggesting I would serve the law even if penalties for breaking it were barbaric?"

"Yes."

"You're mistaken."

"I am not. You confuse modification of punishment with modification of the law."

"Are you suggesting thieves and murderers should go free?"

"I repeat, our views are incompatible. What you might view as a violent attack, I might view as a terrible accident. That's all."

"But I can't make the distinction if I don't have the facts."

"I gave you an outline."

"Give me more details. Thank you," he said to the waitress who laid plates of mixed grill before them.

"And if I do?"

Donaldson hesitated. "Probably I'll close the file."

Arthur sliced meat off the lamb chop, chewed and swallowed it. "It's good," he said, while thinking how he should respond. After a pause, he said, "All right. I'll risk it." He cut the lambs' kidney in half and ate it. "Compson's father was a mini-dictator, a remnant of a slave-owning age, except that the currency the men under his control used to buy jobs was their wives and daughters. He died of heart failure when Compson was an adolescent. Now, where does Laura Dorchester come in?" Arthur cut a piece of calf's liver and smacked his lips after chewing it. "Delicious . . . A doctor once told me liver's the sewage works of the body. Yes. Well. Compson was nineteen. Ignorant. Desperate. But he believed he had the makings of a great writer, though the only evidence was weekly articles about life in the forest, for which he was paid ten shillings each. But what a difference having that money meant to him and his mother! Ah yes, Sylvia. That was Compson's mother's name. After his father's death, they had to move, and when there was no money for rent or food, his mother went a little crazy, which deeply pained Compson because he adored his mother." Arthur picked up and chewed meat off the bone of the lamb chop. "She was probably no prettier than most women, but beauty's always in the eye of beholder, isn't it, especially for a child and more especially for one who suffered from odd, medically inexplicable spells of unconsciousness. Compson's mother took him to specialists, who diagnosed him as having an unknown form of epilepsy, which she didn't accept because the disease was associated in her mind with idiocy. It was years before he realized his mother had traded access to her body for rent and food. They had practically nothing, a tiny army widow's pension, that's all. The father had been a regular soldier, cavalry, a sergeant. "The Sarge," the Asty villagers called him. Compson stole a lined notebook from a stationary shop in Ponnewton and printed his first novel in it. Printed it! I'm amazed when I think of it now. How did he hit on *Tower & Tower*? It doesn't matter. Maybe he was impressed by the name.

Anyway, that's how Laura Dorchester came into Compson's life. She appeared in a car, a rare sight in Hasterley in those days, and walked into their miserable cottage as if she owned it and all the contents. He thought his mother would've knelt and kissed the hem of Laura's skirt as if she were royalty, except for the fact that Laura was prepared to kneel and kiss the ground Compson walked on before taking over his life." Arthur ate a piece of bacon and a mushroom. "To understand, you must first know more about Compson's parents. His mother, a woman with no sexual experience, met and married Compson when he was on sick leave and was overwhelmed by his sexuality. Until the moment of their wedding night, I doubt she had ventured beyond thoughts of sex as hand-holding and decorous kissing, though, later, insanity produced in her a rampant, unappeasable sexuality. Until the day Compson died she had been modest and self-abrogating. After he was buried, she told her son that, though she knew about her husband's other women, she had always welcomed him when he returned to her bed, nor did she condemn her husband for taking his son to the village whore when signs of sexual maturity appeared. So the son replaced the father. Does this shock you?" Donaldson slowly shook his head. "Good. Well. Laura Dorchester enveloped Sylvia and Arthur Compson. She wrapped herself around their lives like a python, then swallowed them. She set up an altar to worship before Compson's genius, at the same time she acquired a house for him and Sylvia and had him slaving on a second, third and fourth novel. He enjoyed being worshipped. He though it a fitting tribute to his talent. Then calamity struck. Compson's mother died and Compson reacted by having a particularly bad spell of illness. Laura found him unconscious at the foot of the stairs. She took over completely. She buried his mother and took him to the Ponnewton hospital. When he was discharged, she took him to a house she'd rented in Ponnewton. She tried to take over his life. Is this tale boring you, Donaldson? Is it too repetitive?"

"No."

"Compson hated the house in Ponnewton. I've told you how one day when Laura was off shopping, Compson slipped out and set off back to the house in the forest. She guessed where he'd gone and followed him. But she wasn't prepared to stay. I've also told you about this. Then she returned with Maria. Compson was never sure if what he felt for Maria was love. As you know, sex wasn't involved. He simply felt contented when he was with her. What a fool he was! His blindness was amazing, but excusable in a way, because the intense nature of his work had forced him to peer into the dark passions consuming other people's lives and prevented him from seeing what was going on in his own. But Maria's death destroyed Compson's grasp on reality and partly explains everything that followed. Laura insisted on nursing Compson back to health at her London home. Her devotion to his well-being can't be faulted, but things between them changed. Laura began using his cock. All Compson had to do was lie still and let her do the work. She said he was the only man who'd ever satisfied her and she wanted to have a child with him more than anything she'd ever wanted in her life. Compson now thinks she must have loved him. The trouble was, he didn't reciprocate her love. Oh, once he'd regained his strength, he supplied her with what she needed for sexual satisfaction, but he would've done the same for any woman. At the time, women were much the same to him, except for Maria, whom he'd idealized as incorruptible and unapproachable. And when Martha entered the picture, he thought, why not join forces? Their love for Maria could hold them together. So they talked themselves into a relationship. Martha tried to turn the young Compson into the father she had never known, so she could play the role of "baby," then "child," then "adolescent" and so on into maturity, though at the time Compson didn't fully grasp what was going on. At first, he thought Martha was tempting him to have sex because she insisted on sleeping with him. How stupid he was. Psychologically, she was still in nappies. She was a needy child who wanted parental love. That was after they'd run away from the house in Hampstead to his place in the forest. Of course, Laura was furious. As I explained last night, she sent two men to take Martha back to Hampstead, but by now Martha hated being a servant in Laura's house, and after some time passed she came back. Martha told Compson that Dorchester had begun to treat her badly. Later Compson understood Laura had become insanely jealous of Martha. Anyway, the first night Martha was back, Laura drove from London to the village and entered the bedroom where Martha and Compson were sleeping. Did I mention their relationship was celibate? You know the rest. Martha was badly bruised and terror-stricken, her back and thighs covered with blood-filled welts. By the time she'd got to Compson's workroom and reached for the typewriter, she feared for her life. She became hysterical. Any independent observer of the scene would have immediately gone to the authorities and reported Laura Dorchester's death, which was the result of Martha defending herself against a savage attack. Later on, after Compson gained a measure of security and could go over the incidents of that awful night without re-experiencing panic, he concluded that when Laura discovered Martha was gone from the London house, she guessed that she had returned to Hasterley, and remembering what Maria had told her about Compson wanting to marry her, she immediately drove to the village and finding Martha in Compson's bed, lost control and tried to beat her to death in a fit of uncontrollable rage. But of course there was no objective witness to the events: only the horrible bruises on Martha, Laura's dead body, and Martha, who couldn't stop shaking, and Compson, in a state of utter panic, though he knew Martha had not intended to kill Laura, only to stop the thrashing. It was a terrible, terrible accident. If Laura had not acted so precipitously, Compson could have explained Martha's presence in his bed, and had she wanted to be truly inquisitorial, she could have spread Martha's thighs, examined her and found her maidenhead still intact. Do you still want to pursue poor Martha? Surely not. When an earthquake shakes the land, or volcanoes erupt, or hurricanes sweep across oceans and lands, people mindlessly run from the fury that pursues them. That's what Compson and Martha did, though in truth Martha was barely aware of what transpired. And if she were to be found alive today, it wouldn't be surprising to find she has no memory of the events. And what would you gain, anyway, if you did find her and drag her through the courts? Tell me. Go on. Tell me. Poor, helpless Martha, who had no choice but to cling to Compson when a cataclysm destroyed the centre of her life. Do you want to apply your laws to her? Eh? Do you?"

"No, only to tie up the loose ends. But I do ask why you returned to England. Was it necessary?"

"Yes, I came to bury Arthur Compson."

"Or lay his ghost to rest."

"Perhaps. "Arthur looked at his watch. "It's ten after two. I have to go."

"If I laid a Bible before you, would you swear you have told me the truth?"

"Seen through the filter of time. Yes." He got up.

"I will need to report to my superior. The decision to continue the search for Martha Sowerton rests with him. But I shall recommend closing the file."

"Do you carry much weight?"

"I think so." Donaldson got up and extended his hand. "Good bye, Mr. Scheiler." Arthur briefly touched the policeman's hand, walked from the restaurant and went to the airline counter for his boarding card. "Scheiler's the name," he said, "Matthew Scheiler."

The ticket agent examined the list. "You have fifteen minutes, Mr. Scheiler. Gate 43."

"Thank you, ma'am," Arthur replied and strode confidently forward, through customs and immigration, down the corridors, up an escalator, finally to present his boarding pass and hurry along the ramp into the pulsing but neutral ambience of the immense aircraft.

He was finally on his way home! At last, he, Matt Scheiler, was going home to Haven.

Later that day, a report circulated on the wire services that a commercial aircraft flying from London to Toronto had exploded and crashed in the mid-Atlantic. Reasons for the explosion were not immediately available. However, the fact that the blast was internal, coupled with the severity of weather and low water temperature in the North Atlantic, led officials to announce that the chance for survival of passengers and crew was low. An ultra-radical wing of the IRA claimed responsibility.

CHAPTER

28

WHEN HE AWAKENED IN THE BED, HE IMMEDIATELY GUESSED where he was and refused to open his eyes because he didn't want to believe that illness had intervened to prevent him from flying home. Yet he couldn't escape the truth: against his closed eyelids he saw an image of himself acknowledging a flight attendant's welcoming smile, walking past the galley and entering the cabin where another smiling attendant waited to direct him to his seat. It was then he saw Laura Dorchester on the other side of the cabin, wearing the dark suit, black shoes and white blouse, which for him had become a publishing hallmark. Her back was to him, and as she slowly turned, his heart momentarily stopped beating, his world swirled and he dropped to the floor. The woman, a Republican member of the U.S. Congress, provided the shocked attendants with the following account: "I had placed my briefcase in the overhead bin and was about to occupy my seat (the Congresswoman always spoke as though addressing an audience, even when talking to her cat) when I saw the gentleman staring wide-eyed at me before he collapsed. Poor fellow. I do hope he recovers. I'm reminded of a colleague—a Democrat— who stood to raise a point of order." She continued for another ten minutes with accounts of men who had collapsed in her presence, which the concerned attendants thought understandable since her presence was formidable and her words unbearably ponderous.

So Arthur knew by scents in the air and odours emanating from clothes worn by people who came to look at him that instead of being winged back to Canada at the rate of many hundreds of miles an hour, he was lying in a hospital bed with monitors attached to his chest and head. He could not believe that after successfully resisting days of pressure from Inspector Donaldson, he had been betrayed by his covert, hidden enemy. Desolation settled over him.

"How do you feel, Mr. Scheiler?" a quiet voice asked. "Why not open your eyes and have a look around?"

"I don't want to see what's in front of them. I was supposed to be looking at the interior of an airplane cabin."

"You're lucky you were taken off the plane. It was blown up over the Atlantic Ocean two days ago. A terrorist group has claimed responsibility for
planting a bomb in the cargo compartment."

He opened his eyes and found he was looking into the dark eyes of a slender, brown-skinned woman. "My God," he said. "Joey . . . my wife . . . she'll
think . . . My God! I have to call her. Get me a telephone."

"Now, now Mr. Scheiler. Don't get excited. Listen to me. The hospital
tried to contact your wife, but no one answered. And I'm sure the airline tried."

"What d'you mean, no answer? She has to be there. Take me to a phone.
I'll call."

"Don't worry Mr. Scheiler. It's probably just a little mix up. Time differ-
ences. You know the sort of thing. When it's noon here . . ." She began singing.
". . . It's midnight in the Rockies."

"For God's sake, shut up. Oh . . . she may have gone down to Los Angeles."

"I have no idea where your wife is Mr. Scheiler," said the nurse, now offended. "I just know we have done everything we can to contact her. Now, I
want you to lie down while I get the doctor."

"I don't want a doctor. I want to use a phone and get out of this place.
Bring my clothes."

"Yes, yes, yes, I'll do that, but for now just lie there. You've been unconscious for two days. You need to rest."

He looked away from her over the empty beds in the ward and felt tears
flowing from his eyes. "Two days," he muttered. "Two days. Oh, my God."

"Let me help you, Mr. Scheiler," she said.

"God . . . what a mess . . . what a mess." The nurse put her arms around
him and helped him lie down. Her arms were thin but strong, and as she slowly
lowered him, his face was pressed between her cone-shaped breasts. "Do you
remember what happened?" she asked.

"I saw . . ." He stopped, licked his lips and continued. "I thought I was
looking at a person who died many years ago. It was a shock. That's all." Her
hand was cool and reminded him of the way Sylvia's hand on his forehead
seemed to quell the throbbing pain in his skull. "Get my clothes, and a couple
of aspirin."

"I can't do that. Only doctors prescribe medication. It won't take long.
Then we'll put you into a wheelchair and take you to a telephone. But promise
you won't try to get up." It was more an appeal than an order, and he guessed
behind it lay a fear she might be blamed if he fell and injured himself.

"You'll bring my things first?"

"As soon as I've told Dr. Evans and Sister McIntyre you're awake." He watched her thin legs and white nurse's shoes disappear and waited for what seemed an eternity before a white-coated man entered the ward, followed by a short plump woman and the nurse.

"So, how are we doing?" Dr. Evans said.

"Who the hell are you?" Arthur rudely asked. He pointed to the nurse. "You said you'd take me to a phone."

"Hold your horses, hold your horses," the physician said. "I'm Dr. Evans. This is Sister McIntyre." He did not acknowledge the presence of the nurse.

"Listen, you sanctimonious lump of medical shit," Arthur began.

"Don't speak to Doctor like that!" Sister McIntyre said.

"I'll say anything I please until you get it through your thick skulls that I have a wife in Canada who probably thinks my cock and balls are feeding mackerel in the Atlantic. I want to let her know they're still intact. Get it?"

"The hospital has made several attempts to get in touch with your wife, Mr. Scheiler," Sister McIntyre snapped. "I will not allow any patient in my wards to insult me or members of my staff. You were unconscious when you were brought here. The least you can do is express some appreciation for what we've done to help you recover."

"All right, all right." Dr. Evans raised a pacifying hand. "Shall we calm down?" He looked at the nurse. "Get a wheelchair for Mr. Scheiler. Now, sir, your business with me won't take long, then you'll be free to do all the telephoning you please. Even to leave the hospital, if that's what you want to do. Okay? So just bear with me. Okay? I'm not trying to prevent you leaving, I just want to make sure you're fit enough to leave. We can deliver you to the front door, but we want to be sure you can function once you're out on the streets. You agree?" He consulted the chart.

"You want an agreement? Fine! I'll get my clothes on while you talk, and after that I'm taken to a phone. Right?"

"Okay. In any event, I already have a pretty clear idea what the problem is. We've run some simple tests, and it looks as if you've got some scar tissue in your brain that every once in a while interrupts the flow of blood and results in unconsciousness. But *why* isn't clear. Naturally, we'd like to conduct further tests. Do you recall ever having had a fall as a child?"

"I've been asked that before. If I did, it's beyond my recall."

"Or perhaps a birth injury, which happens more frequently than you might think. The human female birth canal wasn't designed to pass a fully-formed child's head easily. It's better designed for trapping spermatozoa. If you remain with us, we will utilize radioactive particles— they're quite harmless— and X-ray your brain as the particles circulate through your system."

"No doubt your intentions are good, Doctor, but I don't have time right now. I'll certainly bear it in mind for the future." The doctor shrugged and left the room with Sister McIntyre close behind.

"You put his nose out of joint," the nurse said.

"Good." Arthur replied. He manoeuvred himself into the wheelchair, surprised and disturbed by the effort required to move from the bed to the wheelchair.

"Okay?" she asked.

"Okay," he said. "Will you get my wallet please? My wife must have put some telephone numbers in it. I'll need them."

"You still look pretty weak to me," the nurse commented when she returned with the wallet.

"In half an hour I'll be fine. Now take me to the phone."

She pushed him into a small office near the nurses' station and left him to make the phone calls. When Joey didn't answer at Haven, he went through information and put a call through to the Gambarasi house in Los Angeles. At first, Joey's thick-voice brother Tommy refused to believe his ears when Arthur identified himself and asked to speak to Joey.

"For crissake," Tommy said. "We thought you got blown up in that plane explosion."

"Well, I wasn't," Arthur explained. "I was ill and left the plane before it took off."

"Well, for God's sake," Tommy said. "Why didn't the airline tell Joey you were okay? She thinks you're dead. We heard about the crash on the radio and TV. Nobody was supposed to have survived. Jeez!"

"Can I speak with Joey?"

"She's not here. Boy, oh boy, was she ever cut up when she heard about you being dead! Anyway I brought a friend home, nice guy, knows his way around. He's into financing movies. He thinks Joey should do another movie. You know, get her mind off you being dead."

"Where is she?" Arthur yelled into the receiver.

"He's got a place in Palm Springs."

"You mean you don't know where she is?"

"Of course I know where she is. She and Miracle're at our house in Palm Springs."

"Give me the number."

"Sure. But I got to tell you, Matt, Joey's used to you being dead. Know what I mean?"

"So she'll get used to me being alive again. Right?"

"I'm not so sure. She flew into L.A. the day after you left for England. She got it into her head that she'd had enough of you, Matt. And then she hears about the explosion and no one tells her you're okay, so she sort of thinks that maybe it's a happy ending. Know what I mean? She doesn't have to get a divorce."

"Just give me the number. Everything'll be all right after I talk to Joey."

"Okay, Matt, but it doesn't necessarily follow a guy's welcomed back after he gets resurrected. See what I mean?"

"I get the picture, Tommy. Now give me the goddamn number." Arthur scribbled the number on a pad of paper someone had thoughtfully left next to the phone, hung up, then made a collect call to the Palm Springs house.

Arthur heard Joey's voice say "Hello." When the operator asked if Joey would accept a collect call from Matt Scheiler, he heard her gasp, then say: "No! No! He's dead! He's dead!" before she hung up. Joey's response shocked him, and for a moment or two he couldn't think what to do. He decided to call again and charge the call to the Haven number, and while he waited for it to be completed, he thought of what he should say when Joey answered.

"Hello," Joey said.

"Joey." Arthur swallowed and spoke again. "Joey."

"Who's that?" Joey asked. "Who is it?"

"Matt, Joey. Matt."

"No! It can't be! Matt's dead!" she shrieked, "Go away! Matt is dead!"

"Joey, listen to me. I'm not dead. It's all a big mistake." She seemed far more distant than could be accounted for by the geographic miles that separated them. He recounted what had happened at the airport and told her he was calling from the hospital where he has been taken after his spell; but while Joey did calm down to the extent of objectively accepting the fact that he was actually still alive, he sensed that he was dead to her emotionally and that their life together could not be restored to what it had been, no matter how hard he tried to resuscitate it by speaking of the good time they had shared at Haven, especially since Miracle's birth. he took out the picture of Miracle which Joey had insisted on putting in his wallet, twiddled it in his fingers and told Joey that the happiest moments of his life were watching her nurse the baby. He went overboard and in a delirium of over-exaggeration asserted that if every mother possessed Joey's marvellous, ever-flowing maternal breasts, no pot-bellied, skinny-limbed, vacant-eyed children would ever exist in the world. He then looked around to make sure no one was within hearing range and whispered into the phone that he longed to wipe Miracle's tiny, beautiful bottom, because he'd read somewhere that aboriginal people in the tropical isles of the Pacific Ocean believed that a bond between child and father was forged when his fingers came in contact with the child's feces. Only after he had uttered the words did he think that they might have offended Joey. He tried to make amends, but she remained silent. He then concluded that because she had experienced a double shock, she needed more time to adjust to his renewed presence in her life. He told her he would telephone her the next day and ended the by then one-sided conversation. Badly shaken, he put the phone down, at a loss as to what more he might do other than to keep telephoning, or maybe fly to California and reclaim Joey and Miracle. His fear of seeing Joey's face and hearing her reject any proposal he might make to get them back together forced him into the realization that something would have to change in Joey before he could look her into her face and ask: "Ready to come home?" As he returned the photo to his wallet, he remembered that he had put Martha's address and telephone number into one of its pockets. He took out the piece of paper, unfolded and stared at it while asking himself if it was advisable to contact Martha. After a moment or two, he set caution aside and dialed the number.

When Martha answered, he said, "Martha, this is me. You know who. I've been ill and need a place to stay for a few days. I thought maybe . . ."

"Sure. You can come here. Grab a taxi."

"Thank you, Martha." It was one of the rare occasions when Arthur expressed gratitude to anyone. Like most people whose lives radiate from themselves, he took the assistance of other people, especially women, for granted.

She met him at the door of her small semi-detached house and supported him into a tiny front parlour. "You look wore out," she said. "I'll make a cup of tea." He was so grateful that tears flowed from his eyes and down his cheeks and, forgetting the tea, she sat on the couch to comfort him. "Don't take on so. You'll soon feel better."

In a whisper, he told her all that had happened, and she responded by agreeing his wife was in shock and hadn't known what she was saying or doing. Then, calling him Arthur, Martha told him that the best memories in her life were of Maria and of him. They were the two people she had truly loved other than her own children, and because he had loved Maria, she would help him in any way she could.

Arthur, who had not expected Martha to speak of love, replied that he fondly recalled images of her and appreciated her readiness to step forward now and assist him. They talked in generalities for a while, then moved to the tiny kitchen where Arthur sat at a square table, while Martha cooked scrambled eggs and bacon on a two-burner gas stove. After she had washed and dried the dishes, they returned to the parlour and couch where Martha put her arm around Arthur so that he might cosily recline against her while watching shows on the TV set, which had been a recent gift from her daughters. Although she thought he was being fresh, she didn't protest when his fingers unfastened buttons on her blouse and his hand slipped beneath her clothes to touch her breasts: she buried her doubts beneath the gratitude she felt for his having once looked after her like a real father. During the course of her drab married life she had somehow managed to transform the few days spent with Arthur in Hasterley into a glorious sun-endowed idyll. The few terrible minutes beginning with Miss Dorchester beating her with a belt and, afterward, her smashing the typewriter onto Miss Dorchester's head had vanished into a subterranean vault in her consciousness, so that memories of the event commenced with her leaning out of the railway coach waving goodbye to Arthur. She remembered being an army recruit, learning the drills and how to drive army trucks, which was how she met the man who pulled down her knickers and "did her." He had liked it so much he went on doing it, then finally agreed to marry her when her stomach became too big to be contained within the confines of her uniform.

As mothers go, Martha was adequate, although at the time she was convinced giving birth was a prelude to a painful death. She breast-fed her three children only because the midwife who delivered the babies told her that nursing would serve as a natural contraceptive by preventing a renewal of her menstrual periods. The babies bewildered her and she had no idea what to do with them, apart from putting their pulsing lips to her dripping nipples. However, she guarded them as ferociously as Maria had once protected her. She named her first child Maria and incorporated her sister's name into the names of the other two. For her husband, Martha felt nothing; he was someone who was simply present in her life. She concentrated on raising her children, and especially on embedding into her girls' brains the prohibition that under no circumstances were they ever to give what they had inside their knickers to any man. The girls, who believed everything their mother said and disliked their father's eating habits and continual complaints and the disgusting pubertal inquisitiveness of their younger brother, haughtily rejected the approaches of adolescent youths, and once free of the educational system set about "getting on," as they called it. Maria had taken the latest in secretarial courses and landed a good job with a small business in Knightsbridge, where she rose to become an executive secretary. The younger girl, Mary Margaret, had gone to a teacher's college for two years, then got a position as a pre-school teacher in Manchester. Her son, Marius, had escaped into the army, where his willingness to accept discipline immediately led to promotion. He was presently stationed in Germany. Martha felt guilty knowing she didn't love her son as much as her daughters, but rationalized her lack of affection by telling herself that Marius resembled his father, whereas Maria and Mary Margaret took after her side of the family. Every week, Maria came to drink tea and gossip with her mother and, during the course of their afternoon chats, had heard endless stories about her dead aunt and the marvellous hours her mother had spent with the young man whom her sister had been going to marry, wandering through woodlands and across heaths. "I was just a ignorant girl," Martha told her daughter. "But he looked after me like a real father. I don't know what ever happened to him." She never seemed to get beyond the primroses, bluebell-carpeted woodlands and the bee-loving furze. Maria wondered if her mother had invented the young man, as she herself had invented imaginary friends when she was a child. Maria loved her mother all the more because she had lost the sister she had loved so dearly, and Maria hoped the love she felt for her mother would help to fill in the vast gaps in her mother's life.

"Maria and Mary Margaret are good girls," Martha said. Arthur agreed, adding he was sure Miracle would grow up to be the same. He then inquired if Martha's girls had boyfriends, but Martha, who could not bear the thought of acquisitive men getting around her daughters, ignored the question and asked whether he would like a cup of Ovaltine.

"It's amazing how free young women today are with men," he remarked. "You know, I can still pull up an image of you sleeping in my bed." Martha pushed his hand away and said he had no right to talk like that. "Oh, but I never touched you, Martha. I may have thought of it, but that's as far as it went."

"I don't want to hear about anything you thought," she said and tried to leave the couch, but he held her down.

"I'm a writer, Martha, and that means there's nothing about men and women I haven't thought of."

"Well, I don't want to know about it." She struggled to get up.

"You don't know me very well, Martha."

"I remember you were a decent sort of chap years ago."

"You saw the best side of me. I was an embryo, and so were you." He noticed how upset she was. He kissed her and apologized for his behaviour. "I'm all at sea, Martha," he said. "Half the time I don't know what I'm saying or doing. I'm so mixed up I don't know the day, or time."

"You do look peaked," she commented. "Maybe you should've stayed in hospital for a couple more days. Anyway, it's Friday, and almost ten. See? There's the clock." She pointed to the wall clock over the mantel.

"I should call the airline and arrange a flight."

"I thought you'd stay a few days."

"No. I must get back to Haven. It will easier to call Joey from there."

"But wouldn't you like to meet my girls?"

"If there's time."

"I could call them. Explain you're here. If I called now, Mary Margaret could catch an early train, spend the day with us and go back to Manchester on Sunday. I mean, I used to talk about you when they were little, but I never used your real name. They'll be sorry to miss seeing you."

"There's not much to see. They've probably formed images of me being strong and handsome. You know how children are. They'd be horribly disappointed. Best not to, Martha. Let them keep their illusions about the guy who jaunted around the forest and heaths with their mum when she was a girl."

"You really think so? Honest? They're sensible girls."

"Maybe, but you know as well as I that behind every sensible facade there is a chaos of nonsensical memories."

"I'm sure I don't know anything about that." She glanced at the clock. "It's well past ten." She appeared to have forgotten the Ovaltine and informed Arthur he could sleep in Marius's room.

"Don't shuffle me off into another room, Martha. When you think of the old days when you slept in my bed, shouldn't you think of returning the favour? I'll rest much better if I sleep beside you." Arthur thought that was true and a good night's sleep would help overcome his weakness and exhaustion.

"But this isn't the old days," she said. "Things have changed."

"Maybe. But the girl who slept like a child beside me is still inside you, Martha. And the young chap who sat on his bed and watched you sleeping with your nightgown ruckled up over your pretty little breasts is still inside me. There's unfinished business between us, Martha. That's why you followed me to Harrod's. You want to find out what really happened between us on that bed, don't you?"

"Well . . . maybe."

"You saw the photograph, and you tried to remember, isn't that right?"

"I just wanted to say hello." She turned away.

Arthur looked at her averted face, shrugged and said, "All right. I'll doss down in your son's room."

Martha's face twitched, she reached out to clutch and squeeze his hand while saying, "No. You can sleep in my bed."

He waited while she locked the doors and turned out the lights before following her up the narrow stairs to the bedroom. He stripped down to his shirt and shorts and she put on her nightgown over her underwear. It was or more or less like old times, except that now he kissed her cheek and neck, and after a while she pulled up her nightgown and took off her knickers and bra and he took off his shorts and pulled up his shirt. But when he moved into position between Martha's thighs, it became clear it couldn't be like old times because each had been worn down by time and experience. Martha whispered that she was a "slow coach," and Arthur responded by saying he resembled the "Puffing Billy" that had once chugged from London junction on the single branch line to Ponnewton. He lay there and waited, enjoying the sensation of finally being united with her after so many years, kissing her ears and thrusting his buttocks now and then until she suddenly tensed up, then said, "That's it. You can speed up now, if you want to." It was all very old hat, and Arthur felt as though he had spent his whole life doing it with Martha.

Once it was over, she became talkative and told Arthur that in her opinion it took some people a long time to mature. That was the case with her. She had not grown up until her first baby arrived. Something had clicked in her head when Maria came out and the midwife casually laid her on Martha's stomach while saying, "There you are, dear. There's number one." Martha took this as an omen, a pulsing cranial warning that she mustn't allow her husband do his high-speed thing in her twice a week; if she did, she would be staggering around with a great belly year after year, with one baby nursing and half a dozen more crawling around her feet, making messes in their nappies. She was so scared she told her husband she was through doing it. "Never again," she said. They squabbled over who had what rights, but finally reached a compromise which allowed him to invade her (they used military jargon) but compelled him to retire before firing any ammunition. Her two other children were the outcome of her husband's failure to abandon his advanced position, though he'd done his level best to withhold fire. Still and all, she told Arthur, she loved her children. They showed no inclination to marry, which meant that she might never become a grandmother. As Arthur listened to her talking, he tried to formulate a plan for himself. He must assume that if he telephoned Joey every day, sooner or later everything would return to normal, and he'd even be prepared to fly to California if necessary. He must try to understand that his going to England and then dying (apparently) in a terrible accident had somehow functioned to sever Joey's commitment to him and Haven. Haven! There was no one there protecting Haven! What if vandals had entered the property? Oh God! He clutched Martha as he fought waves of panic.

"What's wrong?" Martha asked.

"I have to get back to Haven, Martha. I have to be there to make sure nothing happens."

"Don't worry." Martha sounded like a mother soothing an agitated child. She even unknowingly cupped a breast ready to pop a nipple into its open mouth.

"Not worry! It's my home! And besides, it's worth a lot of money. Wait until you see it, Martha."

"Me see it!"

"Yes. You can come home with me and stay a while, or until Joey comes back." Arthur manufactured the idea of Martha accompanying him back to Canada as he uttered the words. "It's beautiful, Martha. You'd like it." As he spoke, he thought that he might be able to persuade Martha to take on the running of the household. He wouldn't exploit her, no, nothing like that, but it would be helpful, wouldn't it, and allow him to get on with the novel he was in the midst of finishing before he left for England. And he was fond of Martha, always had been, and once he was physically strong again, he could express it every night in bed. He had noticed in the past year that his cock had a tendency to droop when it was not active, and just in case he wasn't able to convince Joey to return, Martha would be there to keep him in mint condition. No doubt about it, she was an amiable soul. Not bright, but willing. Oh, her breasts sagged a bit and the skin around her neck was loose, but those were minor defects. And he wouldn't have to pay her a wage, would he? No, that would be insulting. He'd just feed and house her, and she could transfer her widow's pension to Canada and that would provide any spare cash she might need. Why, thousands of Americans and Canadians spent big money every year to holiday at the lake. Martha should be grateful for the opportunity he would provide. He moved closer to her.

"You want to again?" she asked.

"Now you know what you missed all those years ago."

Martha shook her head and said it had taken her years to feel anything, and it was quite by chance she had discovered she could, or had the right to, feel anything down there. Although, from overhearing women talking in the local medical clinic, she guessed plenty more women were in the same boat.

"That's not surprising. Until very recently, sexual pleasure was the prerogative of the rich. The working class merely copulated to propagate more working class. By and large, it's still the case," he pompously informed her.

Martha replied she didn't care what other people did or felt. She cared only for herself and daughters. Arthur decided the time had come to present his proposition and he started out by asking if she had a passport.

"Me? A passport? Why ever would I have a passport?"

"Wouldn't you go to Germany to visit your son?"

"He wouldn't be seen traipsing around with his shabby old mum. He's a real sharp chap, he is."

"You'll need a passport if you're going to come and stay with me at Haven. The orchards'll be flowering in a few weeks. Cherry and apple." He thought of the fruit pickers and saw images of the young women and men emerging from the lake, water droplets on their naked bodies reflecting prisms of light. He would encourage Martha to bathe in the nude. She could be a temporary substitute for Joey.

"I don't know if I can leave my girls," Martha said.

"They can visit you at Haven." An image of Martha's two daughters happily splashing and swimming in the cove appeared on his eyelids. Of course they would be bravely naked, and of course before departing, in gratitude for a marvellous holiday, they would gracefully allow him to sample their young, sweet-lipped sexual sheaths. He told himself that his propensity to imagine erotic, even lewd, scenes with girls and young women was increasing and that he must put an end to it. That was the kind of behaviour expected from men who haunted cinemas where pornographic films were screened. Of course, while writing, sexual images involving his characters appeared and were handled according to the demands of the novel's plot; they were the grains that flowed through his authorial mill and he ground and dispatched them expeditiously. But images of Martha's daughters were not in the same category. They were privately exploitive, and that disturbed him because, coupled with his parsimony, was a hidden puritanical streak that allowed him to condemn behaviour in others that he permitted himself. He was like a Victorian judge who condemns a whore for flipping up her skirts, but enjoys watching the beadles strip and tie her hands and feet to the pillory and give her twenty-five good ones on quivering buttocks with the lash. Oh yes, he would never have admitted it, but when the young fruit pickers from Quebec happily splashed in the cove, then emerged like so many white shining inhabitants of Eden, he had looked at the naked women and, way at the back of his mind, thought of them as harlots, who having brazenly exposed themselves in public justly deserved any ill treatment meted out to them. To even momentarily have such a thought shocked him, since he liked to believe he was free of such prejudices. But why hadn't the same thought occurred to him when Joey and Phyllis swam and strolled naked on the headlands and beach? Why indeed? Because way, way down he was infected by class prejudice and, believing himself to be of a superior class, viewed the young pickers as vagrants because in them he saw the scruffy, dirty children in the village of his childhood, and himself always neatly dressed, heeding Sylvia's warning never to play with the running, skipping, half-naked children since he and his family were members of the upper class.

"I must call and arrange my flight. They might even have a seat for you. Think about it. Maybe I should try Joey again too." He left the bed. "Where's your telephone directory?"

"Wait until morning."

"No, I have to. And I'm going to give the airline hell for not contacting Joey. They didn't try hard enough."

"The directory's by the phone." She left the bed and followed him down to the parlour, thinking his skinny legs looked ridiculous as he trotted around her house in nothing but a shirt. In comparison, her husband's legs had been thick and muscular, a soldier's marching legs. He sat on the couch, chewing at a thumbnail, listening to the phone ringing without answer at the Palm Springs house, his legs open so that Martha sitting in the chair opposite had a clear view of his collapsed genitals. She asked herself how it could be that so ugly a contraption only a short time ago had made her tremble with pleasure. It didn't make sense, because she could count on the fingers of one hand the number of times she had felt that way with her husband. But then, except for her daughters, little of what had happened in her life made sense. She never ceased thinking about her two girls and even though they always said, "Don't worry about us, Mum, we're doing fine," anxiety about them ruled her days. She desperately wanted them to have more than she ever had, but, having been tugged at and pushed through life herself, was incapable of formulating methods and rules she could pass on that would enable them to govern their lives successfully. She was like a traveller in a strange land who that knows a wonderful place lies beyond the next mountain range, but, weakened by the struggle to survive, realizes it is unattainable.

"There's no answer. I wonder what's going on? You know, Martha, maybe you should think of coming to Canada for good. I'll buy a car for you. I'll call the airline now, and try Joey again from the airport."

"My girls rely on me being here."

"Yes, yes," he said into the receiver. "Matt Scheiler. You're glad to hear from me? Well, that's one way to think of it. Of course, you didn't do enough to contact my wife. You've caused her unnecessary grief and shock. It's inexcusable. Of course, I want to go home. As soon as possible. Tonight? As you know, I've been ill and I'd like an old friend to accompany me. The problem is, she doesn't have a passport. You don't think so? Too bad. Well, in that case, I'll reserve a seat for a flight next week. That'll give her time to get whatever papers she requires. I'll give you the necessary information when I get to the airport. A complimentary ticket? Yes, that would be appreciated. A red-eye? What's that? Oh, of course. Yes, that'll be fine. I can get to the airport immediately. Oh, you will? Yes, I have my passport. I'll have no trouble with customs and immigration. You do?" He hung up the phone and smiled at Martha. "They kept my bag."

"I can't go. I can't," Martha protested.

"Of course you can. You have time to tell your girls and get a passport. It'll be wonderful to have you at Haven."

"You had no business to make arrangements before I said so," Martha firmly said. "I'm not a servant any more."

"First-class to Vancouver, Martha. You'll love it."

"But what about my girls and my house?"

"Leave it."

"Leave it! This is my home. You make a big song and dance about your house, but for all I know it could be a shack with a tin roof."

"I'm sorry, Martha. I seized the moment. It seemed like a perfect opportunity. I'll cancel the reservation. No harm done."

"You should've asked me first."

They faced each other across the small room, Martha in her nightgown and with corns on her toes, Arthur on the couch, his skin pale, in a striped shirt Joey had bought for the London trip, which was too tight in the neck and too long in the sleeves. "Never do things on the spur of the moment," he said.

"It's not that," Martha explained. "But you just dumped it on me."

"Come on, Martha. Say you'll come." He knelt and put his hands on her knees. "You'll love it."

"I can't afford it," she protested.

"Look Martha, you'll get a free flight. It's the least the airline can do for me. I'll tell you what we'll do, Martha. Come with me now. I'm sure I can talk them into letting you on board without a passport. After all, I'm a sick man. And we'll kiss over the North Pole."

"What's so special about doing that? A kiss is a kiss. Anyway, I'm not going."

"I thought we'd settled it."

"You settled your side. I didn't settle mine. And I'm not leaving my girls. They need me."

"But it would only be for a little while, Martha, though you can stay as long as you want. Your daughters're adults, Martha. They're out in the world. They can look after themselves."

"They come and talk to me. They tell me things about themselves they wouldn't tell other people. I know how they feel because I never had anyone to talk to when I was their age."

"You had me until . . ."

"Until what?" Her fear was evident, though Arthur knew she had nothing to be afraid of now that everything with Inspector Donaldson was settled. After all, he had gone out of his way to help Martha, and he mustn't forget that her killing Laura Dorchester had destroyed his career as an English writer and turned him into a pariah. Maybe he should remind her of the occasion.

"Do you remember the last time you saw Laura Dorchester?" he began.

"I don't know what you're talking about." She pushed him away, went to the parlour door, turned and said, "I don't want you around any more. I'm a respectable woman. I don't want no chap coming here and telling tales." He scrambled to his feet and walked towards her. "Don't come near me!" she shouted.

"But Martha . . ."

"I'm a decent woman. I made sure my children were brought up decent."

He realized he had made a disastrous mistake in raising the spectre of Laura Dorchester and to recover his position of trust was now impossible. He looked at Martha's white defiant face and wondered what kind of story she had fabricated when her own children asked pointed questions about their mother's and aunt's childhood and adolescence and why their mother had joined the army.

"You needn't be afraid of me, Martha," he gently said.

"Maybe. But I'm not going anywhere with you."

"All right. I'll leave. Now, can we make up and be friends again?" He watched her face and decided that although middle-aged now, she was not that much different from what she had been at fourteen and fifteen: stubborn about some things, unpredictable and easy to persuade about others.

"I have to think of my girls."

"Of course, of course," he agreed. "It's right you should."

Martha called a cab for Arthur while he went upstairs and dressed. When he came down and they waited together at the door, she said, "I like you, Arthur. I always shall. But I'd rather like you at a distance. Sometimes a person has to cut things from her life and start over. That's what you did. So you have no right to dig up things I've tried to forget. You can walk away. But I can't. It's wrong of you to come here and upset my apple cart. I thought we could chat and have a nice time together, but that's not good enough for you. You want me to give into you. But I can't do that, because I have my girls to think of. But I do like you. I always told Maria and Mary Margaret you were a real gentleman. The only one I've ever known. You understand?"

"Yes, I think I understand, Martha," he said.

"You could write now and then."

"I'll do that. There's the cab." She kissed him, then stood at the open door waved as he settled into the taxi.

"Take care," he called. She watched until the taxi turned the corner, then went back into the parlour where she sat on the couch and had, as she later described it to her daughters, "a real good cry."

CHAPTER
29

HIS FEARS HAD BEEN GROUNDLESS: HAVEN'S GATES WERE NOT marred by any unsightly *For Sale* signs. Well, thank God (in whom Arthur had never and would never believe) for small mercies. But of course, now that he was back and able to think straight without flying into a panic, he realized that Joey could never have put Haven on the market because he had willed his two-thirds ownership to Miracle on condition she spent at least one summer month of each year there, and if she didn't fulfil the obligation, then Haven would become a refugee for terminally ill people. It was also understood that while trees might be added, none could be removed, and further, all plant life would be allowed to propagate, live and die a natural death. The alternate bequest was made not from compassion for dying people, but as a means of preventing land developers from ripping Haven apart with bulldozers and turning the beautiful little cove into a polluted marina. He had made the will without consulting Joey, and it lay in a conspicuous place on his desk. He paid off the taxi at the gates and walked slowly down the drive, stopping to enjoy the scent of sagebrush, followed by the aroma of the Ponderosa pines, the elusive fragrance of cherry and apple tree blossoms and the sweet, insect-enticing smell of the newly-leafed birches trees he and Joey had planted, which were now mature soaring cones. He visited every room in the house, then went out onto the patio and from there onto the beach. The still beauty surrounding him brought tears to his eyes and because he was alone, tired and still weak, he did not hide them as they slid over his cheeks into his beard. He walked from the beach out onto one of the promontories and watched the sun drop behind the hills on the far side of the lake. He was exhausted from the effects of his London trauma, the air flight and Joey's refusal to return to Haven and asked himself how a man who (in a way) had made more than average contribution to the world's culture could end up being so alone. He looked at the lake and the grey-brown hills and, in a moment of frightening perception, understood that while his love for Haven remained, it was not a necessity now. He was no longer a fugitive and perhaps he only continued to flee because being persecuted provided him with the necessary stimulus to write his novels. He was like an intruder, a spy, who, watching others, looks continually over his own shoulder to see who is watching him. He found the idea so intriguing that he forgot Joey and Martha and the London experience and went back to the house where he spent several hours typing the outline of a story in which an extended circle of people keep watch on each other until each member of the circle becomes so dependent upon what is transmitted from unit to unit that the members of the circle cannot survive if one of them ceases to function. The fascinating part of the story was that the member cells within the circle would eventually receive and unknowingly transmit damning information about themselves. He extended the idea until it embraced a world in which such a vast chain of watchers existed throughout countries and continents that when breaks in the chain occurred, ruinous depressions and calamitous wars resulted. Indeed, he thought he might carry the idea even further and suggest that wars and famines were indirect forms of self-destruction; but he became weary of playing with the notion and finally discarded the extensions, keeping only the original idea. Those who read the story could, if they wished, take up the concept and apply it to the full range of human activity. His job was to write books that would sell and provide him enough money to maintain himself and Haven. After years of depending on Joey to do everything around the house and to provide him with company and sexual pleasure, he was now on his own again.

Before going to bed, he telephoned Palm Springs to tell Joey he was back in Haven. "So?" Joey said.

"We built Haven together," he pleaded. "You, Phyllis and I planned and created it."

"No," Joey said in his right ear. "You did that. Phyllis and I went along with it."

"But you and I lived here for over twenty years. We were happy, Joey."

"You were. I just waited for one o'clock to arrive, when you finished work."

"But Joey, I'd have worked no matter where we lived. Isn't that true? I didn't complain when you were preoccupied with your movie, or pregnant with Miracle. Joey, I miss you so much."

"Then why didn't you ever think about *me* once in a while?"

"I've never stopped thinking about you, Joey."

"You expect me to believe that? You've thought about yourself, and what you want. You want me in your bunker to make meals, clean the place and do what you call 'love-making' at night."

"Oh Christ, Joey. Can you really think that of me? Being with you, lying in

bed with you, being able to touch you was as sacred to me as . . . well, as it is
for a priest when he touches his chalice. That's how I've always felt about you."

"If I mean so much to you, why haven't you come down here? Well?"

How could he answer, except to say that in some inexplicable way he believed that in creating Haven he and Joey had built a temple in which they had
consummated and renewed love; and although, in one conversation, he got
Joey to admit she enjoyed having sex with him, still she conditioned her response by saying it was not the big deal he imagined it to be. She told him it
was all in his head and now that she had Miracle, she saw no reason why she
should continue to live in his stupid bunker. She was going to raise Miracle in
an environment that would offer her every opportunity to get ahead in whatever profession she elected to enter, though Joey already had a pretty clear
idea it would be the movie industry. So, if he wanted to share her bed and
participate in raising Miracle, he could pack his bags and join her in southern
California.

Their telephone conversations followed this pattern, and each evening (long
distance calls were cheaper at night) after Arthur hung up, he would remember something he had intended to say, make a note of it and mention it first
thing when he telephoned the following evening. Thus, during several weeks
of telephoned conversations, almost everything which had occurred in their
years together was resurrected and chewed over, each participant presenting a
different version and interpretation of the incident. For Arthur, listening to
Joey's negative reaction to what he believed to have been high points in their
relationship was excruciatingly painful. In one of their last conversations, Arthur
more or less summarized what Joey apparently thought of him as a man and
husband: He was self-centred and selfish, but no worse than most men; he was
mean and, though he didn't object to spending other people's money, getting a
nickel out of him was worse than extracting a drop of water from a dry rag; he
was mean-spirited, too, and suspicious of other people, which explained why
he had turned himself into a gopher. Joey added her two bits by saying, "as for
sex, well, since you're the only man I've ever had—and likely ever to have—
I'm not an especially good judge, but you're probably no better or worse than
the average guy."

"Is that what you really feel about me, Joey?" he asked.

"That's about it," Joey agreed. "But you helped me make my movie and
finally came through with Miracle, so I'm prepared to pick up where we left
off provided you get out of that bunker."

Arthur said he would consider Joey's proposal, hung up, then remembered
something he had intended to say and telephoned her again to suggest she

would spend the spring-summer-fall months with him in Haven and winters in California. "Forget it," Joey said, and hung up.

At that point, Arthur received a bill from the telephone company. He stared at it, gasped and immediately decided he would change tactics. From now on, he would bombard Joey with a stream on letters filled with words of love and descriptions of the beauties of Haven. However, before a love letter could be read by the person to whom it is mailed, it must first bear a stamp and be dropped into a mail box. When Joey lived with him, she had handled all their mail, which really wasn't much since everything to do with Arthur's novels passed through *Ackroyd and Arnold,* and all Joey did when she wished to communicate with anyone was pick up the phone. Arthur taxied into town where he bought suitable envelopes and stamps for the letters. He then wrote his first letter, called the cab, rode in it to the nearest mailbox, then back home again and, walking down the drive to the front door, calculated the amount of money his daily letters to Joey were going to cost him. Twenty dollars to the mailbox and back, a hundred and forty dollars a week, plus stamps and the cost of envelopes. It was ruinous. For a while, he wondered if getting Joey back justified such an expenditure of money and time. Hours of lying awake at night and remembering the raptures he had experienced with her squashed that notion. He solved the problem by purchasing a bike. The initial outlay of several hundred dollars was painful, but when he tallied up the cost of the daily letters and his weekly cab fare into town to buy groceries and set it against the cost of a bike, a hitch and a trailer in which to carry things he purchased, he found that during the course of a year he would actually save money.

Arthur soon became a fixture on the highway and on town streets where he resolutely ignored red lights at intersections and thoroughly scared elderly pedestrians by careening along sidewalks, until one day he was halted by a starch-faced RCMP officer who lectured him about riding on sidewalks, through red lights at intersections and on the wrong side of the street. His bike, the officer lectured, was a vehicle, not a toy, and therefore must conform to highway rules. He could, the officer threatened, face a stiff fine and have his vehicle confiscated if he didn't start obeying rules of the road. Arthur, who was re-experiencing the thrills of careening down and furiously pedalling up hills, immediately sobered up when faced by the officer in his stiff-peaked hat who was unimpressed by Arthur's name, or the name of his residence. After being told his carelessness might result in a serious automobile or pedestrian accident, Arthur meekly apologized for any inconveniences he may have caused and promised to obey all traffic regulations in the future. But what really scared him was the officer saying he would be "keeping an eye" on him. That aroused old panics, and even though good sense told him it meant nothing more than having the RCMP glance at him while patrolling in their cars, still his first impulse was to turn and run. Of course, the sickening fear disappeared when the officer drove away, but the pleasure he had been experiencing riding the bike to and from town was gone, and cycling to town to mail his letters to Joey became an arduous duty, rather than a pleasure, which resulted in a reduction of the number of letters from one a day to three a week, then finally to one a week.

Nothing came of his outpouring of love and a desire to have Joey with him again. In any case, though he was not to know this, after the first batch, Joey didn't bother to open and read the letters, but simply ripped them in half and dropped the fragments into the litter bag. By that time, any affection she may have felt for Arthur had soured into contempt for the man who persisted in trespassing where he was not wanted. It wasn't that Joey had taken up with men, though they did appear in her life and engagingly offer to alleviate any distress she might be experiencing as a result of separating from the author of her suffering. But Joey ignored them, even those whose virility was apparent in the skimpy swim trunks they wore around her pool. She had made her movie, which was still being screened in art movie houses, and she had Miracle. To produce her movie, cameras, actors and sets had been required and, of course, a man had been needed to make her baby. But now she had fulfilled her two ambitions: she had demonstrated she could direct an original movie under adverse conditions, and after many years of striving, and with the extraterrestrial aid of her best friend Phyllis, had achieved her second goal: to bear a child. One after another male appeared to exhibit his physical, emotional and intellectual (often limited) abilities, and one after another departed after having had more than enough of being asked to interpret Miracle's latest gurgles and attempts to get beyond *Ma-ma, Da-da* and *Ca-ca* while admiring the way she toddled around on the turquoise-coloured pool-side tiles seemingly attempting suicide by tumbling into the deep end of the pool. Their talents were wasted on Joey. She smiled, ignored their departure and immediately forgot them as she had more or less forgotten Arthur now that his letters were reduced to one every other month, and even those she did no more than briefly scan before tearing them in two. It was the cold ripping of Arthur's letters that demonstrated the finality of Joey's resolution to free herself of him, so that within a couple of years, by the time Miracle was walking and talking and ordering Joey to get this or do that, Joey had separated Arthur from the process of conceiving Miracle and had come to regard the child as being engendered solely by herself and Phyllis. But the true miracle of Miracle was not parthenogenesis: it was that she was pretty, intelligent and, despite Joey's perpetual fussing and hovering, a sweet-tempered, happy child. In fact, it was her bubbly, contagious laughter that had landed her first movie role, at age six, and she thereafter rapidly attained stardom as *The Laughing Girl*. (Joey had seen to it that Miracle had singing, dancing and elocution lessons beginning at age three.) But the strangest effect of Miracle's screen presence was that, although a variety of physiologists and psychologists conducted tests on her, no one could explain why, when she laughed, so many people felt inclined to laugh or smile too. The studio, thinking that movie-goers would find the name *Gambarasi* too Mafia-like and the name *Scheiler* too hard on the tongue, finally decided after a series of meetings to bless Miracle with the surname *Shields,* arguing that the combination of *Miracle* and *Shields* would allow moviegoers to feel that looking at the child star and listening to her laugh would not only bring them happiness, but would suggest (at a sub-conscious level) that the little girl was protecting them from evil: a double return on their investment. And oddly enough, it was true that some people, especially those who combined movie and church-going, were always reminded of her whenever they sang "our shield and defender, / the ancient of days, / pavilioned in splendour and girded with praise;" a few even laid greater emphasis on the world "shield" than upon any other word in the oft sung hymn.

"Is Miracle Shields our Miracle?" Arthur had asked in a rare letter to Joey after seeing the name blazoned in extra large print on a poster outside the local movie house where the rushes of Joey's movie had once been screened and the entire film shown to a small select audience made up principally of college students and instructors. When Joey didn't respond to the question, Arthur rode to town one Saturday afternoon, parked his bike across the street from the cinema, bought a ticket and spent the next two hours sitting among several hundred children who shrieked and screamed with laughter every time a laughing girl appeared on the screen. To him, the amazing thing was that Joey had managed, by some mysterious means, to combine the best of her own and his mother's features into their daughter's face. He alone of the entire audience did not laugh. He was too fascinated by the way the little girl, *his daughter,* genuinely laughed at the actors who played clowns in a movie about a circus in which Miracle's parents were high-wire and trapeze performers. He shivered and his heart thumped when the child climbed a rope ladder to the platform, then, holding a tiny, lace-edged umbrella, walked out onto the wire to stand halfway across it and laugh at the upturned, wide-eyed faces sixty feet below her. Of course, he knew the feat was a product of trick photography, a mirage, to terrify and thrill the audience and enhance the glory of Miracle

Shields; but knowing it was all illusion didn't prevent his throat from tightening, his mouth from drying, nor deter what felt like ice cubes roving his spine when Miracle, on reaching the opposite platform and gaily acknowledging the audience's applause, climbed up and rode on her movie-father's shoulders across the wire. But even more frightening was watching her being swung at arms length by her trapeze-dangling movie-father and hurled across space to be caught at trapeze-length by her swinging uncle. Arthur along with the hundreds of children staggered from the cinema, dazed by the talents, courage and daring of Miracle Shields. He crossed the street to where his bike and trailer ought to have been latched to the *No Parking* sign and stared blankly at the severed chain and lock lying on the pavement. The bike and trailer were gone. Why, he demanded from the police constable on duty at the desk in the RCMP building, would anybody steal a cheap bike and trailer? The officer shrugged and said some people would steal anything if they thought they could turn a buck on it, but he quickly lost interest in locating the bicycle when Arthur couldn't tell him the brand name of the bike or supply him with a serial number. He dismissed Arthur with a "it may turn up" and a promise to get in touch by telephone should a bike or trailer be found. Arthur, who regretted his indignant impulse to report his loss to the police, walked to the bike shop where after some discussion and bargaining, he purchased a motor scooter.

"Look, Mr. Scheiler," the bike shop owner had said. "You don't have to work your ass off sweating up hills."

"But I rather enjoy tearing down a hill to see how far I can coast up the other side," Arthur had explained.

"You and the rest of us too," the owner said. "But imagining if you go faster downhill, you can coast further uphill is plain old baloney, Mr. Scheiler. Hell, I'll tell you how it works. The heaviest guy on the most expensive bike goes fastest downhill and the lightest guy on the most expensive bike coasts furthest uphill. Hell, me and my buddies had regular contests on the big hill outside town, the one on the highway out to your place. We had starters, who watched us to make sure none of us pedalled on the downhill. But the winner was always a skinny little guy on a real good bike. Talk about being frustrated! He'd be at the tail-end of the pack going down and then sort of float by us when we'd stopped. Why? Because the guy had an Italian bike, same make as this scooter. Me, I think the Italians is out to lunch when it comes to making autos, same as the French, but they sure know how to make bikes and scooters. Look at this one, a hundred miles to the gallon."

"How much?" Arthur had asked, then, after hearing the price, said he would walk home and wait for the RCMP to locate his bike.

"You got to be joking," the owner said. "Them guys couldn't find nothing, even if it was delivered to their front doorstep. They ain't got no interest in bikes. They're constitutionally constructed to ignore them."

"You mean genetically."

"Same thing. Anyway, let's cut a deal, eh? You get a real good bargain and I make a couple of bucks. Hell, Mr. Scheiler, that's what makes the world go 'round, ain't it?"

And so Arthur switched from pedalling to being propelled along the highway and around town by a popping little motor scooter. Interestingly, the police finally did call to say they believed they had found his bicycle, although when Arthur saw it, he wasn't able to identify it because the bike looked as if it had been run over by an army tank. "In a ditch, on a logging road," the officer told Arthur when he asked where the mashed frame and wheels had been found. "Could be logging trucks ran over it. Those joes are real heavy and the drivers won't stop because of some little ole bike." Arthur agreed there was no good reason why a great truck hauling tons and tons of lumber would, or should, stop to avoid crushing a cheap bike like his. He inquired about the trailer. "It'll show up eventually," the officer said.

"Like a guy who falls into the crevasse of some glacier and is found a hundred years later?" Arthur asked.

"Something like that," the officer agreed. But as a matter of fact, Arthur was sure he had already seen the trailer—repainted and covered with a canvas hood—being towed up a shallow hill by a young woman. Inside it sat two small children and two bags of groceries.

"I'll switch with you," she called when Arthur came abreast with her.

Arthur, who had often towed his laden trailer up the hill, shouted back, "Children included?", then smiled when she firmly shouted: "No way! I worked hard getting them. I'm not exchanging them for a little old scooter." As he crested the hill he looked back in his mirror and saw her turn off the highway into one of the developments (unsightly, Arthur thought) which were replacing orchards on the outskirts of the town.

One afternoon, on his way home from town, he saw her standing at the roadside, examining the rear wheel of her bicycle. He went past, halted and walked back. "Something wrong?" he asked.

"Damn chain's jammed in the gears." She was quite tall, thin, and flushed with rage at a bike that refused to co-operate with her.

"I don't know much about fixing bikes." He looked at the rear wheel and the chain which appeared to jammed between the multiple gears. "You have any tools?" he asked.

"Why the hell would I have tools?" she raged. "For Christ's sake, say something constructive. Sit down!" she barked at one of the children, a boy.

"I have to go, Mom," he whimpered.

"Oh, Jesus!" she exclaimed.

"So do I," the girl said.

"I think I've got some tools somewhere in my saddle pouches," Arthur said. He turned away before she could reply, now wishing he had bowled past her with nothing more than a wave hello. There was indeed a tool kit in one satchel and he returned with it as she marshalled the two children back to the trailer.

"Twins," she said. "If one does something, the other has to do it too." He opened the tool kit and vaguely examined the contents, took out a screwdriver, knelt and levered the chain out. "For Christ's sake, now I feel like a total numbskull," she said.

"Just luck." He put the chain onto a sprocket. "Maybe you should see if it stays on." She swung a leg over the seat and rode a little way along the highway, changing the gears as she went. She drew into the roadside just ahead of his scooter.

"It seems fine, Mr. — ?"

"Scheiler," he said, "Matt Scheiler."

"Oh, you're the guy that lives out . . ." She waved a hand.

"Yes, I do live," he said.

"That's not what I meant. I meant, I've cycled past the place. Stupid of me. Anyway, thanks for the help. Thank Mr. Scheiler, kids. He saved you from having to carry your trailer home."

"Thank you," they piped.

"They're pretty harmless," she said.

"You lived here long?" he asked, as he rolled up and tied the lace around the tool kit.

"Let's see . . . three years. We bought a house in the development just before I had the kids. You been here long?"

"Sometimes I think too long," he said.

"I've tried, but've never been able to see your house," she said.

"It's buried," he said, "under birch trees and sagebrush."

"Oh, neat!" she cried. "When I was a kid I wanted to live in a cave. You mean completely buried?"

"No. The front, facing the cove, is windows and glass doors."

"Sounds wonderful," she said. "Well, I better get going. The dinkies have a dentist appointment. Anyway, thanks again."

"Stop by sometime when you're out my way," he called as she rode away. She gestured an acknowledgement and he went back to his scooter and rode away.

A week or two later, Arthur sat on the patio reading through the manuscript of his latest novel, which, had it been closely examined, would be found
to be little more than a compilation of bits and pieces of his previous novels;
but he wrote from habit, and Betty Arnold passed on his manuscripts to the
publisher, where they were edited and typeset, then printed and distributed to
bookstores and reviewers who commented on Scheiler's unfailing ability to
deliver what his readers had come to expect from him. As before, Arthur never
read any reviews of his books, even though Betty always photocopied and
forwarded them "for his files." (She didn't know he had no files.) He had
nothing else to do, except write, tidy his bed, prepare basic meals, do an occasional laundry and mow the small lawn once a week in the growing season.
That was his unvarying routine, and he was surprised, therefore, one day to
hear voices: "Well, here we are, twins. Let's find out if anybody's home." He
got up and walked along the patio to the corner of the house where he saw the
young woman whose bicycle he had fixed on the roadside. She stood with the
bike, the trailer and the twins. "Hi," she said. "I just came through the gates
and around the orchard. I hope it's okay." She wheeled the bike and trailer
around the end of the patio and parked it on the lawn. "But this is heavenly!
Absolutely heavenly! Isn't it, twins? Oh, our names! I forgot our names! The
twins are Thomas and Thomasina. I call them Tom and Tommie. And I'm Liz.
Liz Osborne." He didn't doubt she meant what she said about the beauty of the
cove, any more than he questioned the pleasure expressed by the children who
raced down to the beach when he invited them to swim. She ran after them to
remove their sandals and, when they pleaded, their shorts and tee shirts. After
fetching his straw hat, Arthur stood beside the young woman and watched the
boy and girl tumbling and rolling in the water. She suddenly frowned and
turned to him. "Is your wife home?" she asked; and Arthur found himself
explaining why Joey and Miracle lived in California and he at Haven.

"You mean Miracle Shields is your daughter?" she cried. "For God's sake,
Miracle Shields! That's too amazing! And to think I'm here because one day I
had trouble with my bloody bike. It doesn't make sense, does it?"

"Sometimes I review what's happened in my life and have to admit when I
started out, I never thought I'd end up here."

"So where did you start?"

He paused, preventing himself from getting caught in the trap he had so
negligently set. "Back east," he said. "A godforsaken place in New England."

"It couldn't be worse than the place in Newfoundland where I was born,"
she said.

"Honestly?"

"Truly."

That, he thought, would explain the edge of brogue in her voice and the steely-eyed, thin-lipped, square-shouldered suggestion of defiance. "Are you ever tempted to go back?"

"Go back! I swore on the family Bible that once I got away I'd never go back."

"I agree. It's unwise, even dangerous, to return to what you have once rejected."

"You bet. I tell my family if they want to see me and the kids, they can visit me here. Come on out, twins, we have to go." Her order seemed abrupt, as though speaking of her distant homeland and memories of the reasons she had left it obliterated her ability to experience present joys. He volunteered to get a towel for her to dry the children, but she refused the offer, and after brushing excess water from the children's heads, dragged shirts and shorts over their damp little bodies and put them into the trailer. Arthur asked how long she had owned the trailer. "Not long. A few weeks. It was advertised in the Buy and Sell. It's changed my life," she said. "I dump the twins in, ride to town, shop and ride back. They get the outing and I get the exercise. Okay, twins, say 'thank you' to Mr. Scheiler for letting you swim on his beach."

They obediently responded, and Arthur murmured they were welcome to come again. As Liz leaned to buckle in the twins, a crucifix slipped from her tee shirt, which made Arthur think she might be from a Catholic family and perhaps would hesitate to bring her little innocents to an isolated house occupied by an aging man, even though he felt certain the trailer in which she hauled her children was his, which she or her husband may have stolen. But then he thought of himself, straw-hatted, standing beside her, watching the deliriously happy children play in the water, and anguish flooded him as he realized what he had lost by not being able to stand with Joey and watch their miracle child jump and flop in the clear, warm water, for while he had stood on the beach, feeling the hot afternoon sun reach beneath his shirt, watching the children's antics, a simple pleasure had displaced his preoccupation with the current novel, and he had felt a surge of contentment as he watched the children's little bodies sinuously rise and fall in the water and heard their high-pitched voices command their mother to admire their proficiency.

He was pleased, therefore, when, one afternoon in the following week, as he sat on the patio he heard her voice: "Here we are again. Anybody home? Are we trespassing where we aren't allowed?"

After he had welcomed her and said he was pleased to see them again, she prodded the children into offering Arthur a paper plate of cookies and a plastic container of what looked like lemonade. "I thought you might like some homemade cookies," she said. "When I was a kid, I adored cookies. I ate tons of them, but still everybody called me Skinny Lizzy."

"Why feel bad about being slender?" he asked.

"I dunno," she said. "I suppose because I've always felt I was supposed to show a return on the food my parents gave me."

"People spend far too much time apologizing for what they are," Arthur grumbled.

"It comes with the turf you're born on," she said. "Do you mind us visiting? I mean, we can pack up and leave if you object."

"I'm glad you came." He had noticed the children had on swimsuits and that she had brought towels. "I'll put the container in the fridge," he said. When he returned, he saw that she was in the water swinging the children around and dipping them into the water. She wore a black bathing suit which drew attention to her thin shoulders and arms. He sat and watched as she dived underwater and listened to the children's shrieks of pleasure combined with fear when she caught their ankles and they collapsed into the water. He wished he hadn't missed playing with Miracle when she still adored him as her father, yet could believe he was a ravenous underwater monster when he caught her. So little was needed to delight a small child, although of course Miracle would be too old for that sort of thing now.

When Liz ushered the twins from the water, she took them to the trailer where she carefully wrapped them in towels, as though to ensure their immature genitals couldn't be seen by him. After they were dressed, she went around the corner of the house to take off her swimsuit and put on her shorts and shirt. She hung the suits on the trailer to dry, then brought the children to the table where he sat and said, "Snack time!"

Arthur brought out the container of lemonade, three glasses and the bag of cookies, and the children perched on chairs, heads just above the table top, solemnly chewing and staring at him. "Tom and Tommie insisted I bring you two cookies," Liz said, so Arthur ate both, appreciatively smacking his lips while intently being watched by four bright blue eyes. "They have no manners," she said, "though I've tried. I was taught never to watch people eat."

"They want to be sure I appreciate your cooking. Don't you?" he said to the twins. They nodded in unison, then the boy left his chair to climb onto his mother's lap and suck a thumb. Liz said they were getting sleepy, and they must leave since it was their nap time. As though to underscore the point, the girl went around the table, got onto Arthur's lap and slipped a thumb into her mouth.

"They've made themselves right at home." She sounded embarrassed. "I'll take her."

"Oh no," he said. "She doesn't weigh much." He could feel the child's heart pumping away on his chest. "It's a funny thing," he added, "but sometimes children settle things for their parents." He nibbled his lips a moment, then said the children could nap in his guest room if she thought they would settle down there.

"They can sleep anywhere," she said, so Arthur lead her to the room which had not been used since Phyllis's last visit, Liz carrying Tom, Arthur carrying Tommie.

This set the pattern, and Liz began coming to Haven every other afternoon. "We don't want to make nuisances of ourselves, do we, twins?" she confessed to Arthur, who assured her that he enjoyed watching the children play in the cove. "But you can never tell when something might become too much of a good thing," she had replied. Still, the visits continued, and each one meant bringing cookies and juice for the children's snack. They even came on cloudy days. "The children love it here, you know," she told Arthur. "They think it's like being on holiday." Weeks passed before she spoke about her husband. The topic arose when Liz offered to vacuum the house for Arthur.

"Vacuum?" he echoed. "Why would you do that?"

"There're dust balls everywhere."

"It's my dust, not yours. You don't have to worry about it."

"It's not healthy," she said. "I'll come over one Saturday afternoon. I can leave the kids with my husband." Arthur was relieved to learn she had a husband and inquired about his work. "He works for the government. Forestry. Don't ask me what he does, I'm not sure, but there's talk of moving him up north someplace. It's a step up, he says, but I'm not too keen on moving. You know, having to sell one house and find another."

"Don't you have friends in the development?" he asked.

"Not really. The people're okay," she said, "but I don't fit in. Maybe it's because I'm a Newfie. I can't get interested in what they do. It strikes me as being petty. Do you get impatient with people?"

"Principally with myself. I don't see many people."

"Do you miss your wife?"

"At first. Now I'm to used to being alone, though I realize how much I've missed when I see your twins playing in the water."

"The twins sure like it here." She looked away as she spoke.

Several weeks went by before she spoke of her husband again, then it was to say his transfer had come through. "In October," she added.

"Well . . . summer'll be over by then," he said.

"He drinks . . ." She stopped, perhaps expecting him to cluck disapproval or say "too bad." "I'm not going with him," she eventually said, which made Arthur uneasy: He wondered if she had hatched a plan to encroach into his life. "I know what you're thinking," she said, "but me leaving him's got nothing to do with you. It's the drink. I thought I'd go on welfare, but then after the twins began napping here, I couldn't stop thinking about being here. I mean, you need somebody to clean the house."

"I don't notice the dust."

"Well, you should. It's a mess. But I didn't plan it."

"It wouldn't work out," he said.

"I'm not much to look at, but I'd clean the house and cook."

"Please . . ."

"Well, I thought I'd give it a try. I mean, nothing risked, nothing gained. Right?"

"Is it that bad? I mean, with your husband?"

"He's not violent. But I don't want the twins . . ." Her voice tailed off, like the after-sound of a gust of wind through trees. Arthur, after instinctively recoiling from her dilemma, now found he didn't know what to say. "You've been very kind," she said. "I've no right . . ."

"No, no. It's just unexpected. But look here, there's something I have to clear up with you."

"About my husband?"

"No. Your trailer."

"Trailer? My *trailer?*"

"It looks very much like my trailer. It was stolen."

"Stolen? You think I stole . . . ?"

"No, no. I just want to be sure you bought it. That's all."

"Of course I bought it. Twenty dollars. But if you say it's yours, you can have it. Oh, for Christ's sake." She covered her face with both hands. "I don't know what I've come to. I'll get the twins and go."

"No. Please, Liz." She was on her way into the house when he managed to get between her and the open glass door. "Come and sit. It's not necessary to leave," he said. "I only wanted to be sure."

"The only thing I ever stole in my life was a lifesaver off my big sister," she said.

"I know. I know." He caught her hand. "Come and sit."

"I'm proud of my honesty."

"Justifiably, I'm sure."

"Not that it's ever brought me one goddamn thing."

"But it's a rare virtue. Now, come and sit." She allowed him to usher her back to the table.

"I began thinking of what could happen to the twins and me. I mean, guys who drink lose control. I don't know why he drinks. I didn't even find out until after we were married. I've thought that maybe it's because I'm not attractive. But I've always done my best. You know what I mean . . . ?"

"I can guess," he said.

"And I've given him two beautiful children."

"Yes, they're lovely," he said.

"I don't know what's wrong with him. I don't know where most of what he earns goes. But it was stupid of me to imagine it could happen. I'll be better off on welfare. But I thought the kids growing up here . . . You know . . ."

"Listen to me, Liz. I've spent years running away from my past. While I was running, I met Joey, fell in love and got her to marry me; then I saw this place and bought it off a man who couldn't bear to live here any longer because it reminded him of his wife who would get up every morning to swim in the cove. For me, this place was, and still is, Haven; but for my wife, it was, and still is, just twenty acres of land on a B.C. lake—any land, any lake, any place. Let me ask you something . . . I've told you what this place means to me. Now you tell me if it means anything to you."

"I . . ." Her thin throat contracted. "I think it's the next best place to paradise," she said.

For a while, Arthur remained silent and still, then said, "We can probably work something out . . . over time."

"But before that, I can vacuum the house?"

"In the afternoons."

"Not ever in the morning?"

"Never in the mornings."

She looked at him, leaned over to kiss his forehead, then they lapsed into in silence, contemplating the future and waiting for the twins to wake from their nap.

CHAPTER
30

WHEN ARTHUR WAS CROTCHETY, WHICH OCCURRED WITH greater frequency as the years passed, he would often glare at Liz and say something like: "I didn't understand what I was getting into when I invited you to live at Haven." From the other side the bed (where Joey had slept) Liz would retaliate with something like this: "Listen Mister, I've cleaned, cooked, mowed the lawn, done laundry, got into this goddamn bed and given you free you-know-what's for umpteen years. That's why you got me here. So don't start complaining at this late date. You've received more than you've spent on me and the kids. And I'm the bigger fool because I've never asked you for a penny."

It was a ritual they engaged in whenever the need to spend money came up. Both hated laying out more money than was absolutely necessary, but both understood that from time to time an outlay was required and imminent (usually clothes for the twins) and so they took to scarifying each other emotionally, hoping to lessen the impending greater pain by ritual infliction of a lesser one, though the sources of their reluctance to spend money were not the same. Arthur was miserly by nature, while Liz, who had been raised in a home where dollars were as rare as jewels, experienced real, nauseating terror when she thought of her twins and herself without money, a home and enough food to eat. She hoarded coins, while he hid statements from banks in the American midwest of which she had never heard. He refused to spend money on clothes for himself and Liz complained he went around looking like a bum. Another way she extracted money was by entering into convoluted agreements whereby at least theoretically, she bought the cherry and apple crops from him, then sold them to whomever offered the best price. She then used the difference between the buy and sell prices to spend on the children and herself. Arthur appeared incapable of grasping that the way children appear before classmates was of far greater importance than the reason why they were attending school and that not wearing brand-new outfits at the commencement of school in September could make or break an entire year; and while Arthur enjoyed inspecting the children in their new outfits and remarking they were getting so big he could hardly recognize them, he still complained about the money spent. "What is this?" he would rhetorically ask. "Eh, who do you think I am? A millionaire?" The unintentional effect of Arthur's rants about money to clothe the natural growth of the twins resulted in their being ashamed of physical gains made during successive years. Tom stooped, and Tommie tried to hide her maturing hips and breasts. Of the two, she suffered most, because she had attached herself to Arthur, much as a lone gosling will attach itself to a species which, if circumstances were normal, would have been alien to it. The recriminations were often quite nasty and bitter.

"Why am I fool enough to spend thousands of dollars on another guy's kids? I must be nuts."

"Don't exaggerate. It's hundreds. Besides, you offered to raise them," Liz would counter. "And don't think I don't know you'd like to do more than just look at Tommie. That is, if you could be sure you would get it up! Men are all the same. They look at a girl and imagine what it would be like to get her into bed." Liz had taken Arthur's measure and concluded he was one of those essentially timid men who, until approached by a woman, committed adultery and fornication in the mind, although the appraisal was not entirely accurate since he had readily ventured forth whenever conquest seemed assured.

"Don't ever say that again! I've never thought of Tommie like that."

"You're always trying to get a look at things you shouldn't."

"Liar!" That usually ended the fight, and after a while Liz would reach across the bed to find and squeeze Arthur's hand.

"I didn't mean it," she would say, or words to that effect. "I know you love Tommie. You love Tom as well, but you feel more strongly about Tommie."

"That's because I associate her with Miracle and a couple of girls I once knew." He sighed. "I wish to God I could stop mixing past and present, though the older I get, the worse the confusion. Maybe my inclination to fuse them," he gloomily continued, "means I'm going to die."

"Don't talk such nonsense!" Anything to do with death frightened Liz because, like some latter-day Eve, she associated death with being driven out of Eden, and of course for her, Eden and Haven were one and the same. She had no idea now much money Arthur had, nor knew anything about the ownership or legal disposition of Haven should he die. Sometimes, when a bitter exchange got out of hand, Arthur would tell her that if Joey ever returned, she and the children would have to go. "How can you say that, Matt! The twins, especially Tommie, think of you as their father!"

"So what! You couldn't stop your husband from seeing the kids, even taking them away."

"Only if they were bottles of rye. That's all he cares about. And what about you? I hear tales of your movie star daughter, but you could be lying for all I know. One day, you tell one story about yourself, the next it's some other story. You manufacture your life as you go along. There's no photos of you and your family. Nothing."

"My work proves I exist."

Once, without warning, during the early years Liz and the twins lived with him, Arthur had collapsed unconscious at the edge of the beach as he was watching the children while Liz vacuumed the house. In the confusion that followed, it was never made clear that the twins probably saved his life, but in fact they had: His head had been submerged in water and the children pulled and rolled him out before they ran screaming to Liz for help. That night, Tommie had crept to his bedside when she heard him huskily cough to clear his throat, and for the remainder of his life Arthur carried in his memory the image of her anxious eyes and parted lips hovering above him. He adored her as he would have adored Miracle had he been given the opportunity, though it didn't prevent him from thinking about her youthful body and imagining what it would be like to make love if only he had the energy for it. Yet he realized that his lustful thoughts about Tommie didn't signify anything in particular, because he always imagined making love with every woman and school girl he saw. He had always been a Don Giovanni of the mind, indulging in speculative lust, but in action cautious to an extreme, such that, except for Joey, if a woman wanted him to make love, she had no choice but to invade his bed. Liz had never received much in the way of sexual pleasure from her husband, but she felt obliged to offer Arthur something in return for his provision of a home for her and the children. Besides, his bed was larger than the one she had originally occupied in the guest room. Of course, adjustments had been necessary because Arthur had more or less talked himself into a state of celibacy, and also because Liz found the entire business of sexual congress embarrassing. Nonetheless, after some fumbling about, they agreed on a routine of once a week or twice every ten days, whichever was more convenient. They had reached the point now where Liz could ask if Arthur was off-colour when he didn't abide by the terms of their informal contract. On every household matter, including sex, Liz laid out routines for each day of the week and went to bed dissatisfied if her round of tasks was not completed. "You're sure?" she asked when he said he was tired and might have more energy in the morning, though that didn't always work out either, for once the twins had discovered their mother was sleeping with Arthur, they took to cuddling in bed with them in the morning. Arthur became accustomed to having Tommie wriggle into the bed and curl up against him, knees butting into his stomach, her blonde hair tickling his chin and her warm breath brushing his neck. He might open his eyes and be disconcerted by the way she impersonally eyed his night-etched face. He thought she was coldly and critically examining him and was surprised when Liz told him that Tommie had told her how much she "really and truly" loved him. He himself could hardly bear to look at his visage in a mirror at any time of the day and thought he must appear grotesque and reptilian to a child, even after Liz patiently explained that physical appearance didn't determine what children felt about a person; what counted was behaviour. A child doesn't know what is beautiful or what is ugly, she explained, which meant that Tom and Tommie had apparently bestowed a face on him which reflected everything about Haven (now their home) and his acceptance of them. But whenever Liz and Arthur did find the time and energy for sex, he always diligently tried to bring her to orgasm, though she never surrendered.

"I won't," she whispered, "I won't give in to a man." When Arthur vindictively reminded her that Tommie's sexual equipment was just like hers and that one day she would have sex, Liz became enraged and demanded to know if he had touched her daughter. That outraged Arthur, though he did try to explain it was a question of logic, not of pederasty. Tommie was a female, he said, therefore it was logical to assume she was anatomically like other females. At such times, Liz felt her respect for Arthur melt away. He was so devious, she thought, and she, who prided herself on her openness and honesty, was invariably shocked by his capacity to deny on a certain day statements he had made the previous day. He was like a chameleon, except you could never predict what colour he would turn. One day, he might go on for hours about rich people and how much he hated them, and the next carry on that the poor had no one to blame but themselves, though he was always careful to conceal that his hatred of wealthy people was rooted in his loathing of the English class system.

Liz would often ask him what he was thinking about when he lay still between her thighs after sex. "Nothing," he would reply, though in fact he was preoccupied with images of childhood people and incidents: of his mother, of his off again-on again pursuit of Heather, of his rewarding but catastrophic relationship with Laura Dorchester, of Maria's slender body at work in the kitchen of the house in Hasterley. He wondered what might have happened if Maria had returned from London and brought Martha with her. An image of Martha sleeping, mouth agape, breathing rapidly as a child does, came to him. Could the three of them ever have been happy together? Would it ever have worked out? Would he have put into practice with Maria, possibly even with

Martha too, what he had learned from Sylvia about women and the ways in which men can satisfy their desires?

"You must be thinking about something," Liz said. "And I'll bet it wasn't me, was it?"

To escape an honest response, Arthur would ask a personal question, knowing that Liz's response would be to push him off and roll away to the far side of their bed. In that way, he could continue to justify being less than truthful with her by telling himself that, though she conveyed an impression of transparency, like everybody else in the world she had her secrets too. Living any life was tantamount to moving through an insect-infected forest, where, regardless of the precautions you took, you ended up accumulating the bites and stings of experience. Once, when Arthur asked Liz how often she'd had sex with her husband, she smacked his face and told him if he ever asked such a personal question again, she would leave him. But curiosity festered in him. He had to know as much about her as he had known about the other women who had played important roles in his life. Having her uncomplainingly accept his efforts in bed wasn't enough. He had to get at the source of her emotions, or lack of them, but since only circumventive routes were available, he either spoke of female characters in his novels or invented women whose experience might have some relevance to her experiences. But it didn't help. Liz listened, stared at him, shrugged and looked over his head at some indistinct object hovering above their bed, so that, through all their years together at Haven, Arthur never did find out much more about Liz than he knew at the beginning.

As he passed into his seventies, Arthur began complaining of assorted aches and pains, although when Liz suggested he consult a physician, he retorted that he was well able to take care of himself and that the shortest path to the grave was to consult a physician. But having less energy and more aches and pains didn't stop Arthur from working, and he continued to spend every morning writing. He also kept a close eye on the development of the twins, and when they reached adolescence, he nagged Liz about giving them too much freedom, especially Tommie. "It only takes five minutes for a girl to get herself knocked up on the back seat of some lout's car," he contended when Tommie started dating high-school youths. "You're worse than a father," Liz argued back. "Don't worry, Matt. I've given her a good talking to. She knows the score."

"Score! What score! There *is* no score when it comes to sex! Just a horny teenager and a sweet girl like Tommie with nothing but thin panties between her and the kid's cock."

Ernest Langford

The way Arthur talked enraged Liz, partly because she felt that his language degraded Tommie, but also because there lingered her fear that what she thought unlikely could in fact happen and that she, Liz, like thousands of other mothers, would have to sit and listen to her miserable, sobbing daughter protesting she hadn't meant to go that far. "For Christ's sake, Matt, what d'you expect me to do? Keep her locked up?" But yes, she *was* worried about the twins' future. Tom had taken to spending weekends drinking beer with friends and telling Liz to cool it when she tried to talk him out of it. "After all, Mom, it's my last year at school. Time for a bit of fun." But Liz endlessly iterated that access to alcohol and sex was too easy for them, and unless they disciplined themselves, they could squander their future in a few hours. She told the twins about their father who had begun his alcoholic career in high school, drinking with so-called pals on Saturday nights, and about her girlfriends who went on jaunts with guys in cars and ended up with brats nobody wanted. And for what? For the guys, so that they could boast they could drink a case of beer and still walk a straight line? And for the girls, so they could transform the sordidness of what had taken place in the back seat of a car into a love affair? Of course it was only natural for the twins to be defiant, but all a person needed was to look at the girls' faces to know what they really felt, and the school dropouts hanging around town told you all you needed to know about them. It was awful, simply awful, and Liz had sworn from the time she was a girl that nothing like that would ever happen to her or her children. But the threat was there, and Liz continually worked on the twins, especially Tom, because she knew Matt was keeping a close watch on Tommie. Oh sure, Matt liked Tom well enough and always listened carefully to everything he said, but the one he really cared about was Tommie. And Tommie had demonstrated her readiness to care for Matt, sitting on his lap when she was a child, crawling into his side of the bed when she awoke from a bad dream, and generally letting him know she was prepared to love and be loved. That's what all little girls were like, wasn't it, but now that Tommie was a teenager she might just succumb to a youth who pleaded that only she could ease his physical pain and suffering. It was an age-old trick which had passed unchanged through generations of men, whereby it was claimed that a woman's denial of access to her body would irrevocably damage a man. In her own adolescence, Liz had heard the same tale and had replied: "Too bad, buster!" She had seen parental rejection and community condemnation of girls who, desiring to prevent the suffering of their boyfriends, had surrendered their chastity, then were made to pay the bill. Liz had so forcibly drummed into Tommie's head the things she must never do that Tommie always came home at the stipulated hour and never allowed her dates to go beyond a clasp of her hand and a kiss on her cheek. Among high-school youths, she was known as "The Lost Cause." It must be said, however, that Tommie had yet to experience the overwhelming effect of impassioned desire. She was still satisfied to shower affection on her mother, brother and Arthur, whom she and Tom called "Mr. Matt."

Late one afternoon in June of the twin's last year at secondary school, the telephone rang and when Tommie answered it, someone asked to speak to Matt Scheiler.

"Who is it?" Arthur called from the patio.

"Don't know, Mr. Matt," Tommie said. "A woman."

"Probably Betty." He grumbled as he left the patio and picked up the phone. "Matt Scheiler here," he said. "That you, Betty?"

"No," the voice said. "It's Miracle."

"Miracle? Miracle. Miracle!" His voice rose from an astounded whisper to a shout.

"We've been shooting scenes in Washington, in the Wenatchee valley, near Spokane. I've got a few weeks before I have to be back in Los Angeles, so I thought I'd come for a visit. Do you mind?"

"Mind? Of course not! I'll be delighted to see you. Liz!" he called. "It's Miracle! She's in town! Miracle, do you have a car?"

"Yes. I rented one in Spokane. I'm in town now."

"Right. I'll tell you how to get here." He gave her directions, then said, "It'll take about half an hour. I'll walk up to the road. When you see an old skinny guy standing by some iron gates, you'll know you've reached Haven."

"I'm looking forward to seeing it."

Tom and Tommie would have accompanied Arthur, except that Liz took them aside and told them to wait at the house. As he stood at the gates, it seemed as though hours had passed and he began to wonder if she had taken the wrong road or been involved in an accident. He behaved like an impatient lover who transforms minutes of waiting to hours, hours to days. Then he saw a car rise over the far ridge, descend into the dip, reappear, roll towards him and stop. He didn't know the make. All he saw was Joey, sitting in a convertible. Only this time the car was red, not white.

"My God," he said, "Joey all over again." He didn't know how to behave, whether to shake her hand or to kiss her. Miracle solved the problem by kissing his cheek, then saying all the right things after he closed the gates and they drove down through the Ponderosas and the orchard. "Oh, how marvellous! How absolutely marvellous," she said when she finally stood on the patio, two suitcases at her feet, looking down at the cove. "And this is where Mom shot her movie. You know, it's quite famous—especially the underwater shots. Mom's told me how you and she came here and transformed everything. I've always wanted to see Haven, but I'm so busy. I've been on location just across the border, so the time seemed right. It's hard to believe that Mom would've given up living here just so I could get my theatrical training." He smiled and wondered if there was some other reason she had suddenly appeared. By this time, the others had come onto the patio, and the twins were immediately enraptured by Miracle who, having been the focal point of a camera lens from childhood on, was well-practised at drawing attention to herself and delivering facile forms of sincerity, so that within an hour Tom had fallen for her and Tommie was in the throes of the adoration adolescent girls often feel for women slightly older than themselves. Even Liz, who could almost be called a professional sceptic, dropped her armour to join the circle of admirers around Miracle. It was so easy to respond to the quick smile she gave whenever one of them looked at her. Her smile masked everything, Arthur thought, though the laughter which had brought her fame had so far been severely rationed. She offered little in the way of conversation, and even that consisted mostly of polite clichés. Whatever she may have thought about the non-movie world, she kept it to herself.

Until evening came no one had given thought to where Miracle might sleep. At first, she said she would drive to town and get a room, but the twins protested she must remain at Haven. Liz suggested Tommie give up her room for one night and sleep on the living room couch.

"Oh, no. I couldn't do that," Miracle cried, to which Tommie countercried, "Oh yes, you can!" Tom said nothing, but looked as though he would be gloriously happy if Miracle would agree to share *his* bed. Arthur settled the matter and said: "Couldn't they both sleep Tommie's bed? It's a double. I remember, because Joey got it for Phyllis Arnold. She said Phyllis needed a large bed."

"If Tommie doesn't object," Miracle said.

"I'd love to," Tommie gushed. She could hardly wait to find out what kind of underwear a glamorous person like Miracle would wear. Tom, who had always loved his older (by one hour) sister and admired her irrepressible vitality, now discovered he disliked her intensely.

"Well, that settles that," Liz said. "We can think about other arrangements tomorrow."

Tommie had rushed through her own undressing in order that she could lie on one side of the bed and observe the famous Miracle Shields remove her clothes, but Tommie was disappointed: the underwear beneath the jeans and sweater was plain white and utilitarian, nothing as lavish as Tommie's own lace-edged panties and bras; and instead of a fancy nightgown, Miracle put on a pair of baggy cotton pyjamas and a scruffy terry-cloth bathrobe. It was a letdown for Tommie, who had expected exotic lingerie. They talked a little to familiarize themselves with each other as bed companions. Miracle said she often slept with her mother, and Tommie replied that she and Tom had slept together as kids and that she had felt deprived when he was given his own room and bed. Miracle agreed that it was comforting when you awoke in the middle of the night and somebody was lying beside you. They asked each other if they snored and when each answered "No," they rolled over onto their sides and went to sleep.

Since the twins had to be positioned at the front gates for the school bus by half-past seven, Tommie was showered and dressed before seven. She was putting on her bra when Miracle poked her head out of the covers to say, "You sure have a cute figure." Tommie blushed and hurriedly fastened the brassiere. She was used to boys ogling her breasts, even Tom, and she now recalled how at thirteen he had invited her to look at his swollen penis, in return demanding to view the buds on her chest and the triangle of hair between her thighs. At the time, they had bitterly resented the intrusion of physical maturity into their lives because they had always been close and it was painful to acknowledge that the thing called "sex" had come between them. Miracle sat up. "I've always been chubby. That was okay when I was little. People like chubby kids, especially little girls. But I'm going to have to fight to keep my weight down. My mom's genes, I guess."

"I think you're lovely," Tommie said.

"Not compared to some stars. I make sure I never get close to them during shots. Never. Why are you up so early?"

"School bus."

"Don't you have an car?"

"Car!" Tommie laughed. She had never thought of herself as having a car.

"Doesn't your brother have one?"

"We have bikes. But it's easier getting to school on the bus. Anyway, I have to run. Did you sleep well?"

"Perfectly. Listen, Tommie. Is the lake cold?"

"Yes. It hasn't warmed up yet."

"Mother always talked about how she'd run to the beach and plunge into the water."

"We do in the summer. But you should try it. You can always come out."

"Tommie!" Tom called from outside the door. "Get a move-on!"

"If you wait, I'll drive you to school," Miracle offered.

"Really? Honest? Classes begin at eight."

"I'm used to being on the set early. Could you find me a cup of coffee?"

"You bet. Oh boy, wait until our friends see us arrive in a convertible! Tom!" she called as she ran from the room.

Everything said and done conspired to solidify the enslavement of Tom and Tommy to Miracle. Directed by Tom, Miracle drove them to the red-brick school where, when she offered to pick them up after classes, they made a point of loudly calling out, "See you at four, Miracle."

"Wow!" one of Tom's pals exclaimed. "Who's that?" "Where'd you find that doll?" another inquired. Tom and his friends habitually gathered as a group at the school entrance to eye passing girls; the youths were crass and ignorant, but that didn't prevent them from collectively thinking they were pretty darn smart as individuals. "Miracle Shields? You mean *the* Miracle Shields, the movie star?" They dug him in the ribs and punched his arm, refusing to believe him, even after he explained she was Mr. Matt's daughter and staying at the house for a few days.

During the morning, Miracle and Liz chatted. Liz, in the role of hostess, asked about the movie Miracle was presently starring in, but Miracle shrugged it off as nothing more than a pot-boiler to keep her name and presence before the public. She told Liz that the last decent movie she had starred in had been filmed on location in England. Arthur, who had finished working for the morning, came onto the patio to allow Liz to make lunch. He asked Miracle how she had liked England.

"You want an honest answer?" Miracle asked.

"Of course," he replied.

"I thought it was a crummy, second-rate place. It rained most of the time."

"That wouldn't help. Did you get to London?"

"Oh no. To tell the truth I was never quite sure where we were. Some town on the English Channel called Ponnewton. Every day we drove from there to the location."

"I see. What was the movie about?"

"You know how the British love to adapt novels to film. Well, this film was an adaptation of a novel written by someone who lived in an old house on the edge of this itty-bitty forest where most of the shooting was done."

"I see."

"A.E. Compson. Ever heard of him?"

"No," Arthur said. "Never." There was a pause in the conversation while he wondered how far he should go in his inquiries about the film. Miracle watched an osprey circle over the lake. "Was the novel any good?" he finally asked.

"I didn't read it. Only the screenplay." Miracle pointed over the lake. "What's that bird?"

"An osprey. Some people call them fish hawks." It was incredible that his daughter had actually acted in a film based on one of his early novels, a coincidence that seemed to defy the laws of probability. The impulse to blurt out his identity as A.E. Compson was momentarily so compelling that Arthur could only avoid doing so by faking a coughing spell. "Sorry," he said after he had calmed down. "You were telling me about the movie."

"Oh yes. It was one of those old-fashioned plots. You know, a married woman meets a worker in the forest and they fall in love, a sort of grand passion. You know the kind of thing. Then war breaks out."

"The last war?"

"No. World War I. The man gets drafted into the army."

"I see. So what happens then?" He remembered it now. The way the passion engendered by the protagonists had swept him to the novel's end.

"He comes back to the forest, recovering from a wound." Arthur thought of Sylvia: how she had dramatized her first encounter with his father. "Instead of going back, he deserts and hides in the forest. The woman takes food to him."

"How does it end?"

"The army finds him when they follow the woman to where he's hiding. When he tries to escape, they shoot him."

"What about her?"

"She drowns herself in a river."

"So what was your role?"

"The woman, Catherine. Edwardian costumes. No sex scenes, just shots of us walking and sitting together. You know, the way people carried on in those days."

"Decorous?"

"The audience was supposed to know what was really going on between the man and woman by the way they looked at each other. Anyway, my contract stipulates no sex. Mother insists on it."

"You disapprove of sex?"

"Sex scenes usually aren't necessary to convey a story." Arthur thought of Sophia Gambarasi looking him over to make sure he could deliver the sexual goods to her daughter.

"What did you think of the setting?"

"It was a joke, but people are always proud of whatever they have. The English think their crummy little cottages are the most beautiful in the world."

"But you enjoyed making the movie?"

"Yes, it was a change and proved I could do drama." He wondered if behind Miracle's glossy facade lay nothing more than movie-world values wherein everything in life was judged by whether it would be viable on film.

Liz appeared with a plate of cheese sandwiches and bowls of cherries she had bottled the previous summer. She put the food on the patio table saying, "Everything here is pretty down-to-earth. Nothing fancy."

"Oh, I adore cheese sandwiches," Miracle said, though Liz doubted this because Miracle ate only one sandwich half, unlike the twins who generally put away five or six. However, she did ask for a second helping of fruit.

"The cherries were canned when they were perfectly ripe. You can't beat that. No sugar added. The sweetness is all in the fruit." Liz continued to explain canning procedures to Miracle who vacantly nodded and smiled.

However, the afternoon passed pleasantly enough. An hour or two after they had eaten lunch, Miracle appeared in a one-piece swimsuit which Arthur thought looked like something an older woman would wear, nothing like the skimpy bits of cloth Tommie and her friends wore. She walked directly down to the beach, waded into the water and swam around a few minutes before she got out and went into the house to change, saying only that the water felt refreshing.

"She isn't like I expected her to be," Liz said.

"What did you expect?"

"Oh, I don't know. Somebody who acts more like a movie star. After all, she is famous."

"Maybe so, but I doubt if she knows much beyond what her mother and the directors tell her."

Liz looked into the house, then leaned over the table to whisper, "Do you think she has many friends? You know, men friends. Lovers?"

"I doubt it. She's like Joey was in her twenties."

"Really!" Liz exclaimed.

"Yes, she's a lot like Joey," he repeated as Miracle joined them. "I was just telling Liz how much you resemble your mother."

"Everybody says that." Miracle spread her wet swimsuit and towel on the grass, then sat. "It's so quiet here, so peaceful. If I stayed long, I'd forget all about Hollywood."

"Isn't it all very exciting there?" Liz asked. "Your name in lights outside the theatres?"

"Not really. It's just a job, like any other."

"You're disillusioning Liz," he said.

"I'm sorry," Miracle said. "Maybe I should go back to my movie-star act." She posed in the chair. "How's that?" she asked.

"As good as Marilyn Monroe," Arthur said.

"Did you ever meet her when you were in Hollywood?" Miracle asked.

"I may have seen her, but no movie star would ever bother with me. I was a mere screenplay writer."

"Mom said you were pretty good."

They continued to chat idly until Miracle remembered she had promised to pick up the twins at school. When she asked the time and was told it was after four, she became upset and ran into the house to get her car keys. "What'll they think of me?"

When she returned, Arthur told her not to worry about it. "They won't mind waiting," he assured her. "They'll have a bunch of other kids waiting with them, all wanting a look at a famous movie star."

"But I said I'd be there at four."

"Blame me for keeping you. I'll come with you and open the gates." As they drove to entrance, Arthur spoke: "There's something I want you to know, Miracle. I didn't ever want to be separated from you. I begged Joey to stay here with me. You should know how much I missed watching you grow and change. That's all. I just want you to know how I feel."

"I guess I understand. It was just one of those things." When Miracle said nothing further, he left the car to open the gates. After she passed through, he stood and watched the car until it passed beyond the brow of the distant hill, overcome with a sense of loss. He then closed the gates and walked back to the house.

At four o'clock, Tom and Tommie and a group of students, mostly male, waited on the pavement outside the school entrance. By twenty past, the audience had thinned, but ten minutes later those who remained were rewarded by the sight of Miracle halting the convertible and waiting for the twins to get in. "Sorry I'm late," Miracle said, "but I was talking with Dad and forgot the time. And you know what? I swam in the lake. The best part was getting out." She laughed, and they laughed with her as they drove off. "It was so cold! But I've felt wonderful all afternoon. Where does this highway lead?"

"I'm not sure," Tommie said.

"Sooner or later, you'd get on the Trans-Canada highway," Tom said, feeling he had let himself and the province down by not knowing where the highway went. "We don't go north much. Mr. Matt doesn't like leaving Haven."

"Well, he needn't come with us if we decide to go for a day trip."

"Mom'd like that. She enjoys getting around. When we were kids, she towed us around in a trailer behind her bike, didn't she, Tom?" Tom nodded. He had managed to slip into the car before his sister and was sitting so close to Miracle that he could feel the warmth of her body and smell her perfume. As they drove to Haven, he promised himself he would never return to the old days (the preceding Saturday) when he had been content to lounge on a broken car seat, swilling beer and discussing the possibility of getting "tail" from certain girls who, so rumour had it, handed it out for free, provided you caught them in the right mood. Tom and his friends hadn't much intelligence, but they recognized that sex functioned as an almost insurmountable barrier to moving ahead in school and that the easiest solution to their problem would be to reduce their permanently stiff male organs to a comfort size by masturbating while imagining possessing a "perfect" woman, like Miracle Shields, or Tom's sister, though it was understood in the group that Tommie was a taboo topic. When a youth once brought up her name, Tom attacked him and, before the rest could drag him off, had broken the youth's nose and knocked out a tooth when he slammed his face against the car frame where the fabric was torn away. While holding the youth down, Tom had shouted that he would kill any guy who talked about Tommie. "For crissake, Tom," the others said. "She's a girl, ain't she? What the hell, you think guys don't talk about her?" "Not while I'm present," Tom had replied. But he had to acknowledge that it was all very difficult, and now caught in a whirlwind of sexual desire as he sat bunched up close to Miracle, he decided it was time to make some changes in his life.

While Tommie opened and closed the gates, Miracle asked Tom about this plans for the future. Tom blushed and said he didn't have any, then added, "But I'm glad you're here."

"Thank you," Miracle said, delivering a practised response. "I'm glad to be here."

"I mean, I like you a lot," Tom mumbled and wished the skirt of her yellow dress would slide further up her thighs, then felt ashamed for acting like his crasser friends while at the same time knowing they would be impressed if he told them he'd seen the colour of Miracle Shield's underpanties.

"I like you and Tommie," she obligingly said as Tommie got in the car. "It's as though I've come home and discovered a brother and sister I didn't know about." They started down to the house. "Your brother's a real sweetheart, Tommie."

"He's okay. Better than the beer-slugging guys he hangs out with."

"I'm not going to hang out with them any more," Tom said.

"Good!" Tommie said as they left the car and walked down the steps to the front door.

"The nice thing about having a family is there's always some other person around who'll listen," Miracle said. "I have nobody but Mom."

"Tommie thinks she's the boss because she's an hour older than me," Tom said.

"Doesn't it amaze you to think you were side by side in your mother's womb?"

"I should have charged him rent," Tommie said.

Miracle laughed and when they entered the living room where Arthur sat, she was still laughing.

"A joke?" Arthur asked.

"Tommie said she should have charged Tom rent for being beside her in Liz's womb." Miracle said.

"Well," Arthur said, "it's not necessarily the first twin out who is the first twin in, if you get my meaning. Anyway, the first time I saw Tom and Tommie they were amicably sharing space in a bike trailer. They complemented each other perfectly. But perhaps they don't remember Liz hauling them around and bringing them here."

"I do," Tommie said,

"So do I," said Tom.

"We swam in our underwear."

"And we brought cookies and something to drink for our snacks."

"And we napped in my bed," Tommie said.

"And Mom told us we couldn't quarrel and fight or say bad words because Haven was heaven on earth."

"And you believed her?" Miracle asked.

"Of course. Why wouldn't we?"

"How sweet of you," Miracle said.

When Liz suggested they go in for a swim, Miracle declined, saying once was enough, but Tom and Tommie went into house and put on swimsuits, then raced each other to the cove and furiously swam to the rock where Joey had once stood in naked glory, as Arthur thought of it. Miracle told Liz that Tommie had a cute little figure, and Liz, after smiling appreciation, left to prepare the evening meal.

"Mother told me you refused to live in California," Miracle said.

"I agreed to spend the winters there," he replied, bending the truth a little. "I want you to know I never rejected you or your mother. I had hoped to watch you playing in the water like those two." He pointed to Tom and Tommie who were standing in shallow water splashing water at each other.

"You could have visited," Miracle said.

"Yes. Or Joey could have brought you here. But we were both pretty hard-nosed about what we wanted. Joey wanted to push you ahead in L.A. I wanted to live here." He smiled apologetically. "I guess your future met head-on with Haven. And in the end Joey and I lost each other."

"You replaced Mom and me with Liz and her kids."

"You could think of it like that. If you stay around, I'll tell you how Liz came to be here." He nodded towards Tom and Tommie now drying themselves on the beach. "I agree she is cute. I'm fond of her . . . and of Tom. Has Joey ever spoken to you about ownership of Haven?"

"No."

"Originally, Haven was owned by Joey and me and our friend Phyllis Ackroyd, who was also my agent, but when she died she left her share to me. I've decided to leave that share to Liz, because I know she'll look after Haven. That'll leave you heir to two-thirds after Joey and I kick the bucket."

"I think it's beautiful. I'll return whenever I have an opportunity."

"Maybe we can talk more before you leave," he said as Tom and Tommie came up from the beach.

"I'd like that," she said.

"It's glorious!" Tommie cried. She got behind Arthur and leaned over to smear her damp hair against his face. "Don't do that!" he yelled. "When she was little, she'd run out of the water, jump into my lap and saturate me."

"Because I wanted you to come and swim with me. You have to force him into the water," she told Miracle as she stood beside Arthur's chair rubbing her thick black hair. Her affection for him was obvious in the way she leaned against him, and Miracle envied the freedom with which she expressed affection for the man Joey had always portrayed as a cold, sickly person, on the lookout only for himself. Tom came from the house with an order from Liz that Tommie was to change, then set the table for dinner. And Tom, now back in jeans and a tee shirt, sat and watched Miracle, following every gesture she made but not saying anything.

When Liz called them to dinner, they filed into the dining room and sat at the round table ("No heads and tails here," Arthur quipped.) to eat baked chicken breasts, vegetables and rice. Before they commenced eating, Arthur raised his glass of water and said, "Health and happiness to all." They repeated the words and began eating. No one could think of anything to say, until Liz asked Miracle if people really ate the food they were served in movies.

"I do," Miracle said. "When it's any good."

"What about wine and things like that?" Tom asked. "You know, champagne?"

"Everything in movies is pretence," Arthur said. "People pretend love and hate, birth and death. They pretend to fight and pretend to get drunk. Not so long ago, Miracle pretended to drown herself. Right, Miracle?"

"I walked up to my knees in a muddy, stinking river and a shot was taken. Then somebody threw the hat I was wearing onto the water and a shot was made of that. That was me dying."

"And movie-goers would know she was drowned because they would see the hat floating away." Arthur grudgingly conceded it wasn't a bad ending because there was something terribly final about a floating hat—it was so irretrievable. What ending had he written? How did he dispose of the woman? Something similar, he recalled. Drowning was an awful way to die, but then any form of death lacked dignity. It was a pity people couldn't just vanish. So much time was spent on death, so much money forked out. In a way, he had already died once and had reincarnated himself as Matt Scheiler; and it was curious that while he associated death with other people, he had, thus far, granted himself immunity to it. Besides, every one of his spells (Arthur calculate that he'd had a couple of hundred in his lifetime, though fewer now than when he was young) could be interpreted as a "little death," though each return to life had been far more painful than all the periodic dyings taken together. So why should he fear the actuality of death when it came his way?

"Did you think about drowning when you were acting the scene?" Tommie asked.

"I was thinking how happy I'd be when I finally got on the plane back to California."

"She was in England," Arthur explained.

"The dreariest location I've ever worked at," Miracle said.

"I thought England was supposed to be a beautiful place," Tommie said.

"Well, it isn't," Miracle said. "I saw a lot of rain falling on a dismal little town and a horrible village stuck off in some place called A.E Compson country. That's the guy who wrote the novel the film is based on."

After a pause Liz said, "It sounds like Newfoundland. That's where I come from. We used to say we lived through three hundred and sixty days of winter to enjoy five days of summer. Most days, the wind just about blows your hair off and it's either raining or snowing, sometimes all three at once."

"What was the movie about?" Tom asked.

"A mixed-up married woman." She went on to give them an outline of the plot. "I thought I did a good job," she said. "I surprised myself, because I'd never had a part before where I was expected to portray deep emotion. The suppressed kind. You know what I mean." They chewed the food and signified they understood how difficult a role it must have been for her by nodding their heads. "The rain loused things up for me. I mean, when you live in Southern California, you're used to sunshine."

"Are we still going for a drive on Saturday?" Tommie asked.

"Why not?" Miracle looked from Tom to Liz.

"Tom and I can pretend we're movie stars too," Tommie said.

"You have the vitality," Miracle said. "That's what I had when I was a girl. I bounced everywhere and laughed at everything. I thought the world was so amusing. Now I hardly laugh, though the world's still much the same—producers grumbling because the movie's behind schedule and over-budget, directors yelling at actors, and actors hoping they won't have to do retakes of the kissing scenes."

"Do you mind doing those?" Tommie asked. Apart from kisses given and received from Liz and a few from Tom before puberty, Tommie had resisted being kissed by boys, except for an occasional peck on the cheek she might allow.

"It comes with the job," Miracle said.

"I couldn't," Tommie shivered.

"So ends your short career in movies," Arthur said. "But you've given me an idea for a short story about a girl who can't kiss." The others laughed, but Tommie protested that she still kissed Arthur every night before she went to bed because she loved him.

Miracle asked, "You really love him?"

Tommie blushed. "Why shouldn't I?" Sometimes Tommie looked at Arthur when he was sitting alone and didn't know she was there and would think he was a truly sad man, though she didn't know why he should be, because he was a successful author with books in shops and even in their school library, and of course he owned Haven. Still, there was something about him she couldn't quite place. It was as if he was a double person who only became single when he was alone, but as soon as anyone came into his presence he would switch to his double-identity. She also thought he was a very shy man who practised congeniality; and there was also a fear, of which she was rather ashamed, that if he suddenly died, her family would be forced to leave Haven, which made her wonder if she fed him affection to prevent that from happening. She remembered her real father disappearing for days and how frightened she had been seeing her mother sitting in the kitchen, biting her lips until they bled, and how relieved she was when she found out that Mr. Matt hardly ever left Haven, so relieved that she had literally thrown herself at him and said she loved him. That being so, she wasn't going to allow his daughter to appear out of the blue and question her attachment to him, even if she was a movie star. But when Miracle smiled at her and said, "He's lucky to have you," the resentment kindling in her evaporated.

"You bet I am," Arthur agreed, then began talking about enlarging the house in order to have a bedroom for Miracle.

"I don't mind occupying half of Tommie's bed. She didn't try to kick me out during the night." She then told them about being on location in Mexico and how the accommodation was so bad there that three girls ended up sleeping in one old bed, and how, being the youngest and smallest, she had been relegated to the outside and had been kicked out by the woman sleeping in the middle. Hearing them laugh was a spur and she reeled off stories which were probably old hat to those in the movie industry, but which amused and fascinated Liz and her teenage children. Miracle even laughed at herself and the misfortunes of others on location. "You either have to laugh or scream with frustration," she said.

And so it went until Tommie began yawning and Liz, after looking at the clock, packed her and Tom off to bed, then began clearing dishes off the table. Miracle offered to help, but Liz said, "Stay and gossip with Matt." But it wasn't long before Miracle excused herself and went off to the bedroom where Tommie lay yawning.

"I thought you'd be asleep," she said.

"I waited for you." Tommie watched Miracle undress. "You seem just like everyone else," she said. "But you're not supposed to. You're supposed to be extra-glamorous. Wonderful clothes and—I dunno, just different. But you aren't. You're like me."

"Of course I'm like you. The difference is that my mother had me trained me as an actor. I'm doing what Mom wanted for herself." She took off her panties and bra and, because of the way she was standing, little dabs of fat were visible around her waist and inner thighs. In ten years' time, Tommie thought, unwanted flesh would cover her body as she had seen lichen blanket the old cherry and apple trees in the orchard.

"Tom's fallen for you," she said.

"He'll recover once I'm gone." Miracle put on a plain white cotton nightgown and got into bed. "He's a nice kid," she said.

"Mom's scared he'll turn out like our real father and take to drinking."

"A director I had when I was a kid was an alcoholic. He drove his car into a bridge abutment. He was a decent man when he was sober."

"I wish you'd tell Tom you like him. It would make him feel good."

"Sure. Why not? And I'll tell him to stay off the booze. I'll say it never got a guy anywhere but onto the streets."

"Have you been married?"

"Married! Heavens no. What gave you that idea?"

"I dunno. I thought all movie stars got married and divorced."

"Some do, some don't. Not me."

"But you have a regular . . . friend?"

"No. If I need an escort to a party or to an Oscar, I just whistle and some guy shows up, hoping to be photographed with me."

"Have you ever won an Oscar?"

"I picked up a special award for my early movies, but I'm not in the running now. My movies are too run-of-the-mill. They'll eventually be shown on late night TV movies. The only good picture I've made lately is the one in England I told you about."

"Was the place really dismal?"

"Yes. It rained a lot and the house where the guy lived who wrote the novel gave me the creeps. Maybe I felt that way because Charles Randle—that's who played the husband, he's an English actor—told me the author had disappeared after a woman was murdered there."

"Did he kill her?"

"I suppose so. Anyway, it's the big local story. Everybody in the town and village told us about it." She imitated the forest dialect. "I 'eard yer wars makin' a movie in the Arthur Compson 'ouse. Yer better be careful, or 'e might whack yer on yer 'ead like 'e done before."

"It sounds scary. Was the actor who played the soldier good-looking?"

"He was okay. I thought I did quite a good job of holding him in my arms after he'd been shot. You should've seen me wading into the river!" Miracle laughed. "It was just an itty-bitty stream near a bridge, but the camera angle made it look wide. It's all deception," she said. "I couldn't believe it was me when I saw the movie. I looked half-crazy when I was drowning myself." They smiled at each other over the gap between their pillows.

"Do you get lots of fan mail?" Tommie asked.

"Probably. But I never see it. It came by the ton when I was a kid. Do you like people?"

"Like them?" The question puzzled Tommie. "I suppose I must. I mean, if I disliked them, then I'd have to dislike myself, wouldn't I? Why do you ask? Don't you like people?"

"I think most women are bitchy, and generally men are vile."

"Tom and Mr. Matt aren't."

"Mother told me your wonderful Mr. Matt didn't treat her with respect."

"What do you mean? Respect?"

"Mother said he sort of raped her."

"I don't believe that," Tommie whispered. "Mr. Matt wouldn't do anything like that."

"Well, only men know what men think, and some times it's too late when the women find out what they're up to."

"He'd never do that," Tommie said again. "He wouldn't. Your mother made that up as an excuse for not staying at Haven."

"You wouldn't be living here if Mother didn't prefer Los Angeles. So thank her and your lucky stars." Tommie glared at Miracle, her face transformed by childish outrage. "Anyway," Miracle said, "don't let's fight their battles." She reached across the bed and touched Tommie's face. "Don't be angry. I liked you the minute I saw you."

"That was a real nasty thing to say."

"I'm sorry. It wasn't intended that way."

"That's how it came out."

Miracle had withdrawn to her pillow. "Still angry?" she asked.

Tommie was slow to respond, but at last she said, "I know we wouldn't be here if your mother had stayed with Mr. Matt. But he's told me that having us living with him was the second most sensible thing he did in his life."

"What was the first?"

"Becoming a writer." Tommie switched off her lamp and turned her back to Miracle, who continued to lie on her side and look at Tommie.

"What about marrying my mother?"

"He said being sensible has nothing to do with love."

After a few minutes passed, Miracle spoke: "Have you ever been to California?"

"I haven't been anywhere except on field trips," Tommie snapped. In general, she was an even-tempered person, but she could not stand being put down, or having to admit that she was not among the most deserving of girls. The slightest reprimand would produce hours of sulking, and girls at school were wary of her because her quick reaction to a reproach might destroy a valued friendship. Now, Miracle couldn't understand what she had said to offend Tommie since she thought she had done no more than simply state a fact. What was so wrong with that? In her line of work, people lived with facts that had to be faced, even when the end products of their labour were illusions. She herself had been told she was coasting along on her childhood reputation, that she wasn't pretty enough as an adult actor, nor did she have sufficient talent to star in blockbuster movies, which were the big money-makers now. Absorbing that fact delivered her by a studio vice-president came close to breaking Miracle's spirit; but she never told her mother, knowing Joey would storm into the studio, throw her weight around and generally make trouble for her. The rejection isolated her, and it was her need to be reassured that had brought her across the U.S.-Canada border to the town where she had nervously telephoned her father. In the few days she'd been at Haven, she'd found she wanted Tommie's friendship and was prepared to do almost anything to retain it. "Would you like to drive back to Los Angeles with me?"

"You told us you were flying back. That's what you said."

"I know. But if you came, we could drive."

"What about Tom?"

"I suppose he could come with us." There was no enthusiasm in Miracle's voice.

"Why don't you like him?"

"Oh I do, I do."

"Well then."

"But I thought just the two of us, would be fun. We could talk about ourselves. Like friends do."

Tommie must have heard the catch in Miracle's voice because she turned and was horrified to see tears streaming down her cheeks. "What is it? What's the matter?" When they were children she, not Liz, had comforted Tom when he cried or was upset. Now she held and kissed Miracle and told her everything would be all right.

"It's nothing," Miracle sniffed. "Sometimes I feel so alone."

"You're with me now," Tommie said.

"But you turned your back to me."

"I didn't mean it that way. I get irritated easily. Mostly with myself. I mean, I admire you and wish I could accomplish what you have, but I know I'll never do anything spectacular. I'll end working in a library, or in some other dull job, like working for the government. That's what C+ people do." She reached out to embrace Miracle and they were reconciled: Tommie offered Miracle admiration and reassurance, while Miracle went to work projecting an exciting future for Tommie. Finally they slept, and when they awoke in the morning, each felt rather ashamed of their emotional outbursts. Miracle drove the twins to school, then returned to Haven where she sat alone on the patio until Liz was freed from housework and could join her.

"He works every day. Nine to one," Liz explained.

"What's he working on?" Miracle asked.

Liz shrugged and said she never poked her nose into his work. "He does his thing, and I do mine. You know, look after the house and whatnot in a half-assed sort of way."

"Everything looks fine to me," Miracle said. Once again, she remarked on the placid beauty of Haven, and Liz responded by telling her how she had first met Matt, then came to the house. "I couldn't believe my eyes," she said. "The cove was so absolutely beautiful, and naturally the twins loved it. I mean, what kid wouldn't? Matt seemed pleased to see us, though probably I wouldn't have come back if the kids hadn't kept bugging me about it. So I came again, and Matt said they could nap in the house if I wanted, which was the first time I'd been inside. What a mess! Dust an inch thick! So I offered to vacuum the place for him. Later on, I told him I was leaving my husband and going on welfare. That was when he said we could live here."

"And were you going to leave your husband?"

"I'd thought about it. His drinking was getting worse. And he'd been transferred, so we would have to move. I didn't want the hassle."

"Did you get a divorce?"

"No. I just moved in with the kids and my belongings."

"And you've slept with him ever since that day?"

"No. Not for several months. Sex doesn't interest me. I thought he was too old to bother with it."

"Does he pay you for being his housekeeper?"

Liz shrugged again, then said she'd managed to scrape together a bit of money for herself, and of course Matt paid for the twins' clothes and general expenses. "He's always been good to the twins, especially Tommie. I think he missed not being able to watch you grow up. And Tommie idolizes him. She's a funny girl. Very impulsive. She either loves or hates people. Nothing in between. I don't know what'll happen when the twins have to go their separate ways, though I don't worry so much about Tommie. It's Tom I worry about. He's getting to act more and more like his dad. Very quiet. Never a squeak out of him, even when he's drinking. Tommie said you'd invited them to drive back with you to Los Angeles."

"Yes, I have," Miracle said.

"How will they get back to B.C.?" Liz asked.

"Fly. I'll pay for the tickets."

"Oh no, I'm sure Matt will want to. How long will it take to go to L.A.?"

"I'm not sure. I have a month before I've got to start another movie. And I'll need to read the screenplay soon."

"So you'll leave right after school is out? That's next week. Let's say two weeks for the whole trip?"

"Something like that."

Liz smiled and got up. "I'll start lunch," she said. "Matt likes to eat as soon as he comes out of his workroom."

"Maybe I'll go for a swim," Miracle said.

Liz went into the house and Miracle walked to the beach, kicked off her sandals and, as she stepped into the water, was reminded of the scene in her mother's film where the young woman grotesquely dances on the beach before tripping and falling. She heard the sand crunch as Arthur came to stand beside her. "I'm thinking about Mother's film," she said. "The way she had the woman dance around to emphasize her dysfunction before she got into the water to swim like a fish."

"You've seen the film?"

"Several times. I've never understood why Mother stopped with one movie."

"I'm not sure either. But it seemed to satisfy her to make just the one. And the odd thing is that the movie works. The screenplay I wrote wasn't much good, but Joey magically turned it into a struggle between the disadvantaged and those who have everything. A universal theme. Even though the film's got plenty of bad parts, it still works, because in the rawest possible sense it states a truth about human behaviour. The disabled woman's dance symbolized her memory of once being whole and capable of giving and receiving love. So long as she remains alone, she can continue to dream, but once a stranger invades her domain, her ability to dance and dream is destroyed. When she attempts to drive him away, he brutally retaliates and does what those in power have always done to those weaker than themselves. He rapes her and in a subtle way lays the foundation for his own destruction. But of course Joey didn't know any of that when she shot the movie; she just wanted to prove she could make a movie. She wanted to get it right. That's what she kept saying: 'I must get everything right'."

"She's still that way."

"Well, I'm glad you're here." He glanced back at the house, as though to make sure no one could hear their conversation. "Tell me about yourself. Do you have a special friend? Would you like to marry and have a family?"

"I have my work. But no special person. Mom says she was like that."

"The resemblance between you is striking."

"Tommie hinted I could have Tom as my special friend."

"What nonsense. He's a rather immature teenager. Tommie should know better than to push him at you."

"Apparently she's afraid he'll turn out like his father."

"That could happen. But Tommie's in no position to forecast what will actually happen to her brother. Life is too unpredictable to prophesy where an individual will end."

"Has Liz told you I've invited the twins to drive back to Los Angeles with me?"

"She mentioned it."

"You don't object?"

"No."

"Is there time for me to swim before lunch?"

"Oh sure. I'll bring you a towel." He went back to the house while she quickly stripped, entered the water, swam to the rock and sat on it with her arms folded across her breasts.

Arthur returned to the house, then walked back to the beach to place a large towel on Miracle's clothes, waved, then returned to sit on the patio with Liz. As Miracle sat on the rock she remembered how, years ago, her mother had explained the origin of her name and had indirectly implied that her father's participation in her generation was minimal, that her conception had occurred through the combined efforts of herself and her great friend, Phyllis Ackroyd. As a child, Miracle believed the story and went around telling everyone that she didn't need a father because her birth was a miracle. Later on, when she understood how profoundly Joey had misled her, she didn't blame her mother, instead she mentally kicked herself for having been so stupid as to take her seriously; and now that she had finally met her father, it seemed to her that there was a great hollow space in her life that could not be filled now, because she would never be able to experience developing from child to adolescent to adult in his presence. Never. She slipped into the water, paddled to the beach and, noticing that both Matt and Liz had their backs to her, she left the water and quickly dried herself, dressed and went to join them at the table under the wide umbrella.

When evening came, Miracle and the twins pored over the road maps Miracle had brought in from the car. They planned where they would go on their trip the next day and the route they would follow when they drove to Los Angeles. They traced secondary roads and interstate highways, and Tommie and Tom had a furious argument whether to follow the old Pacific coast highway, or to go inland and drive south through the inland desert states. When asked for his opinion, Arthur told them that he had travelled both routes by bus. He suggested they go east of the mountains by car and return by bus on the western side.

"I didn't know you'd done that," Liz said.

"I've managed to accomplish a few things you know nothing about," he said. The twins cheered when he added, "I was even in St. John's, Newfoundland for a few hours. Strangely enough, I saw a woman who looked a lot like you. Now that I think of it, she had a squalling baby in a buggy. I politely asked her for directions to the stores, then asked her the baby's name. Guess what she said?"

"Liz! It was Liz!" the twins crowed.

"What a bunch of baloney!" Liz said.

"Prove it," Arthur said. But Liz refused to be drawn into an argument, other than to repeat the word "baloney," until Arthur finally admitted he had concocted the story to tease Liz.

Later that night, just as Tommie was about to fall asleep, she felt Miracle leave the bed, then heard the bedroom door open and close. When Miracle did not return, Tommie knew she had gone to Tom's room. Miracle herself did not know why she had left the bed and crept along the passage to Tom's room. It was dark and she had to feel around the bed frame before she touched his head. She whispered his name, and when he grunted his way out of sleep, she raised the covers and got into the narrow bed with him. At first, he seemed not to understand why she was there, but he quickly became frantic with desire when she began kissing him. His breath smelled of toothpaste and his body of toilet soap. She managed to get beneath him and open her thighs just as he blindly lunged at her and spewed semen over her belly. He then lay upon her, mouthing her breasts, whispering he loved her until he became aroused again and she guided him to her secret place and groaned when she felt him break the fragile barrier and enter. She was not sure what she felt, whether pleasure or mere discomfort at having to lie beneath his body while he recuperated and buckled himself to her again; she merely knew she did not want him to leave and when she felt him shrink and recede, she pressed herself against him and quietly moaned disappointment. She was still there, uncomfortably sleeping, when Liz tapped on the door and said, "Tom. Breakfast. Come on, get up." Miracle felt Tom's mouth move over hers and smelled his sleep-soured breath when he said he would always love her and didn't care about anything else except loving her. She told him he was sweet, but she didn't believe him, already knowing that something so volatile as love and its offspring, desire, could not endure. She showered and returned to Tommie's room, where Tommie glared at her before they went into the kitchen and helped Liz pack sandwiches. By the time everything was loaded in the car, Tommie's resentment of Miracle for spending the night with Tom had faded and was replaced by sadness over leaving Arthur behind.

Arthur stood at the garage and waved goodbye, and as the car passed into the grove of pines, Tommie looked back and began loudly sobbing that she wanted to stay at Haven with Mr. Matt because he looked so sad and alone, but she stopped crying when Liz rebuked her, then cheered up once they were on the road and going north toward their unknown destination.

Much later, Arthur remembered them getting into the car on that Saturday morning—he had forfeited going to his workroom as usual to see them off on their outing—gesturing good-bye and Tommie crying out for him as he point-lessly called: "Take care! Take care!"; and he remembered how in the late afternoon he had walked to the gates to listen for the sound of an approaching car, then gone back to the quiet house to wait and wait through the night until morning when he telephoned the police to tell them his family hadn't returned.

Arthur stood at the window remembering . . .

He remembered watching the twins as children, chasing each other in the shallows of the cove. Tom usually was pursuing Tommie, bent on retaliation for her having splashed water on him. The only bodily difference between them was the variation in the shape of their buttocks, Tommie's being a shade wider and fuller than Tom's. He remembered watching them run from the bathroom to where he waited, ready to hold out their pyjama pants for them to step into. Liz had told him that, being four years old, the twins should do these things for themselves, but he enjoyed having them hold his shoulders while they lifted first one leg, then the other before he pulled the pants up to their navels and bowed the cord. Sometimes he would pretend to mismatch tops with bottoms and they would shriek: "That's boys and this is girls!", then rush off to tell Liz that once again Mr. Matt had put Tommie's top on Tom and Tom's on Tommie. He had never dreamed that he could delight in being around children, that he could relish moments of exquisite pleasure in observing their astonishment when something new entered their lives. At that time, his toler-ance had been general and he made no distinction between the twins, though he had never doubted that Tommie, who epitomized for him the inherent ca-pacity of females to deal with males, had known the effect on him when, fifteen years earlier, she had smudged a kiss on his face and said she loved him. And he had become used to hearing Tommie icily inform her brother that her needs took precedence over his. If three cookies lay on a plate, she had the right to two, though when it came right down to it she shared everything with Tom fifty-fifty. It was more a matter of privilege, a reminder to Tom that she was the kingpin (queen-pin?) who governed his life.

He remembered how he had sensed something out-of-the-ordinary had happened during the night before they had driven off on their doomed day of exploration. Tom had suddenly become cocky and Tommie correspondingly despondent. He suspected that Miracle had gone to Tom's room, and that Tom had emerged from the encounter wearing the cloak of copulatory arrogance put on by young men who foolishly imagine they can reduce every bucking woman to a state of acquiescent docility. No wonder Tommie's nose was out of joint, because it meant the end of her ascendancy over her brother, and she would no longer be able to lift her chin and say: "Since I'm one hour older than you, I know more than you. Right?"

And he remembered Miracle . . . He wished he could have continued their conversations. She would never know that when she had emerged naked from the water, her body had been clearly reflected in the glass doors and he could see it perfectly; nor would she ever know that while watching her dry herself and dress, he had also been watching himself watching Joey swim and dry herself. How dare Joey tell Miracle that her father had more or less raped her! The contrary was true! Joey had teased him and run him around until he did exactly what she wanted. Why else would she wander around the house in her nightie, if not to provoke him into action? Oh yes, Joey, who pretended asexuality, had been the most sensual of all the women he'd known, even Sylvia, and would lie with her eyes closed while he moved his tongue over every part of her, between her toes, inside her ears, there wasn't a spot of her body he hadn't visited. Of course it was pointless to feel anger now.

"Well, it was true," Joey had responded, when Arthur reproached her for palming off the vicious tale of him raping her onto their daughter. Didn't Joey realize she had deprived him of participating in Miracle's childhood? Didn't she understand that in watching Liz's children grow and develop he had relived his own childhood and had understood that, while his first years of life had been restricted by his spells of unconsciousness, comparatively speaking it had been a happy and privileged time. He remembered Tommie once asking him about the most significant events in his life and to avoid embarrassment he had replied that the first was to become a writer and the second was asking her family to live with him at Haven. Lies, lies. He had not consciously decided to become a writer. He had assumed he was one. The first great experience in his life had been discovering he could open a book and read the words in it, although the curious thing was at the time he had not associated his ability to read with the Biblical text and its glossy illustrations. Indeed, the prophets, kings (especially David) and all the others who filled the pages were as real to him as the people who walked along the village lane in Hasterley. It was not until he opened other books that he fully understood that somehow he had learned to decipher their printed symbols by turning pages in the Bible. It was something he just did, much as he rode his pony Mary or walked over Hasterley Common with his mother. The second major experience occurred with the village dressmaker when he discovered that his penis could be put to better use than voiding urine from his bladder. The sensation of his young gut pressing against the dressmaker's soft belly while his penis expanded until it filled the universe had been carried in his memory throughout his life. It was, he thought, something like a child's first lick of an ice cream cone. No matter how much ice cream the person consumes in a lifetime nothing will transcend that first moment when the child's innocent tongue touches the smooth, vanilla-tasting, creamy mixture.

Although why would he now be standing at the window, looking out over the cove to the mountains, remembering Miracle and the twins, months after the terrible calamity which had taken them away from him forever and had finally brought Joey from Los Angeles to stand with him in the crematorium chapel and watch four coffins roll into the furnace behind the curtains. He supposed he was trying to escape the penalty imposed on him by grief, much as he had once bolted to avoid entanglement in the accidental killing of Laura Dorchester.

No one fully explain the deaths, least of all the police, who told Joey (Arthur refused to speak with them) they suspected Miracle had stopped to offer assistance to a man who flagged them down at the side of the road beside a broken-down car. There was almost certainly a second man hiding in the car, though Miracle and her passengers couldn't have known that. The polite theorized that the two men forced Miracle at gun point to drive the car up a disused logging road where they separated Tom from the women and shot him, then sexually assaulted the three women before shooting them too. The discovery of the red convertible near the B.C.-Alberta border, several hundred miles from the place where the crime was committed, had complicated the investigation, because the original search for the missing persons was conducted in the area where the convertible was found, It was not until two men deer-hunting in the fall drove up the little-used road and found the bodies of Miracle, Liz and the twins that the police were finally able to reconstruct the crime and tie it in with the existence of the second car which had been found stripped of its license plates and abandoned in a dried-up a river bed not far from the main road Miracle was driving along.

That's when Joey arrived, heard the police reconstruction the events, which she passed on to Arthur in dribs Joey wanted to know how the police had surmised the women had been raped, and she was informed that forensic evidence conclusively proved it, though she chose not to pass this information on to Arthur. The police assured her that while they had no suspects as yet, they would continue the investigation and sooner or later lay charges.

Joey proved to be the stronger of the two. She did not cry when she and Arthur carried all that remained of the bodies from the crematorium and scattered their ashes among the Ponderosa pines and the old trees in the orchard;

Arthur stumbled over the ground, blinded by his tears, feeling as though he was casting out the remains of his own life.

Each day, Joey said she must get back to Los Angeles, but each day she remained to carry out tasks she had not undertaken in years: preparing meals, making a bed and tidying a house. Her face, due to plastic surgery, was youthful-looking compared to Arthur's, and since she and Arthur had never been divorced, she decided they might as well sleep together, not because she was especially interested in sex, but because it would eliminate the need to make up another bed. He accepted this and did not object when late in the year she telephoned the local goodwill agency and had them send out a truck to collect clothes and other personal possessions. The first indication Arthur had that Joey might stay at Haven for a while came when she taxied to town early in the new year and drove back in a good used car.

During those difficult months, Joey observed that Arthur said little and did nothing except stand at the window and stare down into the cove. She decided to bully him back to work, and in fact he did return to sit in his workroom, though only he knew it was a sham because he could not move beyond the horror of the four deaths. He spent his hours there trying to avoid imagining the final defiling scenes of the tragedy, though he could not escape the images when they returned at night. Then, he would press his face into Joey's breasts and sob, "Oh God, Joey! We have lost so much. We have lost everything. There's nothing left." And Joey would respond, "We can't change what happened, Matt. We have to go on living." "But why, Joey why?" he asked. Joey, who thought Arthur was turning into a self-pitying old man, used her hands to try and get him going. "Come on, Matt," she urged. "It's what you used to live for." Or she might attempt a joke: "Shall I order a splint for you?", which aroused him to retaliate by asking if she'd been doing it with a string of splint-cocked men all those years she'd been living in L.A. But knowing Joey as well as he did, he believed her when she said that no man had touched during the years she'd been away from him. "Had she missed him?" Arthur asked, and she admitted to occasionally wishing he was lying beside her in bed. In turn, she pestered him with questions about Liz and he felt like strangling her when she suggested it would have been in character for him to try to make out with Tommie.

"I thought of Tommie as my daughter!" Arthur snarled. "My daughter! You took my real one away."

"If you loved your daughter, you'd have visited," she said.

"If you loved me, you would have brought Miracle to Haven."

They could neither rid themselves of their past together, nor shut out memories of the calamity that had befallen them. Joey frequently threatened to leave, even packed her bags, then at the last moment found a reason for remaining. "It's no good," she said. "I'd better stay until the guy comes to clean the carpets." Or she would walk around the rooms and tell him that there was no point to having the carpets cleaned, they needed to be replaced, which involved going to stores to look at carpets, then transporting Arthur to town to look at colours and finally having a man come to Haven to measure the floors. "Why am I doing this?" she rhetorically asked, "when I don't intend to stay?"

"I don't know either," he grumbled.

"Tomorrow I'll cancel the order, pack my bags and leave."

"You do that," he agreed, but though she cancelled the order for new carpets, she did not leave. Instead, like a well-trained soldier, she remained on the alert, ready and willing to depart at any time.

One afternoon, when Arthur was late emerging from his workroom, Joey went to the door, opened it and called, "Isn't it time to quit?" When she heard no answer, she entered the room, repeating, "Isn't it time to stop?" At first, she thought he'd had one of his spells, but when she touched his hand and forehead, she realized he was dead. There was a small pile of typescript on one side of the typewriter, a pile of unused paper on the other side, and a piece of paper in the machine on which were typed the words . . . *helpless, like an enslaved Hebrew in Babylon.* She rolled the paper out of the machine, added it to the manuscript pile, then took the papers into the bedroom and put them in a drawer. After this, she found the emergency number in the telephone directory, dialled it, explained her reason for calling and gave directions to Haven. She then looked up funeral services in the yellow pages and telephoned one of the numbers listed there.

Again, she stood in the crematorium chapel and watched an imitation wood coffin glide through the curtains, and once more she walked around the orchard, this time to scatter the ashes of the man she had married, perhaps loved, at least to the extent she was capable, but whom she had never understood any more, perhaps, than he had understood her. Later on, during the evening, she sat in the living room and began reading the typescript: *Who was Sylvia? My memories are filled with her, yet I realize I knew nothing about her, only her movements.* Who was Sylvia? Joey wondered. Who's he talking about? *I remember smiling lips, a voice that expressed love, hands that drew my aching head to rest upon her fine, smooth breasts as if they were my cradle. But who was she? She never spoke of what she thought and felt, but only of distant relatives or of my father Arthur Compson, who, although of no importance in the world at large, was an immensely important person to me. I saw the world through his eyes and wanted to be like him. In this, I was unsuccessful. I believe I more closely resemble my mother, although who was she? Had I been cut from my father's cloth I would not have dallied with Heather.* Women, women, women, always women, Joey thought, and tried to recall if Arthur had ever spoken of a woman named Heather. And what about this man Arthur Compson being Matt's father? *I would have pulled down Heather's knickers and shoved my aching cock into her.* Still at it, Joey muttered. *But I had yet to learn that the possibility of opportunistic copulation is at the back of every woman's mind when she walks in lonely places with a man. Though Father knew this very well; he saw opportunity in every woman or girl in the village.* What village is he talking about? Maybe these pages are the start of a novel about some guy called Arthur Compson. *But if I finally admit how little I know about the people with whom I lived and, at least with Sylvia, intimately knew at a sexual level, how can I possibly claim to know the people who swarm through my books? And if I admit to limited knowledge, where does that place me on the literary scale? Laura Dorchester rated my talents high, but I suspect she flattered me more to heighten her own self-importance than to be truthful about my writing ability. If I turn a sceptical eye on my life's work, I can claim to have produced one novel that will endure and a few short stories that will find their way into anthologies. Can I ask for more? Novelists are lucky to be remembered for having written one good novel in which the characters are not dependent upon what their creator has to say about them.* Lord, why doesn't he say something about me? I was the only woman he truly loved. *My David novel . . . I remember how David's energy, his brutality and sexuality poured into and through me, and although I'm not squeamish, I found myself hating how he treated people dependent upon him and how—I'll never forget this—on finding the small daughter of a maidservant turning over private papers in his office, he first cuffed, then held her over his desk and raped her. Creating David came close to destroying me, but I suspect in some measure to create is to skirt with death. Still, most novels are no more than comments on the times, and I could count the number of characters that live independently on the fingers of both hands. I believe my David exists outside of the novel I wrote about him. He exists outside me. Still, I am a little leery of even saying that. It is all too easy to invest belief in what one has created. After all, while my name is recognized, I am not among the famed. My novels receive respectable notices in respected positions in respectable papers, but my name does not blaze. I think I can truthfully say I chose obscurity, I never did want to be recognized. Perhaps I never wanted anyone to really know me. Could that be true? I'm sure that someone, somewhere has written that for literary works to endure periodic injections of revitalizing reprints are required. But Heather . . . She stripped before me and I, maddened by her whiteness against the green moss, collapsed. Perhaps it was just as well, because she was made to be a warrior, not a lover, not a mistress, not a mother. And yet in my childhood, she personified for me everything desirable in a woman; that is, until I encountered Dot Perks' warm, embracing sheathe.* More about writing novels, and still more women. She'd had only Matt, but maybe he needed to sift through dozens of women before finding her. Losing Miracle made her think she should never had left him. Now, it seemed as though she had wasted all those years. *I am a coward and I shrink from paying the price for my cowardice. I am helpless like an enslaved Hebrew in Babylon. Dare I claim that I am done? Finished with the torturous thing that all my life had me creeping like a slime-covered rat through tunnels in the human house to rooms where I rummaged through skeletons of bleached hopes, ingested rancid hatreds and waded through stagnant pools of morbid images that mirrored age-slackened members momentarily twitching with feeble desires, or to dark closets where insane need seeded itself and reaped illicit fulfilment, and on to passages where facaded faces in dim light paraded, and nothing was what it appeared to be? Am I to bitterly hope that, after being trapped in a maze of creation's illusions, I am at last set free by one final, unexpected, though alas! all too real, at least for me, utterly, senseless tragedy?* That was the last of the copy. Joey reread the pages and when she finished, her only regret was that Matt had not remained alive a little while longer so that he could write something about her and the movie she had made at Haven. She then put the pages back into the drawer and went to bed.

In the morning, after drinking a cup of coffee and eating a piece of toast, she called the town's premier realty office, asked to speak to the manager, identified herself, then said she was putting Haven on the market. After a pause, the manager said: "Thank you for calling, Mrs. Scheiler. I'll be there in half an hour." Joey put down the phone, walked to the windows and looked out onto the lake while waiting for the door chime to sound.

NOTE FROM THE PUBLISHER

Ernest Langford has worked as a full-time author throughout his adult life, creating an impressive array of dramas, short stories, and novels—by any standard, an extraordinary achievement. On the following pages, you will find a list of his literary works.

Langford has never requested or received a government grant, or other cultural subsidy, which may make him unique in contemporary literary life; but what makes his work even more remarkable is the power of its central theme—the revelation of the unseen streams of thought and impulse that lie beneath the monotonous surface of daily life. In his investigation of the human psyche, Langford has created unforgettable characters and deeply moving stories and dramas that are simultaneously rewarding and unsettling.

Several novels and short stories in the list are published works, and some of the dramas have been produced. Others have not yet gained entry into the public domain, though without doubt they merit the attention of readers and theatre-goers. For this reason, we take pleasure in inviting you to visit our home page on the Internet to download onto your PC one or more of Langford's works, or you may wish to purchase a floppy disk of a work directly from us (see pages 526-27).

・ ━◆━ ━

Ernest Langford was born in England. He came to Canada as a young man and lived for a time in Ontario before moving to B.C. He now lives in Kamloops, B.C.

── 523 ──

THE COMPLETE WORKS

of Ernest Langford

THE EARLY YEARS (1950 to 1969)

Novels

The Conquistador
The Span

The Mollusk
Rendezvous at Dieppe

Full-Length Plays

Ellen
The White Hart
Who Stand Alone
The Afternoon Sun
Ollin Wood
Dark Aisles

Bottom of the Well
Death is a Tree
The Fair City of Aipotu
A Summer's Tale
Lament for a Dead
 Flower

The Escarpment
The Snake
The Shaven Poll
Around the Mulberry
 Bush
The Three Shepherds

Short Stage Plays

Drop in a Penny
The Flower-Scented
 Hill
Stepping Stones
General Delivery
Keep the Pot Boiling

The New Life
Rummage Sale
The Unanswerable
 Wind
Stacked Deck
The Contract

A Woman's Touch
Little Boxes
The Perforated
 Encyclopedia
The Rare Flowers

Television/Radio Plays

Boat for Sale
A Bit of Bark
Game
The Choice

Oh, Dream of Fair
 Islands
The Room
To Float Little Corks

The Hunting Spirit
The Three Shepherds
Battle Royal
The Battle of Admiral Bay

Short Stories

The Beginning
Cap Corse
Seaweed
Rabbit
Jackie Kelsey

Mike Christov
The Potlatch and Other
 Stories
Deathless Memories (A
 Collection)

Transformations (A
 Collection)
Old Harry Nobbit
Incident on a Mountain
 Road

Poetry

Poems I

Poems II

THE MIDDLE YEARS (1970 to 1989)

Novels

Assault on Mount
Annapeg
Time to Sow, Time to
Reap

Innocence
The Portuguese Waiter
Funlandia
Betrayal

On the Road to Banff
Show Me the Way, Lord
Prison of Love

Full-Length Plays

The Innocents

The Predators

The Net

Short Stage Plays

The First Link

Voices from the Past

So Many Shadows

Television/Radio Plays

The Way the Cookie
Crumbles

Crabs at the Tail-End of
Burns Night

Something To Do

Short Stories

Never Count Chickens

My Neighbour's Wife

Pink and Blue

Children's Story

Tamara Tiddle and the Diamond-Eyed Warblers

Textbook

The Explorers: Charting the Canadian Wilderness

RECENT WORKS (1990 to the present)

Novels

The Kingdom of
Chombuk
The Ten-Bible Secret
The Apple Eaters

Survival Course
Rosie & Iris
Valley of Shadows
The Wax Key

Necessities of Life
Oh, Patagonia!
The Existentialist

Short Stage Plays

The Valiant Shopper
Breaking the Silence

Bringing Home the
Bacon

Poetry

Poems III

LITERATURE

ON-LINE

Battle Street Books invites you to download
a selection of Langford's novels, short stories and plays on
the INTERNET in the spirit of Shareware.
Here is a sample of what is available:

Novels

The Kingdom of Chombuk

Read the adventures of Crumbthorpe Knottley, funeral director from
Sweet Springs, Saskatchewan, who gets lost in the fog while flying his
plane and discovers *The Kingdom of Chombuk.*

Innocence

Teenager Mary grows up believing if she does what her parents say
she'll have a happy life. But experience destroys her beliefs, and
bitterness replaces hope. She tries to erase painful memories by setting
fire to buildings. When that doesn't help, she travels into the dense bush
of northwest coastal B.C. to make her final escape.

Plays

The Perforated Encyclopedia

A lonely woman meets a salesman peddling the ultimate encyclopedia.

The Snake

Guided by his talisman, a bank teller first gains, then loses a fortune.

Short Stories

The Potlatch and Other Stories

Stories that reveal ways non-aboriginal people interacted with First
Nations people in British Columbia in the 1950s and 1960s.

VISIT

BATTLE STREET BOOKS ON-LINE

Our *NEW* INTERNET address is: http://netpage.bc.ca/battlestreetbooks/

LITERATURE
On Disk

All of the titles listed in The Complete Works are now available on book disk (WordPerfect 5.1/5.2 format), which can be read on IBM and Macintosh computers. If you are a Macintosh user, you require an Apple Superdrive and the Apple File exchange program. To read the files, use a word processing program such as WordPerfect, Microsoft Word, or Claris Works.

Price: $22.95 plus $2.00 handling charge.
(Add 7% sales tax if you are a B.C. resident.)

Send disk to (please print):

Name: _____

Address: _____

City: _____

Province/State: _____

Postal/Zip Code: _____

Book disk requested: _____

Please enclose cheque or
money order, payable to:
Langford Publishing Services
175 Battle Street, Kamloops, BC
Canada V2C 2L1

If you would like further information about our other soft-cover books, you may write to us at the above address.